W9-AMB-782

GULLIVER'S TRAVELS

JONATHAN SWIFT (1667–1745) was born in Dublin, where he was educated at Trinity College, and in 1713 became Dean of St Patrick's Cathedral. While previously living in London, he had made friends with Pope, Gay, and Arbuthnot, formed with them the Scriblerus Club, and written propaganda for the Tory administration of another club member, Robert Harley. He had first made his mark as a satirist with *A Tale of a Tub* and *The Battle of the Books* (1704), and after his return to Dublin (1714) he used his genius for polemical satire to defend Ireland (i.e. Anglo-Irish Protestants) against exploitation by the English Whigs, most sensationally in *A Modest Proposal* (1729). *Gulliver's Travels* is also a powerful political satire. Written when Swift was nearly 60, and first published in 1726, it at once became, quite literally, one of the world's classics.

CLAUDE RAWSON is the Maynard Mack Professor of English at Yale University. He is author of a wide range of books, including *Henry Fielding and the Augustan Ideal under Stress* (1972), *Gulliver and the Gentle Reader* (1973), *Satire and Sentiment, 1660–1830: Stress Points in the English Augustan Tradition* (1994, corrected paperback edition 2000), and, most recently, *God, Gulliver, and Genocide: Barbarism and the European Imagination, 1492–1945* (Oxford University Press, 2001). Both he and Ian Higgins are General Editors of the Cambridge Edition of the Works of Jonathan Swift.

IAN HIGGINS is a Senior Lecturer in English Literature at the Australian National University. He works on British and Irish literature, especially of the early eighteenth century. He is the author of *Swift's Politics: A Study in Disaffection* (1994) and *Jonathan Swift, Writers and their Work* (2004), and of several articles on Swift and his contexts.

OXFORD WORLD'S CLASSICS

*For over 100 years Oxford World's Classics have brought
readers closer to the world's great literature. Now with over 700
titles—from the 4,000-year-old myths of Mesopotamia to the
twentieth century's greatest novels—the series makes available
lesser-known as well as celebrated writing.*

*The pocket-sized hardbacks of the early years contained
introductions by Virginia Woolf, T. S. Eliot, Graham Greene,
and other literary figures which enriched the experience of reading.
Today the series is recognized for its fine scholarship and
reliability in texts that span world literature, drama and poetry,
religion, philosophy and politics. Each edition includes perceptive
commentary and essential background information to meet the
changing needs of readers.*

OXFORD WORLD'S CLASSICS

═══

JONATHAN SWIFT

Gulliver's Travels

═══

Edited with an Introduction by
CLAUDE RAWSON
and Notes by
IAN HIGGINS

OXFORD
UNIVERSITY PRESS

OXFORD
UNIVERSITY PRESS

Great Clarendon Street, Oxford OX2 6DP

Oxford University Press is a department of the University of Oxford.
It furthers the University's objective of excellence in research, scholarship,
and education by publishing worldwide in

Oxford New York

Auckland Cape Town Dar es Salaam Hong Kong Karachi
Kuala Lumpur Madrid Melbourne Mexico City Nairobi
New Delhi Shanghai Taipei Toronto

With offices in

Argentina Austria Brazil Chile Czech Republic France Greece
Guatemala Hungary Italy Japan South Korea Poland Portugal
Singapore Switzerland Thailand Turkey Ukraine Vietnam

Oxford is a registered trade mark of Oxford University Press
in the UK and in certain other countries

Published in the United States
by Oxford University Press Inc., New York

First published as an Oxford World's Classics paperback 1986
Reissued as an Oxford World's Classics paperback 1998
New edition 2005

British Library Cataloguing in Publication Data

Data available

Library of Congress Cataloging-in-Publication Data

Swift, Jonathan, 1667–1745.
Gulliver's travels/Jonathan Swift; edited with an introduction by Claude Rawson
and notes by Ian Higgins.—New ed.
p. cm.—(Oxford world's classics)
Includes bibliographical references.
1. Gullliver, Lemuel (Fictitious character)—Fiction. 2. Voyages, Imaginary—Early
works to 1800. 3. Travelers—Fiction. I. Rawson, Claude Julien. II. Higgins, Ian.
III. Title. IV. Series.
PR3724.G7 2005   823'.5—dc22   2004024295

ISBN–13: 978–0–19–280534–8
ISBN–10: 0–19–280534–7

3

Typeset in Ehrhardt by
RefineCatch Limited, Bungay, Suffolk
Printed in Great Britain by
Clays Ltd, St Ives plc

CONTENTS

GULLIVER'S TRAVELS

LIST OF ILLUSTRATIONS

ABBREVIATIONS

Corr.   *The Correspondence of Jonathan Swift, D.D.*, ed. David Woolley, 4 vols. (Frankfurt am Main: Peter Lang, 1999–   )

Library Dirk F. Passmann and Heinz J. Vienken, *The Library and Reading of Jonathan Swift: A Bio-Bibliographical Handbook, Part 1: Swift's Library*, 4 vols. (Frankfurt am Main: Peter Lang, 2003)

Poems   *The Poems of Jonathan Swift*, ed. Harold Williams, 2nd edn., 3 vols. (Oxford: Clarendon Press, 1958)

PW   *The Prose Writings of Jonathan Swift*, ed. Herbert Davis *et al.*, 16 vols. (Oxford: Basil Blackwell, 1939–74)

INTRODUCTION

JONATHAN SWIFT (1667–1745) was born in Dublin. His English father died before he was born, and he was brought up by relatives in Dublin. He studied (not brilliantly) at Trinity College, Dublin, and was ordained as a priest of the (Anglican) Church of Ireland. In 1713, he became Dean of St Patrick's Cathedral in Dublin, an office he held for the rest of his life. He had always aspired to an English preferment, and hoped to become a bishop. He attributed his failure partly to the reputation for blasphemous unruliness of *A Tale of a Tub* (1704), his first major book and perhaps his most brilliant. He defended the *Tale* against charges of irreligion, but never openly acknowledged the work. This secretiveness over authorship extended, in less extreme form, to many of his other works, including *Gulliver's Travels* (1726).

Though Irish by birth and education, Swift regarded his residence in Ireland as a form of exile. In addition, after the death of Queen Anne in 1714, when Swift's political friends fell from power, Swift found himself in the political wilderness. After several years of pamphleteering for Robert Harley's Tory administration, he now largely ceased to write on English political subjects. Though resentful of his Irish exile, he became very active in Irish politics. From 1720 onwards, he produced a series of historic pamphlets on the political and economic wrongs of Ireland under English rule and on the ineptitude of the Irish at looking after their own interests. Through the *Drapier's Letters* (1724), *A Modest Proposal* (1729), and numerous other writings in verse and prose, he established himself as a 'Hibernian Patriot', and is honoured in the Irish Republic to this day as a founding hero of the modern nation. The Irish interest he defended against rule from London was that of the English settlers, not the 'natives', whom, in common with many English writers of his time, he largely despised. The Yahoos of *Gulliver's Travels* are partly a portrait of these natives. But writing from the perspective of the *colon* or settler, he nevertheless helped to inaugurate a tradition of resistance to metropolitan oppression which created the momentum for the eventual independence of an Irish Republic Swift might not have been altogether happy to see. *Gulliver's Travels*

(1726), his most famous work, is partly fuelled by his perspectives on the Irish situation (in the account of the Flying Island in Book III, for example, as well as the portrayal of the savage Yahoos in Book IV).

Swift's three decades of 'exile' as Dean of St Patrick's were, until he was struck down by painful senile disorders near the end of his life, the most active of his career, both as one of the greatest Anglo-Irish political activists, and as an English writer. It is largely in these years that he established himself as not only one of the most brilliantly versatile and powerful satirists, but as a poet, journalist, and political commentator and activist of extraordinary range, effectiveness, and distinction. He is nevertheless chiefly remembered for *Gulliver's Travels*, which in abridged form became a famous children's book, and is also one of the bleakest satires of the human condition.

Composition and Publication

Gulliver's Travels was written in the years 1721 to 1725, with Book III written last, and published in 1726 by the publisher Benjamin Motte. It was a great success, as Swift's friend John Gay reported, 'universally read, from the Cabinet-council to the Nursery', quickly entering the popular folklore,[1] with some of the impact of a modern soap opera in creating a make-believe world. It was written as a parody of travel books, a genre in which Swift was well read. He owned the great multi-volume travel compendia of Richard Hakluyt and Samuel Purchas, and wrote to his woman friend Vanessa (Esther Vanhomrigh) in 1722 that he had been reading 'I know not how many diverting Books of History and Travells', adding to a male friend a few days later that they were an 'abundance of Trash'.[2]

The travel-book background forms the outward armature of a deep satirical exploration of the human creature. Behind it lies a lifetime of reading in the works of classical and Renaissance ethnographers, from Herodotus and Pliny to Montaigne, and a live interest in the culture, society, and politics of humans in history and in his own time. *Gulliver's Travels* belongs to a species of parody which is not mainly concerned with the books it is ostensibly

---

[1] John Gay to Swift, 7 (or 17) Nov. 1726 (*Corr.*, iii. 47–9).

[2] Swift to Vanessa, 13 July 1722; to Charles Ford, 22 July 1722, *Corr.*, ii. 424, 428. For Swift's copies of Hakluyt and Purchas, see *Library*, ii. 778–83, 1546–51.

mimicking, but uses the medium of parody to explore matters of more central and substantial human import. It purports to be a philosophical response to definitions of man as a 'rational animal'. It flirted with dangerous political allusions, as well as with other shocks to polite sensibilities, and Swift claimed that the publisher Motte had expurgated and sanitized his text. Some corrections were made by Motte in a 'Second Edition' in 1727, but when the work was included in 1735 as volume iii of the edition of Swift's *Works* by the Dublin publisher George Faulkner, it included further revisions, some of them not intended in 1726. There was some mystification over Swift's role in the 1735 edition, from which Swift also pretended to keep his distance, though his involvement in it seems to have been considerable.

Gulliver and Swift, 1726

The book we know as *Gulliver's Travels* first appeared on 28 October 1726 as *Travels into Several Remote Nations of the World*, purportedly written by Lemuel Gulliver, 'first a SURGEON, and then a CAPTAIN of several SHIPS'. There was no overt sign of Swift's authorship. The title of *Gulliver's Travels*, by which the book is nowadays universally known, is a popular piece of shorthand, with no formal authority, though Swift was referring coyly to 'a Book . . . called Gulliver's Travels' as early as 17 November 1726.[3] The frontispiece was a lifelike medallion portrait of '*Captain Lemuel Gulliver, of* Redriff Ætat. suae 58' (i.e. at the age of 58), a hitherto unusual, possibly unprecedented, feature in an imaginary voyage, ostensibly signalling a true account.[4] To a few friends, it was probably evident that the age was also that of Jonathan Swift, whose authorship was not disclosed, and an eagle-eyed reader would be able to report from the text that this cannot have been Gulliver's real age.[5] Some readers may have sensed, or formed the impression, that Gulliver's face 'is

---

[3] Swift to Alexander Pope, *Corr.*, iii. 56.

[4] Jeanne K. Welcher, *Gulliveriana VII: Visual Imitations of Gulliver's Travels 1726–1830* (Delmar, NY: Scholars' Facsimiles & Reprints, 1999), p. xxxiii; the frontispiece portrait of *Robinson Crusoe* (1719) is, by contrast, crowded with fictional detail (p. 4). Welcher gives the most extensive account to date of the frontispiece portraits of *Gulliver's Travels*, pp. xxvi–xxxiii, 1–11 (Figs. 1–2), 143–7 (Fig. 46).

[5] Janine Barchas, *Graphic Design, Print Culture, and the Eighteenth-Century Novel* (Cambridge: Cambridge University Press, 2003), 28, 30.

not unlike that of Swift himself'.[6] To the average reader of the book, the portrait held no secret code. To the knowing reader, the code would not yield all its secrets, for Gulliver is not Swift, although Swift is a lurking presence behind him.

This elusive interchange of identities extended in the opposite direction, to portraits of Swift himself. When, after 1726, the Irish painter Francis Bindon painted what is sometimes thought to be the first of his series of portraits of Swift, now in the National Portrait Gallery, London, the likeness seemed to show a consciousness of the frontispiece Gulliver. The painter is in any case concerned with the book. The portrait shows Swift pointing to the title-page of Book IV, 'A Voyage to the Country of the Houyhnhnms', on a scroll in his hand. In the background is a peaceful Irish landscape, with Houyhnhnm-evoking horses.[7] Both this and the portrait itself thus maintain pictorially a traffic between the fictional Gulliver and Swift himself which conforms closely with the character and early history of the book itself.

In the early editions, this traffic is part of a flaunted mystification, which suggests more than the instinctive secrecy about authorship evident in most of Swift's major works, the product of convention, temperamental guardedness, and the risk of political trouble attendant on subversive writings. There is in addition, throughout the narrative, a protracted tease about the truth content of the work we are reading, and about the character and extent of the 'real' author's commitment to it (whoever he might be). This ostensibly authentic portrait of a mariner-author is followed in the first edition by a foreword from 'The Publisher [i.e. Editor] to the Reader', signed by Gulliver's cousin Richard Sympson. Some of this will not be entirely comprehensible until we have read through the whole work. But it is possible for the reader to remain comfortable (as he or she will not be for long) that nothing more is in the offing than a real travel narrative, or a fiction pretending to be one, like Defoe's *Robinson Crusoe* (1719), a work Swift may have found easier to parody than to admit

---

[6] Robert Halsband, 'Eighteenth-Century Illustrations of *Gulliver's Travels*', in Hermann J. Real and Heinz J. Vienken (eds.), *Proceedings of the First Münster Symposium on Jonathan Swift* (Munich: Wilhelm Fink, 1985), 84; Peter Wagner, 'Captain Gulliver and the Pictures', in *Reading Iconotexts: From Swift to the French Revolution* (London: Reaktion Books, 1995), 46; Welcher, *Gulliveriana VII*, 6.

[7] Welcher, *Gulliveriana VII*, 124–9.

to having read. In an earlier work, Swift had referred to Defoe, a lifelong antagonist, as 'the Fellow that was *pilloryed*, I have forgot his Name', subsequently identifying him (in 1735) in a footnote without removing the pretence of having forgotten him.[8] But in these opening moves of the first edition, the first-time reader has little obvious incentive to detect mystifications and covert agendas.

'The Publisher to the Reader' is followed, after the Table of Contents (not reproduced in this edition), by the famous opening of Gulliver's own autobiographical narrative:

My Father had a small Estate in *Nottinghamshire*; I was the Third of five Sons. He sent me to *Emanuel-College* in *Cambridge*, at Fourteen Years old, where I resided three Years, and applied myself close to my Studies: But the Charge of maintaining me (although I had a very scanty Allowance) being too great for a narrow Fortune; I was bound Apprentice to Mr *James Bates*, an eminent Surgeon in *London*, with whom I continued four Years; and my Father now and then sending me small Sums of Money, I laid them out in learning Navigation, and other Parts of the Mathematicks, useful to those who intend to travel, as I always believed it would be some time or other my Fortune to do. When I left Mr *Bates*, I went down to my Father; where, by the Assistance of him and my Uncle *John*, and some other Relations, I got Forty Pounds, and a Promise of Thirty Pounds a Year to maintain me at *Leyden*: There I studied Physick two Years and seven Months, knowing it would be useful in long Voyages. (I. i)

This plain, matter-of-fact narrative, immediately following the frontispiece and foreword, is said to have deceived some readers into believing they were being offered a true story. One sea captain claimed to be 'very well acquainted with Gulliver, but that the printer had mistaken, that he livd in Wapping, & not at Rotherhith [i.e. the Redriff of the portrait and foreword]'. An old gentleman searched for Lilliput on his map. Best of all, an Irish bishop reportedly preened himself on not being taken in, having been taken in to the extent that he thought he was meant to be taken in. He proudly declared that he thought the 'book was full of improbable lies, and for his part, he hardly believed a word of it'. His triumphalism was

---

[8] *A Letter Concerning the Sacramental Test* (1709), in *PW* ii. 115. A reluctance to mention Defoe by name may or may not lie behind the fact that *Robinson Crusoe* is mentioned three or four times in the *Encyclopédie* of Diderot and d'Alembert, while its author's name does not appear at all: Madeleine Descargues, 'Swift et l'*Encyclopédie*', unpublished lecture, University of Valenciennes, 11 Mar. 2004.

matched by the triumphalism of Swift and his friends over his addlement.[9]

Swift was a consummate hoaxer. He wrote a parody of the astrologer Partridge in 1708, predicting the latter's death, and announcing the event on the due date, to the victim's discomfiture. On another occasion, in 1722, he published some 'last words' of a dead criminal, suggesting that the latter had left behind the names and addresses of all his criminal brethren, thus purportedly reducing the number of street robberies.[10] Such effects of persuading the readers that they are witnessing reality rather than just reading a story came to be valued, by Richardson as by Flaubert, as one of the great achievements of the novel form, and, in our time, connect the novel with soap operas. The readers who begged Richardson or Dickens to spare Clarissa or Paul Dombey look ahead to audiences of *General Hospital* or *Coronation Street*. The compelling intimacy of this 'illusion of life' was, in Swift's lifetime, a cherished objective of Richardson, and perhaps of Defoe, 'the Fellow that was *pilloryed*' for writing *The Shortest-Way with the Dissenters* (1702), a mock extermination proposal which was taken straight, thus variously disturbing the peace; and who later became a founding father of the realist novel.

To Swift, as to his other contemporaries Pope or Fielding (himself a novelist of a different stripe), conditioned by classical or Augustan standards of impersonal seriousness and gentlemanly codes of 'conversational' decorum, such things seemed an in-your-face vulgarity. What would do for an ephemeral *jeu d'esprit* was not suitable for writings of more ambitious purpose. Even a first-time reader of *Gulliver's Travels*, once inside the Gulliverian world of big men and little men, flying islands, and talking horses, might be expected to understand that he or she was reading neither a true story nor a realistic narrative. If they did not, the whole of the work's satirical content would misfire. The sea captain, the old gentleman, the Irish bishop were all very well as gratifying oddities, a tribute to the satirist's power to make fools of obtuse know-alls. But if everyone reacted in this way, the whole point of the book would be lost, as it was lost for those taken in by Defoe's *Shortest-Way*, with nasty consequences for the author to boot.

[9] John Arbuthnot to Swift, 5 Nov. 1726, Swift to Pope, 17 Nov. 1726, *Corr.*, iii. 45, 56.
[10] For the Partridge affair (1708), and *The Last Speech and Dying Words of Ebenezor Elliston* (1722), see *PW* ii. 137–70, 193–231, 269–73, ix. 35–41, 363–7.

The veristic trimmings of the front matter and opening paragraphs of *Gulliver's Travels*, even for first-time readers of the first
edition, ultimately exist in relation to elements in the book which are
designedly so fantastic as to defy any suspension of disbelief. The
deceptive opening partly serves as a guard-lowering ruse, an impression of truth and sympathetic ordinariness, softening the reader into
complacency before assaulting him with a bewildering blend of
unassimilable fantasy and harshly disturbing revelations about the
human creature. This unresolved tension, between an undemand-
ingly genial mode of writing and subsequent assaults on the reader's
expectations and poise, is a characteristic signature of Swift's satiric
manner.

It is evident that Swift had a highly developed sense of the extra-
textual resources of front matter. He went on tinkering with
the frontispiece portrait in the subsequent publication history of
Gulliver's Travels, until it reached, in 1735, the revised version in
which it is most commonly read today (including the present edition).
In a later issue of the first edition, a second state of the portrait
added a Latin quotation from the ending of the second satire of the
Roman poet Persius, protesting the writer's (i.e. Gulliver's) purity of
mind, and 'heart steeped in nobility and honour' (l. 74). If the reader
is seduced by this into thinking of Gulliver as a truthful or reliable
reporter, there will be much in the rest of the work to disabuse or
complicate this impression. The effect of tease and uncertainty
induced by this is something Swift developed and exploited in later
appearances of the portrait, and in other pieces of front matter.[11]

Gulliver, his Cousin Sympson, and Swift, 1735

Swift believed, and made a performance of believing, that the publisher had tampered with his text. He compiled a list of changes,
some of which were added in 1727, and most of which eventually
found their way into the 'final' version. This formed volume iii of a
collected *Works* published in 1735 by the Dublin bookseller George
Faulkner (in four volumes, subsequently expanded over the years).

[11] For some enlightening perceptions into the workings of front matter, and their
bearing on the reliability of the narrator, see Jenny Mezciems, 'Utopia and "The Thing
which is not": More, Swift, and Other Lying Idealists', *University of Toronto Quarterly*,
52 (1982), 40–62, esp. 48–54.

Although the original holograph manuscript of *Gulliver's Travels* no longer survives, the evidence suggests that the later edition is to a greater or lesser extent a revised version rather than a restored original.[12] Swift sometimes pretended that this edition also 'was done utterly against my will' (to Pulteney, 8 March 1735). Faulkner, on the other hand, says Swift worked daily with his publisher and 'corrected every Sheet of the first seven Volumes that were published in his Life Time'.[13] Swift's account is true to character and Faulkner's appears closer to the facts.[14] Indeed the likelihood is that Swift had a hand in preparing Faulkner's prefatory pieces to the volumes of 1735, if these were 'not actually written by him'.[15] Similarly, it is more than likely that Swift was also involved in at least some aspects of the production process, especially those concerning the portraits. Here again, the title-page announces the author as Lemuel Gulliver, although now that the work is included in a collected edition of Swift's work, Swift's initials are on the same title-page, and secrecy of authorship gives way to a more overt tease as to the elusive relationship between the narrator and the real-life author, by no means identical but linked by elusive overlappings and ambiguous distancings.[16] The portrait has changed. Or rather there are two new versions of the portrait, depending on whether the volume belongs to the octavo format of *Works*, 1735, or the smaller duodecimo set.[17]

This time, a resemblance to portraits of Swift becomes overtly paraded. It has been pointed out that 'the oval which frames the portrait is a shape common to both portraits and mirrors',[18] a fact

---

[12] For varying accounts, see F. P. Lock, *The Politics of Gulliver's Travels* (Oxford: Clarendon Press, 1980), 66–88; 'The Text of *Gulliver's Travels*', *Modern Language Review*, 76 (1981), 513–33; Michael Treadwell, 'Benjamin Motte, Andrew Tooke, and *Gulliver's Travels*', *Proceedings of the First Münster Symposium*, 287–304; 'The Text of *Gulliver's Travels*, Again', *Swift Studies*, 10 (1995), 62–79, esp. 74, 78.

[13] Swift to William Pulteney, 8 Mar. 1735, *Correspondence*, ed. Harold Williams, 5 vols. (Oxford: Clarendon Press, 1963–5), iv. 304; George Faulkner, 'To the Reader', *Works* (Dublin, 1763), in *PW* xiii. 203.

[14] For a recent review of the evidence, see James McLaverty, ' "An Evil I could not prevent": Swift's Collusion in his *Works* (1735)', not yet published.

[15] Herbert Davis, introduction to *PW*, xiii. pp. xxxiii–xxxiv; see pp. 179–87 for the 1735 prefaces, and pp. 201–7 for the full text of Faulkner's 'To the Reader'.

[16] See also Welcher, *Gulliveriana VII*, 143–7 (Fig. 46) on the 1735 portraits.

[17] See Barchas, *Graphic Design*, 31–4, on these differences, some of which, however, seem to me over-interpreted; see also the somewhat different account in Teerink and Scouten, *Bibliography*, 25.

[18] Grant Holly, 'Travel and Translation: Textuality in *Gulliver's Travels*', *Criticism*, 21 (1979), 134–52, 149.

which may be apt to the game of identities between narrator and
author. Of the two versions of the Faulkner edition, the octavo especially bears a striking likeness to the portrait of Swift himself which
serves as frontispiece to volume i of the same Faulkner edition, and
which is an engraving based on a portrait by the Irish painter Charles
Jervas, who painted Swift in 1709, and 1716–17 or 1718, and super-
vised engravings, and was also a friend and portraitist of Pope.[19]
Unlike Pope, who sat for many painters throughout his life,[20] Swift
did not like being painted, and was sometimes curmudgeonly about
it. 'I hate to be in Town while [Jervas] is there', he wrote in a letter of
4 October 1716. Many years later, close to the time of Faulkner's
edition, he speaks of having been 'fool enough to sit for my Picture at
full length by Mr Bindon' (15–16 June 1735). Bindon's work was
itself 'very much derived from Jervas's initial effort but with some
adjustments for the advancement of age'.[21] An atmosphere of
irritability surrounds Swift's relations to portraits of himself.

An observant reader would be exercised by the resemblance
between the portraits in volumes i and iii, and, to the extent that he
or she remembers it, would be actively unsettled by the uncertainties
of focus and wavelength which it contributes to a text already heavily
impregnated with elusively aggressive obliquities. In addition, in
both versions of the 1735 Gulliver frontispiece a small new time
bomb has been lobbed at the reader. Gulliver's age and place of
residence, and the quotation from Persius, are dropped. Instead, in
both versions, the caption now merely says 'Capt. Lemuel Gulliver
Splendide Mendax. Hor.' The Latin phrase comes from Horace's
Odes, III. xi. 35, and refers to Hypermestra, the only one of fifty

[19] See David Piper, *Catalogue of Seventeenth-Century Portraits in the National
Portrait Gallery 1625–1714* (Cambridge: Cambridge University Press, 1963), 336–8, pl.
15 (i); Arthur S. Marks, 'Seeking an Enduring Image: Rupert Barber, Jonathan Swift,
and the Profile Portrait', *Swift Studies*, 16 (2001), 31–82, esp. 31–3. Portraits by Jervas
are reproduced in *Corr.*, i (pl. 1), ii (pls. 8–9).
[20] See W. K. Wimsatt's magisterial study, *The Portraits of Alexander Pope*
(New Haven: Yale University Press, 1965). Such a book could not be written about
Swift.
[21] *Corr.*, ii. 182; *Correspondence*, ed. Williams, iv. 352; Marks, 'Seeking an Enduring
Image', 33 and nn. The fullest account of portraits of Swift is still Sir Frederick
Falkiner, 'Of the Portraits, Busts and Engravings of Swift and their Artists', *Prose Works
of Jonathan Swift*, ed. Temple Scott (London: G. Bell, 1897–1908), xii. 3–56. There is a
collection of above two dozen photographs of portraits of Swift, Stella, and Vanessa, in
the Library of the Yale Center for British Art, Jennings Albums, vol. xvi, George I (2),
fos. 151–6.

daughters of Danaus who disobeyed her father in order to save her husband. It is an inversion of the use of Persius in the earlier edition, affirming Gulliver's honour and purity of mind. It means 'lying magnificently', in a good cause, but still lying. Attached prominently to the frontispiece portrait of the narrator, it implies both unreliability and some sort of nobility of purpose.

But perhaps the most disconcerting piece of front-matter in the 1735 edition is the cantankerous letter from Gulliver to his Cousin Sympson, dated '*April* 2, 1727'. In it, Gulliver begins by complaining that the first edition of his book was marred by deletions and additions attributed to Sympson's fear 'of giving Offence' to 'People in Power', as well as by some unacceptable stylistic usages. Gulliver's 'comic dismay' is in many ways a replay of that of Swift himself, so much so that Michael Treadwell, one of the best students of the textual history, speaks of this as 'Gulliver/Swift' writing to 'Sympson/Motte' (i.e. Benjamin Motte, the publisher of the first edition). As always, Gulliver both is and is not Swift, and Swift's complaints about the corruptions of the first edition may have been to some extent 'facetious' or exaggerated in the manner of the letter to Sympson, partly in order to deflect 'onto the poor printers criticism for carelessness which was his own and which he could not otherwise correct', and partly out of mischievous jokerie.[22]

Gulliver explains that he never wanted to publish his book but gave in to pressure from his cousin; that he never expected the book to have any effect since 'the *Yahoos* were a Species of Animals utterly incapable of Amendment'; and yet that 'instead of seeing a full Stop put to all Abuses and Corruptions, . . . as I had Reason to expect: Behold, after above six Months Warning, I cannot learn that my Book hath produced one single Effect according to mine Intentions'. In other words, although he expected no change, he is angry at the absence of changes he 'had Reason to expect'. As a result, he is dismayed to find that six months after publication humanity is still unreformed (the date of 2 April 1727, appended to a letter first published in 1735, happens to be just over five, or very roughly six, months after the original publication of *Gulliver's Travels* on 28 October 1726, as only a very knowing reader would know, though

---

[22] Treadwell, 'Text', 71; Lock, *Politics*, 68, 70.

Gulliver compounds confusion by sliding from 'above six Months Warning' to a remark about 'seven Months' being a 'sufficient Time'):

Behold, after above six Months Warning, I cannot learn that my Book hath produced one single Effect according to mine Intentions: I desired you would let me know by a Letter, when Party and Faction were extinguished; Judges learned and upright; Pleaders honest and modest, with some Tincture of common Sense; and *Smithfield* blazing with Pyramids of Law-Books; the young Nobility's Education entirely changed; the Physicians banished; the female *Yahoos* abounding in Virtue, Honour, Truth and good Sense: Courts and Levees of great Ministers thoroughly weeded and swept; Wit, Merit and Learning rewarded; all Disgracers of the Press in Prose and Verse, condemned to eat nothing but their own Cotten, and quench their Thirst with their own Ink. These, and a Thousand other Reformations, I firmly counted upon by your Encouragement; as indeed they were plainly deducible from the Precepts delivered in my Book. And, it must be owned, that seven Months were a sufficient Time to correct every Vice and Folly to which *Yahoos* are subject; if their Natures had been capable of the least Disposition to Virtue or Wisdom: Yet so far have you been from answering mine Expectation in any of your Letters; that on the contrary, you are loading our Carrier every Week with Libels, and Keys, and Reflections, and Memoirs, and Second Parts; wherein I see myself accused of reflecting upon great States-Folk; of degrading human Nature, (for so they have still the Confidence to stile it) and of abusing the Female Sex. I find likewise, that the Writers of those Bundles are not agreed among themselves; for some of them will not allow me to be Author of mine own Travels; and others make me Author of Books to which I am wholly a Stranger.

The last sentence is one more salvo in the aggressive mystification over authorship, by now largely disposed of by the inclusion of the work in an edition of Swift's *Works*, but still allowed to crackle uncomfortably, and sufficient to sustain a reader's chronic uncertainty as to the relationship and exact roles of Gulliver and the satirist behind him. The language of Gulliver to Sympson bears a disconcerting resemblance both to Swift's own complaints that the first edition of his book had been subjected to deletions, and insertions of 'trash contrary to the Author's manner and Style, and Intention' (to Charles Ford, 9 October 1733); and also to Swift's early disclaimer of involvement in the revised edition of 1735, 'an evil I cannot prevent' (to Pope, 8 July 1733), and which he hasn't 'looked into ... nor I believe ever shall' (to Pulteney, 8 March 1735).[23] You cannot take Swift straight on any such issue, but he doesn't always mean the opposite either.

The traffic between the fictional text and real life is variously carried out in Swift's correspondence, from mixed motives of concealment and play. In Swift's correspondence with his friends, there is the same combination of flaunting and concealment, a continuously nudging and winking *diablerie* as to the Gulliver connection. Letters are signed, by Swift and his friends, with Gulliverian names. One letter, to Mrs Howard (28 November 1726), is signed 'Lemuel Gulliver'. Another, from Mrs Howard, was signed 'Sieve [the term is Lilliputian for a court lady] Yahoo', which Swift made a fussy pretence of not understanding (10, 17 November 1726). Swift also wrote to Pope the same day (17 November) about 'a Letter of Mrs Howard's, writ in such mystical terms, that I should never have found out the meaning, if a Book had not been sent me called Gulliver's Travels', adding 'that if I were Gulliver's friend, I would desire all my acquaintance to give out that his copy was basely mangled, and abused, and added to, and blotted out by the printer'.[24] He also corresponded, directly or by proxy, with the publisher Motte, using the name 'Richard Sympson' (8, 11, 13 August 1726, 27 April 1727),[25] although Sympson partially stands for Motte himself in the book, and sometimes using John Gay's handwriting as a cover.[26]

If Swift often writes in Gulliver-mode, it is not surprising that Gulliver should sometimes write like Swift. Few early readers, and only the most determined readers today, would have, or choose to acquire, sufficient access to Swift's correspondence to recognize its resemblance to Gulliver's cantankerous protestations, but the resemblance reinforces or confirms intimations in the work itself that Gulliver, like others of Swift's derided speakers, is related to, or resembles, his creator. There is a long history of complaints by Swift

[23] *Corr.*, iii. 693, ii. 661; *Correspondence*, ed. Williams, iv. 304.

[24] *Corr.*, iii. 58–9, 49–50, 54–7 (these letters have slightly different dates in Williams's edition of the *Correspondence*, iii. 185–91.

[25] *Corr.*, iii. 9–13, 82. On this, see Treadwell, 'Text', 71–2; Swift remained on good terms with Motte despite his apparent indignation over the corruptions in *Gulliver's Travels*, see A. E. Case, *Four Essays on Gulliver's Travels* (1945; Gloucester, Mass.: 1958), 7–8; Treadwell, 'Benjamin Motte', 300–4.

[26] *Corr.*, iii. 11; Harold Williams, *The Text of Gulliver's Travels* (Cambridge: Cambridge University Press, 1952), 15–19.

about the corruptions in the text of *Gulliver's Travels* of which the
Letter to Sympson provides a grotesque Gulliverian parody.[27] But
even without this doubtless unintended recognition, the letter to
Sympson is a powerful low-key weapon in Swift's wearing down of
his reader's composure. The rest of the passage has a similar effect.
The reader will recognize a familiar rhetoric of satire, showing the
satirist deranged by the disappointment of rational expectations
about humanity's behaviour. The disjunction between ideal and realistic expectation is a staple of satire. In practice it suggests that the
speaker is understood by both author and reader to be antisocial or
even neurotic, but that he is right by a higher standard, and would
not have become unhinged if the world had been a decent place. The
reader seems to be offered the luxury of discounting a character who
(as in Gulliver's case) is driven to excesses of eccentric misanthropy,
and who prefers to spend his time with the horses in his stable rather
than with his wife and family. Such discounting, however, cannot
extend to the balance sheet of human depravity which the entire
fiction has drawn up, and which Gulliver summarizes in this passage,
an indictment which is evidently a principal moral lesson of the
fiction.

How much, and what, to discount is what remains uncertain, a
tease which undermines readerly comfort, and enables the satirist to
make his point without being dismissed as excessive or insane, like
his speaker. And Gulliver himself speaks for his author when he
expresses lack of interest in the reader's good opinion of his person:
'I wrote for their Amendment, and not their Approbation'. The
words prefigure Gulliver's remarks to the reader in the final chapter:
'My principal Design was to inform, and not to amuse thee' (IV. xii).
The testy unfriendliness of this is consonant with Swift's declaration
to Pope on 29 September 1725, as he was finishing writing *Gulliver's
Travels*, that 'the chief end I propose to my self . . . is to vex the
world rather then divert it'.[28] Whichever words were written first,[29] it
is hard to think of them as other than variations on one another, a
further sign of intimate traffic between Swift and Gulliver, and of

[27] For some suggestive remarks on this, see Holly, 'Travel and Translation', 138–9.
[28] *Corr.*, ii. 606.
[29] The natural assumption is that the fictional version was written first, since
the letter speaks of the work as completed, but I am allowing for the possibility of
adjustments and afterthoughts before publication a year later.

the atmosphere Swift was determined to create between his book and his reader.

The first-time reader of the letter to Sympson does not yet know fully why Gulliver likes to be in a stable, but Gulliver's preference for the neighing of his horses to the conversation of his family and neighbours is a hint of disconcerting priorities, to be explained as the narrative reaches its final stages. Indeed, the entire quarrelsome discourse is not easy for a first-time reader to assimilate. It is the language of the later disenchanted Gulliver of Book IV, not that of the innocuously bland narrator whom we are about to meet in the opening chapter of Book I. To understand it fully, one needs to have read the whole book at least once before, like some modern fictions by Conrad, Ford, or William Faulkner, whose time scheme is dislocated in the service of a non-chronological understanding of the events. But this is not, in *Gulliver's Travels*, a matter of manipulating narrative expectation or the presentation of character, but of inducing unease as a tactic of satirical attrition. The simpler satirical effect, of first offering a naïve and guileless narrator ripe for shocks of undeception, gives way to a mood of more continuous undefined foreboding, hard to reconcile with the ensuing accounts of the gullible Gulliver in Book I. The unspecific unease of Gulliver's chatter acquires increasing validation as the evidence of human depravity mounts, and only defines itself fully as an expression of Gulliver's acrimonious 'character' at the end.[30]

Gulliver's Travels is not a novel like those of Conrad, Ford, or Faulkner, of course. But nor is it much like the fictions of its own time, by Defoe, Richardson, or even Fielding, which we agree to call novels. Swift, as I have suggested, would not have been a willing practitioner of the realism or narrative immediacy of Defoe or Richardson. The lifelike unfolding of a personal story is not his purpose. Such realism of notation as he displays is largely a parody of travel books or possibly of travel fictions, and exists in the service of satirical exposure rather than the building of fictional 'illusion'. Though Gulliver has a wife, family, home address, and elements of a biographical record, he does not come over as a fully

---

[30] For fuller treatment of these matters, see Claude Rawson, 'Gulliver and Others: Reflections on Swift's "I" Narrators', in *Gulliver's Travels*, Norton Critical Edition, ed. Albert J. Rivero (New York, 2002), 480–99.

human personality. His progression from acquiescent lover of his
kind to alienated misanthrope is more a satirical awakening to
truth than a significant process of psychological change. Although
he is never the equivalent of Swift, he is always the instrument
of what Swift shows or says through him. It is usually more
natural in the reading, and certainly more productive, to attend to a
Swiftian agenda than to any sort of expression of Gulliverian personality in anything Gulliver says. The shifts and inconsistencies of
Gulliver's point of view are more properly understood as modula-
tions of Swiftian irony than as mental gyrations of the character
himself.

Savages and Imperial Conquest

The most remarkable example of such 'inconsistency' occurs in
Gulliver's anti-imperial outburst at the end of the book, a passage of
great power and interest in its own right. Gulliver has just been
telling the reader that he has decided not to honour his obligation 'as
a Subject of *England*' to report to the government the countries he
has visited, since 'whatever Lands are discovered by a Subject,
belong to the Crown':

To say the Truth, I had conceived a few Scruples with relation to the
distributive Justice of Princes upon those Occasions. For Instance, A Crew
of Pyrates are driven by a Storm they know not whither; at length a Boy
discovers Land from the Top-mast; they go on Shore to rob and plunder;
they see an harmless People, are entertained with Kindness, they give the
Country a new Name, they take formal Possession of it for the King, they
set up a rotten Plank or a Stone for a Memorial, they murder two or three
Dozen of the Natives, bring away a Couple more by Force for a Sample,
return home, and get their Pardon. Here commences a new Dominion
acquired with a Title by *Divine Right*. Ships are sent with the first
Opportunity; the Natives driven out or destroyed, their Princes tortured
to discover their Gold; a free Licence given to all Acts of Inhumanity and
Lust; the Earth reeking with the Blood of its Inhabitants: And this
execrable Crew of Butchers employed in so pious an Expedition, is a
modern Colony sent to convert and civilize an idolatrous and barbarous
People. (IV. xii)

The passage is one of the great denunciations of imperial conquest,
ranking with those of Las Casas and Montaigne, and probably

xxiv   *Introduction*

inspired by the latter.[31] Its eloquent indignation is a set-piece of
Swiftian prose, one of the rare occasions when Swift allowed himself
such accents of lofty fervour, his normal habit being expressed by
the assertion that 'I the lofty Stile decline'.[32] Its vibrant rhetoric is
also, *a fortiori*, outside Gulliver's range as a stylist. But the anger it
expresses confirms what we know of Gulliver's own feelings at this
time.

In the immediately following paragraph, however, Gulliver goes
on to say:

> But this Description, I confess, doth by no means affect the *British*
> Nation, who may be an Example to the whole World for their Wisdom,
> Care, and Justice in planting Colonies; their liberal Endowments for the
> Advancement of Religion and Learning; their Choice of devout and able
> Pastors to propagate *Christianity*; their Caution in stocking their Prov-
> inces with People of sober Lives and Conversations from this the Mother
> Kingdom; their strict Regard to the Distribution of Justice, in supplying
> the Civil Administration through all their Colonies with Officers of the
> greatest Abilities, utter Strangers to Corruption: And to crown all, by
> sending the most vigilant and virtuous Governors, who have no other
> Views than the Happiness of the People over whom they preside, and the
> Honour of the King their Master.

This cannot be the same Gulliver, unless he is being stingingly
ironic. But conscious and stinging ironies are as much outside
Gulliver's stylistic range as the eloquent righteousness of the preceding passage. If we read either passage as mainly expressive of
Gulliver's character, we are confronted by a shocking and implausible inconsistency, in itself almost amounting to cheeky defiance on
the author's part. That option contains its own readerly discomforts.
But it seems more natural to read both passages as ultimately eman-
ating from a Swiftian rather than Gulliverian voice, the first expressing indignation literally, the second doing so ironically, with an
added sarcasm at the species of British complacency frequently

<hr>

[31] Bartolomé de Las Casas, *A Short Account of the Destruction of the Indies* (1552),
trans. Nigel Griffin (London: Penguin, 1992), 3–13; Michel de Montaigne, *Essais*, III. vi
(1588), *Complete Essays*, trans. Donald M. Frame (1958; Stanford, Calif.: Stanford
University Press, 1992), 694–5; see Claude Rawson, *God, Gulliver, and Genocide:
Barbarism and the European Imagination, 1492–1945* (Oxford: Oxford University Press,
2001), 17–24.
[32] Swift, *Epistle to a Lady* (1733), l. 218; see also ll. 140, 260, and *Cadenus and Vanessa*
(1726), ll. 796–7, *Poems*, ii. 634–8, 711.

expressed by travel writers and imperial adventurers before and since.[33]

The latter sarcasm is par for the course, characteristic of Swift's resourcefully incriminating style. If taken straight, it is a return to Gulliver's much earlier manner of complacent acceptance of his country and all its ways. The fact not only evokes the awkwardness of regarding Gulliver as a significant personality in his own right. Since the earlier Gulliver no longer exists, Swift's brief resurrection of him may even be seen as a playful undermining of his own fictional trimmings. That it is Swift's own voice behind his speaker which dominates a reading of both paragraphs, straight and ironic, seems inescapable on any reading.

It is this which makes the fullest sense of the sarcasm of 'British is best', and gives life to other features of both passages. In an equal and opposite way the account of the oppression of harmless natives is not what it seems. The reader comes upon it after a prolonged exposure, in the rest of the book, to the unremitting depravity of humans in all the 'Remote Nations' visited by Gulliver, culminating in the humanoid Yahoos, expressly identified with 'all savage Nations' (IV. ii), and the all too human natives of New Holland who shot Gulliver with an arrow, which Gulliver feared might be poisoned, on his departure from Houyhnhnmland (IV. xi). What is said about the 'harmless People' in Gulliver's speech is spoken with passion, and there is no reason to suppose that Swift didn't 'mean' it. But he meant it in a way that is coloured by an opposite and competing perception, which the volume has been sustaining forcefully throughout.

Even in the speech itself, the 'harmless People' are seen as passive recipients of the cruelty of others rather than as actively virtuous. When it is suggested that they treat their oppressors kindly, the syntax emphasizes that the oppressors 'are entertained with Kindness', so that the only specific record of good action is presented in the passive mode, in the process of being received rather than given. All the active verbs belong to the invading evil-doers. The 'harmless People' exist more to bring out the depravity of these evil-doers than their own virtue or suffering as victims.

Swift detested oppressors. They were an extreme example of a

---

[33] For some examples, see Rawson, *God, Gulliver, and Genocide*, 23, 312–13 n. 13.

human depravity Swift saw as potential in all humans. The oppressed by definition included: 'savages', the Irish, women, to all of whom Swift directed some of his most stinging contempt. Accusations of 'racism' or misogyny are beside the point, not because they are often anachronistic, but because Swift's way with despised subgroups is to say that they are merely human, and that dominant or favoured groups are in fact just as bad. Swift was conscious of being open to charges of misanthropy and misogyny. Gulliver's Letter to Sympson complains of being 'accused . . . of degrading human Nature, (for so they have still the Confidence to stile it) and of abusing the Female Sex'. It is a notable feature of his most memorable disparagements, or apparent disparagements, of the female form divine (the flayed woman of *A Tale of a Tub*, the Brobdingnagian ladies of *Gulliver's Travels*), that they are immediately followed by a male counter-example. Again, this is not to deny aggressive sentiments, and the counter-examples may have a defensive or compensatory element. But they also belong to a persistent effort of reorientation, away from the specific category to the human species itself.

This is especially true of the xenophobic, or what we would call 'racist', aspects of Swift's satire. *A Modest Proposal* is an ironic variation on the old idea that the native Irish were cannibals. But the cannibal slur often directed at the natives is redirected at, or at least extended to, the Anglo-Irish ruling group to which Swift belonged, and also to the ogre nation England, willing to devour Ireland without salt. In the fourth book of *Gulliver's Travels*, what begins as a portrait of humanoid Yahoos who resemble 'all savage Nations', ends up as an anatomy of the entire human race. The language of racial insult is used to attack the species as a whole, much as Augustan satirists used lordly language to attack malefactors, including lords, as low. Humankind is represented as 'low-race' in the way satirized malefactors are made to appear 'low-class'. Arguably, 'racists' are likelier to use the language of misanthropy against specific groups than to allow ethnic slurs to spread to all humans, including themselves.

This is not to sentimentalize Swift's account of 'savages', only to place it in a wider, bleaker, but ultimately less ungenerous perspective. By the time we reach the final chapter, relations between narrator and reader have deteriorated. Gulliver's distaste for humanity is accompanied by an exacerbated quarrelsomeness, very different from the ostensibly guileless geniality of the earliest parts of the work, a quarrelsomeness evident in the letter to Sympson, which was added to the opening pages in 1735. The final chapter opens with an address to the 'gentle Reader':

Thus, gentle Reader, I have given thee a faithful History of my Travels for Sixteen Years, and above Seven Months; wherein I have not been so studious of Ornament as of Truth. I could perhaps like others have aston-ished thee with strange improbable Tales; but I rather chose to relate plain Matter of Fact in the simplest Manner and Style; because my principal Design was to inform, and not to amuse thee. (IV. xii)

The 'familiar' form of the second person singular (thee) is here aggressive, addressed to an inferior, as though familiarity had bred contempt. 'Informing' the reader is, as we saw, the flipside of 'vexing' rather than 'diverting' him. The protestation of strict fac-tual truth is a parody of tall travellers' tales. But coming after a flying island, a visit to the ancient dead, and a land of speaking horses, it strikes a disconcerting note, especially when the extravagant fan-tasies are recognized as in fact enforcing moral truths about humans, which are hard, on the evidence given, to deny. The crackling aggressiveness towards the reader may be detected in *Gulliver's Travels* from the beginning, but its forms are more benign, and more playful, in the earlier books.

Downward Cycles of Human History

The gradual unfolding of human depravity begins with the sche-matic relation between Books I and II. The puniness of the Lilliputians as they re-enact the doings of European societies is a comment on the latter which becomes increasingly stinging as Gulliver realizes that Europeans appear to the Brobdingnagians exactly as Lilliputians appear to him. The schematism is arithmetic-ally very exact, as to the physical proportions between Lilliputians, humans, and Brobdingnagians, but some of its ostensible signals are subjected to disturbance or surprise. The Lilliputians are portrayed almost throughout as unedifyingly similar to corrupt Europeans, but in chapter vi they are suddenly described without warning as a Utopian commonwealth, not in every way appealing to a modern sensibility, but nevertheless recognizably modelled on the ideal commonwealths of Plato and Thomas More, and foreshadowing the ideally ordered Houyhnhnm society of Book IV. This is difficult to square with all previous portrayals of Lilliput, until, after several paragraphs of exposure to the bizarre uncertainty, we get an explanation that the Utopian Lilliput is a thing of the past:

> In relating these and the following Laws, I would only be understood to mean the original Institutions, and not the most scandalous Corruptions into which these People are fallen by the degenerate Nature of Man. For as to that infamous Practice of acquiring great Employments by dancing on the Ropes, or Badges of Favour and Distinction by leaping over Sticks, and creeping under them; the Reader is to observe, that they were first introduced by the Grand-father of the Emperor now reigning; and grew to the present Height, by the gradual Increase of Party and Faction. (I. vi)

The switch is so abrupt that some critics have thought that chapter vi was drafted for some other purpose or context, and eventually inserted into Book I, and that the anomaly had then to be repaired by this explanatory adjustment cobbled for the occasion.[34] In fact, the shock reversal does not seem extraordinary as an example of Swift's way of destabilizing the reading process. It also initiates a series of reflections on historical change which are taken up again in the next two Books.

A parallel situation in reverse occurs in Brobdingnag, a broadly good society whose King is able to denounce the nastiness of Gulliver's compatriots, and whose moral superiority to European humans is reinforced by a gigantic physical stature. Just as the Lilliputians are revealed to have had a constitution of great value before descending to their present state, so the Brobdingnagians, in reverse sequence, were once no better than other nations:

> For, in the Course of many Ages they have been troubled with the same Disease, to which the whole Race of Mankind is Subject; the Nobility often contending for Power, the People for Liberty, and the King for absolute Dominion. All which, however happily tempered by the Laws of that Kingdom, have been sometimes violated by each of the three Parties; and have more than once occasioned Civil Wars, the last whereof was happily put an End to by this Prince's Grandfather by a general Composition . . . (II. vii)

---

[34] Harold Williams, Introduction, *PW* xi. pp. xviii–xix; Ricardo Quintana, *Swift: An Introduction* (1955; London: Oxford University Press, 1962), 146–7.

The passage refers to a technical concern over the propriety of standing armies, but transcends this issue into a wider consideration of processes of political change. Together with the passage from I. vi, it shows an interest in historical cycles. The reference in each case to a change from a royal grandfather to his grandchildren supports not the specific historical allegory of a *roman à clef* (the search for precise correspondences has usually proved futile) so much as a general sense of processes of generational change.

The same generational span is suggested in Book III, when Gulliver, in Glubbdubdrib, is disappointed with his summoning of the famous dead from the past, and desires instead to see the humbler exemplars of defunct English decencies:

I descended so low as to desire that some *English* Yeomen of the old Stamp, might be summoned to appear; once so famous for the Simplicity of their Manners, Dyet and Dress; for Justice in their Dealings; for their true Spirit of Liberty; for their Valour and Love of their Country. Neither could I be wholly unmoved after comparing the Living with the Dead, when I considered how all these pure native Virtues were prostituted for a Piece of Money by their Grand-children; who in selling their Votes, and managing at Elections have acquired every Vice and Corruption that can possibly be learned in a Court. (III. viii)

Again, the local concern with individual issues (corrupt elections) is transcended by a larger interest in historical change. Here the appeal is to an older time of English virtue not easy to identify, and roughly comparable to the Roman past of King Numa or the early Republic, nostalgically evoked in Juvenal's satires. As in the two previous Books, change occurs over a similar generational span, downwards in Books I and III, upwards in Book II. Present-day England is directly parallel to the societies described in Books I and III, to its discredit; it is inversely parallel to the society of Book II, also to its discredit. Historical cycles are often pessimistic concepts. In theory, good and bad succeed one another, but as Plato implies, it is the downward cycles that tend to prevail. The story Swift tells about England, and other human societies, is that they are usually deteriorating.

Little Men, Big Men, and Struldbruggs

A peculiar equivalence establishes itself in Books I and II between size and virtue. It rests on a rhetorical presumption that physical size reflects moral stature. The ill-governed and disagreeable Lilliputians are incrementally contemptible because of their tiny size, while the Brobdingnagians tower above humans in dignity and virtue, their physical height coinciding with their possession of the moral high ground. Characteristically, we are shown Brobdingnagians who do not live up to their best standards, and who are, for example, mercenary or cruel. Moreover, though bigger usually seems best, it is a consequence of size that it magnifies imperfections. The sores and cancers on the breasts of Brobdingnagian women, or the wen on the neck of their male counter-example (II. i, iv, v), are more unsightly to Gulliver than the smooth skins of English ladies, but also tell us that this is how English ladies, and Gulliver himself, would appear to Lilliputians.

These mainly optical examples rest on modern scientific aware-ness, acquired through the invention in the previous century of the telescope and microscope. They show that Swift was not above respecting, and making creative satirical use of, what he recognized as good science, in spite of his well-known contempt for Royal Society experimentation, whose truth and utility seemed opaque to him, and which he attacked in the Academy of Lagado in Book III. But the ironies of size in Books I and II have a further effect. By suggesting that our bodies would look as repulsive in a minuter scale of vision as Brobdingnagian bodies do to Gulliver, Swift is implying a kind of incriminating flaw in the human physique which may be thought of as the physical counterpart of original sin. All humans have it, and there is no way of escaping or eradicating it. The impli-cation is similar to that of the memorable sentence in Swift's earlier masterpiece, *A Tale of a Tub* (1704), 'Last Week I saw a Woman *flay'd*, and you will hardly believe, how much it altered her Person for the worse' (*Tale*, ix).[35]

The context seems to suggest that the woman was a whore being whipped and carted, and that the punishment may be presumed to serve her right. But, as has been pointed out elsewhere, it is also evident that the most virtuous human would similarly appear the worse for being flayed, and there is an ominous subtextual crackle to the effect that every human being is in principle caught up in the predicament of this whore. If the logic of this implication contains escape routes (we don't all deserve flaying), the poetry is clear (we would all look the worse for flaying, no matter who we were or what we did). You cannot unflay a woman, or make her look better flayed than unflayed, any more than you can change the fact of pores or moles. As in *Gulliver's Travels*, the example of the woman is complemented by that of a man whose corpse is being dissected, once again signalling that the reach of the observation is not confined to women.[36] That women are often reported on in such contexts as an initial or initiating instance, may or may not suggest a special Swiftian animus. But, as I have suggested, they are usually quickly redefined as exemplary not of the female sex, but of a Yahoo humanity.

The moral inculpations of physical size, unlike the positive moral stature which runs in some sense against these, remain undeveloped or recessive in the first two books. Nor is there any extension in the rest of *Gulliver's Travels* of the neat schematism that binds these two books together. Book III consists of visits to a number of countries which provide the occasion for extended exposure of the nastiness of totalitarian rule, the oppression of Ireland by England, the depraved folly (intellectual as well as political) of scientific research establishments, and, in the glimpse of otherworldly worthies in Glubbdubdrib, the tarnished stature of several revered figures from the past. The inhabitants of the lands in Book III are of normal human size, though the settings (a flying island, the country of the afterlife) and cultures (conversing with things rather than words) are those of otherworldly or outlandish fantasy. None is a wholly or mainly realistic setting, any more than that of Book IV is, a fact which touches on the mendacity of travel books, and exists in constant friction with the matter of fact narration and Gulliver's protestations of veracity. But the first three books for the most part portray follies and depravities that are specific and self-evidently culpable.

The case of the Brobdingnagian breasts, monstrous and horrifying, is not self-evidently culpable, however. The example implicates all of us, because it is strongly emphasized that we are all included in the phenomenon, since this is how we appear to Lilliputians. If there

---

[36] Swift used 'flayed' elsewhere to mean anatomical dissection, but this does not seem a normal usage (it is not recorded as a definition in its own right in *OED*), and is a deliberately violent metaphor for what satirical surgeons do (*PW* xii. 157–8). In the *Tale*, the reader's first encounter with the flayed woman seems calculated to suggest a painful street scene, only subsequently to be changed by the extended application to an anatomist's dissection.

is no suggestion of active wrongdoing on our part, a touch of unspecific inculpation is clearly sensed. This is compounded by suggestions of secondary culpability (complacent ignorance of human squalor, misplaced pride in the body), but is in itself unspecific and universal, like original sin. *Gulliver's Travels* is a secular book, but its sense of an inherent human depravity acts as a secular analogue to original sin, or draws strength from that doctrine, and the physical marks of a defectiveness that is radical, universal, and incurable, go with the territory.

The intimations of this through most of the first three books remain undeveloped, as I suggested. In all three humanity is portrayed in acts of moral turpitude, political misgovernment, colonial subjugation, legal malpractice, and intellectual folly. We know why they are wrong, and can in principle contemplate the idea of improvement through changes in behaviour or circumstance, though these bad things are so ubiquitous, and their cumulative effect so overwhelming, that it is hard in practice to imagine the likelihood of any change for the better. Towards the end of Book III, however, Gulliver encounters in the land of Luggnagg a small population called the Struldbruggs, who are born with 'a red circular Spot . . . over the left Eye-brow' which eventually grows black, and signifies that they will never die (III. x). It is the last of the exotic groups Gulliver meets before Book IV, and marks a decisive turning point in the work as a whole.

On hearing of the Struldbruggs, Gulliver is full of expectations of the happiness, virtue, and wisdom that he thinks immortality is bound to confer, with its boundless opportunities for acquiring knowledge and experience, in the freedom and disengagement of a mind unencumbered 'by the continual Apprehension of Death'. In fact, the Struldbruggs have perpetual life without perpetual youth, and thus inevitably deteriorate physically, mentally, and morally, once again activating reciprocities of valuation which are already the subject of Books I and II, and here especially evoking a strong resemblance between decrepitude and depravity:

When they came to Fourscore Years, which is reckoned the Extremity of living in this Country, they had not only all the Follies and Infirmities of other old Men, but many more which arose from the dreadful Prospect of never dying. They were not only opinionative, peevish, covetous, morose, vain, talkative; but uncapable of Friendship, and dead to all natural

Affection, which never descended below their Grand-children. Envy and impotent Desires, are their prevailing Passions . . .

At Ninety they lose their Teeth and Hair; they have at that Age no Distinction of Taste, but eat and drink whatever they can get, without Relish or Appetite. The Diseases they were subject to, still continue without encreasing or diminishing. In talking, they forget the common Appellation of Things, and the Names of Persons, even of those who are their nearest Friends and Relations . . .

They were the most mortifying Sight I ever beheld; and the Women more horrible than the Men. Besides the usual Deformities in extreme old Age, they acquired an additional Ghastliness in Proportion to their Number of Years, which is not to be described . . . (III. x)

'The women more horrible than the Men' may be evidence of 'misogyny', or planted for the benefit of those who like collecting such evidence, as Gulliver offered scatological material for those who liked accusing Swift of scatology (I. ii). Gulliver had already told Sympson about seeing himself accused 'of abusing the Female Sex'. Or Gulliver, in Swift's perception, may just have been realistic about the anatomy of the very old. It is possible that all these elements were in play. But the women in this brief incidental comment are merely an extreme example of what is said about all humans, and the strongest charge of feeling in the entire chapter has to do not with any particular sex or category, but with the merciless effect of age on the body, mind, and morals. The depravity of the Struldbruggs is general, not specific; instinctive, not willed; a natural consequence of age and illness, not something they or anyone else can ever have prevented. We are now entering satirical territory of a new kind, in which depravity is not the mark of what people do, but of who they are. The Struldbruggs are a very small group, 'not . . . above Eleven Hundred . . . of both Sexes in the whole Kingdom' (and these are, by definition, the historical grand total), but their sins and nastiness are what flesh is heir to. They sketch out, in a small prophetic way, the guilt of being merely human, and thus prepare us for the Yahoos.

Animal Rationale and the Talking Horse

It is in the much debated Fourth Book that the fiction brings us to a stark and irreducible definition of what humans are (the Yahoos) and are not (rational animals, like the Houyhnhnms). That Swift's concern was a definitional one, to challenge the traditional idea that humans, unlike other beasts, are rational animals, is made clear in the famous letter to Pope of 29 September 1725, written as Swift was completing the work:

I have got Materials Towards a Treatis proving the falsity of that Definition *animal rationale*, and to show it should be only *rationis capax*. Upon this great foundation of Misanthropy (though not Timons manner) the whole building of my Travells is erected.[37]

The 'Definition animal rationale' is the standard textbook proposition that humans, unlike beasts, have an ability to 'reason' or think. Much ink has been spilt on *rationis capax* (capable of reason), but in fact the phrase does not mean anything different from the original 'definition', in its modest textbook sense. Swift's friend Bolingbroke wrote to him on 14 December 1725: 'Your Definition of Animal capax Rationis instead of the Common one Animal Rationale, will not bear examination'.[38]

    In both the letter and the fiction, Swift is engaging in a verbal tease. The absolute rationality of the Houyhnhnms, modelled on Plato's *Republic* and More's *Utopia*, rests on a high or ideal use of the word 'reason' which was never intended in the definition of *animal rationale*. Swift's tactic is to pretend otherwise, in order to say to the reader, 'if you think man is a rational animal, let me show you what a really rational animal is like'. This has no logic as a response to the 'definition', but its poetry, so to speak, carries a cheekily insulting sting. The deadpan violation of logic is elaborately sustained by Swift's attribution of the high rationality to a society of talking horses, since the textbooks which taught the definition habitually gave the horse as the example of choice of a beast possessing all faculties *except* reason. The association was proverbial. The hero of Samuel Butler's *Hudibras* (1663–78), a favourite poem of Swift's, was 'in *Logick* a great Critick', who would

---

[37] *Corr.*, ii. 607.
[38] *Corr.*, ii. 627; see Claude Rawson, *Gulliver and the Gentle Reader: Studies in Swift and Our Time* (London: Routledge, 1973), 24–5, 157 n. 60; Bolingbroke is referring to a conversation in Cicero's *De Natura Deorum*, III. xxvi. 66–xxviii. 71, where reason is said to distinguish man from animals, but can be 'good' or 'bad', depending on its application.

undertake to prove by force
Of Argument, a Man's no Horse.[39]

Swift's use, in the composition of *Gulliver's Travels*, as well as in many details of the letter to Pope, of the textbooks in philosophy habitually taught in the universities of Europe at the time, is now well understood. It establishes that, contrary to the bantering denial in the letter, he is not challenging the truth of the 'definition', for what that was, but rubbing in the fact that humans have no right to pretend to the virtues of high rationality, falling catastrophically short of a noble ideal. It is only by a verbal sleight of hand that this shortfall can be redefined as a lack of 'reason' in the definitional sense. The trick enables Swift to imagine a world in which horses have wisdom while human-shaped creatures are bestial, and pretend that the 'definition' has been rebutted. It is an insulting 'logical' refutation, but it acts only as an imaginative ploy or debating point, and has no substance other than to suggest, again, that if humans are like the Yahoo humanoids, they are no better than their worst sub-groups, 'low-species' or 'low-race', as some people are described as low-class.

Swift's correspondence with Pope is full of bantering tease. Its famous phrases, 'I hate and detest that animal called man', 'this great foundation of Misanthropy (though not Timons manner)', have an air of playful overstatement which distances the writer from the full literal force of his words, without contradicting them: the denial of 'Timons manner' merely means that the 'misanthropy' won't be that of a ranting recluse, like the Timon of Lucian or Shakespeare. Swift's letters about *Gulliver's Travels* are a rich guide to attitudes, so long as the habitual obliquities of his style are taken into proper account. In a subsequent letter to Pope of 26 November 1725, he reversed his acknowledgement of misanthropy by an apparent denial:

I tell you after all that I do not hate Mankind, it is vous autr[e]s who hate them because you would have them reasonable Animals, and are Angry for being disappointed.

---

[39] *Hudibras*, I. i. 65, 71–2. See Rawson, *Gulliver and the Gentle Reader*, 31–2; the seminal study of this question is R. S. Crane, 'The Houyhnhnms, the Yahoos, and the History of Ideas', in J. A. Mazzeo (ed.), *Reason and the Imagination* (New York: Columbia University Press, 1962), 231–53.

It is evident even from this that the supposed denial cannot be taken at face value, though there have been some insistent attempts to do so. At all events, the letter continues:

I have always rejected that Definition and made another of my own. I am no more angry with——[the blank is usually held to refer to Walpole, the prime minister] th[a]n I was with the Kite that last week flew away with one of my Chickins and yet I was pleas'd when one of my Servants shot him two days after.[40]

Nature and Reason

If the letters to Pope, and the portrayal of the Houyhnhnms, rely on an actively unresolved friction between high and low, or ideal and mundane (or technical) senses of the word 'reason', the same is true of the word 'nature' throughout Book IV. The Houyhnhnms' name, we are told, means '*the Perfection of Nature*' (IV. iii), and they live 'according to' Nature and Reason in a high sense in which the two terms coalesce. The Houyhnhnms, who don't have laws, are surprised that Gulliver's countrymen should need them, because, as the master thought, 'Nature and Reason were sufficient Guides for a reasonable Animal, as we pretended to be, in shewing us what we ought to do, and what to avoid' (IV. v). Nature is the term for an ideal order in the sense in which we still speak of a gross misdeed as an 'unnatural act', even if it was committed spontaneously and in conformity with the perpetrator's 'natural' impulses, or his 'nature'. The latter meaning is a lower usage existing in a tension with the higher, a tension which is often present in ordinary speech, and is a matter of systematic awareness and exploitation in Book IV.[41]

This same tension underlies the irony of Gulliver's complaint in the Letter to Sympson that he has been accused of 'degrading human Nature, (for so they have still the Confidence to stile it)'. The remark suggests that 'nature' is a misnomer when applied to humans. In practice, however, Gulliver speaks of our 'natural Vices', reporting for example that the master Houyhnhnm told him

That, although he hated the *Yahoos* of this Country, yet he no more blamed them for their odious Qualities, than he did a *Gnnayh* (a bird of

---

[40] *Corr.*, ii. 623.
[41] For fuller discussion, see Rawson, *Gulliver and the Gentle Reader*, 18–26.

Prey) for its Cruelty, or a sharp Stone for cutting his Hoof. But, when a Creature pretending to Reason, could be capable of such Enormities, he dreaded lest the Corruption of that Faculty might be worse than Brutality itself. He seemed therefore confident, that instead of Reason, we were only possessed of some Quality fitted to increase our natural Vices . . . (IV. v)

The idea of nature is here taken down two successive twists of a descending spiral. The Yahoos have a natural depravity analogous to that of a *Gnnayh* or bird of prey, whom it is appropriate to hate but not to blame, like the kite in Swift's letter of 26 November 1725, which flew away with one of Swift's chickens, and was shot two days later: the *gnnayh* and the kite are evidently echoes of one another, whichever was written first.

The kite in the letter is to some extent like men, whom Swift professes not to hate or be angry with because they know no better. But a further distinction is introduced. It is Yahoos, not us, whom the Houyhnhnm says he hates but does not blame. For 'us' he reserves a further escalation of opprobrium, since we do know better, and since in our case it is reason itself which appears 'to increase our natural Vices'. It is bad enough if vices can be 'natural', but if reason can increase these, a new escalation of depravity has to be conceded. The Houyhnhnm hopes there's another explanation, but the language of Book IV never allows this matter to rest. In a later conversation, about the sexual mores of the Yahoos, and their bearing on our own, Gulliver reports:

I expected every Moment, that my Master would accuse the *Yahoos* of those unnatural Appetites in both Sexes, so common among us. But Nature it seems hath not been so expert a Schoolmistress; and these politer Pleasures are entirely the Productions of Art and Reason, on our Side of the Globe. (IV. vii)

If much of Book IV intimates that humans are essentially the same as Yahoos, and also somewhat superior to them, there is a simultaneous irony to the effect that in some ways humans are worse.

These disconcertingly conflicting signals emerge cumulatively from such passages. In a similar barrage of mixed signals, humans are denied the reason they take pride in, but also have it, and it makes them worse. These are inconsistencies of incrimination, each of them offered as true, and the atmosphere of generalized culpability, of either-way-you-lose, is locked in more tightly with each turn of the screw. The sense that emerges is one of radical incurability of the human condition, grounded in the 'nature' of the human animal, and imprisoningly reaffirmed each time that 'nature' is redefined. That these redefinitions occur in defiance of a local logic (our lack of reason makes us worse than we think we are, but our possession of it makes us even worse than that) causes discomfiture to the reader and is part of what Swift meant when he wrote to Pope that he was determined to 'vex' the world rather than 'divert' it. This satirical manner is the opposite of the one practised by Pope (or Fielding, or Gibbon), which aims to establish solidarity with the reader against a bad world. Swift's way is to disconcert and destabilize, creating a quarrelsome ambience in which the reader is treated as belonging to the enemy.

Swift has been described as a satirist 'of the second person', and it is in the deep logic of his account of humanity that there should be no exceptions. Sniping at the reader may be an expression of temperamental aggressiveness, but it contributes to the suggestion that the reader, if only as a member of the human race, is included in the general inculpation. In that sense, it follows that the narrator and the satirist are similarly included, a fact of which Gulliver is painfully aware, and from which Swift often makes clear (in many of his writings) that he also is not exempt. Whatever improvements are available to humankind from good institutions and laws and the practical accommodations of everyday life, the account of humanity at the essential definitional level is bleak and uncompromising.

'Exterminate from the Face of the Earth'

The universal depravity suggested by the work as a whole may perhaps be compared with the generalized dismay at human doings which God is said to have felt just before he released the deluge: 'I will destroy man whom I have created from the face of the earth' (Genesis 6: 7). The Book of Genesis, which is an important textual presence in Book IV (although *Gulliver's Travels* is not a religious allegory, and its concerns are secular), does not tell us in specific terms what the wickedness was that made God angry. This creates an atmosphere in which the wickedness seems self-evident and comprehensively incriminating, an effect not unlike Swift's, except that Swift's fiction also provides, on another plane, a large documentation of bad doings. It is not a coincidence that when the Houyhnhnm Assembly debates the Yahoos, it does so in the language of scriptural punishment: 'The Question to be debated was, Whether the *Yahoos* should be exterminated from the Face of the Earth' (IV. ix).

This language has led some interpreters to argue that Swift portrayed the Houyhnhnms as genocidal murderers, thus inviting us to read the book as disapproving of them. To this one might answer first that the Yahoos are beasts in the eyes of the Houyhnhnms, so that exterminating them would be no different from exterminating some farmyard pest in the human world. That the Yahoos nevertheless seem human to the reader adds a black humorous touch, no doubt calculated to offend us, but without erasing the main point that in the story they are an alien and unhygienic species. Secondly, the extermination is never carried out. The latest proposal is not said to have been implemented, so that it hangs over the situation as a disturbing possibility, without the potentially alienating shock of an 'actual' extermination, though a selective culling had already been made in the past.

To the extent that a biblical association suggests divine retribution, there is a macabre hint of just deserts. The real difficulty about supposing the Houyhnhnms to be genocidal tyrants is the clear evocation of God's words in Genesis 6: 7. If the Houyhnhnms are genocidal, so is God, and the dominant implication in both the Old Testament and *Gulliver's Travels* is not that a wanton massacre is taking place, but that mankind deserves the punishment. The divine utterance acquired currency, not only in later books of the Old Testament but in more recent history, as a preferred vocabulary of systematic slaughter, recurrently parodied as such in Defoe's *Shortest-Way with the Dissenters*. Ironically, it was used by the Nazis, about whom Swift did not know, but to whom the Houyhnhnms have been compared. Indeed, the arguments as to whether the Yahoos should be killed outright, or castrated (which would have the same result a generation later), and as to how either scheme bears on the fact that Yahoo labour is useful to the Houyhnhnm economy, prefigure the Nazi example with uncanny precision. In an earlier round-up, the Houyhnhnms had once herded the Yahoos in a camp before a selective extermination, and elsewhere in Book IV

useful objects are manufactured by Gulliver from the skins of
Yahoos.

These resemblances speak tellingly to the modern reader. They
show an insight into the mental configurations of violent oppression,
as these inhabit an exploring and creative imagination, or on the
other hand provoke homicidal atrocities in the realm of action. They
have about them the dimension of black humour which the Surrealist
André Breton identified with Swift on the eve of the Second World
War, seeing it as a form of cruel play, in which the imagination is set
free among prohibited or unspeakable matters, without the 'degrading influence' of satirical or moralistic purposes.[42] It is implausible to
think of Swift as jettisoning such purposes, but there is a powerful
sense, recognized by many readers, in which his writing often spills
over its official meaning or tendency, flirting disturbingly with the
forbidden, or indecent, or cruel, and this too is related to his special
interest in his reader's discomfort. This is very different from
having, or endorsing, Nazi characteristics, or from attributing them,
whether in complicity or disparagement, to the Houyhnhnms. Had
Swift known about the Nazis, the example of his treatment of lesser
tyrannies and oppressions makes it clear that he would have
instanced them as a culminating example of Yahoo depravity.

Gulliver and the Gentle Reader

A difficulty for the reader is that all this material is mediated through
a narrator who is variously unreliable, and who in the later parts of
the story, prefigured in the 1735 edition by the Letter to Sympson,
seems actually deranged. The suggestion, as the story unfolds, is that
he has been shattered into total misanthropy by his experience of
human doings and the revelation of the Houyhnhnm Utopia. This
Utopia, like More's commonwealth of that name, and like Plato's
Republic, is a 'no place', a country of the mind, unavailable to human
aspiration except as a notional ideal. The sting is that the 'no place',
which is also (through a pun on two Greek words) a 'good place', is
not for us. But it teaches Gulliver a standard by which humanity falls
short, and he is apparently 'crazed' by the experience. The formula
is a tried way of expressing satirical disaffection. It corresponds in

[42] André Breton, *Anthologie de l'humour noir* (1939), rev. edn. (Paris, 1966), 9–21, esp.
13–14, 19–21.

colloquial speech to the situations in which we say that something 'drives us crazy' or 'makes us mad', but is open to a multitude of fictional elaborations.

One such is the close of the Letter to Sympson:

I must freely confess, that since my last Return, some Corruptions of my *Yahoo* Nature have revived in me by Conversing with a few of your Species, and particularly those of mine own Family, by an unavoidable Necessity; else I should never have attempted so absurd a Project as that of reforming the *Yahoo* Race in this Kingdom; but, I have now done with all such visionary Schemes for ever.

The idea that the world is unmendable, that the satirist is a fool for trying, is one of the oldest in satire, and occurs in various forms in all Swift's major satires from *A Tale of a Tub* to *A Modest Proposal*. It goes with the ambiguous idea that if the world is mad and bad, the satirist's virtue will itself appear mad by that standard, ambiguous because one can be virtuously crazed, like the Modest Proposer, into a vicious alienation, like that of proposing a wholesale cannibal trade, though the latter is itself a reflection of the supposed depravity of the satirized population.

Gulliver's alienations are more benign. He is rude to the Portuguese captain, and prefers the horses in his stable to his wife and family (IV. xi). Some modest accommodations to human society are intimated in the front matter, approvingly by Richard Sympson in 'The Publisher to the Reader', disapprovingly by Gulliver himself, who refers to Yahoo corruptions which 'have revived in me by conversing with a few of your Species, and particularly those of mine own Family'. These changes are reported in prefatory pieces, but they post-date the last words of Book IV, where Gulliver is wholly unreconciled. The last words, after Gulliver's report on human pride, are:

I dwell the longer upon this Subject from the Desire I have to make the Society of an *English Yahoo* by any Means not insupportable; and therefore I here intreat those who have any Tincture of this absurd Vice, that they will not presume to appear in my Sight. (IV. xii)

This is about as unfriendly a treatment of the 'gentle Reader' as anything in Swift's writings. The language is petulantly unsocial, and clearly in breach of polite conversational manners. Any comfort we may take from the thought that Gulliver is deranged must contend with the fact that the reading stops on this sour note, and there is no competing voice offering an alternative point of view.

The reader should have become accustomed by now to a certain withdrawal of conversational good manners. The book's prevailing tone is quarrelsome and disorientating, programmed to 'vex' rather than divert, and it is the antithesis of more conventional satirical styles which purport to engage the reader's solidarity. The fact that Gulliver's attitudes seem unbalanced or unsocial acts not so much to let humankind off the hook as to distance the author from being partially discredited by what appears to be excessive utterance. Since the account of human doings cannot be shrugged off as untrue, Gulliver's response appears 'deranged' only because its truth has made him so, and if Swift has made him act in a comically unbalanced fashion it is clear that Swift is distancing himself from the comedy of excess without conceding any flaw in the diagnosis which brought it about. The lofty accents of Juvenalian denunciation, or the rant of 'Timons manner', are exactly what Swift guarded against. As he said in another context, he declined a lofty style, partly fearing to 'make a Figure scurvy'.[43] If anything, Swift's dissociation from Gulliver's manner rather than his matter (as he told Pope he rejected Timon's manner but not the substantive misanthropy) tends to disconcert rather than to palliate, since the reader may feel entitled to discount something, but cannot be sure what, or how much.

The reader is left, at the end, to negotiate this mood in a void, without support or signposts from the author. Gulliver may be deranged, but there is nobody to tell us any better, or to relieve the discomfort of this 'vexing' alienation. The whole work's radical assault on human nature has settled, in the reverberating afterlife of a reading, on the reader's frayed defences, where in truth it has been all along. This merely accentuates the 'logic' of the general diagnosis, which is that, if humans are what the story says, this includes the reader, along with more passable specimens like the King of Brobdingnag in Book II, Lord Munodi in Book III, the Portuguese Captain in Book IV, and indeed the author himself. Good readers have always understood that Swift is, in clear-eyed mischievousness, implicated in his own satire.

---

[43] *Epistle to a Lady*, l. 219, *Poems*, ii. 637.

Unsurprisingly, he has for some become the type of the demonic, raging misanthrope, best known through Thackeray's famous denunciation.[44] That view ignores Swift's carefully calibrated rejection of the righteous denunciations of 'Timons manner', his persistent preference for working aggressively in a lower key, and his fastidious humour on the subject of Gulliver's eccentric excesses. But Thackeray's view is closer to the truth than that of readers who, in the late Ph.D. era, have seen in Swift a bland model of civic virtue, promoting postcolonial pieties, and repudiating the Houyhnhnms as slave-owners and racists.

Gulliver's Travels is also a very funny book, and a consummate work of other-worldly fiction, operating with a brilliant inventiveness in a mode of science-fiction realism. We should not forget that some early readers took it for real. Swift had the skills, though not, like Defoe, the instincts, of a novelist. He took care, in *Gulliver's Travels* and elsewhere, to disabuse gullible readers of any 'illusion' that they were witnessing life rather than reading fiction. But the power to create what he was eager to neutralize may be part of the appeal of *Gulliver's Travels* as a children's book, usually, in that format, stripped of the bleaker satiric content and the aggressions against the reader. If *Gulliver's Travels* contains parody of Defoe, this necessarily includes mimicry of Defoe's skills as a mimic. The sarcastic idiom which undermines this, to a sensitive reader's discomfort, tends to be dropped in children's adaptations, which perhaps helps partly to explain why one of the world's most disturbing satires has also survived as a children's classic.

[44] W. M. Thackeray, *English Humorists of the Eighteenth Century* (1853), *Works* (London: Everyman, 1949), 3–46, esp. 28–9, 34–5.

First state frontispiece portrait of Gulliver and title-page from the first issue of the first edition, 1726.

Second state frontispiece portrait of Gulliver
from a later issue of the first edition, 1726

Portrait of Gulliver from the duodecimo
edition, 1735

The Reverend
Dr. I. SWIFT D.S.P.D.

Portrait of Jonathan Swift, 1735

NOTE ON THE TEXT

THE text of *Gulliver's Travels* given here is taken from volume xi of Herbert Davis's edition of Swift's *Prose Writings* (1965 reprint). It is based on volume iii of George Faulkner's Dublin edition of Swift's *Works* (1735). This text of 1735 seems to have come closer to what Swift originally wrote than the first edition of 1726, and also to have contained revisions representing his last ideas for the book.

SELECT BIBLIOGRAPHY

Bibliographical Aids

Berwick, Donald M., *The Reputation of Jonathan Swift, 1781–1882* (1941; repr. New York: Haskell, 1965).

Landa, Louis A., and Tobin, James Edward, *Jonathan Swift: A List of Critical Studies Published from 1895 to 1945* (1945; repr. New York: Octagon Books, 1975).

Passman, Dirk F., and Vienken, Heinz J., *The Library and Reading of Jonathan Swift: A Bio-Bibliographical Handbook, Part I: Swift's Library*. 4 vols. (Frankfurt: Peter Lang, 2003).

Rodino, Richard H., *Swift Studies, 1965–1980: An Annotated Bibliography* (New York: Garland, 1984).

Stathis, James J., *A Bibliography of Swift Studies 1945–1965* (Nashville, Tenn.: Vanderbilt University Press, 1967).

Teerink, H., and Scouten, Arthur H. *A Bibliography of the Writings of Jonathan Swift*, 2nd edn. (Philadelphia: University of Pennsylvania Press, 1963).

Vieth, David M., *Swift's Poetry 1900–1980: An Annotated Bibliography of Studies* (New York: Garland, 1982).

Voigt, Milton, *Swift and the Twentieth Century* (Detroit, Mich.: Wayne State University Press, 1964).

Williams, Harold, *Dean Swift's Library* (Cambridge: Cambridge University Press, 1932).

Modern Editions

Correspondence, ed. Harold Williams, 5 vols. (Oxford: Clarendon Press, 1963–5).

Correspondence, ed. David Woolley, 4 vols. (Frankfurt: Peter Lang, 1999–).

Poems, ed. Harold Williams, 2nd edn., 3 vols. (Oxford: Clarendon Press, 1958).

Complete Poems, ed. Pat Rogers (Harmondsworth: Penguin, and New Haven: Yale, 1983).

Prose Writings, ed. Herbert Davis et al., 16 vols. (Oxford: Blackwell, 1939–74). Vol. xiv, Index by Irvin Ehrenpreis et al.; vols. xv–xvi, *Journal to Stella*, ed. Harold Williams. Standard edn. Mainly unannotated. Important introductions.

Basic Writings of Jonathan Swift, selected and with introduction by Claude Rawson and notes by Ian Higgins (New York: Modern Library, 2002). Annotated.

Swift's Irish Pamphlets: An Introductory Selection, ed. Joseph McMinn (Gerrards Cross: C. Smythe, 1991).

The Cambridge Edition of the Works of Jonathan Swift, General Editors Ian Higgins, Claude Rawson, David Womersley, is currently in progress, and will include annotated texts of all Swift's prose and poetry in approximately 16 volumes.

Individual Works

Directions to Servants, ed. Claude Rawson (London: Penguin, 1995).

A Discourse of the Contests and Dissentions between the Nobles and the Commons in Athens and Rome, ed. Frank H. Ellis (Oxford: Clarendon Press, 1967). Annotated.

The Drapier's Letters, ed. Herbert Davis (Oxford: Clarendon Press, 1935). Annotated.

An Enquiry into the Behaviour of the Queen's Last Ministry, ed. Irvin Ehrenpreis (Bloomington: Indiana University Press, 1956). Annotated.

Gulliver's Travels: The Text of the First Edition, ed. Harold Williams (London: First Edition Club, 1926).

Gulliver's Travels, ed. Albert J. Rivero, Norton Critical Edition (New York: Norton, 2002). First edition text. Useful context extracts, and some modern critical discussions.

The Intelligencer, ed. James Woolley (Oxford: Clarendon Press, 1992). Annotated.

Journal to Stella, ed. Harold Williams, 2 vols. (Oxford: Clarendon Press, 1948). Reprinted as vols. xv and xvi of *PW*.

Memoirs of Martinus Scriblerus (with Pope et al.), ed. Charles Kerby-Miller (New Haven: Yale University Press, 1950). Annotated.

A Modest Proposal, ed. Charles Beaumont, Merrill Literary Casebook (Columbus, Oh.: Charles E. Merrill Publishing Company, 1969).

Polite Conversation, ed. Eric Partridge (London: Deutsch, 1963). Annotated.

Swift vs. Mainwaring: The Examiner and the Medley, ed. Frank H. Ellis (Oxford: Clarendon Press, 1985). Annotated.

A Tale of a Tub, ed. A. C. Guthkelch and D. Nichol Smith, 2nd edn. (Oxford: Clarendon Press, 1958). Annotated.

Biography and Criticism

Davis, Herbert, *Jonathan Swift: Essays on His Satire and Other Studies* (New York: Oxford University Press, 1964).

Donoghue, Denis, *Jonathan Swift: A Critical Introduction* (Cambridge: Cambridge University Press, 1969).

Downie, J. A., *Jonathan Swift: Political Writer* (London: Routledge, 1984).

Ehrenpreis, Irvin, *Literary Meaning and Augustan Values* (Charlottesville, Va.: University Press of Virginia, 1974).

—— *The Personality of Jonathan Swift* (London: Methuen, 1958).

—— *Swift: The Man, His Works, and the Age*. Vol. i: *Mr. Swift and His Contemporaries* (London: Methuen, 1962). Vol. ii: *Dr. Swift* (London: Methuen, 1967). Vol. iii: *Dean Swift* (London: Methuen, 1983).

Elliott, Robert C., *The Power of Satire* (Princeton, NJ: Princeton University Press, 1960).

—— *The Literary Persona* (Chicago: University of Chicago Press, 1982).

Fabricant, Carole, *Swift's Landscape* (Baltimore: Johns Hopkins University Press, 1982, paperback 1995).

Ferguson, Oliver W., *Jonathan Swift and Ireland* (Urbana: University of Illinois Press, 1962).

Fox, Christopher (ed.), *The Cambridge Companion to Jonathan Swift* (Cambridge: Cambridge University Press, 2003).

Higgins, Ian, *Jonathan Swift*, Writers and their Work (Horndon, 2004).

—— 'Swift and Sparta: The Nostalgia of *Gulliver's Travels*', *Modern Language Review*, 78 (1983), 513–31.

—— *Swift's Politics: A Study in Disaffection* (Cambridge: Cambridge University Press, 1994).

Johnson, Samuel, 'Swift', in *Lives of the English Poets* (1779–81).

Landa, Louis A., *Essays in Eighteenth-Century Literature* (Princeton, NJ: Princeton University Press, 1980).

Leavis, F. R., 'The Irony of Swift', in *The Common Pursuit* (London: Chatto, 1952; Harmondsworth: Penguin, 1962). Essay frequently reprinted in collections of critical essays on Swift.

Lock, F. P., *Swift's Tory Politics* (London: Duckworth, and Newark: University of Delaware Press, 1983).

Mahony, Robert, *Jonathan Swift: The Irish Identity* (New Haven: Yale University Press, 1995).

Paulson, Ronald, *The Fictions of Satire* (Baltimore: Johns Hopkins Press, 1967).

Price, Martin, *Swift's Rhetorical Art* (New Haven: Yale University Press, 1953; Carbondale: Southern Illinois University Press Arcturus paperback, 1973).

—— *To the Palace of Wisdom: Studies in Order and Energy from Dryden to Blake* (Garden City, NY: Doubleday, 1964).

Quintana, Ricardo, *The Mind and Art of Jonathan Swift* (1936; repr. Gloucester, Mass.: Peter Smith, 1965).

—— *Swift: An Introduction* (London: Oxford University Press, 1955). The best short introductory book, reliable and lively.

—— *Two Augustans: John Locke, Jonathan Swift* (Madison: University of Wisconsin Press, 1978).

Rawson, Claude (ed.), *The Character of Swift's Satire: A Revised Focus* (Newark, Del.: Associated University Presses, 1983).

—— *God, Gulliver and Genocide: Barbarism and the European Imagination, 1492–1945* (Oxford: Oxford University Press, 2001, paperback 2002).

—— *Gulliver and the Gentle Reader: Studies in Swift and Our Time* (London: Routledge, 1973; paperback, Atlantic Highlands, NJ, and London: Humanities Press, 1991).

—— (ed.), *Jonathan Swift: A Collection of Critical Essays* (Englewood Cliffs, NJ: Prentice Hall, 1995); reprints pieces by John Lawlor, Claude Rawson, Robert C. Elliott, Marcus Walsh, Michael Seidel, John F. Tinkler, Christine Rees, Richard Feingold, Penelope Wilson, Ian Higgins, Michael McKeon, Douglas Lane Patey, Jenny Mezciems, A. D. Nuttall, and Oliver Ferguson.

—— *Order from Confusion Sprung: Studies in Eighteenth-Century Literature from Swift to Cowper* (London: Allen & Unwin, 1985; paperback, Atlantic Highlands, NJ, and London: Humanities Press, 1992).

—— *Satire and Sentiment 1660–1830* (Cambridge: Cambridge University Press, 1994; paperback Yale University Press, 2000).

Rogers, Pat, *Grub Street: Studies in a Subculture* (London: Methuen, 1972); abridged as *Hacks and Dunces: Pope, Swift, and Grub Street* (London: Methuen, 1980).

Rosenheim, Edward W., *Swift and the Satirist's Art* (Chicago: University of Chicago Press, 1963).

Steele, Peter, *Jonathan Swift, Preacher and Jester* (Oxford: Clarendon Press, 1978).

Thackeray, W. M. 'Swift', in *English Humorists of the Eighteenth Century* (London, 1853). The best-known and most controversial nineteenth-century discussion.

Williams, Kathleen (ed.), *Swift: The Critical Heritage* (London: Routledge, 1970). Collection of early criticism of Swift.

Gulliver's Travels

Barchas, Janine, *Graphic Design, Print Culture, and the Eighteenth-Century Novel* (Cambridge: Cambridge University Press, 2003).

Brady, Frank (ed.), *Twentieth-Century Interpretations of 'Gulliver's Travels'* (Englewood Cliffs, NJ: Prentice Hall, 1968). Mostly brief extracts rather than complete essays.

Carnochan, W. B., *Lemuel Gulliver's Mirror for Man* (Berkeley and Los Angeles: University of California Press, 1968).

e, Arthur E., *Four Essays on 'Gulliver's Travels'* (1945) (Gloucester, Mass.: P. Smith, 1958).

Crane, R. S., 'The Houyhnhnms, the Yahoos, and the History of Ideas', in J. A. Mazzeo (ed.), *Reason and the Imagination: Studies in the History of Ideas, 1600–1800* (New York: Columbia University Press, 1962). Reprinted in Crane's *The Idea of the Humanities and Other Essays*, 2 vols. (Chicago: University of Chicago Press, 1967). Contains important information crucial to a proper understanding of the Fourth Book.

Eddy, W. A., *'Gulliver's Travels': A Critical Study* (Princeton: Princeton University Press, 1923). Despite its title, concerned mainly with sources.

Elliott, Robert C., *The Power of Satire: Magic, Ritual, Art* (Princeton: Princeton University Press, 1960). A brilliant book in general, with a lively study of *Gulliver* in particular (see Biography and Criticism).

—— *The Shape of Utopia* (Chicago: University of Chicago Press, 1970).

Erskine-Hill, Howard, *Gulliver's Travels*, Landmarks of World Literature (Cambridge, Cambridge University Press, 1993).

Foster, Milton P. (ed.), *A Casebook on Gulliver among the Houyhnhnms* (New York: Crowell, 1961). An important collection of essays on the interpretation of the Fourth Book.

Goldgar, Bertrand A., *Walpole and the Wits: The Relation of Politics to Literature, 1722–1742* (Lincoln: University of Nebraska Press, 1976).

Gravil, Richard (ed.), *'Gulliver's Travels': A Casebook* (London: Macmillan, 1974). Collection of essays that usefully supplements Milton P. Foster, above.

Hammond, Brean, *Gulliver's Travels* (Milton Keynes: Open Guides, 1988).

Keener, Frederick M., *The Chain of Becoming: The Philosophical Tale, the Novel, and a Neglected Realism of the Enlightenment* (New York: Columbia University Press, 1983).

Kenner, Hugh, *The Counterfeiters: An Historical Comedy* (Baltimore: Johns Hopkins University Press, 1985; first published 1968 by Indiana University Press).

Lock, F. P., *The Politics of Gulliver's Travels* (Oxford: Clarendon Press, 1980).

Mezciems, Jenny. ' "'Tis not to divert the Reader": Moral and Literary Determinants in Some Early Travel Narratives', *Prose Studies*, 5 (1982), 1–19; also in *The Art of Travel: Essays on Travel Writing*, ed. Philip Dodd (London: Frank Cass, 1982).

—— 'The Unity of Swift's "Voyage to Laputa": Structure as Meaning in Utopian Fiction', *Modern Language Review*, 72 (1977), 1–21.

—— 'Utopia and "The Thing which is not"': More, Swift, and other Lying Idealists', *University of Toronto Quarterly*, 52 (1982), 40–62.

Orwell, George, 'Politics vs. Literature: An Examination of Gulliver's Travels' (1946), in *Collected Essays, Journalism, and Letters of George Orwell*, ed. Sonia Orwell and Ian Angus, vol. iv (London: Secker & Warburg, 1968). Included in several collections of essays on Swift: see above.

Rawson, Claude, *God, Gulliver and Genocide: Barbarism and the European Imagination, 1492–1945* (see Biography and Criticism).

—— *Gulliver and the Gentle Reader* (see Biography and Criticism).

Rielly, Edward J. (ed.), *Approaches to Teaching Gulliver's Travels* (New York: Modern Language Association of America, 1988).

Smith, Frederik N. (ed.), *The Genres of Gulliver's Travels* (Newark: University of Delaware Press; London: Associated University Presses, 1990). Includes essays by Paul K. Alkon, Louise K. Barnett, J. Paul Hunter, Maximillian E. Novak, William Bowman Piper, and others.

Tippett, Brian, *Gulliver's Travels*, The Critics Debate (Atlantic Highlands, NJ: Humanities Press, 1989).

Traugott, John, 'A Voyage to Nowhere with Thomas More and Jonathan Swift: *Utopia* and *The Voyage to the Houyhnhnms*', *Sewanee Review*, 69 (1961), 534–65.

Welcher, Jeanne K., and Bush, George E., Jr. (eds.), *Gulliveriana*, 8 vols. (Delmar, NY: Scholars' Facsimiles & Reprints, 1970–1999). Contains various contextual materials, sequels, imitations, and other associated works. *Gulliveriana VII* (1999) is a valuable study by Welcher of visual illustrations, 1726–1830.

A CHRONOLOGY OF JONATHAN SWIFT

1660   Restoration of Charles II

1663–4   Samuel Butler, *Hudibras*, i and ii

1667   Birth of Swift in Dublin on 30 November; birth of John
            Arbuthnot; Milton, *Paradise Lost* (1st edition); Thomas Sprat,
            History of the Royal Society

1670   Birth of William Congreve and Bernard Mandeville

1673–82   Swift at school at Kilkenny

1674   Milton, *Paradise Lost* (2nd edition, in 12 books); death of
            Milton

1678   Samuel Butler, *Hudibras*, iii

1679   Birth of Thomas Parnell, poet and friend of Swift and Pope
            and member of Scriblerus Club

1680   Sir William Temple, *Miscellanea*, i

1681   Dryden, *Absalom and Achitophel*

1682–9   Swift attends Trinity College Dublin, BA *speciali gratia* 1686.
            He remains there until the outbreak of war between James II
            and William of Orange.

1682   Dryden, *The Medall, Religio Laici, Mac Flecknoe*, Sir William
            Petty, *Essay Concerning the Multiplication of Mankind; together
            with an Essay on Political Arithmetick* (see 1690)

1685   Death of Charles II, accession of James II; birth of John Gay
            and George Berkeley

1687   Newton, *Principia*; James II's Declaration of Indulgence

1688   Glorious Revolution: William of Orange invades England and
            James II flees to France (transfer of the crown to William and
            Mary in 1689); as civil war breaks out in Ireland, Swift leaves
            for England (in January 1689); birth of Alexander Pope

1689   Swift employed in Sir William Temple's household at Moor
            Park, near Farnham, Surrey; meets Esther Johnson (Stella),
            then 8 years old; accession of William and Mary; John Locke,
            First Letter on Toleration

1690   James II defeated by William III in Ireland (Battle of the
            Boyne) and flees to France; Swift returns to Ireland in May;
            Temple, *Miscellanea*, ii, includes 'An Essay upon the Ancient

and Modern Learning', which triggers Phalaris controversy (rev. 1692); Locke, *Two Treatises of Government, Essay Concerning Human Understanding* (enlarged 1694–1700); *Second Letter on Toleration*; Petty, *Political Arithmetick* (see 1682)

1691   Treaty of Limerick (3 October) ends war in Ireland; Swift, *Ode: To the King on His Irish Expedition*; Swift back in England in August, and returns to Moor Park

1692   Swift obtains MA, Oxford; publishes *Ode to the Athenian Society*; Locke, *Third Letter on Toleration*; death of Shadwell

1693   Dryden, 'Discourse Concerning Satire', prefixed to translation of Juvenal and Persius; Locke, *Thoughts Concerning Education*

1694   Swift returns to Ireland, takes deacon's orders; William Wotton, *Reflections on Ancient and Modern Learning*; death of Mary II; founding of Bank of England; *Dictionary* of French Academy

1695   Swift ordained priest, becomes prebendary of Kilroot, near Belfast; Charles Boyle (ed.), *Epistles of Phalaris*; Locke, *Reasonableness of Christianity, Vindication of the Reasonableness of Christianity* (second *Vindication*, 1697)

1696–9 Swift at Moor Park, at work on *A Tale of a Tub* and related works

1697   Richard Bentley, 'Dissertation upon the *Epistles of Phalaris*' (in 2nd edn. of Wotton's *Reflections*, see 1694); birth of William Hogarth; William Dampier, *New Voyage round the World*

1698   Boyle, *Dr. Bentley's Dissertations on the Epistles of Phalaris and the Fables of Aesop Examin'd*; Jeremy Collier, *Short View of the Immorality and Profaneness of the English Stage* (controversy involving Congreve, Vanbrugh, Dryden and others continues for several years); William Molyneux, *The Case of Ireland Stated*; Dampier, *Voyages and Descriptions*

1699   Sir William Temple dies. Swift returns to Ireland after Temple's death as chaplain to Earl of Berkeley, Lord Justice of Ireland; Bentley, *Dissertation upon the Epistles of Phalaris, with an Answer to the Honourable Charles Boyle*

1700   Swift appointed Vicar of Laracor, Co. Meath, and prebendary of St Patrick's Cathedral, Dublin; death of Dryden; Temple, *Letters*, ed. Swift

1701   Swift goes to England with Lord Berkeley; publishes *Contests*

Addison and Steele start *Spectator*, to which Swift contributes; Shaftesbury, *Characteristics*; Harley becomes Earl of Oxford

1712   Swift, *Proposal for Correcting the English Tongue*; Pope, *Rape of the Locke* (2-canto version); Arbuthnot, *History of John Bull*; Gay, *The Mohocks*

1713   Swift installed as Dean of St Patrick's Cathedral, Dublin, and returns to London; founding of Scriblerus Club (including Swift, Pope, Arbuthnot, Gay, Parnell, and Robert Harley, Earl of Oxford); Swift, *Mr. Collins's Discourse of Free-Thinking*, *Importance of the Guardian Considered*; Pope, *Windsor-Forest*; Gay, *Rural Sports*; Parnell, *Essay on the Different Styles of Poetry*; Addison, *Cato*; Steele, *Guardian*, *Englishman*; Treaty of Utrecht ends War of Spanish Succession

1714   Swift returns to Ireland after fall of Tory government and death of Queen Anne; Swift, *Publick Spirit of the Whigs*, Pope, *Rape of the Lock* (5-canto version); Gay, *Shepherd's Week*; Mandeville, *Fable of the Bees* (expanded 1723); accession of George I

1715   Jacobite Rebellion; impeachment of Earl of Oxford on charges of Jacobite intrigue; death of Louis XIV of France

1715–20 Pope, translation of *Iliad*, 6 vols.

1716   Gossip about possible secret marriage to Stella; Gay, *Trivia*

1717   Earl of Oxford released from impeachment on procedural grounds; Pope, *Works*; Gay, Pope, and Arbuthnot, *Three Hours after Marriage*; Parnell, *Homer's Battle of the Frogs and Mice*

1718   Death of Parnell

1719   Defoe, *Robinson Crusoe*; death of Addison

1720   Swift, *Proposal for the Universal Use of Irish Manufacture; Letter to a Young Gentleman, Lately Entered into Holy Orders*; British House of Lords becomes ultimate court of appeal in Irish cases and British Parliament's right to legislate in Ireland asserted (Declaratory Act); South Sea Bubble

1721–42 Walpole emerges as leading Whig minister (1721)—Britain's first 'prime minister'

1721   Death of Matthew Prior

1722   Parnell, *Poems on Several Occasions*, ed. Pope; Defoe, *Journal of the Plague Year*, *Moll Flanders*, *Colonel Jack*; government discovery of a Jacobite conspiracy, the 'Atterbury Plot'

1723   Death of Vanessa

1724   Swift, *Drapier's Letters*; has popular reputation as Hibernian
            Patriot and government offers reward for 'discovery' of
            Drapier; death of Earl of Oxford

1724–34   Gilbert Burnet, *History of His Own Times*

1725   Pope's edition of Shakespeare (6 vols.)

1725–6   Pope's translation of *Odyssey* (5 vols.)

1726   Swift visits London for several months, stays with Pope,
            has unfruitful meeting with Walpole discussing Irish affairs;
            Gulliver's Travels, Cadenus and Vanessa; Lewis Theobald,
            Shakespeare Restored; Craftsman (opposition paper) started

1727   Swift's final visit to London; death of George I, accession of
            George II

1727–38   Gay, *Fables*

1728   Death of Stella, Swift writes 'On the Death of Mrs. Johnson';
            Short View of the State of Ireland; Swift and Thomas Sheridan,
            Intelligencer; Pope, *Dunciad* (3-book version); Gay, *Beggar's
            Opera*

1728–37   Henry Fielding's career as playwright, over twenty plays acted
            and published

1729   Swift, *Modest Proposal*; Pope, *Dunciad Variorum*, dedicated to
            Swift; death of Congreve, Steele

1730   Colley Cibber, Poet Laureate

1731   Swift writes *Verses on the Death of Dr. Swift* (published 1739)
            and several of the so-called 'scatological poems'; Pope, *Epistle
            to Burlington*; death of Defoe

1732   Pope, *Epistle to Bathurst*; death of Gay

1733   Swift, *On Poetry: A Rapsody, Epistle to a Lady*; Pope, *Epistle to
            Cobham*; death of Mandeville

1733–4   Pope, *Essay on Man, First Satire of the Second Book of Horace,
            Imitated*

1735   Swift, *Works*, Dublin (4 volumes; volume iii includes revised
            version of *Gulliver's Travels*); Pope, *Epistle to Dr. Arbuthnot,
            Epistle to a Lady*; death of Arbuthnot

1736   Swift, *The Legion Club*, attacking members of Irish Parliament

1737   Swift, *A Proposal for Giving Badges to the Beggars*; Stage
            Licensing Act

1738   Swift, *Complete Collection of Genteel and Ingenious Conversation*;
            Pope, *Epilogue to the Satires*; Samuel Johnson, *London*

1739   Swift, *Verses on the Death of Dr. Swift* published

1740   Richardson, *Pamela*, Colley Cibber, *Apology for his Life*; birth
        of James Boswell

1741   Arbuthnot, Pope, and others, *Memoirs of Martinus Scriblerus*;
        Fielding, *Shamela*

1742   Swift declared 'of unsound mind and memory'; Pope, *New
        Dunciad* (Book IV of *Dunciad*); Fielding, *Joseph Andrews*;
        Walpole resigns all offices, is pensioned and created Earl of
        Orford

1743   Pope, *Dunciad* (four-book version, with Cibber replacing
        Theobald as hero); Fielding, *Miscellanies*, 3 vols. (includes
        Jonathan Wild)

1744   Death of Pope

1745   Death of Swift, 19 October; Swift, *Directions to Servants*; death
        of Walpole; Jacobite Rebellion

GULLIVER'S TRAVELS

CAPT. LEMUEL GULLIVER
Splendide Mendax. Hor.

Frontispiece portrait of Gulliver from the octavo edition, 1735

VOLUME III.

Of the Author's

WORKS.

CONTAINING,

TRAVELS

INTO SEVERAL

Remote Nations of the WORLD.

In Four PARTS, *viz.*

I. A Voyage to LIL-
LIPUT.

II. A Voyage to BROB-
DINGNAG.

III. A Voyage to LA-

PUTA, BALNIBARBI,
LUGGNAGG, GLUBB-
DUBDRIB and JAPAN.

IV. A Voyage to the
COUNTRY of the
HOUYHNHNMS.

By *LEMUEL GULLIVER*, first a Surgeon,
and then a CAPTAIN of several SHIPS.

———— *Retroq;*
Vulgus abhorret ab his.

In this Impression several Errors in the *London* and *Dublin*
Editions are corrected.

DUBLIN:

Printed by and for GEORGE FAULKNER, Printer
and Bookseller, in *Essex-Street*, opposite to the
Bridge. MDCCXXXV.

Title-page from the 1735 edition

ADVERTISEMENT*

MR. SYMPSON's *Letter to Captain* Gulliver,* *prefixed to this Volume, will make a long Advertisement unnecessary. Those Interpolations complained of by the Captain, were made by a Person since deceased,* on whose Judgment the Publisher relyed to make any Alterations that might be thought necessary. But, this Person, not rightly comprehending the Scheme of the Author, nor able to imitate his plain simple Style, thought fit among many other Alterations and Insertions, to compliment the Memory* of her late Majesty, by saying,* That she governed without a Chief Minister. We are assured, that the Copy sent to the Bookseller in London, was a Transcript of the Original, which Original being in the Possession of a very worthy Gentleman* in London, and a most intimate Friend of the Authors; after he had bought the Book in Sheets,* and compared it with the Originals, bound it up with blank Leaves, and made those Corrections, which the Reader will find in our Edition. For, the same Gentleman did us the Favour to let us transcribe his Corrections.*

A LETTER FROM CAPT. GULLIVER,* TO HIS COUSIN SYMPSON*

I HOPE you will be ready to own publickly, whenever you shall be called to it, that by your great and frequent Urgency you prevailed on me to publish a very loose and uncorrect Account of my Travels; with Direction to hire some young Gentlemen of either University to put them in Order, and correct the Style, as my Cousin *Dampier** did by my Advice, in his Book called, *A Voyage round the World.* But I do not remember I gave you Power to consent, that any thing should be omitted, and much less that any thing should be inserted: Therefore, as to the latter, I do here renounce every thing of that Kind; particularly a Paragraph* about her Majesty the late Queen *Anne*, of most pious and glorious Memory; although I did reverence and esteem her more than any of human Species. But you, or your Interpolator, ought to have considered, that as it was not my Inclination, so was it not decent to praise any Animal of our Composition* before my Master *Houyhnhnm*:* And besides, the Fact was altogether false; for to my Knowledge, being in *England* during some Part of her Majesty's Reign, she did govern by a chief Minister; nay, even by two successively; the first whereof was the Lord of *Godolphin*, and the second the Lord of *Oxford*;* so that you have made me *say the thing that was not.** Likewise, in the Account of the Academy of Projectors, and several Passages of my Discourse to my Master *Houyhnhnm*, you have either omitted some material Circumstances, or minced or changed them in such a Manner, that I do hardly know mine own Work.* When I formerly hinted to you something of this in a Letter, you were pleased to answer, that you were afraid of giving Offence; that People in Power were very watchful over the Press; and apt not only to interpret, but to punish every thing which looked like an *Inuendo* (as I think you called it.)* But pray, how could that which I spoke so many Years ago, and at about five Thousand Leagues distance, in another Reign, be applyed to any of the *Yahoos*,* who now are said to govern the Herd; especially, at a time when I little thought on or feared the Unhappiness of living under them. Have not I the most Reason to complain, when I see these very *Yahoos* carried by *Houyhnhnms* in a Vehicle, as if these* were Brutes, and those* the rational Creatures? And, indeed, to avoid so monstrous and detestable a Sight, was one principal Motive of my Retirement hither.*

Thus much I thought proper to tell you in Relation to yourself, and to the Trust I reposed in you.

I do in the next Place complain of my own great Want of Judgment, in being prevailed upon by the Intreaties and false Reasonings of you and some others, very much against mine own Opinion, to suffer my Travels to be published. Pray bring to your Mind how often I desired you to consider, when you insisted on the Motive of *publick Good*; that the *Yahoos* were a Species of Animals utterly incapable of Amendment by Precepts or Examples: And so it hath proved; for instead of seeing a full Stop put to all Abuses and Corruptions, at least in this little Island, as I had Reason to expect: Behold, after above six Months Warning, I cannot learn that my Book hath produced one single Effect according to mine Intentions: I desired you would let me know by a Letter, when Party and Faction were extinguished; Judges learned and upright; Pleaders honest and modest, with some Tincture of common Sense; and *Smithfield** blazing with Pyramids of Law-Books; the young Nobility's Education entirely changed; the Physicians banished; the Female *Yahoos* abounding in Virtue, Honour, Truth and good Sense: Courts and Levees of great Ministers thoroughly weeded and swept; Wit, Merit and Learning rewarded; all Disgracers of the Press in Prose and Verse, condemned to eat nothing but their own Cotten* and quench their Thirst with their own Ink. These, and a Thousand other Reformations, I firmly counted upon by your Encouragement; as indeed they were plainly deducible from the Precepts delivered in my Book. And, it must be owned, that seven Months were a sufficient Time to correct every Vice and Folly to which *Yahoos* are subject; if their Natures had been capable of the least Disposition to Virtue or Wisdom: Yet so far have you been from answering mine Expectation in any of your Letters; that on the contrary, you are loading our Carrier every Week with Libels, and Keys, and Reflections, and Memoirs, and Second Parts;* wherein I see myself accused of reflecting upon great States-Folk; of degrading human Nature, (for so they have still the Confidence to stile it), and of abusing the Female Sex. I find likewise, that the Writers of those Bundles are not agreed among themselves; for some of them will not allow me to be Author of mine own Travels; and others make me Author of Books to which I am wholly a Stranger.

I find likewise, that your Printer hath been so careless as to confound the Times,* and mistake the Dates of my several Voyages and Returns; neither assigning the true Year, or the true Month, or Day of the Month: And I hear the original Manuscript is all destroyed,* since the Publication of my Book. Neither have I any Copy left; however, I have sent you some Corrections, which you may insert, if ever there should be a second Edition: And yet I cannot stand to them,* but shall leave that Matter to my judicious and candid Readers, to adjust it as they please.

I hear some of our Sea-*Yahoos* find Fault with my Sea-Language, as not proper in many Parts, nor now in Use.* I cannot help it. In my first Voyages, while I was young, I was instructed by the oldest Mariners, and learned to speak as they did. But I have since found that the Sea-*Yahoos* are apt, like the Land ones, to become new fangled in their Words; which the latter change every Year; insomuch, as I remember upon each Return to mine own Country, their old Dialect was so altered, that I could hardly understand the new. And I observe, when any *Yahoo* comes from *London* out of Curiosity to visit me at mine own House, we neither of us are able to deliver our Conceptions* in a Manner intelligible to the other.

If the Censure of *Yahoos* could any Way affect me, I should have great Reason to complain, that some of them are so bold as to think my Book of Travels a meer Fiction out of mine own Brain; and have gone so far as to drop Hints, that the *Houyhnhnms* and *Yahoos* have no more Existence than the Inhabitants of *Utopia*.*

Indeed I must confess, that as to the people of *Lilliput, Brobdingrag*, (for so the Word should have been spelt, and not erroneously *Brobdingnag*), and *Laputa*, I have never yet heard of any *Yahoo* so presumptuous as to dispute their Being, or the Facts I have related concerning them; because the Truth immediately strikes every Reader with Conviction.* And, is there less Probability in my Account of the *Houyhnhnms* or *Yahoos*, when it is manifest as to the latter, there are so many Thousands even in this City, who only differ from their Brother Brutes in *Houyhnhnmland*, because they use a Sort of *Jabber*, and do not go naked. I wrote for their Amendment, and not their Approbation. The united Praise of the whole Race would be of less Consequence to me, than the neighing of those two degenerate *Houyhnhnms* I keep in my Stable; because, from these, degenerate as they are, I still improve in some Virtues, without any Mixture of Vice.

Do these miserable Animals* presume to think that I am so far degenerated as to defend my Veracity; *Yahoo* as I am, it is well known through all *Houyhnhnmland*, that by the Instructions and Example of my illustrious Master, I was able in the Compass of two Years (although I confess with the utmost Difficulty) to remove that infernal Habit of Lying, Shuffling, Deceiving, and Equivocating, so deeply rooted in the very Souls of all my Species; especially the *Europeans*.

I have other Complaints to make upon this vexatious Occasion; but I forbear troubling myself or you any further. I must freely confess, that since my last Return, some Corruptions of my *Yahoo* Nature have revived in me by conversing with a few of your Species, and particularly those of mine own Family, by an unavoidable Necessity; else I should never have attempted so absurd a Project as that of reforming the *Yahoo* Race in this Kingdom; but I have now done with all such visionary Schemes for ever.

April 2, 1727

THE PUBLISHER TO THE READER*

THE AUTHOR of these Travels, Mr *Lemuel Gulliver*, is my ancient and intimate Friend; there is likewise some Relation between us by the Mother's Side. About three Years ago Mr *Gulliver* growing weary of the Concourse of curious People coming to him at his House in *Redriff*,* made a small Purchase of Land, with a convenient House, near *Newark*, in *Nottinghamshire*, his native Country; where he now lives retired, yet in good Esteem among his Neighbours.

Although Mr *Gulliver* was born in *Nottinghamshire*, where his Father dwelt, yet I have heard him say, his Family came from *Oxfordshire*; to confirm which, I have observed in the Church-Yard at *Banbury*,* in that County, several Tombs and Monuments of the *Gullivers*.

Before he quitted *Redriff*, he left the Custody of the following Papers in my Hands, with the Liberty to dispose of them as I should think fit. I have carefully perused them three Times: The Style is very plain and simple; and the only Fault I find is, that the Author, after the Manner of Travellers, is a little too circumstantial. There is an Air of Truth apparent through the whole; and indeed the Author was so distinguished for his Veracity,* that it became a Sort of Proverb among his Neighbours at *Redriff*, when any one affirmed a Thing, to say, it was as true as if Mr *Gulliver* had spoke it.

By the Advice of several worthy Persons, to whom, with the Author's Permission, I communicated these Papers, I now venture to send them into the World; hoping they may be, at least for some time, a better Entertainment to our young Noblemen, than the common Scribbles of Politicks and Party.

This Volume would have been at least twice as large,* if I had not made bold to strike out innumerable Passages relating to the Winds and Tides,* as well as to the Variations and Bearings in the several Voyages; together with the minute Descriptions of the Management of the Ship in Storms, in the Style of Sailors: Likewise the Account of the Longitudes and Latitudes; wherein I have Reason to apprehend that Mr *Gulliver* may be a little dissatisfied: But I was resolved to fit the Work as much as possible to the general Capacity of Readers. However, if my own Ignorance in Sea-Affairs shall have led me to commit some Mistakes, I alone am answerable for them: And if any Traveller hath a Curiosity to see the whole Work at large, as it came from the Hand of the Author, I will be ready to gratify him.

As for any further Particulars relating to the Author, the Reader will receive Satisfaction from the first Pages of the Book.

Richard Sympson

PART ONE

*A Voyage to Lilliput**

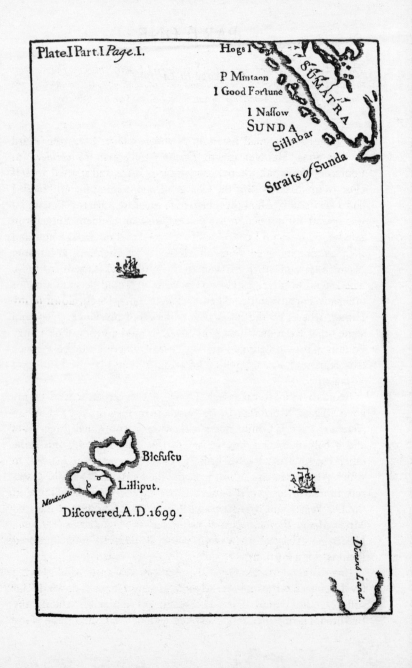

Plate.I Part.I *Page.*I.

Hogs I.

SUMATRA

P Mintaon
I Good Fortune

I Naſſow

SUNDA

Siſſabar

Straits *of* Sunda

Blefuscu

Mendendo

Lilliput.

Diſcovered, A. D. 1699.

Dinards Land.

CHAPTER ONE

The Author giveth some Account of himself and Family; his first Inducements to travel. He is shipwrecked, and swims for his Life; gets safe on shoar in the Country of Lilliput; *is made a Prisoner, and carried up the Country.*

MY father had a small Estate in *Nottinghamshire*; I was the Third of five Sons. He sent me to *Emanuel-College* in *Cambridge*,* at Fourteen* Years old, where I resided three Years, and applied my self close to my Studies: But the Charge of maintaining me (although I had a very scanty Allowance) being too great for a narrow Fortune; I was bound Apprentice to Mr *James Bates*, an eminent Surgeon in *London*, with whom I continued four Years; and my Father now and then sending me small Sums of Money, I laid them out in learning Navigation, and other Parts of the Mathematicks, useful to those who intend to travel, as I always believed it would be some time or other my Fortune to do. When I left Mr *Bates*, I went down to my Father; where, by the Assistance of him and my Uncle *John*, and some other Relations, I got Forty Pounds, and a Promise of Thirty Pounds a Year to maintain me at *Leyden*:* There I studied Physick two Years and seven Months, knowing it would be useful in long Voyages.

Soon after my Return from *Leyden*, I was recommended by my good Master Mr *Bates*, to be Surgeon to the *Swallow*,* Captain *Abraham Pannell* Commander; with whom I continued three Years and a half, making a Voyage or two into the *Levant*,* and some other Parts. When I came back, I resolved to settle in *London*, to which Mr *Bates*, my Master, encouraged me; and by him I was recommended to several Patients. I took Part of a small House in the *Old Jury*;* and being advised to alter my Condition, I married Mrs* *Mary Burton*, second Daughter to Mr *Edmond Burton*, Hosier, in *Newgate-street*, with whom I received four Hundred Pounds* for a Portion.*

But, my good Master *Bates*,* dying in two Years after, and I having few Friends, my Business began to fail; for my Conscience would not suffer me to imitate the bad Practice of too many among my Brethren. Having therefore consulted with my Wife, and some of my

Acquaintance, ~~I determined to go again to Sea~~. I was Surgeon successively in two Ships, and made several Voyages, for six Years, to the *East* and *West-Indies*; by which I got some Addition to my Fortune.* My Hours of Leisure I spent in reading the best Authors, ancient and modern; being always provided with a good Number of Books; and when I was ashore, in observing the Manners and Dispositions of the People, as well as learning their Language; wherein I had a great Facility by the Strength of my Memory.

The last of these Voyages not proving very fortunate, I grew weary of the Sea, and intended to stay at home with my Wife and Family. I removed from the *Old Jury* to *Fetter-Lane*, and from thence to *Wapping*,* hoping to get Business among the Sailors; but it would not turn to account. After three Years Expectation that things would mend, I accepted an advantageous Offer from Captain *William Prichard*, Master of the *Antelope*, who was making a Voyage to the *South-Sea*. We set sail from *Bristol*, *May* 4th, 1699,* and our Voyage at first was very prosperous.

It would not be proper for some Reasons, to trouble the Reader* with the Particulars of our Adventures in those Seas: Let it suffice to inform him, that in our Passage from thence to the *East-Indies*, we were driven by a violent Storm to the North-west of *Van Diemen*'s Land.* By an Observation, we found ourselves in the Latitude of 30 Degrees 2 Minutes South. Twelve of our Crew were dead by immoderate Labour, and ill Food; the rest were in a very weak Condition. On the fifth of *November*,* which was the beginning of Summer in those Parts, the Weather being very hazy, the Seamen spyed a Rock, within half a Cable's length* of the Ship; but the Wind was so strong, that we were driven directly upon it, and immediately split. Six of the Crew, of whom I was one, having let down the Boat into the Sea, made a Shift* to get clear of the Ship, and the Rock. We rowed by my Computation, about three Leagues, till we were able to work no longer, being already spent with Labour while we were in the Ship. We therefore trusted ourselves to the Mercy of the Waves; and in about half an Hour the Boat was overset by a sudden Flurry from the North. What became of my Companions in the Boat, as well as of those who escaped on the Rock, or were left in the Vessel, I cannot tell; but conclude they were all lost. For my own Part, I swam as Fortune directed me, and was pushed forward by Wind and Tide. I often let my Legs drop, and could feel no Bottom: But when I was almost gone, and able to struggle no longer, I found myself within my Depth; and by this Time the Storm was much abated. The Declivity was so small, that I walked near a Mile before I got to the Shore, which I conjectured was about Eight o'Clock in the Evening. I then advanced forward near half a Mile, but could not discover any Sign of Houses or Inhabitants; at least I was in so weak a Condition, that I did not observe them. I was extremely tired, and with that, and the Heat of the Weather, and about half a Pint of Brandy that I drank as I left the Ship, I found my self much inclined to sleep. I lay down on the Grass, which was very short and soft; where I slept sounder than ever I remember to have done in my Life, and as I reckoned, above Nine Hours; for when I awaked,* it was just Day-light. I attempted to rise, but was not able to stir: For as I happened to lie on my Back, I found my Arms and Legs were strongly fastened on each Side to the Ground; and my Hair, which was long and thick, tied down in the same Manner. I likewise felt several slender Ligatures across my Body, from my Armpits to my Thighs. I could only look upwards; the Sun began to grow hot, and the Light offended mine Eyes. I heard a confused Noise about me, but in the Posture I lay, could see nothing except the Sky. In a little time I felt something alive moving on my left Leg, which advancing gently forward over my Breast, came almost up to my Chin; when bending mine Eyes downwards as much as I could, I perceived it to be a human Creature not six Inches high,* with a Bow and Arrow in his Hands, and a Quiver at his Back. In the mean time, I felt at least Forty more of the same Kind (as I conjectured) following the first. I was in the utmost Astonishment, and roared so loud, that they all ran back in a Fright; and some of them, as I was afterwards told, were hurt with the Falls they got by leaping from my Sides upon the Ground. However, they soon returned; and one of them, who ventured so far as to get a full Sight of my Face, lifting up his Hands and Eyes by way of Admiration,* cryed out in a shrill, but distinct Voice, *Hekinah Degul*: The others repeated the same Words several times, but I then knew not what they meant. I lay all this while, as the Reader may believe, in great Uneasiness: At length, struggling to get loose, I had the Fortune to break the Strings, and wrench out the Pegs that fastened my left Arm to the Ground; for, by lifting it up to my Face, I discovered the Methods they had taken to bind me; and, at the same time, with a violent Pull, which gave me excessive Pain, I a little

loosened the Strings that tied down my Hair on the left Side; so that
I was just able to turn my Head about two Inches. But the Creatures
ran off a second time, before I could seize them; whereupon there
was a great Shout in a very shrill Accent; and after it ceased, I heard
one of them cry aloud, *Tolgo Phonac*; when in an Instant I felt above
an Hundred Arrows discharged on my left Hand, which pricked me
like so many Needles; and besides, they shot another Flight into the
Air, as we do Bombs* in *Europe*; whereof many, I suppose, fell on my
Body, (though I felt them not) and some on my Face, which I
immediately covered with my left Hand. When this Shower of
Arrows was over, I fell a groaning with Grief and Pain; and then
striving again to get loose, they discharged another Volly larger than
the first; and some of them attempted with Spears to stick me in the
Sides; but, by good Luck, I had on me a Buff Jerkin,* which they
could not pierce. I thought it the most prudent Method to lie still;
and my Design was to continue so till Night, when my left Hand
being already loose, I could easily free myself: And as for
the Inhabitants, I had Reason to believe I might be a Match for the
greatest Armies they could bring against me, if they were all of the
same Size with him that I saw. But Fortune disposed otherwise of
me. When the People observed I was quiet, they discharged no more
Arrows: But by the Noise increasing, I knew their Numbers were
greater; and about four Yards from me, over-against my right Ear, I
heard a Knocking for above an Hour, like People at work; when
turning my Head that Way, as well as the Pegs and Strings would
permit me, I saw a Stage erected about a Foot and a half from the
Ground, capable of holding four of the Inhabitants, with two or
three Ladders to mount it: From whence one of them, who seemed
to be a Person of Quality, made me a long Speech, whereof I understood not one Syllable. But I should have mentioned, that before the
principal Person began his Oration, he cryed out three times *Langro
Dehul san*: (these Words and the former were afterwards repeated
and explained to me.) Whereupon immediately about fifty of the
Inhabitants came, and cut the Strings that fastened the left side of
my Head, which gave me the Liberty of turning it to the right, and
of observing the Person and Gesture of him who was to speak. He
appeared to be of a middle Age, and taller than any of the other three
who attended him; whereof one was a Page, who held up his Train,
and seemed to be somewhat longer than my middle Finger; the other

two stood one on each side to support him. He acted every part of an Orator; and I could observe many Periods of Threatnings, and others of Promises, Pity, and Kindness. I answered in a few Words, but in the most submissive Manner, lifting up my left Hand and both mine Eyes to the Sun, as calling him for a Witness; and being almost famished with Hunger, having not eaten a Morsel for some Hours before I left the Ship. I found the Demands of Nature so strong upon me, that I could not forbear shewing my Impatience (perhaps against the strict Rules of Decency) by putting my Finger frequently on my Mouth, to signify that I wanted Food. The *Hurgo* (for so they call a great Lord, as I afterwards learnt) understood me very well: He descended from the Stage, and commanded that several Ladders should be applied to my Sides, on which above an hundred of the Inhabitants mounted, and walked towards my Mouth, laden with Baskets full of Meat, which had been provided, and sent thither by the Kings's Orders upon the first Intelligence he received of me. I observed there was the Flesh of several Animals, but could not distinguish them by the Taste. There were Shoulders, Legs, and Loins shaped like those of Mutton, and very well dressed, but smaller than the Wings of a Lark. I eat them by two or three at a Mouthful; and took three Loaves at a time, about the bigness of Musket Bullets. They supplyed me as fast as they could, shewing a thousand Marks of Wonder and Astonishment at my Bulk and Appetite. I then made another Sign that I wanted Drink. They found by my eating that a small Quantity would not suffice me; and being a most ingenious People, they slung up with great Dexterity one of their largest Hogsheads;* then rolled it towards my Hand, and beat out the Top; I drank it off at a Draught, which I might well do, for it hardly held half a Pint, and tasted like a small Wine of *Burgundy*, but much more delicious. They brought me a second Hogshead, which I drank in the same Manner, and made Signs for more, but they had none to give me. When I had performed these Wonders,* they shouted for Joy, and danced upon my Breast, repeating several times as they did at first, *Hekinah Degul*. They made me a Sign that I should throw down the two Hogsheads, but first warned the People below to stand out of the Way, crying aloud, *Borach Mivola*; and when they saw the Vessels in the Air, there was an universal Shout of *Hekinah Degul*. I confess I was often tempted, while they were passing backwards and forwards on my Body, to seize Forty or Fifty of the first that came in my

Reach, and dash them against the Ground. But the Remembrance of what I had felt, which probably might not be the worst they could do; and the Promise of Honour I made them, for so I interpreted my submissive Behaviour, soon drove out those Imaginations. Besides, I now considered my self as bound by the Laws of Hospitality to a People who had treated me with so much Expence and Magnificence. However, in my Thoughts I could not sufficiently wonder at the Intrepidity of these diminutive Mortals, who durst venture to mount and walk on my Body, while one of my Hands was at Liberty, without trembling at the very Sight of so prodigious a Creature as I must appear to them. After some time, when they observed that I made no more Demands for Meat, there appeared before me a Person of high Rank from his Imperial Majesty. His Excellency having mounted on the Small of my Right Leg, advanced forwards up to my Face, with about a Dozen of his Retinue; And producing his Credentials under the Signet Royal, which he applied close to mine Eyes, spoke about ten Minutes, without any Signs of Anger, but with a kind of determinate* Resolution; often pointing forwards, which, as I after-wards found was towards the Capital City, about half a Mile distant, whither it was agreed by his Majesty in Council that I must be conveyed. I answered in few Words, but to no Purpose, and made a Sign with my Hand that was loose, putting it to the other, (but over his Excellency's Head, for Fear of hurting him or his Train) and then to my own Head and Body, to signify that I desired my Liberty. It appeared that he understood me well enough; for he shook his Head by way of Disapprobation, and held his Hand in a Posture to shew that I must be carried as a Prisoner. However, he made other Signs to let me understand that I should have Meat and Drink enough, and very good Treatment. Whereupon I once more thought of attempting to break my Bonds; but again, when I felt the Smart of their Arrows upon my Face and Hands, which were all in Blisters, and many of the Darts still sticking in them; and observing likewise that the Number of my Enemies encreased; I gave Tokens to let them know that they might do with me what they pleased. Upon this, the *Hurgo* and his Train withdrew, with much Civility and chearful Countenances. Soon after I heard a general Shout, with frequent Repetitions of the Words, *Peplom Selan*, and I felt great Numbers of the People on my Left Side relaxing the Cords to such a Degree, that I was able to turn upon my Right, and to ease my self with making Water; which I very plentifully did, to the great Astonishment of the People, who conjecturing by my Motions what I was going to do, immediately opened to the right and left on that Side, to avoid the Torrent which fell with such Noise and Violence from me. But before this, they had dawbed my Face and both my Hands with a sort of Ointment very pleasant to the Smell, which in a few Minutes removed all the Smart of their Arrows. These Circumstances, added to the Refreshment I had received by their Victuals and Drink, which were very nourishing, disposed me to sleep. I slept about eight Hours as I was afterwards assured; and it was no Wonder; for the Physicians, by the Emperor's Order, had mingled a sleeping Potion in the Hogsheads of Wine.

It seems that upon the first Moment I was discovered sleeping on the Ground after my Landing, the Emperor had early Notice of it by an Express;* and determined in Council that I should be tyed in the Manner I have related (which was done in the Night while I slept) that Plenty of Meat and Drink should be sent to me, and a Machine prepared to carry me to the Capital City.

This Resolution perhaps may appear very bold and dangerous, and I am confident would not be imitated by any Prince in *Europe* on the like Occasion; however, in my Opinion it was extremely Prudent as well as Generous. For supposing these People had endeavoured to kill me with their Spears and Arrows while I was asleep; I should certainly have awaked with the first Sense of Smart, which might so far have rouzed my Rage and Strength, as to enable me to break the Strings wherewith I was tyed; after which, as they were not able to make Resistance, so they could expect no Mercy.

These People are most excellent Mathematicians, and arrived to a great Perfection in Mechanicks by the Countenance and Encouragement of the Emperor, who is a renowned Patron of Learning. This Prince hath several Machines fixed on Wheels, for the Carriage of Trees and other great Weights. He often buildeth his largest Men of War, whereof some are Nine Foot long, in the Woods where the Timber grows, and has them carried on these Engines* three or four Hundred Yards to the Sea. Five Hundred Carpenters and Engineers were immediately set at work to prepare the greatest Engine they had. It was a Frame of Wood raised three Inches from the Ground, about seven Foot long and four wide, moving upon twenty-two Wheels. The Shout I heard, was upon the Arrival of this Engine, which, it seems, set out in four Hours after my Landing.

It was brought parallel to me as I lay. But the principal Difficulty was to raise and place me in this Vehicle. Eighty Poles, each of one Foot high, were erected for this Purpose, and very strong Cords of the bigness of Packthread were fastened by Hooks to many Bandages, which the Workmen had girt round my Neck, my Hands, my Body, and my Legs. Nine Hundred of the strongest Men were employed to draw up these Cords by many Pullies fastned on the Poles; and thus in less than three Hours, I was raised and slung into the Engine, and there tyed fast. All this I was told; for while the whole Operation was performing, I lay in a profound Sleep, by the Force of that soporiferous Medicine infused into my Liquor. Fifteen hundred of the Emperor's largest Horses, each about four Inches and a half high, were employed to draw me towards the Metropolis, which, as I said, was half a Mile distant.

About four Hours after we began our Journey, I awaked by a very ridiculous Accident; for the Carriage being stopt a while to adjust something that was out of Order, two or three of the young Natives had the Curiosity to see how I looked when I was asleep; they climbed up into the Engine, and advancing very softly to my Face, one of them, an Officer in the Guards, put the sharp End of his Half-Pike* a good way up into my left Nostril, which tickled my Nose like a Straw, and made me sneeze violently: Whereupon they stole off unperceived; and it was three Weeks before I knew the Cause of my awaking so suddenly. We made a long March the remaining Part of the Day, and rested at Night with Five Hundred Guards on each Side of me, half with Torches, and half with Bows and Arrows, ready to shoot me if I should offer to stir. The next Morning at Sun-rise we continued our March, and arrived within two Hundred Yards of the City-Gates about Noon. The Emperor, and all his Court, came out to meet us; but his great Officers would by no means suffer his Majesty to endanger his Person by mounting on my Body.

At the Place where the Carriage stopt, there stood an ancient Temple, esteemed to be the largest in the whole Kingdom; which having been polluted some Years before by an unnatural Murder,* was, according to the Zeal of those People, looked upon as Prophane, and therefore had been applied to common Use, and all the Ornaments and Furniture carried away. In this Edifice it was deter-mined I should lodge. The great Gate fronting to the North was about four Foot high, and almost two Foot wide, through which I could easily creep. On each Side of the Gate was a small Window not above six Inches from the Ground: Into that on the Left Side, the King's Smiths conveyed fourscore and eleven Chains, like those that hang to a Lady's Watch in *Europe*, and almost as large, which were locked to my Left Leg with six and thirty Padlocks. Over against this Temple, on the other Side of the great Highway, at twenty Foot Distance, there was a Turret at least five Foot high. Here the Emperor ascended with many principal Lords of his Court, to have an Opportunity of viewing me, as I was told, for I could not see them. It was reckoned that above an hundred thousand Inhabitants came out of the Town upon the same Errand; and in spight of my Guards, I believe there could not be fewer than ten thousand, at several Times, who mounted upon my Body by the Help of Ladders. But a Proclamation was soon issued to forbid it, upon Pain of Death. When the Workmen found it was impossible for me to break loose, they cut all the Strings that bound me; whereupon I rose up with as melancholly a Disposition as ever I had in my Life. But the Noise and Astonishment of the People at seeing me rise and walk, are not to be expressed. The Chains that held my left Leg were about two Yards long, and gave me not only the Liberty of walking backwards and forwards in a Semicircle; but being fixed within four Inches of the Gate, allowed me to creep in, and lie at my full Length in the Temple.

CHAPTER TWO

The Emperor of Lilliput, attended by several of the Nobility, comes to see the Author in his Confinement. The Emperor's Person and Habit described. Learned Men appointed to teach the Author their Language. He gains Favour by his mild Disposition. His Pockets are searched, and his Sword and Pistols taken from him.

WHEN I found myself on my Feet, I looked about me, and must confess I never beheld a more entertaining Prospect. The Country round appeared like a continued Garden; and the inclosed Fields, which were generally Forty Foot square, resembled so many Beds of Flowers. These Fields were intermingled with Woods of half a Stang,* and the tallest Trees, as I could judge, appeared to be seven Foot high. I viewed the Town on my left Hand, which looked like the painted Scene of a City in a Theatre.

I had been for some Hours extremely pressed by the Necessities of Nature; which was no Wonder, it being almost two Days since I had last disburthened myself. I was under great Difficulties between Urgency and Shame. The best Expedient I could think on, was to creep into my House, which I accordingly did; and shutting the Gate after me, I went as far as the Length of my Chain would suffer; and discharged my Body of that uneasy Load. But this was the only Time I was ever guilty of so uncleanly an Action; for which I cannot but hope the candid Reader will give some Allowance, after he hath maturely and impartially considered my Case, and the Distress I was in. From this Time my constant Practice was, as soon as I rose, to perform that Business in open Air, at the full Extent of my Chain; and due Care was taken every Morning before Company came, that the offensive Matter should be carried off in Wheel-barrows, by two Servants appointed for that Purpose. I would not have dwelt so long upon a Circumstance, that perhaps at first Sight may appear not very momentous; if I had not thought it necessary to justify my Character in Point of Cleanliness to the World; which I am told, some of my Maligners* have been pleased, upon this and other Occasions, to call in Question.

When this Adventure was at an End, I came back out of my

House, having Occasion for fresh Air. The Emperor was already descended from the Tower, and advancing on Horseback towards me, which had like to have cost* him dear; for the Beast, although very well trained, yet wholly unused to such a Sight, which appeared as if a Mountain moved before him, reared up on his hinder Feet: But that Prince, who is an excellent Horseman, kept his Seat, until his Attendants ran in, and held the Bridle, while his Majesty had Time to dismount. When he alighted, he surveyed me round with great Admiration, but kept beyond the Length of my Chains. He ordered his Cooks and Butlers, who were already prepared, to give me Victuals and Drink, which they pushed forward in a sort of Vehicles upon Wheels until I could reach them. I took those Vehicles, and soon emptied them all; twenty of them were filled with Meat, and ten with Liquor; each of the former afforded me two or three good Mouthfuls, and I emptied the Liquor of ten Vessels, which was contained in earthen Vials, into one Vehicle, drinking it off at a Draught; and so I did with the rest. The Empress, and young Princes of the Blood,* of both Sexes, attended by many Ladies, sate at some Distance in their Chairs; but upon the Accident that happened to the Emperor's Horse, they alighted, and came near his Person; which I am now going to describe. He is taller* by almost the Breadth of my Nail, than any of his Court; which alone is enough to strike an Awe into the Beholders. His Features* are strong and masculine, with an *Austrian* Lip,* and arched Nose,* his Complexion olive, his Countenance* erect, his Body and Limbs well proportioned, all his Motions graceful, and his Deportment majestick. He was then past his Prime,* being twenty-eight Years and three Quarters old, of which he had reigned about seven,* in great Felicity, and generally victorious. For the better Convenience of beholding him, I lay on my Side, so that my Face was parallel to his, and he stood but three Yards off: However, I have had him since many Times in my Hand, and therefore cannot be deceived in the Description. His Dress was very plain and simple, the Fashion of it between the *Asiatick* and the *European*;* but he had on his Head a light Helmet of Gold, adorned with Jewels, and a Plume on the Crest. He held his Sword drawn in his Hand, to defend himself, if I should happen to break loose; it was almost three Inches long, the Hilt and Scabbard were Gold enriched with Diamonds. His Voice was shrill, but very clear and articulate, and I could distinctly hear it when I stood up. The Ladies and

Courtiers were all most magnificently clad, so that the Spot they stood upon seemed to resemble a Petticoat spread on the Ground, embroidered with Figures of Gold and Silver. His Imperial Majesty spoke often to me, and I returned Answers, but neither of us could understand a Syllable. There were several of his Priests and Lawyers present (as I conjectured by their Habits) who were commanded to address themselves to me, and I spoke to them in as many Languages as I had the least Smattering of, which were *High* and *Low Dutch*,* *Latin*, *French*, *Spanish*, *Italian*, and *Lingua Franca*;* but all to no purpose. After about two Hours the Court retired, and I was left with a strong Guard, to prevent the Impertinence, and probably the Malice of the Rabble, who were very impatient to croud about me as near as they durst; and some of them had the Impudence to shoot their Arrows at me as I sate on the Ground by the Door of my House; whereof one very narrowly missed my left Eye. But the Colonel ordered six of the Ring-leaders to be seized, and thought no Punishment so proper as to deliver them bound into my Hands, which some of his Soldiers accordingly did, pushing them forwards with the But-ends of their Pikes into my Reach: I took them all in my right Hand, put five of them into my Coat-pocket; and as to the sixth, I made a Countenance as if I would eat him alive. The poor Man squalled terribly, and the Colonel and his Officers were in much Pain, especially when they saw me take out my Penknife: But I soon put them out of Fear; for, looking mildly, and immediately cutting the Strings he was bound with, I set him gently on the Ground, and away he ran. I treated the rest in the same Manner, taking them one by one out of my Pocket; and I observed, both the Soldiers and People were highly obliged at this Mark of my Clemency, which was represented very much to my Advantage at Court.

Towards Night I got with some Difficulty into my House, where I lay on the Ground, and continued to do so about a Fortnight; during which time the Emperor gave Orders to have a Bed prepared for me. Six Hundred Beds* of the common Measure were brought in Carriages, and worked up in my House; an Hundred and Fifty of their Beds sown together made up the Breadth and Length, and these were four double,* which however kept me but very indifferently from the Hardness of the Floor, that was of smooth Stone. By the same Computation they provided me with Sheets, Blankets, and

Coverlets, tolerable enough for one who had been so long enured to Hardships as I.

As the News of my Arrival spread through the Kingdom, it brought prodigious Numbers of rich, idle, and curious People to see me; so that the Villages were almost emptied, and great Neglect of Tillage and Household Affairs must have ensued, if his Imperial Majesty had not provided by several Proclamations and Orders of State against this Inconveniency. He directed that those, who had already beheld me, should return home, and not presume to come within fifty Yards of my House, without Licence from Court; whereby the Secretaries of State got considerable Fees.

In the mean time, the Emperor held frequent Councils to debate what Course should be taken with me; and I was afterwards assured by a particular Friend, a Person of great Quality, who was as much in the *Secret* as any; that the Court was under many Difficulties concerning me. They apprehended my breaking loose; that my Diet would he very expensive, and might cause a Famine. Sometimes they determined to starve me, or at least to shoot me in the Face and Hands with poisoned Arrows, which would soon dispatch me: But again they considered, that the Stench of so large a Carcase might produce a Plague in the Metropolis, and probably spread through the whole Kingdom. In the midst of these Consultations, several Officers of the Army went to the Door of the great Council-Chamber; and two of them being admitted, gave an Account of my Behaviour to the six Criminals above-mentioned; which made so favourable an Impression in the Breast of his Majesty, and the whole Board, in my Behalf, that an Imperial Commission was issued out, obliging all the Villages nine hundred Yards round the City to deliver in every Morning six Beeves,* forty Sheep, and other Victuals for my Sustenance; together with a proportionable Quantity of Bread and Wine, and other Liquors: For the due Payment of which his Majesty gave Assignments upon his Treasury. For this Prince lives chiefly upon his own Demesnes;* seldom, except upon great Occasions raising any Subsidies* upon his Subjects, who are bound to attend him in his Wars at their own Expence. An Establishment was also made of Six Hundred Persons to be my Domesticks, who had Board-Wages allowed for their Maintenance, and Tents built for them very conveniently on each side of my Door. It was likewise ordered, that three hundred Taylors should make me a Suit of Cloaths after the

Fashion of the Country: That, six of his Majesty's greatest Scholars should be employed to instruct me in their Language: And, lastly, that the Emperor's Horses, and those of the Nobility, and Troops of Guards, should be exercised in my Sight, to accustom themselves to me. All these Orders were duly put in Execution; and in about three Weeks I made a great Progress in Learning their Language; during which Time, the Emperor frequently honoured me with his Visits, and was pleased to assist my Masters in teaching me. We began already to converse together in some Sort; and the first Words I learnt, were to express my Desire, that he would please to give me my Liberty; which I every Day repeated on my Knees. His Answer, as I could apprehend, was, that this must be a Work of Time, not to be thought on without the Advice of his Council; and that first I must *Lumos Kelmin pesso desmar lon Emposo*; that is, *Swear a Peace with him and his Kingdom*. However, that I should be used with all Kindness; and he advised me to acquire by my Patience and discreet Behaviour, the Good opinion of himself and his Subjects. He desired I would not take it ill, if he gave Orders to certain proper Officers to search me; for probably I might carry about me several Weapons,* which must needs be dangerous Things, if they answered the Bulk of so prodigious a Person. I said, his Majesty should be satisfied, for I was ready to strip my self, turn up my Pockets before him. This I delivered, part in Words and part in Signs. He replied, that by the Laws of the Kingdom, I must be searched by two of his Officers: That he knew this could not be done without my Consent and Assistance; that he had so good an Opinion of my Generosity and Justice, as to trust their Persons in my Hands: That whatever they took from me should be returned when I left the Country, or paid for at the Rate which I would set upon them. I took up the two Officers in my Hands, put them first into my Coat-Pockets, and then into every other Pocket about me, except my two Fobs, and another secret Pocket which I had no Mind should be searched, wherein I had some little Necessaries of no Consequence to any but my self. In one of my Fobs there was a Silver Watch, and in the other a small Quantity of Gold in a Purse. These Gentlemen, having Pen, Ink, and Paper about them, made an exact Inventory of every thing they saw, and when they had done, desired I would set them down, that they might deliver it to the Emperor. This Inventory I afterwards translated into *English*, and is Word for Word as follows.

IMPRIMIS,* In the right Coat-Pocket of the *Great Man Mountain* (for so I interpret the Words *Quinbus Flestrin*) after the strictest Search, we found only one great Piece of coarse Cloth, large enough to be a Foot-Cloth* for your Majesty's chief Room of State. In the left Pocket, we saw a huge Silver Chest, with a Cover of the same Metal, which we, the Searchers, were not able to lift. We desired it should be opened; and one of us stepping into it, found himself up to the mid Leg in a sort of Dust, some part whereof flying up to our Faces, set us both a sneezing for several Times together. In his right Waistcoat-Pocket, we found a prodigious Bundle of thin white Substances, folded one above another, about the Bigness of three Men, tied with a strong Cable, and marked with Black Figures; which we humbly conceive to be Writings, every Letter almost half as large as the Palm of our Hands. In the left there was a sort of Engine, from the Back of which were extended twenty long Poles, resembling the Pallisado's before your Majesty's Court; wherewith we conjecture the *Man Mountain* combs his Head; for we did not always trouble him with Questions, because we found it a great Difficulty to make him understand us. In the large Pocket on the right Side of his middle Cover, (so I translate the word *Ranfu-Lo*, by which they meant my Breeches) we saw a hollow Pillar of Iron, about the Length of a Man, fastened to a strong Piece of Timber, larger than the Pillar; and upon one side of the Pillar were huge Pieces of Iron sticking out, cut into strange Figures; which we know not what to make of. In the left Pocket, another Engine of the same kind. In the smaller Pocket on the right Side, were several round flat Pieces of white and red Metal,* of different Bulk: Some of the white, which seemed to be Silver, were so large and heavy, that my Comrade and I could hardly lift them. In the left Pocket were two black Pillars irregularly shaped: we could not, without Difficulty, reach the Top of them as we stood at the Bottom of his Pocket: One of them was covered, and seemed all of a Piece; but at the upper End of the other, there appeared a white round Substance, about twice the bigness of our Heads. Within each of these was inclosed a prodigious Plate of Steel; which, by our Orders, we obliged him to shew us, because we apprehended they might be dangerous Engines. He took them out of their Cases, and told us, that in his own Country his Practice was to shave his Beard with one of these, and to cut his Meat with the other. There were two Pockets which we could not enter:

These he called his Fobs; they were two large Slits cut into the Top
of his middle Cover, but squeezed close by the pressure of his Belly.
Out of the right Fob hung a great Silver Chain, with a wonderful
kind of Engine at the Bottom. We directed him to draw out whatever
was at the End of that Chain; which appeared to be a Globe, half
Silver, and half of some transparent Metal: for on the transparent
Side we saw certain strange Figures circularly drawn, and thought
we could touch them, until we found our Fingers stopped with that
lucid Substance. He put this Engine to our Ears, which made an
incessant Noise like that of a Water-Mill. And we conjecture it is
either some unknown Animal, or the God that he worships: But we
are more inclined to the latter Opinion, because he assured us (if we
understood him right, for he expressed himself very imperfectly)
that he seldom did any Thing without consulting it. He called it his
Oracle, and said it pointed out the Time for every Action of his Life.
From the left Fob he took out a Net almost large enough for a
Fisherman, but contrived to open and shut like a Purse, and served
him for the same Use: We found therein several massy Pieces of
yellow Metal, which if they be real Gold, must be of immense Value.

HAVING thus, in Obedience to your Majesty's Commands, diligently searched all his Pockets; we observed a Girdle about his Waist
made of the Hyde of some prodigious Animal; from which, on the
left Side, hung a Sword of the Length of five Men; and on the right,
a Bag or Pouch divided into two Cells; each Cell capable of holding
three of your Majesty's Subjects. In one of these Cells were several
Globes or Balls of a most ponderous Metal, about the Bigness of our
Heads, and required a strong Hand to lift them: The other Cell contained a Heap of certain black Grains, but of no great Bulk or Weight,
for we could hold above fifty of them in the Palms of our Hands.

THIS is an exact Inventory of what we found about the Body of
the *Man Mountain*; who used us with great Civility, and due Respect
to your Majesty's Commission. Signed and Sealed on the fourth Day
of the eighty ninth Moon of your Majesty's auspicious Reign.

Clefren Frelok, Marsi Frelock.

When this Inventory was read over to the Emperor, he directed
me to deliver up the several Particulars. He first called for my
Scymiter, which I took out, Scabbard and all. In the mean time he
ordered three thousand of his choicest Troops, who then attended

him, to surround me at a Distance, with their Bows and Arrows just ready to discharge: But I did not observe it; for mine Eyes were wholly fixed upon his Majesty. He then desired me to draw my Scymiter, which, although it had got some Rust by the Sea-Water, was in most Parts exceeding bright. I did so, and immediately all the Troops gave a Shout between Terror and Surprize; for the Sun shone clear, and the Reflexion dazzled their Eyes, as I waved the Scymiter to and fro in my Hand. His Majesty, who is a most magnanimous Prince, was less daunted than I could expect; he ordered me to return it into the Scabbard, and cast it on the Ground as gently as I could, about six Foot from the End of my Chain. The next Thing he demanded was one of the hollow Iron Pillars, by which he meant my Pocket-Pistols. I drew it out, and at his Desire, as well as I could, expressed to him the Use of it, and charging it only with Powder, which by the Closeness* of my Pouch, happened to escape wetting in the Sea, (an Inconvenience that all prudent Mariners take special Care to provide against) I first cautioned the Emperor not to be afraid; and then I let it off in the Air. The Astonishment here was much greater than at the Sight of my Scymiter. Hundreds fell down as if they had been struck dead; and even the Emperor, although he stood his Ground, could not recover himself in some time. I delivered up both my Pistols in the same Manner as I had done my Scymiter, and then my Pouch of Powder and Bullets; begging him that the former might be kept from Fire; for it would kindle with the smallest Spark, and blow up his Imperial Palace into the Air. I likewise delivered up my Watch, which the Emperor was very curious to see; and commanded two of his tallest Yeomen of the Guards to bear it on a Pole upon their Shoulders, as Dray-men in *England* do a Barrel of Ale. He was amazed at the continual Noise it made, and the Motion of the Minute-hand, which he could easily discern; for their Sight is much more acute than ours: He asked the Opinions of his learned Men about him, which were various and remote, as the Reader may well imagine without my repeating; although indeed I could not very perfectly understand them. I then gave up my Silver and Copper Money, my Purse with nine large Pieces of Gold, and some smaller ones; my Knife and Razor, my Comb and Silver Snuff-Box, my Handkerchief and Journal Book. My Scymiter, Pistols, and Pouch, were conveyed in Carriages to his Majesty's Stores; but the rest of my Goods were returned me.

I had, as I before observed, one private Pocket which escaped their Search, wherein there was a Pair of Spectacles (which I sometimes use for the Weakness of mine Eyes), a Pocket Perspective,* and several other little Conveniences; which being of no Consequence to the Emperor, I did not think my self bound in Honour to discover; and I apprehended they might be lost or spoiled if I ventured them out of my Possession.

CHAPTER THREE

The Author diverts the Emperor and his Nobility of both Sexes, in a very uncommon Manner. The Diversions of the Court of Lilliput described. The Author hath his Liberty granted him upon certain Conditions.

MY gentleness and good Behaviour had gained so far on the Emperor and his Court, and indeed upon the Army and People in general, that I began to conceive Hopes of getting my Liberty in a short Time. I took all possible Methods to cultivate this favourable Disposition. The Natives came by Degrees to be less apprehensive of any Danger from me. I would sometimes lie down, and let five or six of them dance on my Hand. And at last the Boys and Girls would venture to come and play at Hide and Seek in my Hair. I had now made a good Progress in understanding and speaking their Language. The Emperor had a mind one Day to entertain me with several of the Country Shows; wherein they exceed all Nations I have known, both for Dexterity and Magnificence. I was diverted with none so much as that of the Rope-Dancers,* performed upon a slender white Thread, extended about two Foot, and twelve Inches from the Ground. Upon which, I shall desire Liberty, with the Reader's Patience, to enlarge a little.

This Diversion is only practised by those Persons, who are Candidates for great Employments, and high Favour, at Court. They are trained in this Art from their Youth, and are not always of noble Birth, or liberal Education. When a great Office is vacant, either by Death or Disgrace, (which often happens) five or six of those Candidates petition the Emperor to entertain his Majesty and the Court with a Dance on the Rope; and whoever jumps the highest without falling, succeeds in the Office. Very often the chief Ministers themselves are commanded to shew their Skill, and to convince the Emperor that they have not lost their Faculty. *Flimnap*,* the Treasurer, is allowed to cut a Caper on the strait Rope, at least an Inch higher than any other Lord in the whole Empire. I have seen him do the Summerset* several times together, upon a Trencher fixed on the Rope, which is no thicker than a common Packthread in *England*. My Friend *Reldresal*,* principal Secretary for private

Affairs, is, in my Opinion, if I am not partial, the second after the Treasurer; the rest of the great Officers are much upon a Par.

These Diversions are often attended with fatal Accidents, whereof great Numbers are on Record. I my self have seen two or three Candidates break a Limb. But the Danger is much greater, when the Ministers themselves are commanded to shew their Dexterity: For, by contending to excel themselves and their Fellows, they strain so far, that there is hardly one of them who hath not received a Fall; and some of them two or three. I was assured, that a Year or two before my Arrival, *Flimnap* would have infallibly broke his Neck, if one of the *King's Cushions*,* that accidentally lay on the Ground, had not weakened the Force of his Fall.

There is likewise another Diversion, which is only shewn before the Emperor and Empress, and first Minister, upon particular Occasions. The Emperor lays on a Table three fine silken Threads* of six Inches long. One is Blue, the other Red, and the third Green. These Threads are proposed as Prizes, for those Persons whom the Emperor hath a mind to distinguish by a peculiar Mark of his Favour. The Ceremony is performed in his Majesty's great Chamber of State; where the Candidates are to undergo a Tryal of Dexterity very different from the former; and such as I have not observed the least Resemblance of in any other Country of the old or the new World. The Emperor holds a Stick in his Hands, both ends parallel to the Horizon, while the Candidates advancing one by one, sometimes leap over the Stick, sometimes creep under it backwards and forwards several times, according as the Stick is advanced or depressed. Sometimes the Emperor holds one End of the Stick, and his first Minister the other; sometimes the Minister has it entirely to himself. Whoever performs his Part with most Agility, and holds out the longest in *leaping* and *creeping*, is rewarded with the Blue-coloured Silk; the Red is given to the next, and the Green to the third, which they all wear girt round about the Middle; and you see few great Persons about this Court, who are not adorned with one of these Girdles.

The Horses of the Army, and those of the Royal Stables, having been daily led before me, were no longer shy, but would come up to my very Feet, without starting. The Riders would leap them over my Hand as I held it on the Ground; and one of the Emperor's Huntsmen, upon a large Courser, took my Foot, Shoe and all; which was indeed a prodigious Leap. I had the good Fortune to divert the Emperor one Day, after a very extraordinary Manner. I desired he would order several Sticks of two Foot high, and the Thickness of an ordinary Cane, to be brought me; whereupon his Majesty commanded the Master of his Woods to give Directions accordingly; and the next Morning six Wood-men arrived with as many Carriages, drawn by eight Horses to each. I took nine of these Sticks, and fixing them firmly in the ground in a Quadrangular Figure, two Foot and a half square; I took four other Sticks, and tyed them parallel at each Corner, about two Foot from the Ground; then I fastened my Handkerchief to the nine Sticks that stood erect; and extended it on all Sides, till it was as tight as the Top of a Drum; and the four parallel Sticks rising about five Inches higher than the Handkerchief, served as Ledges on each Side. When I had finished my Work, I desired the Emperor to let a Troop of his best Horse, Twenty-four in Number, come and exercise upon this Plain. His Majesty approved of the Proposal, and I took them up one by one in my Hands, ready mounted and armed, with the proper Officers to exercise them. As soon as they got into Order, they divided into two Parties, performed mock Skirmishes, discharged blunt Arrows, drew their Swords, fled and pursued, attacked and retired; and in short discovered* the best military Discipline I ever beheld. The parallel Sticks secured them and their Horses from falling over the Stage; and the Emperor was so much delighted, that he ordered this Entertainment to be repeated several Days; and once was pleased to be lifted up, and give the Word of Command; and, with great Difficulty, persuaded even the Empress her self to let me hold her in her close Chair,* within two Yards of the Stage, from whence she was able to take a full View of the whole Performance. It was my good Fortune that no ill Accident happened in these Entertainments; only once a fiery Horse that belonged to one of the Captains, pawing with his Hoof struck a Hole in my Handkerchief, and his Foot slipping, he overthrew his Rider and himself; but I immediately relieved them both: For covering the Hole with one Hand, I set down the Troop with the other, in the same Manner as I took them up. The Horse that fell was strained in the left Shoulder, but the Rider got no Hurt; and I repaired my Handkerchief as well as I could: However, I would not trust to the Strength of it any more in such dangerous Enterprizes.

About two or three Days before I was set at Liberty, as I was entertaining the Court with these Kinds of Feats, there arrived an Express to inform his Majesty, that some of his Subjects riding near the Place where I was first taken up, had seen a great black Substance lying on the Ground, very oddly shaped, extending its Edges round as wide as his Majesty's Bedchamber, and rising up in the Middle as high as a Man: That it was no living Creature, as they at first apprehended; for it lay on the Grass without Motion; and some of them had walked round it several Times: That by mounting upon each others Shoulders, they had got to the Top, which was flat and even; and, stamping upon it, they found it was hollow within: That they humbly conceived it might be something belonging to the *Man-Mountain*; and if his Majesty pleased, they would undertake to bring it with only five Horses. I presently knew what they meant; and was glad at Heart to receive this Intelligence. It seems, upon my first reaching the Shore, after our Shipwreck, I was in such Confusion, that before I came to the Place where I went to sleep, my Hat, which I had fastened with a String to my Head while I was rowing, and had stuck on all the Time I was swimming, fell off after I came to Land; the String, as I conjecture, breaking by some Accident which I never observed, but thought my Hat had been lost at Sea. I intreated his Imperial Majesty to give Orders it might be brought to me as soon as possible, describing to him the Use and the Nature of it: And the next Day the Waggoners arrived with it, but not in a very good Condition; they had bored two Holes in the Brim, within an Inch and a half of the Edge, and fastened two Hooks in the Holes; these Hooks were tied by a long Cord to the Harness, and thus my Hat was dragged along for above half an *English* Mile: But the Ground in that Country being extremely smooth and level, it received less Damage than I expected.

Two Days after this Adventure, the Emperor having ordered that Part of his Army, which quarters in and about his Metropolis,* to be in a Readiness, took a fancy of diverting himself in a very singular Manner. He desired I would stand like a *Colossus*,* with my Legs as far asunder as I conveniently could. He then commanded his General (who was an old experienced Leader, and a great Patron of mine) to draw up the Troops in close Order, and march them under me; the Foot by Twenty-four in a Breast,* and the Horse by Sixteen, with Drums beating, Colours flying, and Pikes advanced. This Body consisted of three Thousand Foot, and a Thousand Horse. His Majesty gave Orders, upon Pain of Death, that every Soldier in his March should observe the strictest Decency, with regard to my Person; which, however, could not prevent some of the younger Officers from turning up their Eyes as they passed under me. And, to confess the Truth, my Breeches were at that Time in so ill a Condition, that they afforded some Opportunities for Laughter and Admiration.

I had sent so many Memorials and Petitions for my Liberty, that his Majesty at length mentioned the Matter first in the Cabinet, and then in a full Council; where it was opposed by none, except *Skyresh Bolgolam*,* who was pleased, without any Provocation, to be my mortal Enemy. But it was carried against him by the whole Board, and confirmed by the Emperor. That Minister was *Galbet*, or Admiral of the Realm; very much in his Master's Confidence, and a Person well versed in Affairs, but of a morose and sour Complection. However, he was at length persuaded to comply; but prevailed that the Articles and Conditions upon which I should be set free, and to which I must swear, should be drawn up by himself. These Articles were brought to me by *Skyresh Bolgolam* in Person, attended by two under Secretaries, and several Persons of Distinction. After they were read, I was demanded to swear to the Performance of them; first in the Manner of my own Country, and afterwards in the Method prescribed by their Laws; which was to hold my right Foot in my left Hand, to place the middle Finger of my right Hand on the Crown of my Head, and my Thumb on the Tip of my right Ear. But, because the Reader may perhaps be curious to have some Idea of the Style and Manner of Expression peculiar to that People, as well as to know the Articles upon which I recovered my Liberty; I have made a Translation of the whole Instrument, Word for Word, as near as I was able; which I here offer to the Publick.

GOLBASTO MOMAREN EVLAME GURDILO SHEFIN MULLY ULLY GUE, most Mighty Emperor of *Lilliput*, Delight and Terror of the Universe,* whose Dominions extend five Thousand Blustrugs, (about twelve Miles in Circumference) to the Extremities of the Globe: Monarch of all Monarchs: Taller than the Sons of Men; whose Feet press down to the Center,* and whose Head strikes against the Sun: At whose Nod the Princes of the Earth shake their Knees; pleasant as the Spring, comfortable as the Summer, fruitful as Autumn, dreadful as Winter. His most sublime Majesty proposeth to the *Man-Mountain*, lately arrived at our Celestial Dominions, the following Articles, which by a solemn Oath he shall be obliged to perform.

FIRST, The *Man-Mountain* shall not depart from our Dominions, without our Licence under our Great Seal.

SECONDLY, He shall not presume to come into our Metropolis, without our express Order; at which time, the Inhabitants shall have two Hours Warning, to keep within their Doors.

THIRDLY, The said *Man-Mountain* shall confine his Walks to our principal high Roads; and not offer to walk or lie down in a Meadow, or Field of Corn.

FOURTHLY, As he walks the said Roads, he shall take the utmost Care not to trample upon the Bodies of any of our loving Subjects, their Horses, or Carriages; nor take any of our said Subjects into his Hands, without their own Consent.

FIFTHLY, If an Express require extraordinary Dispatch; the *Man-Mountain* shall be obliged to carry in his Pocket the Messenger and Horse, a six Days journey once in every Moon, and return the said Messenger back (if so required) safe to our Imperial Presence.

SIXTHLY, He shall be our Ally against our Enemies in the Island of *Blefuscu*, and do his utmost to destroy their Fleet, which is now preparing to invade Us.

SEVENTHLY, That the said *Man-Mountain* shall, at his Times of Leisure, be aiding and assisting our Workmen, in helping to raise certain great Stones, towards covering the Wall of the principal Park, and other our Royal Buildings.

EIGHTHLY, That the said *Man-Mountain* shall, in two Moons Time, deliver in an exact Survey of the Circumference of our Dominions, by a Computation of his own Paces round the Coast.

LASTLY, That upon his solemn Oath to observe all the above Articles, the said *Man-Mountain* shall have a daily Allowance of Meat and Drink, sufficient for the Support of 1728 of our Subjects; with free Access to our Royal Person, and other Marks of our Favour. Given at our Palace at *Belfaborac* the Twelfth Day of the Ninety-first Moon of our Reign.

I swore and subscribed to these Articles with great Chearfulness and Content, although some of them were not so honourable as I could have wished; which proceeded wholly from the Malice of

Skyresh Bolgolam the High Admiral: Whereupon my Chains were immediately unlocked, and I was at full Liberty: The Emperor himself, in Person, did me the Honour to be by at the whole Ceremony. I made my Acknowledgments, by prostrating myself at his Majesty's Feet: But he commanded me to rise; and after many gracious Expressions, which, to avoid the Censure of Vanity, I shall not repeat; he added, that he hoped I should prove a useful Servant, and well deserve all the Favours he had already conferred upon me, or might do for the future.

The Reader may please to observe, that in the last Article for the Recovery of my Liberty, the Emperor stipulates to allow me a Quantity of Meat and Drink, sufficient for the Support of 1728 *Lilliputians*. Some time after, asking a Friend at Court how they came to fix on that determinate Number; he told me, that his Majesty's Mathematicians, having taken the Height of my Body by the Help of a Quadrant, and finding it to exceed theirs in the Proportion of Twelve to One, they concluded from the Similarity of their Bodies, that mine must contain at least 1728 of theirs, and consequently would require as much Food as was necessary to support that Number of *Lilliputians*. By which, the Reader may conceive an Idea of the Ingenuity of that People, as well as the prudent and exact Œconomy* of so great a Prince.

CHAPTER FOUR

Milendo, the Metropolis of Lilliput, described, together with the Emperor's Palace. A Conversation between the Author and a principal Secretary, concerning the Affairs of that Empire: The Author's Offers to serve the Emperor in his Wars.

THE first Request I made after I had obtained my Liberty, was, that I might have Licence to see *Mildendo*, the Metropolis; which the Emperor easily granted me, but with a special Charge to do no Hurt, either to the Inhabitants, or their houses. The People had Notice by Proclamation of my Design to visit the Town. The Wall which encompassed it, is two Foot and a half high, and at least eleven Inches broad, so that a Coach and Horses may be driven very safely round it; and it is flanked with strong Towers at ten Foot Distance. I stept over the great *Western* Gate, and passed very gently, and sideling through the two principal Streets, only in my short Waistcoat, for fear of damaging the Roofs and Eves of the Houses with the Skirts of my Coat. I walked with the utmost Circumspection, to avoid treading on any Stragglers, who might remain in the Streets, although the Orders were very strict, that all People should keep in their Houses, at their own Peril. The Garret Windows and Tops of Houses were so crowded with Spectators, that I thought in all my Travels I had not seen a more populous Place. The City is an exact Square, each Side of the Wall being five Hundred Foot long. The two great Streets which run cross and divide it into four Quarters, are five Foot wide. The Lanes and Alleys which I could not enter, but only viewed them as I passed, are from Twelve to Eighteen Inches. The Town is capable of holding five Hundred Thousand Souls. The Houses are from three to five Stories. The Shops and Markets well provided.

The Emperor's Palace is in the Center of the City, where the two great Streets meet. It is inclosed by a Wall of two Foot high, and Twenty Foot distant from the Buildings. I had his Majesty's Permission to step over this Wall; and the Space being so wide between that and the Palace, I could easily view it on every Side. The outward Court is a Square of Forty Foot, and includes two other Courts: In the inmost are the Royal Apartments, which I was very desirous to see, but found it extremely difficult; for the great Gates, from one Square into another, were but Eighteen Inches high, and seven Inches wide. Now the Buildings of the outer Court were at least five Foot high; and it was impossible for me to stride over them, without infinite Damage to the Pile, although the Walls were strongly built of hewn Stone, and four Inches thick. At the same time, the Emperor had a great Desire that I should see the Magnificence of his Palace: But this I was not able to do till three Days after, which I spent in cutting down with my Knife some of the largest Trees in the Royal Park, about an Hundred Yards distant from the City. Of these Trees I made two Stools, each about three Foot high, and strong enough to bear my Weight. The People having received Notice a second time, I went again through the City to the Palace, with my two Stools in my Hands. When I came to the Side of the outer Court, I stood upon one Stool, and took the other in my Hand: This I lifted over the Roof, and gently set it down on the Space between the first and second Court, which was eight Foot wide. I then stept over the Buildings very conveniently from one Stool to the other, and drew up the first after me with a hooked Stick. By this Contrivance I got into the inmost Court; and lying down upon my Side, I applied my Face to the Windows of the middle Stories, which were left open on Purpose, and discovered the most splendid Apartments that can be imagined. There I saw the Empress, and the young Princes in their several Lodgings, with their chief Attendants about them. Her Imperial Majesty was pleased to smile very graciously upon me, and gave me out of the Window her Hand to kiss.

But I shall not anticipate the Reader with farther Descriptions of this Kind, because I reserve them for a greater Work, which is now almost ready for the Press; containing a general Description of this Empire, from its first Erection, through a long Series of Princes, with a particular Account of their Wars and Politicks, Laws, Learning, and Religion; their Plants and Animals, their peculiar Manners and Customs, with other Matters very curious and useful; my chief Design at present being only to relate such Events and Transactions as happened to the Publick, or to my self, during a Residence of about nine Months in that Empire.

One Morning, about a Fortnight after I had obtained my Liberty;

Reldresal, Principal Secretary (as they style him) of private Affairs, came to my House, attended only by one Servant. He ordered his Coach to wait at a Distance, and desired I would give him an Hour's Audience; which I readily consented to, on Account of his Quality, and Personal Merits, as well of the many good Offices he had done me during my Sollicitations at Court. I offered to lie down, that he might the more conveniently reach my Ear; but he chose rather to let me hold him in my Hand during our Conversation. He began with Compliments on my Liberty; said, he might pretend to some Merit in it;* but, however, added, that if it had not been for the present Situation of things at Court, perhaps I might not have obtained it so soon. For, *said he*, as flourishing a Condition as we appear to be in to Foreigners, we labour under two mighty Evils; a violent Faction at home, and the Danger of an Invasion by a most potent Enemy from abroad. As to the first, you are to understand, that for above seventy Moons past, there have been two struggling Parties in this Empire, under the Names of *Tramecksan*, and *Slamecksan*,* from the high and low Heels on their Shoes, by which they distinguish themselves.

It is alledged indeed, that the high Heels are most agreeable to our ancient Constitution: But however this be, his Majesty hath determined to make use of only low Heels in the Administration* of the Government, and all Offices in the Gift of the Crown; as you cannot but observe; and particularly, that his Majesty's Imperial Heels are lower at least by a *Drurr* than any of his Court; (*Drurr* is a Measure about the fourteenth Part of an Inch.) The Animosities* between these two Parties run so high, that they will neither eat nor drink, nor talk with each other. We compute the *Tramecksan*, or High-Heels, to exceed us in Number; but the Power is wholly on our Side. We apprehend his Imperial Highness, the Heir to the Crown, to have some Tendency towards the High-Heels;* at least we can plainly discover one of his Heels higher than the other; which gives him a Hobble in his Gait. Now, in the midst of these intestine Disquiets, we are threatened with an Invasion from the Island of *Blefuscu*, which is the other great Empire of the Universe, almost as large and powerful as this of his Majesty. For as to what we have heard you affirm, that there are other Kingdoms and States in the World, inhabited by human Creatures as large as your self, our Philosophers are in much Doubt; and would rather conjecture that you dropt from the Moon, or one of the Stars; because it is certain, than an hundred Mortals of your Bulk, would, in a short Time, destroy all the Fruits and Cattle of his Majesty's Dominions. Besides, our Histories of six Thousand Moons make no Mention of any other Regions, than the two great Empires of *Lilliput* and *Blefuscu*. Which two mighty Powers have, as I was going to tell you, been engaged in a most obstinate War for six and thirty Moons* past. It began upon the following Occasion. It is allowed on all Hands, that the primitive Way of breaking Eggs before we eat them, was upon the larger End: But his present Majesty's Grand-father, while he was a Boy, going to eat an Egg, and breaking it according to the ancient Practice, happened to cut one of his Fingers. Whereupon the Emperor, his Father, published an Edict, commanding all his Subjects, upon great Penalties, to break the smaller End of their Eggs. The People so highly resented this Law, that our Histories tell us, there have been six Rebellions raised on that Account; wherein one Emperor lost his Life, and another his Crown.* These civil Commotions were constantly fomented by the Monarchs of *Blefuscu*; and when they were quelled, the Exiles always fled for Refuge to that Empire.* It is computed, that eleven Thousand Persons have, at several Times, suffered Death, rather than submit to break their Eggs at the smaller End. Many hundred large Volumes have been published upon this Controversy: But the Books of the *Big-Endians* have been long forbidden, and the whole Party rendred incapable by Law* of holding Employments. During the Course of these Troubles, the Emperors of *Blefuscu* did frequently expostulate by their Ambassadors, accusing us of making a Schism in Religion, by offending against a fundamental Doctrine of our great Prophet *Lustrog*, in the fifty-fourth Chapter of the *Brundrecal*, (which is their *Alcoran**). This, however, is thought to be a meer Strain upon the Text: For the Words are these; *That all true Believers shall break their Eggs at the convenient End*: and which is the convenient End, seems, in my humble Opinion, to be left to every Man's Conscience, or at least in the Power of the chief Magistrate* to determine. Now the *Big-Endian* Exiles have found so much Credit in the Emperor of *Blefuscu's* Court; and so much private Assistance and Encouragement from their Party here at home, that a bloody War hath been carried on between the two Empires for six and thirty Moons with various Success; during which Time we have lost Forty Capital Ships, and a much greater Number of smaller

Vessels, together with thirty thousand of our best Seamen and Soldiers; and the Damage received by the Enemy is reckoned to be somewhat greater than ours. However, they have now equipped a numerous Fleet, and are just preparing to make a Descent upon us: And his Imperial Majesty, placing great Confidence in your Valour and Strength, hath commanded me to lay this Account of his Affairs before you.

I desired the Secretary to present my humble Duty to the Emperor, and to let him know, that I thought it would not become me, who was a Foreigner, to interfere with Parties; but I was ready, with the Hazard of my Life, to defend his Person and State against all Invaders.

CHAPTER FIVE

The Author by an extraordinary Stratagem prevents an Invasion. A high Title of Honour is conferred upon him. Ambassadors arrive from the Emperor of Blefuscu *and sue for Peace. The Empress's Apartment on fire by an Accident; the* Author *instrumental in saving the rest of the Palace.*

THE Empire of *Blefuscu*, is an Island situated to the North North-East Side of *Lilliput*, from whence it is parted only by a Channel of eight Hundred Yards wide. I had not yet seen it, and upon this Notice of an intended Invasion, I avoided appearing on that Side of the Coast, for fear of being discovered by some of the Enemies Ships, who had received no Intelligence of me; all intercourse between the two Empires having been strictly forbidden during the War, upon Pain of Death; and an Embargo laid by our Emperor upon all Vessels whatsoever. I communicated to his Majesty a Project I had formed of seizing the Enemies whole Fleet; which, as our Scouts assured us, lay at Anchor in the Harbour ready to sail with the first fair Wind. I consulted the most experienced Seamen, upon the Depth of the Channel, which they had often plummed; who told me, that in the Middle at high Water it was seventy *Glumgluffs* deep, which is about six Foot of *European* Measure; and the rest of it fifty *Glumgluffs* at most. I walked to the North-East Coast over against *Blefuscu*; where, lying down behind a Hillock, I took out my small Pocket Perspective Glass, and viewed the Enemy's Fleet at Anchor, consisting of about fifty Men of War, and a great Number of Transports: I then came back to my House, and gave Order (for which I had a Warrant) for a great Quantity of the strongest Cable and Bars of Iron. The Cable was about as thick as Packthread, and the Bars of the Length and Size of a Knitting-Needle. I trebled the Cable to make it stronger; and for the same Reason I twisted three of the Iron Bars together, bending the Extremities into a Hook. Having thus fixed fifty Hooks to as many Cables, I went back to the North-East Coast, and putting off my Coat, Shoes, and Stockings, walked into the Sea in my Leathern Jerken, about half an Hour before high Water. I waded with what Haste I could, and swam in the Middle about thirty Yards until I felt the Ground; I arrived at the Fleet in

less than half an Hour. The Enemy was so frighted when they saw
me, that they leaped out of their Ships, and swam to Shore; where
there could not be fewer than thirty thousand Souls. I then took my
Tackling, and fastning a Hook to the Hole at the Prow of each, I
tyed all the Cords together at the End. While I was thus employed,
the Enemy discharged several Thousand Arrows, many of which
stuck in my Hands and Face; and besides the excessive Smart, gave
me much Disturbance in my Work. My greatest Apprehension
was for mine Eyes, which I should have infallibly lost, if I had not
suddenly thought of an Expedient. I kept, among other little Necessaries, a Pair of Spectacles in a private Pocket, which, as I observed
before, had escaped the Emperor's Searchers. These I took out, and
fastened as strongly as I could upon my Nose; and thus armed went
on boldly with my Work in spight of the Enemy's Arrows; many of
which struck against the Glasses of my Spectacles, but without any
other Effect, further than a little to discompose them. I had now
fastened all the Hooks, and taking the Knot in my Hand, began to
pull; but not a Ship would stir, for they were all too fast held by
their Anchors; so that the boldest Part of my Enterprize remained. I
therefore let go the Cord, and leaving the Hooks fixed to the Ships, I
resolutely cut with my Knife the Cables that fastened the Anchors;
receiving above two hundred Shots in my Face and Hands: Then I
took up the knotted End of the Cables to which my Hooks were
tyed; and with great Ease drew fifty of the Enemy's largest Men of
War after me.*

The *Blefuscudians*, who had not the least Imagination of what I
intended, were at first confounded with Astonishment. They had
seen me cut the Cables, and thought my Design was only to let the
Ships run a-drift, or fall foul on each other: But when they perceived
the whole Fleet moving in Order, and saw me pulling at the End,
they set up such a Scream of Grief and Dispair, that it is almost
impossible to describe or conceive. When I had got out of Danger, I
stopt a while to pick out the Arrows that stuck in my Hands and
Face, and rubbed on some of the same Ointment that was given me
at my first Arrival, as I have formerly mentioned. I then took off my
Spectacles, and waiting about an Hour until the Tyde was a little
fallen, I waded through the Middle with my Cargo, and arrived safe
at the Royal Port of *Lilliput*.

The Emperor and his whole Court stood on the Shore, expecting the Issue of this great Adventure. They saw the Ships move forward in a large Half-Moon, but could not discern me, who was up to my Breast in Water. When I advanced to the Middle of the Channel, they were yet more in Pain because I was under Water to my Neck. The Emperor concluded me to be drowned, and that the Enemy's Fleet was approaching in a hostile Manner: But he was soon eased of his Fears; for the Channel growing shallower every Step I made, I came in a short Time within Hearing; and holding up the End of the Cable by which the Fleet was fastened, I cryed in a loud Voice, *Long live the most puissant Emperor of Lilliput!* This great Prince received me at my Landing with all possible Encomiums, and created me a *Nardac* upon the Spot, which is the highest Title of Honour among them.

His Majesty desired I would take some other Opportunity of bringing all the rest of his Enemy's Ships into his Ports. And so unmeasurable is the Ambition of Princes, that he seemed to think of nothing less than reducing the whole Empire of *Blefuscu* into a Province, and governing it by a Viceroy;* of destroying the *Big-Endian* Exiles, and compelling that People to break the smaller End of their Eggs; by which he would remain sole Monarch of the whole World. But I endeavoured to divert him from this Design, by many Arguments drawn from the Topicks* of Policy as well as Justice: And I plainly protested, that I would never be an Instrument of bringing a free and brave People into Slavery: And when the Matter was debated in Council, the wisest Part of the Ministry were of my Opinion.

This open bold Declaration of mine was so opposite to the Schemes and Politicks of his Imperial Majesty, that he could never forgive me: He mentioned it in a very artful Manner at Council, where, I was told, that some of the wisest appeared, at least by their Silence, to be of my Opinion; but others, who were my secret Enemies, could not forbear some Expressions, which by a Side-wind reflected on me. And from this Time began an Intrigue between his Majesty, and a Junta* of Ministers maliciously bent against me, which broke out in less than two Months, and had like to have ended in my utter Destruction. Of so little Weight are the greatest Services to Princes, when put into the Balance with a Refusal to gratify their Passions.

About three Weeks after this Exploit, there arrived a solemn

Embassy from *Blefuscu*, with humble Offers of a Peace; which was soon concluded upon Conditions very advantageous to our Emperor; wherewith I shall not trouble the Reader. There were six Ambassadors, with a Train of about five Hundred Persons; and their Entry was very magnificent, suitable to the Grandeur of their Master, and the Importance of their Business. When their Treaty was finished, wherein I did them several good Offices by the Credit I now had, or at least appeared to have at Court; their Excellencies, who were privately told how much I had been their Friend, made me a Visit in Form.* They began with many Compliments upon my Valour and Generosity; invited me to that Kingdom in the Emperor their Master's Name; and desired me to shew them some Proofs of my prodigious Strength, of which they had heard so many Wonders; wherein I readily obliged them, but shall not interrupt the Reader with the Particulars.

When I had for some time entertained their Excellencies to their infinite Satisfaction and Surprize, I desired they would do me the Honour to present my most humble Respects to the Emperor their Master, the Renown of whose Virtues had so justly filled the whole World with Admiration, and whose Royal Person I resolved to attend before I returned to my own Country. Accordingly, the next time I had the Honour to see our Emperor, I desired his general Licence to wait on the *Blefuscudian* Monarch, which he was pleased to grant me, as I could plainly perceive, in a very cold Manner; but could not guess the Reason, till I had a Whisper from a certain Person, that *Flimnap* and *Bolgolam* had represented my Intercourse with those Ambassadors, as a Mark of Disaffection,* from which I am sure my Heart was wholly free. And this was the first time I began to conceive some imperfect Idea of Courts and Ministers.

It is to be observed, that these Ambassadors spoke to me by an Interpreter; the Languages of both Empires differing as much from each other as any two in *Europe*, and each Nation priding itself upon the Antiquity, Beauty, and Energy of their own Tongues, with an avowed Contempt for that of their Neighbour: Yet our Emperor standing upon the Advantage he had got by the Seizure of their Fleet, obliged them to deliver their Credentials, and make their Speech in the *Lilliputian* Tongue. And it must be confessed, that from the great Intercourse of Trade and Commerce between both

Realms; from the continual Reception of Exiles, which is mutual among them; and from the Custom in each Empire to send their young Nobility and richer Gentry to the other, in order to polish themselves, by seeing the World, and understanding Men and Manners; there are few Persons of Distinction, or Merchants, or Seamen, who dwell in the Maritime Parts, but what can hold Conversation in both Tongues; as I found some Weeks after, when I went to pay my Respects to the Emperor of *Blefuscu*, which in the Midst of great Misfortunes, through the Malice of my Enemies, proved a very happy Adventure to me, as I shall relate in its proper Place.

The Reader may remember, that when I signed those Articles upon which I recovered my Liberty, there were some which I disliked upon Account of their being too servile, neither could any thing but an extreme Necessity have forced me to submit. But being now a *Nardac*, of the highest Rank in that Empire, such Offices were looked upon as below my Dignity; and the Emperor (to do him Justice) never once mentioned them to me. However, it was not long before I had an Opportunity of doing his Majesty, at least, as I then thought, a most signal Service. I was alarmed at Midnight with the Cries of many Hundred People at my Door; by which being suddenly awaked, I was in some Kind of Terror. I heard the Word *Burglum* repeated incessantly; several of the Emperor's Court making their Way through the Croud, intreated me to come immediately to the Palace, where her Imperial Majesty's Apartment was on fire, by the Carelessness of a Maid of Honour, who fell asleep while she was reading a Romance.* I got up in an Instant; and Orders being given to clear the Way before me; and it being likewise a Moon-shine Night, I made a shift to get to the Palace without trampling on any of the People. I found they had already applied Ladders to the Walls of the Apartment, and were well provided with Buckets, but the Water was at some Distance. These Buckets were about the Size of a large Thimble, and the poor People supplied me with them as fast as they could; but the Flame was so violent, that they did little Good. I might easily have stifled it with my Coat, which I unfortunately left behind me for haste, and came away only in my Leathern Jerkin. The Case seemed wholly desperate and deplorable; and this magnificent Palace would have infallibly been burnt down to the Ground, if, by a Presence of Mind, unusual to me, I had not suddenly thought of an Expedient. I had the Evening before drank plentifully of a most delicious Wine, called *Glimigrim*, (the *Blefuscudians* call it *Flunec*, but ours is esteemed the better Sort) which is very diuretick. By the luckiest Chance in the World, I had not discharged myself of any Part of it. The Heat I had contracted by coming very near the Flames, and by my labouring to quench them, made the Wine begin to operate by Urine; which I voided in such a Quantity, and applied so well to the proper Places, that in three Minutes the Fire was wholly extinguished;* and the rest of that noble Pile, which had cost so many Ages in erecting, preserved from Destruction.

It was now Day-light, and I returned to my House, without waiting to congratulate with the Emperor; because, although I had done a very eminent Piece of Service, yet I could not tell how his Majesty might resent the Manner by which I had performed it: For, by the fundamental Laws of the Realm, it is Capital* in any Person, of what Quality soever, to make water within the Precincts of the Palace. But I was a little comforted by a Message from his Majesty, that he would give Orders to the Grand Justiciary for passing my Pardon in Form; which, however, I could not obtain. And I was privately assured, that the Empress conceiving the greatest Abhorrence of what I had done, removed to the most distant Side of the Court, firmly resolved that those Buildings should never be repaired for her Use; and, in the Presence of her chief Confidents, could not forbear vowing Revenge.

CHAPTER SIX

Of the Inhabitants of Lilliput; *their Learning, Laws, and Customs. The Manner of Educating their Children. The Author's Way of living in that Country. His Vindication of a great Lady.*

ALTHOUGH I intend to leave the Description of this Empire to a particular Treatise, yet in the mean time I am content to gratify the curious Reader with some general Ideas.* As the common Size of the Natives is somewhat under six Inches, so there is an exact Proportion in all other Animals, as well as Plants and Trees: For Instance, the tallest Horses and Oxen are between four and five Inches in Height, the Sheep an Inch and a half, more or less; their Geese about the Bigness of a Sparrow; and so the several Gradations downwards, till you come to the smallest, which, to my Sight, were almost invisible; but Nature hath adapted the Eyes of the *Lilliputians* to all Objects proper for their View: They see with great Exactness, but at no great Distance. And to show the Sharpness of their Sight towards Objects that are near, I have been much pleased with observing a Cook pulling a Lark,* which was not so large as a common Fly; and a young Girl threading an invisible Needle with invisible Silk. Their tallest Trees are about seven Foot high; I mean some of those in the great Royal Park, the Tops whereof I could but just reach with my Fist clinched.* The other Vegetables are in the same Proportion: But this I leave to the Reader's Imagination.

I shall say but little at present of their Learning, which for many Ages hath flourished in all its Branches among them: But their Manner of Writing* is very peculiar; being neither from the Left to the Right, like the *Europeans*; nor from the Right to the Left, like the *Arabians*; nor from up to down, like the *Chinese*; nor from down to up, like the *Cascagians*; but aslant from one Corner of the Paper to the other, like Ladies in *England*.

They bury their Dead with their Heads directly downwards;* because they hold an Opinion, that in eleven Thousand Moons they are all to rise again; in which Period, the Earth (which they conceive to be flat) will turn upside down, and by this Means they shall, at their Resurrection, be found ready standing on their

Feet. The Learned among them confess the Absurdity of this Doctrine; but the Practice still continues, in Compliance to the Vulgar.

There are some Laws and Customs in this Empire very peculiar; and if they were not so directly contrary to those of my own dear Country, I should be tempted to say a little in their Justification. It is only to be wished, that they were as well executed. The first I shall mention, relateth to Informers. All Crimes against the State, are punished here with the utmost Severity; but if the Person accused make his Innocence plainly to appear upon his Tryal, the Accuser is immediately put to an ignominious Death; and out of his Goods or Lands, the innocent Person is quadruply recompensed for the Loss of his Time, for the Danger he underwent, for the Hardship of his Imprisonment, and for all the Charges he hath been at* in making his Defence. Or, if that Fund be deficient, it is largely supplyed by the Crown. The Emperor doth also confer on him some publick Mark of his Favour; and Proclamation is made of his Innocence through the whole City.

They look upon Fraud as a greater Crime than Theft, and therefore seldom fail to punish it with Death: For they alledge, that Care and Vigilance, with a very common understanding, may preserve a Man's Goods from Thieves; but Honesty hath no Fence against superior Cunning: And since it is necessary that there should be a perpetual Intercourse of buying and selling, and dealing upon Credit; where Fraud is permitted or connived at, or hath no Law to punish it, the honest Dealer is always undone, and the Knave gets the Advantage. I remember when I was once interceeding with the King for a Criminal who had wronged his Master of a great Sum of Money, which he had received by Order, and ran away with; and happening to tell his Majesty, by way of Extenuation, that it was only a Breach of Trust; The Emperor thought it monstrous in me to offer, as a Defence, the greatest Aggravation of the Crime: And truly, I had little to say in Return, farther than the common Answer, that different Nations had different Customs;* for, I confess, I was heartily ashamed.

Although we usually call Reward and Punishment, the two Hinges* upon which all Government turns; yet I could never observe this Maxim to be put in Practice by any Nation, except that of *Lilliput*.* Whoever can there bring sufficient Proof that he hath strictly observed the Laws of his Country for Seventy-three Moons, hath a Claim to certain Privileges, according to his Quality and Condition of Life, with a proportionable Sum of Money out of a Fund appropriated for that Use: He likewise acquires the Title of *Snilpall*, or *Legal*, which is added to his Name, but doth not descend to his Posterity. And these People thought it a prodigious Defect of Policy among us, when I told them that our Laws were enforced only by Penalties, without any Mention of Reward. It is upon this account that the Image of Justice, in their Courts of Judicature, is formed with six Eyes, two before, as many behind, and on each Side one, to signify Circumspection; with a Bag of Gold open in her right Hand, and a Sword sheathed in her left, to shew she is more disposed to reward than to punish.

In chusing Persons* for all Employments, they have more Regard to good Morals than to great Abilities: For, since Government is necessary to Mankind, they believe that the common Size of human Understandings, is fitted to some Station or other; and that Providence never intended to make the Management of publick Affairs a Mystery, to be comprehended only by a few Persons of sublime Genius, of which there seldom are three born in an Age: But, they suppose Truth, Justice, Temperance, and the like, to be in every Man's Power; the Practice of which Virtues, assisted by Experience and a good Intention, would qualify any Man for the Service of his Country, except where a Course of Study is required. But they thought the Want of Moral Virtues was so far from being supplied by superior Endowments of the Mind, that Employments could never be put into such dangerous Hands as those of Persons so qualified; and at least, that the Mistakes committed by Ignorance in a virtuous Disposition, would never be of such fatal Consequence to the Publick Weal, as the Practices* of a Man, whose Inclinations led him to be corrupt, and had great Abilities to manage, to multiply, and defend his Corruptions.

In like Manner, the Disbelief of a Divine Providence renders a Man uncapable of holding any publick Station:* For, since Kings avow themselves to be the Deputies of Providence, the *Lilliputians* think nothing can be more absurd than for a Prince to employ such Men as disown the Authority under which he acteth.

In relating these and the following Laws, I would only be understood to mean the original Institutions, and not the most scandalous

Corruptions into which these People are fallen by the degenerate Nature of Man. For as to that infamous Practice of acquiring great Employments by dancing on the Ropes, or Badges of Favour and Distinction by leaping over Sticks, and creeping under them; the Reader is to observe, that they were first introduced by the Grandfather of the Emperor now reigning; and grew to the present Height, by the gradual Increase of Party and Faction.

Ingratitude is among them a capital Crime,* as we read it to have been in some other Countries: For they reason thus; that whoever makes ill Returns to his Benefactor, must needs be a common Enemy to the rest of Mankind, from whom he hath received no Obligation; and therefore such a Man is not fit to live.

Their Notions relating to the Duties of Parents and Children differ extremely from ours.* For, since the Conjunction of Male and Female is founded upon the great Law of Nature, in order to propagate and continue the Species; the *Lilliputians* will needs have it, that Men and Women are joined together like other Animals, by the Motives of Concupiscence; and that their Tenderness towards their Young, proceedeth from the like natural Principle: For which Reason they will never allow, that a Child is under any Obligation to his Father for begetting him, or to his Mother for bringing him into the World;* which, considering the Miseries of human Life, was neither a Benefit in itself, nor intended so by his Parents, whose Thoughts in their Love-encounters were otherwise employed. Upon these, and the like Reasonings, their Opinion is, that Parents are the last of all others to be trusted with the Education of their own Children:* And therefore they have in every Town publick Nurseries, where all Parents, except Cottagers and Labourers, are obliged to send their Infants of both Sexes to be reared and educated when they come to the Age of twenty Moons; at which Time they are supposed to have some Rudiments of Docility. These Schools are of several kinds, suited to different Qualities, and to both Sexes. They have certain Professors* well skilled in preparing Children for such a Condition of Life as befits the Rank of their Parents, and their own Capacities as well as Inclinations. I shall first say something of the Male Nurseries, and then of the Female.

The Nurseries for Males of Noble or Eminent Birth, are provided with grave and learned Professors, and their several Deputies. The Clothes and Food of the Children are plain and simple. They are bred up in the Principles of Honour, Justice, Courage, Modesty, Clemency, Religion, and Love of their Country: They are always employed* in some Business, except in the Times of eating and sleeping, which are very short, and two Hours for Diversions, consisting of bodily Exercises. They are dressed by Men until four Years of Age, and then are obliged to dress themselves, although their Quality be ever so great; and the Women Attendants, who are aged proportionably to ours at fifty, perform only the most menial Offices. They are never suffered to converse with Servants, but go together in small or greater Numbers to take their Diversions, and always in the Presence of a Professor, or one of his Deputies; whereby they avoid those early bad Impressions of Folly and Vice to which our Children are subject. Their Parents are suffered to see them only twice a Year; the Visit is not to last above an Hour; they are allowed to kiss the Child at Meeting and Parting; but a Professor, who always standeth by on those Occasions, will not suffer them to whisper, or use any fondling Expressions, or bring any presents of Toys, Sweet-meats, and the like.*

The Pension from each Family for the Education and Entertainment of a Child, upon Failure of due Payment, is levyed by the Emperor's Officers.

The Nurseries for Children of ordinary Gentlemen, Merchants, Traders, and Handicrafts, are managed proportionably after the same Manner; only those designed for Trades, are put out Apprentices at seven Years old; whereas those of Persons of Quality continue in their Exercises until Fifteen, which answers to One and Twenty with us: But the Confinement is gradually lessened for the last three Years.

In the Female Nurseries, the young Girls of Quality are educated much like the Males, only they are dressed by orderly Servants of their own Sex, but always in the Presence of a Professor or Deputy, until they come to dress themselves, which is at five Years old. And if it be found that these Nurses ever presume to entertain the Girls with frightful or foolish Stories,* or the common Follies practised by Chamber-Maids among us; they are publickly whipped thrice about the City, imprisoned for a Year, and banished for Life to the most desolate Part of the Country. Thus the young Ladies there are as much ashamed of being Cowards and Fools, as the Men; and despise all personal Ornaments* beyond Decency and Cleanliness; neither did I perceive any Difference* in their Education, made by their Difference of Sex, only that the Exercises of the Females were not altogether so robust; and that some Rules were given them relating to domestick Life, and a smaller Compass of Learning was enjoyned them: For, their Maxim is, that among People of Quality, a Wife should be always a reasonable and agreeable Companion, because she cannot always be young.* When the Girls are twelve Years old, which among them is the marriageable Age, their Parents or Guardians take them home, with great Expressions of Gratitude to the Professors, and seldom without Tears of the young Lady and her Companions.

In the Nurseries of Females of the meaner Sort, the Children are instructed in all Kinds of Works proper for their Sex, and their several Degrees: Those intended for Apprentices are dismissed at seven Years old, the rest are kept to eleven.

The meaner Families who have Children at these Nurseries, are obliged, besides their annual Pension, which is as low as possible, to return to the Steward of the Nursery a small Monthly Share of their Gettings, to be a Portion for the Child; and therefore all Parents are limited in their Expences by the Law. For the *Lilliputians* think nothing can be more unjust, than that People, in Subservience to their own Appetites, should bring Children into the World, and leave the Burthen of supporting them on the Publick. As to Persons of Quality, they give Security to appropriate a certain Sum for each Child, suitable to their Condition; and these Funds are always managed with good Husbandry, and the most exact Justice.

The Cottagers and Labourers keep their Children at home, their Business being only to till and cultivate the Earth; and therefore their Education is of little Consequence to the Publick; but the Old and Diseased among them are supported by Hospitals: For begging is a Trade unknown in this Empire.

And here it may perhaps divert the curious Reader, to give some Account of my Domestick,* and my Manner of living in this Country, during a Residence of nine Months and thirteen Days. Having a Head mechanically turned,* and being likewise forced by Necessity, I had made for myself a Table and Chair convenient enough, out of the largest Trees in the Royal Park. Two hundred Sempstresses were employed to make me Shirts, and Linnen for my Bed and Table, all of the strongest and coarsest kind they could get; which, however, they were forced to quilt together in several Folds; for the thickest was some Degrees finer than Lawn. Their Linnen is usually three Inches wide, and three Foot make a Piece. The Sempstresses took my Measure as I lay on the Ground, one standing at my Neck, and another at my Mid-Leg, with a strong Cord extended, that each held by the End, while the third measured the Length of the Cord with a Rule of an Inch long. Then they measured my right Thumb, and desired no more; for by a mathematical Computation, that twice round the Thumb is once round the Wrist, and so on to the Neck and the Waist; and by the Help of my old Shirt, which I displayed on the Ground before them for a Pattern, they fitted me exactly. Three hundred Taylors were employed in the same Manner to make me Clothes; but they had another Contrivance for taking my Measure. I kneeled down, and they raised a Ladder from the Ground to my Neck; upon this Ladder one of them mounted, and let fall a Plum-Line from my Collar to the Floor, which just answered the Length of my Coat; but my Waist and Arms I measured myself. When my Cloaths were finished, which was done in my House, (for the largest of theirs would not have been able to hold them) they looked like the Patch-work made by the Ladies in *England*, only that mine were all of a Colour.

I had three hundred Cooks to dress my Victuals, in little convenient Huts built about my House, where they and their Families lived, and prepared me two Dishes a-piece. I took up twenty Waiters in my Hand, and placed them on the Table; an hundred more attended below on the Ground, some with Dishes of Meat, and some with Barrels of Wine, and other Liquors, slung on their Shoulders; all which the Waiters above drew up as I wanted, in a very ingenious Manner, by certain Cords, as we draw the Bucket up a Well in *Europe*. A Dish of their Meat was a good Mouthful, and a Barrel of their Liquor a reasonable Draught. Their Mutton yields to ours,* but their Beef is excellent. I have had a Sirloin so large, that I have been forced to make three Bits* of it; but this is rare. My Servants were astonished to see me eat it Bones and all, as in our Country we do the Leg of a Lark. Their Geese and Turkeys I usually eat at a Mouthful, and I must confess they far exceed ours. Of their smaller Fowl I could take up twenty or thirty at the End of my Knife.

One Day his Imperial Majesty being informed of my Way of living, desired that himself, and his Royal Consort; with the young Princes of the Blood of both Sexes, might have the Happiness (as he was pleased to call it) of dining with me. They came accordingly, and I placed them upon Chairs of State on my Table, just over against me, with their Guards about them. *Flimnap* the Lord High Treasurer attended there likewise, with his white Staff;* and I observed he often looked on me with a sour Countenance, which I would not seem to regard, but eat more than usual, in Honour to my dear Country, as well as to fill the Court with Admiration. I have some private Reasons to believe, that this Visit from his Majesty gave *Flimnap* an Opportunity of doing me ill Offices to his Master. That Minister had always been my secret Enemy, although he outwardly caressed* me more than was usual to the Moroseness of his Nature. He represented to the Emperor the low Condition of his Treasury; that he was forced to take up Money at great Discount;* that Exchequer Bills would not circulate under nine *per Cent.* below Par; that I had cost his Majesty above a Million and a half of *Sprugs*, (their greatest Gold Coin, about the Bigness of a Spangle;) and upon the whole, that it would be adviseable in the Emperor to take the first fair Occasion of dismissing me.

I am here obliged to vindicate the Reputation of an excellent Lady, who was an innocent Sufferer upon my Account. The Treasurer took a Fancy to be jealous of his Wife, from the Malice of some evil Tongues, who informed him that her Grace had taken a violent Affection for my Person; and the Court-Scandal ran for some Time that she once came privately to my Lodging. This I solemnly declare to be a most infamous Falshood, without any Grounds, farther than that her Grace was pleased to treat me with all innocent Marks of Freedom and Friendship. I own she came often to my House, but always publickly, nor ever without three more in the Coach, who were usually her Sister, and young Daughter, and some particular Acquaintance; but this was common to many other Ladies of the Court. And I still appeal to my Servants round, whether they at any Time saw a Coach at my Door without knowing what Persons were in it. On those Occasions, when a Servant had given me Notice, my Custom was to go immediately to the Door; and after paying my Respects, to take up the Coach and two Horses very carefully in my Hands, (for if there were six Horses, the Postillion always unharnessed four) and place them on a Table, where I had fixed a moveable Rim quite round, of five Inches high, to prevent Accidents. And I have often had four Coaches and Horses at once on my Table full of Company, while I sat in my Chair leaning my Face towards them; and when I was engaged with one Sett, the Coachmen would gently drive the others round my Table. I have passed many an Afternoon very agreeably in these Conversations: But I defy the Treasurer, or his two Informers, (I will name them, and let them make their best of it) *Clustril* and *Drunlo*, to prove that any Person ever came to me *incognito*,* except the Secretary *Reldresal*, who was sent by express Command of his Imperial Majesty, as I have before related. I should not have dwelt so long upon this Particular, if it had not been a Point wherein the Reputation of a great Lady is so nearly concerned; to say nothing of my own; although I had the Honour to be a *Nardac*, which the Treasurer himself is not; for all the World knows he is only a *Clumglum*, a Title inferior by one Degree, as that of a Marquess is to a Duke in *England*; yet I allow he preceded me in right of his Post. These false Informations, which I afterwards came to the Knowledge of, by an Accident not proper to mention, made the Treasurer shew his Lady for some Time an ill Countenance, and me a worse: For although he were at last undeceived and reconciled to her, yet I lost all Credit with him; and found my Interest decline very fast with the Emperor himself, who was indeed too much governed by that Favourite.

CHAPTER SEVEN

The Author being informed of a Design to accuse him of High Treason, makes his Escape to Blefuscu. *His Reception there.*

BEFORE I proceed to give an Account of my leaving this Kingdom, it may be proper to inform the Reader of a private Intrigue which had been for two Months forming against me.

I had been hitherto all my Life a Stranger to Courts, for which I was unqualified by the Meanness of my Condition. I had indeed heard and read enough of the Dispositions of great Princes and Ministers; but never expected to have found such terrible Effects of them in so remote a Country,* governed, as I thought, by very different Maxims from those in *Europe*.

When I was just preparing to pay my Attendance on the Emperor of *Blefuscu*; a considerable Person at Court (to whom I had been very serviceable at a time when he lay under the highest Displeasure of his Imperial Majesty) came to my House very privately at Night in a close Chair, and without sending his Name, desired Admittance: The Chair-men were dismissed; I put the Chair, with his Lordship in it, into my Coat-Pocket; and giving Orders to a trusty Servant to say I was indisposed and gone to sleep, I fastened the Door of my House, placed the Chair on the Table, according to my usual Custom, and sat down by it. After the common Salutations were over, observing his Lordship's Countenance full of Concern; and enquiring into the Reason, he desired I would hear him with Patience, in a Matter that highly concerned my Honour and my Life. His Speech was to the following Effect, for I took Notes of it as soon as he left me.

You are to know, said he, that several Committees of Council have been lately called in the most private Manner on your Account: And it is but two Days since his Majesty came to a full Resolution.

You are very sensible that *Skyris Bolgolam* (*Galbet*, or High Admiral) hath been your mortal Enemy almost ever since your Arrival. His original Reasons I know not; but his Hatred is much encreased since your great Success against *Blefuscu*, by which his

Glory, as Admiral, is obscured. This Lord, in Conjunction with *Flimnap* the High Treasurer, whose Enmity against you is notorious on Account of his Lady; *Limtoc* the General, *Lalcon* the Chamberlain, and *Balmuff* the grand Justiciary, have prepared Articles of Impeachment against you, for Treason, and other capital Crimes.

This Preface made me so impatient, being conscious of my own Merits and Innocence, that I was going to interrupt; when he intreated me to be silent; and thus proceeded.

Out of Gratitude of the Favours you have done me, I procured Information of the whole Proceedings, and a Copy of the Articles, wherein I venture my Head for your Service.

Articles of Impeachment against* Quinbus Flestrin, (*the* Man-Mountain.)

ARTICLE I.

Whereas, by a Statute made in the Reign of his Imperial Majesty *Calin Deffar Plune*, it is enacted, That whoever shall make water within the Precincts of the Royal Palace, shall be liable to the Pains and Penalties of High Treason: Notwithstanding, the said *Quinbus Flestrin*, in open Breach of the said Law, under Colour* of extinguishing the Fire kindled in the Apartment of his Majesty's most dear Imperial Consort, did maliciously, traitorously, and devilishly, by discharge of his Urine, put out the said Fire kindled in the said Apartment, lying and being within the Precincts of the said Royal Palace; against the Statute in that Case provided, &c. against the Duty, &c.

ARTICLE II.

That the said *Quinbus Flestrin* having brought the Imperial Fleet of *Blefuscu* into the Royal Port, and being afterwards commanded by his Imperial Majesty to seize all the other Ships of the said Empire of *Blefuscu*, and reduce that Empire to a Province, to be governed by a Vice-Roy from hence; and to destroy and put to death not only all the *Big-Endian Exiles*, but likewise all the People of that Empire, who would not immediately forsake the *Big-Endian* Heresy: He the said *Flestrin*, like a false Traitor against his most Auspicious, Serene,*

Imperial Majesty, did petition to be excused from the said Service, upon Pretence of Unwillingness to force the Consciences, or destroy the Liberties and Lives of an innocent People.

ARTICLE III.

That, whereas certain Embassadors arrived from the Court of *Blefuscu* to sue for Peace in his Majesty's Court: He the said *Flestrin* did, like a false Traitor, aid, abet, comfort, and divert the said Embassadors; although he knew them to be Servants to a Prince who was lately an open Enemy to his Imperial Majesty, and in open War against his said Majesty.

ARTICLE IV.

That the said *Quinbus Flestrin*, contrary to the Duty of a faithful Subject, is now preparing to make a Voyage to the Court and Empire of *Blefuscu*, for which he hath received only verbal Licence from his Imperial Majesty; and under Colour of the said Licence, doth falsely and traitorously intend to take the said Voyage, and thereby to aid, comfort, and abet the Emperor of *Blefuscu*, so late an Enemy, and in open War with his Imperial Majesty aforesaid.

There are some other Articles, but these are the most important, of which I have read you an Abstract.

In the several Debates upon this Impeachment, it must be confessed that his Majesty gave many Marks of his great *Lenity*; often urging the Services you had done him, and endeavouring to extenuate your Crimes. The Treasurer and Admiral insisted that you should be put to the most painful and ignominious Death, by setting Fire on your House at Night; and the General was to attend with Twenty Thousand Men armed with poisoned Arrows, to shoot you on the Face and Hands. Some of your Servants were to have private Orders to strew a poisonous Juice on your Shirts* and Sheets, which would soon make you tear your own Flesh, and die in the utmost Torture. The General came into the same Opinion; so that for a long time there was a Majority against you. But his Majesty, resolving, if possible, to spare your Life, at last brought off* the Chamberlain.

Upon this Incident, *Reldresal*, principal Secretary for private Affairs, who always approved himself your true Friend, was commanded by the Emperor to deliver his Opinion, which he accordingly did; and therein justified the good Thoughts you have of him. He allowed your Crimes to be great; but that still there was room for Mercy, the most commendable Virtue in a Prince, and for which his Majesty was so justly celebrated. He said, the Friendship between you and him was so well known to the World, that perhaps the most honourable Board might think him partial: However, in Obedience to the Command he had received, he would freely offer his Sentiments. That if his Majesty, in Consideration of your Services, and pursuant to his own merciful Disposition, would please to spare your Life, and only give order to put out both your Eyes;* he humbly conceived, that by this Expedient, Justice might in some measure be satisfied, and all the World would applaud the *Lenity* of the Emperor, as well as the fair and generous Proceedings of those who have the Honour to be his Counsellors. That the Loss of your Eyes would be no Impediment to your bodily Strength,* by which you might still be useful to his Majesty. That Blindness is an Addition to Courage, by concealing Dangers from us; that the Fear you had for your Eyes, was the greatest Difficulty in bringing over the Enemy's Fleet; and it would be sufficient for you to see by the Eyes of the Ministers, since the greatest Princes do no more.*

This Proposal was received with the utmost Disapprobation by the whole Board. *Bolgolam*, the Admiral, could not preserve his Temper; but rising up in Fury, said, he wondered how the Secretary durst presume to give his Opinion for preserving the Life of a Traytor: That the Services you had performed, were, by all Reasons of State,* the great Aggravation of your Crimes; that you, who were able to extinguish the Fire, by discharge of Urine in her Majesty's Apartment (which he mentioned with Horror) might, at another time, raise an Inundation by the same Means, to drown the whole Palace; and the same Strength which enabled you to bring over the Enemy's Fleet, might serve, upon the first Discontent, to carry it back: That he had good Reasons to think you were a *Big-Endian* in your Heart; and as Treason begins in the Heart before it appears in Overt-Acts; so he accused you as a Traytor on that Account, and therefore insisted you should be put to death.

The Treasurer was of the same Opinion; he shewed to what Streights his Majesty's Revenue was reduced by the Charge of maintaining you, which would soon grow insupportable: That the

Secretary's Expedient of putting out your Eyes, was so far from being a Remedy against this Evil, that it would probably increase it; as it is manifest from the common Practice of blinding some Kind of Fowl, after which they fed the faster, and grew sooner fat: That his sacred Majesty, and the Council, who are your Judges, were in their own Consciences fully convinced of your Guilt; which was a sufficient Argument to condemn you to death, without the *formal Proofs* *required by the strict Letter of the Law.*

But his Imperial Majesty fully determined against capital Punishment, was graciously pleased to say, that since the Council thought the Loss of your Eyes too easy a Censure, some other may be inflicted hereafter. And your Friend the Secretary humbly desiring to be heard again, in Answer to what the Treasurer had objected concerning the great Charge his Majesty was at in maintaining you; said, that his Excellency, who had the sole Disposal of the Emperor's Revenue, might easily provide against this Evil, by gradually lessening your Establishment; by which, for want of sufficient Food, you would grow weak and faint, and lose your Appetite, and consequently decay and consume in a few Months; neither would the Stench of your Carcass be then so dangerous, when it should become more than half diminished; and immediately upon your Death, five or six Thousand of his Majesty's Subjects might, in two or three Days, cut your Flesh from your Bones, take it away by Cart-loads, and bury it in distant Parts to prevent Infection; leaving the Skeleton as a Monument of Admiration to Posterity.

Thus by the great Friendship of the Secretary, the whole Affair was compromised. It was strictly enjoined, that the Project of starving you by Degrees should be kept a Secret; but the Sentence of putting out your Eyes was entered on the Books; none dissenting except *Bolgolam* the Admiral, who being a Creature of the Empress, was perpetually instigated by her Majesty to insist upon your Death; she having born perpetual Malice against you, on Account of that infamous and illegal Method you took to extinguish the Fire in her Apartment.

In three Days your Friend the Secretary will be directed to come to your House, and read before you the Articles of Impeachment; and then to signify the great *Lenity* and Favour of his Majesty and Council; whereby you are only condemned to the Loss of your Eyes, which his Majesty doth not question you will gratefully and humbly submit to; and Twenty of his Majesty's Surgeons will attend, in order to see the Operation well performed, by discharging very sharp pointed Arrows into the Balls of your Eyes, as you lie on the Ground.

I leave to your Prudence what Measures you will take; and to avoid Suspicion, I must immediately return in as private a Manner as I came.

His Lordship did so, and I remained alone, under many Doubts and Perplexities of Mind.

It was a Custom introduced by this Prince and his Ministry, (very different, as I have been assured, from the Practices of former Times) that after the Court had decreed any cruel Execution, either to gratify the Monarch's Resentment, or the Malice of a Favourite; the Emperor always made a Speech to his whole Council, expressing his *great Lenity and Tenderness, as Qualities known and confessed by all the World.* This Speech was immediately published through the Kingdom; nor did any thing terrify the People so much as those Encomiums on his Majesty's Mercy;* because it was observed, that the more these Praises were enlarged and insisted on, the more *inhuman* was the Punishment, and the *Sufferer more innocent.* Yet, as to myself, I must confess, having never been designed for a Courtier, either by my Birth or Education, I was so ill a Judge of Things, that I could not discover the *Lenity* and Favour of this Sentence; but conceived it (perhaps erroneously) rather to be rigorous than gentle. I sometimes thought of standing my Tryal; for although I could not deny the Facts alledged in the several Articles, yet I hoped they would admit of some Extenuations. But having in my Life perused many State-Tryals, which I ever observed to terminate as the Judges thought fit to direct; I durst not rely on so dangerous a Decision, in so critical a Juncture, and against such powerful Enemies.* Once I was strongly bent upon Resistance: For while I had Liberty, the whole Strength of that Empire could hardly subdue me, and I might easily with Stones pelt the Metropolis to Pieces: But I soon rejected that Project with Horror, by remembering the Oath* I had made to the Emperor, the Favours I received from him, and the high Title of *Nardac* he conferred upon me. Neither had I so soon learned the Gratitude of Courtiers, to persuade myself that his Majesty's *present Severities acquitted me of all past Obligations.*

At last I fixed upon a Resolution, for which it is probable I may incur some Censure, and not unjustly; for I confess I owe the preserving mine Eyes, and consequently my Liberty, to my own great

Rashness and Want of Experience: Because if I had then known the
Nature of Princes and Ministers, which I have since observed in
many other Courts, and their Methods of treating Criminals less
obnoxious than myself; I should with great Alacrity and Readiness
have submitted to so *easy* a Punishment. But hurried on by the
Precipitancy of Youth; and having his Imperial Majesty's Licence to
pay my Attendance upon the Emperor of *Blefuscu*; I took this
Opportunity, before the three Days were elapsed, to send a Letter to
my Friend the Secretary, signifying my Resolution of setting out that
Morning for *Blefuscu*, pursuant to the Leave I had got; and without
waiting for an Answer, I went to that Side of the Island where our
Fleet lay. I seized a large Man of War, tied a Cable to the Prow, and
lifting up the Anchors, I stript myself, put my Cloaths (together with
my Coverlet, which I carryed under my Arm) into the Vessel; and
drawing it after me, between wading and swimming, arrived at the
Royal Port of *Blefuscu*, where the People had long expected me:
They lent me two Guides to direct me to the Capital City, which is of
the same Name; I held them in my Hands until I came within two
Hundred Yards of the Gate; and desired them to signify my Arrival
to one of the Secretaries, and let him know, I there waited his
Majesty's Commands. I had an Answer in about an Hour, that his
Majesty, attended by the Royal Family, and great Officers of the
Court, was coming out to receive me. I advanced a Hundred Yards;
the Emperor, and his Train, alighted from their Horses, the Empress
and Ladies from their Coaches; and I did not perceive they were in
any Fright or Concern. I lay on the Ground to kiss his Majesty's and
the Empress's Hand. I told his Majesty, that I was come according to
my Promise, and with the Licence of the Emperor my Master, to
have the Honour of seeing so mighty a Monarch, and to offer him
any Service in my Power, consistent with my Duty to my own
Prince; not mentioning a Word of my Disgrace, because I had hitherto no regular Information of it, and might suppose myself wholly
ignorant of any such Design; neither could I reasonably conceive
that the Emperor would discover the Secret while I was out of his
Power: Wherein, however, it soon appeared I was deceived.

I shall not trouble the Reader with the particular Account of my
Reception at this Court, which was suitable to the Generosity of so
great a Prince; nor of the Difficulties I was in for want of a House and
Bed, being forced to lie on the Ground, wrapt up in my Coverlet.

CHAPTER EIGHT

The Author, by a lucky Accident, finds Means to leave Blefuscu; *and, after some Difficulties, returns safe to his Native Country.*

THREE DAYS after my Arrival, walking out of Curiosity to the North-East Coast of the Island; I observed, about half a League off, in the Sea, somewhat that looked like a Boat overturned: I pulled off my Shoes and Stockings, and wading two or three Hundred Yards, I found the Object to approach nearer by Force of the Tide; and then plainly saw it to be a real Boat, which I supposed might, by some Tempest, have been driven from a Ship. Where-upon I returned immediately towards the City, and desired his Imperial Majesty to lend me Twenty of the tallest Vessels he had left after the Loss of his Fleet, and three Thousand Seamen under the Command of his Vice-Admiral. This Fleet sailed round, while I went back the shortest Way to the Coast where I first discovered the Boat; I found the Tide had driven it still nearer; the Seamen were all provided with Cordage, which I had beforehand twisted to a sufficient Strength. When the Ships came up, I stript myself, and waded till I came within an Hundred Yards of the Boat; after which I was forced to swim till I got up to it. The Seamen threw me the End of the Cord, which I fastened to a Hole in the forepart of the Boat, and the other End to a Man of War: But I found all my Labour to little Purpose; for being out of my Depth, I was not able to work. In this Necessity, I was forced to swim behind, and push the Boat forwards as often as I could, with one of my Hands; and the Tide favouring me, I advanced so far, that I could just hold up my Chin and feel the Ground. I rested two or three Minutes, and then gave the Boat another Shove, and so on till the Sea was no higher than my Arm-pits. And now the most laborious Part being over, I took out my other Cables which were stowed in one of the Ships, and fastening them first to the Boat, and then to nine of the Vessels which attended me; the Wind being favourable, the Seamen towed, and I shoved till we arrived within forty Yards of the Shore; and waiting till the Tide was out, I got dry to the Boat, and by the Assistance of two Thousand Men, with Ropes and

Engines, I made a shift to turn it on its Bottom, and found it was but little damaged.

I shall not trouble the Reader with the Difficulties I was under by the Help of certain Paddles, which cost me ten Days making, to get my Boat to the Royal Port of *Blefuscu*; where a mighty Concourse of People appeared upon my Arrival, full of Wonder at the Sight of so prodigious a Vessel. I told the Emperor, that my good Fortune had thrown this Boat in my Way, to carry me to some Place from whence I might return into my native Country; and begged his Majesty's Orders for getting Materials to fit it up; together with his Licence to depart; which, after some kind Expostulations, he was pleased to grant.

I did very much wonder, in all this Time, not to have heard of any Express relating to me from our Emperor to the Court of *Blefuscu*. But I was afterwards given privately to understand, that his Imperial Majesty, never imagining I had the least Notice of his Designs, believed I was only gone to *Blefuscu* in Performance of my Promise, according to the Licence he had given me, which was well known at our Court; and would return in a few Days when that Ceremony was ended. But he was at last in pain at my long absence; and, after consulting with the Treasurer, and the rest of that Cabal; a Person of Quality* was dispatched with the Copy of the Articles against me. This Envoy had Instructions to represent to the Monarch of *Blefuscu*, the great *Lenity* of his Master, who was content to punish me no further than with the Loss of mine Eyes: That I had fled from Justice, and if I did not return in two Hours, I should be deprived of my Title of *Nardac*, and declared a Traitor. The Envoy further added; that in order to maintain the Peace and Amity between both Empires, his Master expected, that his Brother of *Blefuscu* would give Orders to have me sent back to *Lilliput*, bound Hand and Foot, to be punished as a Traitor.

The Emperor of *Blefuscu* having taken three Days to consult, returned an Answer consisting of many Civilities and Excuses. He said, that as for sending me bound, his Brother knew it was Impossible; that although I had deprived him of his Fleet, yet he owed great Obligations to me for many good Offices I had done him in making the Peace. That however, both their Majesties would soon be made easy; for I had found a prodigious Vessel on the Shore, able to carry me on the Sea, which he had given order to fit up with my own

Assistance and Direction; and he hoped in a few Weeks both Empires would be freed from so insupportable an Incumbrance.

With this Answer the Envoy returned to *Lilliput*, and the Monarch of *Blefuscu* related to me all that had past; offering me at the same time (but under the strictest Confidence) his gracious Protection, if I would continue in his Service; wherein although I believed him sincere, yet I resolved never more to put any Confidence in Princes or Ministers, where I could possibly avoid it; and therefore, with all due Acknowledgements for his favourable Intentions, I humbly begged to be excused. I told him, that since Fortune, whether good or evil, had thrown a Vessel in my Way; I was resolved to venture myself in the Ocean, rather than be an Occasion of Difference between two such mighty Monarchs. Neither did I find the Emperor at all displeased; and I discovered by a certain Accident, that he was very glad of my Resolution, and so were most of his Ministers.

These Considerations moved me to hasten my Departure somewhat sooner than I intended; to which the Court, impatient to have me gone, very readily contributed. Five hundred Workmen were employed to make two Sails to my Boat, according to my Directions, by quilting thirteen fold of their strongest Linnen together. I was at the Pains of making Ropes and Cables, by twisting ten, twenty or thirty of the thickest and strongest of theirs. A great Stone that I happened to find, after a long Search by the Sea-shore, served me for an Anchor. I had the Tallow of three hundred Cows for greasing my Boat, and other Uses. I was at incredible Pains in cutting down some of the largest Timber Trees for Oars and Masts, wherein I was, however, much assisted by his Majesty's Ship-Carpenters, who helped me in smoothing them, after I had done the rough Work.

In about a Month, when all was prepared. I sent to receive his Majesty's Commands, and to take my leave. The Emperor and Royal Family came out of the Palace: I lay down on my Face to kiss his Hand, which he very graciously gave me; so did the Empress, and young Princes of the Blood. His Majesty presented me with fifty Purses of two hundred *Sprugs* a-piece, together with his Picture at full length, which I put immediately into one of my Gloves, to keep it from being hurt. The Ceremonies at my Departure were too many to trouble the Reader with at this time.

I stored the Boat with the Carcasses of an hundred Oxen, and three hundred Sheep, with Bread and Drink proportionable, and as much Meat ready dressed as four hundred Cooks could provide. I took with me six Cows and two Bulls alive, with as many Yews and Rams, intending to carry them into my own Country, and propagate the Breed. And to feed them on board, I had a good Bundle of Hay, and a Bag of Corn. I would gladly have taken a Dozen of the Natives; but this was a thing the Emperor would by no Means permit; and besides a diligent Search into my Pockets, his Majesty engaged my Honour not to carry away any of his Subjects, although with their own Consent and Desire.

Having thus prepared all things as well as I was able; I set sail on the Twenty-fourth Day of *September* 1701, at six in the Morning; and when I had gone about four Leagues to the Northward, the Wind being at South-East; at six in the Evening, I descryed a small Island about half a League to the North West. I advanced forward, and cast Anchor on the Lee-side of the Island, which seemed to be uninhabited. I then took some Refreshment, and went to my Rest. I slept well, and as I conjecture at least six Hours; for I found the Day broke in two Hours after I awaked. It was a clear Night; I eat my Breakfast before the Sun was up; and heaving Anchor, the Wind being favourable, I steered the same Course that I had done the Day before, wherein I was directed by my Pocket-Compass. My Intention was to reach, if possible, one of those Islands, which I had reason to believe lay to the North-East of *Van Diemen*'s Land. I discovered nothing all that Day; but upon the next, about three in the After-noon, when I had by my Computation made Twenty-four Leagues from *Blefuscu*, I descryed a Sail steering to the South-East; my Course was due East. I hailed her, but could get no Answer; yet I found I gained upon her, for the Wind slackened. I made all the Sail I could, and in half an Hour she spyed me, then hung out her Antient,* and discharged a Gun. It is not easy to express the joy I was in upon the unexpected Hope of once more seeing my beloved Country, and the dear Pledges I had left in it. The Ship slackned her Sails, and I came up with her between five and six in the Evening, *September* 26; but my Heart leapt within me to see her *English* Colours. I put my Cows and Sheep into my Coat-Pockets, and got on board with all my little Cargo of Provisions. The Vessel was an *English* Merchant-man, returning from *Japan* by the *North* and

*South Seas;** the Captain, Mr *John Biddel* of *Deptford*, a very civil
Man, and an excellent Sailor. We were now in the Latitude of
30 Degrees South; there were about fifty Men in the Ship; and here I
met an old Comrade of mine, one *Peter Williams*, who gave me a
good Character to the Captain. This Gentleman treated me with
Kindness, and desired I would let him know what Place I came from
last, and whither I was bound; which I did in few Words; but he
thought I was raving, and that the Dangers I underwent had disturbed my Head; whereupon I took my black Cattle and Sheep out
of my Pocket, which, after great Astonishment, clearly convinced
him of my Veracity.* I then shewed him the Gold given me by the
Emperor of *Blefuscu*, together with his Majesty's Picture at full
Length, and some other Rarities of that Country. I gave him two
Purses of two Hundred *Sprugs* each, and promised, when we arrived
in *England*, to make him a Present of a Cow and a Sheep big with
Young.

I shall not trouble the Reader with a particular Account of this
Voyage, which was very prosperous for the most Part. We arrived in
the *Downs** on the 13th of *April* 1702. I had only one Misfortune, that
the Rats on board carried away one of my Sheep; I found her Bones
in a Hole, picked clean from the Flesh. The rest of my Cattle I
got safe on Shore, and set them a grazing in a Bowling-Green at
Greenwich, where the Fineness of the Grass made them feed very
heartily, although I had always feared the contrary: Neither could I
possibly have preserved them in so long a Voyage, if the Captain had
not allowed me some of his best Bisket, which rubbed to Powder, and
mingled with Water, was their constant Food. The short Time I
continued in *England*, I made a considerable Profit by shewing my
Cattle to many Persons of Quality, and others: And before I began
my second Voyage, I sold them for six Hundred Pounds. Since my
last Return, I find the Breed is considerably increased, especially the
Sheep; which I hope will prove much to the Advantage of the Woollen
Manufacture, by the Fineness of the Fleeces.*

I stayed two Months with my Wife and Family; for my insatiable
Desire of seeing foreign Countries* would suffer me to continue no
longer. I left fifteen Hundred Pounds with my Wife, and fixed her in
a good House at *Redriff*. My remaining Stock I carried with me, Part
in Money, and Part in Goods, in Hopes to improve my Fortunes. My
eldest Uncle, *John*, had left me an Estate in Land, near *Epping*, of

about Thirty Pounds a Year; and I had a long Lease of the *Black-Bull* in *Fetter-Lane*,* which yielded me as much more: So that I was not in any Danger of leaving my Family upon the Parish.* My Son *Johnny*, named so after his Uncle, was at the Grammar School, and a towardly* Child. My Daughter *Betty* (who is now well married, and has Children) was then at her Needle-Work. I took Leave of my Wife, and Boy and Girl, with Tears on both Sides; and went on board the *Adventure*,* a Merchant-Ship of three Hundred Tons, bound for *Surat*,* Captain *John Nicholas* of *Liverpool*, Commander. But my Account of this Voyage must be referred to the second part of my Travels.

The End of the First Part.

PART TWO

A Voyage to Brobdingnag

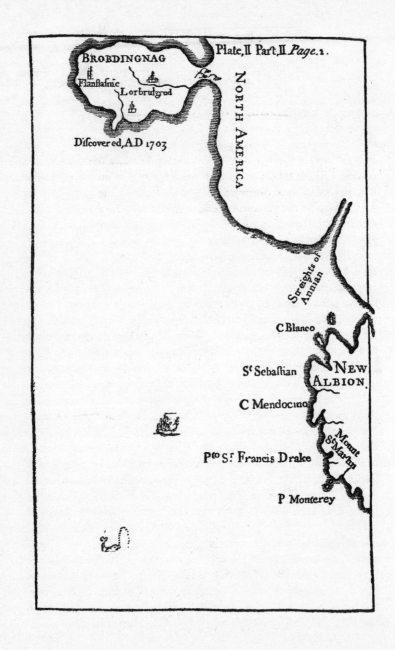

Plate, II Part II *Page.* 1.

BROBDINGNAG

Flanflasnic

Lorbrulgrud

Discovered, AD 1703

NORTH AMERICA

Streights of Annian

C. Blanco

St Sebastian

C Mendocino

NEW ALBION.

Mount St Martin

Pto St Francis Drake

P Monterey

CHAPTER ONE

A great Storm described, The long Boat sent to fetch Water, the Author goes with it to discover the Country. He is left on Shoar, is seized by one of the Natives, and carried* to a Farmer's House. His Reception there, with several Accidents that happened there. A Description of the Inhabitants.

Back to england.

HAVING BEEN condemned by Nature and Fortune to an active and restless Life; in two Months after my Return, I again left my native Country, and took Shipping in the *Downs* on the 20th Day of *June*, 1702, in the *Adventure*, Capt. *John Nicholas*, a *Cornish* Man, Commander, bound for *Surat*. We had a very prosperous Gale till we arrived at the *Cape* of *Good-hope*,* where we landed for fresh Water; but discovering a Leak we unshipped our Goods, and wintered there; for the Captain falling sick of an Ague, we could not leave the *Cape* till the End of *March*. We then set sail, and had a good Voyage till we passed the *Streights of Madagascar*; but having got Northward of that Island, and to about five Degrees South Latitude, the Winds, which in those Seas are observed to blow a constant equal Gale between the North and West, from the Beginning of *December* to the Beginning of *May*, on the 19th of *April* began to blow with much greater Violence, and more Westerly than usual; continuing so for twenty Days together, during which time we were driven a little to the East of the *Molucca* Islands, and about three Degrees Northward of the Line, as our Captain found by an Observation he took the 2d of *May*, at which time the Wind ceased, and it was a perfect Calm, whereat I was not a little rejoyced. But he being a Man well experienced in the Navigation of those Seas, bid us all prepare against a Storm, which accordingly happened the Day following: For a Southern Wind, called the Southern *Monsoon*,* began to set in.

Finding it was like to overblow,* we took in our Sprit-sail,* and stood by to hand* the Fore-sail; but making* foul Weather, we looked the Guns were all fast,* and handed the Missen.* The Ship lay very broad off,* so we thought it better spooning* before the Sea, than trying* or hulling.* We reeft the Foresail and set him, we hawled aft the Fore-sheet;* the Helm was hard a Weather.* The Ship wore*

bravely. We belay'd the Foredown-hall;* but the Sail was split, and we hawl'd down the Yard,* and got the Sail into the Ship, and unbound all the things clear of it. It was a very fierce Storm; the Sea broke strange and dangerous.* We hawl'd off upon the Lanniard of the Wipstaff,* and helped the Man at Helm. We would not get down our Top-Mast, but let all stand, because She scudded before the Sea very well,* and we knew that the Top-Mast being aloft, the Ship was the wholesomer,* and made better way through the Sea, seeing we had Sea room. When the Storm was over, we set Fore-sail and Main-sail, and brought the Ship to.* Then we set the Missen, Maintop-Sail and the Foretop-Sail. Our Course was East North-east, the Wind was at South-West. We got the Star-board Tacks aboard,* we cast off our Weather-braces and Lifts;* we set in the Lee-braces,* and hawl'd forward by the Weather-bowlings,* and hawl'd them tight, and belayed them, and hawl'd over the Missen Tack to Windward, and kept her full and by as near as she would lye.*

During this Storm, which was followed by a strong Wind West South-west, we were carried by my Computation about five hundred Leagues to the East, so that the oldest Sailor on Board could not tell in what part of the World we were. Our Provisions held out well, our Ship was staunch, and our Crew all in good Health; but we lay in the utmost Distress for Water. We thought it best to hold on the same Course rather than turn more Northerly, which might have brought us to the North-west Parts of the great *Tartary*, and into the frozen Sea.*

On the 16*th* Day of *June*, 1703, a Boy on the Top-mast discovered Land. On the 17*th* we came in full View of a great Island or Continent, (for we knew not whether*) on the South-side whereof was a small Neck of Land jutting out into the Sea, and a Creek too shallow to hold a Ship of above one hundred Tuns. We cast Anchor within a League of this Creek, and our Captain sent a dozen of his Men well armed in the Long Boat, with Vessels for Water if any could be found. I desired his leave to go with them, that I might see the Country, and make what Discoveries I could. When we came to Land we saw no River or Spring, nor any Sign of Inhabitants. Our Men therefore wandered on the Shore to find out some fresh Water near the Sea, and I walked alone about a Mile on the other side, where I observed the Country all barren and rocky. I now began to be weary, and seeing nothing to entertain my Curiosity, I returned gently down towards the Creek; and the Sea being full in my View, I saw our Men already got into the Boat, and rowing for Life to the Ship. I was going to hollow* after them, although it had been to little purpose, when I observed a huge Creature walking after them in the Sea,* as fast as he could: He waded not much deeper than his Knees, and took prodigious strides: But our Men had the start of him half a League, and the Sea thereabouts being full of sharp pointed Rocks, the Monster was not able to overtake the Boat. This I was afterwards told, for I durst not stay to see the Issue of that Adventure; but ran as fast as I could the Way I first went; and then climbed up a steep Hill, which gave me some Prospect of the Country. I found it fully culti-vated; but that which first surprised me was the Length of the Grass, which in those Grounds that seemed to be kept for Hay, was about twenty Foot high.

I fell into a high Road, for so I took it to be, although it served to the Inhabitants only as a foot Path through a Field of Barley. Here I walked on for sometime, but could see little on either Side, it being now near Harvest, and the Corn rising at least forty Foot. I was an Hour walking to the end of this Field, which was fenced in with a Hedge of at least one hundred and twenty Foot high, and the Trees so lofty that I could make no Computation of their Altitude. There was a Stile to pass from this Field into the next: It had four Steps, and a Stone to cross over when you came to the uppermost. It was impossible for me to climb this Stile, because every Step was six Foot high, and the upper Stone above twenty. I was endeavouring to find some Gap in the Hedge; when I discovered one of the Inhabitants in the next Field advancing towards the Stile, of the same Size with him whom I saw in the Sea pursuing our Boat. He appeared as Tall as an ordinary Spire-steeple; and took about ten Yards at every Stride,* as near as I could guess. I was struck with the utmost Fear and Astonishment, and ran to hide my self in the Corn, from whence I saw him at the Top of the Stile, looking back into the next Field on the right Hand; and heard him call in a Voice many Degrees louder than a speaking Trumpet; but the Noise was so High in the Air, that at first I certainly thought it was Thunder. Whereupon seven Monsters like himself came towards him with Reaping-Hooks in their Hands, each Hook about the largeness of six Scythes. These People were not so well clad as the first, whose Servants or Labour-ers they seemed to be. For, upon some Words he spoke, they went to reap the Corn in the Field where I lay. I kept from them at as great a Distance as I could, but was forced to move with extream Difficulty; for the Stalks of the Corn were sometimes not above a Foot distant, so that I could hardly squeeze my Body betwixt them. However, I made a shift to go forward till I came to a part of the Field where the Corn had been laid by the Rain and Wind: Here it was impossible for me to advance a step; for the Stalks were so interwoven that I could not creep through, and the Beards of the fallen Ears so strong and pointed, that they pierced through my Cloaths into my Flesh. At the same time I heard the Reapers not above an hundred Yards behind me. Being quite dispirited with Toil, and wholly overcome by Grief and Despair, I lay down between two Ridges, and heartily wished I might there end my Days. I bemoaned my desolate Widow, and Fatherless Children: I lamented my own Folly and Wilfulness in attempting a second Voyage against the Advice of all my Friends and Relations. In this terrible Agitation of Mind I could not forbear thinking of *Lilliput*, whose Inhabitants looked upon me as the great-est Prodigy that ever appeared in the World; where I was able to draw an Imperial Fleet in my Hand, and perform those other Actions which will be recorded for ever in the Chronicles of that Empire, while Posterity shall hardly believe them, although attested by Millions. I reflected what a Mortification it must prove to me to appear as inconsiderable in this Nation, as one single *Lilliputian* would be among us. But, this I conceived was to be the least of my Misfortunes: For, as human Creatures are observed to be more Savage and cruel in Proportion to their Bulk;* what could I expect but to be a Morsel in the Mouth of the first among these enormous Barbarians that should happen to seize me? Undoubtedly Philo-sophers* are in the Right when they tell us, that nothing is great or little otherwise than by Comparison: It might have pleased Fortune to let the *Lilliputians* find some Nation, where the People were as diminutive with respect to them, as they were to me. And who knows but that even this prodigious Race of Mortals might be equally overmatched in some distant Part of the World, whereof we have yet no Discovery?

Scared and confounded as I was, I could not forbear going on with these Reflections; when one of the Reapers approaching within ten Yards of the Ridge where I lay, made me apprehend that with the next Step I should be squashed to Death under his Foot, or cut in two with his Reaping Hook. And therefore when he was again about to move, I screamed as loud as Fear could make me. Whereupon the huge Creature trod short, and looking round about under him for some time, at last espied me as I lay on the Ground. He considered a while with the Caution of one who endeavours to lay hold on a small dangerous Animal in such a Manner that it shall not be able either to scratch or to bite him; as I my self have sometimes done with a *Weasel* in *England*. At length he ventured to take me up behind by the middle between his Fore-finger and Thumb, and brought me within three Yards of his Eyes, that he might behold my Shape more perfectly. I guessed his Meaning; and my good Fortune gave me so much Presence of Mind, that I resolved not to struggle in the least as he held me in the Air about sixty Foot from the Ground; although he grievously pinched my Sides, for fear I should slip through his Fingers. All I ventured was to raise my Eyes towards the Sun, and place my Hands together in a supplicating Posture, and to speak some Words in a humble melancholy Tone, suitable to the Condition I then was in. For, I apprehended every Moment that he would dash me against the Ground, as we usually do any little hateful Animal which we have a Mind to Destroy. But my good Star would have it, that he appeared pleased with my Voice and Gestures, and began to look upon me as a Curiosity; much wondering to hear me pronounce articulate Words, although he could not understand them. In the mean time I was not able to forbear Groaning and shedding Tears, and turning my Head towards my Sides; letting him know, as well as I could, how cruelly I was hurt by the Pressure of his Thumb and Finger. He seemed to apprehend my Meaning; for, lifting up the Lappet* of his Coat, he put me gently into it, and immediately ran along with me to his Master, who was a substantial Farmer, and the same Person I had first seen in the Field.

The Farmer having (as I supposed by their Talk) received such an Account of me as his Servant could give him, took a piece of a small Straw, about the Size of a walking Staff, and therewith lifted up the Lappets of my Coat; which it seems he thought to be some kind of Covering that Nature had given me. He blew my Hairs aside to take a better View of my Face. He called his Hinds* about him, and asked them (as I afterwards learned) whether they had ever seen in the Fields any little Creature that resembled me. He then placed me softly on the Ground upon all four; but I got immediately up, and

walked slowly backwards and forwards, to let those People see I had
no Intent to run away. They all sate down in a Circle about me, the
better to observe my Motions. I pulled off my Hat, and made a low
Bow towards the Farmer. I fell on my Knees, and lifted up my Hands
and Eyes, and spoke several Words as loud as I could: I took a Purse
of Gold out of my Pocket, and humbly presented it to him. He
received it on the Palm of his Hand, then applied it close to his Eye,
to see what it was, and afterwards turned it several times with the
Point of a Pin (which he took out of his Sleeve,) but could make
nothing of it. Whereupon I made a Sign that he should place his
Hand on the Ground: I then took the Purse, and opening it, poured
all the Gold into his Palm. There were six *Spanish*-Pieces of four
Pistoles* each, besides twenty or thirty smaller Coins. I saw him wet
the Tip of his little Finger upon his Tongue, and take up one of my
largest Pieces, and then another; but he seemed to be wholly ignorant
what they were. He made me a Sign to put them again into my
Purse, and the Purse again into my Pocket; which after offering to
him several times, I thought it best to do.

The Farmer by this time was convinced I must be a rational
Creature. He spoke often to me, but the Sound of his Voice pierced
my Ears like that of a Water-Mill;* yet his Words were articulate
enough. I answered as loud as I could in several Languages; and he
often laid his Ear within two Yards of me, but all in vain, for we were
wholly unintelligible to each other. He then sent his Servants to their
Work, and taking his Handkerchief out of his Pocket, he doubled and
spread it on his Hand, which he placed flat on the Ground with the
Palm upwards, making me a Sign to step into it, as I could easily do,
for it was not above a Foot in thickness. I thought it my part to
obey; and for fear of falling, laid myself at full Length upon the
Handkerchief, with the Remainder of which he lapped me up to the
Head for further Security; and in this Manner carried me home to
his House. There he called his Wife, and shewed me to her; but she
screamed and ran back as Women in *England* do at the Sight of a
Toad or a Spider. However, when she had a while seen my
Behaviour, and how well I observed the Signs her Husband made,
she was soon reconciled, and by Degrees grew extremely tender
of me.

It was about twelve at Noon, and a Servant brought in Dinner. It
was only one substantial Dish of Meat (fit for the plain Condition of

an Husband-Man) in a Dish of about four and twenty Foot Diameter. The Company were the Farmer and his Wife, three Children, and an old Grandmother: When they were sat down, the Farmer placed me at some Distance from him on the Table, which was thirty Foot high from the Floor. I was in a terrible Fright, and kept as far as I could from the Edge, for fear of falling. The Wife minced a bit of Meat, then crumbled some Bread on a Trencher, and placed it before me. I made her a low Bow, took out my Knife and Fork, and fell to eat; which gave them exceeding Delight. The Mistress sent her Maid for a small Dram-cup, which held about two Gallons, and filled it with Drink: I took up the Vessel with much difficulty in both Hands, and in a most respectful Manner drank to her Ladyship's Health, expressing the Words as loud as I could in *English*; which made the Company laugh so heartily, that I was almost deafened with the Noise. This Liquor tasted like a small Cyder, and was not unpleasant. Then the Master made me a Sign to come to his Trencher side; but as I walked on the Table, being in great surprize* all the time, as the indulgent Reader will easily conceive and excuse, I happened to stumble against a Crust, and fell flat on my Face, but received no hurt. I got up immediately, and observing the good People to be in much Concern, I took my Hat (which I held under my Arm out of good Manners) and waving it over my Head, made three Huzza's, to shew I had got no Mischief by the Fall. But advancing forwards toward my Master (as I shall henceforth call him) his youngest Son who sate next to him, an arch* Boy of about ten Years old, took me up by the Legs, and held me so high in the Air, that I trembled every Limb; but his Father snatched me from him; and at the same time gave him such a Box on the left Ear, as would have felled an *European* Troop of Horse to the Earth; ordering him to be taken from the Table. But, being afraid the Boy might owe me a Spight; and well remembering how mischievous all Children among us naturally are to Sparrows, Rabbits, young Kittens, and Puppy-Dogs; I fell on my Knees, and pointing to the Boy, made my Master to understand, as well as I could, that I desired his Son might be pardoned. The Father complied, and the Lad took his seat again; whereupon I went to him and kissed his Hand, which my Master took, and made him stroak me gently with it.

In the Midst of Dinner my Mistress's favourite Cat leapt into her Lap. I heard a Noise behind me like that of a Dozen

Stocking-Weavers* at work; and turning my Head, I found it proceeded from the Purring of this Animal, who seemed to be three Times larger than an Ox, as I computed by the View of her Head, and one of her Paws, while her Mistress was feeding and stroking her. The Fierceness of this Creature's Countenance altogether discomposed me; although I stood at the further End of the Table, above fifty Foot off; and although my Mistress held her fast for fear she might give a Spring, and seize me in her Talons. But it happened there was no Danger; for the Cat took not the least Notice of me when my Master placed me within three Yards of her. And as I have been always told, and found true by Experience in my Travels, that flying, or discovering Fear before a fierce Animal, is a certain Way to make it pursue or attack you; so I resolved in this dangerous Juncture to shew no Manner of Concern. I walked with Intrepidity five or six Times before the very Head of the Cat, and came within half a Yard of her; whereupon she drew her self back, as if she were more afraid of me: I had less Apprehension concerning the Dogs, whereof three or four came into the Room, as it is usual in Farmers Houses; one of which was a Mastiff equal in Bulk to four Elephants, and a Greyhound, somewhat taller than the Mastiff, but not so large.

When Dinner was almost done, the Nurse came in with a Child of a Year old in her Arms; who immediately spied me, and began a Squall that you might have heard from *London-Bridge* to *Chelsea*; after the usual Oratory of Infants, to get me for a Play-thing. The Mother out of pure Indulgence took me up, and put me towards the Child, who presently seized me by the Middle, and got my Head in his Mouth, where I roared so loud that the Urchin was frighted, and let me drop; and I should infallibly have broken my Neck, if the Mother had not held her Apron under me. The Nurse to quiet her Babe made use of a Rattle, which was a Kind of hollow Vessel filled with great Stones, and fastned by a Cable to the Child's Waist: But all in vain, so that she was forced to apply the last Remedy by giving it suck. I must confess no Object ever disgusted me so much as the Sight of her monstrous Breast, which I cannot tell what to compare with, so as to give the curious Reader an Idea of its Bulk, Shape and Colour. It stood prominent six Foot, and could not be less than sixteen in Circumference. The Nipple was about half the Bigness of my Head, and the Hue both of that and the Dug so varified with Spots, Pimples and Freckles, that nothing could appear more nauseous: For I had a near Sight of her, she sitting down the more conveniently to give Suck, and I standing on the Table. This made me reflect upon the fair Skins of our *English* Ladies, who appear so beautiful to us, only because they are of our own Size, and their Defects not to be seen but through a magnifying Glass,* where we find by Experiment that the smoothest and whitest Skins look rough and coarse, and ill coloured.

I remember when I was at *Lilliput*, the Complexions of those diminutive People appeared to me the fairest in the World: And talking upon this Subject with a Person of Learning there, who was an intimate Friend of mine; he said, that my Face appeared much fairer and smoother when he looked on me from the Ground, than it did upon a nearer View when I took him up in my Hand, and brought him close; which he confessed was at first a very shocking Sight. He said, he could discover great Holes in my Skin; that the Stumps of my Beard were ten Times stronger than the Bristles of a Boar; and my Complexion made up of several Colours altogether disagreeable: Although I must beg Leave to say for my self, that I am as fair as most of my Sex and Country, and very little Sunburnt by all my Travels. On the other Side, discoursing of the Ladies in that Emperor's Court, he used to tell me, one had Freckles, another too wide a Mouth, a third too large a Nose; nothing of which I was able to distinguish. I confess this Reflection was obvious enough; which, however, I could not forbear, lest the Reader might think those vast Creatures were actually deformed: For I must do them Justice to say they are a comely Race of People; and particularly the Features of my Master's Countenance, although he were but a Farmer, when I beheld him from the Height of sixty Foot, appeared very well proportioned.

When Dinner was done, my Master went out to his Labourers; and as I could discover by his Voice and Gesture, gave his Wife a strict Charge to take Care of me. I was very much tired and disposed to sleep, which my Mistress perceiving, she put me on her own Bed, and covered me with a clean white Handkerchief, but larger and coarser than the Main Sail of a Man of War.

I slept about two Hours, and dreamed I was at home with my Wife and Children, which aggravated my Sorrows when I awakened and found my self alone in a vast Room, between two and three Hundred Foot wide, and above two Hundred high; lying in a Bed twenty Yards wide. My Mistress was gone about her household Affairs, and had locked me in. The Bed was eight Yards from the Floor. Some natural Necessities required me to get down: I durst not presume to call, and if I had, it would have been in vain with such a Voice as mine at so great a Distance from the Room where I lay, to the Kitchen where the Family kept. While I was under these Circumstances, two Rats* crept up the Curtains, and ran Smelling backwards and forwards on the Bed: One of them came up almost to my Face; whereupon I rose in a Fright, and drew out my Hanger* to defend my self. These horrible Animals had the Boldness to attack me on both Sides, and one of them held his Fore-feet at my Collar; but I had the good fortune to rip up his Belly before he could do me any Mischief. He fell down at my Feet; and the other seeing the Fate of his Comrade, made his Escape, but not without one good Wound on the Back, which I gave him as he fled, and made the Blood run trickling from him. After this Exploit I walked gently to and fro on the Bed, to recover my Breath and Loss of Spirits. These Creatures were of the Size of a large Mastiff, but infinitely more nimble and fierce; so that if I had taken off my Belt before I went to sleep, I must have infallibly been torn to Pieces and devoured. I measured the Tail of the dead Rat, and found it to be two Yards long, wanting an Inch; but it went against my Stomach to drag the Carcass off the Bed, where it lay still bleeding; I observed it had yet some Life, but with a strong Slash cross the Neck, I thoroughly dispatched it.

Soon after, my Mistress came into the Room, who seeing me all bloody, ran and took me up in her Hand. I pointed to the dead *Rat*, smiling and making other Signs to shew I was not hurt; whereat she was extremely rejoyced, calling the Maid to take up the dead *Rat* with a Pair of Tongs, and throw it out of the Window. Then she set me on a Table, where I shewed her my Hanger all bloody, and wiping it on the Lappet of my Coat, returned it to the Scabbard. I was pressed to do more than one Thing, which another could not do for me; and therefore endeavoured to make my Mistress understand that I desired to be set down on the Floor; which after she had done, my Bashfulness would not suffer me to express my self farther than by pointing to the Door, and bowing several Times. The good Woman with much Difficulty at last perceived what I would be at; and taking me up again in her Hand, walked into the Garden, where she set me down. I went on one Side about two Hundred Yards; and beckoning to her not to look or to follow me, I hid myself between two Leaves of Sorrel, and there discharged the Necessities of Nature.

I hope, the gentle Reader will excuse me for dwelling on these and the like Particulars; which however insignificant they may appear to grovelling vulgar Minds, yet will certainly help a Philosopher to enlarge his Thoughts and Imagination, and apply them to the Benefit of publick as well as private Life; which was my sole Design in presenting this and other Accounts of my Travels to the World;* wherein I have been chiefly studious of Truth, without affecting any Ornaments of Learning, or of Style.* But the whole Scene of this Voyage made so strong an Impression on my Mind, and is so deeply fixed in my Memory, that in committing it to Paper, I did not omit one material Circumstance: However, upon a strict Review, I blotted out several Passages of less Moment which were in my first Copy, for fear of being censured as tedious and trifling, whereof Travellers are often, perhaps not without Justice, accused.

CHAPTER TWO

A Description of the Farmer's Daughter. The Author carried to a Market-Town, and then to the Metropolis. The Particulars of his Journey.

M Y mistress had a daughter of nine Years old, a Child of towardly Parts* for her Age, very dextrous at her Needle, and skilful in dressing her Baby.* Her Mother and she contrived to fit up the Baby's Cradle for me against Night: The Cradle was put into a small Drawer of a Cabinet, and the Drawer placed upon a hanging Shelf for fear of the *Rats.* This was my Bed all the Time I stayed with those People, although made more convenient by Degrees, as I began to learn their Language, and make my Wants known. This young Girl was so handy, that after I had once or twice pulled off my Cloaths before her, she was able to dress and undress me, although I never gave her that Trouble when she would let me do either my self.* She made me seven Shirts, and some other Linnen of as fine Cloth as could be got, which indeed was coarser than Sackcloth; and these she constantly washed for me with her own Hands. She was likewise my School-Mistress to teach me the Language: When I pointed to any thing, she told me the Name of it in her own Tongue, so that in a few Days I was able to call for whatever I had a mind to. She was very good natured, and not above forty Foot high, being little for her Age. She gave me the Name of *Grildrig*, which the Family took up, and afterwards the whole Kingdom. The Word imports what the *Latins* call *Nanunculus*,* the *Italians Homunceletino*,* and the *English Mannikin*. To her I chiefly owe my Preservation in that Country: We never parted while I was there; I called her my *Glumdalclitch*,* or little Nurse: And I should be guilty of great Ingratitude if I omitted this honourable Mention of her Care and Affection towards me, which I heartily wish it lay in my Power to requite as she deserves, instead of being the innocent but unhappy Instrument of her Disgrace, as I have too much Reason to fear.

It now began to be known and talked of in the Neighbourhood, that my Master had found a strange Animal in the Field, about the Bigness of a *Splacknuck*, but exactly shaped in every Part like a human Creature; which it likewise imitated in all its actions; seemed to speak in a little Language* of its own, had already learned several Words of theirs, went erect upon two Legs, was tame and gentle, would come when it was called, do whatever it was bid, had the finest Limbs in the World, and a Complexion fairer than a Nobleman's Daughter of three Years old. Another Farmer who lived hard by, and was a particular Friend of my Master, came on a Visit on Purpose to enquire into the Truth of this Story. I was immediately produced, and placed upon a Table; where I walked as I was commanded, drew my Hanger, put it up again, made my Reverence to my Master's Guest, asked him in his own Language how he did, and told him he was welcome; just as my little Nurse had instructed me. This Man, who was old and dim-sighted, put on his Spectacles to behold me better, at which I could not forbear laughing very heartily; for his Eyes appeared like the Full-Moon shining into a Chamber at two Windows. Our People, who discovered the Cause of my Mirth, bore me Company in Laughing; at which the old Fellow was Fool enough to be angry and out of Countenance. He had the Character of a great Miser; and to my Misfortune he well deserved it by the cursed Advice he gave my Master, to shew me as a Sight upon a Market-Day in the next Town, which was half an Hour's Riding, about two and twenty Miles from our House. I guessed there was some Mischief contriving, when I observed my Master and his Friend whispering long together, sometimes pointing at me; and my Fears made me Fancy that I overheard and understood some of their Words. But, the next Morning *Glumdalclitch* my little Nurse told me the whole Matter, which she had cunningly picked out from her Mother. The poor Girl laid me on her Bosom, and fell a weeping with Shame and Grief. She apprehended some Mischief would happen to me from rude vulgar Folks, who might Squeeze me to Death, or break one of my Limbs by taking me in their Hands. She had also observed how modest I was in my Nature, how nicely I regarded my Honour; and what an Indignity I should conceive it to be exposed for Money as a publick Spectacle to the meanest of the People. She said, her *Papa* and *Mamma* had promised that *Grildrig* should be hers; but now she found they meant to serve her as they did last Year, when they pretended to give her a Lamb; and yet, as soon as it was fat, sold it to a Butcher. For my own Part, I may truly affirm that I was less concerned than my Nurse. I had a strong Hope which never left me, that I should one Day recover my Liberty;

and as to the Ignominy of being carried about for a Monster,* I considered my self to be a perfect Stranger in the Country; and that such a Misfortune could never be charged upon me as a Reproach if ever I should return to *England*; since the King of *Great Britain* himself, in my Condition, must have undergone the same Distress.*

My Master, pursuant to the Advice of his Friend, carried me in a Box* the next Market-Day to the neighbouring Town; and took along with him his little Daughter my Nurse upon a Pillion behind him. The Box was close* on every Side, with a little Door for me to go in and out, and a few Gimlet-holes to let in Air. The Girl had been so careful to put the Quilt of her Baby's Bed into it, for me to lye down on. However, I was terribly shaken and discomposed in this Journey, although it were but of half an Hour. For the Horse went about forty Foot at every Step; and trotted so high, that the Agitation was equal to the rising and falling of a Ship in a great Storm, but much more frequent: Our Journey was somewhat further than from *London* to St *Albans*.* My Master alighted at an Inn which he used to frequent; and after consulting a while with the Inn-keeper, and making some necessary Preparations, he hired the *Grultrud*, or Cryer, to give Notice through the Town, of a strange Creature to be seen at the Sign of the Green *Eagle*,* not so big as a *Splacknuck*, (an Animal in that Country very finely shaped, about six Foot long) and in every Part of the Body resembling an human Creature; could speak several Words, and perform a Hundred diverting Tricks.

I was placed upon a Table in the largest Room of the Inn, which might be near three Hundred Foot square. My little Nurse stood on a low Stool close to the Table, to take care of me, and direct what I should do. My Master, to avoid a Croud, would suffer only Thirty People at a Time to see me. I walked about on the Table as the Girl commanded; she asked me Questions as far as she knew my Understanding of the Language reached, and I answered them as loud as I could. I turned about several Times to the Company, paid my humble Respects, said they were welcome; and used some other Speeches I had been taught. I took up a Thimble filled with Liquor, which *Glumdalclitch* had given me for a Cup, and drank their Health. I drew out my Hanger, and flourished it after the Manner of Fencers in *England*. My Nurse gave me part of a Straw, which I exercised as a Pike, having learned the Art in my Youth. I was that Day shewn to twelve Sets of Company; and as often forced to go over again with the same Fopperies,* till I was half dead with Weariness and Vexation. For, those who had seen me, made such wonderful Reports, that the People were ready to break down the Doors to come in. My Master for his own Interest would not suffer any one to touch me, except my Nurse; and, to prevent Danger, Benches were set around the Table at such a Distance, as put me out of every Body's Reach. However, an unlucky* School-Boy aimed a Hazel Nut directly at my Head, which very narrowly missed me; otherwise, it came with so much Violence, that it would have infallibly knocked out my Brains; for it was almost as large as a small Pumpion:* But I had the Satisfaction to see the young Rogue well beaten, and turned out of the Room.

My Master gave publick Notice, that he would shew me again the next Market-Day: And in the mean time, he prepared a more convenient Vehicle for me, which he had Reason enough to do; for I was so tired with my first Journey, and with entertaining Company for eight Hours together, that I could hardly stand upon my Legs, or speak a Word. It was at least three Days before I recovered my Strength; and that I might have no rest at home, all the neighbouring Gentlemen from a Hundred Miles round, hearing of my Fame, came to see me at my Master's own House. There could not be fewer than thirty Persons with their Wives and Children; (for the Country is very populous;) and my Master demanded the Rate of a full Room whenever he shewed me at Home, although it were only to a single Family. So that for some time I had but little Ease every Day of the Week, (except *Wednesday*, which is their Sabbath) although I were not carried to the Town.

My Master finding how profitable I was likely to be, resolved to carry me to the most considerable Cities of the Kingdom. Having therefore provided himself with all things necessary for a long Journey, and settled his Affairs at Home; he took Leave of his Wife, and upon the 17*th* of *August* 1703, about two Months after my Arrival, we set out for the Metropolis, situated near the Middle of that Empire, and about three Thousand Miles distance from our House: My Master made his Daughter *Glumdalclitch* ride behind him. She carried me on her Lap in a Box tied about her Waist. The Girl had lined it on all Sides with the softest Cloth she could get, well quilted underneath; furnished it with her Baby's Bed, provided me with Linnen and other Necessaries; and made every thing as convenient as she could. We had no other Company but a Boy of the House, who rode after us with the Luggage.

My Master's Design was to shew me in all the Towns by the Way, and to step out of the Road for Fifty or an Hundred Miles, to any Village or Person of Quality's House where he might expect Custom. We made easy Journies of not above seven or eight Score Miles a Day: For *Glumdalclitch*, on Purpose to spare me, complained she was tired with the trotting of the Horse. She often took me out of my Box at my own Desire, to give me Air and shew me the Country; but always held me fast by Leading-strings. We passed over five or six Rivers many Degrees broader and deeper than the *Nile* or the *Ganges*; and there was hardly a Rivulet so small as the *Thames* at *London-Bridge*. We were ten Weeks in our Journey; and I was shewn in Eighteen large Towns, besides many Villages and private Families.

On the 26th Day of *October*, we arrived at the Metropolis, called in their Language *Lorbrulgrud*, or *Pride of the Universe*. My Master took a Lodging in the principal Street of the City, not far from the Royal Palace; and put out Bills in the usual Form, containing an exact Description of my Person and Parts. He hired a large Room between three and four Hundred Foot wide. He provided a Table sixty Foot in Diameter, upon which I was to act my Part; and pallisadoed it around three Foot from the Edge, and as many high, to prevent my falling over. I was shewn ten Times a Day to the Wonder and Satisfaction of all People. I could now speak the Language tolerably well; and perfectly understood every Word that was spoken to me. Besides, I had learned their Alphabet, and could make a shift to explain a Sentence here and there; for *Glumdalclitch* had been my Instructer while we were at home, and at leisure Hours during our Journey. She carried a little Book in her Pocket, not much larger than a *Sanson*'s *Atlas*;* it was a common Treatise for the use of young Girls, giving a short Account of their Religion; out of this she taught me my Letters, and interpreted the Words.

CHAPTER THREE

The Author sent for to Court. The Queen buys him of his Master the Farmer, and presents him to the King. He disputes with his Majesty's great Scholars. An Apartment at Court provided for the Author. He is in high Favour with the Queen. He stands up for the Honour of his own Country. His Quarrels with the Queen's Dwarf.

THE frequent Labours I underwent every Day, made in a few Weeks a very considerable Change in my Health: The more my Master got by me, the more unsatiable he grew. I had quite lost my Stomach,* and was almost reduced to a Skeleton. The Farmer observed it; and concluding I soon must die, resolved to make as good a Hand of* me as he could. While he was thus reasoning and resolving with himself; a *Slardral*, or Gentleman Usher, came from Court, commanding my Master to bring me immediately thither for the Diversion of the Queen and her Ladies. Some of the latter had already been to see me; and reported strange Things of my Beauty, Behaviour, and good Sense. Her Majesty and those who attended her, were beyond Measure delighted with my Demeanor. I fell on my Knees, and begged the Honour of kissing her Imperial Foot;* but this Gracious Princess held out her little Finger towards me (after I was set on a Table) which I embraced in both my Arms, and put the Tip of it with the utmost Respect, to my Lip. She made me some general Questions about my Country and my Travels, which I answered as distinctly and in as few Words as I could. She asked, whether I would be content to live at Court. I bowed down to the Board of the Table, and humbly answered, that I was my Master's Slave; but if I were at my own Disposal, I should be proud to devote my Life to her Majesty's Service. She then asked my Master whether he were willing to sell me at a good Price. He, who apprehended I could not live a Month, was ready enough to part with me; and demanded a Thousand Pieces of Gold; which were ordered him on the Spot, each Piece being about the Bigness of eight Hundred Moydores:* But, allowing for the Proportion of all Things between that Country and *Europe*, and the high Price of Gold among them; was hardly so great a Sum as a Thousand Guineas would be in *England*. I then said to the

Queen; since I was now her Majesty's most humble Creature and Vassal, I must beg the Favour, that *Glumdalclitch*, who had always tended me with so much Care and Kindness, and understood to do it so well, might be admitted into her Service, and continue to be my Nurse and Instructor. Her Majesty agreed to my Petition; and easily got the Farmer's Consent, who was glad enough to have his Daughter preferred at Court: And the poor Girl herself was not able to hide her Joy. My late Master withdrew, bidding me farewell, and saying he had left me in a good Service; to which I replyed not a Word, only making him a slight Bow.

The Queen observed my Coldness; and when the Farmer was gone out of the Apartment, asked me the Reason. I made bold to tell her Majesty, that I owed no other Obligation to my late Master, than his not dashing out the Brains of a poor harmless Creature found by Chance in his Field; which Obligation was amply recompensed by the Gain he had made in shewing me through half the Kingdom, and the Price he had now sold me for. That the Life I had since led, was laborious enough to kill an Animal of ten Times my Strength. That my Health was much impaired by the continual Drudgery of entertaining the Rabble every Hour of the Day; and that if my Master had not thought my Life in Danger, her Majesty perhaps would not have got so cheap a Bargain. But as I was out of all fear of being ill treated under the Protection of so great and good an Empress, the Ornament of Nature, the Darling of the World, the Delight of her Subjects, the Phoenix of the Creation; so, I hoped my late Master's Apprehensions would appear to be groundless; for I already found my Spirits to revive by the Influence of her most August Presence.

This was the Sum of my Speech, delivered with great Improprieties and Hesitation; the latter Part was altogether framed in the Style peculiar to that People, whereof I learned some Phrases from *Glumdalclitch*, while she was carrying me to Court.

The Queen giving great Allowance for my Defectiveness in speaking, was however surprised at so much Wit and good Sense in so diminutive an Animal. She took me in her own Hand, and carried me to the King, who was then retired to his Cabinet. His Majesty,* a Prince of much Gravity, and austere Countenance, not well observing my Shape at first View, asked the Queen after a cold Manner, how long it was since she grew fond of a *Splacknuck*; for such it seems he took me to be, as I lay upon my Breast in her Majesty's right Hand. But this Princess, who hath an infinite deal of Wit and Humour, set me gently on my Feet upon the Scrutore;* and commanded me to give His Majesty an Account of my self, which I did in a very few Words; and *Glumdalclitch*, who attended at the Cabinet Door, and could not endure I should be out of her Sight, being admitted; confirmed all that had passed from my Arrival at her Father's House.

The King, although he be as learned a Person* as any in his Dominions and had been educated in the Study of Philosophy, and particularly Mathematicks; yet when he observed my Shape exactly, and saw me walk erect, before I began to speak, conceived I might be a piece of Clock-work,* (which is in that Country arrived to a very great Perfection) contrived by some ingenious Artist.* But, when he heard my Voice, and found what I delivered to be regular and rational, he could not conceal his Astonishment. He was by no means satisfied with the Relation I gave him of the Manner I came into his Kingdom; but thought it a Story concerted between *Glumdalclitch* and her Father, who had taught me a Sett of Words to make me sell at a higher Price. Upon this Imagination he put several other Questions to me, and still received rational Answers, no otherwise defective than by a Foreign Accent, and an imperfect Knowledge in the Language; with some rustick Phrases which I had learned at the Farmer's House, and did not suit the polite Style of a Court.

His Majesty sent for three great Scholars who were then in their weekly waiting* (according to the Custom in that Country.) These Gentlemen, after they had a while examined my Shape with much Nicety, were of different Opinions concerning me. They all agreed that I could not be produced according to the regular Laws of Nature;* because I was not framed with a Capacity of preserving my Life, either by Swiftness, or climbing of Trees, or digging Holes in the Earth. They observed by my Teeth, which they viewed with great Exactness, that I was a carnivorous Animal; yet most Quadrupeds being an Overmatch for me; and Field-Mice, with some others, too nimble, they could not imagine how I should be able to support my self, unless I fed upon Snails and other Insects;* which they offered by many learned Arguments to evince that I could not possibly do. One of them seemed to think that I might be an Embrio, or abortive Birth. But this Opinion was rejected by the other two, who observed my Limbs to be perfect and finished; and that I had lived several Years, as it was manifested from my Beard; the Stumps whereof they plainly discovered through a Magnifying-Glass. They would not allow me to be a Dwarf, because my Littleness was beyond all Degrees of Comparison; for the Queen's favourite Dwarf, the smallest ever known in that Kingdom, was nearly thirty Foot high. After much Debate, they concluded unanimously that I was only *Relplum Scalcath*, which is interpreted literally *Lusus Naturæ*;* a Determination exactly agreeable to the Modern Philosophy of *Europe*: whose Professors,* disdaining the old Evasion of *occult Causes*, whereby the Followers of *Aristotle* endeavour in vain to disguise their Ignorance; have invented this wonderful Solution of all Difficulties, to the unspeakable Advancement of human Knowledge.

After this decisive Conclusion, I entreated to be heard a Word or two. I applied my self to the King, and assured His Majesty, that I came from a Country which abounded with several Millions of both Sexes, and of my own Stature; where the Animals, Trees, and Houses were all in Proportion; and where by Consequence I might be as able to defend my self, and to find Sustenance, as any of his Majesty's Subjects could do here; which I took for a full Answer to those Gentlemens Arguments. To this they only replied with a Smile of Contempt,* saying, that the Farmer had instructed me very well in my Lesson. The King, who had a much better Understanding, dismissing his learned Men, sent for the Farmer, who by good Fortune was not yet gone out of Town: Having therefore first examined him privately, and then confronted him with me and the young Girl; his Majesty began to think that what we told him might possibly be true. He desired the Queen to order, that a particular Care should be taken of me; and was of Opinion, that *Glumdalclitch* should still continue in her Office of tending me, because he observed we had a great Affection for each other. A convenient Apartment was provided for her at Court; she had a sort of Governess appointed to take care of her Education, a Maid to dress her, and two other Servants for menial Offices; but the Care of me was wholly appropriated to her self. The Queen commanded her own Cabinet-maker to contrive a Box that might serve me for a Bed-chamber, after the Model that *Glumdalclitch* and I should agree upon. This Man was a most ingenious Artist; and according to my Directions, in three Weeks finished for me a wooden Chamber of sixteen Foot square, and twelve High;

with Sash Windows, a Door, and two Closets, like a *London* Bed-chamber. The Board that made the Cieling was to be lifted up and down by two Hinges, to put in a Bed ready furnished by her Majesty's Upholsterer; which *Glumdalclitch* took out every Day to air, made it with her own Hands, and letting it down at Night, locked up the Roof over me. A Nice* Workman, who was famous for little Curiosities, undertook to make me two Chairs, with Backs and Frames, of a Substance not unlike Ivory; and two Tables, with a Cabinet to put my Things in. The Room was quilted on all Sides, as well as the Floor and the Cieling, to prevent any Accident from the Carelessness of those who carried me; and to break the Force of a Jolt when I went in a Coach. I desired a Lock for my Door to prevent Rats and Mice from coming in: The Smith after several Attempts made the smallest that was ever seen among them; for I have known a larger at the Gate of a Gentleman's House in *England*. I made a shift to keep the Key in a Pocket of my own, fearing *Glumdalclitch* might lose it. The Queen likewise ordered the thinnest Silks that could be gotten, to make me Cloaths, not much thicker than an *English* Blanket, very cumbersome till I was accustomed to them. They were after the Fashion of the Kingdom, partly resembling the *Persian*, and partly the *Chinese*; and are a very grave and decent Habit.

The Queen became so fond of my Company, that she could not dine without me. I had a Table placed upon the same at which her Majesty eat, just at her left Elbow; and a Chair to sit on. *Glumdalclitch* stood upon a Stool on the Floor, near my Table, to assist and take Care of me. I had an entire set of Silver Dishes and Plates, and other Necessaries, which in Proportion to those of the Queen, were not much bigger than what I have seen in a *London* Toy-shop, for the Furniture of a Baby-house:* These my little Nurse kept in her Pocket in a Silver Box, and gave me at Meals as I wanted them; always cleaning them her self. No Person dined with the Queen but the two Princesses Royal; the elder sixteen Years old, and the younger at that time thirteen and a Month. Her Majesty used to put a Bit of Meat upon one of my Dishes, out of which I carved for my self, and her Diversion was to see me eat in Miniature. For the Queen (who had indeed but a weak Stomach) took up at one Mouthful, as much as a dozen *English* Farmers could eat at a Meal, which to me was for some time a very nauseous Sight. She would craunch* the Wing of a Lark, Bones and all, between her Teeth, although it were nine Times as large as that of a full grown Turkey; and put a Bit of Bread in her Mouth, as big as two twelve-penny Loaves. She drank out of a golden Cup, above a Hogshead at a Draught. Her Knives were twice as long as a Scythe set straight upon the Handle. The Spoons, Forks, and other Instruments were all in the same Proportion. I remember when *Glumdalclitch* carried me out of Curiosity to see some of the Tables at Court, where ten or a dozen of these enormous Knives and Forks were lifted up together; I thought I had never till then beheld so terrible a Sight.

It is the Custom, that every *Wednesday*, (which as I have before observed, was their Sabbath) the King and Queen, with the Royal Issue of both Sexes, dine together in the Apartment of his Majesty; to whom I was now become a Favourite; and at these Times my little Chair and Table were placed at his left Hand before one of the Salt-sellers. This Prince took a Pleasure in conversing with me; enquiring into the Manners, Religion, Laws, Government, and Learning of *Europe*, wherein I gave him the best Account I was able. His Apprehension was so clear, and his Judgment so exact, that he made very wise Reflections and Observations upon all I said. But, I confess, that after I had been a little too copious in talking of my own beloved Country; of our Trade, and Wars by Sea and Land, of our Schisms in Religion, and Parties in the State; the Prejudices of his Education prevailed so far, that he could not forbear taking me up in his right Hand, and stroaking me gently with the other; after an hearty Fit of laughing, asked me whether I were a *Whig* or a *Tory*.* Then turning to his first Minister, who waited behind him with a white Staff, near as tall as the Main-mast of the Royal *Sovereign*;* he observed, how contemptible a Thing was human Grandeur, which could be mimicked by such diminutive Insects as I; And yet, said he, I dare engage, these Creatures have their Titles and Distinctions of Honour; they contrive little Nests and Burrows, that they call Houses and Cities;* they make a Figure in Dress and Equipage; they love, they fight, they dispute, they cheat, they betray. And thus he continued on, while my Colour came and went several Times, with Indignation to hear our noble Country, the Mistress of Arts and Arms, the Scourge of *France*, the Arbitress of *Europe*, the Seat of Virtue, Piety, Honour and Truth, the Pride and Envy of the World, contemptuously treated.

But, as I was not in a Condition to resent Injuries, so, upon mature

Thoughts, I began to doubt whether I were injured or no. For, after having been accustomed several Months to the Sight and Converse of this People, and observed every Object upon which I cast my Eyes, to be of proportionable Magnitude; the Horror I had first conceived from their Bulk and Aspect was so far worn off, that if I had then beheld a Company of *English* Lords and Ladies in their Finery and Birth-day Cloaths,* acting their several Parts in the most courtly Manner of Strutting, and Bowing and Prating; to say the Truth, I should have been strongly tempted to laugh as much at them as the King and his Grandees did at me. Neither indeed could I forbear smiling at my self, when the Queen used to place me upon her Hand towards a Looking-Glass, by which both our Persons appeared before me in full View together; and there could nothing be more ridiculous than the Comparison: So that I really began to imagine my self dwindled many Degrees below my usual Size.

Nothing angered and mortified me so much as the Queen's Dwarf,* who being of the lowest Stature that was ever in that Country, (for I verily think he was not full Thirty Foot high) became insolent at seeing a Creature so much beneath him, that he would always affect to swagger and look big as he passed by me in the Queen's Antichamber, while I was standing on some Table talking with the Lords or Ladies of the Court; and he seldom failed of a smart Word or two upon my Littleness; against which I could only revenge my self by calling him *Brother*, challenging him to wrestle; and such Repartees as are usual in the Mouths of *Court Pages*. One Day at Dinner, this malicious little Cubb was so nettled with something I had said to him, that raising himself upon the Frame of her Majesty's Chair, he took me up by the Middle, as I was sitting down, not thinking any Harm, and let me drop into a large Silver Bowl of Cream;* and then ran away as fast as he could. I fell over Head and Ears, and if I had not been a good Swimmer, it might have gone very hard with me; for *Glumdalclitch* in that Instant happened to be at the other End of the Room; and the Queen was in such a Fright, that she wanted Presence of Mind to assist me. But my little Nurse ran to my Relief; and took me out, after I had swallowed above a Quart of Cream. I was put to Bed; however I received no other Damage than the loss of a Suit of Cloaths, which was utterly spoiled. The Dwarf was soundly whipped, and as a further Punishment, forced to drink up the Bowl of Cream, into which he had thrown me; neither was he ever restored to Favour: For, soon after the Queen bestowed him to a Lady of high Quality; so that I saw him no more, to my very great Satisfaction; for I could not tell to what Extremity such a malicious Urchin might have carried his Resentment.

He had before served me a scurvy Trick, which set the Queen a laughing, although at the same time she was heartily vexed, and would have immediately cashiered him, if I had not been so generous as to intercede. Her Majesty had taken a Marrow-bone upon her Plate; and after knocking out the Marrow, placed the Bone again in the Dish erect as it stood before; the Dwarf watching his Opportunity, while *Glumdalclitch* was gone to the Sideboard, mounted the Stool she stood on to take care of me at Meals; took me up in both Hands, and squeezing my Legs together, wedged them into the Marrow-bone above my Waist; where I stuck for some time, and made a very ridiculous Figure. I believe it was near a Minute before any one knew what was become of me; for I thought it below me to cry out. But, as Princes seldom get their Meat hot, my Legs were not scalded, only my Stockings and Breeches in a sad Condition. The Dwarf at my Entreaty had no other Punishment than a sound whipping.

I was frequently raillied by the Queen upon Account of my Fearfulness; and she used to ask me whether the People of my Country were as great Cowards as my self. The Occasion was this. The Kingdom is much pestered with Flies in Summer; and these odious Insects, each of them as big as a *Dunstable* Lark,* hardly gave me any Rest while I sat at Dinner, with their continual Humming and Buzzing about mine Ears. They would sometimes alight upon my Victuals, and leave their Loathsome Excrement or Spawn behind, which to me was very visible, although not to the Natives of that Country, whose large Opticks were not so acute as mine in viewing smaller Objects. Sometimes they would fix upon my Nose or Forehead, where they stung me to the Quick, smelling very offensively; and I could easily trace that viscous Matter, which our Naturalists tell us enables those Creatures to walk with their Feet upwards upon a Ceiling. I had much ado to defend my self against these detestable Animals, and could not forbear starting when they came on my Face. It was the common Practice of the Dwarf to catch a Number of these Insects in his Hand, as School-boys do among us, and let them out suddenly under my Nose, on Purpose to frighten me, and divert the

Queen. My Remedy was to cut them in Pieces with my Knife as they flew in the Air; wherein my Dexterity was much admired.

I remember one Morning when *Glumdalclitch* had set me in my Box upon a Window, as she usually did in fair Days to give me Air, (for I durst not venture to let the Box be hung on a Nail out of the Window, as we do with Cages in *England*) after I had lifted up one of my Sashes, and sat down at my Table to eat a Piece of Sweet-Cake for my Breakfast; above twenty Wasps, allured by the Smell, came flying into the Room, humming louder than the Drones of as many Bagpipes. Some of them seized my Cake, and carried it piecemeal away; others flew about my Head and Face, confounding me with the Noise, and putting me in the utmost Terror of their Stings. However I had the Courage to rise and draw my Hanger, and attack them in the Air. I dispatched four of them, but the rest got away, and I presently shut my Window. These Insects were as large as Partridges; I took out their Stings, found them an Inch and a half long, and as sharp as Needles. I carefully preserved them all, and having since shewn them with some other Curiosities in several Parts of *Europe*, upon my Return to *England* I gave three of them to *Gresham College*,* and kept the fourth for my self.

CHAPTER FOUR

The Country described. A Proposal for correcting modern Maps. The King's Palace, and some Account of the Metropolis. The Author's Way of travelling. The chief Temple described.

I NOW intend to give the Reader a short Description of this Country, as far as I travelled in it, which was not above two thousand Miles round *Lorbrulgrud* the Metropolis. For, the Queen, whom I always attended, never went further when she accompanied the King in his Progresses; and there staid till his Majesty returned from viewing his Frontiers. The whole Extent of this Prince's Dominions reacheth about six thousand Miles in Length, and from three to five in Breadth. From whence I cannot but conclude, that our Geographers of *Europe* are in a great Error, by supposing nothing but Sea between *Japan* and *California*: For it was ever my Opinion, that there must be a Balance of Earth to counterpoise the great Continent of *Tartary*; and therefore they ought to correct their Maps and Charts, by joining this vast Tract of Land to the North-west Parts of *America*; wherein I shall be ready to lend them my Assistance.

The Kingdom is a Peninsula,* terminated to the North-east by a Ridge of Mountains thirty Miles high which are altogether impassable by Reason of the Volcanoes upon the Tops. Neither do the most Learned know what sort of Mortals inhabit beyond those Mountains, or whether they be inhabited at all. On the three other Sides it is bounded by the Ocean. There is not one Sea-port in the whole Kingdom; and those Parts of the Coasts into which the Rivers issue, are so full of pointed Rocks, and the Sea generally so rough, that there is no venturing with the smallest of their Boats; so that these People are wholly excluded from any Commerce with the rest of the World.* But the large Rivers are full of Vessels, and abound with excellent Fish; for they seldom get any from the Sea, because the Sea-fish are of the same Size with those in *Europe*, and consequently not worth catching; whereby it is manifest, that Nature, in the Production of Plants and Animals of so extraordinary a Bulk, is wholly confined to this Continent; of which I leave the Reasons to be determined by Philosophers. However, now and then they take a

Whale that happens to be dashed against the Rocks, which the common People feed on heartily. These Whales I have known so large that a Man could hardly carry one upon his Shoulders; and sometimes for Curiosity they are brought in Hampers to *Lorbrulgrud*: I saw one of them in a Dish at the King's Table, which passed for a Rarity; but I did not observe he was fond of it; for I think indeed the Bigness disgusted him, although I have seen one somewhat larger in *Greenland*.

The Country is well inhabited, for it contains fifty-one Cities,* near an hundred walled Towns, and a great Number of Villages. To satisfy my curious Reader, it may be sufficient to describe *Lorbrulgrud*.* This City stands upon almost two equal Parts on each Side the River that passes through. It contains above eighty thousand Houses. It is in Length three *Glonglungs** (which make about fifty four English Miles) and two and a half in Breadth, as I measured it myself in the Royal Map made by the King's Order, which was laid on the Ground on purpose for me, and extended an hundred Feet; I paced the Diameter and Circumference several times Bare-foot, and computing by the Scale, measured it pretty exactly.

The King's Palace is no regular Edifice, but an Heap of Buildings about seven Miles round: The chief Rooms are generally two hundred and forty Foot high, and broad and long in Proportion. A Coach was allowed to *Glumdalclitch* and me, wherein her Governess frequently took her out to see the Town, or go among the Shops; and I was always of the Party, carried in my Box; although the Girl at my own Desire would often take me out, and hold me in her Hand, that I might more conveniently view the Houses and the People as we passed along the Streets. I reckoned our Coach to be about a Square of *Westminster-Hall*, but not altogether so High; however, I cannot be very exact. One Day the Governess ordered our Coachman to stop at several Shops; where the Beggars watching their Opportunity, crouded to the Sides of the Coach, and gave me the most horrible Spectacles that ever an *European* Eye beheld. There was a Woman with a Cancer in her Breast, swelled to a monstrous Size, full of Holes, in two or three of which I could have easily crept, and covered my whole Body. There was a Fellow with a Wen in his Neck, larger than five Woolpacks; and another with a couple of wooden Legs, each about twenty Foot high. But, the most hateful Sight of all was the Lice crawling on their Cloathes: I could see distinctly the Limbs of these Vermin with my naked Eye, much better than those of an *European* Louse through a Microscope; and their Snouts with which they rooted like Swine. They were the first I had ever beheld; and I should have been curious enough to dissect one of them, if I had proper Instruments (which I unluckily left behind me in the Ship) although indeed the Sight was so nauseous, that it perfectly turned my Stomach.

Beside the large Box in which I was usually carried, the Queen ordered a smaller one to be made for me, of about twelve Foot Square, and ten high, for the Convenience of Travelling; because the other was somewhat too large for *Glumdalclitch*'s Lap, and cumbersom in the Coach; it was made by the same Artist, whom I directed in the whole Contrivance. This travelling Closet was an exact Square with a Window in the Middle of three of the Squares, and each Window was latticed with Iron Wire on the outside, to prevent Accidents in long Journeys. On the fourth Side, which had no Window, two strong Staples were fixed, through which the Person that carried me, when I had a Mind to be on Horseback, put in a Leathern Belt, and buckled it about his Waist. This was always the Office of some grave trusty Servant in whom I could confide, whether I attended the King and Queen in their Progresses, or were disposed to see the Gardens, or pay a Visit to some great Lady or Minister of State in the Court, when *Glumdalclitch* happened to be out of Order: For I soon began to be known and esteemed among the greatest Officers, I suppose more upon Account of their Majesty's Favour, than any Merit of my own. In Journeys, when I was weary of the Coach, a Servant on Horseback would buckle my Box, and place it on a Cushion before him; and there I had a full Prospect of the Country on three Sides from my three Windows. I had in this Closet a Field-Bed and a Hammock hung from the Ceiling, two Chairs and a Table, neatly screwed to the Floor, to prevent being tossed about by the Agitation of the Horse or the Coach. And having been long used to Sea-Voyages, those Motions, although sometimes very violent, did not much discompose me.

Whenever I had a Mind to see the Town, it was always in my Travelling-Closet; which *Glumdalclitch* held in her Lap in a kind of open Sedan, after the Fashion of the Country, born by four Men, and attended by two others in the Queen's Livery. The People who had often heard of me, were very curious to croud about the Sedan;

and the Girl was complaisant enough to make the Bearers stop, and to take me in her Hand that I might be more conveniently seen.

I was very desirous to see the chief Temple, and particularly the Tower belonging to it, which is reckoned the highest in the Kingdom. Accordingly one Day my Nurse carried me thither, but I may truly say I came back disappointed; for, the Height is not above three thousand Foot, reckoning from the Ground to the highest Pinnacle top; which allowing for the Difference between the Size of those People, and us in *Europe*, is no great matter for Admiration, nor at all equal in Proportion (if I rightly remember) to *Salisbury* Steeple.* But, not to detract from a Nation to which during my Life I shall acknowledge myself extremely obliged; it must be allowed, that whatever this famous Tower wants in Height, is amply made up in Beauty and Strength. For the Walls are near an hundred Foot thick, built of hewn Stone, whereof each is about forty Foot square, and adorned on all Sides with Statues of Gods and Emperors cut in Marble larger than the Life, placed in their several Niches. I measured a little Finger which had fallen down from one of these Statues, and lay unperceived among some Rubbish; and found it exactly four Foot and an Inch in Length. *Glumdalclitch* wrapped it up in a Handkerchief, and carried it home in her Pocket to keep among other Trinkets, of which the Girl was very fond, as Children at her Age usually are.

The King's Kitchen is indeed a noble Building, vaulted at Top, and about six hundred Foot high. The great Oven is not so wide by ten Paces as the Cupola at St *Paul*'s:* For I measured the latter on purpose after my Return. But if I should describe the Kitchen-grate, the prodigious Pots and Kettles, the Joints of Meat turning on the Spits, with many other Particulars; perhaps I should be hardly believed;* at least a severe Critick would be apt to think I enlarged a little, as Travellers are often suspected to do. To avoid which Censure, I fear I have run too much into the other Extream; and that if this Treatise should happen to be translated into the Language of *Brobdingnag*, (which is the general Name of that Kingdom) and transmitted thither; the King and his People would have Reason to complain; that I had done them an Injury by a false and diminutive Representation.

His Majesty seldom keeps above six hundred Horses in his Stables: They are generally from fifty-four to sixty Foot high. But, when he goes abroad on solemn Days, he is attended for State by a Militia Guard of five hundred Horse, which indeed I thought was the most splendid Sight that could be ever beheld, till I saw part of his Army in Battalia:* whereof I shall find another Occasion to speak.

CHAPTER FIVE

Several Adventures that happened to the Author. The Execution of a Criminal. The Author shews his Skill in Navigation.

I SHOULD have lived happy enough in that Country, if my Littleness had not exposed me to several ridiculous and troublesome Accidents; some of which I shall venture to relate. *Glumdalclitch* often carried me into the Gardens of the Court in my smaller Box, and would sometimes take me out of it and hold me in her Hand, or set me down to walk. I remember, before the Dwarf left the Queen, he followed us one Day into those Gardens; and my Nurse having set me down, he and I being close together, near some Dwarf Apple-trees, I must need shew my Wit by a silly Allusion between him and the Trees, which happens to hold in their Language as it doth in ours. Whereupon, the malicious Rogue watching his Opportunity, when I was walking under one of them, shook it directly over my Head, by which a dozen Apples, each of them near as large as a *Bristol* Barrel, came tumbling about my Ears; one of them hit me on the Back as I chanced to stoop, and knocked me down flat on my Face, but I received no other Hurt; and the Dwarf was pardoned at my Desire, because I had given the Provocation.

Another Day, *Glumdalclitch* left me on a smooth Grass-plot to divert my self while she walked at some Distance with her Governess. In the mean time there suddenly fell such a violent Shower of Hail, that I was immediately by the Force of it struck to the Ground: And when I was down, the Hail-stones gave me such cruel Bangs all over the Body, as if I had been pelted with Tennis-Balls; however I made a Shift to creep on all four, and shelter my self by lying flat on my Face on the Lee-side of a Border of Lemmon Thyme; but so bruised from Head to Foot, that I could not go abroad in ten Days. Neither is this at all to be wondered at; because Nature in that Country observing the same Proportion through all her Operations, a Hail-stone is near Eighteen Hundred Times as large as one in *Europe*; which I can assert upon Experience, having been so curious to weigh and measure them.

But, a more dangerous Accident happened to me in the same

Garden, when my little Nurse, believing she had put me in a secure Place, which I often entreated her to do, that I might enjoy my own Thoughts; and having left my Box at home to avoid the Trouble of carrying it, went to another Part of the Garden with her Governess and some Ladies of her Acquaintance. While she was absent and out of hearing, a small white Spaniel belonging to one of the chief Gardiners, having got by Accident into the Garden, happened to range near the Place where I lay. The Dog following the Scent, came directly up, and taking me in his Mouth, ran strait to his Master, wagging his Tail, and set me gently on the Ground. By good Fortune he had been so well taught, that I was carried between his Teeth without the least Hurt, or even tearing my Cloaths. But, the poor Gardiner, who knew me well, and had a great Kindness for me, was in a terrible Fright. He gently took me up in both his Hands, and asked me how I did; but I was so amazed* and out of Breath, that I could not speak a Word. In a few Minutes I came to my self, and he carried me safe to my little Nurse, who by this time had returned to the Place where she left me, and was in cruel Agonies when I did not appear, nor answer when she called; she severely reprimanded the Gardiner on Account of his Dog. But, the Thing was hushed up, and never known at Court; for the Girl was afraid of the Queen's Anger; and truly as to my self, I thought it would not be for my Reputation that such a Story should go about.

This Accident absolutely determined *Glumdalclitch* never to trust me abroad for the future out of her Sight. I had been long afraid of this Resolution; and therefore concealed from her some little unlucky Adventures that happened in those Times when I was left by my self. Once a Kite hovering over the Garden, made a Stoop at me, and if I had not resolutely drawn my Hanger, and run under a thick Espalier, he would have certainly carried me away in his Talons. Another time, walking to the Top of a fresh Mole-hill, I fell to my Neck in the Hole through which that Animal had cast up the Earth; and coined some Lye not worth remembering, to excuse my self for spoiling my cloaths. I likewise broke my right Shin against the Shell of a Snail, which I happened to stumble over, as I was walking alone, and thinking on poor *England*.

I cannot tell whether I were more pleased or mortified, to observe in those solitary Walks, that the smaller Birds did not appear to be at all afraid of me; but would hop about within a Yard Distance, looking for Worms, and other Food, with as much Indifference and Security as if no Creature at all were near them. I remember, a Thrush had the Confidence to snatch out of my Hand with his Bill, a Piece of Cake that *Glumdalclitch* had just given me for my Breakfast. When I attempted to catch any of these Birds, they would boldly turn against me, endeavouring to pick my Fingers, which I durst not venture within their Reach; and then they would hop back unconcerned to hunt for Worms or Snails, as they did before. But, one Day I took a thick Cudgel, and threw it with all my Strength so luckily at a Linnet, that I knocked him down, and seizing him by the Neck with both my Hands, ran with him in Triumph to my Nurse. However, the Bird who had only been stunned, recovering himself, gave me so many Boxes with his Wings on both Sides of my Head and Body, although I held him at Arms Length, and was out of the Reach of his Claws, that I was twenty Times thinking to let him go. But I was soon relieved by one of our Servants, who wrung off the Bird's Neck; and I had him next Day for Dinner by the Queen's Command. This Linnet, as near as I can remember, seemed to be somewhat larger than an *English* Swan.

The Maids of Honour* often invited *Glumdalclitch* to their Apartments, and desired she would bring me along with her, on Purpose to have the Pleasure of seeing and touching me. They would often strip me naked from Top to Toe, and lay me at full Length in their Bosoms; wherewith I was much disgusted; because, to say the Truth, a very offensive Smell came from their Skins; which I do not mention or intend to the Disadvantage of those excellent Ladies, for whom I have all Manner of Respect: But, I conceive, that my Sense was more acute in Proportion to my Littleness; and that those illustrious Persons were no more disagreeable to their Lovers, or to each other, than People of the same Quality are with us in *England*. And, after all, I found their natural Smell was much more supportable than when they used Perfumes, under which I immediately swooned away. I cannot forget, that an intimate Friend of mine in *Lilliput* took the Freedom in a warm Day, when I had used a good deal of Exercise, to complain of a strong Smell about me; although I am as little faulty that way as most of my Sex: But I suppose, his Faculty of Smelling was as nice with regard to me, as mine was to that of this People. Upon this Point, I cannot forbear doing Justice to the Queen

my Mistress, and *Glumdalclitch* my Nurse; whose Persons were as
sweet as those of any Lady in *England*.

That which gave me most Uneasiness among these Maids of
Honour, when my Nurse carried me to visit them, was to see them
use me without any Manner of Ceremony, like a Creature who had
no Sort of Consequence. For, they would strip themselves to the
Skin, and put on their Smocks in my Presence, while I was placed on
their Toylet* directly before their naked Bodies; which, I am sure, to
me was very far from being a tempting Sight, or from giving me any
other Motions* than those of Horror and Disgust. Their Skins
appeared so coarse and uneven, so variously coloured when I saw
them near, with a Mole here and there as broad as a Trencher, and
Hairs hanging from it thicker than Pack-threads; to say nothing
further concerning the rest of their Persons. Neither did they at all
scruple while I was by, to discharge what they had drunk, to the
Quantity of at least two Hogsheads, in a Vessel that held above three
Tuns.* The handsomest among these Maids of Honour, a pleasant*
frolicsome Girl of sixteen, would sometimes set me astride upon one
of her Nipples; with many other Tricks, wherein the Reader will
excuse me for not being over particular. But, I was so much displeased, that I entreated *Glumdalclitch* to contrive some excuse for
not seeing that young Lady any more.

One Day, a young Gentleman who was a Nephew to my Nurse's
Governess, came and pressed them both to see an Execution. It was
of a Man who had murdered one of that Gentleman's intimate
Acquaintance. *Glumdalclitch* was prevailed on to be of the Company,
very much against her Inclination, for she was naturally tender
hearted: And, as for my self, although I abhorred such Kind of
Spectacles; yet my Curiosity tempted me to see something that I
thought must be extraordinary. The Malefactor was fixed in a Chair
upon a Scaffold erected for the Purpose; and his Head cut off at one
Blow with a Sword of about forty Foot long. The Veins and Arteries
spouted up such a prodigious Quantity of Blood, and so high in the
Air, that the great *Jet d'Eau* at *Versailles** was not equal for the Time it
lasted; and the Head when it fell on the Scaffold Floor, gave such a
Bounce, as made me start, although I were at least an *English* Mile
distant.

The Queen, who often used to hear me talk of my Sea-Voyages,
and took all Occasions to divert me when I was melancholy, asked me

whether I understood how to handle a Sail or an Oar; and whether a little Exercise of Rowing might not be convenient for my Health. I answered, that I understood both very well. For although my proper Employment had been to be Surgeon or Doctor to the Ship; yet often upon a Pinch, I was forced to work like a common Mariner. But I could not see how this could be done in their Country, where the smallest Wherry was equal to a first Rate Man of War among us; and such a Boat as I could manage, would never live in any of their Rivers: Her Majesty said, if I would contrive a Boat, her own Joyner should make it, and she would provide a Place for me to sail in. The Fellow was an ingenious Workman, and by my Instructions in ten Days finished a Pleasure-Boat with all its Tackling, able conveniently to hold eight *Europeans*. When it was finished, the Queen was so delighted, that she ran with it in her Lap to the King, who ordered it to be put in a Cistern full of Water, with me in it, by way of Tryal; where I could not manage my two Sculls or little Oars for want of Room. But, the Queen had before contrived another Project. She ordered the Joyner to make a wooden Trough of three Hundred Foot long, fifty broad, and eight deep; which being well pitched to prevent leaking, was placed on the Floor along the Wall, in an outer Room of the Palace. It had a Cock near the Bottom, to let out the Water when it began to grow stale; and two Servants could easily fill it in half an Hour. Here I often used to row for my own Diversion, as well as that of the Queen and her Ladies, who thought themselves agreeably entertained with my Skill and Agility. Sometimes I would put up my Sail, and then my Business was only to steer, while the Ladies gave me a Gale with their Fans; and when they were weary, some of the Pages would blow my Sail forward with their Breath, while I shewed my Art steering Starboard or Larboard as I pleased. When I had done, *Glumdalclitch* always carried my Boat into her Closet, and hung it on a Nail to dry.

In this Exercise I once met an Accident which had like to have cost me my Life. For, one of the Pages having put my Boat into the Trough; the Governess who attended *Glumdalclitch*, very officiously lifted me up to place me in the Boat; but I happened to slip through her Fingers, and should have infallibly fallen down forty Foot upon the Floor, if by the luckiest Chance in the World, I had not been stop'd by a Corking-pin that stuck in the good Gentlewoman's Stomacher;* the Head of the Pin passed between my Shirt and the

Waistband of my Breeches; and thus I was held by the Middle in the Air, till *Glumdalclitch* ran to my Relief.

Another time, one of the Servants, whose Office it was to fill my Trough every third Day with fresh Water; was so careless to let a huge Frog (not perceiving it) slip out of his Pail. The Frog lay concealed till I was put into my Boat, but then seeking a resting Place, climbed up, and made it lean so much on one Side, that I was forced to balance it with all my Weight on the other, to prevent overturning. When the Frog got in, it hopped at once half the Length of the Boat, and then over my Head, backwards and forwards, daubing my Face and Cloaths with its odious Slime. The Largeness of its Features made it appear the most deformed Animal that can be conceived. However, I desired *Glumdalclitch* to let me deal with it alone. I banged it a good while with one of my Sculls, and at last forced it to leap out of the Boat.

But, the greatest Danger I ever underwent in that Kingdom, was from a Monkey, who belonged to one of the Clerks of the Kitchen. *Glumdalclitch* had locked me up in her Closet, while she went somewhere upon Business, or a Visit. The Weather being very warm, the Closet Window was left open, as well as the Windows and the Door of my bigger Box, in which I usually lived, because of its Largeness and Conveniency. As I sat quietly meditating at my Table, I heard something bounce in at the Closet Window, and skip about from one Side to the other; whereat, although I were much alarmed, yet I ventured to look out, but not stirring from my Seat; and then I saw this frolicksome Animal, frisking and leaping up and down, till at last he came to my Box, which he seemed to view with great Pleasure and Curiosity, peeping in at the Door and every Window. I retreated to the farther Corner of my Room, or Box; but the Monkey looking in at every Side, put me into such a Fright, that I wanted Presence of Mind to conceal myself under the Bed, as I might easily have done. After some time spent in peeping, grinning, and chattering, he at last espyed me; and reaching one of his Paws in at the Door, as a Cat does when she plays with a Mouse, although I often shifted Place to avoid him; he at length seized the Lappet of my Coat (which being made of that Country Silk, was very thick and strong) and dragged me out. He took me up in his right Fore-foot, and held me as a Nurse doth a Child she is going to suckle; just as I have seen the same Sort of Creature do with a Kitten in *Europe*: and when I offered to struggle, he squeezed me so hard, that I thought it more prudent to submit. I have good Reason to believe that he took me for a young one of his own Species, by his often stroaking my Face very gently with his other Paw. In these Diversions he was interrupted by a Noise at the Closet Door, as if some Body were opening it; whereupon he suddenly leaped up to the Window at which he had come in, and thence upon the Leads and Gutters, walking upon three Legs, and holding me in the fourth, till he clambered up to a Roof* that was next to ours. I heard *Glumdalclitch* give a Shriek at the Moment he was carrying me out. The poor Girl was almost distracted: That Quarter of the Palace was all in an Uproar; the Servants ran for Ladders; the Monkey was seen by Hundreds in the Court, sitting upon the Ridge of a Building, holding me like a Baby in one of his Fore-Paws, and feeding me with the other, by cramming into my Mouth some Victuals he had squeezed out of the Bag on one side of his Chaps, and patting me when I would not eat; whereat many of the Rabble below could not forbear laughing; neither do I think they justly ought to be blamed; for without Question, the Sight was ridiculous enough to every Body but my self. Some of the People threw up Stones, hoping to drive the Monkey down; but this was strictly forbidden, or else very probably my Brains had been dashed out.

The Ladders were now applied, and mounted by several Men; which the Monkey observing, and finding himself almost encompassed; not being able to make Speed enough with his three Legs, let me drop on a Ridge-Tyle, and made his Escape. Here I sat for some time five Hundred Yards from the Ground, expecting every Moment to be blown down by the Wind, or to fall by my own Giddiness, and come tumbling over and over from the Ridge to the Eves. But an honest Lad, one of my Nurse's Footmen, climbed up, and putting me into his Breeches Pocket, brought me down safe.

I was almost choaked with the filthy Stuff the Monkey had crammed down my Throat; but, my dear little Nurse picked it out of my Mouth with a small Needle; and then I fell to vomiting, which gave me great Relief. Yet I was so weak and bruised in the Sides with the Squeezes given me by this odious Animal, that I was forced to keep my Bed a Fortnight. The King, Queen, and all the Court, sent every Day to enquire after my Health; and her Majesty made me several Visits during my Sickness. The Monkey was killed, and an Order made that no such Animal should be kept about the Palace.

When I attended the King after my Recovery, to return him Thanks for his Favours, he was pleased to railly me a good deal upon this Adventure. He asked me what my Thoughts and Speculations were while I lay in the Monkey's Paw; how I liked the Victuals he gave me, his Manner of Feeding; and whether the fresh Air on the Roof had sharpened my Stomach. He desired to know what I would have done upon such an Occasion in my own Country. I told his Majesty, that in *Europe* we had no Monkies, except such as were brought for Curiosities from other Places, and so small, that I could deal with a Dozen of them together, if they presumed to attack me. And as for that monstrous Animal with whom I was so lately engaged, (it was indeed as large as an Elephant) if my Fears had suffered me to think so far as to make Use of my Hanger (looking fiercely, and clapping my Hand upon the Hilt as I spoke) when he poked his Paw into my Chamber, perhaps I should have given him such a Wound, as would have made him glad to withdraw it with more Haste than he put it in. This I delivered in a firm Tone, like a Person who was jealous lest his Courage should be called in Question. However, my Speech produced nothing else besides a loud Laughter; which all the Respect due to his Majesty from those about him, could not make them contain. This made me reflect, how vain an Attempt it is for a Man to endeavour doing himself Honour among those who are out of all Degree of Equality or Comparison with him. And yet I have seen the Moral of my own Behaviour very frequent in *England* since my Return; where a little contemptible Varlet, without the least Title to Birth, Person, Wit, or common Sense, shall presume to look with Importance, and put himself upon a Foot with the greatest Persons of the Kingdom.

I was every Day furnishing the Court with some ridiculous Story; and *Glumdalclitch*, although she loved me to Excess, yet was arch enough to inform the Queen, whenever I committed any Folly that she thought would be diverting to her Majesty. The Girl who had been out of Order, was carried by her Governess to take the Air about an Hour's Distance, or thirty Miles from Town. They alighted out of the Coach near a small Footpath in a Field; and *Glumdalclitch* setting down my travelling Box, I went out of it to walk. There was a Cow-dung* in the Path, and I must needs try my Activity by attempt-ing to leap over it. I took a Run, but unfortunately jumped short, and found myself just in the Middle up to my Knees. I waded through with some Difficulty, and one of the Footmen wiped me as clean as he could with his Handkerchief; for I was filthily bemired, and my Nurse confined me to my Box until we returned home; where the Queen was soon informed of what had passed, and the Footmen spread it about the Court; so that all the Mirth, for some Days, was at my Expence.

CHAPTER SIX

Several Contrivances of the Author to please the King and Queen. He shews his Skill in Musick. The King enquires into the State of Europe, *which the Author relates to him. The King's Observations thereon.*

I USED to attend the King's Levee* once or twice a Week, and had often seen him under the Barber's Hand, which indeed was at first very terrible to behold. For, the Razor was almost twice as long as an ordinary Scythe. His Majesty, according to the Custom of the Country, was only shaved twice a Week. I once prevailed on the Barber to give me some of the Suds or Lather, out of which I picked Forty or Fifty of the strongest Stumps of Hair. I then took a Piece of fine Wood, and cut it like the Back of a Comb, making several Holes in it at equal Distance with as small a Needle as I could get from *Glumdalclitch.* I fixed in the Stumps so artificially,* scraping and sloping them with my Knife toward the Points, that I made a very tolerable Comb; which was a seasonable Supply,* my own being so much broken in the Teeth, that it was almost useless; Neither did I know any Artist in that Country so nice and exact, as would undertake to make me another.

And this puts me in mind of an Amusement wherein I spent many of my leisure Hours. I desired the Queen's Woman to save for me the Combings of her Majesty's Hair, whereof in time I got a good Quantity; and consulting with my Friend the Cabinet-maker, who had received general Orders to do little Jobbs for me; I directed him to make two Chair-frames, no larger than those I had in my Box, and then to bore little Holes with a fine Awl round those Parts where I designed the Backs and Seats; through these Holes I wove the strongest Hairs I could pick out, just after the Manner of Cane-chairs in *England.* When they were finished, I made a Present of them to her Majesty, who kept them in her Cabinet, and used to shew them for Curiosities; as indeed they were the Wonder of every one who beheld them. The Queen would have had me sit upon one of these Chairs, but I absolutely refused to obey her; protesting I would rather die a Thousand Deaths than place a dishonourable Part of my Body on those precious Hairs that once adorned her Majesty's Head.*

Of these Hairs (as I had always a Mechanical Genius*) I likewise made a neat little Purse about five Foot long, with her Majesty's Name decyphered* in Gold Letters; which I gave to *Glumdalclitch*, by the Queen's Consent. To say the Truth, it was more for Shew than Use, being not of Strength to bear the Weight of the larger Coins; and therefore she kept nothing in it, but some little Toys that Girls are fond of.

The King, who delighted in Musick, had frequent Consorts* at Court, to which I was sometimes carried, and set in my Box on a Table to hear them: But, the Noise was so great, that I could hardly distinguish the Tunes. I am confident, that all the Drums and Trumpets of a Royal Army, beating and sounding together just at your Ears, could not equal it. My Practice was to have my Box removed from the Places where the Performers sat, as far as I could; then to shut the Doors and Windows of it, and draw the Window-Curtains; after which I found their Musick not disagreeable.*

I had learned in my Youth to play a little upon the Spinet; *Glumdalclitch* kept one in her Chamber, and a Master attended twice a Week to teach her: I call it a Spinet, because it somewhat resembled that Instrument, and was play'd upon in the same Manner. A Fancy came into my Head, that I would entertain the King and Queen with an *English* Tune upon this Instrument. But this appeared extremely difficult: For, the Spinet was near sixty Feet long, each Key being almost a Foot wide; so that, with my Arms extended, I could not reach to above five Keys; and to press them down required a good smart stroak with my Fist, which would be too great a Labour, and to no purpose. The Method I contrived was this. I prepared two round Sticks about the Bigness of common Cudgels; they were thicker at one End than the other; and I covered the thicker Ends with a Piece of a Mouse's Skin, that by rapping on them, I might neither Damage the Tops of the Keys, nor interrupt the Sound. Before the Spinet, a Bench was placed, about four Foot below the Keys, and I was put upon the Bench. I ran sideling upon it that way and this, as fast as I could, banging the proper Keys with my two Sticks; and made a shift to play a Jigg to the great Satisfaction of both their Majesties: But, it was the most violent Exercise I ever underwent, and yet I could not strike above sixteen Keys, nor, consequently, play the Bass and Treble together, as other Artists do; which was a great Disadvantage to my Performance.

The King, who as I before observed, was a Prince of excellent Understanding, would frequently order that I should be brought in my Box, and set upon the Table in his Closet. He would then command me to bring one of my Chairs out of the Box, and sit down within three Yards Distance upon the Top of the Cabinet; which brought me almost to a Level with his Face. In this Manner I had several Conversations with him. I one Day took the Freedom to tell his Majesty, that the Contempt he discovered towards *Europe*, and the rest of the World, did not seem answerable to those excellent Qualities of the Mind, that he was Master of. That, Reason did not extend itself with the Bulk of the Body: On the contrary, we observed in our Country, that the tallest Persons were usually least provided with it. That among other Animals, Bees and Ants had the Reputation of more Industry, Art, and Sagacity than many of the larger Kinds. And that, as inconsiderable as he took me to be, I hoped I might live to do his Majesty some signal Service. The King heard me with Attention; and began to conceive a much better Opinion of me than he had ever before. He desired I would give him as exact an Account of the Government of *England* as I possibly could; because, as fond as Princes commonly are of their own Customs (for so he conjectured of other Monarchs by my former Discourses) he should be glad to hear of any thing that might deserve Imitation.

Imagine with thy self, courteous Reader, how often I then wished for the Tongue of *Demosthenes* or *Cicero*,* that might have enabled me to celebrate the Praise of my own dear native Country in a Style equal to its Merits and Felicity.

I began my Discourse by informing his Majesty, that our Dominions consisted of two Islands, which composed three mighty Kingdoms* under one Sovereign, beside our Plantations* in *America*. I dwelt long upon the Fertility of our Soil, and the Temperature of our Climate. I then spoke at large upon the Constitution of an *English* Parliament, partly made up of an illustrious Body called the House of Peers, Persons of the noblest Blood, and of the most ancient and ample Patrimonies. I described that extraordinary Care always taken of their Education* in Arts and Arms, to qualify them for being Counsellors born* to the King and Kingdom; to have a Share in the Legislature, to be Members of the highest Court of Judicature from whence there could be no Appeal;* and to be Champions always ready for the Defence of their Prince and Country by their Valour, Conduct and Fidelity. That these were the Ornament and Bulwark of the Kingdom; worthy Followers of their most renowned Ancestors, whose Honour had been the Reward of their Virtue; from which their Posterity were never once known to degenerate.* To these were joined several holy Persons, as part of that Assembly, under the Title of Bishops; whose peculiar Business it is, to take care of Religion, and of those who instruct the People therein. These were searched and sought out through the whole Nation, by the Prince and his wisest Counsellors, among such of the Priesthood, as were most deservedly distinguished by the Sanctity of their Lives, and the Depth of their Erudition; who were indeed the spiritual Fathers of the Clergy and the People.*

That, the other Part of the Parliament consisted of an Assembly called the House of Commons; who were all principal Gentlemen, *freely* picked and culled out by the People themselves, for their great Abilities, and Love of their Country, to represent the Wisdom of the whole Nation. And, these two Bodies make up the most august Assembly in *Europe*; to whom, in Conjunction with the Prince, the whole Legislature is committed.

I then descended to the Courts of Justice, over which the Judges, those venerable Sages and Interpreters of the Law, presided, for determining the disputed Rights and Properties of Men, as well as for the Punishment of Vice, and Protection of Innocence. I mentioned the prudent Management of our Treasury; the Valour and Atchievements of our Forces by Sea and Land. I computed the Number of our People, by reckoning how many Millions there might be of each Religious Sect, or Political Party amongst us. I did not omit even our Sports and Pastimes, or any other Particular which I thought might redound to the Honour of my Country. And, I finished all with a brief historical Account of Affairs and Events in *England* for about an hundred Years past.

This Conversation was not ended under five Audiences, each of several Hours; and the King heard the whole with great Attention; frequently taking Notes of what I spoke, as well as Memorandums of several Questions he intended to ask me.

When I had put an End to these long Discourses, his Majesty in a sixth Audience consulting his Notes, proposed many Doubts, Queries, and Objections, upon every Article.* He asked, what Methods were used to cultivate the Minds and Bodies of our young

Nobility; and in what kind of Business they commonly spent the first and teachable Part of their Lives. What Course was taken to supply that Assembly, when any noble Family became extinct. What Qualifications were necessary in those who were to be created new Lords: Whether the Humour of the Prince, a Sum of Money to a Court-Lady, or a Prime Minister; or a Design of strengthening a Party opposite to the publick Interest, ever happened to be Motives in those Advancements. What Share of Knowledge these Lords had in the Laws of their Country, and how they came by it, so as to enable them to decide the Properties of their Fellow-Subjects in the last Resort. Whether they were always so free from Avarice, Partialities, or Want, that a Bribe, or some other sinister View, could have no Place among them. Whether those holy Lords I spoke of, were always promoted to that Rank upon Account of their Knowledge in religious Matters, and the Sanctity of their Lives, had never been Compliers with the Times, while they were common Priests; or slavish prostitute Chaplains to some Nobleman,* whose Opinions they continued servilely to follow after they were admitted into that Assembly.

He then desired to know, what Arts were practiced in electing those whom I called Commoners. Whether, a Stranger with a strong Purse might not influence the vulgar Voters to chuse him before their own Landlord, or the most considerable Gentleman in the Neighbourhood. How it came to pass, that People were so violently bent upon getting into this Assembly, which I allowed to be a great Trouble and Expence, often to the Ruin of their Families, without any Salary or Pension: Because this appeared such an exalted Strain of Virtue and publick Spirit, that his Majesty seemed to doubt it might possibly not be always sincere: And he desired to know, whether such zealous Gentlemen could have any Views of refunding themselves for the Charges and Trouble they were at, by sacrificing the publick Good to the Designs of a weak and vicious Prince, in Conjunction with a corrupted Ministry. He multiplied his Questions, and sifted* me thoroughly upon every Part of this Head; proposing numberless Enquiries and Objections, which I think it not prudent or convenient to repeat.

Upon what I said in relation to our Courts of Justice, his Majesty desired to be satisfied in several Points: And this I was the better able to do, having been formerly almost ruined by a long Suit in

Chancery, which was decreed for me with Costs. He asked, what Time was usually spent in determining between Right and Wrong; and what Degree of Expence. Whether Advocates and Orators had Liberty to plead in Causes manifestly known to be unjust, vexatious, or oppressive. Whether Party in Religion or Politicks were observed to be of any Weight in the Scale of Justice. Whether those pleading Orators were Persons educated in the general Knowledge of Equity; or only in provincial, national, and other local Customs. Whether they or their Judges had any Part in penning those Laws, which they assumed the Liberty of interpreting and glossing upon at their Pleasure. Whether they had ever at different Times pleaded for and against the same Cause, and cited Precedents to prove contrary Opinions. Whether they were a rich or a poor Corporation. Whether they received any pecuniary Reward for pleading or delivering their Opinions. And particularly whether they were ever admitted as Members in the lower Senate.

He fell next upon the Management of our Treasury; and said, he thought my Memory had failed me, because I computed our Taxes at about five or six Millions a Year; and when I came to mention the Issues,* he found they sometimes amounted to more than double; for, the Notes he had taken were very particular in this Point; because he hoped, as he told me, that the Knowledge of our Conduct might be useful to him; and he could not be deceived in his Calculations. But, if what I told him were true, he was still at a Loss how a Kingdom could run out of its Estate like a private Person.* He asked me, who were our Creditors? and, where we found Money to pay them? He wondered to hear me talk of such chargeable* and extensive Wars; that, certainly we must be a quarrelsome People, or live among very bad Neighbours; and that our Generals must needs be richer than our Kings.* He asked, what Business we had out of our own Islands, unless upon the Score of Trade or Treaty, or to defend the Coasts with our Fleet. Above all, he was amazed to hear me talk of a mercenary standing Army* in the Midst of Peace, and among a free People. He said, if we were governed by our own Consent in the Persons of our Representatives, he could not imagine of whom we were afraid, or against whom we were to fight; and would hear my Opinion, whether a private Man's House might not better be defended by himself, his Children, and Family; than by half a Dozen Rascals picked up at a Venture in the Streets, for small

Wages, who might get an Hundred Times more by cutting their Throats.

He laughed at my odd Kind of Arithmetick* (as he was pleased to call it) in reckoning the Numbers of our People by a Computation drawn from the several Sects among us in Religion and Politicks. He said, he knew no Reason,* why those who entertain Opinions preju- dicial to the Publick, should be obliged to change, or should not be obliged to conceal them. And, as it was Tyranny in any Government to require the first, so it was Weakness not to enforce the second: For, a Man may be allowed to keep Poisons in his Closet, but not to vend them about as Cordials.*

He observed, that among the Diversions of our Nobility and Gentry, I had mentioned Gaming.* He desired to know at what Age this Entertainment was usually taken up, and when it was laid down. How much of their Time it employed; whether it ever went so high as to affect their Fortunes. Whether mean vicious People, by their Dexterity in that Art, might not arrive at great Riches, and some- times keep our very Nobles in Dependance, as well as habituate them to vile Companions; wholly take them from the Improvement of their Minds, and force them by the Losses they have received, to learn and practice that infamous Dexterity upon others.

He was perfectly astonished with the historical Account I gave him of our Affairs during the last Century; protesting it was only an Heap of Conspiracies, Rebellions, Murders, Massacres, Revolutions, Banishments; the very worst Effects that Avarice, Faction, Hypocrisy, Perfidiousness, Cruelty, Rage, Madness, Hatred, Envy, Lust, Malice, and Ambition could produce.

His Majesty in another Audience, was at the Pains to recapitulate the Sum of all I had spoken; compared the Questions he made, with the Answers I had given; then taking me into his Hands, and stroak- ing me gently, delivered himself in these Words, which I shall never forget, nor the Manner he spoke them in. My little Friend *Grildrig*; you have made a most admirable Panegyric upon your Country. You have clearly proved that Ignorance, Idleness, and Vice are the proper Ingredients for qualifying a Legislator. That Laws are best explained, interpreted, and applied by those whose Interest and Abilities lie in perverting, confounding, and eluding them. I observe among you some Lines of an Institution, which in its Original might have been tolerable; but these half erased, and the rest wholly blurred and blotted by Corruptions. It doth not appear from all you have said, how any one Perfection is required towards the Procurement of any one Station among you; much less that Men are ennobled on Account of their Virtue, that Priests are advanced for their Piety or Learning, Soldiers for their Conduct or Valour, Judges for their Integrity, Senators for the Love of their Country, or Counsellors for their Wisdom. As for yourself (continued the King) who have spent the greatest Part of your Life in travelling; I am well disposed to hope you may hitherto have escaped many Vices of your Country. But, by what I have gathered from your own Relation, and the Answers I have with much Pains wringed and extorted from you; I cannot but conclude the Bulk of your Natives, to be the most pernicious Race of little odious Vermin that Nature ever suffered to crawl upon the Surface of the Earth.*

CHAPTER SEVEN

The Author's Love of his Country. He makes a Proposal of much Advantage to the King; which is rejected. The King's great Ignorance in Politicks. The Learning of that Country very imperfect and confined. Their Laws, and military Affairs, and Parties in the State.

NOTHING but an extreme Love of Truth could have hindered me from concealing this Part of my Story. It was in vain to discover my Resentments, which were always turned into Ridicule: And I was forced to rest with Patience, while my noble and most beloved Country was so injuriously treated. I am heartily sorry as any of my Readers can possibly be, that such an Occasion was given: But this Prince happened to be so curious and inquisitive upon every Particular, that it could not consist either with Gratitude or good Manners to refuse giving him what Satisfaction I was able. Yet thus much I may be allowed to say in my own Vindication; that I artfully eluded many of his Questions, and gave to every Point a more favourable turn by many Degrees than the strictness of Truth would allow. For, I have always born that laudable Partiality to my own Country, which *Dionysius Halicarnassensis** with so much Justice recommends to an Historian. I would hide the Frailties and Deformities of my Political Mother, and place her Virtues and Beauties in the most advantageous Light. This was my sincere Endeavour in those many Discourses I had with that Monarch, although it unfortunately failed of Success.

But, great Allowances should be given to a King who lives wholly secluded from the rest of the World, and must therefore be altogether unacquainted with the Manners and Customs that most prevail in other Nations: The want of which Knowledge will ever produce many *Prejudices,** and a certain *Narrowness of Thinking*; from which we and the politer Countries of *Europe* are wholly exempted. And it would be hard indeed, if so remote a Prince's Notions of Virtue and Vice were to be offered as a Standard for all Mankind.

To confirm what I have now said, and further to shew the miserable Effects of a *confined Education*; I shall here insert a Passage which will hardly obtain Belief. In hopes to ingratiate my self farther into his Majesty's Favour, I told him of an Invention discovered between three and four hundred Years ago,* to make a certain Powder; into an heap of which the smallest Spark of Fire falling, would kindle the whole in a Moment, although it were as big as a Mountain; and make it all fly up in the Air together, with a Noise and Agitation greater than Thunder. That, a proper Quantity of this Powder rammed into a hollow Tube of Brass or Iron, according to its Bigness, would drive a Ball of Iron or Lead with such Violence and Speed, as nothing was able to sustain its Force. That, the largest Balls thus discharged, would not only Destroy whole Ranks of an Army at once; but batter the strongest Walls to the Ground; sink down Ships with a thousand Men in each, to the Bottom of the Sea; and when linked together by a Chain, would cut through Masts and Rigging; divide Hundreds of Bodies in the Middle, and lay all Waste before them. That we often put this Powder into large hollow Balls of Iron, and discharged them by an Engine into some City we were besieging; which would rip up the Pavement, tear the Houses to Pieces, burst and throw Splinters on every Side, dashing out the Brains of all who came near. That I knew the Ingredients very well, which were Cheap, and common; I understood the Manner of compounding them, and could direct his Workmen how to make those Tubes of a Size proportionable to all other Things in his Majesty's Kingdom; and the largest need not be above a hundred Foot long; twenty or thirty of which Tubes, charged with the proper Quantity of Powder and Balls, would batter down the Walls of the strongest Town in his Dominions in a few Hours; or destroy the whole Metropolis, if ever it should pretend to dispute his absolute Commands. This I humbly offered to his Majesty, as a small Tribute of Acknowledgment in return of so many Marks that I had received of his Royal Favour and Protection.

The King was struck with Horror at the Description I had given of those terrible Engines, and the Proposal I had made. He was amazed how so impotent and groveling an Insect as I (these were his Expressions) could entertain such inhuman Ideas, and in so familiar a Manner as to appear wholly unmoved at all the Scenes of Blood and Desolation, which I had painted as the common Effects of those destructive Machines; whereof he said, some evil Genius, Enemy to Mankind, must have been the first

Contriver. As for himself, he protested that although few Things delighted him so much as new Discoveries in Art or in Nature; yet he would rather lose Half his Kingdom than be privy to such a Secret; which he commanded me, as I valued my Life, never to mention any more.

A strange Effect of *narrow Principles* and *short Views!* that a Prince possessed of every Quality which procures Veneration, Love and Esteem; of strong Parts, great Wisdom and profound Learning; endued with admirable Talents for Government, and almost adored by his Subjects; should from a *nice unnecessary Scruple*, whereof in *Europe* we can have no Conception, let slip an Opportunity to put into his Hands, that would have made him absolute Master of the Lives, the Liberties, and the Fortunes of his People. Neither do I say this with the least Intention to detract from the many Virtues of that excellent King; whose Character I am sensible will on this Account be very much lessened in the Opinion of an *English* Reader: But, I take this Defect among them to have risen from their Ignorance; they not having hitherto reduced *Politicks* into a *Science,** as the more acute Wits of *Europe* have done. For, I remember very well, in a Discourse one Day with the King; when I happened to say, there were several thousand Books among us written upon the *Art of Government*; it gave him (directly contrary to my Intention) a very mean Opinion of our Understandings. He professed both to abominate and despise all *Mystery, Refinement*, and *Intrigue*, either in a Prince or a Minister. He could not tell what I meant by *Secrets of State*, where an Enemy or some Rival Nation were not in the Case. He confined the Knowledge of governing within very *narrow Bounds*; to common Sense and Reason, to Justice and Lenity, to the Speedy Determination of Civil and criminal Causes; with some other obvious Topicks which are not worth considering. And, he gave it for his Opinion;* that whoever could make two Ears of Corn, or two Blades of Grass to grow upon a Spot of Ground where only one grew before; would deserve better of Mankind, and do more essential Service to his Country, than the whole Race of Politicians put together.

The Learning of this People is very defective; consisting only in Morality, History, Poetry and Mathematicks; wherein they must be allowed to excel. But, the last of these is wholly applied to what may be useful in Life; to the Improvement of Agriculture and all mechanical Arts; so that among us it would be little esteemed. And as to

Ideas,* Entities,* Abstractions and Transcendentals,* I could never drive the least Conception into their Heads.*

No Law* of that Country must exceed in Words the Number of Letters in their Alphabet; which consists only of two and twenty. But indeed, few of them extend even to that Length. They are expressed in the most plain and simple Terms, wherein those People are not Mercurial enough to discover above one Interpretation. And, to write a Comment upon any Law, is a capital Crime. As to the Decision of civil Causes, or Proceedings against Criminals, their Precedents are so few, that they have little Reason to boast of any extraordinary Skill in either.

They have had the Art of Printing,* as well as the *Chinese*, Time out of Mind. But their Libraries are not very large;* for that of the King's which is reckoned the largest, doth not amount to above a thousand Volumes; placed in a Gallery of twelve hundred Foot long; from which I had Liberty to borrow what Books I pleased. The Queen's Joyner had contrived in one of *Glumdalclitch*'s Rooms a Kind of wooden Machine five and twenty Foot high, formed like a standing Ladder; the steps were each fifty Foot long: It was indeed a moveable Pair of Stairs, the lowest End placed at ten Foot Distance from the Wall of the Chamber. The Book I had a Mind to read was put up leaning against the Wall. I first mounted to the upper Step of the Ladder, and turning my Face towards the Book, began at the Top of the Page, and so walking to the Right and Left about eight or ten Paces according to the Length of the Lines, till I had gotten a little below the Level of mine Eyes; and then descending gradually till I came to the Bottom: After which I mounted again, and began the other Page in the same Manner, and so turned over the Leaf, which I could easily do with both my Hands, for it was as thick and stiff as Paste-board, and in the largest Folio's not above eighteen or twenty Foot long.

Their Stile* is clear, masculine, and smooth, but not Florid; for they avoid nothing more than multiplying unnecessary Words, or using various Expressions. I have perused many of their Books, especially those in History and Morality. Among the latter I was much diverted with a little old Treatise, which always lay in *Glumdalclitch*'s Bedchamber, and belonged to her Governess, a grave elderly Gentlewoman, who dealt in Writings of Morality and Devotion. The Book treats of the Weakness of Human kind; and is in little Esteem except among the Women and the Vulgar. However, I was curious to see what an Author of that Country could say upon such a Subject. This Writer went through all the usual Topicks of *European* Moralists; shewing how diminutive, contemptible, and helpless an Animal was Man in his own Nature; how unable to defend himself from the Inclemencies of the Air, or the Fury of wild Beasts: How much he was excelled by one Creature in Strength, by another in Speed, by a third in Foresight, by a fourth in Industry. He added, that Nature was degenerated* in these latter declining Ages of the World, and could now produce only small abortive Births in Comparison of those in ancient Times. He said, it was very reasonable to think, not only that the Species of Men were originally much larger, but also that there must have been Giants in former Ages; which, as it is asserted by History and Tradition, so it has been confirmed by huge Bones and Sculls casually dug up* in several Parts of the Kingdom, far exceeding the common dwindled Race of Man in our Days. He argued, that the very Laws of Nature absolutely required we should have been made in the Beginning, of a Size more large and robust, not so liable to Destruction from every little Accident of a Tile falling* from an House, or a Stone cast from the Hand of a Boy, or of being drowned in a little Brook. From this Way of Reasoning the Author drew several moral Applications useful in the Conduct of Life, but needless here to repeat. For my own Part, I could not avoid reflecting how universally this Talent was spread of drawing Lectures in Morality, or indeed rather Matter of Discontent and repining, from the Quarrels we raise with Nature. And, I believe upon a strict Enquiry, those Quarrels might be shewn as ill-grounded among us, as they are among that People.

As to their military Affairs; they boast that the King's Army consists of a hundred and seventy six thousand Foot, and thirty two thousand Horse: If that may be called an Army which is made up of Tradesmen* in the several Cities, and Farmers in the Country, whose Commanders are only the Nobility and Gentry, without Pay or Reward. They are indeed perfect enough in their Exercises; and under very good Discipline, wherein I saw no great Merit: For, how should it be otherwise, where every Farmer is under the Command of his own Landlord, and every Citizen under that of the principal Men in his own City, chosen after the Manner of *Venice** by *Ballot*?

I have often seen the Militia of *Lorbrulgrud* drawn out to Exercise in a great Field near the City, of twenty Miles Square. They were in all not above twenty five thousand Foot, and six thousand Horse; but it was impossible for me to compute their Number, considering the Space of Ground they took up. A *Cavalier* mounted on a large Steed might be about Ninety Foot high. I have seen this whole Body of Horse upon a Word of Command draw their Swords at once, and brandish them in the Air. Imagination can Figure nothing so Grand,* so surprising and so astonishing. It looked as if ten thousand Flashes of Lightning were darting at the same time from every Quarter of the Sky.

I was curious to know how this Prince, to whose Dominions there is no Access from any other Country, came to think of Armies, or to teach his People the Practice of military Discipline. But I was soon informed, both by Conversation, and Reading their Histories. For, in the Course of many Ages they have been troubled with the same Disease,* to which the whole Race of Mankind is Subject; the Nobility often contending for Power, the People for Liberty, and the King for absolute Dominion. All which, however happily tempered by the Laws of that Kingdom, have been sometimes violated by each of the three Parties; and have once or more occasioned Civil Wars, the last whereof was happily put an End to by this Prince's Grandfather by a general Composition;* and the Militia then settled with common Consent has been ever since kept in the strictest Duty.

CHAPTER EIGHT

*The King and Queen make a Progress to the Frontiers. The Author attends
them. The Manner in which he leaves the Country very particularly related.
He returns to* England.

I HAD always a strong Impulse that I should some time recover my
Liberty, although it were impossible to conjecture by what Means, or
to form any Project with the least Hope of succeeding. The Ship in
which I sailed was the first ever known to be driven within Sight of
that Coast; and the King had given strict Orders, that if at any Time
another appeared, it should be taken ashore, and with all its Crew
and Passengers brought in a Tumbril to *Lorbrulgrud.* He was
strongly bent to get me a Woman of my own Size, by whom I might
propagate the Breed: But I think I should rather have died than
undergone the Disgrace of leaving a Posterity to be kept in Cages
like tame Canary Birds,* and perhaps in time sold about the Kingdom
to Persons of Quality for Curiosities. I was indeed treated with much
Kindness; I was the Favourite of a great King and Queen, and the
Delight of the whole Court; but it was upon such a Foot as ill became
the Dignity of human Kind. I could never forget those domestick
Pledges I had left behind me. I wanted to be among People with
whom I could converse upon even* Terms; and walk about the Streets
and Fields without Fear of being trod to Death like a Frog or a young
Puppy. But, my Deliverance came sooner than I expected, and in a
Manner not very common: The whole Story and Circumstances of
which I shall faithfully relate.

I had now been two Years in this Country; and, about the
Beginning of the third, *Glumdalclitch* and I attended the King and
Queen in a Progress to the South Coast of the Kingdom. I was
carried as usual in my Travelling-Box, which, as I have already
described, was a very convenient Closet of twelve Foot wide. And
I had ordered a Hammock to be fixed by silken Ropes from the
four Corners at the Top; to break the Jolts, when a Servant carried
me before him on Horseback, as I sometimes desired; and would
often sleep in my Hammock while we were upon the Road. On the
Roof of my Closet, set not directly over the Middle of the

Hammock, I ordered the Joyner to cut out a Hole of a Foot square to give me Air in hot Weather as I slept; which Hole I shut at pleasure with a Board that drew backwards and forwards through a Groove.

When we came to our Journey's End, the King thought proper to pass a few Days at a Palace he has near *Flanflasnic*, a City within eighteen *English* Miles of the Sea-side. *Glumdalclitch* and I were much fatigued: I had gotten a small Cold; but the poor Girl was so ill as to be confined to her Chamber. I longed to see the Ocean, which must be the only scene of my Escape, if ever it should happen. I pretended to be worse than I really was; and desired leave to take the fresh Air of the Sea, with a Page whom I was very fond of, and who had sometimes been trusted with me. I shall never forget with what Unwillingness *Glumdalclitch* consented; nor the strict Charge she gave the Page to be careful of me; bursting at the same time into a Flood of Tears, as if she had some Foreboding of what was to happen. The Boy took me out in my Box about Half an Hour's Walk from the Palace, towards the Rocks on the Sea-shore. I ordered him to set me down; and lifting up one of my Sashes, cast many a wistful melancholy Look towards the Sea.* I found myself not very well; and told the Page that I had a Mind to take a Nap in my Hammock, which I hoped would do me good. I got in, and the Boy shut the Window close down, to keep out the Cold. I soon fell asleep: And all I can conjecture is, that while I slept, the Page thinking no Danger could happen, went among the Rocks to look for Birds Eggs; having before observed him from my Window searching about, and picking up one or two in the Clefts. Be that as it will; I found myself suddenly awaked with a violent Pull upon the Ring which was fastened at the Top of my Box, for the Conveniency of Carriage. I felt my Box raised very high in the Air, and then born forward with prodigious Speed. The first Jolt had like to have shaken me out of my Hammock; but afterwards the Motion was easy enough. I called out several times as loud as I could raise my Voice, but all to no purpose. I looked towards my Windows, and could see nothing but the Clouds and Sky. I heard a Noise just over my Head like the clapping of Wings; and then began to perceive the woful Condition I was in; that some Eagle* had got the Ring of my Box in his Beak, with an Intent to let it fall on a Rock, like a Tortoise* in a Shell, and then pick out my Body and devour it. For the Sagacity and Smell of this Bird enable him to discover his Quarry at a great Distance, though better concealed than I could be within a two Inch Board.

In a little time I observed the Noise and flutter of Wings to encrease very fast; and my Box was tossed up and down like a Signpost on a windy Day. I heard several Bangs or Buffets, as I thought, given to the Eagle (for such I am certain it must have been that held the Ring of my Box in his Beak) and then all on a sudden felt my self falling perpendicularly down for above a Minute; but with such incredible Swiftness that I almost lost my Breath. My Fall was stopped by a terrible Squash,* that sounded louder to mine Ears than the Cataract of *Niagara*; after which I was quite in the Dark for another Minute, and then my Box began to rise so high that I could see Light from the Tops of my Windows. I now perceived that I was fallen into the Sea.* My Box, by the Weight of my Body, the Goods that were in, and the broad Plates of Iron fixed for Strength at the four Corners of the Top and Bottom, floated five Foot deep in Water. I did then, and do now suppose, that the Eagle which flew away with my Box was pursued by two or three others, and forced to let me drop while he was defending himself against the Rest, who hoped to share in the Prey. The Plates of Iron fastned at the Bottom of the Box, (for those were the strongest) preserved the Balance while it fell; and hindred it from being broken on the Surface of the Water. Every Joint of it was well grooved, and the Door did not move on Hinges, but up and down like a Sash; which kept my Closet so tight that very little Water came in. I got with much Difficulty out of my Hammock, having first ventured to draw back the Slip board on the Roof already mentioned, contrived on purpose to let in Air; for want of which I found myself almost stifled.

How often did I then wish my self with my dear *Glumdalclitch*, from whom one single Hour had so far divided me! And I may say with Truth, that in the midst of my own Misfortune, I could not forbear lamenting my poor Nurse, the Grief she would suffer for my Loss, the Displeasure of the Queen, and the Ruin of her Fortune. Perhaps many Travellers have not been under greater Difficulties and Distress than I was at this Juncture; expecting every Moment to see my Box dashed in Pieces, or at least overset by the first violent Blast, or a rising Wave. A Breach in one single Pane of Glass would have been immediate Death: Nor could any thing have preserved the Windows but the strong Lattice Wires placed on the outside against

Accidents in Travelling. I saw the Water ooze in at several Crannies, although the Leaks were not considerable; and I endeavoured to stop them as well as I could. I was not able to lift up the Roof of my Closet, which otherwise I certainly should have done, and sat on the Top of it, where I might at least preserve myself from being shut up, as I may call it, in the Hold. Or, if I escaped these Dangers for a Day or two, what could I expect but a miserable Death of Cold and Hunger! I was four Hours under these Circumstances, expecting and indeed wishing every Moment to be my last.

I have already told the Reader, that there were two strong Staples fixed upon that Side of my Box which had no Window, and into which the Servant, who used to carry me on Horseback, would put a Leathern Belt, and buckle it about his Waist. Being in this disconsolate State, I heard, or at least thought I heard some kind of grating Noise on that Side of my Box where the Staples were fixed; and soon after I began to fancy that the Box was pulled, or towed along in the Sea; for I now and then felt a sort of tugging, which made the Waves rise near the Tops of my Windows, leaving me almost in the Dark. This gave me some faint Hopes of Relief, although I were not able to imagine how it could be brought about. I ventured to unscrew one of my Chairs, which were always fastned to the Floor; and having made a hard shift to screw it down again directly under the Slipping-board that I had lately opened; I mounted on the Chair, and putting my Mouth as near as I could to the Hole, I called for Help in a loud Voice, and in all the Languages I understood. I then fastned my Handkerchief to a Stick I usually carried, and thrusting it up the Hole, waved it several times in the Air; that if any Boat or Ship were near, the Seamen might conjecture some unhappy Mortal to be shut up in the Box.

I found no Effect from all I could do, but plainly perceived my Closet to be moved along; and in the Space of an Hour, or better,* that Side of the Box where the Staples were, and had no Window, struck against something that was hard. I apprehended it to be a Rock, and found my self tossed more than ever. I plainly heard a Noise upon the Cover of my Closet, like that of a Cable, and the grating of it as it passed through the Ring. I then found my self hoisted up by Degrees at least three Foot higher than I was before. Whereupon, I again thrust up my Stick and Handkerchief, calling for Help till I was almost hoarse. In return to which, I heard a great

Shout repeated three times, giving me such Transports of Joy as are not to be conceived but by those who feel them. I now heard a trampling over my Head; and somebody calling through the Hole with a loud Voice in the *English* Tongue: *If there be any Body below, let them speak.* I answered, I was an *Englishman*, drawn by ill Fortune into the greatest Calamity that ever any Creature underwent; and begged, by all that was moving,* to be delivered out of the Dungeon I was in. The Voice replied, I was safe, for my Box was fastned to their Ship; and the Carpenter should immediately come, and saw an Hole in the Cover, large enough to pull me out. I answered, that was needless, and would take up too much Time; for there was no more to be done, but let one of the Crew put his Finger into the Ring, and take the Box out of the Sea into the Ship, and so into the Captain's Cabbin. Some of them upon hearing me talk so wildly, thought I was mad; others laughed; for indeed it never came into my Head, that I was now among People of my own Stature and Strength. The Carpenter came, and in a few Minutes sawed a Passage about four Foot square; then let down a small Ladder, upon which I mounted, and from thence was taken into the Ship in a very weak Condition.

The Sailors were all in Amazement, and asked me a thousand Questions, which I had no Inclination to answer. I was equally confounded at the Sight of so many Pigmies; for such I took them to be, after having so long accustomed mine Eyes to the monstrous Objects I had left. But the Captain, Mr *Thomas Wilcocks*, an honest worthy *Shropshire* Man, observing I was ready to faint, took me into his Cabbin, gave me a Cordial to comfort me, and made me *turn in* upon his own Bed; advising me to take a little Rest, of which I had great need. Before I went to sleep I gave him to understand, that I had some valuable Furniture in my Box too good to be lost; a fine Hammock, an handsome Field-Bed, two Chairs, a Table, and a Cabinet: That my Closet was hung on all Sides, or rather quilted, with Silk and Cotton: That if he would let one of the Crew bring my Closet into his Cabbin, I would open it there before him, and shew him my Goods. The Captain hearing me utter these Absurdities, concluded I was raving: However, (I suppose to pacify me) he promised to give Order as I desired; and going upon Deck, sent some of his Men down into my Closet, from whence (as I afterwards found) they drew up all my Goods, and stripped off the Quilting; but the Chairs, Cabinet, and Bed-sted being screwed to the Floor, were much damaged by the Ignorance of the Seamen, who tore them up by Force. Then they knocked off some of the Boards for the Use of the Ship; and when they had got all they had a Mind for, let the Hulk drop into the Sea, which by Reason of many Breaches made in the Bottom and Sides, sunk *to rights*.* And indeed I was glad not to have been a Spectator of the Havock they made; because I am confident it would have sensibly touched me, by bringing former Passages* into my Mind, which I had rather forget.

I slept some Hours, but perpetually disturbed with Dreams of the Place I had left, and the Dangers I had escaped. However, upon waking I found myself much recovered. It was now about eight a Clock at Night, and the Captain ordered Supper immediately, thinking I had already fasted too long. He entertained me with great Kindness, observing me not to look wildly, or talk inconsistently; and when we were left alone, desired I would give him a Relation of my Travels, and by what Accident I came to be set adrift in that monstrous wooden Chest. He said, that about twelve a Clock at Noon, as he was looking through his Glass, he spied it at a Distance, and thought it was a Sail, which he had a Mind to make;* being not much out of his Course, in hopes of buying some Biscuit, his own beginning to fall short. That, upon coming nearer, and finding his Error, he sent out his Long-boat to discover what I was; that his Men came back in a Fright, swearing they had seen a swimming House. That he laughed at their Folly, and went himself in the Boat, ordering his Men to take a strong Cable along with them. That the Weather being calm, he rowed round me several times, observed my Windows, and the Wire Lattices that defended them. That he discovered two Staples upon one Side, which was all of Boards, without any Passage for Light. He then commanded his Men to row up to that Side; and fastning a Cable to one of the Staples, ordered his Men to tow my Chest (as he called it) towards the Ship. When it was there, he gave Directions to fasten another Cable to the Ring fixed in the Cover, and to raise up my Chest with Pullies, which all the Sailors were not able to do above two or three Foot. He said, they saw my Stick and Handkerchief thrust out of the Hole, and concluded, that some unhappy Men must be shut up in the Cavity. I asked whether he or the Crew had seen any prodigious Birds in the Air about the Time he first discovered me: To which he answered, that discoursing this Matter with the Sailors while I was asleep, one of them said he had *observed* three Eagles flying towards the North: but remarked nothing of their being larger than the usual Size; which I suppose must be imputed to the great Height they were at: And he could not guess the Reason of my Question. I then asked the Captain how far he reckoned we might be from Land; he said, by the best Computation he could make, we were at least a hundred Leagues. I assured him, that he must be mistaken by almost half; for I had not left the Country from whence I came, above two Hours before I dropt into the Sea. Whereupon he began again to think that my Brain was disturbed, of which he gave me a Hint, and advised me to go to Bed in a Cabin he had provided. I assured him I was well refreshed with his good Entertainment and Company, and as much in my Senses as ever I was in my Life. He then grew serious, and desired to ask me freely whether I were not troubled in Mind by the Consciousness of some enormous Crime, for which I was punished at the Command of some Prince, by exposing me in that Chest; as great Criminals in other Countries have been forced to Sea in a leaky Vessel without Provisions: For, although he should be sorry to have taken so ill a Man into his Ship, yet he would engage his Word to set me safe on Shore in the first Port where we arrived. He added, that his Suspicions were much increased by some very absurd Speeches I had delivered at first to the Sailors, and afterwards to himself, in relation to my Closet or Chest, as well as by my odd Looks and Behaviour while I was at Supper.

I begged his Patience to hear me tell my Story; which I faithfully did from the last Time I left *England*, to the Moment he first dis-covered me. And, as Truth always forceth its Way into rational Minds; so, this honest worthy Gentleman, who had some Tincture of Learning, and very good Sense, was immediately convinced of my Candor and Veracity. But, further to confirm all I had said, I entreated him to give Order that my Cabinet should be brought, of which I had the Key in my Pocket, (for he had already informed me of how the Seamen disposed of my Closet) I opened it in his Presence, and shewed him the small Collection of Rarities I made in the Coun-try from whence I had been so strangely delivered. There was a Comb I had contrived out of the Stumps of the King's Beard; and another of the same Materials, but fixed into a paring of her Majesty's Thumb-nail, which served for the Back. There was a Collection of Needles and Pins from a Foot to half a Yard long. Four

Wasp-Stings, like Joyners Tacks: Some Combings of the Queen's Hair: A Gold Ring which one Day she made me a Present of in a most obliging Manner, taking it from her little Finger, and throwing it over my Head like a Collar. I desired the Captain would please to accept this Ring in Return of his Civilities; which he absolutely refused. I shewed him a Corn that I had cut off with my own Hand from a Maid of Honour's Toe; it was about the Bigness of a *Kentish* Pippin, and grown so hard, that when I returned to *England*, I got it hollowed into a Cup and set in Silver. Lastly, I desired him to see the Breeches I had then on, which were made of a Mouse's Skin.

I could force nothing on him but a Footman's Tooth, which I observed him to examine with great Curiosity, and found he had a Fancy for it. He received it with abundance of Thanks, more than such a Trifle could deserve. It was drawn by an unskilful Surgeon in a Mistake from one of *Glumdalclitch*'s Men, who was afflicted with the Tooth-ach; but it was as sound as any in his Head. I got it cleaned, and put it into my Cabinet. It was about a Foot long, and four Inches in Diameter.

The Captain was very well satisfied with this plain Relation I had given him; and said, he hoped when we returned to *England*, I would oblige the World by putting it in Paper, and making it publick. My Answer was, that I thought we were already over-stocked with Books of Travels: That nothing could now pass which was not extraordinary; wherein I doubted, some Authors less consulted Truth than their own Vanity or Interest, or the Diversion of ignorant Readers. That my Story could contain little besides common Events, without those ornamental Descriptions of strange Plants, Trees, Birds, and other Animals; or the barbarous Customs and Idolatry of savage People, with which most Writers abound. However, I thanked him for his good Opinion, and promised to take the matter into my Thoughts.

He said, he wondered at one Thing very much; which was, to hear me speak so loud; asking me whether the King or Queen of that Country were thick of Hearing. I told him it was what I had been used to for above two Years past; and that I admired as much at the Voices of him and his Men, who seemed to me only to whisper, and yet I could hear them well enough. But, when I spoke in that Country, it was like a Man talking in the Street to another looking out from the Top of a Steeple, unless when I was placed on a Table,

or held in any person's Hand. I told him, I had likewise observed
another Thing; that when I first got into the Ship, and the Sailors
stood all about me, I thought they were the most little contemptible
Creatures I had ever beheld. For, indeed, while I was in that Prince's
Country, I could never endure to look in a Glass after mine Eyes had
been accustomed to such prodigious Objects; because the Comparison gave me so despicable a Conceit of my self. The Captain
said, that while we were at Supper, he observed me to look at every
thing with a Sort of Wonder; and that I often seemed hardly able to
contain my Laughter; which he knew not well how to take, but
imputed it to some Disorder in my Brain. I answered, it was very
true; and I wondered how I could forbear, when I saw his Dishes of
the Size of a Silver Three-pence, a Leg of Pork hardly a Mouthful, a
Cup not so big as a Nutshell: And so I went on, describing the rest of
his Household-stuff and Provisions after the same Manner. For
although the Queen had ordered a little Equipage of all Things
necessary for me while I was in her Service; yet my Ideas were
wholly taken up with what I saw on every Side of me; and I winked
at my own Littleness, as People do at their own Faults. The Captain
understood my Raillery very well, and merrily replied with the
old *English* proverb, that he doubted, mine Eyes were bigger than
my Belly; for he did not observe my Stomach so good, although I
had fasted all Day: And continuing in his Mirth, protested he would
have gladly given a Hundred Pounds to have seen my Closet in
the Eagle's Bill, and afterwards in its Fall from so great a Height
into the Sea; which would certainly have been a most astonishing
Object, worthy to have the Description of it transmitted to future
Ages: And the Comparison of *Phaeton** was so obvious, that he could
not forbear applying it, although I did not much admire the Conceit.

The Captain having been at *Tonquin,** was in his Return to *England*
driven North Eastward to the Latitude of 44 Degrees, and of
Longitude 143. But meeting a Trade Wind two Days after I came on
board him, we sailed Southward a long Time, and coasting
*New-Holland,** kept our Course West-south-west, and then South-
south-west till we doubled the *Cape of Good Hope*. Our Voyage was
very prosperous, but I shall not trouble the Reader with a Journal of
it. The Captain called in at one or two Ports, and sent in his Long-
boat for Provisions and fresh Water; but I never went out of the Ship
till we came into the *Downs*, which was on the 3d Day of *June* 1706,

about nine Months after my Escape. I offered to leave my Goods in Security for Payment of my Freight; but the Captain protested he would not receive one Farthing. We took kind Leave of each other; and I made him promise he would come to see me at my House in *Redriff*. I hired a Horse and Guide for five Shillings, which I borrowed of the Captain.

As I was on the Road; observing the Littleness of the Houses, the Trees, the Cattle and the People, I began to think my self in *Lilliput*. I was afraid of trampling on every Traveller I met; and often called aloud to have them stand out of the Way; so that I had like to have gotten one or two broken heads for my Impertinence.

When I came to my own House, for which I was forced to enquire, one of the Servants opening the Door, I bent down to go in (like a Goose under a Gate) for fear of striking my Head. My Wife ran out to embrace me, but I stooped lower than her Knees, thinking she could otherwise never be able to reach my Mouth. My Daughter kneeled to ask my Blessing, but I could not see her till she arose; having been so long used to stand with my Head and Eyes erect to above Sixty Foot; and then I went to take her up with one Hand, by the Waist. I looked down upon the Servants, and one or two Friends who were in the House, as if they had been Pigmies, and I a Giant. I told my wife, she had been too thrifty, for I found she had starved herself and her Daughter to nothing. In short, I behaved myself so unaccountably, that they were all of the Captain's Opinion when he first saw me; and concluded I had lost my Wits. This I mention as an Instance of the great Power of Habit and Prejudice.

In a little Time I and my Family and Friends came to a right Understanding: But my Wife protested I should never go to Sea any more; although my evil Destiny so ordered, that she had not Power to hinder me; as the Reader may know hereafter. In the mean Time, I here conclude the second Part of my unfortunate Voyages.

The End of the Second Part.

PART THREE

A Voyage to Laputa, Balnibarbi,
Luggnagg, Glubbdubdrib, and Japan*

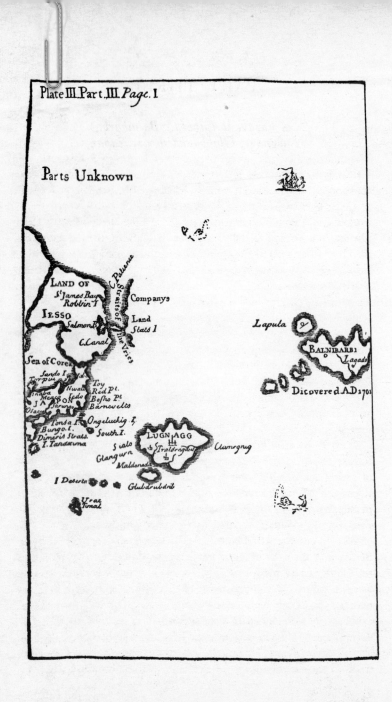

Plate III.Part.III. *Page.* 1

Parts Unknown

LAND OF
St James Bay
Robbin I
IESSO
SalmonB
C. Canal

C. Patience
Straits of The Vries

Company's
Land
Stats I

Lapula

BALNIBARBI
Lagado

Sea of Corea
Sando I
Torpui
Inaba
Meaco Iedo
Jacca
Saringa
Tonsa I
Bungo I
Dimeri's Strats
I. Tanaxuma

Nwall
Toy
Red Pt.
Bosho Pt
Barnevelts

Ongeluckig I
South I

Discovered A.D.1701

LUGN AGG
Traldragdrub

Clumegnug

S ialo
Glangurn
Maldonada

I Deserta

Glubdubdrib

Ur at
Timal

CHAPTER ONE

The Author sets out on his Third Voyage. Is taken by Pyrates. The Malice of a Dutchman. *His Arrival at an Island. He is received into* Laputa.

I HAD not been at home above ten Days, when Captain *William Robinson*, a *Cornish* Man, Commander of the *Hopewell*,* a stout Ship of three Hundred Tuns, came to my House. I had formerly been Surgeon of another Ship where he was Master, and a fourth Part Owner, in a Voyage to the *Levant*. He had always treated me more like a Brother than an inferior Officer; and hearing of my Arrival made me a Visit, as I apprehended only out of Friendship, for nothing passed more than what is usual after long Absence. But repeating his Visits often, expressing his Joy to find me in good Health, asking whether I were now settled for Life, adding that he intended a Voyage to the *East-Indies*, in two Months, at last he plainly invited me, although with some Apologies, to be Surgeon of the Ship. That I should have another Surgeon under me besides our two Mates; that my Sallary should be double to the usual Pay; and that having experienced my Knowledge in Sea-Affairs to be at least equal to his, he would enter into any Engagement to follow my Advice, as much as if I had Share in the Command.

He said so many other obliging things, and I knew him to be so honest a Man, that I could not reject his Proposal; the Thirst I had of seeing the World,* notwithstanding my past Misfortunes, continuing as violent as ever. The only Difficulty that remained, was to persuade my Wife, whose Consent however I at last obtained, by the Prospect of Advantage she proposed* to her Children.

We set out the 5th Day of *August*, 1706, and arrived at Fort St *George*,* the 11th of *April* 1707. We stayed there three Weeks to refresh our Crew, many of whom were sick. From thence we went to *Tonquin*, where the Captain resolved to continue some time; because many of the Goods he intended to buy were not ready, nor could he expect to be dispatched in several Months. Therefore in hopes to defray some of the Charges he must be at, he bought a Sloop, loaded it with several Sorts of Goods, wherewith the *Tonquinese* usually trade to the neighbouring Islands; and putting Fourteen Men on

Board, whereof three were of the Country, he appointed me Master of the Sloop, and gave me Power to traffick, while he transacted his affairs at *Tonquin*.

We had not sailed above three Days, when a great Storm arising, we were driven five Days to the North-North-East, and then to the East; after which we had fair Weather, but still with a pretty strong Gale from the West. Upon the tenth Day we were chased by two Pyrates, who soon overtook us; for my Sloop was so deep loaden, that she sailed very slow; neither were we in a Condition to defend our selves.

We were boarded about the same Time by both the Pyrates, who entered furiously at the Head of their Men; but finding us all prostrate upon our Faces, (for so I gave Order,) they pinioned us with strong Ropes, and setting a Guard upon us, went to search the Sloop.

I observed among them a *Dutchman*, who seemed to be of some Authority, although he were not Commander of either Ship. He knew us by our Countenances to be *Englishmen*, and jabbering to us in his own Language, swore we should be tyed Back to Back,* and thrown into the Sea. I spoke *Dutch* tolerably well; I told him who we were, and begged him in Consideration of our being Christians and Protestants, of neighbouring Countries, in strict Alliance,* that he would move the Captains to take some pity on us. This inflamed his Rage; he repeated his Threatnings, and turning to his Companions, spoke with great Vehemence, in the *Japanese* Language, as I suppose; often using the Word *Christianos*.

The largest of the two Pyrate Ships was commanded by a *Japanese* Captain, who spoke a little *Dutch*, but very imperfectly. He came up to me, and after several Questions, which I answered in great Humility, he said we should not die. I made the Captain a very low Bow, and then turning to the *Dutchman*, said, I was sorry to find more Mercy in a Heathen, than in a Brother Christian. But I had soon Reason to repent those foolish Words; for that malicious Reprobate, having often endeavoured in vain to persuade both the Captains that I might be thrown into the Sea, (which they would not yield to after the Promise made me, that I should not die) however prevailed so far as to have a Punishment inflicted on me, worse in all human Appearance than Death it self. My Men were sent by an equal Division into both the Pyrate-Ships, and my Sloop new manned. As to my self, it was determined that I should be set a-drift, in a small Canoe, with Paddles and a Sail, and four Days Provisions; which last the *Japanese* Captain was so kind to double out of his own Stores, and would permit no Man to search me. I got down into the Canoe, while the *Dutchman* standing upon the Deck, loaded me with all the Curses and injurious Terms his Language could afford.

About an Hour before we saw the Pyrates, I had taken an Observation, and found we were in the Latitude of 46 N. and of Longitude 183.* When I was at some Distance from the Pyrates, I discovered by my Pocket-Glass several Islands to the South-East. I set up my Sail, the Wind being fair, with a Design to reach the nearest of those Islands, which I made a Shift to do in about three Hours. It was all rocky; however I got many Birds Eggs; and striking Fire, I kindled some Heath and dry Sea Weed, by which I roasted my Eggs. I eat no other Supper, being resolved to spare my Provisions as much as I could. I passed the Night under the Shelter of a Rock, strowing some Heath under me, and slept pretty well.

The next Day I sailed to another Island, and thence to a third and fourth, sometimes using my Sail, and sometimes my Paddles. But not to trouble the Reader with a particular Account of my Distresses; let it suffice, that on the 5th Day, I arrived at the last Island in my Sight, which lay South-South-East to the former.

This island was at a greater Distance than I expected, and I did not reach it in less than five Hours. I encompassed it almost round before I could find a convenient Place to land in, which was a small Creek, about three Times the Wideness of my Canoe. I found the Island to be all rocky, only a little intermingled with Tufts of Grass, and sweet smelling Herbs. I took out my small Provisions, and after having refreshed myself, I secured the Remainder in a Cave, whereof there were great Numbers. I gathered Plenty of Eggs upon the Rocks, and got a Quantity of dry Seaweed, and parched Grass, which I designed to kindle the next Day, and roast my Eggs as well as I could. (For I had about me my Flint, Steel, Match, and Burning-glass.) I lay all Night in the Cave where I had lodged my Provisions. My Bed was the same dry Grass and Sea-weed which I intended for Fewel. I slept very little; for the Disquiets of my Mind prevailed over my Wearyness, and kept me awake. I considered how impossible it was to preserve my Life, in so desolate a Place, and how miserable my End must be. Yet I found my self so listless and desponding, that

I had not the Heart to rise; and before I could get Spirits enough to creep out of my Cave, the Day was far advanced. I walked a while among the Rocks, the Sky was perfectly clear, and the Sun so hot, that I was forced to turn my Face from it: When all on a Sudden it became obscured, as I thought, in a Manner very different from what happens by the Interposition of a Cloud. I turned back, and perceived a vast Opake Body* between me and the Sun, moving forwards towards the Island: It seemed to be about two Miles high, and hid the Sun six or seven Minutes, but I did not observe the Air to be much colder, or the Sky more darkened, than if I had stood under the Shade of a Mountain. As it approached nearer over the Place where I was, it appeared to be a firm Substance, the Bottom flat, smooth, and shining very bright* from the Reflexion of the Sea below. I stood upon a Height about two Hundred Yards from the Shoar, and saw this vast Body descending almost to a Parallel with me, at less than an *English* Mile Distance. I took out my Pocket-Perspective, and could plainly discover Numbers of People moving up and down the Sides of it, which appeared to be sloping, but what those People were doing, I was not able to distinguish.

The natural Love of Life gave me some inward Motions of Joy; and I was ready to entertain a Hope, that this Adventure might some Way or other help to deliver me from the desolate Place and Condition I was in. But, at the same Time, the Reader can hardly conceive my Astonishment, to behold an Island in the Air, inhabited by Men, who were able (as it should seem) to raise, or sink, or put it into a progressive Motion, as they pleased.* But not being, at that Time, in a Disposition to philosophise upon this Phænomenon, I rather chose to observe what Course the Island would take; because it seemed for a while to stand still. Yet soon after it advanced nearer, and I could see the Sides of it, encompassed with several Gradations of Galleries and Stairs, at certain Intervals, to descend from one to the other. In the lowest Gallery, I beheld some People fishing with long Angling Rods, and others looking on. I waved my Cap (for my Hat was long since worn out,) and my Handkerchief towards the Island; and upon its nearer Approach, I called and shouted with the utmost Strength of my Voice; and then looking circumspectly, I beheld a Crowd gathered to that Side which was most in my View. I found by their pointing towards me and to each other, that they plainly discovered me, although they made no Return to my Shouting: But I could see four or five Men running in great Haste up the Stairs to the Top of the Island, who then disappeared. I happened rightly to conjecture, that these were sent for Orders to some Person in Authority upon this Occasion.

The Number of People increased; and in less than Half an Hour, the Island was moved and raised in such a Manner, that the lowest Gallery appeared in a Parallel of less than an Hundred Yards Distance from the Height where I stood. I then put my self into the most supplicating Postures, and spoke in the humblest Accent, but received no Answer. Those who stood nearest over-against me, seemed to be Persons of Distinction, as I supposed by their Habit. They conferred earnestly with each other, looking often upon me. At length one of them called out in a clear, polite,* smooth Dialect, not unlike in Sound to the *Italian*;* and therefore I returned an Answer in that Language, hoping at least that the Cadence might be more agreeable to his Ears. Although neither of us understood the other, yet my Meaning was easily known, for the People saw the Distress I was in.

They made Signs for me to come down from the Rock, and go towards the Shoar, which I accordingly did; and the flying Island being raised to a convenient Height, the Verge directly over me, a Chain was let down from the lowest Gallery, with a Seat fastned to the Bottom, to which I fixed my self, and was drawn up by Pullies.

CHAPTER TWO

The Humours and Dispositions of the Laputians *described. An Account of their Learning. Of the King and his Court. The Author's Reception there. The Inhabitants subject to Fears and Disquietudes. An Account of the Women.*

AT my alighting I was surrounded by a Crowd of People, but those who stood nearest seemed to be of better Quality. They beheld me with all the Marks and Circumstances of Wonder; neither indeed was I much in their Debt,* having never till then seen a Race of Mortals so singular* in their Shapes, Habits, and Countenances. Their Heads were all reclined either to the Right or the Left; one of their Eyes turned inward, and the other directly up to the Zenith. Their outward Garments were adorned with the Figures of Suns, Moons, and Stars, interwoven with those of Fiddles, Flutes, Harps, Trumpets, Guittars, Harpsichords, and many more Instruments of Musick, unknown to us in *Europe*. I observed here and there many in the Habit of Servants, with a blown Bladder fastned like a Flail to the End of a short Stick, which they carried in their Hands. In each Bladder was a small Quantity of dried Pease, or little Pebbles (as I was afterwards informed). With these Bladders they now and then flapped the Mouths and Ears of those who stood near them, of which Practice I could not then conceive the Meaning. It seems, the Minds of these People are so taken up with intense Speculations, that they neither can speak, nor attend to the Discourses of others, without being roused by some external Taction* upon the Organs of Speech and Hearing; for which Reason, those Persons who are able to afford it, always keep a *Flapper*, (the Original is *Climenole*) in their Family, as one of their Domesticks; nor ever walk abroad or make Visits without him. And the Business of this Officer is, when two or more Persons are in Company, gently to strike with his Bladder the Mouth of him who is to speak, and the Right Ear of him or them to whom the Speaker addresseth himself. This *Flapper* is likewise employed diligently to attend his Master in his Walks, and upon Occasion to give him a soft Flap on his Eyes; because he is always so wrapped up* in Cogitation, that he is in manifest Danger of falling down every Precipice, and bouncing his Head against every Post; and in the Streets, of jostling others, or being jostled himself into the Kennel.*

It was necessary to give the Reader this Information, without which he would be at the same Loss with me, to understand the Proceedings of these People, as they conducted me up the Stairs, to the Top of the Island, and from thence to the Royal Palace. While we were ascending, they forgot several Times what they were about, and left me to my self, till their Memories were again rouzed by their *Flappers*; for they appeared altogether unmoved by the Sight of my foreign Habit and Countenance, and by the Shouts of the Vulgar, whose Thoughts and Minds were more disengaged.

At last we entered the Palace, and proceeded into the Chamber of Presence; where I saw the King seated on his Throne, attended on each Side by Persons of prime Quality. Before the Throne, was a large Table filled with Globes and Spheres, and Mathematical Instruments* of all Kinds. His Majesty took not the least Notice of us, although our Entrance were not without sufficient Noise, by the Concourse of all Persons belonging to the Court. But, he was then deep in a Problem, and we attended at least an Hour, before he could solve it. There stood by him on each Side, a young Page, with Flaps in their Hands; and when they saw he was at Leisure, one of them gently struck his Mouth, and the other his Right Ear; at which he started like one awakened on the sudden, and looking towards me, and the Company I was in, recollected the Occasion of our coming, whereof he had been informed before. He spoke some Words; whereupon immediately a young Man with a Flap came up to my Side, and flapt me gently on the Right Ear; but I made Signs as well as I could, that I had no Occasion for such an Instrument; which as I afterwards found, gave his Majesty and the whole Court a very mean Opinion of my Understanding. The King, as far as I could con-jecture, asked me several Questions, and I addressed my self to him in all the Languages I had. When it was found, that I could neither understand nor be understood, I was conducted by his Order to an Apartment in his Palace, (this Prince being distinguished above all his Predecessors for his Hospitality to Strangers,*) where two Servants were appointed to attend me. My Dinner was brought, and four Persons of Quality, whom I remembered to have seen very near the King's Person, did me the Honour to dine with me. We had two Courses, of three Dishes each. In the first Course, there was a

Shoulder of Mutton, cut into an Æquilateral Triangle; a Piece of Beef into a Rhomboides; and a Pudding into a Cycloid. The second Course was two Ducks, trussed up into the Form of Fiddles; Sausages and Puddings resembling Flutes and Haut-boys, and a Breast of Veal in the Shape of a Harp. The Servants cut our Bread into Cones, Cylinders, Parallelograms, and several other Mathematical Figures.

While we were at Dinner, I made bold to ask the Names of several Things in their Language; and those noble Persons, by the Assistance of their *Flappers*, delighted to give me Answers, hoping to raise my Admiration of their great Abilities, if I could be brought to converse with them. I was soon able to call for Bread, and Drink, or whatever else I wanted.

After Dinner my Company withdrew, and a Person was sent to me by the King's Order, attended by a *Flapper*. He brought with him Pen, Ink, and Paper, and three or four Books; giving me to understand by Signs, that he was sent to teach me the Language. We sat together four Hours, in which Time I wrote down a great Number of Words in Columns, with the Translations over against them. I likewise made a Shift to learn several short Sentences. For my Tutor would order one of my Servants to fetch something, to turn about, to make a Bow, to sit, or stand, or walk, and the like. Then I took down the Sentence in Writing. He shewed me also in one of his Books, the Figures of the Sun, Moon, and Stars, the Zodiack, the Tropics, and Polar Circles, together with the Denominations of many Figures of Planes and Solids. He gave me the Names and Descriptions of all the Musical Instruments, and the general Terms of Art in playing on each of them. After he had left me, I placed all my Words with their Interpretations in alphabetical Order. And thus in a few Days, by the Help of a very faithful Memory, I got some Insight into their Language.

The Word, which I interpret the *Flying* or *Floating Island*,* is in the Original *Laputa*, whereof I could never learn the true Etymology.* *Lap* in the old obsolete Language signifies *High*, and *Untuh*, a *Governor*, from which they say by Corruption was derived *Laputa* from *Lapuntuh*. But I do not approve of this Derivation, which seems to be a little strained. I ventured to offer to the Learned among them a Conjecture of my own, that *Laputa* was *quasi Lap outed*; *Lap* signifying properly the dancing of the Sun Beams in the Sea; and *outed* a Wing, which however I shall not obtrude, but submit to the judicious Reader.

Those to whom the King had entrusted me, observing how ill I was clad, ordered a Taylor to come next Morning, and take my Measure for a Suit of Cloths. This Operator did his Office after a different Manner from those of his Trade in *Europe*. He first took my Altitude by a Quadrant, and then with a Rule and Compasses, described the Dimensions and Out-Lines of my whole Body; all which he entered upon Paper, and in six Days brought my Cloths very ill made, and quite out of Shape, by happening to mistake a Figure* in the Calculation. But my Comfort was, that I observed such Accidents very frequent, and little regarded.

During my Confinement for want of Cloaths, and by an Indisposition that held me some Days longer, I much enlarged my Dictionary; and when I went next to Court, was able to understand many Things the King spoke, and to return him some Kind of Answers. His Majesty had given Orders, that the Island should move North-East and by East, to the vertical Point over *Lagado*, the Metropolis of the whole Kingdom, below upon the firm Earth. It was about Ninety Leagues distant, and our Voyage lasted four Days and an Half. I was not in the least sensible of the progressive Motion made in the Air by the Island. On the second Morning, about Eleven o'Clock, the King himself in Person, attended by his Nobility, Courtiers, and Officers, having prepared all their Musical Instruments,* played on them for three Hours without Intermission; so that I was quite stunned with the Noise; neither could I possibly guess the Meaning, till my Tutor informed me. He said, that the People of their Island had their Ears adapted to hear the Musick of the Spheres,* which always played at certain Periods; and the Court was now prepared to bear their Part in whatever Instrument they most Excelled.

In our Journey towards *Lagado*, the Capital City, his Majesty ordered that the Island should stop over certain Towns and Villages, from whence he might receive the Petitions of his Subjects. And to this Purpose, several Packthreads were let down* with small Weights at the Bottom. On these Packthreads the People strung their Petitions, which mounted up directly like the Scraps of Paper fastned by School-boys at the End of the String that holds their Kite. Sometimes we received Wine and Victuals from below, which were drawn up by Pullies.

The Knowledge I had in Mathematicks gave me great Assistance in acquiring their Phraseology, which depended much upon that Science and Musick; and in the latter I was not unskilled. Their Ideas are perpetually conversant in Lines and Figures. If they would, for Example, praise the Beauty of a Woman, or any other Animal, they describe it by Rhombs, Circles, Parallelograms, Ellipses, and other Geometrical Terms; or else by Words of Art drawn from Musick, needless here to repeat. I observed in the King's Kitchen all Sorts of Mathematical and Musical Instruments, after the Figures of which they cut up the Joynts that were served to his Majesty's Table.

Their Houses are very ill built, the Walls bevil without one right Angle in any Apartment; and this Defect ariseth from the Contempt they bear to practical Geometry; which they despise as vulgar and mechanick, those Instructions they give being too refined for the Intellectuals* of their Workmen; which occasions perpetual Mistakes. And although they are dexterous enough upon a Piece of Paper in the Management of the Rule, the Pencil, and the Divider, yet in the common Actions and Behaviour of Life, I have not seen a more clumsy, awkward, and unhandy People, nor so slow and perplexed in their Conceptions upon all other Subjects, except those of Mathematicks and Musick. They are very bad Reasoners, and vehemently given to Opposition, unless when they happen to be of the right Opinion, which is seldom their Case. Imagination, Fancy, and Invention, they are wholly Strangers to, nor have any Words in their Language by which those Ideas can be expressed; the whole Compass of their Thoughts and Mind, being shut up within the two forementioned Sciences.

Most of them, and especially those who deal in the Astronomical Part, have great Faith in judicial Astrology,* although they are ashamed to own it publickly. But, what I chiefly admired, and thought altogether unaccountable, was the strong Disposition I observed in them towards News and Politicks,* perpetually enquiring into publick Affairs, giving their Judgments in Matters of State; and passionately disputing every Inch of a Party Opinion. I have indeed observed the same Disposition among most of the Mathematicians* I have known in *Europe*; although I could never discover the least Analogy between the two Sciences; unless those People suppose, that because the smallest Circle hath as many Degrees as the largest, therefore the Regulation and Management of the World require no more Abilities than the handling and turning of a Globe. But, I rather take this Quality to spring from a very common Infirmity of human Nature, inclining us to be more curious and conceited* in Matters where we have least Concern, and for which we are least adapted either by Study or Nature.

These People are under continual Disquietudes, never enjoying a Minute's Peace of Mind; and their Disturbances proceed from Causes which very little affect the rest of Mortals. Their Apprehensions arise from several Changes they dread in the Celestial Bodies. For Instance; that the Earth by the continual Approaches of the Sun towards it, must in Course of Time be absorbed or swallowed up.* That the Face of the Sun will by Degrees be encrusted with its own Effluvia,* and give no more Light to the World. That, the Earth very narrowly escaped a Brush from the Tail of the last Comet,* which would have infallibly reduced it to Ashes; and that the next, which they have calculated for One and Thirty years hence, will probably destroy us.* For, if in its Perihelion* it should approach within a certain Degree of the Sun, (as by their Calculations they have Reason to dread) it will conceive a Degree of Heat ten Thousand Times more intense than that of red hot glowing Iron; and in its Absence from the Sun, carry a blazing Tail Ten Hundred Thousand and Fourteen Miles long; through which if the Earth should pass at the distance of one Hundred Thousand Miles from the *Nucleus*, or main Body of the Comet, it must in its Passage be set on Fire, and reduced to Ashes. That the Sun daily spending its Rays without any Nutriment to supply them, will at last be wholly consumed and annihilated;* which must be attended with the Destruction of this Earth, and of all the Planets that receive their Light from it.

They are so perpetually alarmed with the Apprehensions of these and the like impending Dangers, that they can neither sleep quietly in their Beds, nor have any Relish for the common Pleasures or Amusements of Life. When they meet an Acquaintance in the Morning, the first Question is about the Sun's Health; how he looked at his Setting and Rising, and what Hopes they have to avoid the Stroak of the approaching Comet. This Conversation they are apt to run into with the same Temper that Boys discover, in delighting to hear terrible Stories of Sprites and Hobgoblins, which they greedily listen to, and dare not go to Bed for fear.

The Women of the Island have Abundance of Vivacity; they

contemn their Husbands, and are exceedingly fond of Strangers, whereof there is always a considerable Number from the Continent below, attending at Court, either upon Affairs of the several Towns and Corporations, or their own particular Occasions; but are much despised, because they want the same Endowments.* Among these the Ladies chuse their Gallants: But the Vexation is, that they act with too much Ease and Security; for the Husband is always so rapt in Speculation, that the Mistress and Lover may proceed to the greatest Familiarities before his Face, if he be but provided with Paper and Implements,* and without his *Flapper* at his Side.

The Wives and Daughters lament their Confinement to the Island, although I think it the most delicious Spot of Ground in the World; and although they live here in the greatest Plenty and Magnificence, and are allowed to do whatever they please: They long to see the World, and take the Diversions of the Metropolis, which they are not allowed to do without a particular Licence from the King; and this is not easy to be obtained, because the People of Quality have found by frequent Experience, how hard it is to persuade their Women to return from below. I was told, that a great Court Lady, who had several Children, is married to the prime Minister,* the richest Subject in the Kingdom, a very graceful Person, extremely fond of her, and lives in the finest Palace of the Island; went down to *Lagado*, on the Pretence of Health, there hid her self for several Months, till the King sent a Warrant to search for her; and she was found in an obscure Eating-House all in Rags, having pawned her Cloths to maintain an old deformed Footman, who beat her every Day, and in whose Company she was taken much against her Will. And although her Husband received her with all possible Kindness, and without the least Reproach; she soon after contrived to steal down again with all her Jewels, to the same Gallant, and hath not been heard of since.

This may perhaps pass with the Reader rather for an *European* or *English* Story,* than for one of a Country so remote. But he may please to consider, that the Caprices of Womankind are not limited by any Climate or Nation; and that they are much more uniform than can be easily imagined.

In about a Month's Time I had made a tolerable Proficiency in their Language, and was able to answer most of the King's Questions, when I had the Honour to attend him. His Majesty discovered not the least Curiosity to inquire into the Laws, Government, History, Religion, or Manners of the Countries where I had been; but confined his Questions to the State of Mathematicks, and received the Account I gave him, with great Contempt and Indifference, though often roused by his *Flapper* on each Side.

CHAPTER THREE

A Phænomenon solved by modern Philosophy and Astronomy. The Laputians *great Improvements in the latter. The King's Method of suppressing Insurrections.*

I DESIRED Leave of this Prince to see the Curiosities of the Island; which he was graciously pleased to grant, and ordered my Tutor to attend me. I chiefly wanted to know to what Cause in Art or in Nature, it owed its several Motions; whereof I will now give a philosophical Account to the Reader.

The flying or floating Island is exactly circular; its Diameter* 7837 Yards, or about four Miles and a Half, and consequently contains ten Thousand Acres. It is three Hundred Yards thick. The Bottom, or under Surface, which appears to those who view it from below, is one even regular Plate of Adamant, shooting up to the Height of about two Hundred Yards. Above it lye the several Minerals in their usual Order; and over all is a Coat of rich Mould ten or twelve Foot deep. The Declivity of the upper Surface, from the Circumference to the Center, is the natural Cause why all the Dews and Rains which fall upon the Island, are conveyed in small Rivulets toward the Middle, where they are emptied into four large Basons, each of about Half a Mile in Circuit, and two Hundred Yards distant from the Center. From these Basons the Water is continually exhaled by the Sun in the Day-time, which effectually prevents their overflowing. Besides, as it is in the Power of the Monarch to raise the Island above the Region of Clouds and Vapours, he can prevent the falling of Dews and Rains whenever he pleases. For the highest Clouds cannot rise above two Miles, as Naturalists agree,* at least they were never known to do so in that Country.

At the Center of the Island there is a Chasm about fifty Yards in Diameter, from whence the Astronomers descend into a large Dome, which is therefore called *Flandona Gagnole*, or the *Astronomers Cave*;* situated at the Depth of an Hundred Yards beneath the upper Surface of the Adamant. In this Cave are Twenty Lamps continually burning, which from the Reflection of the Adamant cast a strong Light into every Part. The Place is stored with great Variety of

Sextants, Quadrants, Telescopes, Astrolabes, and other Astronomical Instruments. But the greatest Curiosity, upon which the Fate of the Island depends, is a Load-stone* of a prodigious Size, in Shape resembling a Weaver's Shuttle.* It is in Length six Yards, and in the thickest Part at least three Yards over. This Magnet is sustained by a very strong Axle of Adamant, passing through its Middle, upon which it plays, and is poized so exactly that the weakest Hand can turn it. It is hooped round with a hollow Cylinder of Adamant, four Foot deep, as many thick, and twelve Yards in Diameter, placed horizontally, and supported by Eight Adamantine feet, each Six Yards high. In the Middle of the Concave Side there is a Groove Twelve Inches deep, in which the Extremities of the Axle are lodged, and turned round as there is Occasion.

This Stone cannot be moved from its Place by any Force, because the Hoop and its Feet are one continued Piece with that Body of Adamant which constitutes the Bottom of the Island.

By Means of this Load-stone, the Island is made to rise and fall, and move from one Place to another. For, with respect to that Part of the Earth over which the Monarch presides, the Stone is endued at one of its Sides with an attractive Power, and at the other with a repulsive. Upon placing the Magnet erect with its attracting End towards the Earth, the Island descends; but when the repelling Extremity points downwards, the Island mounts directly upwards. When the Position of the Stone is oblique, the Motion of the Island is so too. For in this Magnet the Forces always act in Lines parallel to its Direction.

By this oblique Motion the Island is conveyed to different Parts of the Monarch's Dominions. To explain the Manner of its Progress, let *A B* represent a Line drawn cross the Dominions of *Balnibarbi*; let the Line *c d* represent the Load-stone, of which let *d* be the repelling End, and *c* the attracting End, the Island being over *C*; let the Stone be placed in the Position *c d*, with its repelling End downwards; then the Island will be driven upwards obliquely towards *D*. When it is arrived at *D*, let the Stone be turned upon its Axle, till its attracting End points towards *E*, and then the Island will be carried obliquely towards *E*; where if the Stone be again turned upon its Axle till it stands in the Position *E F*, with its repelling Point downwards, the Island will rise obliquely towards *F*, where by directing the attracting End towards *G*, the Island may be carried to *G*, and

Plate IIII. Part.III.

Page.39

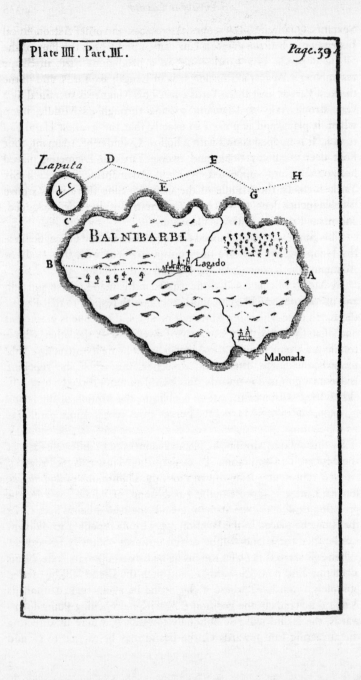

from *G* to *H*, by turning the Stone, so as to make its repelling Extremity point directly downwards. And thus by changing the Situation of the Stone as often as there is Occasion, the Island is made to rise and fall by Turns in an oblique Direction; and by those alternate Risings and Fallings (the Obliquity being not Considerable) is conveyed from one Part of the Dominions to the other.

But it must be observed, that this Island cannot move beyond the Extent of the Dominions below; nor can it rise above the Height of four Miles. For which the Astronomers (who have written large Systems concerning the Stone) assign the following Reason: That the Magnetick Virtue does not extend beyond the Distance of four Miles, and that the Mineral which acts upon the Stone in the Bowels of the Earth, and in the Sea about six Leagues distant from the Shoar, is not diffused through the whole Globe, but terminated with the Limits of the King's Dominions: And it was easy from the great Advantage of such a superior Situation, for a Prince to bring under his Obedience whatever Country lay within the Attraction of that Magnet.

When the Stone is put parallel to the Plane of the Horizon, the Island standeth still; for in that Case, the Extremities of it being at equal Distance from the Earth, act with equal Force, the one in drawing downwards, the other in pushing upwards; and consequently no Motion can ensue.

This Load-stone is under the Care of certain Astronomers, who from Time to Time give it such Positions as the Monarch directs. They spend the greatest Part of their Lives in observing the celestial Bodies, which they do by the Assistance of Glasses, far excelling ours in Goodness. For, although their largest Telescopes do not exceed three Feet, they magnify much more than those of a Hundred with us, and shew the Stars with greater Clearness.* This Advantage hath enabled them to extend their Discoveries much farther than our Astronomers in *Europe*. They have made a Catalogue of ten Thousand fixed Stars,* whereas the largest of ours do not contain above one third Part of that Number. They have likewise discovered two lesser Stars, or *Satellites*,* which revolve about *Mars*; whereof the innermost is distant from the Center of the primary Planet exactly three of his Diameters, and the outermost five; the former revolves in the Space of ten Hours, and the latter in

Twenty-one and a Half; so that the Squares of their periodical
Times, are very near in the same Proportion with the Cubes of their
Distance from the Center of *Mars*; which evidently shews them to be
governed by the same Law of Gravitation, that influences the other
heavenly Bodies.

They have observed Ninety-three different Comets,* and settled
their Periods with great Exactness. If this be true, (and they affirm it
with great Confidence) it is much to be wished that their Observations
were made publick; whereby the Theory of Comets, which at present
is very lame and defective, might be brought to the same Perfection
with other Parts of Astronomy.

The King would be the most absolute Prince in the Universe, if he
could but prevail on a Ministry to join with him; but these having
their Estates* below on the Continent, and considering that the Office
of a Favourite hath a very uncertain Tenure, would never consent to
the enslaving their Country.

If any Town should engage in Rebellion or Mutiny, fall into
violent Factions, or refuse to pay the usual Tribute; the King hath
two Methods of reducing them to Obedience. The first and the
mildest Course by keeping the Island hovering over such a Town,
and the lands about it; whereby he can deprive them of the Benefit of
the Sun* and the Rain, and consequently afflict the Inhabitants with
Dearth and Diseases. And if the Crime deserve it, they are at the
same time pelted from above with great Stones, against which they
have no Defence, but by creeping into Cellars or Caves, while the
Roofs of their Houses are beaten to Pieces. But if they still continue
obstinate, or offer to raise Insurrections; he proceeds to the last
Remedy, by letting the Island drop directly upon their Heads, which
makes a universal Destruction both of Houses and Men. However,
this is an Extremity to which the Prince is seldom driven, neither
indeed is he willing, to put it in Execution; nor dare his Ministers
advise him to an Action, which as it would render them odious to the
People, so it would be a great Damage to their own Estates that lie all
below; for the Island is the King's Demesn.

But there is still indeed a more weighty Reason, why the Kings of
this Country have been always averse from executing so terrible an
Action, unless upon the utmost Necessity. For if the Town intended
to be destroyed should have in it any tall Rocks, as it generally falls
out in the larger Cities; a Situation probably chosen at first with a

View to prevent such a Catastrophe: Or if it abound in high Spires or Pillars of Stone, a sudden Fall might endanger the Bottom or under Surface of the Island, which although it consists as I have said, of one entire Adamant two hundred Yards thick, might happen to crack by too great a Choque, or burst by approaching too near the Fires from the Houses below; as the Backs both of Iron and Stone will often do in our Chimneys. Of all this the People are well apprized, and understand how far to carry their Obstinacy, where their Liberty or Property is concerned. And the King, when he is highest provoked, and most determined to press a City to Rubbish, orders the Island to descend with great Gentleness, out of a Pretence of Tenderness to his People, but indeed for fear of breaking the Adamantine Bottom; in which Case it is the Opinion of all their Philosophers, that the Load-stone could no longer hold it up, and the whole Mass would fall to the Ground.

[About three years* before my Arrival among them, while the King was in his Progress over his Dominions, there happened an extraordinary Accident which had like to have put a Period to the Fate of that Monarchy, at least as it is now instituted. Lindalino* the second City in the Kingdom was the first his Majesty visited in his Progress. Three Days after his Departure, the Inhabitants who had often complained of great Oppressions, shut the Town Gates, seized on the Governor, and with incredible Speed and Labour erected four large Towers, one at every Corner of the City (which is an exact Square) equal in Heigth to a strong pointed Rock that stands directly in the Center of the City. Upon the Top of each Tower, as well as upon the Rock, they fixed a great Loadstone, and in case their Design should fail, they had provided a vast Quantity of the most combustible Fewel, hoping to burst therewith the adamantine Bottom of the Island, if the Loadstone Project should miscarry.

It was eight Months before the King had perfect Notice that the Lindalinians were in Rebellion. He then commanded that the Island should be wafted over the City. The People were unanimous, and had laid in Store of Provisions, and a great River runs through the middle of the Town. The King hovered over them several Days to deprive them of the Sun and the Rain. He ordered many Packthreads to be let down, yet not a Person offered to send up a Petition, but instead thereof, very bold Demands, the Redress of all their Greivances, great Immunitys,* the Choice of their own Governor,* and other the like Exorbitances. Upon which his Majesty commanded all the Inhabitants of the Island to cast great Stones from the lower Gallery into the Town; but the Citizens had provided against this Mischief by conveying their Persons and Effects into the four Towers, and other strong Buildings, and Vaults under Ground.

The King being now determined to reduce this proud People, ordered that the Island should descend gently within fourty Yards of the Top of the Towers and Rock. This was accordingly done; but the Officers employed in that Work found the Descent much speedier than usual, and by turning the Loadstone could not without great Difficulty keep it in a firm Position, but found the Island inclining to fall. They sent the King immediate Intelligence of this astonishing Event, and begged his Majesty's Permission to raise the Island higher; the King consented, a general Council was called, and the Officers of the Loadstone ordered to attend. One of the oldest and expertest among them obtained Leave to try an Experiment. He took a strong Line of an hundred Yards, and the Island being raised over the Town above the attracting Power they had felt, He fastened a Piece of Adamant to the End of his Line which had in it a Mixture of Iron mineral, of the same Nature with that whereof the Bottom or lower Surface of the Island is composed, and from the lower Gallery let it down slowly towards the Top of the Towers. The Adamant was not descended four Yards, before the Officer felt it drawn so strongly downwards, that he could hardly pull it back. He then threw down several small Pieces of Adamant, and observed that they were all violently attracted by the Top of the Tower. The same Experiment was made on the other three Towers, and on the Rock with the same Effect.

This Incident broke entirely the King's Measures and (to dwell no longer on other Circumstances) he was forced to give the Town their own Conditions.

I was assured by a great Minister, that if the Island had descended so near the Town, as not to be able to raise it self, the Citizens were determined to fix it for ever, to kill the King and all his Servants, and entirely change the Government.]*

By a fundamental Law of this Realm, neither the King nor either of his two elder Sons, are permitted to leave the Island; nor the Queen till she is past Child-bearing.*

CHAPTER FOUR

The Author leaves Laputa, *is conveyed to* Balnibarbi, *arrives at the Metropolis. A Description of the Metropolis and the Country adjoining. The Author hospitably received by a great Lord. His Conversation with that Lord.*

ALTHOUGH I cannot say that I was ill treated in this Island, yet I must confess I thought myself too much neglected, not without some Degree of Contempt. For neither Prince nor People appeared to be curious in any Part of Knowledge, except Mathematicks and Musick, wherein I was far their inferior, and upon that Account very little regarded.

On the other Side, after having seen all the Curiosities of the Island, I was very desirous to leave it, being heartily weary of those People.* They were indeed excellent in two Sciences for which I have great Esteem, and wherein I am not unversed; but at the same time so abstracted and involved in Speculation, that I never met with such disagreeable Companions. I conversed only with Women, Tradesmen, *Flappers*, and Court-Pages, during two Months of my Abode there; by which at last I rendered myself extremely contemptible; yet these were the only People from whom I could ever receive a reasonable Answer.

I had obtained by hard Study a good Degree of Knowledge in their Language: I was weary of being confined to an Island where I received so little Countenance;* and resolved to leave it with the first Opportunity.

There was a great Lord at Court, nearly related to the King, and for that Reason alone used with respect. He was universally reckoned the most ignorant and stupid Person among them. He had performed many eminent Services for the Crown, had great natural and acquired Parts, adorned with Integrity and Honour; but so ill an Ear for Musick, that his Detractors reported he had been often known to beat Time in the wrong Place; neither could his Tutors without extreme Difficulty teach him to demonstrate the most easy Proposition in the Mathematicks. He was pleased to shew me many Marks of Favour, often did me the Honour of a Visit, desired to be informed in the Affairs of *Europe*, the Laws and Customs, the

Manners and Learning of the several Countries where I had travelled. He listened to me with great Attention, and made very wise Observations on all I spoke. He had two *Flappers* attending him for State, but never made use of them except at Court, and in Visits of Ceremony, and would always command them to withdraw when we were alone together.

I intreated this illustrious Person to intercede in my Behalf with his Majesty for Leave to depart; which he accordingly did, as he was pleased to tell me, with Regret: For, indeed he had made me several Offers very advantageous, which however I refused with Expressions of the highest Acknowledgment.

On the 16th Day of *February*, I took Leave of his Majesty and the Court. The King made me a Present to the Value of about two Hundred Pounds *English*; and my Protector his Kinsman as much more, together with a Letter of Recommendation to a friend of his in *Lagado*, the Metropolis. The Island being then hovering over a Mountain about two Miles from it, I was let down from the lowest Gallery, in the same Manner as I had been taken up.

The Continent, as far as it is subject to the Monarch of the *Flying Island*, passeth under the general Name of *Balnibarbi*; and the Metropolis, as I said before, is called *Lagado*. I felt some little Satisfaction in finding myself on firm Ground. I walked to the City without any Concern, being clad like one of the Natives, and sufficiently instructed to converse with them. I soon found out the Person's House to whom I was recommended; presented my Letter from his Friend the Grandee in the Island, and was received with much Kindness. This great Lord, whose Name was *Munodi*,* ordered me an Apartment in his own House, where I continued during my Stay, and was entertained in a most hospitable Manner.

The next Morning after my Arrival, he took me in his Chariot to see the Town, which is about half the Bigness of *London*; but the Houses very strangely built, and most of them out of Repair. The People in the Streets walked fast, looked wild, their Eyes fixed, and were generally in Rags. We passed through one of the Town Gates, and went about three Miles into the Country, where I saw many Labourers working with several Sorts of Tools in the Ground, but was not able to conjecture what they were about; neither did I observe any Expectation either of Corn or Grass, although the Soil appeared to be excellent. I could not forbear admiring at these odd

Appearances both in Town and Country; and I made bold to desire my Conductor, that he would be pleased to explain to me what could be meant by so many busy Heads, Hands and Faces, both in the Streets and the Fields, because I did not discover any good Effects they produced; but on the contrary, I never knew a Soil so unhappily cultivated, Houses so ill contrived and so ruinous, or a People whose Countenances and Habit expressed so much Misery and Want.*

This Lord *Munodi* was a Person of the first Rank, and had been some Years Governor of *Lagado*; but by a Cabal of Ministers was discharged for Insufficiency.* However the King treated him with Tenderness, as a well-meaning Man, but of a low contemptible Understanding.

When I gave that free Censure of the Country and its Inhabitants, he made no further Answer than by telling me, that I had not been long enough among them to form a Judgment; and that the different Nations of the World had different Customs; with other common Topicks to the same Purpose. But when we returned to his Palace, he asked me how I liked the Building, what Absurdities I observed, and what Quarrel I had with the Dress or Looks of his Domesticks. This he might safely do; because every Thing about him was magnificent, regular, and polite.* I answered that his Excellency's Prudence, Quality, and Fortune, had exempted him from those Defects which Folly and Beggary had produced in others. He said if I would go with him to his Country House, about Twenty Miles distant, where his Estate lay, there would be more Leisure for this Kind of Conversation. I told his Excellency, that I was entirely at his Disposal; and accordingly we set out next Morning.

During our Journey, he made me observe the several Methods used by Farmers in managing their Lands; which to me were wholly unaccountable: For except in some very few Places I could not discover one Ear of Corn, or Blade of Grass. But, in three Hours travelling, the Scene was wholly altered; we came into a most beautiful Country; Farmers Houses at small Distances, neatly built, the Fields enclosed, containing Vineyards, Corngrounds and Meadows. Neither do I remember to have seen a more delightful Prospect. His Excellency observed my Countenance to clear up; he told me with a Sigh, that there his Estate began, and would continue the same till we should come to his House. That his

Countrymen ridiculed and despised him for managing his Affairs no better, and for setting so ill an Example to the Kingdom; which however was followed by very few, such as were old, and wilful, and weak like himself.

We came at length to the House, which was indeed a noble Structure, built according to the best Rules of ancient Architecture. The Fountains, Gardens, Walks, Avenues, and Groves were all disposed with exact Judgment and Taste. I gave due Praises to every Thing I saw, whereof his Excellency took not the least Notice till after Supper; when, there being no third Companion, he told me with a very melancholy Air, that he doubted he must throw down his Houses in Town and Country, to rebuild them after the present Mode; destroy all his Plantations, and cast others into such a Form as modern Usage required; and give the same Directions to all his Tenants, unless he would submit to incur the Censure of Pride, Singularity, Affectation, Ignorance, Caprice; and perhaps increase his Majesty's Displeasure.

That the Admiration I appeared to be under, would cease or diminish when he had informed me of some Particulars, which probably I never heard of at Court, the People there being too much taken up in their own Speculations, to have Regard to what passed here below.

The Sum of his Discourse was to this Effect. That about Forty Years ago* certain Persons went up to *Laputa*, either upon Business or Diversion; and after five Months Continuance, came back with a very little Smattering in Mathematicks, but full of Volatile Spirits acquired in that Airy Region. That these Persons upon their Return, began to dislike the Management of every Thing below; and fell into Schemes of putting all Arts, Sciences, Languages, and Mechanicks upon a new Foot. To this End they procured a Royal Patent for erecting an Academy of PROJECTORS* in *Lagado*: and the Humour prevailed so strongly among the People, that there is not a Town of any Consequence in the Kingdom without such an Academy. In these Colleges, the Professors contrive new Rules and Methods of Agriculture and Building, and new Instruments and Tools for all Trades and Manufactures, whereby, as they undertake, one Man shall do the Work of Ten; a Palace may be built in a Week, of Materials so durable as to last for ever without repairing. All the Fruits of the Earth shall come to Maturity at whatever Season we think fit to chuse,* and increase an Hundred Fold more than they do at present; with innumerable other happy Proposals. The only Inconvenience is, that none of these Projects are yet brought to Perfection; and in the mean time, the whole Country lies miserably waste, the Houses in Ruins, and the People without Food or Cloaths. By all which, instead of being discouraged, they are Fifty Times more violently bent upon prosecuting their Schemes, driven equally on by Hope and Despair: That, as for himself, being not of an enterprizing Spirit, he was content to go on in the old Forms; to live in the Houses his Ancestors had built, and act as they did in every Part of Life without Innovation. That, some few other Persons of Quality and Gentry had done the same; but were looked on with an Eye of Contempt and ill Will, as Enemies to Art, ignorant, and ill Commonwealthsmen,* preferring their own Ease and Sloth before the general Improvement of their Country.

His Lordship added, that he would not by any further Particulars prevent the Pleasure I should certainly take in viewing the grand Academy, whither he was resolved I should go. He only desired me to observe a ruined Building* upon the Side of a Mountain about three Miles distant, of which he gave me this Account. That he had a very convenient Mill within Half a Mile of his House, turned by a Current from a large River, and sufficient for his own Family as well as a great Number of his Tenants. That, about seven Years ago, a Club of those Projectors came to him with Proposals to destroy this Mill, and build another on the Side of that Mountain, on the long Ridge whereof a long Canal must be cut for a Repository of Water, to be conveyed up by Pipes and Engines to supply the Mill: Because the Wind and Air upon a Height agitated the Water, and thereby made it fitter for Motion: And because the Water descending down a Declivity would turn the Mill with half the Current of a River whose Course is more upon a Level. He said, that being then not very well with the Court, and pressed by many of his Friends, he complied with the Proposal; and after employing an Hundred Men for two Years, the Work miscarryed, the Projectors went off, laying the blame intirely upon him; railing at him ever since, and putting others upon the same Experiment, with equal Assurance of Success, as well as equal Disappointment.

In a few Days we came back to Town; and his Excellency, considering the bad Character he had in the Academy, would not go

with me himself, but recommended me to a Friend of his to bear me
Company thither. My Lord was pleased to represent me as a great
Admirer of Projects, and a Person of much Curiosity and easy Belief;
which indeed was not without Truth, for I had my self been a Sort of
Projector in my younger Days.*

CHAPTER FIVE

The Author permitted to see the grand Academy of Lagado.* *The Academy largely* described. The Arts wherein the Professors employ themselves.*

THIS Academy is not an entire single Building, but a Continuation of several Houses* on both Sides of a Street; which growing waste,* was purchased and applyed to that Use.

I was received very kindly by the Warden, and went for many Days to the Academy. Every Room hath in it one or more Projectors; and I believe I could not be in fewer than five Hundred Rooms.*

The first Man I saw was of a meagre Aspect, with sooty Hands and Face, his Hair and Beard long, ragged and singed in several Places. His Clothes, Shirt, and Skin were all of the same Colour. He had been Eight Years upon a Project for extracting Sun-Beams out of Cucumbers,* which were to be put into Vials hermetically sealed, and let out to warm the Air in raw inclement Summers. He told me, he did not doubt in Eight Years more, he should be able to supply the Governors Gardens with Sun-shine at a reasonable Rate; but he complained that his stock was low, and intreated me to give him something as an Encouragement to Ingenuity, especially since this had been a very dear Season for Cucumbers. I made him a small Present, for my Lord had furnished me with Money on purpose, because he knew their Practice of begging from all who go to see them.

I went into another Chamber, but was ready to hasten back, being almost overcome with a horrible Stink.* My Conductor pressed me forward, conjuring me in a Whisper to give no Offence, which would be highly resented; and therefore I durst not so much as stop my Nose. The Projector of this Cell was the most ancient Student of the Academy. His Face and Beard were of a pale Yellow; his Hands and Clothes dawbed over with Filth. When I was presented to him, he gave me a close Embrace, (a Compliment I could well have excused.) His Employment from his first coming into the Academy, was an Operation to reduce human Excrement to its original Food, by separating the several Parts, removing the Tincture which it receives from the Gall, making the Odour exhale, and scumming off the Saliva. He had a weekly Allowance from the Society, of a Vessel filled with human Ordure, about the Bigness of a *Bristol* Barrel.

I saw another at work to calcine Ice into Gunpowder; who likewise shewed me a Treatise he had written concerning the Malleability of Fire,* which he intended to publish.

There was a most ingenious Architect who had contrived a new Method for building Houses, by beginning at the Roof, and working downwards to the Foundation; which he justified to me by the like Practice of those two prudent Insects the Bee and the Spider.*

There was a Man born blind,* who had several Apprentices in his own Condition: Their Employment was to mix Colours for Painters, which their Master taught them to distinguish by feeling and smelling. It was indeed my Misfortune to find them at that Time not very perfect in their Lessons; and the Professor himself happened to be generally mistaken: This Artist is much encouraged and esteemed by the whole Fraternity.

In another Apartment I was highly pleased with a Projector, who had found a Device of plowing the Ground with Hogs,* to save the Charges of Plows, Cattle, and Labour. The Method is this: In an Acre of Ground you bury at six Inches Distance and eight deep, a Quantity of Acorns, Dates, Chestnuts, and other Maste* or Vegetables whereof these Animals are fondest; then you drive six Hundred or more of them into the Field, where in a few Days they will root up the whole Ground in search of their Food, and make it fit for sowing, at the same time manuring it with their Dung. It is true, upon Experiment they found the Charge and Trouble very great, and they had little or no Crop. However, it is not doubted that this Invention may be capable of great Improvement.

I went into another Room, where the Walls and Ceiling were all hung round with Cobwebs, except a narrow Passage for the Artist* to go in and out. At my Entrance he called aloud to me not to disturb his Webs. He lamented the fatal Mistake the World had been so long in of using Silk-Worms, while we had such plenty of domestick Insects, who infinitely excelled the former, because they understood how to weave as well as spin. And he proposed farther, that by employing Spiders, the Charge of dying Silks would be wholly saved; whereof I was fully convinced when he shewed me a vast Number of Flies most beautifully coloured, wherewith he fed his Spiders; assuring us, that the Webs would take a Tincture from them; and as he had them of all Hues, he hoped to fit every Body's Fancy, as soon as he could find proper Food for the Flies, of certain Gums, Oyls, and other glutinous Matter, to give a Strength and Consistence to the Threads.

There was an Astronomer who had undertaken to place a Sun-Dial* upon the great Weather-Cock on the Town-House,* by adjusting the annual and diurnal Motions of the Earth and Sun, so as to answer and coincide with all accidental Turnings of the Wind.

I was complaining of a small Fit of the Cholick;* upon which my Conductor led me into a Room, where a great Physician resided, who was famous for curing that Disease by contrary Operations from the same Instrument. He had a large Pair of Bellows,* with a long slender Muzzle of Ivory. This he conveyed eight Inches up the Anus, and drawing in the Wind, he affirmed he could make the Guts as lank as a dried Bladder. But when the Disease was more stubborn and violent, he let in the Muzzle while the Bellows were full of Wind, which he discharged into the Body of the Patient; then withdrew the Instrument to replenish it, clapping his Thumb strongly against the Orifice of the Fundament; and this being repeated three or four Times, the adventitious Wind would rush out, bringing the noxious along with it (like Water put into a Pump) and the Patient recovers. I saw him try both Experiments upon a Dog,* but could not discern any Effect from the former. After the latter, the Animal was ready to burst, and made so violent a Discharge, as was very offensive to me and my Companions. The Dog died on the Spot, and we left the Doctor endeavouring to recover him by the same Operation.

I visited many other Apartments, but shall not trouble my Reader with all the Curiosities I observed, being studious of Brevity.

I had hitherto seen only one Side of the Academy, the other being appropriated to the Advancers of speculative Learning; of whom I shall say something when I have mentioned one illustrious Person more, who is called among them *the universal Artist.** He told us, he had been Thirty Years employing his Thoughts for the Improvement of human Life. He had two large Rooms full of wonderful Curiosities, and Fifty Men at work. Some were condensing Air into a dry tangible Substance, by extracting the Nitre, and letting the

Plate.V.Part.III.

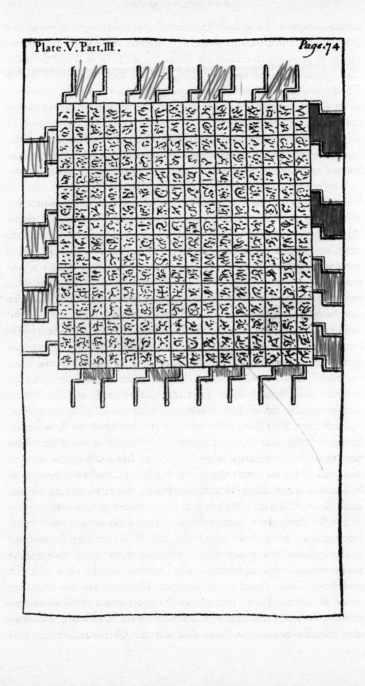

aqueous or fluid Particles percolate: Others softening Marbles for Pillows and Pin-cushions; others petrifying the Hoofs of a living Horse to preserve them from foundering. The Artist himself was at that Time busy upon two great designs: The first, to sow Land with Chaff,* wherein he affirmed the true seminal Virtue* to be contained, as he demonstrated by several Experiments which I was not skilful enough to comprehend. The other was, by a certain Composition of Gums, Minerals, and Vegetables outwardly applied, to prevent the Growth of Wool upon two young Lambs; and he hoped in a reasonable Time to propagate the Breed of naked Sheep* all over the Kingdom.

We crossed a Walk to the other Part of the Academy, where, as I have already said, the Projectors in speculative Learning resided.

The first Professor I saw was in a very large Room, with Forty Pupils about him. After Salutation, observing me to look earnestly upon a Frame,* which took up the greatest Part of both the Length and Breadth of the Room; he said, perhaps I might wonder to see him employed in a Project for improving speculative Knowledge by practical and mechanical Operations. But the World would soon be sensible of its Usefulness; and he flattered himself, that a more noble exalted Thought never sprang in any other Man's Head. Every one knew how laborious the usual Method is of attaining to Arts and Sciences; whereas by his Contrivance, the most ignorant Person* at a reasonable Charge, and with a little bodily Labour, may write Books in Philosophy, Poetry, Politicks, Law, Mathematicks and Theology, without the least Assistance from Genius or Study. He then led me to the Frame, about the Sides whereof all his Pupils stood in Ranks. It was Twenty Foot square, placed in the Middle of the Room. The Superficies was composed of several Bits of Wood, about the Bigness of a Dye, but some larger than others. They were all linked together by slender Wires. These Bits of Wood were covered on every Square with Paper pasted on them; and on these Papers were written all the Words of their Language in their several Moods, Tenses, and Declensions, but without any Order. The Professor then desired me to observe, for he was going to set his Engine at work. The Pupils at his Command took each of them hold of an Iron Handle, whereof there were Forty Fixed round the Edges of the Frame; and giving them a sudden Turn, the whole Disposition of the Words was entirely changed. He then commanded Six and Thirty of the Lads to read the several Lines softly as they appeared upon the Frame; and where they found three or four Words together that might make Part of a Sentence, they dictated to the four remaining Boys who were Scribes. This Work was repeated three or four Times, and at every Turn the Engine was so contrived, that the Words shifted into new Places, as the square Bits of Wood moved upside down.

Six Hours a-Day the young Students were employed in this Labour; and the Professor shewed me several Volumes in large Folio already collected, of broken Sentences, which he intended to piece together; and out of those rich Materials to give the World a complete Body of all Arts and Sciences, which however might be still improved, and much expedited, if the Publick would raise a Fund for making and employing five Hundred such Frames in *Lagado*, and oblige the Managers to contribute in common their several Collections.

He assured me, that this Invention had employed all his Thoughts from his Youth; that he had emptyed the whole Vocabulary into his frame, and made the strictest Computation of the general Proportion there is in Books between the Numbers of Particles, Nouns, and Verbs, and other Parts of Speech.

I made my humblest Acknowledgments to this illustrious Person for his great Communicativeness; and promised if ever I had the good Fortune to return to my native Country, that I would do him Justice, as the sole Inventor of this wonderful Machine; the Form and Contrivance of which I desired Leave to delineate upon Paper as in the Figure here annexed. I told him, although it were the Custom of our Learned in *Europe* to steal Inventions from each other,* who had thereby at least this Advantage, that it became a Controversy which was the right Owner; yet I would take such Caution, that he should have the Honour entire without a Rival.

We next went to the School of Languages,* where three Professors sat in Consultation upon improving that of their own Country.

The first Project was to shorten Discourse* by cutting Polysyllables into one, and leaving out Verbs and Participles; because in Reality all things imaginable are but Nouns.

The other, was a Scheme for entirely abolishing all Words whatsoever: And this was urged as a great Advantage in Point of Health as well as Brevity. For, it is plain, that every Word we speak is in some Degree a Diminution of our Lungs* by Corrosion; and consequently contributes to the shortning of our Lives. An Expedient was therefore offered, that since Words are only Names for *Things*,* it would be more convenient for all Men to carry about them, such *Things* as were necessary to express the particular Business they are to discourse on. And this Invention would certainly have taken Place, to the great Ease as well as Health of the Subject, if the Women in Conjunction with the Vulgar and Illiterate, had not threatened to raise a Rebellion, unless they might be allowed the Liberty to speak with their Tongues, after the Manner of their Forefathers: Such constant irreconcilable Enemies to Science are the common People.* However, many of the most Learned and Wise adhere to the new Scheme of expressing themselves by *Things*; which hath only this Inconvenience attending it; that if a Man's Business be very great, and of various Kinds, he must be obliged in Proportion to carry a greater Bundle of *Things* upon his Back, unless he can afford one or two strong Servants to attend him. I have often beheld two of those Sages almost sinking under the Weight of their Packs, like Pedlars among us; who, when they met in the Streets, would lay down their Loads, open their Sacks, and hold Conversation for an Hour together; then put up their Implements, help each other to resume their Burthens, and take their Leave.

But, for short Conversations a Man may carry Implements in his Pockets and under his Arms, enough to supply him, and in his House he cannot be at a Loss; therefore the Room where Company meet who practice this Art, is full of all *Things* ready at Hand, requisite to furnish Matter for this Kind of artificial Converse.

Another great Advantage proposed by this Invention, was, that it would serve as an universal Language* to be understood in all civil-ized Nations, whose Goods and Utensils are generally of the same Kind, or nearly resembling, so that their Uses might easily be comprehended. And thus, Embassadors would be qualified to treat with foreign Princes or Ministers of State, to whose Tongues they were utter Strangers.

I was at the Mathematical School, where the Master taught his Pupils after a Method scarce imaginable to us in *Europe*. The Proposition and Demonstration were fairly written on a thin Wafer, with Ink composed of a Cephalick Tincture.* This the Student was to swallow upon a fasting Stomach, and for three Days following eat nothing but Bread and Water. As the Wafer digested, the Tincture mounted to his Brain, bearing the Proposition along with it. But the

Success has not hitherto been answerable, partly by some Error in
the *Quantum** or Composition, and partly by the Perverseness of
Lads; to whom this Bolus* is so nauseous, that they generally
steal aside, and discharge it upwards before it can operate; neither
have they been yet persuaded to use so long an Abstinence as the
Prescription requires.

CHAPTER SIX

A further Account of the Academy. The Author proposeth some Improvements, which are honourably received.

IN the School of political Projectors I was but ill entertained; the Professors appearing in my Judgment wholly out of their Senses;* which is a Scene that never fails to make me melancholy. These unhappy People were proposing Schemes for persuading Monarchs to chuse Favourites upon the Score of their Wisdom, Capacity and Virtue; of teaching Ministers to consult the publick Good; of rewarding Merit, great Abilities, and eminent Services; of instructing Princes to know their true Interest, by placing it on the same Foundation with that of their People: Of chusing for Employments Persons qualified to exercise them; with many other wild impossible Chimæras, that never entered before into the Heart of Man to conceive; and confirmed in me the old Observation, that there is nothing so extravagant and irrational which some Philosophers have not maintained for Truth.

But, however I shall so far do Justice to this Part of the Academy, as to acknowledge that all of them were not so visionary. There was a most ingenious Doctor who seemed to be perfectly versed in the whole Nature and System of Government. This illustrious Person had very usefully employed his Studies in finding out effectual Remedies for all Diseases and Corruptions, to which the several Kinds of publick Administration are subject by the Vices or Infirmities of those who govern, as well as by the Licentiousness of those who are to obey. For Instance: Whereas all Writers and Reasoners have agreed, that there is a strict universal Resemblance between the natural and the political Body; can there be anything more evident, than that the Health of both must be preserved, and the Diseases cured by the same Prescriptions? It is allowed, that Senates and great Councils are often troubled with redundant, ebullient,* and other peccant Humours;* with many Diseases of the Head, and more of the Heart; with strong Convulsions, with grievous Contractions of the Nerves and Sinews in both Hands, but especially the Right:* With Spleen, Flatus,* Vertigoes, and Deliriums; with scrophulous Tumours full of fœtid purulent Matter; with sower frothy Ructations;* with Canine Appetites* and Crudeness of Digestion;* besides many others needless to mention. This Doctor therefore proposed, that upon the meeting of a Senate, certain Physicians should attend at the three first Days of their sitting, and at the Close of each Day's Debate, feel the Pulses of every Senator; after which having maturely considered, and consulted upon the Nature of the several Maladies, and the Methods of Cure; they should on the fourth Day return to the Senate-House, attended by their Apothecaries stored with proper Medicines; and before the Members sat, administer to each of them Lenitives, Aperitives, Abstersives, Corrosives, Restringents, Palliatives, Laxatives, Cephalalgicks, Ictericks, Apophlegmaticks, Acousticks, as their several Cases required,* and according as these Medicines should operate, repeat, alter, or omit them at the next Meeting.

This Project could not be of any great Expence to the Publick; and might, in my poor Opinion, be of much Use for the Dispatch of Business in those Countries where Senates have any Share in the legislative Power; beget Unanimity, shorten Debates, open a few Mouths which are now closed, and close many more which are now open; curb the Petulancy of the Young, and correct the Positiveness of the Old; rouze the Stupid, and damp the Pert.

Again; Because it is a general Complaint that the Favourites of Princes are troubled with short and weak Memories; the same Doctor proposed, that whoever attended a first Minister, after having told his Business with the utmost Brevity, and in the plainest Words; should at his Departure give the said Minister a Tweak by the Nose, or a Kick in the Belly, or tread on his Corns, or lug him thrice by both Ears, or run a Pin into his Breech, or pinch his Arm black and blue; to prevent Forgetfulness: And at every Levee Day repeat the same Operation, till the Business were done or absolutely refused.

He likewise directed, that every Senator in the great Council of a Nation, after he had delivered his Opinion, and argued in the Defence of it, should be obliged to give his Vote directly contrary; because if that were done, the Result would infallibly terminate in the Good of the Publick.

When Parties in a State are violent, he offered a wonderful Contrivance to reconcile them. The Method is this. You take an

Hundred Leaders of each Party; you dispose them into Couples of such whose Heads are nearest of a Size; then let two nice Operators saw off the *Occiput* of each Couple at the same Time, in such a Manner that the Brain may be equally divided. Let the *Occiputs* thus cut off be interchanged, applying each to the Head of his opposite Party-man. It seems indeed to be a Work that requireth some Exactness; but the Professor assured us, that if it were dexterously performed, the Cure would be infallible. For he argued thus; that the two half Brains being left to debate the Matter between themselves within the Space of one Scull, would soon come to a good Under-standing, and produce that Moderation as well as Regularity of Thinking, so much to be wished for in the Heads of those, who imagine they came into the World only to watch and govern its Motion: And as to the Difference of Brains in Quantity or Quality, among those who are Directors in Faction; the Doctor assured us from his own Knowledge, that it was a perfect Trifle.

I heard a very warm Debate between two Professors, about the most commodious and effectual Ways and Means of raising Money without grieving the Subject. The first affirmed, the justest Method would be to lay a certain Tax upon Vices and Folly; and the sum fixed upon every Man, to be rated after the fairest Manner by a Jury of his Neighbours. The second was of an Opinion dir-ectly contrary; to tax those Qualities of Body and Mind for which Men chiefly value themselves; the Rate to be more or less accord-ing to the Degrees of excelling; the Decision whereof should be left entirely to their own Breast. The highest Tax was upon Men, who are the greatest Favourites of the other Sex; and the Assess-ments according to the Number and Natures of the Favours they have received; for which they are allowed to be their own Vouchers. Wit, Valour, and Politeness were likewise proposed to be largely taxed, and collected in the same Manner, by every Person giving his own Word for the Quantum of what he possessed. But, as to Honour, Justice, Wisdom and Learning, they should not be taxed at all; because they are Qualifications of so singular a Kind, that no Man will either allow them in his Neighbour, or value them in himself.

The Women were proposed to be taxed according to their Beauty and Skill in Dressing; wherein they had the same Privilege with the Men, to be determined by their own Judgment. But Constancy,

Chastity, good Sense, and good Nature were not rated, because they would not bear the Charge of Collecting.

To keep Senators in the Interest of the Crown, it was proposed that the Members should raffle for Employments; every Man first taking an Oath, and giving Security that he would vote for the Court, whether he won or no; after which the Losers had in their Turn the Liberty of raising upon the next Vacancy. Thus, Hope and Expectation would be kept alive; none would complain of broken Promises, but impute their Disappointments wholly to Fortune, whose Shoulders are broader and stronger than those of a ministry.

Another Professor shewed me a large Paper of Instructions for discovering Plots and Conspiracies against the Government. He advised great Statesmen to examine into the Dyet of all suspected Persons; their Times of eating; upon which Side they lay in Bed; with which Hand they wiped their Posteriors; to take a strict View of their Excrements,* and from the Colour, the Odour, the Taste, the Consistence, the Crudeness, or Maturity of Digestion, form a Judgment of their Thoughts and Designs: Because Men are never so serious, thoughtful, and intent, as when they are at Stool; which he found by frequent Experiment: for in such Conjunctures,* when he used merely as a Trial to consider which was the best Way of murdering the King, his Ordure would have a Tincture of Green; but quite different when he thought only of raising an Insurrection, or burning the Metropolis.

The whole Discourse was written with great Acuteness, containing many Observations both curious and useful for Politicians, but as I conceived not altogether compleat. This I ventured to tell the Author, and offered if he pleased to supply him with some Additions. He received my Proposition with more Compliance than is usual among Writers, especially those of the Projecting Species; professing he would be glad to receive farther Information.

I told him, that in the Kingdom of *Tribnia*,* by the Natives called *Langden*,* where I had sojourned, the Bulk of the People consisted wholly of Discoverers, Witnesses, Informers, Accusers, Prosecutors, Evidences,* Swearers; together with their several subservient and subaltern Instruments; all under the Colours, the Conduct, and pay of Ministers and their Deputies. The Plots in that Kingdom* are usually the Workmanship of those Persons who desire to raise their own Characters of profound Politicians; to restore new Vigour to a crazy Administration; to stifle or divert general Discontents; to fill their Coffers with Forfeitures;* and raise or sink the Opinion of publick Credit,* as either shall best answer their private Advantage. It is first agreed and settled among them, what suspected Persons shall be accused of a Plot: Then, effectual Care is taken to secure all their Letters and other Papers, and put the Owners in Chains. These Papers are delivered to a Set of Artists very dextrous in finding out the mysterious Meanings of Words, Syllables and Letters. For Instance, they can decypher a Close-stool to signify a Privy-Council; a Flock of Geese, a Senate; a lame Dog,* an Invader;* the Plague, a standing Army;* a Buzard,* a Minister; the Gout, a High Priest;* a Gibbet, a Secretary of State; a Chamber pot, a Committee of Grandees; a Sieve,* a Court Lady; a Broom, a Revolution; a Mouse-trap, an Employment;* a bottomless Pit, the Treasury; a Sink, a C——t;* a Cap and Bells, a Favourite; a broken Reed, a Court of Justice; an empty Tun, a General; a running Sore, the Administration.

When this Method fails, they have two others more effectual; which the Learned among them call Acrosticks, and Anagrams. *First*, they can decypher all initial Letters into political Meanings: Thus, *N*, shall signify a Plot; *B*, a Regiment of Horse: *L*, a Fleet at Sea; Or, *secondly*, by transposing the Letters of the Alphabet, in any suspected Paper, they can lay open the deepest Designs of a dis-contented Party. So for Example, if I should say in a Letter to a Friend, *Our Brother* Tom *has just got the Piles*;* a Man of Skill in this Art would discover how the same Letters which compose that Sentence, may be analysed into the following words; *Resist,——a Plot is brought home——The Tour.** And this is the Anagrammatick Method.

The Professor made me great Acknowledgments for communicating these Observations, and promised to make honourable mention of me in his Treatise.

I saw nothing in this Country that could invite me to a longer Continuance; and began to think of returning home to *England*.

CHAPTER SEVEN

The Author leaves Lagado, *arrives at* Maldonada. *No Ship ready. He takes a Short Voyage to* Glubbdubdrib. *His Reception by the Governor.*

THE Continent of which this Kingdom is a part, extends itself, as I have Reason to believe, Eastward to that unknown Tract of *America*, Westward to *California*, and North to the Pacifick Ocean, which is not above an hundred and fifty Miles from *Lagado*; where there is a good Port and much Commerce with the great Island of *Luggnagg*, situated to the North-West* about 29 Degrees North Latitude, and 140 Longitude. The Island of *Luggnagg* stands South Eastward of *Japan*, about an hundred leagues distant. There is a strict Alliance between the *Japanese* Emperor and the King of *Luggnagg*, which affords frequent Opportunities of sailing from one Island to the other. I determined therefore to direct my Course this Way, in order to my Return to *Europe*. I hired two Mules with a Guide to shew me the Way, and carry my small Baggage. I took leave of my noble Protector, who had shewn me so much Favour and made me a generous Present at my Departure.

My Journey was without any Accident or Adventure worth relating. When I arrived at the Port of *Maldonada*, (for so it is called) there was no Ship in the Harbour bound for *Luggnagg*, nor like to be in some Time. The Town is about as large as *Portsmouth*. I soon fell into some Acquaintance, and was very hospitably received. A Gentleman of Distinction said to me, that since the Ships bound for *Luggnagg* could not be ready in less than a Month, it might be no disagreeable Amusement for me to take a Trip to the little Island of *Glubbdubdrib*, about five Leagues to the South-West. He offered himself and a Friend to accompany me, and that I should be provided with a small convenient Barque for the Voyage.

GLUBBDUBDRIB,* as nearly as I can interpret the Word, signifies the Island of *Sorcerers* or *Magicians*. It is about one-third as large as the Isle of *Wight*, and extreamly fruitful: It is governed by the Head of a certain Tribe, who are all Magicians. This Tribe marries only among each other; and the eldest in Succession is

Prince or Governor. He hath a noble Palace, and a Park of about three thousand Acres, surrounded by a Wall of hewn Stone twenty Foot high. In this Park are several small Inclosures for Cattle, Corn and Gardening.

The Governor and his Family are served and attended by Domesticks of a Kind somewhat unusual. By his Skill in Necromancy, he hath Power of calling whom he pleaseth from the Dead, and commanding their Service for twenty-four Hours, but no longer; nor can he call the same Persons up again in less than three Months, except upon very extraordinary Occasions.

When we arrived at the Island, which was about Eleven in the Morning, one of the Gentlemen who accompanied me, went to the Governor, and desired Admittance for a Stranger, who came on purpose to have the Honour of attending on his Highness. This was immediately granted, and we all three entered the Gate of the Palace between two Rows of Guards, armed and dressed after a very antick* Manner, and something in their Countenances that made my Flesh creep with a Horror I cannot express. We passed through several Apartments, between Servants of the same Sort, ranked on each Side as before, till we came to the Chamber of Presence, where after three profound Obeysances, and a few general Questions, we were permitted to sit on three Stools near the lowest Step of his Highness's Throne. He understood the Language of *Balnibarbi*, although it were different from that of his Island. He desired me to give him some Account of my Travels; and to let me see that I should be treated without Ceremony, he dismissed all his Attendants with a Turn of his Finger, at which to my great Astonishment they vanished in an Instant, like Visions in a Dream, when we awake on a sudden. I could not recover myself in some Time, till the Governor assured me that I should receive no Hurt; and observing my two Companions to be under no Concern, who had been often entertained in the same Manner, I began to take Courage; and related to his Highness a short History of my several Adventures, yet not without some Hesitation, and frequently looking behind me to the Place where I had seen those domestick Spectres. I had the Honour to dine with the Governor, where a new Set of Ghosts served up the Meat, and waited at Table. I new observed myself to be less terrified than I had been in the Morning. I stayed till Sun-set, but humbly desired his Highness to excuse me for not accepting his Invitation of lodging in the Palace. My two Friends and I lay at a private House in the Town adjoining, which is the Capital of this little Island; and the next Morning we returned to pay our Duty to the Governor, as he was pleased to command us.

After this Manner we continued in the Island for ten Days, most Part of every Day with the Governor, and at Night in our Lodging. I soon grew so familiarized to the Sight of Spirits, that the third or fourth Time they gave me no Emotion at all; or if I had any Apprehensions left, my Curiosity prevailed over them. For his Highness the Governor ordered me to call up whatever Persons I would chuse to name,* and in whatever Numbers among all the Dead from the Beginning of the World to the present Time, and command them to answer any Questions I should think fit to ask; with this Condition, that my Questions must be confined within the Compass of the Times they lived in. And one Thing I might depend upon, that they would certainly tell me Truth, for Lying was a Talent of no Use in the lower World.

I made my humble Acknowledgments to his Highness for so great a Favour. We were in a Chamber, from whence there was a fair Prospect into the Park. And because my first Inclination was to be entertained with Scenes of Pomp and Magnificence. I desired to see *Alexander* the Great, at the Head of his Army just after the Battle of Arbela; which upon a Motion of the Governor's Finger immediately appeared in a large Field under the Window, where we stood. *Alexander* was called up into the Room; It was with great Difficulty that I understood his *Greek*, and had but little of my own. He assured me upon his Honour that he was not poisoned, but dyed of a Fever by excessive Drinking.*

Next I saw *Hannibal* passing the *Alps*, who told me he had not a Drop of Vinegar* in his Camp.

I saw *Cæsar* and *Pompey* at the Head of their Troops, just ready to engage.* I saw the former in his last great Triumph.* I desired that the Senate of *Rome* might appear before me in one large Chamber, and a modern Representative, in Counterview, in another. The first seemed to be an Assembly of Heroes and Demy-Gods; the other a Knot of Pedlars, Pickpockets, Highwaymen and Bullies.

The Governor at my Request gave the Sign for *Cæsar* and *Brutus* to advance towards us. I was struck with a profound Veneration at the Sight of *Brutus*;* and could easily discover the most consummate

Virtue, the greatest Intrepidity, and Firmness of Mind, the truest Love of his Country, and general Benevolence for Mankind in every Lineament of his Countenance. I observed with much Pleasure that these two Persons were in good Intelligence* with each other; and *Cæsar* freely confessed to me, that the greatest Actions of his own Life were not equal by many Degrees to the Glory of taking it away. I had the Honour to have much Conversation with *Brutus*; and was told that his Ancestor *Junius*,* *Socrates*,* *Epaminondas*,* *Cato the Younger*,* *Sir Thomas More*,* and himself, were perpetually together: A *Sextumvirate* to which all the Ages of the World cannot add a Seventh.

It would be tedious to trouble the Reader with relating what vast Numbers of illustrious Persons were called up, to gratify that insatiable Desire I had to see the World in every Period of Antiquity placed before me. I chiefly fed mine Eyes with beholding the Destroyers of Tyrants and Usurpers, and the Restorers of Liberty to oppressed and injured Nations. But it is impossible to express the Satisfaction I received in my own Mind, after such a Manner as to make it a suitable Entertainment to the Reader.

CHAPTER EIGHT

A further Account of Glubbdubdrib. *Antient and Modern History corrected.*

HAVING a Desire to see those Antients, who were most renowned for Wit and Learning, I set apart one Day on purpose. I proposed that *Homer** and *Aristotle* might appear at the Head of all their Commentators; but these were so numerous that some Hundreds were forced to attend in the Court and outward Rooms of the Palace. I knew and could distinguish those two Heroes at first Sight, not only from the Croud, but from each other. *Homer* was the taller and comelier Person of the two, walked very erect for one of his Age, and his Eyes were the most quick and piercing* I ever beheld. *Aristotle* stooped much, and made use of a Staff. His Visage was meager, his Hair lank and thin, and his Voice hollow. I soon discovered that both of them were perfect Strangers to the rest of the Company, and had never seen or heard of them before. And I had a Whisper from a Ghost, who shall be nameless, that these Commentators always kept in the most distant Quarters from their Principals in the lower World, through a Consciousness of Shame and Guilt, because they had so horribly misrepresented the Meaning of those Authors to Posterity. I introduced *Didymus** and *Eustathius** to *Homer*, and prevailed on him to treat them better than perhaps they deserved; for he soon found they wanted a Genius to enter into the Spirit of a Poet.* But *Aristotle* was out of all Patience* with the Account I gave him of *Scotus** and *Ramus*,* as I presented them to him; and he asked them whether the rest of the Tribe were as great Dunces as themselves.

I then desired the Governor to call up *Descartes** and *Gassendi*,* with whom I prevailed to explain their Systems to *Aristotle*. This great Philosopher freely acknowledged his own Mistakes in Natural Philosophy, because he proceeded in many things upon Conjecture, as all Men must do; and he found, that *Gassendi*, who had made the Doctrine of *Epicurus* as palatable as he could, and the *Vortices* of *Descartes*, were equally exploded. He predicted the same fate to *Attraction*,* whereof the present Learned are such zealous Asserters. He said that new Systems of Nature were but new Fashions, which would vary in every Age; and even those who pretend to demon-strate them from Mathematical Principles,* would flourish but a short Period of Time, and be out of Vogue when that was determined.

I spent five Days in conversing with many others of the antient Learned. I saw most of the first *Roman* Emperors. I prevailed on the Governor to call up *Eliogabalus*'s* Cooks to dress us a Dinner; but they could not shew us much of their Skill, for want of Materials. A *Helot** of *Agesilaus** made us a Dish of *Spartan* Broth,* but I was not able to get down a second *Spoonful*.

The two Gentlemen who conducted me to the Island were pressed by their private Affairs to return in three Days, which I employed in seeing some of the modern Dead, who had made the greatest Figure for two or three Hundred Years past in our own and other Countries of *Europe*; and having been always a great Admirer of old illustrious Families,* I desired the Governor would call up a Dozen or two of Kings with their Ancestors in order, for eight or nine Generations. But my Disappointment was grievous and unexpected. For, instead of a long Train with Royal Diadems, I saw in one Family two Fiddlers, three spruce Courtiers, and an *Italian* Prelate. In another, a Barber, an Abbot, and two Cardinals. I have too great a Veneration for crowned Heads to dwell any longer on so nice a Subject: But as to Counts, Marquesses, Dukes, Earls, and the like, I was not so scrupulous. And I confess it was not without some Pleasure that I found myself able to trace the particu-lar Features, by which certain Families are distinguished up to their Originals. I could plainly discover from whence one family derives a long Chin; why a second hath abounded with Knaves for two Generations, and Fools for two more; why a third happened to be crack-brained, and a fourth to be Sharpers. Whence it came, what *Polydore Virgil** says of a certain great House, *Nec Vir fortis, nec Fœmina Casta*.* How Cruelty, Falsehood, and Cowardice grew to be Characteristicks by which certain Families are distinguished as much as by their Coat of Arms. Who first brought the *Pox** into a noble House, which has lineally descended in scrophulous Tumours to their Posterity. Neither could I wonder at all this, when I saw such an Interruption of Lineages by Pages, Lacqueys, Valets, Coachmen, Gamesters, Fidlers, Players, Captains, and Pick-pockets.

I was chiefly disgusted with modern History. For having strictly examined all the Persons of greatest Name in the Courts of Princes for an Hundred Years past, I found how the World had been misled by prostitute Writers, to ascribe the greatest Exploits in War to Cowards, the wisest Counsel to Fools, Sincerity to Flatterers, *Roman* Virtue to Betrayers of their Country, Piety to Atheists, Chastity to Sodomites, Truth to Informers. How many innocent and excellent Persons had been condemned to Death or Banishment, by the practising of great Ministers upon the Corruption of Judges, and the Malice of Factions. How many Villains had been exalted to the highest Places of Trust, Power, Dignity, and Profit: How great a Share in the Motions and Events of Courts, Councils, and Senates might be challenged by Bawds, Whores, Pimps, Parasites, and Buffoons: How low an Opinion I had of human Wisdom and Integrity, when I was truly informed of the Springs and Motives of great Enterprizes and Revolutions in the World, and of the contemptible Accidents* to which they owed their Success.

Here I discovered the Roguery and Ignorance of those who pretend to write *Anecdotes*, or secret History;* who send so many Kings to their Graves with a Cup of Poison; will repeat the Discourse between a Prince and chief Minister, where no Witness was by; unlock the Thoughts and Cabinets of Embassadors and Secretaries of State; and have the perpetual Misfortune to be mistaken. Here I discovered the true Causes of many great Events that have surprized the World: How a Whore can govern the Back-stairs, the Back-stairs a Council, and the Council a Senate. A General confessed in my Presence, that he got a Victory purely by the Force of Cowardice and ill Conduct: And an Admiral,* that for want of proper Intelligence, he beat the Enemy to whom he intended to betray the Fleet. Three Kings protested to me, that in their whole Reigns they never did once prefer any Person of Merit, unless by Mistake or Treachery of some Minister in whom they confided: Neither would they do it if they were to live again; and they shewed with great Strength of Reason that the Royal Throne could not be supported without Corruption; because that positive, confident, restive Temper, which Virtue infused into Man, was a perpetual Clog to publick Business.

I had the Curiosity to enquire in a particular Manner, by what Method great Numbers had procured to themselves high Titles of

Honour, and prodigious Estates; and I confined my Enquiry to a very modern Period: However, without grating upon present Times, because I would be sure to give no Offence even to Foreigners, (for I hope the Reader need not be told that I do not in the least intend my own Country in what I say upon this Occasion) a great Number of Persons concerned were called up, and upon a very slight Examination, discovered such a Scene of Infamy, that I cannot reflect upon it without some Seriousness. Perjury, Oppression, Subornation, Fraud, Panderism, and the like *Infirmities* were amongst the most excusable Arts they had to mention; and for these I gave, as it was reasonable, due Allowance. But when some confessed they owed their Greatness and Wealth to Sodomy or Incest; others to the prostituting of their own Wives and Daughters; others to the betraying their Country or their Prince; some to poisoning, more to the perverting of Justice in order to destroy the Innocent: I hope I may be pardoned if these Discoveries inclined me little to abate of that profound Veneration which I am naturally apt to pay to Persons of high Rank, who ought to be treated with the utmost Respect due to their sublime Dignity, by us their Inferiors.

I had often read of some great Services done to Princes and States, and desired to see the Persons by whom those Services were performed. Upon Enquiry I was told, that their Names were to be found on no Record, except a few of them whom History hath represented as the vilest Rogues and Traitors. As to the rest, I had never once heard of them. They all appeared with dejected Looks, and in the meanest Habit; most of them telling me they died in Poverty and Disgrace, and the rest on a Scaffold or a Gibbet.

Among the rest there was one Person whose Case appeared a little singular. He had a Youth about Eighteen Years old standing by his Side. He told me, he had for many Years been Commander of a Ship; and in the Sea Fight of *Actium*,* had the good Fortune to break through the Enemy's great Line of Battle, sink three of their Capital Ships, and take a fourth, which was the sole Cause of *Antony's* Flight,* and of the Victory that ensued: That the Youth standing by him, his only Son, was killed in the Action. He added, that upon the Confidence of some Merit, the War being at an End, he went to *Rome*, and solicited at the Court of *Augustus** to be preferred to a greater Ship, whose Commander had been killed; but without any regard to his Pretensions, it was given to a Boy who had never seen the Sea, the son of a *Libertina*,* who waited on one of the Emperor's Mistresses. Returning back to his own Vessel, he was charged with Neglect of Duty, and the Ship given to a favourite Page of *Publicola** the Vice-Admiral; whereupon he retired to a poor Farm, at a great Distance from *Rome*, and there ended his Life. I was so curious to know the Truth of this Story, that I desired *Agrippa** might be called, who was Admiral in that Fight. He appeared, and confirmed the whole Account, but with much more Advantage to the Captain, whose Modesty had extenuated or concealed a great Part of his Merit.

I was surprized to find Corruption grown so high and so quick in that Empire, by the Force of Luxury so lately introduced; which made me less wonder at many parallel Cases in other Countries, where Vices of all Kinds have reigned so much longer, and where the whole Praise as well as Pillage hath been engrossed by the chief Commander,* who perhaps had the least Title to either.

As every Person called up made exactly the same Appearance he had done in the World, it gave me melancholy Reflections to observe how much the Race of human Kind was degenerate among us, within these Hundred Years past. How the Pox under all its Consequences and Denominations had altered every Lineament of an *English* Countenance: shortened the Size of Bodies, unbraced the Nerves, relaxed the Sinews and Muscles, introduced a sallow Complexion, and rendered the Flesh loose and *rancid*.

I descended so low as to desire that some *English* Yeomen of the old Stamp,* might be summoned to appear; once so famous for the Simplicity of their Manners, Dyet and Dress; for Justice in their Dealings; for their true Spirit of Liberty; for their Valour and Love of their Country. Neither could I be wholly unmoved after comparing the Living with the Dead, when I considered how all these pure native Virtues were prostituted for a Piece of Money by their Grand-children; who in selling their Votes, and managing at Elections* have acquired every Vice and Corruption that can possibly be learned in a Court.

CHAPTER NINE

The Author's Return to Maldonada. *Sails to the Kingdom of* Luggnagg. *The Author confined. He is sent for to Court. The Manner of his Admittance. The King's great Lenity to his Subjects.*

THE day of our Departure being come, I took leave of his Highness the Governor of *Glubbdubdrib*, and returned with my two companions to *Maldonada*, where after a Fortnight's waiting, a Ship was ready to sail for *Luggnagg*. The two Gentlemen and some others were so generous and kind as to furnish me with Provisions, and see me on Board. I was a Month in this Voyage. We had one violent Storm, and were under a Necessity of steering Westward to get into the Trade-Wind, which holds for above sixty Leagues. On the 21st of *April*, 1708, we sailed into the River of *Clumegnig*, which is a Seaport Town, at the South-East Point of *Luggnagg*. We cast Anchor within a League of the Town, and made a Signal for a Pilot. Two of them came on Board in less than half an Hour, by whom we were guided between certain Shoals and Rocks, which are very dangerous in the Passage, to a large Basin, where a Fleet may ride in Safety within a Cable's Length of the Town-Wall.

Some of our Sailors, whether out of Treachery or Inadvertence, had informed the Pilots that I was a Stranger and a great Traveller, whereof these gave Notice to a Custom-House Officer, by whom I was examined very strictly upon my landing. This Officer spoke to me in the Language of *Balnibarbi*, which by the Force of much Commerce is generally understood in that Town, especially by Seamen, and those employed in the Customs. I gave him a short Account of some Particulars, and made my Story as plausible and consistent as I could; but I thought it necessary to disguise my Country, and call myself an *Hollander*; because my Intentions were for Japan, and I knew the *Dutch* were the only *Europeans* permitted to enter into that Kingdom.* I therefore told the Officer, that having been shipwrecked on the Coast of *Balnibarbi*, and cast on a Rock, I was received up into *Laputa*, or the flying Island (of which he had often heard) and was now endeavouring to get to *Japan*, from whence I might find a Convenience of returning to my own

Country. The Officer said, I must be confined till he could receive Orders from Court, for which he would write immediately, and hoped to receive an Answer in a Fortnight. I was carried to a convenient Lodging, with a Centry placed at the Door; however I had the Liberty of a large Garden, and was treated with Humanity enough, being maintained all the Time at the King's Charge. I was visited by several Persons, chiefly out of Curiosity, because it was reported that I came from Countries very remote, of which they had never heard.

I hired a young Man who came in the same Ship to be an Interpreter; he was a Native of *Luggnagg*, but had lived some Years at *Maldonada*, and was a perfect Master of both Languages. By his Assistance I was able to hold a Conversation with those who came to visit me; but this consisted only of their Questions and my Answers.

The Dispatch came from Court about the Time we expected. It contained a Warrant for conducting me and my Retinue to *Traldragdubb* or *Trildrogdrib*, (for it is pronounced both Ways as near as I can remember) by a Party of Ten Horse. All my Retinue was that poor Lad for an Interpreter, whom I persuaded into my Service. And at my humble Request we had each of us a Mule to ride on. A Messenger was dispatched half a Day's Journey before us, to give the King Notice of my Approach, and to desire that his Majesty would please appoint a Day and Hour, when it would be his gracious Pleasure that I might have the Honour to *lick the Dust* before his Footstool*. This is the Court Style, and I found it to be more than Matter of Form: For upon my Admittance two Days after my Arrival, I was commanded to crawl on my Belly, and lick the Floor as I advanced; but on account of my being a Stranger, Care was taken to have it so clean that the Dust was not offensive. However, this was a peculiar Grace, not allowed to any but Persons of the highest Rank, when they desire an Admittance: Nay, sometimes the Floor is strewed with Dust on purpose, when the Person to be admitted happens to have powerful Enemies at Court: And I have seen a great Lord with his Mouth so crammed, that when he had crept to the proper Distance from the Throne, he was not able to speak a Word. Neither is there any Remedy, because it is capital for those who receive an Audience to spit or wipe their Mouths in his Majesty's Presence. There is indeed another Custom, which I cannot altogether approve of. When the King hath a Mind to put any of his Nobles to Death in a gentle indulgent Manner; he commands to have the Floor strowed with a certain brown Powder, of a deadly Composition, which being licked up infallibly kills him in twenty-four Hours. But in Justice to this Prince's great Clemency, and the Care he has of his Subjects Lives, (wherein it were much to be wished that the Monarchs of *Europe* would imitate him) it must be mentioned for his Honour, that strict Orders are given to have the infected Parts of the Floor well washed after every such Execution; which if his Domesticks neglect, they are in Danger of incurring his Royal Displeasure. I my self heard him give Directions, that one of his Pages should be whipt, whose Turn it was to give Notice about washing the Floor after an Execution, but maliciously had omitted it; by which Neglect a young Lord of great Hopes coming to an Audience, was unfortunately poisoned, although the King at that Time had no Design against his Life. But this good Prince was so gracious, as to forgive the poor Page his Whipping, upon Promise that he would do so no more, without special Orders.

To return from this Digression; when I had crept within four Yards of the Throne, I raised my self gently upon my Knees, and then striking my Forehead seven Times against the Ground, I pronounced the following Words, as they had been taught me the Night before, *Ickpling Gloffthrobb Squutserumm blhiop Mlashnalt Zwin tnodbalkguffh Slhiophad Gurdlubh Asht.* This is the Compliment established by the Laws of the Land for all Persons admitted to the King's Presence. It may be rendered into *English* thus: *May your cœlestial Majesty out-live the Sun, eleven Moons and an half.* To this the King returned some Answer, which although I could not understand, yet I replied as I had been directed: *Fluft drin Yalerick Dwuldum prastrad mirplush*, which properly signifies, *My Tongue is in the Mouth of my Friend*; and by this Expression was meant that I desired leave to bring my Interpreter; whereupon the young Man already mentioned was accordingly introduced; by whose Intervention I answered as many Questions as his Majesty could put in above an Hour. I spoke in the *Balnibarbian* Tongue, and my Interpreter delivered my Meaning in that of *Luggnagg*.

The King was much delighted with my Company, and ordered his *Bliffmarklub* or High Chamberlain to appoint a Lodging in the Court for me and my Interpreter, with a daily Allowance for my Table, and a large Purse of Gold for my common Expences.

I stayed three Months in this Country out of perfect Obedience to his Majesty, who was pleased highly to favour me, and made me very honourable Offers. But I thought it more consistent with Prudence and Justice to pass the Remainder of my Days with my Wife and Family.

CHAPTER TEN

The Luggnuggians *commended. A particular Description of the* Struldbrugs*
*with many Conversations between the Author and some eminent Persons upon
that Subject.*

THE Luggnuggians are a polite and generous People, and although
they are not without some Share of that Pride which is peculiar to all
Eastern Countries, yet they shew themselves courteous to Strangers,
especially such who are countenanced by the Court. I had many
Acquaintance among Persons of the best Fashion, and being always
attended by my Interpreter, the Conversation we had was not
disagreeable.

One Day in much good Company, I was asked by a Person of
Quality, whether I had seen any of their *Struldbrugs* or *Immortals*. I
said I had not; and desired he would explain to me what he meant by
such an Appellation, applyed to a mortal Creature. He told me, that
sometimes, although very rarely, a Child happened to be born in a
Family with a red circular Spot in the Forehead, directly over the left
Eye-brow, which was an infallible Mark that it should never dye. The
Spot, as he described it, was about the Compass of a Silver Three-
pence, but in the Course of Time grew larger, and changed its
Colour; for at Twelve Years old it became green, so continued till Five
and Twenty, then turned to a deep blue; at Five and Forty it grew
coal black, and as large as an *English* Shilling; but never admitted
any farther Alteration. He said these Births were so rare, that he did
not believe there could be above Eleven Hundred *Struldbrugs* of
both Sexes in the whole Kingdom, of which he computed about
Fifty in the Metropolis, and among the rest a young Girl born
about three Years ago. That, these Productions were not peculiar to
any Family, but a mere Effect of Chance; and the Children of
the *Struldbrugs* themselves, were equally mortal with the rest of the
People.

I freely own myself to have been struck with inexpressible Delight
upon hearing this Account: And the Person who gave it me happening to understand the *Balnibarbian* Language, which I spoke very
well, I could not forbear breaking out into Expressions perhaps a

little too extravagant. I cryed out as in a Rapture; Happy Nation, where every Child hath at least a Chance for being immortal! Happy People who enjoy so many living Examples of antient Virtue, and have Masters ready to instruct them in the Wisdom of all former Ages! But, happiest* beyond all Comparison are those excellent *Struldbrugs*, who being born exempt from that universal Calamity of human Nature, have their Minds free and disingaged, without the Weight and Depression of Spirits caused by the continual Apprehension of Death. I discovered my Admiration that I had not observed any of these illustrious Persons at Court; the black Spot on the Fore-head, being so remarkable a Distinction, that I could not have easily overlooked it: And it was impossible that his Majesty, a most judicious Prince, should not provide himself with a good Number of such wise and able Counsellors. Yet perhaps the Virtue of those Reverend Sages was too strict for the corrupt and libertine Manners of a Court. And we often find by Experience, that young Men are too opinionative and volatile to be guided by the sober Dictates of their Seniors. However, since the King was pleased to allow me Access to his Royal Person, I was resolved upon the very first Occasion to deliver my Opinion to him on this Matter freely and at large, by the Help of my Interpreter; and whether he would please to take my Advice or no, yet in one Thing I was determined, that his Majesty having frequently offered me an Establishment in this Country, I would with great Thankfulness accept the Favour, and pass my Life here in the Conversation of those superiour Beings the *Struldbrugs*, if they would please to admit me.

The Gentleman to whom I addressed my Discourse, because (as I have already observed) he spoke the Language of *Balnibarbi*, said to me with a Sort of a Smile, which usually ariseth from Pity to the Ignorant, that he was glad of any Occasion to keep me among them, and desired my Permission to explain to the Company what I had spoke. He did so; and they talked together for some time in their own Language, whereof I understood not a Syllable, neither could I observe by their Countenances what Impression my Discourse had made on them. After a short Silence, the same Person told me, that his Friends and mine (so he thought fit to express himself) were very much pleased with the judicious Remarks I had made on the great Happiness and Advantages of immortal Life; and they were desirous to know in a particular Manner, what Scheme of Living I should have formed to myself, if it had fallen to my Lot to have been born a *Struldbrug*.

I answered, it was easy to be eloquent on so copious and delightful a Subject, especially to me who have been often apt to amuse myself with Visions of what I should do if I were a King, a General, or a great Lord: and upon this very Case I had frequently run over the whole System how I should employ myself, and pass the Time if I were to live for ever.

That, if it had been my good Fortune to come into the World a *Struldbrug*; as soon as I could discover my own Happiness by understanding the Difference between Life and Death, I would first resolve by all Arts and Methods whatsoever to procure myself Riches: In the Pursuit of which, by Thrift and Management, I might reasonably expect in about two Hundred Years to be the wealthiest Man in the Kingdom. In the second Place, I would from my earliest Youth apply myself to the Study of Arts and Sciences, by which I should arrive in time to excel all others in Learning. Lastly, I would carefully record every Action and Event of Consequence that happened in the Publick, impartially draw the Characters of the several Successions of Princes, and great Ministers of State; with my own Observations on every Point. I would exactly set down the several Changes in Customs, Language, Fashion of Dress, Dyet and Diversions. By all which Acquirements, I should be a living Treasury of Knowledge and Wisdom, and certainly become the Oracle of the Nation.

I would never marry after Threescore,* but live in an hospitable Manner, yet still on the saving Side. I would entertain myself in forming and directing the Minds of hopeful young Men, by convincing them from my own Remembrance, Experience and Observation, fortified by numerous Examples, of the Usefulness of Virtue in publick and private Life. But, my choise and constant Companions should be a Sett of my own immortal Brotherhood, among whom I would elect a Dozen from the most ancient down to my own Contemporaries. Where any of these wanted Fortunes, I would provide them with convenient Lodges round my own Estate, and have some of them always at my Table, only mingling a few of the most valuable among you Mortals, whom Length of Time would harden me to lose with little or no Reluctance, and treat your Posterity after the same Manner; just as a Man diverts himself with the annual

Succession of Pinks and Tulips in his Garden, without regretting the Loss of those which withered the preceding Year.

These *Struldbrugs* and I would mutually communicate our Observations and Memorials through the Course of Time; remark the several Gradations by which Corruption steals into the World, and oppose it in every Step, by giving perpetual Warning and Instruction to Mankind; which, added to the strong Influence of our own Example, would probably prevent that continual Degeneracy of human Nature, so justly complained of in all Ages.

Add to all this, the Pleasure of seeing the various Revolutions of States and Empires; the Changes in the lower and upper World;* antient Cities in Ruins, and obscure Villages become the Seats of Kings. Famous Rivers lessening into shallow Brooks; the Ocean leaving one Coast dry, and overwhelming another: The Discovery of many Countries yet unknown. Barbarity over-running the politest Nations, and the most barbarous becoming civilized. I should then see the Discovery of the *Longitude*,* the *perpetual Motion*,* the *universal Medicine*,* and many other great Inventions brought to the utmost Perfection.

What wonderful Discoveries should we make in Astronomy, by outliving and confirming our own Predictions; by observing the Progress and Returns of Comets, with the Changes of Motion in the Sun, Moon and Stars.

I enlarged upon many other Topicks, which the natural Desire of endless Life and sublunary Happiness could easily furnish me with. When I had ended, and the Sum of my Discourse had been interpreted as before, to the rest of the Company, there was a good Deal of Talk among them in the Language of the Country, not without some Laughter at my Expence. At last the same Gentleman who had been my Interpreter, said, he was desired by the rest to set me right in a few Mistakes, which I had fallen into through the common Imbecility of human Nature, and upon that Allowance was less answerable for them. That, this Breed of *Struldbrugs* was peculiar to their Country, for there were no such People either in *Balnibarbi* or *Japan*, where he had the Honour to be Embassador from his Majesty, and found the Natives in both those Kingdoms very hard to believe that the Fact was possible; and it appeared from my Astonishment when he first mentioned the Matter to me, that I received it as a Thing wholly new, and scarcely to be credited. That in the two Kingdoms above-mentioned, where during his Residence he had conversed very much, he observed long Life to be the universal Desire and Wish of Mankind. That, whoever had one foot in the Grave, was sure to hold back the other as strongly as he could. That the oldest had still Hopes of living one Day longer, and looked on Death as the greatest Evil, from which Nature always prompted him to retreat; only in this Island of *Luggnagg*, the Appetite for living was not so eager, from the continual Example of the *Struldbrugs* before their Eyes.

That the System of Living contrived by me was unreasonable and unjust, because it supposed a Perpetuity of Youth, Health, and Vigour, which no Man could be so foolish to hope, however extravagant he may be in his Wishes. That, the Question therefore was not whether a Man would chuse to be always in the Prime of Youth, attended with Prosperity and Health; but how he would pass a perpetual Life under all the usual Disadvantages which old Age brings along with it. For although few Men will avow their Desires of being immortal upon such hard Conditions, yet in the two Kingdoms before-mentioned of *Balnibarbi* and *Japan*, he observed that every Man desired to put off Death for some time longer, let it approach ever so late; and he rarely heard of any Man who died willingly, except he were incited by the Extremity of Grief or Torture. And he appealed to me whether in those Countries I had travelled as well as my own, I had not observed the same general Disposition.

After this Preface, he gave me a particular Account of the *Struldbrugs* among them. He said they commonly acted like Mortals, till about Thirty Years old, after which by Degrees they grew melancholy and dejected, increasing in both till they came to Fourscore. This he learned from their own Confession; for otherwise there not being above two or three of that Species born in an Age, they were too few to form a general Observation by. When they came to Fourscore Years, which is reckoned the Extremity of living in this Country, they had not only all the Follies and Infirmities of other old Men, but many more which arose from the dreadful Prospect of never dying. They were not only opinionative, peevish, covetous, morose, vain, talkative; but uncapable of Friendship, and dead to all natural Affection, which never descended below their Grandchildren. Envy and impotent Desires, are their prevailing Passions. But those Objects against which their Envy seems principally directed, are the Vices of the younger Sort, and the Deaths of the old. By reflecting on the former, they find themselves cut off from all Possibility of Pleasure; and whenever they see a Funeral, they lament and repine that others have gone to an Harbour of Rest, to which they themselves never can hope to arrive. They have no Remembrance of any thing but what they learned and observed in their Youth and middle Age, and even that is very imperfect: And for the Truth or Particulars of any Fact, it is safer to depend on common Traditions than upon their best Recollections. The least miserable among them, appear to be those who turn to Dotage, and entirely lose their Memories; these meet with more Pity and Assistance, because they want many bad Qualities which abound in others.

If a *Struldbrug* happen to marry one of his own Kind, the Marriage is dissolved of Course by the Courtesy of the Kingdom,* as soon as the younger of the two comes to be Fourscore. For the Law thinks it a reasonable Indulgence, that those who are condemned without any Fault of their own to a perpetual Continuance in the World, should not have their Misery doubled by the Load of a Wife.

As soon as they have completed the Term of Eighty Years, they are looked on as dead in Law; their Heirs immediately succeed to their Estates, only a small Pittance is reserved for their Support; and the poor ones are maintained at the publick Charge. After that Period they are held incapable of any Employment of Trust or Profit; they cannot purchase Lands, or take Leases, neither are they allowed to be Witnesses in any Cause, either Civil or Criminal, not even for the Decision of Meers* and Bounds.

At Ninety* they lose their Teeth and Hair; they have at that Age no Distinction of Taste, but eat and drink whatever they can get, without Relish or Appetite. The Diseases they were subject to, still continue without encreasing or diminishing. In talking they forget the common Appellation of Things, and the Names of Persons, even of those who are their nearest Friends and Relations. For the same Reason they never can amuse themselves with reading, because their Memory will not serve to carry them from the Beginning of a Sentence to the End; and by this Defect they are deprived of the only Entertainment whereof they might otherwise be capable.

The Language of this Country being always upon the Flux,* the *Struldbrugs* of one Age do not understand those of another; neither are they able after two Hundred Years to hold any Conversation (farther than by a few general Words) with their Neighbours the Mortals; and thus they lye under the Disadvantage of living like Foreigners in their own Country.

This was the Account given me of the *Struldbrugs*, as near as I can remember. I afterwards saw five or six of different Ages, the youngest not above two Hundred Years old, who were brought to me at several Times by some of my Friends; but although they were told that I was a great Traveller, and had seen all the World, they had not the least Curiosity to ask me a Question; only desired I would give them *Slumskudask*, or a Token of Remembrance; which is a modest Way of begging, to avoid the Law that strictly forbids it, because they are provided for by the Publick, although indeed with a very scanty Allowance.

They are despised and hated by all Sorts of People: When one of them is born, it is reckoned ominous, and their Birth is recorded very particularly; so that you may know their Age by consulting the Registry, which however hath not been kept above a Thousand Years past, or at least hath been destroyed by Time or publick Disturbances. But the usual Way of computing how old they are, is by asking them what Kings or great Persons they can remember, and then consulting History; for infallibly the last Prince in their Mind did not begin his Reign after they were Fourscore Years old.

They were the most mortifying Sight I ever beheld; and the Women more horrible than the Men. Besides the usual Deformities in extreme old Age, they acquired an additional Ghastliness in Proportion to their Number of Years, which is not to be described; and among half a Dozen I soon distinguished which was the eldest, although there were not above a Century or two between them.

The Reader will easily believe, that from what I had heard and seen, my keen Appetite for Perpetuity of Life was much abated. I grew heartily ashamed of the pleasing Visions I had formed; and thought no Tyrant could invent a Death into which I would not run with Pleasure from such a Life. The King heard of all that had passed between me and my Friends upon this Occasion, and rallied me very pleasantly; wishing I would send a Couple of *Struldbrugs* to my own Country, to arm our People against the Fear of Death; but this it seems is forbidden by the fundamental Laws of the Kingdom; or else I should have been well content with the Trouble and Expence of transporting them.

I could not but agree, that the Laws of this Kingdom relating to the *Struldbrugs*, were founded upon the strongest Reasons, and such as any other Country would be under the Necessity of enacting in the like Circumstances. Otherwise, as Avarice is the necessary Consequent of old Age, those Immortals would in time become Proprietors of the whole Nation, and engross the Civil Power; which, for want of Abilities to manage, must end in the Ruin of the Publick.

CHAPTER ELEVEN

The Author leaves Luggnugg *and sails to* Japan. *From thence he returns in a* Dutch *Ship to* Amsterdam, *and from* Amsterdam *to* England.

I THOUGHT this Account of the *Struldbrugs* might be some Entertainment to the Reader, because it seems to be a little out of the common Way; at least, I do not remember to have met the like in any Book of Travels* that hath come to my Hands: And if I am deceived, my Excuse must be, that it is necessary for Travellers, who describe the same Country, very often to agree in dwelling on the same Particulars, without deserving the Censure of having borrowed or transcribed from those who wrote before them.

There is indeed a perpetual Commerce between this Kingdom and the great Empire of *Japan*; and it is very probable that the *Japanese* Authors may have given some Account of the *Struldbrugs*; but my Stay in *Japan* was so short, and I was so entirely a Stranger to the Language, that I was not qualified to make any Enquiries. But I hope the *Dutch** upon this Notice will be curious and able enough to supply my Defects.

His Majesty having often pressed me to accept some Employment in his Court, and finding me absolutely determined to return to my Native Country; was pleased to give me his Licence to depart; and honoured me with a Letter of Recommendation under his own Hand to the Emperor of *Japan*. He likewise presented me with four Hundred and forty-four large Pieces of Gold (this Nation delighting in even Numbers) and a red Diamond* which I sold in *England* for Eleven Hundred Pounds.

On the 6th Day of *May*, 1709, I took a solemn Leave of his Majesty, and all my Friends. This Prince was so gracious as to order a Guard to conduct me to *Glanguenstald*, which is a Royal Port to the *South-West* Part of the Island. In six Days I found a Vessel ready to carry me to *Japan*; and spent fifteen Days in the Voyage. We landed at a small Port-Town called *Xamoschi*,* situated on the *South-East* Part of *Japan*. The Town lies on the *Western* Part, where there is a narrow Streight, leading *Northward* into a long Arm of the Sea, upon the *North-West* Part of which, *Yedo** the Metropolis stands. At landing, I

shewed the Custom-House Officers my Letter from the King of
Luggnagg to his Imperial Majesty: They knew the Seal perfectly well;
it was as broad as the Palm of my Hand. The Impression was, *A King
lifting up a lame Beggar from the Earth*. The Magistrates of the Town
hearing of my Letter, received me as a publick Minister; they provided me with Carriages and Servants, and bore my Charges to *Yedo*,
where I was admitted to an Audience, and delivered my Letter; which
was opened with great Ceremony, and explained to the Emperor by
an Interpreter, who then gave me Notice of his Majesty's Order, that
I should signify my Request; and whatever it were, it should be
granted for the sake of his Royal Brother of *Luggnagg*. This Interpreter was a Person employed to transact Affairs with the *Hollanders*:
He soon conjectured by my Countenance that I was a *European*, and
therefore repeated his Majesty's Commands in *Low-Dutch*,* which
he spoke perfectly well. I answered, (as I had before determined) that
I was a *Dutch* Merchant, shipwrecked in a very remote Country, from
whence I travelled by Sea and Land to *Luggnagg*, and then took
Shipping for *Japan*, where I knew my Countrymen often traded, and
with some of these I hoped to get an Opportunity of returning into
Europe: I therefore most humbly entreated his Royal Favour to give
Order, that I should be conducted in Safety to *Nangasac*.* To this I
added another Petition, that for the sake of my Patron the King of
Luggnagg, his Majesty would condescend to excuse my performing
the Ceremony imposed on my Countrymen, of *trampling upon the
Crucifix*;* because I had been thrown into his Kingdom by my
Misfortunes, without any Intention of trading. When this latter Petition was interpreted to the Emperor, he seemed a little surprised;
and said, he believed I was the first of my Countrymen who ever
made any Scruple in this Point; and that he began to doubt whether I
was a real *Hollander* or no; but rather suspected I must be a CHRISTIAN.
However, for the Reasons I had offered, but chiefly to gratify the
King of *Luggnagg*, by an uncommon Mark of his Favour, he would
comply with the *singularity* of my Humour; but the Affair must be
managed with Dexterity, and his Officers should be commanded to
let me pass as it were by Forgetfulness. For he assured me, that if the
Secret should be discovered by my Countrymen, the *Dutch*, they
would cut my Throat in the Voyage. I returned my Thanks by the
Interpreter for so unusual a Favour; and some Troops being at that
Time on their March to *Nangasac*, the Commanding Officer had

Orders to convey me safe thither, with particular Instructions about the Business of the *Crucifix*.

On the 9th Day of *June*, 1709, I arrived at *Nangasac*, after a very long and troublesome Journey. I soon fell into the Company of some *Dutch* Sailors belonging to the *Amboyna** of *Amsterdam*, a stout Ship of 450 Tuns. I had lived long in *Holland*, pursuing my Studies at *Leyden*, and I spoke *Dutch* well: The Seamen soon knew from whence I came last; they were curious to enquire into my Voyages and Course of Life. I made up a Story as short and probable as I could, but concealed the greatest Part. I knew many Persons in *Holland*; I was able to invent Names for my Parents, whom I pretended to be obscure People in the Province of *Guelderland*. I would have given the Captain (one *Theodorus Vangrult**) what he pleased to ask for my Voyage to *Holland*; but, understanding I was a Surgeon, he was contented to take half the usual Rate, on Condition that I would serve him in the Way of my Calling. Before we took Shipping, I was often asked by some of the Crew, whether I had performed the Ceremony above-mentioned? I evaded the Question by general Answers, that I had satisfied the Emperor and Court in all Particulars. However, a malicious Rogue of a Skipper* went to an Officer, and pointing to me, told him, I had not yet *trampled on the Crucifix*: But the other, who had received Instructions to let me pass, gave the Rascal twenty Strokes on the Shoulders with a Bamboo; after which I was no more troubled with such Questions.

Nothing happened worth mentioning in this Voyage. We sailed with a fair Wind to the *Cape of Good Hope*, where we stayed only to take in fresh Water. On the 6th of *April* we arrived safe at *Amsterdam*, having lost only three Men by Sickness in the Voyage, and a fourth who fell from the Fore-mast into the Sea, not far from the Coast of *Guinea*. From *Amsterdam* I soon after set sail for *England* in a small Vessel belonging to that City.

On the 10th of *April*, 1710, we put in at the *Downs*. I landed the next Morning, and saw once more my Native Country after an Absence of five Years and six Months compleat. I went straight to *Redriff*, where I arrived the same Day at two in the Afternoon, and found my Wife and Family in good Health.

The End of the Third Part.

PART FOUR

*A Voyage to the Country of The Houyhnhnms**

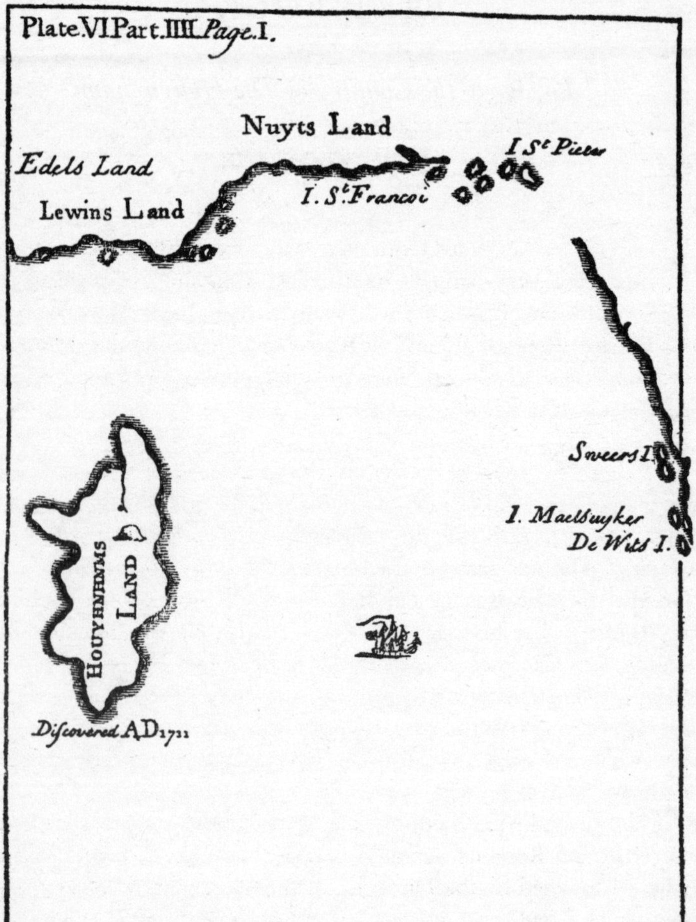

Plate.VI.Part.IIII.*Page*.I.

Nuyts Land

Edels Land

Lewins Land

I. St Francoi

I St Pieter

Sweers I.

I. Maetsuyker

De Wits I.

HOUYHNHNMS LAND

Discovered A.D. 1711

CHAPTER ONE

The Author sets out as Captain of a Ship. His Men conspire* against him, confine him a long Time to his Cabbin, set him on Shore in an unknown Land. He travels up into the Country. The Yahoos,* *a strange Sort of Animal, described. The Author meets two* Houyhnhnms.

I CONTINUED at home with my Wife and Children about five Months in a very happy Condition, if I could have learned the Lesson of knowing when I was well. I left my poor Wife big with Child, and accepted an advantageous Offer made me to be Captain of the *Adventure,** a stout Merchant-man of 350 Tuns: for I understood Navigation well, and being grown weary of a Surgeon's Employment at Sea, which however I could exercise upon Occasion, I took a skilful young Man of that Calling, one *Robert Purefoy*, into my Ship. We set sail from *Portsmouth* upon the 7th Day of *September*, 1710; on the 14th we met with Captain *Pocock** of *Bristol*, at *Tenariff*, who was going to the Bay of *Campeachy*, to cut Logwood.* On the 16th he was parted from us by a Storm: I heard since my Return, that his Ship foundered, and none escaped, but one Cabbin-Boy. He was an honest Man, and a good Sailor, but a little too positive in his own Opinions,* which was the Cause of his Destruction, as it hath been of several others. For if he had followed my Advice, he might at this Time have been safe at home with his Family as well as my self.

I had several Men died in my Ship of Calentures,* so that I was forced to get Recruits out of *Barbadoes,** and the *Leeward Islands*, where I touched by the Direction of the Merchants who employed me; which I had soon too much Cause to repent; for I found afterwards that most of them had been Buccaneers. I had fifty Hands on Board; and my Orders were, that I should trade with the *Indians* in the *South-Sea*, and make what Discoveries I could. These Rogues whom I had picked up, debauched my other Men, and they all formed a Conspiracy to seize the Ship and secure me; which they did one Morning, rushing into my Cabbin, and binding me Hand and Foot, threatening to throw me overboard, if I offered to stir. I told them, I was their Prisoner, and would submit. This they made me swear to do, and then unbound me, only fastening one of my Legs with a Chain near my Bed; and placed a Centry at my Door with his Piece* charged, who was commanded to shoot me dead if I attempted my Liberty. They sent me down Victuals and Drink, and took the Government of the Ship to themselves. Their Design was to turn Pirates, and plunder the *Spaniards*, which they could not do, till they got more Men. But first they resolved to sell the Goods in the Ship, and then go to *Madagascar** for Recruits, several among them having died since my Confinement. They sailed many Weeks, and traded with the *Indians*; but I knew not what Course they took, being kept close Prisoner in my Cabbin, and expecting nothing less than to be murdered, as they often threatened me.

Upon the 9th Day of *May*, 1711, one *James Welch* came down to my Cabbin; and said he had Orders from the Captain to set me ashore. I expostulated with him, but in vain; neither would he so much as tell me who their new Captain was. They forced me into the Long-boat, letting me put on my best Suit of Cloaths, which were as good as new, and a small Bundle of Linnen, but no Arms except my Hanger; and they were so civil as not to search my Pockets, into which I conveyed what Money I had, with some other little Necessaries. They rowed about a League; and then set me down on a Strand. I desired them to tell me what Country it was: They all swore, they knew no more than my self, but said, that the Captain (as they called him) was resolved, after they had sold the Lading, to get rid of me in the first Place where they discovered Land. They pushed off immediately, advising me to make haste, for fear of being overtaken by the Tide; and so bade me farewell.

In this desolate Condition I advanced forward, and soon got upon firm Ground, where I sat down on a Bank to rest my self, and consider what I had best to do. When I was a little refreshed, I went up into the Country, resolving to deliver my self to the first Savages I should meet; and purchase my Life from them by some Bracelets, Glass Rings, and other Toys,* which Sailors usually provide themselves with in those Voyages, and whereof I had some about me: The Land was divided by long Rows of Trees, not regularly planted, but naturally growing; there was great Plenty of Grass, and several Fields of Oats. I walked very circumspectly for fear of being surprised, or suddenly shot with an Arrow from behind, or on either Side. I fell into a beaten Road, where I saw many Tracks of human

Feet, and some of Cows, but most of Horses. At last I beheld several
Animals in a Field,* and one or two of the same Kind sitting in Trees.
Their Shape was very singular, and deformed, which a little
discomposed me, so that I lay down behind a Thicket to observe
them better. Some of them coming forward near the Place where I
lay, gave me an Opportunity of distinctly marking their Form. Their
Heads and Breasts were covered with a thick Hair, some frizzled and
others lank; they had Beards like Goats, and a Long Ridge of Hair
down their Backs, and the fore Parts of their Legs and Feet; but the
rest of their Bodies were bare, so that I might see their Skins, which
were of a brown Buff Colour. They had no Tails, nor any Hair at all
on their Buttocks, except about the *Anus*; which, I presume Nature
had placed there to defend them as they sat on the Ground; for this
Posture they used, as well as lying down, and often stood on their
hind Feet. They climbed high Trees, as nimbly as a Squirrel, for
they had strong extended Claws before and behind, terminating in
sharp Points, and hooked. They would often spring, and bound, and
leap with prodigious Agility. The Females were not so large as the
Males; they had long lank Hair on their Heads, and only a Sort of
Down on the rest of their Bodies, except about the *Anus*, and
Pudenda. Their Dugs hung between their fore Feet, and often
reached almost to the Ground as they walked.* The Hair of both
Sexes was of several Colours, brown, red, black and yellow. Upon the
whole, I never beheld in all my Travels so disagreeable an Animal, or
one against which I naturally conceived so strong an Antipathy. So
that thinking I had seen enough, full of Contempt and Aversion, I
got up and pursued the beaten Road, hoping it might direct me to
the Cabbin of some *Indian*. I had not gone far when I met one of
these Creatures full in my Way, and coming up directly to me. The
ugly Monster, when he saw me, distorted several Ways every Feature
of his Visage, and stared as at an Object he had never seen before;
then approaching nearer, lifted up his fore Paw, whether out of
Curiosity or Mischief, I could not tell: But I drew my Hanger, and
gave him a good Blow with the flat Side of it; for I durst not strike
him with the Edge, fearing the Inhabitants might be provoked
against me, if they should come to know, that I had killed or maimed
any of their Cattle.* When the Beast felt the Smart, he drew back, and
roared so loud, that a Herd of at least forty came flocking about me
from the next Field, howling and making odious Faces; but I ran to

the Body of a Tree, and leaning my Back against it, kept them off, by waving my Hanger. Several of this cursed Brood getting hold of the Branches behind, leaped up into the Tree, from whence they began to discharge their Excrements on my Head:* However, I escaped pretty well, by sticking close to the Stem of the Tree, but was almost stifled with the Filth, which fell about me on every Side.

In the Midst of this Distress, I observed them all to run away on a sudden as fast as they could; at which I ventured to leave the Tree, and pursue the Road, wondering what it was that could put them into this Fright. But looking on my Left-Hand, I saw a Horse walking softly in the Field; which my Persecutors having sooner discovered, was the Cause of their Flight. The Horse started a little when he came near me, but soon recovering himself, looked full in my Face with manifest Tokens of Wonder: He viewed my Hands and Feet, walking round me several times. I would have pursued my Journey, but he placed himself directly in the Way, yet looking with a very mild Aspect, never offering the least Violence. We stood gazing at each other for some time; at last I took the Boldness to reach my Hand towards his Neck, with a Design to stroak it; using the common Style and Whistle of Jockies when they are going to handle a strange Horse. But, this Animal seeming to receive my Civilities with Disdain, shook his Head, and bent his Brows, softly raising up his Left Fore-Foot to remove my Hand. Then he neighed three or four times, but in so different a Cadence, that I almost began to think he was speaking to himself in some Language of his own.

While He and I were thus employed, another Horse came up; who applying himself to the first in a very formal Manner, they gently struck each others Right Hoof before, neighing several times by Turns, and varying the Sound, which seemed to be almost articulate. They went some Paces off, as if it were to confer together, walking Side by Side, backward and forward, like Persons deliberating upon some Affair of Weight; but often turning their Eyes towards me, as it were to watch that I might not escape. I was amazed to see such Actions and Behavior in Brute Beasts; and concluded with myself, that if the Inhabitants of this Country were endued with a pro-portionable Degree of Reason, they must needs be the wisest People upon Earth. This Thought gave me so much Comfort, that I resolved to go forward until I could discover some House or Village, or meet with any of the Natives; leaving the two Horses to discourse together as they pleased. But the first, who was a Dapple-Grey, observing me to steal off, neighed after me in so expressive a Tone, that I fancied myself to understand what he meant; whereupon I turned back, and came near him, to expect his farther Commands; but concealing my Fear as much as I could; for I began to be in some Pain, how this Adventure might terminate: and the Reader will easily believe I did not much like my present Situation.

The two Horses came up close to me, looking with great Earnestness upon my Face and Hands. The grey Steed rubbed my Hat all round with his Right Fore-hoof, and discomposed it so much, that I was forced to adjust it better, by taking it off, and settling it again; whereat both he and his Companion (who was a brown Bay) appeared to be much surprized; the latter felt the Lappet of my Coat, and finding it to hang loose about me, they both looked with new Signs of Wonder. He stroked my Right Hand, seeming to admire the Softness, and Colour; but he squeezed it so hard between his Hoof and his Pastern, that I was forced to roar; after which they both touched me with all possible Tenderness. They were under great Perplexity about my Shoes and Stockings, which they felt very often, neighing to each other, and using various Gestures, not unlike those of a Philosopher, when he would attempt to solve some new and difficult Phænomenon.

Upon the whole, the Behaviour of these Animals was so orderly and rational, so acute and judicious, that I at last concluded, they must needs be Magicians, who had thus metamorphosed* themselves upon some Design; and seeing a Stranger in the Way, were resolved to divert themselves with him; or perhaps were really amazed at the Sight of a Man so very different in Habit, Feature and Complexion from those who might probably live in so remote a Climate. Upon the Strength of this Reasoning, I ventured to address them in the following Manner: Gentlemen, if you be Conjurers, as I have good Cause to believe, you can understand any Language; therefore I make bold to let your Worships know, that I am a poor distressed *Englishman*, driven by his Misfortunes upon your Coast; and I entreat one of you, to let me ride upon his Back, as if he were a real Horse, to some House or Village, where I can be relieved. In return of which Favour, I will make you a Present of this Knife and Bracelet, (taking them out of my Pocket.) The two Creatures stood silent while I spoke, seeming to listen with great Attention; and when I had ended, they neighed frequently towards each other, as if they were engaged in serious Conversation. I plainly observed, that their Language expressed the Passions* very well, and the Words might with little Pains be resolved into an Alphabet more easily than the *Chinese*.*

I could frequently distinguish the Word *Yahoo*, which was repeated by each of them several times; and although it were impossible for me to conjecture what it meant, yet while the two Horses were busy in Conversation, I endeavoured to practice this Word upon my Tongue; and as soon as they were silent, I boldly pronounced *Yahoo* in a loud Voice, imitating, at the same time, as near as I could, the Neighing of a Horse; at which they were both visibly surprized,* and the Grey repeated the same Word twice, as if he meant to teach me the right Accent, wherein I spoke after him as well as I could, and found myself perceivably to improve every time, although very far from any Degree of Perfection. Then the Bay tried me with a second Word, much harder to be pronounced; but reducing it to the *English Orthography*, may be spelt thus, *Houyhnhnm*. I did not succeed in this so well as the former, but after two or three farther Trials, I had better Fortune; and they both appeared amazed at my Capacity.

After some farther Discourse, which I then conjectured might relate to me, the two Friends took their Leaves, with the same Compliment of striking each other's Hoof; and the Grey made me Signs that I should walk before him; wherein I thought it prudent to comply, till I could find a better Director. When I offered to slacken my Pace, he would cry *Hhuun, Hhuun*; I guessed his Meaning, and gave him to understand, as well as I could, that I was weary, and not able to walk faster; upon which, he would stand a while to let me rest.

CHAPTER TWO

The Author conducted by a Houyhnhnm *to his House. The House described.
The Author's Reception. The Food of the* Houyhnhnms. *The Author in
Distress for want of Meat, is at last relieved. His Manner of feeding in that
Country.*

HAVING travelled about three Miles, we came to a long Kind of
Building, made of Timber, stuck in the Ground, and wattled a-cross;
the Roof was low, and covered with Straw. I now began to be a little
comforted; and took out some Toys, which Travellers usually carry
for Presents to the Savage *Indians* of *America* and other Parts, in
hopes the People of the House would be thereby encouraged to
receive me kindly. The Horse made me a Sign to go in first; it was a
large Room with a smooth Clay Floor, and a Rack and Manger
extending the whole Length on one Side. There were three Nags,
and two Mares, not eating, but some of them sitting down upon their
Hams, which I very much wondered at; but wondered more to see
the rest employed in domestick Business: The last seemed but
ordinary Cattle; however this confirmed my first Opinion, that a
People who could so far civilize brute Animals, must needs excel in
Wisdom all the Nations of the World. The Grey came in just after,
and thereby prevented any ill Treatment, which the others might
have given me. He neighed to them several times in a Style of
Authority, and received Answers.

Beyond this Room there were three others, reaching the Length of
the House, to which you passed through three Doors, opposite to
each other, in the Manner of a Vista: We went through the second
Room towards the third; here the Grey walked in first, beckoning me
to attend: I waited in the second Room, and got ready my Presents,
for the Master and Mistress of the House: They were two Knives,
three Bracelets of false Pearl, a small Looking Glass and a Bead
Necklace. The Horse neighed three or four Times, and I waited to
hear some Answers in a human Voice, but I heard no other Returns
than in the same Dialect, only one or two a little shriller than his. I
began to think that this House must belong to some Person of great
Note among them, because there appeared so much ceremony before

I could gain Admittance. But, that a Man of Quality should be served all by Horses, was beyond my Comprehension. I feared my Brain was disturbed by my Sufferings and Misfortunes: I roused my self, and looked about me in the Room where I was left alone; this was furnished as the first, only after a more elegant Manner. I rubbed mine Eyes often, but the same Objects still occurred. I pinched my Arms and Sides, to awake my self, hoping I might be in a Dream. I then absolutely concluded, that all these Appearances could be nothing else but Necromancy and Magick. But I had no Time to pursue these Reflections; for the Grey Horse came to the Door, and made me a Sign to follow him into the third Room; where I saw a very comely Mare, together with a Colt and Fole, sitting on their Haunches, upon Mats of Straw, not unartfully made, and perfectly neat and clean.

The Mare soon after my Entrance, rose from her Mat, and coming up close, after having nicely observed my Hands and Face, gave me a most contemptuous Look; then turning to the Horse, I heard the Word *Yahoo* often repeated betwixt them; the meaning of which Word I could not then comprehend, although it were the first I had learned to pronounce; but I was soon better informed, to my ever-lasting Mortification: For the Horse beckoning to me with his Head, and repeating the Word *Hhuun, Hhuun*, as he did upon the Road, which I understood was to attend him, led me out into a kind of Court, where was another Building at some Distance from the House. Here we entered, and I saw three of those detestable Crea-tures, which I first met after my landing, feeding upon Roots, and the Flesh of some Animals, which I afterwards found to be that of Asses and Dogs, and now and then a Cow dead by Accident or Disease.* They were all tied by the Neck with strong Wyths,* fastened to a Beam; they held their Food between the Claws of their fore Feet, and tore it with their Teeth.

The Master Horse ordered a Sorrel Nag, one of his Servants, to untie the largest of these Animals, and take him into the Yard. The Beast and I were brought close together; and our Countenances diligently compared, both by Master and Servant, who thereupon repeated several Times the Word *Yahoo.* My Horror and Astonish-ment are not to be described, when I observed, in this abominable Animal, a perfect human Figure; the Face of it indeed was flat and broad, the Nose depressed, the Lips large, and the Mouth wide: But these Differences are common to all savage Nations, where the Lineaments of the Countenance are distorted by the Natives suffering their Infants to lie grovelling on the Earth, or by carrying them on their Backs, nuzzling with their Face against the Mother's Shoulders. The Fore-feet of the *Yahoo* differed from my Hands in nothing else, but the Length of the Nails, the Coarseness and Brownness of the Palms, and the Hairiness on the Backs. There was the same Resemblance between our Feet, with the same Differences, which I knew very well, although the Horses did not, because of my Shoes and Stockings; the same in every Part of our Bodies, except as to Hairiness and Colour, which I have already described.

The great Difficulty that seemed to stick with the two Horses, was, to see the rest of my Body so very different from that of a *Yahoo*, for which I was obliged to my Cloaths, whereof they had no Conception:* The Sorrel Nag offered me a Root, which he held (after their Manner, as we shall describe in its proper Place) between his Hoof and Pastern; I took it in my Hand, and having smelt it, returned it to him again as civilly as I could. He brought out of the *Yahoo*'s Kennel a Piece of Ass's Flesh, but it smelt so offensively that I turned from it with loathing; he then threw it to the *Yahoo*, by whom it was greedily devoured. He afterwards shewed me a Wisp of Hay, and a Fettlock full of Oats; but I shook my Head, to signify, that neither of these were Food for me. And indeed, I now apprehended, that I must absolutely starve, if I did not get to some of my own Species: For as to those filthy *Yahoos*, although there were few greater Lovers of Mankind, at that time, than myself; yet I confess I never saw any sensitive Being so detestable on all Accounts; and the more I came near them, the more hateful they grew, while I stayed in that Country. This the Master Horse observed by my Behaviour, and therefore sent the *Yahoo* back to his Kennel. He then put his Fore-hoof to his Mouth, at which I was much surprized, although he did it with Ease, and with a Motion that appear'd perfectly natural; and made other Signs to know what I would eat; but I could not return him such an Answer as he was able to apprehend; and if he had understood me I did not see how it was possible to contrive any way for finding myself Nourishment. While we were thus engaged, I observed a Cow passing by; whereupon I pointed to her, and expressed a Desire to let me go and milk her. This had its Effect; for he led me back into the House, and ordered a Mare-servant to open a

Room, where a good Store of Milk lay in Earthen and Wooden Vessels, after a very orderly and cleanly Manner. She gave me a large Bowl full, of which I drank very heartily, and found myself well refreshed.

About Noon I saw coming towards the House a Kind of Vehicle, drawn like a Sledge* by four *Yahoos*. There was in it an old Steed,* who seemed to be of Quality; he alighted with his Hind-feet forward, having by Accident got a Hurt in his Left Fore-foot. He came to dine with our Horse, who received him with great Civility. They dined in the best Room, and had Oats boiled in Milk for the second Course, which the old Horse eat warm, but the rest cold. Their Mangers were placed circular in the Middle of the Room, and divided into several Partitions, round which they sat on their Haunches upon Bosses of Straw. In the Middle was a large Rack with Angles answering to every Partition of the Manger. So that each Horse and Mare eat their own Hay, and their own Mash of Oats and Milk, with much Decency and Regularity. The Behaviour of the young Colt and Foal appeared very modest; and that of the Master and Mistress extremely chearful and complaisant* to their Guest. The Grey ordered me to stand by him; and much Discourse passed between him and his Friend concerning me, as I found by the Stranger's often looking on me, and the frequent Repetition of the Word *Yahoo*.

I happened to wear my Gloves; which the Master Grey observing, seemed perplexed; discovering Signs of Wonder what I had done to my Fore-feet; he put his Hoof three or four times to them, as if he would signify, that I should reduce them to their former Shape, which I presently did, pulling off both my Gloves, and putting them into my Pocket. This occasioned farther Talk, and I saw the Company was pleased with my Behaviour, whereof I soon found the good Effects. I was ordered to speak the few Words I understood; and while they were at Dinner, the Master taught me the Names for Oats, Milk, Fire, Water, and some others; which I could readily pronounce after him; having from my Youth a great Facility in learning Languages.

When Dinner was done, the Master Horse took me aside, and by Signs and Words made me understand the Concern he was in, that I had nothing to eat. Oats in their Tongue are called *Hlunnh*. This Word I pronounced two or three times; for although I had refused them at first, yet upon second Thoughts, I considered that I could contrive to make of them a Kind of Bread, which might be sufficient with Milk to keep me alive, till I could make my Escape to some other Country, and to Creatures of my own Species. The Horse immediately ordered a white Mare-servant of his Family to bring me a good Quantity of Oats in a Sort of wooden Tray. These I heated before the Fire as well as I could, and rubbed them till the Husks came off, which I made a shift to winnow from the Grain; I ground and beat them between two Stones, then took Water, and made them into a Paste or Cake, which I toasted at the Fire, and eat warm with Milk. It was at first a very insipid Diet, although common enough in many Parts of *Europe*, but grew tolerable by Time; and having been often reduced to hard Fare in my Life, this was not the first Experiment I had made how easily Nature is satisfied.* And I cannot but observe, that I never had one Hour's Sickness, while I staid in this Island. It is true, I sometimes made a shift to catch a Rabbet, or Bird, by Springes made of *Yahoos* Hairs; and I often gathered wholesome Herbs, which I boiled, or eat as Salades with my Bread; and now and then, for a Rarity, I made a little Butter, and drank the Whey. I was at first at a great Loss for Salt; but Custom soon reconciled the Want of it; and I am confident that the frequent Use of Salt among us is an Effect of Luxury, and was first introduced only as a Provocative to Drink; except where it is necessary for preserving of Flesh in long Voyages, or in Places remote from great Markets. For we observe no Animal to be fond of it but Man:* And as to myself, when I left this Country, it was a great while before I could endure the Taste of it in any thing that I eat.

This is enough to say upon the Subject of my Dyet, wherewith other Travellers fill their Books, as if the Readers were personally concerned, whether we fare* well or ill. However, it was necessary to mention this Matter, lest the World should think it impossible that I could find Sustenance for three Years in such a Country, and among such Inhabitants.

When it grew towards Evening, the Master Horse ordered a Place for me to lodge in; it was but Six Yards from the House, and separated from the Stable of the *Yahoos*. Here I got some Straw, and covering myself with my own Cloaths, slept very sound. But I was in a short time better accommodated, as the Reader shall know hereafter, when I come to treat more particularly about my Way of living.

CHAPTER THREE

The Author studious to learn Language, the Houyhnhnm *his Master assists in teaching him. The Language described. Several* Houyhnhnms *of Quality come out of Curiosity to see the Author. He gives his Master a short Account of his Voyage.*

MY principal Endeavour was to learn the Language, which my Master* (for so I shall henceforth call him) and his Children, and every Servant of his House were desirous to teach me. For they looked upon it as a Prodigy, that a brute Animal should discover such Marks of a rational Creature. I pointed to every thing, and enquired the Name of it, which I wrote down in my *Journal Book* when I was alone, and corrected my bad Accent, by desiring those of the Family to pronounce it often. In this Employment, a Sorrel Nag, one of the under Servants, was very ready to assist me.

In speaking, they pronounce through the Nose and Throat, and their Language approaches nearest to the *High Dutch* or *German*, of any I know in *Europe*; but is much more graceful and significant. The Emperor *Charles* V. made almost the same Observation* when he said, That if he were to speak to his Horse, it should be in *High Dutch*.

The Curiosity and Impatience of my Master were so great, that he spent many Hours of his Leisure to instruct me. He was convinced (as he afterwards told me) that I must be a *Yahoo*, but my Teachableness, Civility and Cleanliness astonished him; which were Qualities altogether so opposite to those Animals. He was most perplexed about my Cloaths, reasoning sometimes with himself, whether they were a Part of my Body; for I never pulled them off till the Family were asleep, and got them on before they waked in the Morning. My Master was eager to learn from whence I came; how I acquired those Appearances of Reason, which I discovered in all my Actions; and to know my Story from my own Mouth, which he hoped he should soon do by the great Proficiency I made in learning and pronouncing their Words and Sentences. To help my Memory, I formed all I learned into the *English* Alphabet, and writ the Words down with the Translations. This last, after some time, I ventured to do in my

Master's Presence. It cost me much Trouble to explain to him what I was doing; for the Inhabitants have not the least Idea of Books or Literature.*

In about ten Weeks time I was able to understand most of his Questions; and in three Months could give him some tolerable Answers. He was extremely curious to know from what Part of the Country I came, and how I was taught to imitate a rational Creature; because the *Yahoos*, (whom he saw I exactly resembled in my Head, Hands and Face, that were only visible,) with some Appearance of Cunning, and the strongest Disposition to Mischief, were observed to be the most unteachable of all Brutes. I answered; that I came over the Sea, from a far Place, with many others of my own Kind, in a great hollow Vessel made of the Bodies of Trees: That, my Companions forced me to land on this Coast, and then left me to shift for myself. It was with some Difficulty, and by the Help of many Signs, that I brought him to understand me. He replied, that I must needs be mistaken, or that I *said the thing which was not*. (For they have no Word in their Language to express Lying or Falshood.) He knew it was impossible* that there could be a Country beyond the Sea, or that a Parcel of Brutes could move a wooden Vessel whither they pleased upon Water. He was sure no *Houyhnhnm* alive could make such a Vessel, or would trust *Yahoos* to manage it.

The Word *Houyhnhnm*, in their Tongue, signifies a *Horse*; and in its Etymology, *the Perfection of Nature*.* I told my Master, that I was at a Loss for Expression, but would improve as fast as I could; and hoped in a short time I would be able to tell him Wonders: He was pleased to direct his own Mare, his Colt and Fole, and the Servants of the Family, to take all Opportunities of instructing me; and every Day for two or three Hours, he was at the same Pains himself: Several Horses and Mares of Quality in the Neighbourhood came often to our House, upon the Report spread of a wonderful *Yahoo*, that could speak like a *Houyhnhnm*, and seemed in his Words and Actions to discover some Glimmerings of Reason. These delighted to converse with me; they put many Questions, and received such Answers, as I was able to return. By all which Advantages, I made so great a Progress, that in five Months from my Arrival, I understood whatever was spoke, and could express myself tolerably well.

The *Houyhnhnms* who came to visit my Master, out of a Design of seeing and talking with me, could hardly believe me to be a right*

Yahoo, because my Body had a different Covering from others of my Kind. They were astonished to observe me without the usual Hair or Skin, except on my Head, Face and Hands: but I discovered that Secret to my Master, upon an Accident, which happened about a Fortnight before.

I have already told the Reader, that every Night when the Family were gone to Bed, it was my Custom to strip and cover myself with my Cloaths: It happened one Morning early, that my Master sent for me, by the Sorrel Nag, who was his Valet; when he came, I was fast asleep, my Cloaths fallen off on one Side, and my Shirt above my Waste. I awaked at the Noise he made, and observed him to deliver his Message in some Disorder; after which he went to my Master, and in a great Fright gave him a very confused Account of what he had seen: This I presently discovered; for going as soon as I was dressed, to pay my Attendance upon his Honour, he asked me the Meaning of what his Servant had reported; that I was not the same Thing when I slept as I appeared to be at other times; that his Valet assured him, some Part of me was white, some yellow, at least not so white, and some brown.

I had hitherto concealed the Secret of my Dress, in order to distinguish myself as much as possible, from that cursed Race of *Yahoos*; but now I found it in vain to do so any longer. Besides, I considered that my Cloaths and Shoes would soon wear out, which already were in a declining Condition, and must be supplied by some Contrivance from the Hides of *Yahoos**, or other Brutes; whereby the whole Secret would be known. I therefore told my Master, that in the Country from whence I came, those of my Kind always covered their Bodies with the Hairs of certain Animals prepared by Art, as well for Decency, as to avoid Inclemencies of Air both hot and cold; of which, as to my own Person I would give him immediate Conviction, if he pleased to command me; only desiring his Excuse, if I did not expose those Parts that Nature taught us to conceal. He said, my Discourse was all very strange, but especially the last Part; for he could not understand why Nature should teach us to conceal what Nature had given.* That neither himself nor Family were ashamed of any Parts of their Bodies; but however I might do as I pleased. Whereupon I first unbuttoned my Coat, and pulled it off. I did the same with my Wastecoat; I drew off my Shoes, Stockings and Breeches. I let my Shirt down to my Waste, and drew up the Bottom, fastening it like a Girdle about my Middle to hide my Nakedness.

My Master observed the whole Performance with great Signs of Curiosity and Admiration. He took up all my Cloaths in his Pastern, one Piece after another, and examined them diligently; he then stroked my Body very gently, and looked round me several Times; after which he said, it was plain I must be a perfect *Yahoo*; but that I differed very much from the rest of my Species, in the Whiteness, and Smoothness of my Skin, my want of Hair in several Parts of my Body, the Shape and Shortness of my Claws behind and before, and my Affectation of walking continually on my two hinder Feet. He desired to see no more; and gave me leave to put on my Cloaths again, for I was shuddering with Cold.

I expressed my Uneasiness at his giving me so often the Appellation of *Yahoo*, an odious Animal, for which I had so utter an Hatred and Contempt. I begged he would forbear applying that Word to me, and take the same Order in his Family, and among his Friends whom he suffered to see me. I requested likewise, that the Secret of my having a false Covering to my Body might be known to none but himself, at least as long as my present Cloathing should last: For as to what the Sorrel Nag his Valet had observed, his Honour might command him to conceal it.

All this my Master very graciously consented to;* and thus the Secret was kept till my Cloaths began to wear out, which I was forced to supply by several Contrivances, that shall hereafter be mentioned. In the mean Time, he desired I would go on with my utmost Diligence to learn their Language, because he was more astonished at my Capacity for Speech and Reason, than at the Figure of my Body, whether it were covered or no; adding, that he waited with some Impatience to hear the Wonders which I promised to tell him.

From thenceforward he doubled the Pains he had been at to instruct me; he brought me into all Company, and made them treat me with Civility, because, as he told them privately, this would put me into good Humour, and make me more diverting.

Every Day when I waited on him, beside the Trouble he was at in teaching, he would ask me several Questions concerning my self, which I answered as well as I could; and by those Means he had already received some general Ideas, although very imperfect. It would be tedious to relate the several Steps, by which I advanced to a more regular Conversation: But the first Account I gave of my self in any Order and Length, was to this Purpose:

That, I came from a very far Country, as I already had attempted to tell him, with about fifty more of my own Species; that we travelled upon the Seas, in a great hollow Vessel made of Wood, and larger than his Honour's House. I described the Ship to him in the best Terms I could; and explained by the Help of my Handkerchief displayed, how it was driven forward by the Wind. That, upon a Quarrel among us, I was set on Shoar on this Coast, where I walked forward without knowing whither, till he delivered me from the Persecution of those execrable *Yahoos*. He asked me, Who made the Ship, and how it was possible that the *Houyhnhnms* of my Country would leave it to the Management of Brutes? My Answer was, that I durst proceed no farther in my Relation, unless he would give me his Word and Honour that he would not be offended; and then I would tell him the Wonders I had so often promised. He agreed; and I went on by assuring him, that the Ship was made by Creatures like myself, who in all the Countries I had travelled, as well as in my own, were the only governing, rational Animals; and that upon my Arrival hither, I was as much astonished to see the *Houyhnhnms* act like rational Beings, as he or his friends could be in finding some Marks of Reason in a Creature he was pleased to call a *Yahoo*; to which I owned my Resemblance in every Part, but could not account for their degenerate and brutal Nature. I said farther, That if good Fortune ever restored me to my native Country, to relate my Travels hither, as I resolved to do; every Body would believe that I *said the Thing which was not*; that I invented the Story out of my own Head: And with all possible respect to Himself, his Family, and Friends, and under his Promise of not being offended, our Countrymen would hardly think it probable, that a *Houyhnhnm* should be the presiding Creature of a Nation, and a *Yahoo* the brute.

CHAPTER FOUR

The Houyhnhnms *Notion of Truth and Falshood. The Author's Discourse disapproved by his Master. The Author gives a more particular Account of himself, and the Accidents of his Voyage.*

MY Master heard me with great Appearances of Uneasiness in his Countenance; because *Doubting* or *not believing*, are so little known in this Country, that the Inhabitants cannot tell how to behave themselves under such Circumstances. And I remember in frequent Discourses with my Master concerning the Nature of Manhood,* in other Parts of the World; having Occasion to talk of *Lying*, and *false Representation*, it was with much Difficulty that he comprehended what I meant; although he had otherwise a most acute Judgment. For he argued thus; That the Use of Speech was to make us understand one another, and to receive Information of Facts; now if any one *said the Thing which was not*, these Ends were defeated; because I cannot properly be said to understand him; and I am so far from receiving Information, that he leaves me worse than in Ignorance; for I am led to believe a Thing *Black* when it is *White*, and *Short* when it is *Long*. And these were all the Notions he had concerning that Faculty of *Lying*, so perfectly well understood, and so universally practised among human Creatures.

To return from this Digression; when I asserted that the *Yahoos* were the only governing Animals in my Country, which my Master said was altogether past his Conception, he desired to know, whether we had *Houyhnhnms* among us, and what was their Employment: I told him, we had great Numbers; that in Summer they grazed in the Fields, and in Winter were kept in Houses, with Hay and Oats, where *Yahoo*-Servants were employed to rub their Skins smooth, comb their Manes, pick their Feet, serve them with Food, and make their Beds. I understand you well, said my Master; it is now very plain from all you have spoken, that whatever Share of Reason the *Yahoos* pretend to, the *Houyhnhnms* are your Masters; I heartily wish our *Yahoos* would be so tractable. I begged his Honour would please to excuse me from proceeding any farther, because I was very certain that the Account he expected from me would be highly displeasing.

But he insisted in commanding me to let him know the best and the worst: I told him he should be obeyed. I owned, that the *Houyhnhnms* among us, whom we called *Horses*, were the most generous and comely Animal we had; that they excelled in Strength and Swiftness; and when they belonged to Persons of Quality, employed in Travelling, Racing, and drawing Chariots, they were treated with much Kindness and Care, till they fell into Diseases, or became foundered in the Feet; but then they were sold, and used to all kind of Drudgery till they died; after which their Skins were stripped and sold for what they were worth, and their Bodies left to be devoured by Dogs and Birds of Prey.* But the common Race of Horses had not so good Fortune, being kept by Farmers and Carriers, and other mean People, who put them to great Labour, and feed them worse. I described as well as I could, our Way of Riding; the Shape and Use of a Bridle, a Saddle, a Spur, and a Whip; of Harness and Wheels. I added, that we fastened Plates of a certain hard Substance called *Iron* at the Bottom of their Feet, to preserve their Hoofs from being broken by the Stony Ways on which we often travelled.

My Master, after some Expressions of great Indignation, wondered how we dared to venture upon a *Houyhnhnm*'s Back; for he was sure, that the weakest Servant in his House would be able to shake off the strongest *Yahoo*; or by lying down, and rolling upon his Back, squeeze the Brute to Death. I answered, That our Horses were trained up from three or four Years old to the several Uses we intended them for; That if any of them proved intolerably vicious, they were employed for Carriages; that they were severely beaten while they were young for any mischievous Tricks: That the Males, designed for the common Use of Riding or Draught, were generally *castrated* about two Years after their Birth, to take down their Spirits, and make them more tame and gentle: That they were indeed sensible of Rewards and Punishments; but his Honour would please to consider, that they had not the least Tincture of Reason any more than the *Yahoos* in this Country.

It put me to the Pains of many Circumlocutions to give my Master a right Idea of what I spoke; for their Language doth not abound in Variety of Words, because their Wants and Passions are fewer* than among us. But it is impossible to express his noble Resentment at our savage Treatment of the *Houyhnhnm* Race;* particularly after I had explained the Manner and Use of *Castrating* Horses among us, to hinder them from propagating their Kind, and to render them more servile. He said, if it were possible there could be any Country where *Yahoos* alone were endued with Reason, they certainly must be the governing Animal, because Reason will in Time always prevail against Brutal Strength. But, considering the Frame of our Bodies, and especially of mine, he thought no Creature of equal Bulk was so ill-contrived, for employing that Reason in the common Offices of Life; whereupon he desired to know whether those among whom I lived, resembled me or the *Yahoos* of his Country. I assured him, that I was as well shaped as most of my Age; but the younger and the Females were much more soft and tender, and the Skins of the latter generally as white as Milk. He said, I differed indeed from other *Yahoos*, being much more cleanly, and not altogether so deformed; but in point of real Advantage, he thought I differed for the worse. That my Nails were of no Use either to my fore or hinder Feet: As to my fore Feet, he could not properly call them by that Name, for he never observed me to walk upon them; that they were too soft to bear the Ground; that I generally went with them uncovered, neither was the Covering I sometimes wore on them, of the same Shape or so strong as that on my Feet behind. That I could not walk with any Security; for if either of my hinder Feet slipped, I must inevitably fall. He then began to find fault with other Parts of my Body; the Flatness of my Face, the Prominence of my Nose, mine Eyes placed directly in Front, so that I could not look on either Side without turning my Head: That I was not able to feed my self, without lifting one of my fore Feet to my Mouth: And therefore Nature had placed those Joints to answer that Necessity. He knew not what could be the Use of these several Clefts and Divisions in my Feet behind; that these were too soft to bear the Hardness and Sharpness of Stone without a Covering made from the Skin of some other Brute; that my whole Body wanted a Fence against Heat and Cold, which I was forced to put on and off every Day with Tediousness and Trouble. And lastly, that he observed every Animal in this Country naturally to abhor the *Yahoos*, whom the Weaker avoided, and the Stronger drove from them. So that supposing us to have the Gift of Reason, he could not see how it were possible to cure that natural Antipathy which every Creature discovered against us; nor consequently, how we could tame and render them serviceable. However, he would (as he said) debate the Matter no farther, because he was more desirous to know my own Story, the Country, where I was born, and the several Actions and Events of my Life before I came hither.

I assured him, how extreamly desirous I was that he should be satisfied on every Point; but I doubted much, whether it would be possible for me to explain my self on several Subjects whereof his Honour could have no Conception, because I saw nothing in his Country to which I could resemble them. That however, I would do my best, and strive to express my self by Similitudes, humbly desiring his Assistance when I wanted proper Words; which he was pleased to promise me.

I said, my Birth was of honest Parents, in an Island called *England*, which was remote from this Country, as many Days Journey as the strongest of his Honour's Servants could travel in the Annual Course of the Sun. That I was bred a Surgeon, whose Trade it is to cure Wounds and Hurts in the Body, got by Accident or Violence. That my Country was governed by a Female Man, whom we called a *Queen*. That I left it to get Riches, whereby I might maintain my self and Family when I should return. That in my last Voyage, I was Commander of the Ship and had about fifty *Yahoos* under me, many of which died at Sea, and I was forced to supply them by others picked out from several Nations. That our Ship was twice in Danger of being sunk; the first Time by a great Storm, and the second, by striking against a Rock. Here my Master interposed, by asking me, How I could persuade Strangers out of different Countries to venture with me, after the Losses I had sustained, and the Hazards I had run. I said, they were Fellows of desperate Fortunes, forced to fly from the Places of their Birth, on Account of their Poverty or their Crimes. Some were undone by Law-suits; others spent all they had in Drinking, Whoring and Gaming; others fled for Treason; many for Murder, Theft, Poysoning, Robbery, Perjury, Forgery, Coining false Money; for committing Rapes or Sodomy; for flying from their Colours,* or deserting to the Enemy; and most of them had broken Prison. None of these durst return to their native Countries for fear of being hanged, or of starving in a Jail; and therefore were under a Necessity of seeking a Livelihood in other Places.

During this Discourse, my Master was pleased often to interrupt me. I had made Use of many Circumlocutions in describing to him the Nature of the several Crimes, for which most of our Crew had been forced to fly their Country. This Labour took up several Days Conversation before he was able to comprehend me. He was wholly at a Loss to know what could be the Use or Necessity of practising those Vices. To clear up which I endeavored to give him some Ideas of the Desire of Power and Riches; of the terrible Effects of Lust, Intemperance, Malice, and Envy. All this I was forced to define and describe by putting of Cases, and making Suppositions. After which, like one whose Imagination was struck with something never seen or heard of before, he would lift up his Eyes with Amazement and Indignation. Power, Government, War, Law, Punishment, and a Thousand other Things had no Terms, wherein that Language could express them; which made the Difficulty almost insuperable to give my Master any Conception of what I meant: But being of an excellent Understanding, much improved by Contemplation and Converse, he at last arrived at a competent Knowledge of what human Nature in our Parts of the World is capable to perform; and desired I would give him some particular Account of that Land, which we call *Europe*, especially, of my own Country.

CHAPTER FIVE

The Author at his Master's Commands informs him of the State of England. The Causes of War among the Princes of Europe. The Author begins to explain the English Constitution.

THE Reader may please to observe, that the following Extract of many Conversations I had with my Master, contains a Summary of the most material Points, which were discoursed at several times for above two Years; his Honour often desiring fuller Satisfaction as I farther improved in the *Houyhnhnm* Tongue. I laid before him, as well as I could, the whole State of *Europe*; I discoursed of Trade and Manufactures, of Arts and Sciences; and the Answers I gave to all the Questions he made, as they arose upon several Subjects, were a Fund of Conversation not to be exhausted. But I shall here only set down the Substance of what passed between us concerning my own Country, reducing it into Order as well as I can, without any Regard to Time or other Circumstances, while I strictly adhere to Truth. My only Concern is, that I shall hardly be able to do Justice to my Master's Arguments and Expressions, which must needs suffer by my Want of Capacity, as well as by a Translation into our barbarous *English*.*

In Obedience therefore to his Honour's Commands, I related to him the *Revolution** under the Prince of *Orange*; the long War* with *France* entered into by the said Prince, and renewed by his Successor the present Queen; wherein the greatest Powers of *Christendom* were engaged, and which still continued: I computed at his Request, that about a Million of *Yahoos* might have been killed in the whole Progress of it; and perhaps a Hundred or more Cities taken, and five times as many Ships burnt or sunk.

He asked me what were the usual Causes or Motives that made one Country go to War with another. I answered, they were innumerable; but I should only mention a few of the chief. Sometimes the Ambition of Princes, who never think they have Land or People enough to govern:* Sometimes the Corruption of Ministers, who engage their Master in a War in order to stifle or divert the Clamour of the Subjects against their evil Administration. Difference in Opinions* hath cost many Millions of Lives: For Instance, whether *Flesh* be *Bread*, or *Bread* be *Flesh:** Whether the Juice of a certain *Berry* be *Blood* or *Wine*: Whether *Whistling* be a Vice or a Virtue:* Whether it be better to *kiss a Post*,* or throw it into the Fire: What is the best colour for a *Coat*,* whether *Black*, *White*, *Red*, or *Grey*; and whether it should be *long* or *short*, *narrow* or *wide*, *dirty* or *clean*; with many more. Neither are any Wars so furious and bloody, or of so long Continuance, as those occasioned by Difference in Opinion, especially if it be in things indifferent.*

Sometimes the Quarrel between two Princes is to decide which of them shall dispossess a Third of his Dominions, where neither of them pretend to any Right.* Sometimes one Prince quarrelleth with another, for fear the other should quarrel with him. Sometimes a War is entered upon, because the Enemy is too *strong*, and sometimes because he is too *weak*. Sometimes our Neighbours *want* the *Things* which we *have*, or *have* the Things which we want; and we both fight, till they take ours or give us theirs. It is a very justifiable Cause of War to invade a Country after the People have been wasted by Famine, destroyed by Pestilence, or embroiled by Factions amongst themselves. It is justifiable to enter into War against our nearest Ally, when one of his Towns lies convenient for us, or a Territory of Land, that would render our Dominions round and compact.* If a Prince send Forces into a Nation, where the People are poor and ignorant, he may lawfully put half of them to Death, and make Slaves of the rest, in order to civilize and reduce* them from their barbarous Way of Living. It is a very kingly, honourable, and frequent Practice, when one Prince desires the Assistance of another to secure him against an Invasion, that the Assistant, when he hath driven out the Invader, should seize on the Dominions himself, and kill, imprison or banish the Prince he came to relieve. Allyance by Blood or Marriage, is a sufficient Cause of War between Princes; and the nearer the Kindred is, the greater is their Disposition to quarrel: *Poor* Nations are *hungry*, and *rich* Nations are *proud*; and Pride and Hunger will ever be at Variance. For these Reasons, the Trade of a *Soldier* is held the most honourable of all others: Because a *Soldier* is a *Yahoo* hired to kill in cold Blood as many of his own Species, who have never offended him, as possibly he can.

There is likewise a Kind of beggarly Princes in *Europe*, not able to make War by themselves, who hire out their Troops to richer

Nations for so much a Day to each Man; of which they keep three
Fourths to themselves, and it is the best Part of their Maintenance;
such are those in many *Northern* Parts of *Europe.**

What you have told me, (said my Master) upon the Subject of
War, doth indeed discover most admirably the Effects of that Reason
you pretend to: However, it is happy that the *Shame* is greater than
the *Danger*; and that Nature hath left you utterly uncapable of doing
much Mischief: For your Mouths lying flat with your Faces, you can
hardly bite each other to any Purpose, unless by Consent. Then, as
to the Claws upon your Feet before and behind, they are so short and
tender, that one of our *Yahoos* would drive a Dozen of yours before
him. And therefore in recounting the Numbers of those who have
been killed in Battle, I cannot but think that you have *said the Thing
which is not.*

I could not forbear shaking my Head and smiling a little at his
Ignorance.* And, being no Stranger to the Art of War,* I gave him a
Description of Cannons, Culverins,* Muskets, Carabines,* Pistols,
Bullets, Powder, Swords, Bayonets, Sieges, Retreats, Attacks,
Undermines,* Countermines,* Bombardments, Sea-fights; Ships
sunk with a Thousand Men; twenty Thousand killed on each Side;
dying Groans, Limbs flying in the Air: Smoak, Noise, Confusion,
trampling to Death under Horses Feet: Flight, Pursuit, Victory;
Fields strewed with Carcases left for Food to Dogs, and Wolves, and
Birds of Prey; Plundering, Stripping, Ravishing, Burning and
Destroying. And, to set forth the Valour of my own dear Country-
men, I assured him, that I had seen them blow up a Hundred
Enemies at once in a Siege, and as many in a Ship; and beheld the
dead Bodies drop down in Pieces from the Clouds, to the great
Diversion of all the Spectators.

I was going on to more Particulars, when my Master commanded
me Silence. He said, whoever understood the Nature of *Yahoos*
might easily believe it possible for so vile an Animal, to be capable of
every Action I had named, if their Strength and Cunning equalled
their Malice. But, as my Discourse had increased his Abhorrence of
the whole Species, so he found it gave him a Disturbance in his
Mind, to which he was wholly a Stranger before. He thought his
Ears being used to such abominable Words, might by Degrees admit
them with less Detestation. That, although he hated the *Yahoos* of
this Country, yet he no more blamed them for their odious Qualities,

than he did a *Gnnayh* (a Bird of Prey) for its Cruelty, or a sharp Stone for cutting his Hoof.* But, when a Creature pretending to Reason, could be capable of such Enormities, he dreaded lest the Corruption of that Faculty might be worse than Brutality itself. He seemed therefore confident, that instead of Reason, we were only possessed of some Quality fitted to increase our natural Vices; as the Reflection from a troubled Stream returns the Image of an ill-shapen Body, not only *larger*, but more *distorted*.

He added, That he had heard too much upon the Subject of War, both in this, and some former Discourses. There was another Point which a little perplexed him at present. I had said, that some of our Crew left their Country on Account of being ruined by *Law*: That I had already explained the Meaning of the Word; but he was at a Loss how it should come to pass, that the *Law* which was intended for *every* Man's Preservation, should be any Man's Ruin. Therefore he desired to be farther satisfied what I meant by *Law*, and the Dispensers thereof, according to the present Practice in my own Country: Because he thought, Nature and Reason were sufficient Guides for a reasonable Animal,* as we pretended to be, in shewing us what we ought to do, and what to avoid.

I assured his Honour, that *Law* was a Science wherein I had not much conversed, further than by employing Advocates, in vain, upon some Injustices that had been done me. However, I would give him all the Satisfaction I was able.

I said there was a Society of Men among us,* bred up from their Youth in the Art of proving by Words multiplied for the Purpose, that *White* is *Black*, and *Black* is *White*, according as they are paid. To this Society all the rest of the People are Slaves.

For Example. If my Neighbour hath a mind to my *Cow*, he hires a Lawyer to prove that he ought to have my *Cow* from me. I must then hire another to defend my Right; it being against all Rules of *Law* that any Man should be allowed to speak for himself.* Now in this Case, I who am the true Owner lie under two great Disadvantages. First, my Lawyer being practiced almost from his Cradle in defending Falshood; is quite out of his Element when he would be an Advocate for Justice, which as an Office unnatural, he always attempts with great Awkwardness, if not with Ill-will. The second Disadvantage is, that my Lawyer must proceed with great Caution: Or else he will be reprimanded by the Judges, and abhorred by his

Brethren, as one who would lessen the Practice* of the Law. And therefore I have but two Methods to preserve my *Cow*. The first is, to gain over my Adversary's Lawyer with a double Fee; who will then betray his Client, by insinuating that he hath Justice on his Side. The second Way is for my Lawyer to make my Cause appear as unjust as he can; by allowing the *Cow* to belong to my Adversary; and this if it be skilfully done, will certainly bespeak the Favour of the Bench.

Now, your Honour is to know, that these Judges are Persons appointed to decide all Controversies of Property, as well as for the Tryal of Criminals; and picked out from the most dexterous Lawyers who are grown old or lazy: And having been byassed all their Lives against Truth and Equity, are under such a fatal Necessity of favouring Fraud, Perjury and Oppression; that I have known some of them to have refused a large Bribe from the Side where Justice lay, rather than injure the *Faculty*,* by doing any thing unbecoming their Nature or their Office.

It is a Maxim among these Lawyers, that whatever hath been done before, may legally be done again: And therefore they take special Care to record all the Decisions formerly made against common Justice and the general Reason of Mankind. These, under the Name of *Precedents*, they produce as Authorities to justify the most iniquitous Opinions; and the Judges never fail of decreeing accordingly.

In pleading, they studiously avoid entering into the *Merits* of the Cause; but are loud, violent and tedious in dwelling upon all *Circumstances* which are not to the Purpose. For Instance, in the Case already mentioned: They never desire to know what Claim or Title my Adversary hath to my *Cow*; but whether the said *Cow* were Red or Black; her Horns long or short; whether the Field I graze her in be round or square; whether she were milked at home or abroad; what Diseases she is subject to, and the like. After which they consult *Precedents*, adjourn the Cause, from Time to Time, and in Ten, Twenty, or Thirty Years come to an Issue.

It is likewise to be observed, that this Society hath a peculiar Cant and Jargon of their own, that no other Mortal can understand, and wherein all their Laws are written, which they take special Care to multiply; whereby they have wholly confounded the very Essence of Truth and Falshood, of Right and Wrong; so that it will take Thirty

Years to decide whether the Field, left me by my Ancestors for six Generations, belong to me, or to a Stranger three Hundred Miles off.

In the Tryal of Persons accused for Crimes against the State, the Method is much more short and commendable: The Judge first sends to sound the Disposition of those in Power,* after which he can easily hang or save the Criminal, strictly preserving all the Forms of Law.

Here my Master interposing, said it was a Pity, that Creatures endowed with such prodigious Abilities of Mind as these Lawyers, by the Description I gave of them must certainly be, were not rather encouraged to be Instructors of others in Wisdom and Knowledge. In Answer to which, I assured his Honour, that in all Points out of their own Trade, they were usually the most ignorant and stupid Generation among us, the most despicable in common Conversation, avowed Enemies to all Knowledge and Learning; and equally disposed to pervert the general Reason of Mankind, in every other Subject of Discourse, as in that of their own Profession.

CHAPTER SIX

A Continuation of the State of England, *under Queen* Anne.* *The Character of a first Minister in the Courts of* Europe.

MY Master was yet wholly at a Loss to understand what Motives could incite this Race of Lawyers to perplex, disquiet, and weary themselves by engaging in a Confederacy of Injustice, merely for the Sake of injuring their Fellow-Animals; neither could he comprehend what I meant in saying they did it for *Hire.* Whereupon I was at much Pains to describe to him the Use of *Money*, the Materials it was made of, and the Value of the Metals:* That when a *Yahoo* had got a great Store of this precious Substance, he was able to purchase whatever he had a mind to; the finest Cloathing, the noblest Houses, great Tracts of Land, the most costly Meats and Drinks; and have his Choice of the most beautiful Females. Therefore since *Money* alone, was able to perform all these Feats, our *Yahoos* thought, they could never have enough of it to spend or to save, as they found themselves inclined from their natural Bent either to Profusion or Avarice. That, the rich Man enjoyed the Fruit of the poor Man's Labour, and the latter were a Thousand to One in Proportion to the former. That the Bulk of our People was forced to live miserably, by labouring every Day for small Wages to make a few live plentifully.* I enlarged myself much on these and many other Particulars to the same Purpose: But his Honour was still to seek:* For he went upon a Supposition that all Animals had a Title to their Share in the Productions of the Earth; and especially those who presided over the rest. Therefore he desired I would let him know, what these costly Meats were, and how any of us happened to want them. Whereupon I enumerated as many Sorts as came into my Head, with the Various Methods of dressing them, which could not be done without sending Vessels by Sea to every Part of the World, as well for Liquors to drink, as for Sauces, and innumerable other Conveniences. I assured him, that this whole Globe of Earth must be at least three Times gone round,* before one of our better Female *Yahoos* could get her Breakfast, or a Cup to put it in. He said, That must needs be a miserable Country which cannot furnish Food for its own Inhabitants.

But what he chiefly wondered at, was how such vast Tracts of Ground as I described, should be wholly without *Fresh water*, and the People put to the Necessity of sending over the Sea for Drink. I replied, that *England* (the dear Place of my Nativity) was computed to produce three Times the Quantity of Food, more than its Inhabitants are able to consume, as well as Liquors extracted from Grain, or pressed out of the Fruit of certain Trees, which made excellent Drink; and the same Proportion in every other Convenience of Life. But, in order to feed the Luxury and Intemperance of the Males, and the Vanity of the Females, we sent away the greatest Part of our necessary Things to other Countries, from whence in Return we brought the Materials of Diseases, Folly, and Vice, to spend among ourselves. Hence it follows of Necessity, that vast Numbers of our People are compelled to seek their Livelihood by Begging, Robbing, Stealing, Cheating, Pimping, Forswearing, Flattering, Suborning, Forging, Gaming, Lying, Fawning, Hectoring, Voting, Scribbling, Stargazing, Poisoning, Whoring, Canting, Libelling, Free-thinking, and the like Occupations: Every one of which Terms, I was at much Pains to make him understand.

That, *Wine* was not imported among us from foreign Countries, to supply the Want of Water or other Drinks, but because it was a Sort of Liquid which made us merry, by putting us out of our Senses; diverted all melancholy Thoughts, begat wild extravagant Imaginations in the Brain, raised our Hopes, and banished our Fears; suspended every Office of Reason for a Time, and deprived us of the Use of our Limbs, untill we fell into a profound Sleep; although it must be confessed, that we always awaked sick and dispirited; and that the Use of this Liquor filled us with Diseases, which made our Lives uncomfortable and short.*

But beside all this, the Bulk of our People supported themselves by furnishing the Necessities or Conveniences of Life to the Rich, and to each other. For Instance, when I am at home and dressed as I ought to be, I carry on my Body the Workmanship of a Hundred Tradesmen,* the Building and Furniture of my House employ as many more; and five Times the Number to adorn my Wife.

I was going on to tell him of another Sort of People, who get their Livelihood by attending the Sick having upon some Occasions informed his Honour that many of my Crew had died of Diseases.

But here it was with the utmost Difficulty, that I brought him to
apprehend what I meant. He could easily conceive, that a *Houyhnhnm*
grew weak and heavy a few Days before his Death; or by some
Accident might hurt a Limb. But that Nature, who worketh all
things to Perfection, should suffer any Pains to breed in our Bodies,
he thought impossible; and desired to know the Reason of so
unaccountable an Evil. I told him, we fed on a Thousand Things
which operated contrary to each other; that we eat when we were not
hungry, and drank without the Provocation of Thirst: That we sat
whole Nights drinking strong Liquors without eating a Bit; which
disposed us to Sloth, enflamed our Bodies, and precipitated or
prevented Digestion. That, prostitute Female *Yahoos* acquired a
certain Malady, which bred Rottenness in the Bones of those, who
fell into their Embraces: That this and many other Diseases, were
propagated from Father to Son; so that great Numbers come into
the World with complicated Maladies upon them: That, it would be
endless to give him a Catalogue of all Diseases incident to human
Bodies; for they could not be fewer than five or six Hundred, spread
over every Limb, and Joynt: In short, every Part, external and intestine, having Diseases appropriated to each. To remedy which, there
was a Sort of People bred up among us, in the Profession or Pretence
of curing the Sick. And because I had some Skill in the Faculty, I
would in Gratitude to his Honour, let him know the whole Mystery*
and Method by which they proceed.

   Their Fundamental is, that all Diseases arise from *Repletion*; from
whence they conclude, that a great *Evacuation* of the Body is necessary, either through the natural Passage, or upwards at the Mouth.
Their next Business is, from Herbs, Minerals, Gums, Oyls, Shells,
Salts, Juices, Sea-weed, Excrements, Barks of Trees, Serpents,
Toads, Frogs, Spiders, dead Mens Flesh and Bones, Birds, Beasts
and Fishes, to form a Composition for Smell and Taste the most
abominable, nauseous and detestable, that they can possibly contrive,
which the Stomach immediately rejects with Loathing: and this they
call *a Vomit.** Or else from the same Store-house, with some other
poysonous Additions, they command us to take in at the Orifice
above or *below*, (just as the Physician then happens to be disposed) a
Medicine equally annoying and disgustful to the Bowels; which
relaxing the Belly, drives down all before it: And this they call a
Purge, or a *Clyster.** For Nature (as the Physicians alledge) having

intended the superior anterior Orifice only for the *Intromission* of Solids and Liquids, and the inferior Posterior for Ejection; these Artists ingeniously considering that in all Diseases Nature is forced out of her Seat; therefore to replace her in it, the Body must be treated in a Manner directly contrary, by interchanging the Use of each Orifice; forcing Solids and Liquids in at the *Anus*, and making Evacuations at the Mouth.

But, besides real Diseases, we are subject to many that are only imaginary, for which the Physicians have invented imaginary Cures; these have their several Names, and so have the Drugs that are proper for them; and with these our Female *Yahoos* are always infested.

One great Excellency in this Tribe is their Skill at *Prognosticks*, wherein they seldom fail; their Predictions in real Diseases, when they rise to any Degree of Malignity, generally portending *Death*, which is always in their Power, when Recovery is not: And therefore, upon any unexpected Signs of Amendment, after they have pronounced their Sentence, rather than be accused as false Prophets, they know how to approve their Sagacity to the World by a seasonable Dose.*

They are likewise of special Use to Husbands and Wives, who are grown weary of their Mates; to eldest Sons, to great Ministers of State, and often to Princes.

I had formerly upon Occasion discoursed with my Master upon the Nature of *Government* in general, and particularly of our own *excellent Constitution*, deservedly the Wonder and Envy of the whole World. But having here accidentally mentioned a *Minister of State*; he commanded me some Time after to inform him, what Species of *Yahoo* I particularly meant by that Appellation.

I told him, that a *First* or *Chief Minister of State*, whom I intended to describe, was a Creature wholly exempt from Joy and Grief, Love and Hatred, Pity and Anger; at least makes use of no other Passions but a violent Desire of Wealth, Power, and Titles: That he applies his Words to all Uses, except to the Indication of his Mind;* That he never tells a *Truth*, but with an Intent that you should take it for a *Lye*; nor a *Lye*, but with a Design that you should take it for a *Truth*; That those he speaks worst of behind their Backs, are in the surest way to Preferment; and whenever he begins to praise you to others or to your self, you are from that Day forlorn.* The worst Mark you can receive is a *Promise*, especially

when it is confirmed with an Oath;* after which every wise Man
retires, and gives over all Hopes.

There are three Methods by which a Man may rise to be Chief
Minister: The first is, by knowing how with Prudence to dispose of a
Wife, a Daughter, or a Sister: The second, by betraying or under-
mining his Predecessor: And the third is, by a *furious Zeal* in publick
Assemblies against the Corruptions of the Court. But a wise Prince
would rather chuse to employ those who practise the last of these
Methods; because such Zealots prove always the most obsequious
and subservient to the Will and Passions of their Master. That, these
Ministers having all Employments at their Disposal, preserve
themselves in Power by bribing the Majority of a Senate or great
Council; and at last by an Expedient called an *Act of Indemnity**
(whereof I described the Nature to him) they secure themselves
from After-reckonings, and retire from the Publick, laden with the
Spoils of the Nation.

The Palace of a *Chief Minister*, is a Seminary to breed up others in
his own Trade: The Pages, Lacquies, and Porter, by imitating their
Master, become *Ministers of State* in their several Districts, and learn
to excel in the three principal *Ingredients*, of *Insolence*, *Lying*, and
Bribery. Accordingly, they have a *Subaltern* Court paid to them by
Persons of the best Rank; and sometimes by the Force of Dexterity
and Impudence, arrive through several Gradations to be Successors
to their Lord.

He is usually governed by a decayed Wench, or favourite Footman,
who are the Tunnels* through which all Graces are conveyed, and
may properly be called, *in the last Resort*, the Governors of the
Kingdom.

One Day, my Master, having heard me mention the *Nobility* of my
Country, was pleased to make me a Compliment which I could not
pretend to deserve: That, he was sure, I must have been born of
some Noble Family, because I far exceeded in Shape, Colour, and
Cleanliness, all the *Yahoos* of his Nation, although I seemed to fail in
Strength, and Agility, which must be imputed to my different Way
of Living from those other Brutes; and besides, I was not only
endowed with the Faculty of Speech, but likewise with some
Rudiments of Reason, to a Degree, that with all his Acquaintance I
passed for a Prodigy.

He made me observe, that among the *Houyhnhnms*, the *White*, the

Sorrel, and the *Iron-grey*, were not so exactly shaped as the *Bay*, the *Dapple-grey*, and the *Black*; nor born with equal Talents of Mind, or a Capacity to improve them; and therefore continued always in the Condition of Servants, without ever aspiring to match out of their own Race, which in that Country would be reckoned monstrous and unnatural.*

I made his Honour my most humble Acknowledgements for the good Opinion he was pleased to conceive of me; but assured him at the same Time, that my Birth was of the lower Sort, having been born of plain, honest Parents, who were just able to give me a tolerable Education: That, *Nobility* among us was altogether a different Thing from the Idea he had of it; That, our young *Noblemen* are bred from their Childhood in Idleness and Luxury; that, as soon as Years will permit, they consume their Vigour, and contract odious Diseases among lewd Females; and when their Fortunes are almost ruined, they marry some Woman of mean Birth, disagreeable Person, and unsound Constitution, merely for the sake of Money, whom they hate and despise. That, the Productions of such Marriages are generally scrophulous, rickety or deformed Children; by which Means the Family seldom continues above three Generations, unless the Wife take Care to provide a healthy Father among her Neighbours or Domesticks, in order to improve and continue the Breed. That, a weak diseased Body, a meagre Countenance, and sallow Complexion, are the true Marks of *noble Blood*; and a healthy robust Appearance is so disgraceful in a Man of Quality, that the World concludes his real Father to have been a Groom or a Coachman. The Imperfections of his Mind run parallel with those of his Body; being a Composition of Spleen, Dulness, Ignorance, Caprice, Sensuality and Pride.

Without the Consent of this illustrious Body, no Law can be enacted, repealed, or altered: And these Nobles have likewise the Decision of all our Possessions without Appeal.

CHAPTER SEVEN

The Author's great Love of his Native Country. His Master's Observations upon the Constitution and Administration of England, *as described by the Author, with parallel Cases and Comparisons. His Master's Observations upon human Nature.*

THE Reader may be disposed to wonder how I could prevail on my self to give so free a Representation of my own Species, among a Race of Mortals who were already too apt to conceive the vilest Opinion of Human Kind, from that entire Congruity betwixt me and their *Yahoos.* But I must freely confess, that the many Virtues of those excellent *Quadrupeds* placed in opposite View to human Corruptions, had so far opened my Eyes, and enlarged my Understanding, that I began to view the Actions and Passions of Man in a very different Light; and to think the Honour of my own Kind not worth managing;* which, besides, it was impossible for me to do before a Person of so acute a Judgment as my Master, who daily convinced me of a thousand Faults in my self, whereof I had not the least Perception before, and which with us would never be numbered even among human Infirmities. I had likewise learned from his Example an utter Detestation of all Falsehood or Disguise; and *Truth* appeared so amiable to me,* that I determined upon sacrificing every thing to it.

Let me deal so candidly with the Reader, as to confess, that there was yet a much stronger Motive for the Freedom I took in my Representation of Things. I had not been a Year in this Country, before I contracted such a Love and Veneration for the Inhabitants, that I entered on a firm Resolution never to return to human Kind, but to pass the rest of my Life among these admirable *Houyhnhnms* in the Contemplation and Practice of every Virtue; where I could have no Example or Incitement to Vice. But it was decreed by Fortune, my perpetual Enemy, that so great a Felicity should not fall to my Share. However, it is now some Comfort to reflect, that in what I said of my Countrymen, I *extenuated* their Faults as much as I durst before so strict an Examiner; and upon every Article, gave as *favourable* a Turn as the Matter would bear. For, indeed, who is there alive that will not be swayed by his Byass and Partiality to the Place of his Birth?

I have related the Substance of several Conversations I had with my Master, during the greatest Part of the Time I had the Honour to be in his Service; but have indeed for Brevity sake omitted much more than is here set down.

When I had answered all his Questions, and his Curiosity seemed to be fully satisfied; he sent for me one Morning early, and commanding me to sit down at some Distance, (an Honour which he had never before conferred upon me) He said, he had been very seriously considering my whole Story, as far as it related both to my self and my Country: That, he looked upon us as a Sort of Animals to whose Share, by what Accident he could not conjecture, some small Pittance of *Reason* had fallen, whereof we made no other Use than by its Assistance to aggravate our *natural* Corruptions, and to acquire new ones which Nature had not given us. That, we disarmed our selves of the few Abilities she had bestowed; had been very successful in multiplying our original Wants, and seemed to spend our whole Lives in vain Endeavours to supply them by our own Inventions. That, as to my self, it was manifest I had neither the Strength or Agility of a common *Yahoo*; that I walked infirmly on my hinder Feet; had found out a Contrivance to make my Claws of no Use or Defence, and to remove the Hair from my Chin, which was intended as a Shelter from the Sun and the Weather. Lastly, that I could neither run with Speed, nor climb Trees like my *Brethren* (as he called them) the *Yahoos* in this Country.

That, our Institutions of *Government* and *Law* were plainly owing to our gross Defects in *Reason,* and by consequence, in *Virtue*; because *Reason* alone is sufficient to govern a *Rational* Creature; which was therefore a Character we had no Pretence to challenge,* even from the Account I had given of my own People; although he manifestly perceived, that in order to favour them, I had concealed many Particulars, and often *said the Thing which was not.*

He was the more confirmed in this Opinion, because he observed, that as I agreed in every Feature of my Body with other *Yahoos*, except where it was to my real Disadvantage in point of Strength, Speed and Activity, the Shortness of my Claws, and some other Particulars where Nature had no Part; so, from the Representation I had given him of our Lives, our Manners, and our Actions, he found as near a Resemblance in the Disposition of our Minds. He said, the *Yahoos* were known to hate one another more than they did any different Species of Animals; and the Reason usually assigned, was, the Odiousness of their own Shapes, which all could see in the rest, but not in themselves. He had therefore begun to think it not unwise in us to *cover* our Bodies, and by that Invention, conceal many of our Deformities from each other, which would else be hardly supportable. But, he now found he had been mistaken; and that the Dissentions of those Brutes in his Country were owing to the same Cause with ours, as I had described them. For, if (said he) you throw among five *Yahoos* as much Food as would be sufficient for fifty, they will, instead of eating peaceably, fall together by the Ears, each single one impatient to *have all to it self*; and therefore a Servant was usually employed to stand by while they were feeding abroad, and those kept at home were tied at a Distance from each other. That, if a Cow died of Age or Accident, before a *Houyhnhnm* could secure it for his own *Yahoos*, those in the Neighbourhood would come in Herds to seize it, and then would ensue such a Battle as I had described, with terrible Wounds made by their Claws on both Sides, although they seldom were able to kill one another, for want of such convenient Instruments of Death as we had invented. At other Times the like Battles have been fought between the *Yahoos* of several Neighbourhoods without any visible Cause: Those of one District watching all Opportunities to surprise the next before they are prepared. But if they find their Project hath miscarried, they return home, and for want of Enemies, engage in what I call a *Civil War* among themselves.

That, in some Fields of his Country, there are certain *shining Stones* of several Colours,* whereof the *Yahoos* are violently fond; and when Part of these *Stones* are fixed in the Earth, as it sometimes happeneth, they will dig with their Claws for whole Days to get them out, then carry them away, and hide them by Heaps in their Kennels; but still looking round with great Caution, for fear their Comrades should find out their Treasure. My master said, he could never discover the Reason of this unnatural Appetite, or how these *Stones* could be of any Use to a *Yahoo*; but now he believed it might proceed from the same Principle of *Avarice*, which I had ascribed to Mankind. That he had once by way of Experiment,* privately removed a Heap of these *Stones* from the Place where one of his *Yahoos* had buried it: Whereupon, the sordid* Animal missing his Treasure, by his loud lamenting brought the whole Herd to the Place, there miserably howled, then fell to biting and tearing the rest; began to pine away, would neither eat nor sleep, nor work, till he ordered a Servant privately to convey the *Stones* into the same Hole, and hide them as before; which when his *Yahoo* had found, he presently recovered his Spirits and good Humour; but took Care to remove them to a better hiding Place; and hath ever since been a very serviceable Brute.

My Master farther assured me, which I also observed my self; That in the Fields where the *shining Stones* abound, the fiercest and most frequent Battles are fought, occasioned by perpetual Inroads of the neighbouring *Yahoos*.

He said, it was common when two *Yahoos* discovered such a *Stone* in a Field, and were contending which of them should be the Proprietor, a third would take the Advantage, and carry it away from them both; which my Master would needs contend to have some Resemblance with our *Suits at Law*; wherein I thought it for our Credit not to undeceive him; since the Decision he mentioned was much more equitable than many Decrees among us: Because the Plaintiff and Defendant there lost nothing beside the *Stone* they contended for; whereas our *Courts of Equity*,* would never have dismissed the Cause while either of them had any thing left.

My Master continuing his Discourse, said, There was nothing that rendered the *Yahoos* more odious, than their undistinguishing Appetite* to devour every thing that came in their Way, whether Herbs, Roots, Berries, the corrupted Flesh of Animals, or all mingled together: And it was peculiar in their Temper, that they were fonder of what they could get by Rapine or Stealth at a greater Distance, than much better Food provided for them at home. If their Prey held out, they would eat till they were ready to burst, after which Nature had pointed out to them a certain *Root* that gave them a general Evacuation.

There was also another Kind of *Root* very *juicy*, but something rare and difficult to be found, which the *Yahoos* sought for with much Eagerness, and would suck it with great Delight: It produced the same Effects that Wine hath upon us. It would make them sometimes hug, and sometimes tear one another; they would howl and grin, and chatter, and reel, and tumble, and then fall asleep in the Mud.

I did indeed observe, that the *Yahoos* were the only Animals in his Country subject to any Diseases; which however, were much fewer than Horses have among us, and contracted not by any ill Treatment they meet with, but by the Nastiness and Greediness of that sordid Brute. Neither has their Language* any more than a general Appellation for those Maladies; which is borrowed from the Name of the Beast, and called *Hnea Yahoo*, or the *Yahoo's-Evil*; and the Cure prescribed is a Mixture of *their own Dung* and *Urine*, forcibly put down the *Yahoo*'s Throat. This I have since often known to have been taken with Success: And do here freely recommend it to my Countrymen, for the publick Good, as an admirable Specifick against all diseases produced by Repletion.

As to Learning, Government, Arts, Manufactures, and the like; my Master confessed he could find little or no Resemblance between the *Yahoos* of that Country and those in ours. For, he only meant to observe what Parity there was in our Natures. He had heard indeed some curious *Houyhnhnms* observe, that in most Herds there was a Sort of ruling *Yahoo*, (as among us there is generally some leading or principal Stag in a Park) who was always more *deformed* in Body, and *mischievous in Disposition,* than any of the rest. That, this *Leader* had usually a Favourite as *like himself* as he could get, whose Employment was to *lick his Master's Feet and Posteriors, and drive the Female* Yahoos *to his Kennel*; for which he was now and then rewarded with a Piece of Ass's Flesh. This *Favourite* is hated by the whole Herd; and therefore to protect himself, keeps always *near the Person of his Leader.* He usually continues in Office till worse can be found; but the very Moment he is discarded, his Successor, at the Head of all the *Yahoos* in that District, Young and Old, Male and Female, come in a Body, and discharge their Excrements upon him from Head to Foot. But how far this might be applicable to our *Courts* and *Favourites,* and *Ministers of State,* my Master said I could best determine.

I durst make no Return to this malicious Insinuation, which debased human Understanding below the Sagacity of a common *Hound,* who hath Judgment enough to distinguish and follow the Cry of the *ablest Dog in the Pack*, without being ever mistaken.

My Master told me, there were some Qualities remarkable in the *Yahoos,* which he had not observed me to mention, or at least very slightly, in the Accounts I had given him of human Kind. He said, those Animals, like other Brutes, had their Females in common;* but in this they differed, that the She-*Yahoo* would admit the Male, while she was pregnant; and that the Hees would quarrel and fight with the Females as fiercely as with each other. Both which Practices were such Degrees of infamous Brutality, that no other sensitive Creature ever arrived at.

Another Thing he wondered at in the *Yahoos*, was their strange Disposition to Nastiness and Dirt; whereas there appears to be a natural Love of Cleanliness in all other Animals. As to the two former Accusations, I was glad to let them pass without any Reply, because I had not a Word to offer upon them in Defence of my Species, which otherwise I certainly had done from my own Inclinations. But I could have easily vindicated human Kind from the Imputation of Singularity upon the last Article, if there had been any *Swine* in that Country, (as unluckily for me there were not) which although it may be a *sweeter Quadruped* than a *Yahoo*, cannot I humbly conceive in Justice pretend to more Cleanliness; and so his Honour himself must have owned, if he had seen their filthy Way of feeding, and their Custom of wallowing and sleeping in the Mud.

My Master likewise mentioned another Quality which his Servants had discovered in several *Yahoos*, and to him was wholly unaccountable. He said, a Fancy would sometimes take a *Yahoo* to retire into a Corner, to lie down and howl, and groan, and spurn away all that came near him, although he were young and fat, wanted neither Food nor Water; nor did the Servants imagine what could possibly ail him. And the only Remedy they found was to set him to hard Work, after which he would infallibly come to himself. To this I was silent out of Partiality to my own Kind; yet here I could plainly discover the true Seeds of *Spleen*,* which only seizeth on the *Lazy*, the *Luxurious*, and the *Rich*; who, if they were forced to undergo the *same Regimen*, I would undertake for the Cure.

His Honour had farther observed, that a Female *Yahoo** would often stand behind a Bank or a Bush, to gaze on the young Males passing by, and then appear, and hide, using many antick Gestures and Grimaces; at which time it was observed, that she had a most *offensive Smell*; and when any of the Males advanced, would slowly retire, looking often back, and with a counterfeit Shew of Fear, run off into some convenient Place where she knew the Male would follow her.

At other times, if a Female Stranger came among them, three or four of her own Sex would get about her, and stare and chatter, and grin, and smell her all over; and then turn off with Gestures that seemed to express Contempt and Disdain.

Perhaps my Master might refine a little in these Speculations, which he had drawn from what he observed himself, or had been told him by others: However, I could not reflect without some Amazement, and much Sorrow, that the Rudiments of *Lewdness*, *Coquetry*, *Censure*, and *Scandal*, should have Place by Instinct in Womankind.

I expected every Moment, that my Master would accuse the *Yahoos* of those unnatural Appetites in both Sexes, so common among us. But Nature it seems hath not been so expert a School-mistress; and these politer Pleasures* are entirely the Productions of Art and Reason, on our Side of the Globe.

CHAPTER EIGHT

The Author relateth several Particulars of the Yahoos. *The great Virtues of the* Houyhnhnms. *The Education and Exercise of their Youth. Their general Assembly.*

As I ought to have understood human Nature much better than I supposed it possible for my Master to do, so it was easy to apply the Character he gave of the *Yahoos* to myself and my Countrymen; and I believed I could yet make farther Discoveries from my own Observation. I therefore often begged his Honour to let me go among the Herds of *Yahoos* in the Neighbourhood; to which he always very graciously consented, being perfectly convinced that the Hatred I bore those Brutes would never suffer me to be corrupted by them; and his Honour ordered one of his Servants, a strong Sorrel Nag,* very honest and good-natured, to be my Guard; without whose Protection I durst not undertake such Adventures. For I have already told the Reader how much I was pestered by those odious Animals upon my first Arrival. I afterwards failed very narrowly three or four times of falling into their Clutches, when I happened to stray at any Distance without my Hanger. And I have Reason to believe, they had some Imagination that I was of their own Species, which I often assisted myself, by stripping up my Sleeves, and shewing my naked Arms and Breast in their Sight, when my Protector was with me: At which times they would approach as near as they durst, and imitate my Actions after the Manner of Monkeys, but ever with great Signs of Hatred; as a tame *Jack Daw* with Cap and Stockings, is always persecuted by the wild ones, when he happens to be got among them.

They are prodigiously nimble from their Infancy; however, I once caught a young Male of three Years old, and endeavoured by all Marks of Tenderness to make it quiet; but the little Imp fell a squalling, and scratching, and biting with such Violence, that I was forced to let it go; and it was high time, for a whole Troop of old ones came about us at the Noise; but finding the Cub was safe, (for away it ran) and my Sorrel Nag being by, they durst not venture near us. I observed the young Animal's Flesh to smell very rank, and the Stink was somewhat between a *Weasel* and a *Fox*, but much more disagreeable. I forgot another Circumstance, (and perhaps I might have the Reader's Pardon, if it were wholly omitted) that while I held the odious Vermin in my Hands, it voided its filthy Excrements of a yellow liquid Substance, all over my Cloaths; but by good Fortune there was a small Brook hard by, where I washed myself as clean as I could; although I durst not come into my Master's Presence, until I were sufficiently aired.

By what I could discover, the *Yahoos* appear to be the most unteachable of all Animals, their Capacities never reaching higher than to draw or carry Burthens. Yet I am of Opinion, this Defect ariseth chiefly from a perverse, restive Disposition. For they are cunning, malicious, treacherous and revengeful. They are strong and hardy, but of a cowardly Spirit, and by Consequence insolent, abject, and cruel. It is observed that, the *Red-haired* of both Sexes are more libidinous and mischievous than the rest,* whom yet they much exceed in Strength and Activity.

The *Houyhnhnms* keep the *Yahoos* for present* Use in Huts not far from the House; but the rest are sent abroad to certain Fields, where they dig up Roots, eat several Kinds of Herbs, and search about for Carrion, or sometimes catch *Weasels* and *Luhimuhs* (a Sort of *wild* Rat) which they greedily devour. Nature has taught them to dig deep Holes with their Nails on the Side of a rising Ground, wherein they lie by themselves; only the Kennels of the Females are larger, sufficient to hold two or three Cubs.

They swim from their Infancy like Frogs, and are able to continue long under Water, where they often take Fish, which the Females carry home to their Young. And upon this Occasion, I hope the Reader will pardon my relating an odd Adventure.

Being one Day abroad with my Protector the Sorrel Nag, and the Weather exceeding hot, I entreated him to let me bathe in a River that was near. He consented, and I immediately stripped myself stark naked, and went down softly* into the Stream. It happened that a young Female *Yahoo** standing behind a Bank, saw the whole Proceeding; and inflamed by Desire, as the Nag and I conjectured, came running with all Speed, and leaped into the Water within five Yards of the Place where I bathed. I was never in my Life so terribly frighted; the Nag was grazing at some Distance, not suspecting any Harm: She embraced me after a most fulsome Manner; I roared as loud as I could, and the Nag came galloping towards me, whereupon she quitted her Grasp, with the utmost Reluctancy, and leaped upon the opposite Bank, where she stood gazing and howling all the time I was putting on my Cloaths.

This was Matter of Diversion to my Master and his Family, as well as of Mortification to my self. For now I could no longer deny, that I was a real *Yahoo*, in every Limb and Feature, since the Females had a natural Propensity to me as one of their own Species: Neither was the Hair of this Brute of a Red Colour, (which might have been some Excuse for an Appetite a little irregular) but black as a Sloe, and her Countenance did not make an Appearance altogether so hideous as the rest of the Kind; for, I think, she could not be above Eleven Years old.*

Having already lived three Years in this Country, the Reader I suppose will expect, that I should, like other Travellers, give him some Account of the Manners and Customs of its Inhabitants, which it was indeed my principal Study to learn.

As these noble *Houyhnhnms* are endowed by Nature with a general Disposition to all Virtues, and have no Conceptions or Ideas of what is evil in a rational Creature, so their grand Maxim is, to cultivate *Reason*, and to be wholly governed by it. Neither is *Reason* among them a Point problematical as with us, where Men can argue with Plausibility on both Sides of a Question; but strikes you with immediate Conviction;* as it must needs do where it is not mingled, obscured, or discoloured by Passion and Interest. I remember it was with extreme Difficulty that I could bring my Master to understand the Meaning of the Word *Opinion*, or how a Point could be disputable; because *Reason* taught us to affirm or deny only where we are certain; and beyond our Knowledge we cannot do either. So that Controversies, Wranglings, Disputes, and Positiveness in false or dubious Propositions, are Evils unknown among the *Houyhnhnms*.* In the like Manner when I used to explain to him our several Systems of *Natural Philosophy*, he would laugh that a Creature pretending to *Reason*, should value itself upon the Knowledge of other Peoples Conjectures, and in Things, where that Knowledge, if it were certain, could be of no Use. Wherein he agreed entirely with the Sentiments of *Socrates*,* as *Plato* delivers them; which I mention as the highest Honour I can do that Prince of Philosophers. I have often since reflected what Destruction such a Doctrine would make in the

Libraries of *Europe*; and how many Paths to Fame would be then shut up in the Learned World.

Friendship and *Benevolence* are the two principal Virtues among the *Houyhnhnms*; and these not confined to particular Objects, but universal to the whole Race. For, a Stranger from the remotest Part, is equally treated with the nearest Neighbour, and where-ever he goes, looks upon himself as at home.* They preserve *Decency* and *Civility* in the highest Degrees, but are altogether ignorant of *Ceremony*.* They have no Fondness* for their Colts or Foles; but the Care they take in educating them proceedeth entirely from the Dictates of *Reason*. And, I observed my Master to shew the same Affection to his Neighbour's Issue that he had for his own.* They will have it that *Nature* teaches them to love the whole *Species*,* and it is *Reason* only that maketh a Distinction of Persons, where there is a superior Degree of Virtue.*

When the Matron *Houyhnhnms* have produced one of each Sex, they no longer accompany with their Consorts,* except they lose one of their Issue by some Casualty, which very seldom happens: But in such a Case they meet again; or when the like Accident befalls a Person, whose Wife is past bearing, some other Couple bestow on him one of their own Colts, and then go together a second Time, until the Mother be pregnant. This Caution is necessary to prevent the Country from being over-burthened with Numbers.* But the Race of inferior *Houyhnhnms* bred up to be Servants is not so strictly limited upon this Article; these are allowed to produce three of each Sex, to be Domesticks in the Noble Families.

In their Marriages they are exactly careful to chuse such Colours as will not make any disagreeable Mixture in the Breed.* *Strength* is chiefly valued in the Male, and *Comeliness* in the Female; not upon the Account of *Love*, but to preserve the Race from degenerating: For, where a Female happens to excel in *Strength*, a Consort is chosen with regard to *Comeliness*. Courtship, Love, Presents, Joyntures, Settlements, have no place in their Thoughts; or Terms whereby to express them in their Language. The young Couple meet and are joined, merely because it is the Determination of their Parents and Friends: It is what they see done every Day; and they look upon it as one of the necessary Actions in a reasonable Being.* But the Violation of Marriage, or any other Unchastity, was never heard of:* And the married Pair pass their Lives with the same

Friendship, and mutual Benevolence that they bear to all others of the same Species, who come in their Way; without Jealousy, Fondness, Quarrelling, or Discontent.

In educating the Youth of both Sexes, their Method is admirable, and highly deserveth our Imitation. These are not suffered to taste a Grain of *Oats*, except upon certain Days, till Eighteen Years old; nor *Milk*, but very rarely; and in Summer they graze two Hours in the Morning, and as many in the Evening, which their Parents likewise observe; but the Servants are not allowed above half that Time; and a great Part of their Grass is brought home, which they eat at the most convenient Hours, when they can be best spared from Work.

Temperance, *Industry*, *Exercise* and *Cleanliness*, are the Lessons equally enjoyned to the young ones of both Sexes: And my Master thought it monstrous in us to give the Females a different Kind of Education from the Males,* except in some Articles of Domestick Management; whereby, as he truly observed, one Half of our Natives were good for nothing but bringing Children into the World: And to trust the Care of their Children to such useless Animals, he said was yet a greater Instance of Brutality.

But the *Houyhnhnms* train up their Youth to Strength, Speed, and Hardiness, by exercising them in running Races up and down steep Hills, and over hard stony Grounds; and when they are all in a Sweat, they are ordered to leap over Head and Ears into a Pond or a River. Four times a Year the Youth of certain Districts meet to shew their Proficiency in Running, and Leaping, and other Feats of Strength or Agility; where the Victor is rewarded with a Song made in his or her Praise. On this Festival the Servants drive a Herd of *Yahoos* into the Field, laden with Hay, and Oats, and Milk for a Repast to the *Houyhnhnms*; after which, these Brutes are immediately driven back again, for fear of being noisome to the Assembly.

Every fourth Year, at the *Vernal Equinox*, there is a Representative Council of the whole Nation,* which meets in a Plain about twenty Miles from our House, and continueth about five or six Days. Here they inquire into the State and Condition of the several Districts; whether they abound or be deficient in Hay or Oats, or Cows or *Yahoos*? And where-ever there is any Want (which is but seldom) it is immediately supplied by unanimous Consent and

Contribution. Here likewise the Regulation of Children is settled: As for instance, if a *Houyhnhnm* hath two Males, he changeth one of them with another who hath two Females: and when a Child hath been lost by any Casualty, where the Mother is past Breeding, it is determined what Family shall breed another to supply the Loss.

CHAPTER NINE

A grand Debate at the General Assembly of the Houyhnhnms; *and how it was determined. The Learning of the* Houyhnhnms. *Their Buildings. Their Manner of Burials. The Defectiveness of their Language.*

ONE of these Grand Assemblies was held in my time, about three Months before my Departure, whither my Master went as the Representative of our District. In this Council was resumed their old Debate, and indeed, the only Debate that ever happened in their Country; whereof my Master after his Return gave me a very particular Account.

The Question to be debated was, Whether the *Yahoos* should be exterminated from the Face of the Earth.* One of the *Members* for the Affirmative offered several Arguments of great Strength and Weight; alledging, That, as the *Yahoos* were the most filthy, noisome, and deformed Animal which Nature ever produced, so they were the most restive and indocible, mischievous and malicious: They would privately suck the Teats of the *Houyhnhnms* Cows; kill and devour their Cats, trample down their Oats and Grass, if they were not continually watched; and commit a Thousand other Extravagancies. He took Notice of a general Tradition, that *Yahoos* had not been always in their Country: But, that many Ages ago, two of these Brutes appeared together upon a Mountain;* whether produced by the Heat of the Sun upon corrupted Mud and Slime, or from the Ooze and Froth of the Sea,* was never known. That these *Yahoos* engendered, and their Brood in a short time grew so numerous as to overrun and infest the whole Nation. That the *Houyhnhnms* to get rid of this Evil, made a general Hunting, and at last inclosed the whole Herd; and destroying the Older, every *Houyhnhnm* kept two young Ones in a Kennel, and brought them to such a Degree of Tameness, as an Animal so savage by Nature can be capable of acquiring; using them for Draught and Carriage. That, there seemed to be much Truth in this Tradition, and that those Creatures could not be *Ylnhniamshy* (or *Aborigines* of the Land) because of the violent Hatred the *Houyhnhnms* as well as all other Animals, bore them; which although their evil Disposition sufficiently deserved, could never have arrived at so high a Degree, if they had been *Abori-gines*, or else they would have long since been rooted out. That, the Inhabitants taking a Fancy to use the Service of the *Yahoos*, had very imprudently neglected to cultivate the Breed of *Asses*,* which were a comely Animal, easily kept, more tame and orderly, without any offensive Smell, strong enough for Labour, although they yield to the other in Agility of Body; and if their Braying be no agreeable Sound, it is far preferable to the horrible Howlings of the *Yahoos*.

Several others declared their Sentiments to the same purpose; when my Master proposed an Expedient to the Assembly, whereof he had indeed borrowed the Hint from me. He approved of the Tradition, mentioned by the *Honourable Member*, who spoke before; and affirmed that the two *Yahoos* said to be first seen among them, had been driven thither over the Sea; that coming to Land, and being forsaken by their Companions, they retired to the Mountains, and degenerating by Degrees, became in Process of Time, much more savage than those of their own Species in the Country from whence these two Originals came. The Reason of his Assertion was, that he had now in his Possession, a certain wonderful *Yahoo* (mean-ing myself) which most of them had heard of, and many of them had seen. He then related to them, how he first found me; that, my Body was all covered with an artificial Composure of the Skins and Hairs of other Animals: That, I spoke in a Language of my own, and had thoroughly learned theirs: That, I had related to him the Accidents which brought me thither: That, when he saw me without my Covering, I was an exact *Yahoo* in every Part, only of a whiter Colour, less hairy, and with shorter Claws. He added, how I had endeavoured to persuade him, that in my own and other Countries the *Yahoos* acted as the governing, rational Animal, and held the *Houyhnhnms* in Servitude: That, he observed in me all the Qualities of a *Yahoo*, only a little more civilized by some Tincture of Reason; which however was in a Degree as far inferior to the *Houyhnhnm* Race, as the *Yahoos* of their Country were to me: That, among other things, I mentioned a Custom we had of *castrating Houyhnhnms* when they were young, in order to render them tame; that the Operation was easy and safe; that it was no Shame to learn Wisdom from Brutes, as Industry is taught by the Ant, and Building by the Swallow. (For so I translate the Word *Lyhannh*, although it be a much larger Fowl) That, this Invention* might be practiced upon the younger *Yahoos* here, which, besides rendering them tractable and fitter for Use, would in an Age put an End to the whole Species without destroying Life. That, in the mean time the *Houyhnhnms* should be *exhorted* to cultivate the Breed of Asses, which, as they are in all respects more valuable Brutes; so they have this Advantage, to be fit for Service at five Years old, which the others are not till Twelve.

This was all my Master thought fit to tell me at that Time, of what passed in the Grand Council. But he was pleased to conceal* one Particular, which related personally to myself, whereof I soon felt the unhappy Effect, as the Reader will know in its proper Place, and from whence I date all the succeeding Misfortunes of my Life.

The *Houyhnhnms* have no Letters, and consequently, their Knowledge is all traditional. But there happening few Events of any Moment among a People so well united, naturally disposed to every Virtue, wholly governed by Reason, and cut off from all Commerce with other Nations; the historical Part is easily preserved without burthening their Memories. I have already observed, that they are subject to no Diseases, and therefore can have no Need of Physicians. However, they have excellent Medicines composed of Herbs, to cure accidental Bruises and Cuts in the Pastern or Frog of the Foot by sharp Stones, as well as other Maims and Hurts in the several Parts of the Body.

They calculate the Year by the Revolution of the Sun and the Moon, but use no Subdivisions into Weeks. They are well enough acquainted with the Motions of those two Luminaries, and understand the Nature of *Eclipses*; and this is the utmost Progress of their *Astronomy*.

In *Poetry* they must be allowed to excel all other Mortals;* wherein the Justness of their Similes, and the Minuteness, as well as Exactness of their Descriptions, are indeed inimitable. Their Verses abound very much in both of these; and usually contain either some exalted Notions of Friendship and Benevolence, or the Praises of those who were Victors in Races, and other bodily Exercises. Their Buildings, although very rude and simple, are not inconvenient, but well contrived to defend them from all Injuries of Cold and Heat. They have a Kind of Tree, which at Forty Years old loosens in the Root, and falls with the first Storm; it grows very strait, and being pointed like Stakes with a sharp Stone, (for the *Houyhnhnms* know not the Use of Iron) they stick them erect in the Ground about ten Inches asunder, and then weave in Oat-straw, or sometimes Wattles betwixt them. The Roof is made after the same Manner, and so are the Doors.

The *Houyhnhnms* use the hollow Part between the Pastern and the Hoof of their Fore-feet, as we do our Hands, and this with greater Dexterity, than I could at first imagine. I have seen a white Mare of our Family thread a Needle (which I lent her on Purpose) with that Joynt. They milk their Cows, reap their Oats, and do all the Work which requires Hands, in the same Manner. They have a Kind of hard Flints, which by grinding against other Stones, they form into Instruments, that serve instead of Wedges, Axes, and Hammers. With Tools made of these Flints they likewise cut their Hay, and reap their Oats, which there groweth naturally in several Fields: The *Yahoos* draw home the Sheaves in Carriages, and the Servants tread them in certain covered Hutts, to get out the Grain, which is kept in Stores. They make a rude Kind of earthen and wooden Vessels, and bake the former in the Sun.

If they can avoid Casualties, they die only of old Age, and are buried in the obscurest Places that can be found, their Friends and Relations expressing neither Joy nor Grief* at their Departure; nor does the dying Person discover the least Regret that he is leaving the World, any more than if he were upon returning* home from a Visit to one of his Neighbours: I remember, my Master having once made an Appointment with a Friend and his family to come to his House upon some Affair of Importance; on the Day fixed, the Mistress and her two Children came very late; she made two Excuses, first for her Husband, who, as she said, happened that very Morning to *Lhnuwnh*. The Word is strongly expressive in their Language, but not easily rendered into *English*; it signifies, *to retire to his first Mother*. Her Excuse for not coming sooner, was, that her Husband dying late in the Morning, she was a good while consulting her Servants about a convenient Place where his Body should be laid; and I observed she behaved herself at our House, as chearfully as the rest: She died about three Months after.*

They live generally to Seventy or Seventy-five Years, very seldom to Fourscore: Some Weeks before their Death they feel a gradual Decay, but without Pain. During this time they are much visited by their Friends, because they cannot go abroad with their usual Ease and Satisfaction. However, about ten Days before their Death, which they seldom fail in computing they return the Visits that have been made them by those who are nearest in the Neighbourhood, being carried in a convenient Sledge drawn by *Yahoos*; which Vehicle they use, not only upon this Occasion, but when they grow old, upon long Journeys, or when they are lamed by any Accident. And therefore when the dying *Houyhnhnms* return those Visits, they take a solemn Leave of their Friends, as if they were going to some remote Part of the Country, where they designed to pass the rest of their Lives.

I know not whether it may be worth observing, that the *Houyhnhnms* have no Word in their Language to express any thing that is *evil*, except what they borrow from the Deformities or ill Qualities of the *Yahoos*. Thus they denote the Folly of a Servant, an Omission of a Child, a Stone that cuts their Feet, a Continuance of foul or unseasonable Weather, and the like, by adding to each the Epithet of *Yahoo*. For Instance, *Hhnm Yahoo*, *Whnaholm Yahoo*, *Ynlhmnawihlma Yahoo*, and an ill contrived House *Ynholmhnmrohlnw Yahoo*.

I could with great Pleasure enlarge further upon the Manners and Virtues of this excellent People; but intending in a short time to publish a Volume by itself expressly upon that Subject, I refer the Reader thither. And in the mean time, proceed to relate my own sad Catastrophe.

CHAPTER TEN

The Author's Oeconomy and happy Life among the Houyhnhnms. *His great Improvement in Virtue, by conversing with them. Their Conversations. The Author hath Notice given him by his Master that he must depart from the Country. He falls into a Swoon for Grief, but submits. He contrives and finishes a Canoo, by the Help of a Fellow-Servant, and puts to Sea at a Venture.*

I HAD settled my little Oeconomy to my own Heart's Content. My Master had ordered a Room to be made for me after their Manner, about six Yards from the House; the Sides and Floors of which I plaistered with Clay, and covered with Rush-mats of my own contriving: I had beaten Hemp, which there grows wild, and made of it a Sort of Ticking: This I filled with the Feathers of several Birds I had taken with Springes made of *Yahoos* Hairs; and were excellent Food. I had worked two Chairs with my Knife, the Sorrel Nag helping me in the grosser and more laborious Part. When my Cloaths were worn to Rags, I made my self others with the Skins of Rabbets, and of a certain beautiful Animal about the same Size, called *Nnuhnoh,* the Skin of which is covered with a fine Down. Of these I likewise made very tolerable Stockings. I soaled my Shoes with Wood which I cut from a Tree, and fitted to the upper Leather, and when this was worn out, I supplied it with the Skins of *Yahoos,* dried in the Sun. I often got Honey out of hollow Trees, which I mingled with Water,* or eat it with my Bread. No Man could more verify the Truth of these two Maxims, *That, Nature is very easily satisfied*; and, *That, Necessity is the Mother of Invention.* I enjoyed perfect Health of Body, and Tranquillity of Mind; I did not feel the Treachery or Inconstancy of a Friend, nor the Injuries of a secret or open Enemy.* I had no Occasion of bribing, flattering or pimping, to procure the Favour of any great Man, or of his Minion. I wanted no Fence against Fraud or Oppression: Here was neither Physician to destroy my Body, nor Lawyer to ruin my Fortune: No Informer to watch my Words and Actions, or forge Accusations against me for Hire; Here were no Gibers, Censurers, Backbiters, Pickpockets, Highwaymen, House-breakers, Attorneys, Bawds, Buffoons, Gamesters, Politicians, Wits, Spleneticks, tedious Talkers, Controvertists,*

Ravishers, Murderers, Robbers, Virtuoso's;* no Leaders or Followers of Party and Faction; no Encouragers to Vice, by Seducement or
Examples: No Dungeon, Axes, Gibbets, Whipping-posts, or Pillor-
ies; No cheating Shopkeepers or Mechanicks:* No Pride, Vanity or
Affectation: No Fops, Bullies, Drunkards, strolling Whores, or
Poxes: No ranting, lewd, expensive Wives: No stupid, proud Ped-
ants: No importunate, over-bearing, quarrelsome, noisy, roaring,
empty, conceited, swearing Companions: No Scoundrels, raised
from the Dust upon the Merit of their Vices; or Nobility thrown into
it on account of their Virtues: No Lords, Fiddlers,* Judges or
Dancing-masters.

I had the Favour of being admitted to several *Houyhnhnms*, who
came to visit or dine with my Master; where his Honour graciously
suffered me to wait in the Room, and listen to their Discourse. Both
he and his Company would often descend* to ask me Questions, and
receive my Answers. I had also sometimes the Honour of attending
my Master in his Visits to others. I never presumed to speak, except
in answer to a Question; and then I did it with inward Regret,
because it was a Loss of so much Time for improving my self: But I
was infinitely delighted with the Station of an humble Auditor in
such Conversations, where nothing passed but what was useful,
expressed in the fewest and most significant Words:* Where (as I have
already said) the greatest *Decency* was observed, without the least
Degree of Ceremony; where no Person spoke without being pleased
himself, and pleasing his Companions: Where there was no Interruption, Tediousness, Heat, or Difference of Sentiments. They have
a Notion, That when People are met together, a short Silence doth
much improve Conversation: This I found to be true; for during
those little Intermissions of Talk, new Ideas would arise in their
Minds, which very much enlivened the Discourse. Their Subjects*
are generally on Friendship and Benevolence, or Order and
Oeconomy; sometimes upon the visible Operations of Nature, or
ancient Traditions; upon the Bounds and Limits of Virtue; upon the
unerring Rules of Reason; or upon some Determinations, to be taken
at the next great Assembly; and often upon the various Excellencies
of *Poetry.* I may add, without Vanity, that my Presence often gave
them sufficient Matter for Discourse, because it afforded my Master
an Occasion of letting his Friends into the History of me and my
Country, upon which they were all pleased to discant in a Manner

not very advantageous to human Kind; and for that Reason I shall not repeat what they said: Only I may be allowed to observe, That his Honour, to my great Admiration, appeared to understand the Nature of *Yahoos* much better than my self. He went through all our Vices and Follies, and discovered many which I had never mentioned to him; by only supposing what Qualities a *Yahoo* of their Country, with a small Proportion of Reason, might be capable of exerting: And concluded, with too much Probability, how vile as well as miserable such a Creature must be.

I freely confess, that all the little Knowledge I have of any Value, was acquired by the Lectures I received from my Master, and from hearing the Discourses of him and his Friends; to which I should be prouder to listen, than to dictate to the greatest and wisest Assembly in *Europe.* I admired the Strength, Comeliness and Speed of the Inhabitants; and such a Constellation of Virtues in such amiable Persons produced in me the highest Veneration. At first, indeed, I did not feel that natural Awe which the *Yahoos* and all other Animals bear towards them; but it grew upon me by Degrees, much sooner than I imagined, and was mingled with a respectful Love and Gratitude, that they would condescend to distinguish me from the rest of my Species.

When I thought of my Family, my Friends, my Countrymen, or human Race in general, I considered them as they really were, *Yahoos* in Shape and Disposition, perhaps a little more civilized, and qualified with the Gift of Speech; but making no other Use of Reason, than to improve and multiply those Vices, whereof their Brethren in this Country had only the Share that Nature allotted them. When I happened to behold the Reflection of my own Form in a Lake or Fountain, I turned away my Face in Horror and detestation of my self;* and could better endure the Sight of a common *Yahoo*, than of my own Person. By conversing with the *Houyhnhnms*, and looking upon them with Delight, I fell to imitate their Gait and Gesture, which is now grown into a Habit; and my Friends often tell me in a blunt Way, that *I trot like a Horse*; which, however, I take for a great Compliment: Neither shall I disown, that in speaking I am apt to fall into the Voice and manner of the *Houyhnhnms*, and hear my self ridiculed on that Account without the least Mortification.

In the Midst of all this Happiness, when I looked upon my self to be fully settled for Life, my Master sent for me one Morning a little earlier than his usual Hour. I observed by his Countenance that he was in some Perplexity, and at a Loss how to begin what he had to speak. After a short Silence, he told me, he did not know how I would take what he was going to say: That, in the last general Assembly, when the Affair of the *Yahoos* was entered upon, the Representatives had taken Offence at his keeping a *Yahoo* (meaning my self) in his Family more like a *Houyhnhnm* than a Brute Animal. That, he was known frequently to converse with me, as if he could receive some Advantage or Pleasure in my Company: That, such a Practice was not agreeable to Reason or Nature, nor a thing ever heard of before among them. The Assembly did therefore *exhort* him, either to employ me like the rest of my Species, or command me to swim back to the Place from whence I came. That, the first of these Expedients was utterly rejected by all the *Houyhnhnms*, who had ever seen me at his House or their own: For, they alledged, That because I had some Rudiments of Reason, added to the natural Pravity of those Animals, it was to be feared, I might be able to seduce them into the woody and mountainous Parts of the Country, and bring them in Troops by Night to destroy the *Houyhnhnms* Cattle, as being naturally of the ravenous* Kind, and averse from Labour.

My Master added, That he was daily pressed by the *Houyhnhnms* of the Neighbourhood to have the Assembly's *Exhortation* executed, which he could not put off much longer. He doubted, it would be impossible for me to swim to another Country; and therefore wished I would contrive some Sort of Vehicle* resembling those I had described to him, that might carry me on the Sea; in which Work I should have the Assistance of his own Servants, as well as those of his Neighbours. He concluded, that for his own Part he could have been content to keep me in this Service as long as I lived; because he found I had cured myself of some bad Habits and Dispositions, by endeavouring, as far as my inferior Nature was capable, to imitate the *Houyhnhnms*.

I should here observe to the Reader, that a Decree of the general Assembly in this Country, is expressed by the Word *Hnhloayn*, which signifies an *Exhortation*; as near as I can render it: For they have no Conception how a rational Creature can be *compelled*, but only advised, or *exhorted*; because no Person can disobey Reason, without giving up his Claim to be a rational Creature.

I was struck with the utmost Grief and Despair at my Master's Discourse; and being unable to support the Agonies I was under, I fell into a Swoon at his Feet: When I came to myself, he told me, that he concluded I had been dead. (For these People are subject to no such Imbecillities of Nature.) I answered, in a faint Voice, that Death would have been too great an Happiness; that although I could not blame the Assembly's *Exhortation*, or the Urgency of his Friends; yet in my weak and corrupt Judgment, I thought it might consist with Reason to have been less rigorous. That, I could not swim a League, and probably the nearest Land to theirs might be distant above an Hundred: That, many Materials, necessary for making a small Vessel to carry me off, were wholly wanting in this Country, which however, I would attempt in Obedience and Gratitude to his Honour, although I concluded the thing to be impossible, and therefore looked on myself as already devoted to Destruction. That, the certain Prospect of an unnatural Death, was the least of my Evils: For, supposing I should escape with Life by some strange Adventure, how could I think with Temper, of passing my Days among *Yahoos*, and relapsing into my old Corruptions, for want of Examples to lead and keep me within the Paths of Virtue. That, I knew too well upon what solid Reasons all the Determinations of the wise *Houyhnhnms* were founded, not to be shaken by Arguments of mine, a miserable *Yahoo*; and therefore, after presenting him with my humble Thanks for the Offer of his Servants Assistance in making a Vessel, and desiring a reasonable Time for so difficult a Work, I told him, I would endeavour to preserve a wretched Being; and, if ever I returned to *England*, was not without Hopes of being useful to my own Species, by celebrating the Praises of the renowned* *Houyhnhnms*, and proposing their Virtues to the Imitation of Mankind.

My Master in a few Words made me a very gracious Reply, allowed me the Space of two *Months* to finish my Boat; and ordered the Sorrel Nag, my Fellow-Servant, (for so at this Distance I may presume to call him) to follow my Instructions, because I told my Master, that his Help would be sufficient, and I knew he had a Tenderness for me.

In his Company my first Business was to go to that Part of the Coast, where my rebellious Crew had ordered me to be set on Shore. I got upon a Height, and looking on every Side into the Sea, fancied I saw a small Island, towards the *North-East*: I took out my

Pocket-glass, and could then clearly distinguish it about five Leagues off, as I computed; but it appeared to the Sorrel Nag to be only a blue Cloud: For, as he had no Conception of any Country beside his own, so he could not be as expert in distinguishing remote Objects at Sea, as we who so much converse in that Element.

After I had discovered this Island, I considered no farther; but resolved, it should, if possible, be the first Place of my Banishment, leaving the Consequence to Fortune.

I returned home, and consulting with the Sorrel Nag, we went into a Copse at some Distance, where I with my Knife, and he with a sharp Flint fastened very artificially, after their Manner, to a wooden Handle, cut down several oak Wattles* about the Thickness of a Walking-staff, and some larger Pieces. But I shall not trouble the Reader with a particular Description of my own Mechanicks: let it suffice to say, that in six Weeks time, with the Help of the Sorrel Nag, who performed the Parts that required most Labour, I finished a Sort of *Indian* Canoo, but much larger, covering it with the Skins of *Yahoos*, well stitched together, with hempen Threads of my own making. My Sail was likewise composed of the Skins of the same Animal; but I made use of the youngest I could get, the older being too tough and thick; and I likewise provided myself with four Paddles. I laid in a Stock of boiled Flesh, of Rabbets and Fowls; and took with me two Vessels, one filled with Milk, and the other with Water.

I tried my Canoo in a large Pond near my Master's House, and then corrected in it what was amiss; stopping all the Chinks with *Yahoos* Tallow, till I found it stanch,* and able to bear me, and my Freight. And when it was as compleat as I could possibly make it, I had it drawn on a Carriage very gently by *Yahoos*, to the Sea-side, under the Conduct of the Sorrel Nag, and another Servant.

When all was ready, and the Day came for my Departure, I took Leave of my Master and Lady, and the whole Family, mine Eyes flowing with Tears, and my Heart quite sunk with Grief. But his Honour, out of Curiosity, and perhaps (if I may speak it without Vanity) partly out of Kindness, was determined to see me in my Canoo; and got several of his neighbouring Friends to accompany him. I was forced to wait above an Hour for the Tide, and then observing the Wind very fortunately bearing towards the Island, to which I intended to steer my Course, I took a second Leave of my

Master: But as I was going to prostrate myself to kiss his Hoof, he did me the Honour to raise it gently to my Mouth.* I am not ignorant how much I have been censured for mentioning this last Particular. Detractors are pleased to think it improbable, that so illustrious a Person should descend to give so great a Mark of Distinction to a Creature so inferior as I. Neither have I forgot, how apt some Travellers are to boast of extraordinary Favours they have received. But, if these Censurers were better acquainted with the noble and courteous Disposition of the *Houyhnhnms*, they would soon change their Opinion.

I paid my Respects to the rest of the *Houyhnhnms* in his Honour's Company; then getting into my Canoo, I pushed off from Shore.

CHAPTER ELEVEN

The Author's dangerous Voyage. He arrives at New-Holland, *hoping to settle there. Is wounded with an Arrow by one of the Natives. Is seized and carried by Force into a* Portugueze Ship. *The great Civilities of the Captain. The Author arrives at* England.

I BEGAN this desperate Voyage on *February* 15, 171$\frac{4}{5}$,* at 9 o'Clock in the Morning. The Wind was very favourable; however, I made use at first only of my Paddles; but considering I should soon be weary, and that the Wind might probably chop about, I ventured to set up my little Sail; and thus, with the Help of the Tide, I went at the Rate of a League and a Half an Hour, as near as I could guess. My Master and his Friends continued on the Shoar, till I was almost out of Sight; and I often heard the Sorrel Nag (who always loved me) crying out, *Hnuy illa nyha maiah Yahoo*, Take Care of thy self, gentle *Yahoo*.

My Design was, if possible, to discover some small Island uninhabited, yet sufficient by my Labour to furnish me with Necessaries of Life, which I would have thought a greater Happiness than to be first Minister in the politest Court of *Europe*; so horrible was the Idea I conceived of returning to live in the Society and under the Government of *Yahoos*. For in such a Solitude* as I desired, I could at least enjoy my own Thoughts, and reflect with Delight on the Virtues of those inimitable *Houyhnhnms*, without any Opportunity of degenerating into the Vices and Corruptions of my own Species.

The Reader may remember what I related when my Crew conspired against me, and confined me to my Cabbin. How I continued there several Weeks, without knowing what Course we took; and when I was put ashore in the Long-boat, how the Sailors told me with Oaths, whether true or false, that they knew not in what Part of the World we were. However, I did then believe us to be about ten Degrees *Southward* of the *Cape of Good Hope*, or about 45 Degrees *Southern* Latitude, as I gathered from some general Words I overheard among them, being I supposed to the *South-East* in their intended Voyage to *Madagascar*. And although this were but little better than Conjecture, yet I resolved to steer my Course *Eastward*,

hoping to reach the *South-West* Coast of *New-Holland*, and perhaps
some such Island as I desired, lying *Westward* of it. The Wind was
full *West*, and by six in the Evening I computed I had gone *Eastward*
at least eighteen Leagues; when I spied a very small Island about half
a League off, which I soon reached. It was nothing but a Rock with
one Creek, naturally arched by the Force of Tempests. Here I put in
my Canoo, and climbing a Part of the Rock, I could plainly discover
Land to the *East*, extending from *South* to *North*. I lay all Night in
my Canoo; and repeating my Voyage early in the Morning, I arrived
in seven Hours to the *South-East* Point of *New-Holland*.* This confirmed me in the Opinion I have long entertained, that the *Maps* and
Charts place this Country at least three Degrees more to the *East*
than it really is;* which Thought I communicated many Years ago to
my worthy Friend Mr *Herman Moll*,* and gave him my Reasons for
it, although he hath rather chosen to follow other Authors.

I saw no Inhabitants in the Place where I landed; and being
unarmed, I was afraid of venturing far into the Country. I found
some Shell-Fish on the Shore, and eat them raw, not daring to kindle
a Fire, for fear of being discovered by the Natives. I continued three
Days feeding on Oysters and Limpets, to save my own Provisions;
and I fortunately found a Brook of excellent Water, which gave me
great Relief.

On the fourth Day, venturing out early a little too far, I saw twenty
or thirty Natives upon a Height, not above five hundred Yards from
me. They were stark naked, Men, Women and Children round a
Fire, as I could discover by the Smoke. One of them spied me, and
gave Notice to the rest; five of them advanced towards me, leaving
the Women and Children at the Fire. I made what haste I could to
the Shore, and getting into my Canoo, shoved off: The Savages
observing me retreat, ran after me; and before I could get far enough
into the Sea, discharged an Arrow, which wounded me deeply on the
Inside of my left Knee* (I shall carry the Mark to my Grave.) I
apprehended the Arrow might be poisoned; and paddling out of the
Reach of their Darts (being a calm Day) I made a shift to suck the
Wound, and dress it as well as I could.

I was at a Loss what to do, for I durst not return to the same
Landing-place, but stood to* the *North*, and was forced to paddle;
for the Wind, although very gentle, was against me, blowing *North-
West*. As I was looking about for a secure Landing-place, I saw a Sail

to the *North North-East*, which appearing every Minute more visible, I was in some Doubt, whether I should wait for them or no; but
at last my Detestation of the *Yahoo* Race prevailed; and turning my
Canoo, I sailed and paddled together to the *South*, and got into the
same Creek from whence I set out in the Morning; choosing rather
to trust my self among these *Barbarians*, than live with *European
Yahoos*. I drew up my Canoo as close as I could to the Shore, and hid
my self behind a Stone by the little Brook, which, as I have already
said, was excellent Water.

The Ship came within half a League of this Creek, and sent out
her Long-Boat with Vessels to take in fresh Water (for the Place it
seems was very well known) but I did not observe it until the Boat
was almost on Shore; and it was too late to seek another
Hiding-Place. The Seamen at their landing observed my Canoo, and
rummaging it all over, easily conjectured that the Owner could not
be far off. Four of them well armed searched every Cranny and
Lurking-hole, till at last they found me flat on my Face behind the
Stone. They gazed a while in Admiration at my strange uncouth
Dress; my Coat made of Skins, my wooden-soaled Shoes, and my
furred Stockings; from whence, however, they concluded I was not a
Native of the Place, who all go naked. One of the Seamen in *Portugueze*
bid me rise, and asked who I was. I understood that Language very
well, and getting upon my Feet, said, I was a poor *Yahoo*, banished
from the *Houyhnhnms*, and desired they would please to let me
depart. They admired to hear me answer them in their own Tongue,
and saw by my Complection I must be an European; but were at a
Loss to know what I meant by *Yahoos* and *Houyhnhnms*, and at the
same Time fell a laughing at my strange Tone in speaking, which
resembled the Neighing of a Horse. I trembled all the while betwixt
Fear and Hatred: I again desired Leave to depart, and was gently
moving to my Canoo; but they laid hold on me, desiring to know
what Country I was of? whence I came? with many other Questions.
I told them, I was born in *England*, from whence I came about five
Years ago, and then their Country and ours were at Peace. I therefore
hoped they would not treat me as an Enemy, since I meant them no
Harm, but was a poor *Yahoo*, seeking some desolate Place where to
pass the Remainder of his unfortunate Life.

When they began to talk, I thought I never heard or saw any thing
so unnatural; for it appeared to me as monstrous as if a Dog or a Cow

should speak in *England*, or a *Yahoo* in *Houyhnhnm-Land*. The honest Portuguese were equally amazed at my strange Dress, and the odd Manner of delivering my Words, which however they understood very well. They spoke to me with great Humanity, and said they were sure their Captain would carry me *gratis* to *Lisbon*, from whence I might return to my own Country; that two of the Seamen would go back to the Ship, to inform the Captain of what they had seen, and receive his Orders; in the mean Time, unless I would give my solemn Oath not to fly, they would secure me by Force. I thought it best to comply with their Proposal. They were very curious to know my Story, but I gave them very little Satisfaction; and they all conjectured, that my Misfortunes had impaired my Reason. In two Hours the Boat, which went loaden with Vessels of Water, returned with the Captain's Commands to fetch me on Board. I fell on my Knees to preserve my Liberty; but all was in vain, and the Men having tied me with Cords, heaved me into the Boat, from whence I was taken into the Ship, and from thence into the Captain's Cabbin.

His Name was *Pedro de Mendez*;* he was a very courteous and generous Person; he entreated me to give some Account of my self, and desired to know what I would eat or drink; said, I should be used as well as himself, and spoke so many obliging Things, that I wondered to find such Civilities from a *Yahoo*. However, I remained silent and sullen; I was ready to faint at the very Smell of him and his Men. At last I desired something to eat out of my own Canoo; but he ordered me a Chicken and some excellent Wine, and then directed that I should be put to Bed in a very clean Cabbin. I would not undress my self, but lay on the Bed-cloaths; and in half an Hour stole out, when I thought the Crew was at Dinner; and getting to the Side of the Ship, was going to leap into the Sea, and swim for my Life, rather than continue among *Yahoos*. But one of the Seamen prevented me, and having informed the Captain, I was chained to my Cabbin.

After Dinner *Don Pedro* came to me, and desired to know my Reason for so desperate an Attempt; assured me he only meant to do me all the Service he was able; and spoke so very movingly, that at last I descended to treat him like an Animal which had some little Portion of Reason. I gave him a very short Relation of my Voyage; of the Conspiracy against me by my own Men; of the Country where they set me on Shore, and of my five Years Residence there. All which he looked upon as if it were a Dream or a Vision; whereat I took great Offence: For I had quite forgotten the Faculty of Lying, so peculiar to *Yahoos* in all Countries where they preside, and, consequently the Disposition of suspecting Truth in others of their own Species. I asked him, Whether it were the Custom of his Country to *say the Thing that was not?* I assured him I almost forgot what he meant by Falshood; and if I had lived a thousand Years in *Houyhnhnmland*, I should never have heard a Lie from the meanest Servant. That I was altogether indifferent whether he believed me or no; but however, in return for his Favours, I would give so much Allowance to the Corruption of his Nature, as to answer any Objection he would please to make; and he might easily discover the Truth.

The Captain, a wise Man, after many Endeavours to catch me tripping in some Part of my Story, at last began to have a better Opinion of my Veracity.* But he added, that since I professed so inviolable an Attachment to Truth, I must give him my Word of Honour to bear him Company in this Voyage without attempting any thing against my Life; or else he would continue me a Prisoner till we arrived at *Lisbon*. I gave him the Promise he required; but at the same time protested that I would suffer the greatest Hardships rather than return to live among *Yahoos*.

Our Voyage passed without any considerable Accident. In Gratitude to the Captain I sometimes sate with him at his earnest Request, and strove to conceal my Antipathy against human Kind, although it often broke out; which he suffered to pass without Observation. But the greatest Part of the Day, I confined myself to my Cabbin, to avoid seeing any of the Crew. The Captain had often intreated me to strip myself of my savage Dress, and offered to lend me the best Suit of Cloaths he had. This I would not be prevailed on to accept, abhorring to cover myself with any thing that had been on the Back of a *Yahoo*. I only desired he would lend me two clean Shirts, which having been washed since he wore them, I believed would not so much defile me. These I changed every second Day, and washed them myself.

We arrived at *Lisbon*, *Nov.* 5, 1715. At our landing, the Captain forced me to cover myself with his Cloak, to prevent the Rabble from crouding about me. I was conveyed to his own House; and at my earnest Request, he led me up to the highest Room backwards.* I conjured him to conceal from all Persons what I had told him of the *Houyhnhnms*; because the least Hint of such a Story would not only draw Numbers of People to see me, but probably put me in Danger of being imprisoned, or burnt by the *Inquisition*.* The Captain persuaded me to accept a Suit of Cloaths newly made; but I would not suffer the Taylor to take my Measure; however, Don *Pedro* being almost of my Size, they fitted me well enough. He accoutred me with other Necessaries all new, which I aired for Twenty-four Hours before I would use them.

The Captain had no Wife, nor above three Servants, none of which were suffered to attend at Meals; and his whole Deportment was so obliging, added to very good *human* Understanding, that I really began to tolerate his Company. He gained so far upon me, that I ventured to look out of the back Window. By Degrees I was brought into another Room, from whence I peeped into the Street, but drew my Head back in a Fright. In a Week's Time he seduced me down to the Door. I found my Terror gradually lessened, but my Hatred and Contempt seemed to increase. I was at last bold enough to walk the Street in his Company, but kept my Nose well stopped with Rue, or sometimes with Tobacco.*

In ten Days, Don *Pedro*, to whom I had given some Account of my domestick Affairs, put it upon me as a Point of Honour and Conscience, that I ought to return to my native Country, and live at home with my Wife and Children. He told me, there was an *English* Ship in the Port just ready to sail, and he would furnish me with all things necessary. It would be tedious to repeat his Arguments, and my Contradictions. He said, it was altogether impossible to find such a solitary Island as I had desired to live in; but I might command in my own House, and pass my time in a Manner as recluse as I pleased.

I complied at last, finding I could not do better. I left *Lisbon* the 24th Day of *November*, in an *English* Merchant-man, but who was the Master I never inquired. Don *Pedro* accompanied me to the Ship, and lent me Twenty Pounds. He took kind Leave of me, and embraced me at parting; which I bore as well as I could. During this last Voyage I had no Commerce* with the Master, or any of his Men; but pretending I was sick kept close in my Cabbin. On the Fifth of *December*, 1715, we cast Anchor in the *Downs* about Nine in the

Morning, and at Three in the Afternoon I got safe to my House at *Redriff*.

My Wife and Family received me with great Surprize and Joy, because they concluded me certainly dead; but I must freely confess, the Sight of them filled me only with Hatred, Disgust, and Contempt; and the more, by reflecting on the near Alliance I had to them. For, although since my unfortunate Exile from the *Houyhnhnm* Country, I had compelled myself to tolerate the Sight of *Yahoos*, and to converse with Don *Pedro de Mendez*; yet my Memory and Imaginations were perpetually filled with the Virtues and Ideas of those exalted *Houyhnhnms*. And when I began to consider, that by copulating with one of the *Yahoo*-Species, I had become a Parent of more; it struck me with the utmost Shame, Confusion and Horror.

As soon as I entered the House, my Wife took me in her Arms, and kissed me; at which, having not been used to the Touch of that odious Animal for so many Years, I fell in a Swoon for almost an Hour.* At the Time I am writing, it is five Years since my last Return to *England*: During the first Year I could not endure my Wife or Children in my Presence, the very Smell of them was intolerable; much less could I suffer them to eat in the same Room. To this Hour they dare not presume to touch my Bread, or drink out of the same Cup; neither was I ever able to let one of them take me by the Hand.* The first Money I laid out was to buy two young Stone-Horses,* which I keep in a good Stable, and next to them the Groom is my greatest Favourite; for I feel my Spirits revived by the Smell he contracts in the Stable. My Horses understand me tolerably well; I converse with them at least four Hours every Day. They are Strangers to Bridle or Saddle; they live in great Amity with me, and Friendship to each other.

CHAPTER TWELVE

The Author's Veracity. His Design in publishing this Work. His Censure of those Travellers who swerve from the Truth. The Author clears himself from any sinister Ends in writing. An Objection answered. The Method of planting Colonies. His Native Country commended. The Right of the Crown to those Countries described by the Author, is justified. The Difficulty of conquering them. The Author takes his last Leave of the Reader; proposeth his Manner of Living for the future; gives good Advice, and concludeth.

THUS, gentle Reader, I have given thee a faithful History* of my Travels for Sixteen Years, and above Seven Months; wherein I have not been so studious of Ornament as of Truth. I could perhaps like others have astonished thee with strange improbable Tales; but I rather chose to relate plain Matter of Fact in the simplest Manner and Style; because my principal Design was to inform, and not to amuse thee.

It is easy for us who travel into remote Countries, which are seldom visited by *Englishmen* or other *Europeans*, to form Descriptions of wonderful Animals both at Sea and Land. Whereas, a Traveller's chief Aim should be to make Men wiser and better, and to improve their Minds by the bad, as well as good Example of what they deliver concerning foreign Places.*

I could heartily wish a Law was enacted, that every Traveller, before he were permitted to publish his Voyages, should be obliged to make Oath before the *Lord High Chancellor*, that all he intended to print was absolutely true to the best of his Knowledge; for then the World would no longer be deceived as it usually is, while some Writers, to make their Works pass the better upon the Publick, impose the grossest Falsities on the unwary Reader. I have perused several Books of Travels with great Delight in my younger Days; but, having since gone over most Parts of the Globe, and been able to contradict many fabulous Accounts from my own Observation; it hath given me a great Disgust against this Part of Reading, and some Indignation to see the Credulity of Mankind so impudently abused. Therefore since my Acquaintance were pleased to think my poor Endeavours might not be unacceptable to my Country; I imposed on myself as a Maxim, never to be swerved from, that I would *strictly adhere to Truth*; neither indeed can I be ever under the least Temptation to vary from it, while I retain in my Mind the Lectures and Example of my noble Master, and the other illustrious *Houyhnhnms*, of whom I had so long the Honour to be an humble Hearer.

——*Nec si miserum Fortuna Sinonem*
Finxit, vanum etiam, mendacemque improba finget. *

I know very well, how little Reputation is to be got by Writings which require neither Genius nor Learning, nor indeed any other Talent, except a good Memory, or an exact *Journal*.* I know likewise that Writers of Travels, like *Dictionary*-Makers, are sunk into Oblivion by the Weight and Bulk of those who come last, and therefore lie uppermost: And it is highly probable, that such Travellers who shall hereafter visit the Countries described in this Work of mine, may by detecting my Errors, (if there be any) and adding many new Discoveries of their own, jostle me out of Vogue, and stand in my Place; making the World forget that I was ever an Author. This indeed would be too great a Mortification if I wrote for Fame: But, as my sole Intention was the PUBLICK GOOD, I cannot be altogether disappointed. For, who can read of the Virtues I have mentioned in the glorious *Houyhnhnms*, without being ashamed of his own Vices, when he considers himself as the reasoning, governing Animal of his Country? I shall say nothing of those remote Nations where *Yahoos* preside; amongst which the least corrupted are the *Brobdingnagians*, whose wise Maxims in Morality and Government, it would be our Happiness to observe. But I forbear descanting further, and rather leave the judicious Reader to his own Remarks and Applications.

I am not a little pleased that this Work of mine can possibly meet with no Censurers: For what Objections can be made against a Writer who relates only plain Facts that happened in such distant Countries, where we have not the least Interest with respect either to Trade or Negotiations? I have carefully avoided every Fault with which common Writers of Travels are often too justly charged. Besides, I meddle not the least with any *Party*, but write without Passion, Prejudice, or Ill-will against any Man or Number of Men whatsoever. I write for the noblest End, to inform and instruct

Mankind, over whom I may, without Breach of Modesty, pretend to some Superiority, from the Advantages I received by conversing so long among the most accomplished *Houyhnhnms*. I write without any View towards Profit or Praise. I never suffer a Word to pass that may look like Reflection, or possibly give the least Offence even to those who are most ready to take it. So that, I hope, I may with Justice pronounce myself an Author perfectly blameless; against whom the Tribes of Answerers, Considerers, Observers, Reflecters, Detecters, Remarkers, will never be able to find Matter for exercising their Talents.

I confess, it was whispered to me, that I was bound in Duty as a Subject of *England*, to have given in a Memorial to a Secretary of State, at my first coming over; because, whatever Lands are discovered by a Subject, belong to the Crown. But I doubt, whether our Conquests in the Countries I treat of, would be as easy as those of *Ferdinando Cortez** over the naked *Americans*. The *Lilliputians* I think, are hardly worth the Charge of a Fleet and Army to reduce them; and I question whether it might be prudent or safe to attempt the *Brobdingnagians*: Or, whether an *English* Army would be much at their Ease with the Flying Island over their Heads. The *Houyhnhnms*, indeed, appear not to be so well prepared for war, a Science to which they are perfect Strangers, and especially against missive Weapons.* However, supposing myself to be a Minister of State, I could never give my Advice for invading them. Their Prudence, Unanimity, Unacquaintedness with Fear, and their Love of their Country would amply supply all Defects in the military Art. Imagine twenty Thousand of them breaking into the Midst of an *European* Army, confounding the Ranks, overturning the Carriages, battering the Warriors Faces into Mummy,* by terrible Yerks* from their hinder Hoofs: For they would well deserve the Character given to *Augustus*; *Recalcitrat undique tutus.** But instead of Proposals for conquering that magnanimous Nation, I rather wish they were in a Capacity or Disposition to send a sufficient Number of their Inhabitants for civilizing *Europe*; by teaching us the first Principles of Honour, Justice, Truth, Temperance, publick Spirit, Fortitude, Chastity, Friendship, Benevolence, and Fidelity. The *Names* of all which Virtues are still retained among us in most Languages, and are to be met with in modern as well as ancient Authors; which I am able to assert from my own small Reading.

But, I had another Reason which made me less forward to enlarge his Majesty's Dominions by my Discoveries: To say the Truth, I had conceived a few Scruples with relation to the distributive* Justice of Princes upon those Occasions. For Instance, A Crew of Pyrates are driven by a Storm they know not whither; at length a Boy discovers Land from the Top-mast; they go on Shore to rob and plunder; they see an harmless People, are entertained with Kindness, they give the Country a new Name, they take formal Possession of it for the King, they set up a rotten Plank or a Stone for a Memorial, they murder two or three Dozen of the Natives, bring away a Couple more by Force for a Sample, return home, and get their Pardon. Here commences a new Dominion acquired with a Title by *Divine Right*. Ships are sent with the first Opportunity; the Natives driven out or destroyed, their Princes tortured to discover their Gold;* a free Licence given to all Acts of Inhumanity and Lust; the Earth reeking with the Blood of its Inhabitants: And this execrable Crew of Butchers employed in so pious an Expedition, is a *modern Colony* sent to convert* and civilize an idolatrous and barbarous People.

But this Description,* I confess, doth by no means affect the *British* Nation, who may be an Example to the whole World for their Wisdom, Care, and Justice in planting Colonies; their liberal Endowments* for the Advancement of Religion and Learning; their Choice of devout and able Pastors to propagate *Christianity*; their Caution in stocking their Provinces with People of sober Lives and Conversations from this the Mother Kingdom; their strict Regard to the Distribution of Justice, in supplying the Civil Administration through all their Colonies with Officers of the greatest Abilities, utter Strangers to Corruption: And to crown all, by sending the most vigilant and virtuous Governors, who have no other Views than the Happiness of the People over whom they preside, and the Honour of the King their Master.

But, as those Countries which I have described do not appear to have a Desire of being conquered, and enslaved, murdered or driven out by Colonies; nor abound either in Gold, Silver, Sugar or Tobacco; I did humbly conceive they were by no Means proper Objects of our Zeal, our Valour, or our Interest. However, if those whom it more concerns, think fit to be of another Opinion, I am ready to depose, when I shall be lawfully called, That no *European* did ever visit these Countries before me. I mean, if the Inhabitants ought to be believed.*

But, as to the Formality of taking Possession in my Sovereign's Name, it never came once into my Thoughts; and if it had, yet as my Affairs then stood, I should perhaps in point of Prudence and Self-Preservation have, put it off to a better Opportunity.

Having thus answered the *only* Objection that can be raised against me as a Traveller; I here take a final Leave of my Courteous Readers, and return to enjoy my own Speculations in my little Garden at *Redriff*; to apply those excellent Lessons of Virtue which I learned among the *Houyhnhnms*; to instruct the *Yahoos* of my own Family as far as I shall find them docible Animals; to behold my Figure often in a Glass, and thus if possible habituate my self by Time to tolerate the Sight of a human Creature: To lament the Brutality of *Houyhnhnms* in my own Country, but always treat their Persons with Respect, for the Sake of my noble Master, his Family, his Friends, and the whole *Houyhnhnm* Race, whom these of ours have the Honour to resemble in all their Lineaments, however their Intellectuals came to degenerate.

I began last Week to permit my Wife to sit at Dinner with me, at the farthest End of a long Table; and to answer (but with the utmost Brevity) the few Questions I asked her. Yet the Smell of a *Yahoo* continuing very offensive, I always keep my Nose well stopt with Rue, Lavender, or Tobacco-Leaves. And although it be hard for a Man late in Life to remove old Habits; I am not altogether out of Hopes in some Time to suffer a Neighbour *Yahoo* in my Company, without the Apprehensions I am yet under of his Teeth or his Claws.

My Reconcilement to the *Yahoo*-kind in general might not be so difficult, if they would be content with those Vices and Follies only which Nature hath entitled them to. I am not in the least provoked at the Sight of a Lawyer, a Pick-pocket, a Colonel, a Fool, a Lord, a Gamester, a Politician, a Whoremunger, a Physician, an Evidence,* a Suborner, an Attorney, a Traytor, or the like: This is all according to the due Course of Things: But, when I behold a Lump of Deformity, and Diseases both in Body and Mind, smitten with *Pride*, it immediately breaks all the Measures of my Patience; neither shall I ever be able to comprehend how such an Animal and such a Vice could tally together. The wise and virtuous *Houyhnhnms*, who abound in all Excellencies that can adorn a rational Creature, have no Name for this Vice in their Language, which hath no Terms to express any thing that is evil, except those whereby they describe the detestable Qualities of their *Yahoos*; among which they were not able to distinguish this of Pride, for want of thoroughly understanding Human Nature, as it sheweth it self in other Countries, where that Animal presides. But I, who had more Experience, could plainly observe some Rudiments of it among the wild *Yahoos*.

But the *Houyhnhnms*, who live under the Government of Reason, are no more proud of the good Qualities they possess, than I should be for not wanting a Leg or an Arm, which no Man in his Wits would boast of, although he must be miserable without them. I dwell the longer upon this Subject from the Desire I have to make the Society of an *English Yahoo* by any Means not insupportable; and therefore I here intreat those who have any Tincture of this absurd Vice, that they will not presume to appear in my Sight.*

FINIS.

EXPLANATORY NOTES

The notes in this edition are indebted to Paul Turner, editor of the Oxford University Press edition of *Gulliver's Travels* in 1971 (published as a World's Classics paperback in 1986). Paul Turner's notes are the basis for the annotation in this new edition and many of Turner's glosses, and extensive notes (identified as PT) remain unchanged or only slightly altered here. There is a vast scholarly commentary on *Gulliver's Travels* and its contexts, and many sources, analogues, and allusions have been discovered. A comprehensive handbook of Swift's library and reading identifying where Swift is known to have quoted from, referred to, or alluded to an author in his writings is Dirk F. Passmann and Heinz J. Vienken, *The Library and Reading of Jonathan Swift: A Bio-Bibliographical Handbook* (Frankfurt am Main: Peter Lang, 2003–). These notes attempt to focus on essential explanation indicating sources, allusions, and analogues which seem particularly germane to an understanding of the meaning and resonance of a passage. Words and phrases defined in standard dictionaries such as the *Concise Oxford Dictionary* are not normally glossed here.

All references to classical texts are taken from the relevant volume in the Loeb Classical Library (Cambridge: Harvard University Press) unless otherwise stated. Biblical references are to the King James Authorized Version. References to Shakespeare are to *The Oxford Shakespeare*, General Editor Stanley Wells (Oxford University Press).

Abbreviations

Bacon	Francis Bacon, *The Advancement of Learning and New Atlantis*, ed. Arthur Johnston (Oxford: Clarendon Press, 1974)
Boccalini	*Advertisements from Parnassus. Written Originally in Italian. By the Famous Trajano Boccalini. Newly Done into English, and adapted to the Present Times . . . By N.N. Esq* (London: Printed for Richard Smith, 1704)
Bonner	Willard Hallam Bonner, *Captain William Dampier: Buccaneer-Author* (Stanford, Calif.: Stanford University Press, 1934)
Burton	Robert Burton, *The Anatomy of Melancholy*, ed. Thomas C. Faulkner, Nicolas K. Kiessling, Rhonda L. Blair, introd. J. B. Bamborough, 6 vols. (Oxford: Clarendon Press, 1989–2000). Reference is by partition, section, member, subsection, and page number
Cervantes	Miguel de Cervantes Saavedra, *The Ingenious Hidalgo Don Quixote de la Mancha*, trans. John Rutherford (London: Penguin, 2000, repr. 2003)
Companion	*The Cambridge Companion to Jonathan Swift*, ed. Christopher Fox (Cambridge: Cambridge University Press, 2003)

Constitution	Xenophon, *Constitution of the Lacedaemonians*, in *Scripta Minora*, trans. E. C. Marchant, Loeb Classical Library, supplemented edition (London: William Heinemann; Cambridge, Mass.: Harvard University Press, 1968)
Corr.	*The Correspondence of Jonathan Swift, D.D.*, ed. David Woolley, 4 vols. (Frankfurt am Main: Peter Lang, 1999–)
Cruickshanks	Eveline Cruickshanks, *The Glorious Revolution* (Houndmills: Macmillan, 2000)
Cyrus	Andrew Michael Ramsay, *The Travels of Cyrus*, 2 vols. (London, 1727)
Dryden	*The Works of John Dryden*, ed. H. T. Swedenberg, Jr., et al., 20 vols. (Berkeley and Los Angeles: University of California Press, 1956–2000)
Eddy	W. A. Eddy, *Gulliver's Travels: A Critical Study* (Princeton: Princeton University Press, 1923)
Ehrenpreis	Irvin Ehrenpreis, *Swift: The Man, His Works, and the Age*, 3 vols. (London: Methuen, 1962–83)
ELN	*English Language Notes*
Englishman	Richard Steele, *The Englishman: A Political Journal*, ed. Rae Blanchard (Oxford: Clarendon Press, 1955)
Firth	Sir Charles Firth, 'The Political Significance of "Gulliver's Travels" ', in *Essays Historical & Literary* (Oxford, 1938), 210–41
Frantz	R. W. Frantz, 'Swift's Yahoos and the Voyagers', *Modern Philology*, 29 (1931), 49–57
GGG	Claude Rawson, *God, Gulliver, and Genocide: Barbarism and the European Imagination, 1492–1945* (Oxford: Oxford University Press, 2001)
Gough	Jonathan Swift, *Gulliver's Travels*, ed. A. B. Gough (Oxford: Clarendon Press, 1915)
GT	*Gulliver's Travels*
Hakluyt	Richard Hakluyt, *The Principal Navigations, Voyages, Traffiques & Discoveries of the English Nation*, 12 vols. (Glasgow: James MacLehose, 1903–5)
Histoire	Cyrano de Bergerac, *Histoire comique des états et empires de la lune et du soleil*, ed. P. L. Jacob (Paris: Adolphe Delahays, 1858)
HLQ	*Huntington Library Quarterly*
Hudibras	Samuel Butler, *Hudibras*, ed. John Wilders (Oxford: Clarendon Press, 1967)
JHI	*Journal of the History of Ideas*
Key	*A Key, Being Observations and Explanatory Notes, upon the Travels of Lemuel Gulliver. By Signor Corolini, a noble Venetian now residing in London. In a Letter to Dean Swift. Translated from the Italian Original*. 4 Parts (London: [Edmund Curll], 1726)

Lansdowne	George Granville, Baron Lansdowne, *A Letter from a Noble-Man Abroad, to his Friend in England* (London, 1722)
Library	Dirk F. Passmann and Heinz J. Vienken, *The Library and Reading of Jonathan Swift: A Bio-Bibliographical Handbook, Part I: Swift's Library in Four Volumes* (Frankfurt am Main: Peter Lang, 2003)
Linschoten	*John Huyghen Van Linschoten. His Discours of Voyages into ye Easte & West Indies* (London, 1598)
Lock	F. P. Lock, *The Politics of Gulliver's Travels* (Oxford: Clarendon Press, 1980)
Lucian	Lucian, *Satirical Sketches*, trans. Paul Turner (Harmondsworth: Penguin, 1968)
'Lycurgus'	Plutarch, 'Lycurgus', in *Plutarch's Lives*, trans. Bernadotte Perrin, 11 vols. (Cambridge, Mass.: Harvard University Press; London: William Heinemann, 1914, 1967 repr.), vol. i.
Memoirs	*The Memoirs of the Extraordinary Life, Works, and Discoveries of Martinus Scriblerus*, ed. Charles Kerby-Miller (New Haven: Yale University Press, 1950; repr. Oxford: Oxford University Press, 1988)
MLN	*Modern Language Notes*
MLR	*Modern Language Review*
Montaigne	*The Complete Essays of Montaigne*, trans. Donald M. Frame (Stanford, Calif.: Stanford University Press, 1958)
Nicolson	Marjorie Nicolson, *Science and Imagination* (Ithaca, NY: Cornell University Press, 1956)
N&Q	*Notes and Queries*
OED	*Oxford English Dictionary*
Paradise Lost	John Milton, *Paradise Lost*, ed. Alastair Fowler, 2nd edn. (London: Longman, 1998)
Passmann	Dirk F. Passmann, 'Gulliver's "Temple of Fame": Glubbdubdrib Revisited', in Hermann J. Real and Helgard Stöver-Leidig (eds.), *Reading Swift: Papers from the Fourth Münster Symposium on Jonathan Swift* (Munich: Wilhelm Fink, 2003), 329–48
POAS	*Poems on Affairs of State*, ed. G. deF. Lord and others, 7 vols. (New Haven, 1963–75)
Poems	*The Poems of Jonathan Swift*, ed. Harold Williams, 2nd edn., 3 vols. (Oxford: Clarendon Press, 1958)
PQ	*Philological Quarterly*
PT	Paul Turner's annotation in Jonathan Swift, *Gulliver's Travels*, ed. with an Introduction and Notes by Paul Turner, Oxford World's Classics (Oxford: Oxford University Press, 1986; repr. 1998)
PTA	*The Philosophical Transactions Abridg'd and Dispos'd under General Heads*, vols. iv, v: *1700–20*, ed. B. Motte (1721); vol. vi: *1719–33*, ed. J. Eames and J. Martyn (1734)

Purchas	Samuel Purchas, *Hakluytus Posthumus or Purchas His Pilgrimes*, 20 vols. (Glasgow: James MacLehose, 1905–7)
PW	*The Prose Writings of Jonathan Swift*, ed. Herbert Davis et al., 16 vols. (Oxford: Basil Blackwell, 1939–74)
Quinlan	Maurice J. Quinlan, 'Lemuel Gulliver's Ships', *Philological Quarterly*, 46 (1967), 412–17
Rabelais	François Rabelais, *The Histories of Gargantua and Pantagruel*, trans. J. M. Cohen (Harmondsworth: Penguin, 1955)
Rawson	Claude Rawson, *Gulliver and the Gentle Reader: Studies in Swift and Our Time* (London: Routledge & Kegan Paul, 1973)
Reading Swift	Hermann J. Real and Helgard Stöver-Leidig (eds.), *Reading Swift: Papers from the Fourth Münster Symposium on Jonathan Swift* (Munich: Wilhelm Fink, 2003)
Real/Vienken	H. J. Real and H. J. Vienken, 'Lemuel Gulliver's Ships Once More', *N&Q*, NS 30 (1983), 518–19
Somers Tracts	*A Collection of Scarce and Valuable Tracts*, ed. Walter Scott, 2nd edn., 13 vols. (London, 1809–15)
SP	*Studies in Philology*
Spectator	*The Spectator*, ed. Donald F. Bond, 5 vols. (Oxford: Clarendon Press, 1965)
Teerink	*A Bibliography of the Writings of Jonathan Swift*, 2nd edn., revised and corrected by H. Teerink, ed. Arthur H. Scouten (Philadelphia: University of Pennsylvania Press, 1963)
Temple	*The Works of Sir William Temple*, 2 vols. (London, 1740)
TSE	*Tulane Studies in English*
TSLL	*Texas Studies in Literature and Language*
Utopia	Thomas More, *Utopia*, ed. George M. Logan and Robert M. Adams, rev. edn., Cambridge Texts in the History of Political Thought (Cambridge: Cambridge University Press, 2002)
Voyages	*Dampier's Voyages*, ed. John Masefield, 2 vols. (London: E. Grant Richards, 1906)
Wafer	Lionel Wafer, *A New Voyage and Description of the Isthmus of America*, ed. L. E. Elliott Joyce (Oxford: Hakluyt Society, 1934)
Ward	Ned Ward, *The London Spy*, ed. Paul Hyland from the Fourth Edition of 1709 (East Lansing: Colleagues Press, 1993)
Wharton	*The Duke of Wharton's Reasons for Leaving his native Country, and espousing the Causes of his Royal Majesty King James III. in a Letter to his Friends in Great Britain and Ireland* [1726]
Williams	*The Correspondence of Jonathan Swift*, ed. Harold Williams, 5 vols. (Oxford: Clarendon Press, 1963–5)

2 *Frontispiece portrait. Splendide Mendax*: Gloriously False. The phrase from Horace *Odes*, III. xi. 35 is positive. The motto presents Gulliver as a magnificent liar for noble ends.

5 *Advertisement.* First added in Faulkner's edition of 1735.

Mr. Sympson's Letter to Captain Gulliver: in fact, it is Captain Gulliver's letter to his Cousin Sympson. See the discussion of the front matter, Introduction, pp. xv–xxii.

Interpolations . . . made by a Person since deceased: Swift complained that the Reverend Andrew Tooke (d. 1732), a silent partner and mentor of the London publisher Benjamin Motte, had altered the manuscript of the *Travels* before publication. In October 1733, preparing for the new edition to be published in Dublin by George Faulkner, Swift reminded his friend Charles Ford 'how much I complained of Motts suffering some friend of his (I suppose it was Mr Took a Clergy-man now dead) not onely to blot out some things that he thought might give offence, but to insert a good deal of trash contrary to the Author's manner and Style, and Intention' (*Corr.*, iii. 693. For Swift's complaints that his satire in the first edition of 1726 had been altered by Motte and Tooke, see also *Corr.*, iii. 57, 66–69, 708)

compliment the Memory: Part IV, chapter vi of Motte's first edition contains an extended passage that was cut from the revised edition published by Faulkner in Dublin in 1735. The passage contains a panegyric of Queen Anne that is also a transparent attack by innuendo on the honour of King George I and imputes a connection between the monarch and his corrupt ministry. The passage was specifically disclaimed as an interpolated paragraph by Charles Ford, writing to Motte, as a friend of the author, on 3 January 1727 (*Corr.*, iii. 66). In 'A Letter from Capt. Gulliver, to his Cousin Sympson', Swift has Gulliver 'renounce' all interpolations, 'particularly a Paragraph about her Majesty the late Queen *Anne*'. The chapter heading in the Motte edition provocatively praised Queen Anne, reading in part: '*A Continuation of the State of* England, *so well governed by a Queen as to need no first Minister*'. The 'interpolation' reads as follows: 'I TOLD him, that our She Governor or Queen having no Ambition to gratify, no Inclination to satisfy of extending her Power to the Injury of her Neighbours, or the Prejudice of her own Subjects, was therefore so far from needing a corrupt Ministry to carry on or cover any sinister Designs, that She not only directs her own Actions to the Good of her People, conducts them by the Direction, and restrains them within the Limitation of the Laws of her own Country; but submits the Behaviour and Acts of those She intrusts with the Administration of Her Affairs to the Examination of Her great Council, and subjects them to the Penalties of the Law; and therefore never puts any such Confidence in any of her Subjects as to entrust them with the whole and entire Administration of her Affairs: But I added, that in some former Reigns here, and in many other Courts of *Europe* now, where Princes grew indolent and careless of their own Affairs through a constant Love and Pursuit of Pleasure, they made use of such an Administrator, as I had mentioned, under the Title of *first* or *chief Minister of State*, the Description of which, as far as it may be collected not only from their Actions, but from the Letters, Memoirs, and Writings published by themselves, the Truth of which has not yet been disputed, may be allowed to be as follows: That he is a Person' (*PW* xi. 318). Approval of Queen Anne would certainly have been objectionable to the Hanoverian Whig government which had prosecuted the leaders of Queen Anne's Tory ministry for treason. The prosecutions of Jacobite publicists during the reigns of George I and II show that the Whig government was willing and able to punish reflections on the ruling dynasty. It seems unlikely that Motte would have inserted a passage that increased the offensiveness of Swift's satire and the risk of prosecution by attacking the King as well as his '*First* or *Chief Minister of State*'. The awkwardly composed passage may well have been Tooke's inadequate attempt to soften the anti-Hanoverian satire he may have found in Swift's original manuscript. In Faulkner's 1735 edition the scathing satire is aimed at Robert Walpole as '*First* or *Chief Minister of State*' not, as in 1726, at the King and Walpole.

a very worthy Gentleman: Swift's friend Charles Ford, whose interleaved copy of the first edition of *GT* with manuscript corrections in his hand is now in the National Art Library in the Victoria and Albert Museum in London.

Book in Sheets: books were often bought with the pages unbound.

7 *Gulliver*: the choice of name for the putative author of the *Travels* seems to have been made at a late stage. Swift first names Lemuel Gulliver in a letter to Benjamin Motte of 8 August 1726 (see *Corr.*, iii. 9–12). The name Captain Lemuel Gulliver appears in the paratexts of the book (on the frontispiece, title-page, Advertisement, 'The Publisher to the Reader', and in this prefatory Letter to Sympson) but the voyager is not named in the main text. The first name 'Lemuel', which means 'dedicated to God' in Hebrew, may allude to the biblical King Lemuel (Proverbs 31: 1–9). The prophetic words of King Lemuel in Proverbs might be thought relevant to some of the targets of Swift's satire. They include: 'Give not thy strength unto women, nor thy ways to that which destroyeth kings' (31: 3); 'Open thy mouth for the dumb in the cause of all such as are appointed to destruction' (31: 8); and 'Open thy mouth, judge righteously, and plead the cause of the poor and needy' (31: 9). The view of King Lemuel in Proverbs 31: 6, 7: 'Give strong drink unto him that is ready to perish, and wine unto those that be of heavy hearts'; 'Let him drink, and forget his poverty, and remember his misery no more' was shared by Swift (a wine lover) in his Irish pamphleteering against an additional duty on wine. Swift argued that wine is essential for the singularly impoverished and miserable Irish people, it was the only thing that made life in Hanoverian Ireland endurable: 'there is no nation yet known, in either hemisphere, where the people of all conditions are more in want of some cordial, to keep up their spirits, than in this of ours. I am not in jest' (*PW* xii. 124). Swift, also like King Lemuel (Proverbs 31: 4–5), could warn against strong drink, and Gulliver under Houyhnhnm

influence in Part IV, chapter vi attacks the use of wine because it puts people out of their senses.

The first syllable of Lemuel's last name, Gulliver, might suggest the character's gullibility. A 'gull' is a dupe or fool. The final syllable 'ver' might signify veracity or truth. Gulliver is 'the dupe of truth', the cipher of the truth-telling satirist (see Cecil C. Seronsy, 'Some Proper Names in "Gulliver's Travels" ', *N&Q* 202 (1957), 471).

7 *Sympson*: the pseudonym used by Swift when negotiating with Motte before and after the publication of *GT*. Swift has given a fictitious after-life to a real Richard Sympson, one of the copyright holders of Sir William Temple's writings which Swift had edited and prepared for the press in the 1690s. Richard Sympson has become Gulliver's cousin, copy-editor, and agent (see *Corr.*, i. 119, n. 4). The name is probably also part of the joke that Gulliver is a fiction and *GT* is a mock travel book. Sympson might be recalling William Symson, the fictitious author of *A New Voyage to the East-Indies* (1715) which was a plagiarism from an earlier travel book. This spurious voyage book is one of the sources Swift draws upon in *GT* (see R. W. Frantz, 'Gulliver's "Cousin Sympson" ', *HLQ* 1 (1938), 329–34).

A Letter from Capt. Gulliver to His Cousin Sympson. First published in 1735 but apparently intended for an earlier revised second edition in 1727. The Letter is dated '*April* 2, 1727', the day after April Fool's Day, perhaps a wry reference to the fact that this travel book is a hoax. Swift pulled off some brilliant April Fool's Day hoaxes during his career. It was an important date in his calendar.

Dampier: William Dampier (1652–1715), naval captain, buccaneer, privateer, circumnavigator, hydrographer, and author. His voyage writings, such as *A New Voyage Round the World* (1697) mentioned here, are among the travel books parodied by Swift. Dampier admitted that what he wrote was corrected by friends (*Voyages*, ii. 342).

a Paragraph: the passage is complained about in the Advertisement, see the fourth note to the Advertisement, above.

of our Composition: made like us, that is, a human being.

my Master Houyhnhnm: the horse that takes charge of Gulliver in Part IV. Gulliver's references to Part IV are bewildering to a first-time reader.

Godolphin . . . and . . . Oxford: Sidney Godolphin (1645–1712) was Lord Treasurer from 1702 until 1710. He was succeeded by Robert Harley (1661–1724), Lord Treasurer 1710–14, made first Earl of Oxford in 1711.

say the thing that was not: the Houyhnhnms' expression for lying or falsehood.

I do hardly know mine own Work: Swift complained of the 'mangled and murdered Pages' of the Motte edition (*Corr.*, iii. 693).

Inuendo (as I think you called it.): as defined in the *OED* an innuendo is an oblique hint, indirect suggestion; an allusive remark concerning a person or thing, especially of a depreciatory kind. It was a legal term for the construction put upon a word or expression, especially an injurious or libellous meaning or signification alleged of words not in themselves injurious or actionable. It was very much a vogue term for what the government regarded as seditious indirect hints and allusions. In a work attributed to Daniel Defoe an '*Innuendo*' is described as 'a rare new *Law-figure*' used in Charles II's reign (*An Account of the Late Horrid Conspiracy to Depose Their Present Majesties K. William and Q. Mary* (London, 1691), 29–30). The Walpolean Administration was said to be destroying the liberty of the press in its punishment of writers allegedly using seditious and treasonable innuendo (see *The Doctrine of Innuendo's Discuss'd, or the Liberty of the Press Maintain'd: Being some Thoughts upon the present Treatment of the Printer and Publishers of the Craftsman* (London, 1731)).

Yahoos: brutish humanoid species in Part IV.

these: the Houyhnhnms.

those: the Yahoos.

8 *Retirement hither*: readers are informed in 'The Publisher to the Reader' that Gulliver now lives retired near Newark in Nottinghamshire.

Smithfield: an open area north-west of St Paul's Cathedral where heretics or martyrs and their books were burned in the sixteenth century.

Cotten: cotton was used to make paper.

Libels . . . Keys . . . Reflections . . . Memoirs . . . Second Parts: the popularity and provocation of *GT* generated a range of responses in print including lampoons, explanatory keys, pamphlet attacks, continuations, and adaptations. The list of 'Gulliveriana' given in the standard Teerink-Scouten bibliography (see Teerink, 244–52; 34 items up to 1735) vastly understates the phenomenal response to *GT*. For a comprehensive record, see Jeanne K. Welcher (ed.), *Gulliveriana VIII: An Annotated List of Gulliveriana, 1721–1800* (Delmar, NY: Scholars' Facsimiles & Reprints, 1988). For modern facsimile reproductions of 'Gulliveriana', see *Swiftiana*, V–VIII (New York: Garland, 1974) and Jeanne K. Welcher et al. (eds.), *Gulliveriana*, I–VIII (Gainesville, Fla., and Delmar, NY: Scholars' Facsimiles & Reprints, 1970–88).

9 *confound the Times*: Gulliver's complaints are a typical author's cant, blaming the printer for all mistakes. There is evidence that the printers of the early editions tried to fix discrepancies in the times and dates which were almost certainly the result of Swift's own carelessness. The time scheme in Faulkner's 1735 edition is generally consistent. On this textual issue, see Michael Treadwell, 'The Text of *Gulliver's Travels*, Again', *Swift Studies*, 10 (1995), 62–79 (p. 71).

Manuscript . . . destroyed: the printer's copy, a transcript of the original manuscript, was destroyed by Motte, thus removing incriminating evidence, a routine practice among eighteenth-century publishers, especially of politically sensitive works. Swift's holograph, in the safe custody of his friend Charles Ford, seems to have survived into the second half of the eighteenth century, see David Woolley, 'The Stemma of *Gulliver's Travels*: A Second Note', *Swift Studies*, 17 (2002), 75–87.

9 *stand to them*: insist on them.

nor now in Use: indeed, as Swift largely took the nautical language from Samuel Sturmy's *The Mariner's Magazine* published in 1669.

deliver our Conceptions: express our thoughts.

Utopia: the word was first coined by Sir Thomas More as the name for the imaginary island described in his book of 1516. 'Utopia' means 'no place', but the word also puns on 'eutopia', meaning happy or fortunate place, and has come to mean a perfect society. Sir Thomas More's *Utopia* (1516) is one of Swift's sources. More's Utopians like Swift's Houyhnhnms live according to reason and nature. Swift's Houyhnhnmland like More's Utopia exhibits, at least for many modern readers, both attractive and unattractive features. No one starves there but there is little personal freedom.

Truth immediately . . . Conviction: a Houyhnhnm doctrine.

10 *these miserable Animals*: Gulliver's human critics.

11 *The Publisher to the Reader*: this was the preface to the text proper in Motte's first edition of 1726. Publisher here means 'editor'.

Redriff: Rotherhithe.

Banbury: the town of Banbury in Oxfordshire was associated with Puritan fanaticism. Swift refers to 'a *Banbury Saint*' in his satire on Puritan Enthusiasm in *A Discourse Concerning the Mechanical Operation of the Spirit* (*PW* i. 184). PT notes that several Gulliver tombstones are still legible in the churchyard of St Mary's, and the parish register records the burial of a Samuel Gulliver on 17 Aug. 1728. Like Lemuel, Samuel was an innkeeper, and the name of his inn, the 'Dolphin' (on the south side of the Horsefair), had associations with seafaring. Samuel's wife, like Lemuel's daughter, was called Elizabeth. There is a local tradition that Swift once lodged on the opposite side of the Horsefair, probably at 'The Three Tuns', the principal inn at Banbury during the eighteenth century. He may have passed through the town in the summer of 1726, on his way to visit his old friend William Rollinson, whose family home was at Chadlington, about 15 miles south-west of Banbury. PT (see *Corr.*, iii. 7 n. 2; 11 n. 1).

Veracity: the word repeats the irony of 'true' in Lucian's *True History*, a deliberately fantastic traveller's tale which was one of Swift's sources. PT.

twice as large: a parody of Dampier, who claimed to have often omitted 'Sea Phrases, to gratify the Land Reader', and excluded enough nautical information from *A New Voyage* to make up another whole book, *Voyages and Descriptions* (Bonner, 162–3). PT.

Winds and Tides: Dampier wrote *A Discourse of the Trade-Winds, Breezes, Storms, Seasons of the Year, Tides and Currents of the Torrid Zone throughout the World* (see *Voyages*, ii. 227–321).

Part I. A Voyage to Lilliput

13 *Lilliput*: there have been ingenious attempts to decipher the fictional place names and languages in *GT*. Many of these suggested decodings are recorded in the explanatory notes of Paul Turner's Oxford edition of *GT* and in studies such as Paul Odell Clark, 'A Gulliver Dictionary', *Studies in Philology*, 50 (1953), 592–624. While many of Swift's invented words may teasingly suggest puns, anagrams, and language games involving letter substitutions, on the whole, the invented words and languages seem to be mainly delightful nonsense. Swift's linguistic playfulness on display in *GT* is also evidenced in the 'little language' used in his correspondence with Esther Johnson (known as the *Journal to Stella*, see *PW* xv and xvi) and in the punning language games he enjoyed with his friend Thomas Sheridan. *GT* has given several words to the language, including 'lilliputian' meaning a little or diminutive person or thing.

15 *My father . . . Cambridge*: the details here seem to suggest that Gulliver is an average Englishman: the middle son of a father of middling social estate, born in the English midlands. He is educated at a Cambridge college of Puritan foundation implying perhaps that he is solidly Whiggish and Protestant. The opening reads like a parody of the manner of voyage authors reporting personal details, and of the start of the Protestant Dissenter Daniel Defoe's *Robinson Crusoe* in particular. Defoe's fictional voyage hero is also a third son.

Fourteen: Swift entered Trinity College Dublin at 14 years of age.

Leyden: Leiden in the Netherlands. The university was famous for teaching medicine ('Physick') and was also a natural educational destination abroad for Dissenting Protestants in England.

Swallow: with the exception of the Dutch ship the 'Amboyna' in Part III, all of Gulliver's ships have the names recorded of real contemporary ships in the *Calendar of Treasury Books* (Quinlan, 412–17) and in the huge voyage collections of Richard Hakluyt and Samuel Purchas (Real/Vienken, 518–19). Swift's library contained Hakluyt's *Principal Navigations* (either in the 1589 or the 1598–1600 edition, see *Library*, Part I, vol. ii, 778–83) and *Hakluytus Posthumous, or Purchas His Pilgrimes* (1625, see *Library*, Part I, vol. ii, 1546–51). Ships called *Swallow*, *Adventure*, *Antelope*, and *Hopewell* are recorded several times in a number of London newspapers in the single month of August 1722 (Real/Vienken, 519). A '*Swallow*, was among the vessels with which Sir John Hawkins conducted a profitable slave trade in Guinea in the 1560s' and other ships with this name are mentioned in Purchas (Real/Vienken, 518) and in the *Calendar of Treasury Books* (Quinlan, 412–13).

15 *Levant*: eastern Mediterranean, the Near East.

Old Jury: Old Jewry, in the City of London, the commercial and legal centre of London.

Mrs: a polite title used for single and married women.

four Hundred Pounds: a substantial amount but very difficult to relate to modern money. It was estimated that a contemporary eighteenth-century tradesman's family and servants could live comfortably for a year on about £350. Gulliver as a student in Leiden was expected to maintain himself on 'Thirty Pounds a Year'.

I married . . . Portion: possibly a veiled reference to Defoe, who had started life as a hosier, married an heiress called Mary Tuffley, rapidly spent her dowry of nearly £4,000, and passed five months in Newgate Prison. PT. Swift affected not to know Defoe's name, referring to the notorious Dissenter and Whig author in one pamphlet as 'the Fellow that was *pilloryed*, I have forgot his Name' (*PW* ii. 113).

Master Bates: it is sometimes suggested that the possible pun on the surgeon's name, elaborately built up with earlier references to 'Mr *James Bates*', 'Mr *Bates*', 'my good Master Mr *Bates*', and 'Mr *Bates*, my Master', alludes to the panic about masturbation generated by sensational contemporary publications such as the best-selling *Onania, or The Heinous Sin of Self-Pollution, and All Its Frightful Consequences, in Both Sexes, Considered* (in its eighth edition in 1723). The concern about 'Masturbation' among young men is amusingly exploited in Bernard Mandeville's *A Modest Defence of Public Stews* (London, 1724): 'they are every Day committing *Rapes* upon their own Bodies' with 'the Agility of their Wrists' and 'laying *violent Hands* upon themselves' (pp. 30, 31). The reader may already be beginning to suspect that this voyage book will be giving details not found in real voyage books or in fictional works like Defoe's *Robinson Crusoe*.

16 *I was Surgeon . . . to the East and West-Indies . . . Addition to my Fortune*: Gulliver is vague about the nature of his profitable voyages but he is almost certainly involved in the slave–sugar trade in the West Indies. One of the surgeon's tasks on slaving voyages was the selection of slaves.

Wapping: a dockland district, on the north side of the Thames.

Antelope . . . May 4th, 1699: on 3 June 1699, off the Cape of Good Hope, Dampier met the *Antelope* of London, bound for the East Indies (*Voyages*, ii. 416; Bonner, 168). PT.

trouble the Reader: one of Dampier's favourite phrases (Bonner, 164). PT.

Van Diemen's Land: the old name for Tasmania.

fifth of November: an important date on the Protestant and Whig calendar. The anniversary of the discovery of the Gunpowder Plot in 1605, and the day of the Prince of Orange's landing in England with a Dutch army in 1688 assisted, it was said, by a Providential Protestant wind. For Swift here it is the date of a shipwreck. Curll's *Key* finds in

Gulliver's shipwreck and misfortunes in the South Seas an allusion to the South Sea Bubble, a financial market crash in 1720 which saw a speculative boom in South Sea stock collapse, citing Swift's satiric poem 'The Bubble' where the bankrupt 'plunges in the Southern waves' (line 23, see *Poems*, 207–14; *Key*, Part I, p. 7).

a Cable's length: a nautical measure, 200 yards or 600 feet.

made a Shift: managed with difficulty.

17 *when I awaked*: Gulliver is perhaps imagined like Hercules being attacked by pygmies (Philostratus, *Imagines*, ii. 22) or like Samson being bound and imprisoned (Judges 15: 14; 16: 7–30). The Philistines 'put out' Samson's eyes, the Lilliputians later plan such a fate for Gulliver.

not six Inches high: Lilliputians are one-twelfth the size of humans, the scale of proportion in Lilliput is one to twelve, and since we are three dimensional, humans are therefore 1,728 times as large as Lilliputians. The scale is reversed in Brobdingnag, twelve to one. Powerfully used by Swift for purposes of satiric reduction and aggrandisement, the use of and interest in perspective also reflect the recent discovery of the microscope and the telescope.

Admiration: astonishment.

18 *Bombs*: shells.

Buff Jerkin: close-fitting leather jacket.

19 *Hogsheads*: large casks or barrels.

Wonders: Gulliver's gigantic exploits in eating, drinking, urinating, and defecating recall Gargantua's feats in Rabelais's *Gargantua and Pantagruel*, a favourite work of Swift's and an important source for *GT* (see *Library*, iii. 1559–70).

20 *determinate*: determined.

21 *Express*: special messenger.

Engines: machines.

22 *Half-Pike*: short pike carried by infantry officers.

an ancient Temple . . . polluted . . . by an unnatural Murder: 'bears so near a Resemblance to the *Banquetting-House* at *White-Hall*, before which Structure, King CHARLES I was Beheaded' (*Key*, Part I, pp. 7–8). Swift venerated the 'memory of that excellent King and blessed Martyr CHARLES I' describing the regicide in 1649 as a murder, for example, in a sermon preached in 1726, the year of the publication of *GT* (see *PW* ix. 219–31). The allusion to the martyrdom of Charles I is a sign of the political satire's High Church Tory rather than dissident Old Whig provenance as Old Whigs hated the Stuart king. Swift also honoured the memory of the executed Earl of Strafford 'that illustrious Earl who dyed to preserve The Church, his King and the old Constitution, so shattered and crazy almost ever since' (see Hermann J. Real, 'A New Letter from Swift: His Answer to the Earl of Strafford, 29 March 1735, Recovered', *Swift Studies*, 18 (2003), 20–5).

24 *Stang*: a rood or quarter of an acre.

my Maligners: this remark, though said by Gulliver, seems to come from Swift, whose writings, and especially *A Tale of a Tub*, had been accused of 'Filthiness', 'Lewdness', 'Immodesty', and of using 'the Language of the Stews' (Rawson, 7).

25 *had like to have cost*: very nearly cost.

Princes of the Blood: members of the royal family.

He is taller: in Joseph Addison's Latin mock-epic of 1699 'The Battle between the Pygmies and the Cranes' the pygmy monarch towers over his subjects rising to a height of almost 2 feet (the possible reminiscence is noted in *Key*, Part I, pp. 13–14).

His Features: the description of the Emperor of Lilliput's features is a sardonic allusion to George I with seditious innuendo. In sarcastic contrast George cut a short, thick, and awkward figure.

Austrian Lip: the thick underlip typical of the Habsburgs. George was neither Austrian nor a Habsburg but German. Contemporary Jacobite pamphleteers, however, attempted to discredit George's Protestant credentials by claiming that he was secretly pro-Catholic and in league with the Catholic House of Austria (see e.g. [Matthias Earbery], *An Historical Account of the Advantages that have Accrued to England by the Succession in the Illustrious House of Hanover, Part II* (London, 1722), 20, 37).

arched Nose: invokes the memory of William III who had an arched nose (*Key*, Part I, pp. 8–9), perhaps a reference to the fact that George I and the Hanoverian dynasty's right to rule derived from the Revolution settlement that followed William's invasion of England.

Countenance: bearing.

past his Prime: as was George I who was 66 when *GT* was published.

reigned about seven: George I had reigned seven years when Swift began writing *GT* in 1721.

between the Asiatick and the European: suggesting that he appears Turkish. George I had Turkish servants and was depicted as a Turkish-style oriental despot in Tory and Jacobite opposition propaganda (see e.g. [Francis Atterbury], *English Advice, to the Freeholders of England* [London, 1715], 24; *The Character of Sultan Galga, the present Cham of Tartary . . .* [*c.*1720].

26 *High and Low Dutch*: German and Dutch.

Lingua Franca: a mixture of Italian, French, Spanish, Greek, and Arabic used in the eastern Mediterranean where Gulliver had been in his earlier voyages.

Six Hundred Beds: mattresses.

four double: four deep.

27 *Beeves*: mature cattle. The details of Gulliver's gargantuan gastronomy here are an instance of the influence of Rabelais.

upon his own Demesnes: on the income from the Crown lands.

Subsidies: taxes levied for particular purposes.

28 *search me . . . Weapons*: a contemporary satiric application would be to activities of the Committee set up by the Whigs in 1715 to investigate members of Queen Anne's Tory government of 1710–14 for Jacobite conspiracy and to searches and confiscations during the Jacobite rebellion of 1715. 'The *Inventory* here given, of the *Effects* found about Mr. *Gulliver* by the *State-Officers*, is extremely entertaining, and the Application would have been easily made in the Time of the *Preston* Rebellion' (*Key*, Part I, p. 9).

29 *IMPRIMIS*: first of all (a legal term).

Foot-Cloth: carpet.

red Metal: copper.

31 *Closeness*: density and impermeability of its materials.

32 *Perspective*: telescope.

33 *Rope-Dancers*: a popular contemporary entertainment. Swift had already used rope-dancing as a satiric trope in his hostile 'Remarks' (*c.*1708) upon the anticlerical Whig Matthew Tindal's *The Rights of the Christian Church*: 'Put the Case, that walking on the slack Rope were the only Talent required by Act of Parliament for making a Man a Bishop; no Doubt, when a Man had done his Feat of Activity in Form, he might sit in the House of Lords, put on his Robes and his Rotchet, go down to his Palace, receive and spend his Rents; but it requireth very little Christianity to believe this Tumbler to be one whit more a Bishop than he was before' (*PW* ii. 75).

Flimnap: this satiric paradigm of a Royal favourite and first minister was seen by contemporaries as alluding to the Whig statesman Robert Walpole, Chancellor of the Exchequer in 1715 and a principal champion of the post-1688 settlement and supporter of the Hanoverian dynasty. Walpole took a severe line on Jacobite disaffection, vigorously pursuing Queen Anne's Tory ministers for treason, was active in the suppression of the 1715 Jacobite Rising, and led proceedings against Francis Atterbury, the Bishop of Rochester, for Jacobite conspiracy in 1722–3. Although he lost power during the Whig split of 1717, he emerged after the South Sea crisis in 1720 and following the deaths of the Whig leaders Sunderland and Stanhope in 1721–2 as the leading Whig minister. He was, in effect, the Whig prime minister of both George I and George II from 1721–2 to 1742. His political management secured the Hanoverian dynasty through a number of crises (including the controversy over the affair of Wood's halfpence in which Swift was one of Walpole's principal Irish polemical antagonists) and maintained Whig hegemony and the Tory party's proscription from office. Swift opposed him on religious, political, economic, and Irish issues. In an explicit, unpublished political allegory, *An Account of the Court and Empire of Japan* (written in 1728),

Swift satirized Walpole's government as arbitrary and corrupt and referred to Walpole as 'perfectly skilled, by long practice' in parliamentary management 'and dextrous in the purchasing of votes' (*PW* v. 101), recalling the references to Flimnap's skill and dexterity in *GT*. The Opposition press alluded to Walpole as a brazen man who made '*Britannia*' turn '*Rope-Dancer*' (*Robin's Panegyrick. Or, The Norfolk Miscellany* (London, [1729]), 81–4).

33 *Summerset*: somersault.

Reldresal: a type of the false friend and trimming politician, identified in modern commentary with various Whigs who, unlike Walpole, sometimes seemed disposed either to the Tories or to Swift: Lord Carteret, a Whig Secretary of State and Lord Lieutenant of Ireland, and the Earl of Stanhope, head of the Whig government in 1717–21 and a rival to Walpole, have been suggested. The *Key* linked Flimnap and Reldresal with Walpole and Lord Townshend, a Whig Secretary of State and Walpole's close political ally in the 1720s although their relationship deteriorated (*Key*, Part I, p. 13).

34 *one of the King's Cushions*: in the fifth *Drapier's Letter* (1724), an eastern king is said to put an unjust judge to death and stuff his hide into a cushion. Swift wonders 'what Number of such *Cushions*' the king had (*PW* x. 92). The satire in *GT* suggests that the corrupt and dexterous Flimnap (innuendo Walpole) has his neck saved at the court of an arbitrary oriental despot, the Emperor of Lilliput (innuendo King George).

three fine silken Threads: the colours correspond with the British Order of the Garter (blue), given to Walpole, May 1726; the Order of the Bath (red), revived by George I, May 1725; and the Order of the Thistle (green), revived by Queen Anne, 1703. The colours in the first edition of 1726 were purple, yellow, and white. Nevertheless, it was recognized that the 'Intent could be no other than to ridicule our *three* most noble Orders of the *Garter*, the *Thistle* and the *Bath*' (*Key*, Part I, p. 16; see also Mrs Howard to Swift, *c*.10 November 1726, *Corr.*, iii. 50). In the 1735 edition Swift is more specific. The 1735 text either restores the original colours that Motte may have altered in 1726 believing the satire to be too dangerous, or revises the colours to blue, red, and green since the satiric allusion had been recognized in 1726 without provoking a government prosecution. The seditious point of Swift's satire was noted, for example, in Curll's *Key* where it is loyally answered: 'But indeed the Meannesses to which the *Lilliputians* are subjected by an Arbitrary Prince can never be the fate of *Britons* thanks to the Happiness of our admirable Constitution!' (*Key*, Part I, p. 16).

35 *discovered*: revealed.

close Chair: sedan chair.

36 *the Emperor . . . Metropolis*: the militaristic Emperor, like George I, has a large standing army which was the object of Swiftian and Opposition antipathy. The Whig government ordered troops to be camped in Hyde

Park in 1722 during the Jacobite emergency after the discovery of the Atterbury Plot.

Colossus: the statue that stood astride the harbour entrance at Rhodes, one of the Seven Wonders of the Ancient World. The behaviour of the younger officers seems to recall Shakespeare, *Julius Caesar*, I. ii. 135–7: 'Why, man, he doth bestride the narrow world | Like a colossus, and we petty men | Walk under his huge legs and peep about.' PT.

in a Breast: abreast.

37 *Skyresh Bolgolam*: a type of the implacable and malignant courtier. A topical application might have been to the Earl of Nottingham, a former first Lord of the Admiralty, who was called 'Dismal' because of his 'dark and dismal Countenance' (*PW* vi. 139; 'Toland's Invitation to Dismal, to Dine with the Calves-Head Club', *Poems*, i. 161–6). Skyresh Bolgolam has 'a morose and sour Complection'. Although a High Churchman, Nottingham was a Hanoverian Tory. He did not support the Tory Peace policy, siding with the Whigs on the peace and succession issues in the last years of Anne's reign. Swift savaged him as an apostate, a selfish unprovoked wrecker of the Tory government, and in effect a true Whig (see e.g. 'An Excellent New Song, Being the Intended Speech of a Famous Orator against Peace', *Poems*, i. 141–5).

Delight . . . of the Universe: compare Suetonius on the Emperor Titus: 'the delight and darling of the human race' (Suetonius, 'The Deified Titus', I, in *The Lives of the Caesars*, Book VIII). King George was praised in the Old Whig journal *Cato's Letters* as 'the favourite of heaven, and the darling of all good men' (no. 18, 25 February 172[1]).

Center: of the earth.

39 *Oeconomy*: rules for domestic living.

42 *Tramecksan, and Slamecksan*: the contemporary topical application would be to the High Church Tory and the Low Church Whig parties.

his Majesty hath . . . Administration: the Tory party was proscribed from office under George I (1714–27), a proscription continued under George II.

Animosities: Swift described the party-political strife in London in 1703 (roughly contemporaneous with Gulliver's stay in Lilliput; Gulliver returns from Lilliput in 1702) as follows: 'I wish you had been here for ten days during the highest and warmest reign of party and faction that I ever knew or read of . . . It was so universal, that I observed the dogs in the streets much more contumelious and quarrelsome than usual . . . a committee of Whig and Tory cats had a very warm and loud debate upon the roof of our house. But why should we wonder at that, when the very ladies are split asunder into High Church and Low, and, out of zeal for religion, have hardly time to say their prayers?' (Swift to the Revd William Tisdall, 16 December 1703, *Corr.*, i. 147).

Tendency towards the High-Heels: there was a hope among the Tories,

shared by Swift, that the Prince of Wales on becoming George II would
show favour to the Tories.

43 *two mighty Powers . . . for six and thirty Moons*: England was at war with
Catholic France from 1689 (36 years before 1725 when Swift was preparing GT) until 1697 (the War of the League of Augsburg), and again in
1701–13 (War of the Spanish Succession).

one Emperor lost his Life, and another his Crown: Charles I was executed in
1649 and James II was deposed in 1689. An application for the entire
passage would be the conflict between Catholics (Big Endians) and
Protestants (Little Endians) since the Henrician Reformation, and
between Roman Catholics, Anglicans, and Puritans from the time of the
Civil Wars.

fled for Refuge to that Empire: an analogy for Swift's contemporaries
would have been with France which gave asylum to Royalists during the
Commonwealth, and to Jacobites after the Revolution of 1688–9.

rendred incapable by Law: an analogy would be with the Test Acts passed
after the Restoration which required public office-holders to demon-
strate their conformity to the established Church of England by taking
the sacrament according to Anglican rites.

Alcoran: Koran.

Conscience . . . Magistrate: Swift wrote in favour of public conformity in a
confessional Anglican state (see e.g. *The Sentiments of a Church of
England Man*, *PW* ii. 4–13).

46 *Men of War after me*: Gulliver's naval victory reflects contemporary Tory
preference for naval defence rather than land war.

47 *governing it by a Viceroy*: as Ireland was under British rule.

Topicks: maxims.

Junta: political clique or cabal.

48 *Visit in Form*: formal visit.

Mark of Disaffection: a satiric reflection on the Walpolean Whig government's readiness to suspect the Tories of Jacobitism. Disaffection meant
disloyalty to the ruling dynasty and establishment. Swift's satire invites
us to believe that such charges are baseless and politically motivated, and
that the accused, like Gulliver, are essentially innocent. Swift wrote to
Pope in 1723: 'I have often made the same remark with you of my
Infelicity in being so strongly attached to Traytors (as they call them) and
Exiles, and State Criminalls' (*Corr.*, ii. 468). In 1735 he tells Pope: 'I
heartily wish you were what they call disaffected, as I, who detest abominate & abhor every Creature who hath a dram of Power in either
Kingdom' (Williams, iv. 383). In 1737 Lord Bathurst described Swift as
'a disaffected person' who would be reputed so for as long as Swift lived
(Williams, v. 79).

49 *reading a Romance*: contemporary newspapers reported fires caused by
the carelessness of servants. Swift particularly disapproved of romances

and their alleged pernicious effects on women readers. In unpublished manuscript notes entitled 'Hints: Education of Ladyes' Swift wrote: 'No French Romances, and few plays for young Ladyes' (*PW* xii. 308). In *A Letter to a Young Lady, on her Marriage* (written in 1723, published 1727) Swift recommends 'a Match of Prudence, and common Good-liking, without any Mixture of that ridiculous Passion which hath no Being, but in Play-Books and Romances' (*PW* ix. 89).

50 *Urine . . . Fire . . . extinguished*: compare the exploits of Gargantua in Rabelais, *Gargantua and Pantagruel*, Book I, chapter xvii. Gargantua decides to give the people of Paris 'some wine' so he 'pissed on them so fiercely that he drowned two hundred and sixty thousand, four hundred and eighteen persons, not counting the women and small children. A number of them, however, were quick enough on their feet to escape this piss-flood; and when they reached the top of the hill above the University, sweating, coughing, spitting, and out of breath, they began to swear and curse, some in a fury and others in sport' (p. 74).

Capital: a capital crime, that is, punishable by death.

51 *general Ideas*: the account of original Lilliput draws on several sources, including accounts of remote peoples in voyage literature (for some of the more far-fetched customs), and descriptions of classical utopias, particularly the social models expounded in Plato's *Republic* and in Plutarch's *Life of Lycurgus* (for the admirable aspects of a pre-degenerate social order).

pulling a Lark: plucking the lark's feathers.

clinched: clenched.

Manner of Writing: analogues for Gulliver's observations on Lilliputian writing style have been found in several works, fictitious and genuine. William Symson wrote of the East Indians in *A New Voyage to the East-Indies*: 'Their Way of Writing, is not like the *Europeans*, in a Line from the Left to the Right; nor like the *Hebrews*, from the Right to the Left; nor yet like the *Chinese*, from the Top of the Paper strait down to the Bottom; but from the Left Corner down to the Right, slanting downwards' (pp. 35–6). This passage was stolen and adapted from a real voyage book, John Ovington's *Voyage to Suratt* (1696) (R. W. Frantz, 'Gulliver's "Cousin Sympson" ', *HLQ* 1 (1938), 331–3). Other analogues include a passage on Chinese writing in Swift's first patron, Sir William Temple's essay 'Of Heroic Virtue' (1690; Temple, ii. 201). Swift has invented the 'Cascagians', and given this passage of Lilliputian exotica a satiric inflection with the reference to the handwriting of English ladies. A joke reanimated in the correspondence between Mrs Howard and Swift, Mrs Howard writing aslant to Swift 'downwards to the right on one Page, and upwards in the two others' (*Corr.*, iii. 51, 54).

They bury their Dead . . . downwards: Swift draws on actual voyage accounts for this Lilliputian custom. In Part II Gulliver will join a voyage bound for Surat. In Jean de Thevenot's *Voyages* (Paris, 1684) there is an account of a burial site near Surat where the dead are 'interred with the Head down and the Feet upwards' (see Dirk Passmann, 'Jean De Thevenot and Burials in Lilliput', *N&Q*, NS 33 (March 1986), 50–1). There are accounts of upright burials in voyage books Swift owned, see Linschoten, 263, and Thomas Herbert, *A Relation of Some Yeares Travaile, Begunne Anno 1626. Into Afrique and the greater Asia* (London, 1634), 89. An illustration in Herman Moll's *Atlas* (1709) shows Laplanders buried standing upright, see Ellen D. Leyburn, *Satiric Allegory: Mirror of Man* (New Haven: Yale University Press, 1956), 74. PT observes that 'Swift's parody of literal-minded piety is in the tradition of satirical Utopian fiction'. It also recalls the satire of Jack's literal-minded religious enthusiasm in Swift's *A Tale of a Tub*.

52 *Charges he hath been at*: expenses incurred.

different Nations ... different Customs: proverbial. Swift's satire rejects cultural relativism insisting on universal truths about human nature and societies. Swift shares the view of his first patron, Sir William Temple, who after a consideration of Peruvian religion and government wrote in his essay 'Of Heroic Virtue' (1690): 'it must, I think, be allowed, that human Nature is the same in these Remote, as well as the other more known and celebrated Parts of the World' (Temple, ii. 210; see also Temple, i. 95).

two Hinges: an image found in Temple's essay 'Of Heroic Virtue' in a passage about China: 'The two great Hinges of all Governments, Reward and Punishment, are no where turned with greater Care, nor exercised with more Bounty and Severity' (Temple, ii. 203).

except that of Lilliput: in More's *Utopia*: 'They not only deter people from crime by penalties, but they incite them to virtue by public honours' (*Utopia*, 82).

53 *In chusing Persons*: compare Swift's *A Project for the Advancement of Religion, and the Reformation of Manners* (1709): 'For if Piety and Virtue were once reckoned Qualifications necessary to Preferment ... Things would soon take a new Face, and Religion receive a mighty Encouragement: Nor would the publick Weal be less advanced; since of nine Offices in ten that are ill executed, the Defect is not in Capacity or Understanding, but in common Honesty' (*PW* ii. 48–9).

Practices: schemes, intrigues, manœuvres.

Disbelief ... Station: in Utopia a person who denies the immortality of the soul and divine providence is not considered a citizen 'since he would openly despise all the laws and customs of society, if not prevented by fear' and such a person 'is offered no honours, entrusted with no offices, and given no public responsibility' (*Utopia*, 95).

54 *Ingratitude ... capital Crime*: cf. Chevalier Ramsay's *The Travels of Cyrus*, i. 5: 'The chief Aim of the Laws in antient *Persia*, was to prevent the Corruption of the Heart: And for this Reason, the *Persians* punish'd Ingratitude, a Vice against which there is no Provision made by the Laws

of other Nations. Whoever was capable of forgetting a Benefit, or of refusing to do a good Office when it was in his Power, was looked upon as an Enemy to Society'. In Utopia a relapse into the crime of adultery after being pardoned for the first offence 'is punished by death' (*Utopia*, 81). PT observes that moral failings are treated as crimes in Utopian societies.

Their Notions . . . differ extremely from ours: education in pre-degenerate Lilliput, as in Houyhnhnmland, is modelled on the laws of Lycurgus in ancient Sparta as described by Xenophon and Plutarch and mediated as an important presence in the (for Swift) charismatic utopias of Plato's *Republic* and More's *Utopia*. Xenophon set out to explain the educational system of Lycurgus and how it differed from other systems (*Constitution*, ii. 1).

will never allow . . . World: the same point is made in Cyrano de Bergerac's *Histoire comique de la lune* (1657) (Eddy, 112–13; PT).

Parents are the last . . . Children: in ancient Sparta the state had control over the education of children and parental involvement was not permitted (Plutarch, 'Lycurgus', xvi; Xenophon, *Constitution*, ii).

Professors: teachers.

55 *They are always employed*: Lycurgus imposed on Spartan youth a constant round of work and occupation (Xenophon, *Constitution*, iii. 1–4). A principle adopted in More's Utopia (*Utopia*, 50).

Professor . . . the like: Lycurgus ensured that nurses exercised care and skill in the nurture of children (Plutarch, 'Lycurgus', xvi. 3–4). One of Swift's hopes in 'When I come to be old' (1699) was 'Not to be fond of Children, or let them come near me hardly' (*PW* i. p. xxxvii). In Part IV the Houyhnhnms 'have no Fondness for their Colts or Foles' (p. 250).

frightful or foolish Stories: in Plato's *Republic* children's stories and fables are censored and nurses and mothers are induced to tell stories only from the state's prescribed list in order to cultivate virtue in the young (*Republic*, 376E–379).

despise . . . Ornaments: in Utopia gems are the playthings of small children and put aside as shameful when the children grow older (*Utopia*, 61).

56 *neither . . . any Difference*: in Lycurgan Sparta the education and training of women was taken as seriously as that of the men (*Constitution*, i. 3–5; Plutarch, 'Lycurgus', xiv). Education of both sexes is a feature of Plato's Republic (*Republic*, 451E–452B) and More's Utopia (*Utopia*, 50, 63–4).

cannot always be young: compare Swift's didacticism in *A Letter to a Young Lady, on her Marriage* (1723): 'You have but a very few Years to be young and handsome in the Eyes of the World; and as few Months to be so in the Eyes of a Husband, who is not a Fool . . . You must, therefore, use all Endeavours to attain to some Degree of those Accomplishments, which your Husband most values in other People . . . You must improve your Mind, by closely pursuing such a Method of Study, as I shall direct or approve of. You must get a Collection of History and Travels, which I will recommend to you; and spend some Hours every Day in reading them.' Swift is progressive in supporting female education, but a principal purpose of female education is for the woman 'to become a reasonable and agreeable Companion' (*PW* ix. 89–90).

56 *Domestick*: domestic arrangements.

   mechanically turned: with a turn for handicraft or practical contrivance.

57 *yields to ours*: is not so good as ours.

   Bits: bites, mouthfuls.

58 *white Staff*: symbol of the office of Lord High Treasurer.

   caressed: treated with favour or kindness.

   at great Discount: at a greatly reduced price. He had to borrow money by issuing government bonds ('Exchequer Bills') which nobody would buy except at a price reduced by at least 9 per cent; i.e. 100-Sprug bills were selling at 91 Sprugs. PT.

59 *ever came to me incognito*: amusingly, Gulliver's strident protestation of innocence is rendered suspect by the revelation in the next chapter that 'a considerable Person at Court . . . came to my House very privately at Night in a close Chair' (p. 60).

60 *so remote a Country*: Swift presents a positive, quasi-Utopian society in the account of pre-degenerate Lilliput in chapter vi and satirizes European society in the depiction of corrupt modern Lilliput.

61 *Articles of Impeachment*: a topical application of the satire was the impeachment of the Tory leaders Oxford, Bolingbroke, and Ormonde by George I's Whig government on charges of high treason in 1715. Bolingbroke and Ormonde fled to France just as Gulliver escapes to Blefuscu. Curll's *Key* commented that 'the Severities threatned against poor *Lemuel*, some here have resembled to the late Earl of *O[xfor]d*'s Sufferings' (*Key*, Part I, p. 26). The effect of the satire is to suggest the innocence of those accused of treason by the Whig government.

   under Colour: on the pretext.

   Serene: the German dynasty was described as the Serene House of Hanover.

62 *Juice on your Shirts*: recalls the fate of Hercules who died in agony when his shirt was smeared with the poisoned blood of the Centaur Nessus.

   brought off: won over.

63 *put out both your Eyes*: a court custom of the island kingdom of Ormus reported in Linschoten, 14. Biblical analogues include the fate of Zedekiah in Jeremiah 52: 11 and Samson in Judges 16: 21. A literary analogue is the blinding of Gloucester and the fear of such a fate for Lear in Shakespeare's *King Lear*. Gulliver has been particularly concerned about protecting his eyes and may be, as Pat Rogers observes, 'the first bespectacled hero in English Literature' (Pat Rogers, 'Gulliver's

Glasses', in Clive T. Probyn (ed.), *The Art of Jonathan Swift* (London: Vision Press, 1978), 179–88 (p. 179).

no Impediment . . . Strength: compare the fate of Samson: 'the Philistines took him, and put out his eyes . . . and bound him with fetters of brass; and he did grind in the prison house' (Judges 16: 21). In a letter of October 1722 Swift refers to the Whig prosecutors of Tories accused of Jacobite plotting as 'uncircumcised Philistines' (*Corr.*, ii. 432).

greatest Princes do no more: compare Boccalini, Advertisement I ('*The Politicians open their Warehouse at* Parnassus; *An Account of what is to be sold there.*'): 'You may buy . . . *true human Eyes* . . . *For Politicians affirm, Men look much better into their Affairs, when they see with other folks Eyes, than while they make use of their own*. Yet have a care of throwing away your own, when you buy a Pair of these Eyes, lest you be serv'd as the Unfortunate *James* the II. was' (p. 3). The biblical King Zedekiah 'with his Eyes put out' by the King of Babylon (Jeremiah 52: 11) was paralleled with the fate of James II in 1688 in the Jacobite Matthias Earbery's edition of *Advices from Parnassus. By Trajano Boccalini*, no. III (May 1727), Advice XII, p. 52. PT and Gough note that in Herodotus a minister of the King of Persia is known as 'the King's Eye' (Herodotus, i. 114).

Reasons of State: political considerations. The phrase echoes the Italian *ragioni di stato*, associated with the unscrupulous methods of government advocated by Machiavelli. PT.

64 *without the formal Proofs*: a topical allusion to the trial and attainder of Francis Atterbury the Bishop of Rochester who had been arrested and sent to the Tower in 1722 on a charge of high treason for Jacobite plotting. With insufficient evidence to secure a legal conviction Walpole's Whig government prosecuted him by parliamentary means in the House of Lords bringing in a bill of pains and penalties. Atterbury was exiled to France in 1723.

65 *Encomiums . . . Mercy*: the sardonic satire on the Emperor of Lilliput's mercy alludes to George I's speeches declaring his mercy and lenity in his treatment of the Jacobite prisoners who surrendered after the 1715 Rebellion (many of whom were executed or transported) and to the Whig government's proclamation of George's clemency. The division in the Lilliputian court between the ministers calling for immediate capital punishment and the Emperor and Secretary Reldresal who think 'there was room for Mercy' alludes to a division in the Whig court in 1723. Whether or not Atterbury should receive the death penalty 'divided the Court much and made the leaders very uneasy who were for tempering justice with mercy as the prudenter way' (entry for March 1723 in Sir Edward Knatchbull's *Parliamentary Diary* quoted in Romney Sedgwick (ed.), *The History of Parliament: The House of Commons 1715–54*, 2 vols. (London, 1970), i. 66). In October 1722 Swift wrote sarcastically of George I and Whig encomiums on the King's clemency: 'It is a wonderful thing to see the Tories provoking his present majesty, whose clemency,

mercy, and forgiving temper, have been so signal, so extraordinary, so more than humane during the whole course of his reign; which plainly appears, not only from his own speeches and declarations, but also from a most ingenious pamphlet just come over, relating to the wicked Bishop of Rochester' (*Corr.*, ii. 432). The euphemistic clemency of the Emperor of Lilliput (innuendo George I) is probably also meant to recall the cruelty of the Roman Emperor Domitian described by Suetonius in his *The Lives of the Caesars*: '[Domitian] never pronounced an unusually dreadful sentence without a preliminary declaration of clemency, so that there came to be no more certain indication of a cruel death than the leniency of his preamble' (Suetonius, *Domitian*, xi. 2; R. F. Kennedy in *N&Q*, 214 (1969), 340–1). Jacobite polemicists cast George I as an oriental despot, as for example, in *The Character of Sultan Galga, the present Cham of Tartary* (*c.*1720), 2: 'the distinguishing Part of *GALGA*'s Character, is, his cruel Disposition . . . Yet he talks every Day very gravely of his great Clemency and Lenity . . . the most bitter Curse . . . in Tartary . . . is, "May God's Curse and *Galga*'s Mercy light upon you." '

65 *But having . . . Enemies*: an apologia for the conduct of the Tory Lords Bolingbroke and Ormonde who fled to France rather than stand trial for treason in England.

Oath: Gulliver performs the subject's duty of passive obedience and non-resistance to the sovereign power, but the satire encourages sympathy for the subject who might revolt against such a monarch. Commenting on the obligation of the oath of allegiance to King George I, Swift wrote: 'Suppose a King grows a Beast, or a Tyrant, after I have taken an Oath: a'prentice takes an Oath; but if his Master useth him barbarously, the lad may be excused if he wishes for a Better' (*PW* v. 252).

68 *A Person of Quality*: a topical allusion to diplomatic protests made to France about the asylum given to Jacobites. Gulliver is in an analogous role to a Jacobite seeking refuge in France.

70 *Antient*: ensign or flag.

71 *North and South Seas*: North and South Pacific.

my Veracity: since the reader cannot see the sheep and cattle, this proof of veracity is equivalent to Lucian's when, after telling some very tall stories about lunar society, he concludes: 'Well, that is what it was like on the Moon. If you do not believe me, go and see for yourself' (Lucian, 262). Until 20 July 1969 no one was in a position to refute him. PT.

the Downs: an open roadstead off the coast of Kent, partly sheltered by the Goodwin Sands. It is so named because it lies opposite the North Downs (Gough, 362). Dampier ended his voyage round the world at 'the Downs' (*Voyages*, i. 529). PT.

Fineness of the Fleeces: Gulliver's concern for the advantage of the English woollen manufacture was not shared by Swift, who championed the Irish woollen manufacture and wrote against the Irish Woollens Act (1699) which forbade the export of Irish woollen products in order to protect the English wool industry. As PT observes Swift is also, like More in *Utopia*, satirizing the fashionable taste for fine wool. More's Utopians 'do not value fineness of texture' in linen and wool cloth (*Utopia*, 53).

insatiable Desire ... Countries: PT compares Lucian's *wanderlust* which sends him off on a voyage across the Atlantic (Lucian, 250).

72 *Black-Bull in Fetter-Lane*: there was an inn of this name in Holborn, opposite Fetter Lane (Gough, 362).

upon the Parish: before the nineteenth-century Poor Law the destitute depended on the parish for charity.

towardly: promising.

Adventure: the name of contemporary ships including that of the notorious pirate Captain Kidd.

Surat: a port city on the west coast of India, near Bombay. The East India Company had a factory in Surat.

Part II. A Voyage to Brobdingnag

75 *carried*: the reader will not suspect at this point that Gulliver is to be seized by the hand and carried in a coat. The word could also mean 'transported' or 'conveyed' by a vehicle or on horseback, or 'conducted' or 'escorted'. Jeoly, a captive native Dampier brought back to England, 'was carried about to be shown as a Sight' (*Voyages*, i. 528).

Cape of Good-hope: cf. Dampier's account of his voyage under Captain Heath to the Cape of Good Hope, an important way station in voyages to and from the East Indies. The crew, suffering from illness caused by 'the badness of the Water' on board, sought refreshment there. 'The Cape of Good Hope is the utmost Bounds of the Continent of Africa towards the South, lying in 34 d. 30 m. S. lat. in a very temperate Climate.' After arriving at the Cape, the Captain 'took an House to live in, in order to recover his health' (*Voyages*, i. 506, 511, 522).

the Wind ceased ... perfect calm ... prepare against a Storm ... Monsoon: cf. William Dampier's account of a violent storm in *A New Voyage Round the World*: 'we had some signs of an approaching Storm; this being the time of the Year ... for the S.W. Monsoon, but the Wind had been whiffling about from one part of the Compass to another for two or three Days, and sometimes it would be quite calm ... such flattering Weather is commonly the fore-runner of a Tempest' (*Voyages*, i. 408–9).

like to overblow: to blow too hard for the sails. Gulliver's account follows to the letter the instructions on how to negotiate a storm at sea in *The Mariners Magazine; or, Sturmy's Mathematical and Practical Arts ... By Capt. Samuel Sturmy* (London, 1669), Book I, chapter ii, pp. 17–18. Swift's plagiarism was first noticed by E. H. Knowles in an article in *N&Q* in 1868. The plagiarism becomes a Swiftian parody of nautical jargon (a specific target may have been Dampier's account of how he negotiated a violent storm at sea in *A New Voyage Round the World*, see *Voyages*, i. 409–11), and an instance of Gulliver's old-fashioned 'Sea-Language', much of which, Gulliver complains, his publisher cut out. See also Eddy, 143–4.

75 *Sprit-sail*: a sail attached to a yard slung under the bowsprit of large vessels (*OED*).

hand: take in, furl.

making: meeting with.

looked the Guns were all fast: secured so they would not move during the storm.

Missen: mizzen-sail, a fore- and aft-sail set on the after side of the mizzen-mast (the aftermost mast of a three-master). The 'mizen trysail' is set in stormy weather (*OED*; PT).

very broad off: well away from the wind.

spooning: running.

trying: lying to. The sails are set so as to keep the ship's bow to sea.

hulling: driving with all sails furled.

Fore-sheet: the rope by which the lee corner of the foresail is kept in place (*OED*).

a Weather: towards the windward side.

wore: came round.

76 *belay'd the Foredown-hall*: made fast the rope used to pull down the foresail. PT.

Yard: a long wooden or steel spar, slung at its centre from a mast serving to support and extend a square sail.

the Sea broke strange and dangerous: although the words are from Sturmy's *Mariners Magazine* ('The Sea breaks strange and dangerous', Bk I, ch. ii, p. 17), compare Dampier: 'the Sea seemed all of a Fire about us; for every Sea that broke sparkled like lightning' (*Voyages*, i. 409).

hawl'd off upon the Lanniard of the Wipstaff: pulled away at the short rope attached to the tiller on the head of the rudder (so helping the helmsman).

She scudded before the Sea very well: *Mariners Magazine*, i. ii. 17: 'She scuds before the Sea very well'; Dampier: 'We continued scudding right before the Wind and Sea . . . we scudded, and run before the Wind very swift' (*Voyages*, i. 411).

wholesomer: steadier.

brought the Ship to: brought the ship to a standstill.

got the Star-board Tacks aboard: hauled the tacks (ropes used to secure to the ship's side the windward corners of the lower square sails) into such a position as to trim the sails to a wind on the starboard side. PT.

cast off our Weather-braces and Lifts: loosened the braces or ropes attached to the yards on the windward side of the ship and the lifts (ropes reaching from the masthead to the yardarms to steady and support their ends). PT.

set in the Lee-braces: shortened the ropes or braces on the side of the ship away from the wind.

hawl'd forward by the Weather-bowlings: pulled forward the windward side of the square sails by the bowlines (ropes reaching from the perpendicular edges of the sails to the port or starboard bow, to keep the edges of the sails steady). PT.

kept her full and by as near as she would lye: kept the ship sailing close-hauled to the wind, and heading as near as possible to the direction from which the wind was blowing. PT.

great Tartary . . . frozen Sea: Siberia and the Arctic ocean.

whether: which of the two.

77 *hollow*: shout.

walking after them in the Sea: as PT observes, in Virgil's *Aeneid*, iii. 664–5 the Cyclops Polyphemus 'strides through the open sea' after the terrified men on Aeneas's ship, the waves not wetting 'his towering sides'. The men on the ship escape from the monster having rescued a man who, like Gulliver, had been left behind by his companions (*Aeneid*, iii. 616–17).

ten Yards at every Stride: since the average pace is 30 inches, this gives a 12 to 1 scale for Brobdingnag (Eddy, 136).

78 *more Savage . . . Bulk*: the traditional view implied in Shakespeare's 'O, it is excellent | To have a giant's strength, but it is tyrannous | To use it like a giant' (*Measure for Measure*, II. ii. 108–10) and in Milton's use of the giant analogy for the rebel angels in *Paradise Lost* (i. 197–200), and illustrated by the behaviour of the Giants and of Cyclops in Greek mythology. Swift's conventional usage of giants as bad can be seen in an attack on the Earl of Wharton in the *Examiner* (*PW* iii. 9). As PT observes, Swift produces a surprise effect in *GT* by making the Brobdingnagians the most humane and 'the least corrupted' of the nations Gulliver visits. Gulliver was a humane giant in Lilliput.

Philosophers: Swift's friend George Berkeley (1685–1753) was one of these philosophers, especially in his *Essay towards a New Theory of Vision* (1709).

79 *Lappet*: lapel.

Hinds: labourers.

80 *Pistoles*: Spanish gold coins worth from 16 to 18 shillings.

pierced my Ears . . . Water-Mill: Swift suffered from Ménière's syndrome, a disease of the inner ear, and in 1724 he wrote that 'I have the Noise of seven Watermills in my Ears' (*Corr.*, ii. 524; see Ehrenpreis, iii. 319–20).

81 *surprize*: perplexity, alarm, terror.

arch: mischievous.

82 *Stocking-Weavers*: stocking-frames, a kind of knitting machine.

83 *magnifying Glass*: cf. 'The Virtues we must not let pass, | Of *Celia*'s magnifying Glass. | When frighted *Strephon* cast his Eye on't | It shew'd the Visage of a Gyant. | A Glass that can to Sight disclose, | The smallest Worm in *Celia*'s Nose' ('The Lady's Dressing Room' (1730); *Poems*, ii. 527).

84 *Rats*: the habitation of the marooned contemporary mariner Alexander Selkirk 'was extreamly pester'd with Rats, which gnaw'd his Cloaths and Feet when sleeping' (Richard Steele, *The Englishman*, no. 26 (3 December 1713), *Englishman*, 108).

    Hanger: short sword.

85 *my sole Design . . . World*: as in Part I, Gulliver presents particular details (such as these on urination and defecation) that other over-particular voyagers leave out. As PT observes, Swift is parodying Dampier among others. Dampier states in the dedication of *A New Voyage Round the World*: 'I have not so much of the Vanity of a Traveller, as to be fond of telling Stories, especially of this kind . . . Yet dare I avow, according to my narrow Sphere and poor Abilities, a hearty Zeal for the promoting of useful Knowledge, and of any thing that may never so remotely tend to my Countries Advantage' (*Voyages*, i. 17).

    without affecting . . . Style: a parody of Dampier who defends 'this plain Piece of mine' (*Voyages*, i. 17): 'As to my Stile, it cannot be expected, that a Seaman should affect Politeness . . . for I am perswaded, that if what I say be intelligible, it matters not greatly in what words it is express'd' (*Voyages*, i. 20).

86 *towardly Parts*: promising abilities.

    Baby: doll.

    This young Girl . . . self: analogues for giant women having affection for men occur in Cyrano de Bergerac, *Histoire comique de la lune* (1657) and in the *Arabian Nights* (Eddy, 128–30; PT).

    Nanunculus: a portmanteau word (from *nanus*, dwarf, and *homunculus*, manikin). PT observes that there are similar games of word invention in the proper names in *Utopia*.

    Homunceletino: a similar coinage, from homunculus with a quasi-Italian diminutive suffix.

    Glumdalclitch: Gulliver's nurse has been thought 'a meditation, wholly or partly unconscious' upon the infant Swift's nurse (Margaret Anne Doody, 'Swift and Women' in *Companion*, 91) and to have 'touches of Esther Johnson', Swift's companion 'Stella' (Ehrenpreis, iii. 457).

87 *little Language*: Swift's name for the invented language in his letters to Esther Johnson (see *Journal to Stella*, in *PW* xv and xvi).

88 *Monster*: freak, monstrosity. The details of Gulliver's tour as a public spectacle and his performances draw on the actual public sights and

shows and sensational newspaper advertisements in contemporary Britain and Ireland (see Aline Mackenzie Taylor, 'Sights and Monsters and Gulliver's *Voyage to Brobdingnag*', *TSE* 7 (1957), 29–82, and Dennis Todd, 'The Hairy Maid at the Harpsichord: Some Speculations on the Meaning of *Gulliver's Travels*', *TSLL* 34 (Summer 1992), 239–83. Gulliver finds himself shown as a sight, the role suffered by natives brought back to Britain by voyagers like Dampier. Cf. Dampier's account of Jeoly, 'the Painted Prince' who 'was shown for a Sight in England'. Dampier 'proposed no small advantage to my self from my Painted Prince' although 'I was no sooner arrived in the Thames, but he was sent ashore to be seen by some eminent Persons; and I being in want of Money, was prevailed upon to sell first, part of my share in him, and by degrees all of it. After this I heard he was carried about to be shown as a Sight, and that he died of the Small-pox at Oxford' (see *Voyages*, i. 494–500, 502, 528). A literary analogue is in Cyrano performing as a circus dwarf in *Histoire comique de la lune* (Eddy, 21; PT).

since the King . . . Distress: the reader is prompted to regard the Hanoverian King as a freak.

in a Box: a famous Swiss dwarf, John Wormberg (or Hans Worrenbergh), 31 inches high, was carried around in a box (A. M. Taylor, *TSE* 7 (1957), 30). PT.

close: without any openings except the door and the gimlet-holes.

London to St Albans: 20 miles.

at the Sign of the Green Eagle: in the Armagh copy of *GT* the name of the inn is altered in ink to 'Horn and Crown' an unmistakable allusion to George I as a royal cuckold (*PW* xi. 306; the manuscript variant is discussed in Michael Treadwell, 'The Text of *Gulliver's Travels*, Again', *Swift Studies*, 10 (1995), 69–70).

89 *Fopperies*: silly tricks.

unlucky: probably in the obsolete sense of 'mischievous, malicious'. Cyrano also has to dodge a huge nut thrown by a spectator (*Histoire*, 142; Eddy, 127–8). PT.

Pumpion: pumpkin.

90 *Sanson's Atlas*: Nicolas Sanson (1600–67), French cartographer, founder of the Sanson firm. He produced a pocket atlas in four parts (1656–1705). His atlases were published in folio, the largest book size. Sanson's cartographic material was incorporated into large-scale atlases.

91 *Stomach*: appetite.

make as good a Hand of: make as much profit out of.

kissing her Imperial Foot: Swift is deflating the hubris of contemporary voyagers in Gulliver's prostration and abjection. Lionel Wafer, for example, in his *A New Voyage and Description of the Isthmus of America* (London, 1699), one of Swift's sources (see *Library*, Part I, vol. iii, p. 1948), reported how a native King 'bowed, and kiss'd my Hand' and 'the rest came thick about me, and some kissed my Hand, others my Knee, and some my Foot . . . the *Indians* . . . in a manner ador'd me' (Wafer, 19).

91 *Moydores*: Portuguese gold coins.

92 *His Majesty*: the King of Brobdingnag is primarily the paradigm of the good King and offers a positive contrast to the Emperor of Lilliput (see Lock, 16–17, 131–2, 138). However, the king and his views had seditious political resonance. The Stuart Pretender or 'James III' is 'a huge Giant' across the sea in a political allegory printed in Dublin in 1714 (*The Life of Aristides, the Athenian; Who was Decreed to be Banish'd for His Justice* . . . (Dublin: Printed by Daniel Tompson, 1714), 25). The King of Brobdingnag's views on England's taxes, national debt, wars, foreign deployment of the fleet, and mercenary standing army were understood by contemporary readers as 'a common *Jacobite* Insinuation' (*Gulliver Decypher'd* (London, n.d.), 38). The hereditary King of Brobdingnag's political philosophy and polity may be indebted to one of the most widely read contemporary French works in the genre of the imaginary voyage, Francois de Fenélon's *Télémaque* (1699; see *Telemachus, son of Ulysses*, ed. and trans. Patrick Riley (Cambridge: Cambridge University Press, 1994)). Fénelon's work theorized a combination of monarchisn with the virtues of ancient Lycurgan Sparta, attacked luxury and militarism, and valued simplicity and the virtues of agriculture. Fénelon was profoundly admired by the Stuart Pretender or 'King James III'. The Jacobite Charles Wogan refers to Swift as 'Mentor', Telemachus' sage companion (actually Minerva in disguise), in a letter to Swift in 1733 (*Corr.*, iii. 590–3). For Whigs the Pretender was a 'fictitious Monarch' (Thomas Burnett, *The British Bulwark* (London, 1715), 42). In having a fictional king articulate what could be understood as a Jacobite political critique of the Hanoverian Whig regime, Swift gives his satire the atmosphere of a dynastic challenge. There are parallels between the whiggish Gulliver's conversation with His Majesty of Brobdingnag and the (former Whig now Jacobite convert) Duke of Wharton's account of his interview with the Pretender in a sensational political work of 1726, *The Duke of Wharton's Reasons for Leaving his native Country, and espousing the Causes of his Royal Majesty King James III. in a Letter to his Friends in Great Britain and Ireland*. Swift denied the charge of Jacobitism that was often levelled at him by his Whig enemies. However, he thought that the threat of a revolt to a pretender might oblige ruling princes to govern well, although he lamented that it had 'not succeeded in mending Kings' (*PW* v. 292).

93 *Scrutore*: escritoire, writing-desk.

The King . . . as learned a Person: Wharton on meeting the Pretender refers to 'the Politeness of his Education, illustrating the Majesty of his Person' (Wharton, 3)

Clock-work: clockwork automata were popular exhibits in Swift's time. This may be a hostile allusion to René Descartes and his description of humans in mechanistic terms in *L'Homme* (1664).

Artist: craftsman.

waiting: attendance at court.

They all agreed . . . Nature: Cyrano is similarly discussed by lunar philosophers, who agree that he must be a *lusus naturae* (*Histoire*, 117, 142, 277: Eddy, 126–7). PT.

Insects: it was formerly applied more widely to include earthworms, snails, and some small vertebrates, such as frogs and tortoises (*OED*).

94 *Lusus Naturæ*: frolic or freak of nature, an exception to the general laws of nature.

whose Professors: an oblique attack on Sir Isaac Newton (who received the patronage of King George I). In his *Opticks* (1704) Newton had argued that modern science, with its general laws of nature, was more useful than Aristotelianism with its reference to occult qualities (Gough, 369; PT).

To this they only replied . . . Contempt: in satirizing the ignorant dogmatism of scientists, Swift follows the Lucianic tradition: 'in spite of the difficulty of ascertaining the facts, they never put forward a theory as a tentative hypothesis. On the contrary, they struggled desperately to prove that no other theory could possibly be true' (*Icaromenippus*, Lucian, 115). PT.

95 *Nice*: capable of fine, delicate, or intricate work.

Baby-house: doll's house.

craunch: crunch.

96 *a Whig or a Tory*: cf. *The Sentiments of a Church-of-England Man* (written 1708): 'in order to find out the Character of a Person; instead of enquiring whether he be a Man of Virtue, Honour, Piety, Wit, good Sense, or Learning; the modern Question is only, Whether he be a *Whig* or a *Tory*' (*PW* ii. 24). In *A Short Character of His Excellency Thomas Earl of Wharton*, Swift reports how the Whig Lord Lieutenant of Ireland refused the promotion of a chaplain, an esteemed gentleman of 'good Birth', decency, 'Wit', 'Learning' and experience, because 'he had the original Sin of being a reputed Tory' (*PW* iii. 183). In his partisan Tory *History of the Four Last Years of the Queen* Swift refers to Whig and Tory as 'those Fantastick Words' which should have been dropped in favour of other names 'to distinguish Lovers of Peace [Tories] from Lovers of War [Whigs]' (*PW* vii. 3). Whig and Tory was the primary party-political division in Swift's lifetime. Tory originally derived from the name of Irish Catholic bandits or rapparees. The Tories supported King Charles II and the hereditary succession in the Exclusion Crisis (1679–81). Swift called them the 'Church Party' and the defence of the exclusive position of the Church of England was fundamental to their political ideology. The Tory party after the Revolution of 1688–9 had a Jacobite wing. In Ireland the appellation 'Tory' denoted a supporter of the Jacobite succession, so Swift rarely uses the term for his side of politics since it signified

treason. After Queen Anne's Tory ministry of 1710–14, which Swift served as propagandist, the Tories never again formed a government in Swift's lifetime, being proscribed under George I and George II. The name Whig originally derived from whiggamore, a name for Scottish Puritan rebels in the Civil War. The Whigs supported the exclusion of the Catholic Duke of York from the throne in the Exclusion crisis. They supported the Revolution of 1688–9 and were the political party perceived as most sympathetic to Protestant Dissenters from the Established Church of England supporting Protestant religious freedom and toleration. They had an anticlerical, crypto-republican wing. The Whig party was entrenched in government after 1714.

96 *Royal Sovereign*: Charles I's warship, launched in 1637; it was one of the largest of its time with 106 guns and a main mast of about 110 feet. (Gough, 370; PT).

Nest and Burrows . . . Cities: the diminution of human grandeur when viewed from a great height has a long literary history. PT cites Lucian, *Icaromenippus* (Lucian, 123) and Cicero, *Somnium Scipionis*, viii.

97 *Birth-day Cloaths*: fine clothes worn at court on royal birthdays.

Queen's Dwarf: dwarfs were often members of royal households. Charles I's Queen, Henrietta Maria, kept three at her court, one of whom, Jeffery Hudson, was said to be only 18 inches high, one of the smallest on record (Gough, 368).

let me drop . . . Cream: in the sixteenth-century Irish story 'Aidedh Ferghusa', Esirt is picked up by the King's cupbearer and dropped into a wine goblet, where he is nearly drowned; he also slips into a porridge-bowl and gets stuck to his middle (cf. next paragraph; A. C. L. Brown, *MLN* 19 (1904), 46). PT.

98 *Flies . . . Dunstable Lark*: Swift parodies Dampier's accounts of the annoying flies in New Holland (*Voyages*, i. 453; ii. 442). Larks for the London market were caught in large numbers on the downs around the market town of Dunstable in Bedfordshire (Gough, 370).

99 *Gresham College*: location of the Royal Society and its collections. Swift visited Gresham College in a day of London sight-seeing which included the Tower, Bedlam, and a puppet show on 13 December 1710 (*PW* xv. 122). PT observes that the 'unpleasant picture of enormously magnified insects was possibly intended as a satire on such members of the Royal Society as Robert Hooke, whose *Micrographia* (1665) contained some striking micrographical illustrations of fleas and flies'.

100 *a Peninsula*: Utopia was an isthmus until a channel was cut where the land joined the continent (*Utopia*, 42).

excluded from any Commerce . . . World: which is why we have not heard of them before Gulliver's account. But the fact that it is a closed society is significant. Lycurgus ensured through his laws that Sparta was cut off from commerce with the world as a means of preventing the introduction of luxury into the pristine agrarian community. Swift's Brobdingnag and Houyhnhnmland, like Sparta (see 'Lycurgus', xxvii. 3–4), are isolated communities without commerce and foreign contact. The Houyhnhnms are without luxury and Brobdingnag is said to be 'the least corrupted' of the human societies Gulliver visits. China, highly esteemed by Swift's contemporaries and by his first employer Sir William Temple as an apogee of civilization, was isolated from the outside world by its rulers.

101 *fifty-one Cities*: there are 'fifty-four cities' in Utopia (*Utopia*, 43).

sufficient to describe Lorbrulgrud: similarly one city, Amaurot, is described as representative of all the cities in Utopia, and as with Swift's Lorbrulgrud, More's Amaurot is like London in several ways (cf. *Utopia*, 44–5).

Glonglungs: apparently derived from English *long*, Italian *lungo*, plus the g (= great?) which seems as characteristic of Brobdingnagian as *h* is of Houyhnhnm-language. PT.

103 *Salisbury Steeple*: 404 feet high, the equivalent of 4,848 feet in Brobdingnag. PT.

Cupola at St Paul's: 122 feet in interior diameter and, like Salisbury steeple, 404 feet in height (hence, perhaps, Swift's train of thought from the one building to the other). Gulliver arrived home from Brobdingnag in 1706; St Paul's was completed in 1710. PT.

I should be hardly believed: as PT observes Swift parodies a familiar formula in the mock-traveller's tale (cf. Lucian, *The True History*, Lucian, 261; More, *Utopia*, 59).

104 *Battalia*: battle-order.

106 *amazed*: dazed, stupefied.

107 *The Maids of Honour*: a literary standard in indecency had been set by the giant princess in the *Arabian Nights* (see Eddy, 129–31), presumably one of those proscribed romances with which Swift is nevertheless apparently familiar and young women are advised not to be. Amusingly, Swift presents Gulliver in the prefatory 'Letter to Sympson' as in denial about 'abusing the Female Sex' in his book. A joke he continued outside the book in his correspondence with Mrs Howard, a Bed-Chamber Woman at Court, see the letter of ' "Lemuel Gulliver" to Mrs. Howard' from 'Newark in Nottinghamshire' of 28 November 1726 where 'Gulliver' begs Howard to reconcile him 'to the Maids of Honour, whom they say I have most greviously offended. I am so stupid as not to find out how I have disobliged them; Is there any harm in a young Ladys reading of Romances? Or did I make use of an improper Engine to extinguish a fire that was kindled by a Maid of Honour? And I will venture to affirm, that if ever the Young Ladies at your Court, should meet with a man of as little consequence in this country, as I was in Brobdingnag, they would use him with as much contempt' (*Corr.*, iii. 58–9).

108 *Toylet*: dressing-table.

108 *Motions*: emotions.

three Tuns: equal to 12 hogsheads, or at least 1,200 wine-gallons. Ovid (*Remedia Amoris*, 437–40) suggests this type of spectacle as a possible remedy for love. PT. Variants on this scene occur in Swift's scatological or excremental verse. Cf. 'Strephon and Chloe' where Chloe a 'Maid in Thought, and Word, and Deed' drinks 'TWELVE Cups of Tea', details of her urination and flatulence and Strephon's feats follow (*Poems*, ii. 588–90).

pleasant: humorous, jocular.

great Jet d'Eau at Versailles: famous water fountain at Louis XIV's palace.

109 *Stomacher*: an ornamental covering for the chest worn by women under the lacing of the bodice (*OED*).

111 *clambered up to a Roof*: this episode must have been written by June 1722 since Esther Vanhomrigh ('Vanessa') alludes to it in a letter to Swift at that time (*Corr.*, ii. 423).

112 *Cow-dung*: as PT observes Gulliver's humiliation recalls *Iliad*, xxiii. 774–84, where Ajax slips on cow dung, falls flat on his face in it, and is laughed at.

114 *Levee*: morning receptions.

artificially: skilfully.

seasonable Supply: opportune replacement.

dishonourable Part . . . Head: in Part I, Gulliver urinates on a palace offending the Lilliputian empress. In Part II, he will not sit on a chair made of the hairs from the Queen's head.

115 *Mechanical Genius*: talent for handicraft.

decyphered: represented by a cipher or monogram.

Consorts: concerts.

Musick not disagreeable: Swift claimed to 'know musick no more than an ass' ('The Dean to himself on St. Cecilia's day', l. 2 (*Poems*, ii. 522). He said that 'I know nothing of music . . . I would not give a farthing for all the musick in the universe' (Patrick Delany, *Observations upon Lord Orrery's Remarks in the Life and Writings of Dr Jonathan Swift* (London, 1754), 189). Hyperbolic hostility to fiddlers, for instance, is ubiquitous in Swift's writing.

116 *Tongue of Demosthenes or Cicero*: Swift remembers Juvenal, *Satires*, x. 114, referring to the famous eloquence of Cicero and Demosthenes. Gulliver's loyal Whig eulogy of his country will be interrogated with Juvenalian ferocity in Swift's satire.

three mighty Kingdoms: England, Scotland, and Ireland. Gulliver is in Brobdingnag before the Union of 1707 which united England and Scotland. Swift was hostile to the Anglo-Scottish Union (see *Poems*, i. 95–6; *PW* ix. 3–12) and to the English Whig government's treatment of Ireland 'as if it had been one of their *Colonies* of *Out-casts* in *America*' (*PW* ix. 20–1). The Declaratory Act, 'an act for the better securing of the dependency of the kingdom of Ireland upon the crown of Great Britain', had asserted the British parliament's right to pass legislation binding on Ireland. Gulliver's (pre-1707) praise of a three-kingdom monarchy may have had seditious resonance for readers in 1726 as the Jacobite Pretender's Declarations promised to abolish the Union and envisaged that a restored Stuart dynasty would rule a multi-kingdom monarchy.

Plantations: colonies.

extraordinary Care . . . Education: Swift asserted that the opposite was the case (see *The Intelligencer*, no. IX (1728), *PW* xii. 46–53).

Counsellors born: hereditary advisers.

highest Court . . . Appeal: Swift protested against the English House of Lords being the final court of appeal for Ireland (*PW* xii. 6). The Declaratory Act of 1720 had denied that the Irish House of Lords had any jurisdiction over appeals from the courts and Swift opposed it telling Charles Ford in a letter of 4 April 1720: 'I believe my self not guilty of too much veneration for the Irish H[ouse] of L[ords], but . . . the Question is whether People ought to be Slaves or no' (*Corr.*, ii. 327).

117 *never once known to degenerate*: the degeneracy of the aristocracy was a traditional satiric topos and Juvenal, *Satires*, viii, was an important model. The degeneration of the hereditary nobility was a virulent theme in Jacobite writing against the Williamite and Hanoverian regimes. Swift traced the degeneration of the nobility to the 'Rebellion and Usurpation' of the 1640s and 1650s (*PW* xii. 47) and to the Revolution of 1688–9 and the Williamite Whig creations (*PW* vii. 19, 21). In Ireland, Swift wrote, the Lords were 'a mungril Breed' and 'Peerage is a wither'd Flower' (*Poems*, ii. 570).

These were searched . . . People: although Swift was strident in defence of episcopacy he rarely has a good word for contemporary bishops. Cf. his observation on the Revd Thomas Sawbridge, Dean of Ferns, in a letter to the Earl of Oxford in 1730: 'There is a fellow here from England one Sawbridge, he was last term indited for a Rape. The Plea he intended was his being drunk when he forced the woman; but he bought her off; He is a Dean and I name him to your Lordship, because I am confident you will hear of his being a Bishop' (*Corr.*, iii. 322; *Poems*, ii. 516–20). A contemporary story has it that when 'King George . . . made several odd and illiterate English Clergymen Bishops in Ireland' his choice was freely condemned when they came over to Ireland. 'Upon which Swift said with a grave face, ye are in the wrong to blame his Majesty before you know the truth: He sent us over very good and great Men, but they were murder'd by a parcell of highway Men between Chester and London, who slipping on their gowns and Cassocks here pretend to pass for those Bishops' (Ehrenpreis, ii. 771; iii. 168). The failure of the Dean of St Patrick's to become a bishop clearly rankled; he wrote in *Verses on the Death of Dr. Swift* that 'HAD he but spar'd his Tongue and Pen, | He might have rose like other Men', observing 'While Numbers to Preferment rose; | Whose Merits were, to be his Foes' (ll. 355–6, 401–2, *Poems*, ii. 567, 569).

117 *When I had put an End . . . upon every Article*: the King's critique of Gulliver's account of his country is a combination of traditional satiric themes and contemporary opposition politics. The attack on a degenerate nobility, unfree elections, a corrupt legal system, criminal mismanagement of the treasury, and a mercenary standing army were prominent themes in Jacobite propaganda against the Hanoverian Whig state. Cf. the Duke of Wharton's critique of Hanoverian England and account of his interview with the Stuart Pretender, 'James III', published in 1726: 'the Triennial Act repelled, standing Armies and martial Law established by Authority of Parliament, the Convocation of the Clergy prevented from meeting, the orthodox Members of the Church discouraged, Schism, Ignorance and Atheism become the only Recommendations to Ecclesiastical Benefices; both Houses filled with the corrupt Tools of the Court, the Nation overwhelmed with exorbitant Taxes, the Honour and Treasure of *England* sacrificed to enlarge the Dominions of *Hanover*, and *German* beggarly Favourites trampling on the ancient Nobility; the Act of Limitation disregarded, the Liberty of the Press abolished, and the Constitution of *England* thrown into the Mould of Corruption, to be modelled according to arbitrary Pleasure and Usurpation . . . I was surprised to find ['his Majesty'] pointing out each particular Misfortune that Usurpation had introduced into his native Country; and thus preventing me from enumerating the long Catalogue of Calamities that I had prepared to be the Subject of my melancholly Story. Throughout his Majesty's whole Discourse, he appeared . . . like a Patriot weeping over the Ruins of his Country . . . His Resolutions to preserve inviolably the established Church of *England*, his just Sense of the Necessity of frequent Parliaments, his generous Desire of freeing his Subjects from the unnecessary Burden of Taxes, his Abhorrence of Corruption, his Detestation of Tyranny . . . SINCE that happy Interview with the King, I have directed all my Thoughts to his Majesty's Service . . . in Defence of . . . the Liberty of *Old England* . . .' (Wharton, 2, 3–4, 7; see also Lansdowne, *passim*).

118 *slavish prostitute Chaplains . . . Nobleman*: Swift alleged in his *Short Character* of the Earl of Wharton that the Whig Earl had tried to make his sycophantic chaplain a bishop as a reward for marrying one of the Earl's cast-off mistresses (*PW* iii. 182–3). In *Some Arguments against Enlarging the Power of Bishops*, Swift wrote that Irish Bishoprics will be left 'to the Disposal of a chief Governor, who can never fail of some worthless illiterate Chaplain, fond of a Title and Precedence. Thus will that whole Bench, in an Age or two, be composed of mean, ignorant, fawning Gown-men, humble Suppliants and Dependents upon the *Court* for a Morsel of Bread, and ready to serve every Turn that shall be demanded from them' (*PW* ix. 53).

sifted: closely questioned.

119 *Issues*: expenditure.

he was still at a Loss . . . Person: the King articulates Tory criticism of the financial revolution under William III which saw the institutionalization of a permanent national debt (Firth, 223–4; PT).

chargeable: expensive.

Wars . . . Kings: cf. Swift's Tory pro-Peace pamphlet *The Conduct of the Allies* (1711) attacking Whig war policy, the Dutch, and the Duke of Marlborough: 'THOSE who are fond of continuing the War cry up our constant Success at a most prodigious rate . . . Getting into the Enemy's Lines, passing Rivers, and taking Towns, may be Actions attended with many glorious Circumstances: But when all this brings no real solid Advantage to us, when it hath no other End than to enlarge the Territories of the *Dutch*, and encrease the Fame and Wealth of our *General*, I conclude, however it comes about, that Things are not as they should be; and that surely our Forces and Money might be better employed . . .'. The 'true Spring or Motive' of the war against France 'was the aggrandizing a particular Family, and in short, a War of the *General* and the *Ministry*, and not of the *Prince* or *People*' (*PW*, vi. 19–20, 41).

mercenary standing Army: the King of Brobdingnag's observations recall the argument against standing armies in *Utopia* comparing mercenary soldiers to thieves (*Utopia*, 17). Swift's first patron Sir William Temple argued against a standing army in *An Essay upon the Original and Nature of Government* (Temple, i. 102) and used the same family metaphor of father–children–servant as Swift does in his anti-army writings (see Robert C. Steensma, 'Swift on Standing Armies: A Possible Source', *N&Q*, NS 10 (1963), 215–16). Opposition to standing armies was a popular theme of Old Whigs and Tories during William III's reign. After the Hanoverian accession, total opposition to standing armies was a Jacobite theme. Charles Leslie set the tone in 1715: 'For when he [the 'Elector of Brunswick' i.e. George I] has an army, he may augment it to a number that shall make you hewers of wood and drawers of water; which deserves the notice of whig as well as tory, for the calamity will be general, and therefore equally affect both' (*The Church of England's Advice to her Children, and to all Kings, Princes, and Potentates*, in *Somers Tracts*, xiii. 699). The Jacobite George Flint was 'amaz'd, astonish'd' how any man with a family and property could be 'pleased to see a standing Army' (*The Shift Shifted*, no. 7 (16 June 1716), 41). As propagandist for Queen Anne's Tory government in the *Examiner* of 21 December 1710 Swift considered 'a Kingdom as a great Family, whereof the Prince is the Father; and it will appear plainly, that Mercenary Troops are only *Servants armed*' and associated standing armies with the military tyranny of Caesar in Rome and Cromwell in England (*PW* iii. 41, 44). In 1722 Swift denounced the mercenary standing army kept up by King George I and his Whig ministry (*PW* ix. 31–2). In a bleak description of Hanoverian Ireland (written *c.*1730), Swift computed that the impoverished and starving Irish population was almost doubled by 'a Standing Army of Twenty Thousand *English* . . . together with their Trulls, their Bastards, and their Horse-Boys' ('The Answer to the Craftsman', *PW* xii. 175). Swift opposed a standing army in England whether in time of peace or war (*PW* v. 80). See also Lock, 138–40.

120 *odd Kind of Arithmetick*: alludes to statistical studies of population and political economy which Swift also parodied in works such as *A Modest Proposal* and 'The Answer to the Craftsman' and which is a subject of satire in the *Memoirs of Martinus Scriblerus* (*Memoirs*, 167–8, 341–2). Swift's library contained the English statistician and political economist Sir William Petty's *Several Essays in Political Arithmetick* (1699), see *Library*, Part I, vol. ii, 1413–16.

he knew no Reason: cf. Swift's 'Thoughts on Religion': 'You may force men, by interest or punishment, to say or swear they believe, and to act as if they believed: You can go no further. Every man, as a member of the commonwealth, ought to be content with the possession of his own opinion in private, without perplexing his neighbour or disturbing the public' (*PW* ix. 261).

vend them about as Cordials: in his 'Remarks' upon Matthew Tindal's *The Rights of the Christian Church asserted*, Swift wrote: 'Men must be governed in Speculations, at least not suffered to vent them' (*PW* ii. 99).

Gaming: gambling. Also queried and rejected in More's Utopia (*Utopia*, pp. 20, 50, 70).

121 *Surface of the Earth*: cf. Apollo's reaction and judgement in Boccalini, Advertisement XLVI: 'his Majesty being mightily troubled, That the Art of Destruction, the Art of War, should be improved of late to such a degree of wicked Excellence' declares that 'Since Men were grown so wretchedly Foolish and Wicked . . . He desired . . . to rid the World of such Vermin . . . That a second Deluge might at once sweep 'em off the Face of the Earth' (pp. 173, 176).

122 *Dionysius Halicarnassensis*: a Greek writer (*fl. c.*25 BC) who lived in and eulogized Rome. In ch. 3 of his *Letter to Pompeius* (774) he judges Thucydides inferior to Herodotus as a historian, because Thucydides showed 'a bitter and resentful attitude towards his country, for sending him into exile. Thus he very accurately lists all her wrongdoings, but when she does right, he either ignores it completely, or mentions it with obvious reluctance'. PT.

Prejudices: Gulliver is in true Whig mode. Opposition to 'prejudices' was a shibboleth of anticlerical Whigs. In 'Thoughts on Various Subjects', Swift wrote: 'SOME Men, under the Notions of weeding out Prejudices; eradicate Religion, Virtue, and common Honesty' (*PW* i. 243). The putative author of *A Tale of a Tub*, the mad hack, thinks it best 'to remove Prejudices'; Swift, in his authorial 'Apology' for the book writes that '*under the Notion of Prejudices, he knew to what dangerous Heights some Men have proceeded*' (*PW* i. 101, 1).

123 *between three and four hundred Years ago*: as early as 1242 Roger Bacon was aware of the explosive power of a mixture of saltpetre, charcoal, and sulphur. An illustration of a gun appears in an Oxford manuscript of 1325 and guns are known to have been used in Florence in 1326. Gunpowder was said to have been invented by a German monk Bertholdus or Michael Schwarz in about 1320 (Gough, 376; PT). The gunpowder revolution in military technology had begun in Europe over three centuries earlier, however the Chinese had the technology from the ninth century.

124 *reduced Politicks into a Science*: an approach associated with Machiavelli's *The Prince* (1513).

he gave it for his Opinion: it was also Swift's opinion, cf. *The Drapier's Letters*, Letter VII: 'An Humble Address to Both Houses of Parliament': 'I shall never forget what I once ventured to say to a great Man in *England*; That few *Politicians*, with all their Schemes, are half so useful Members of a Commonwealth, as an *honest Farmer*; who, by skilfully draining, fencing, manuring and planting, hath increased the intrinsick Value of a Piece of Land; and thereby done a *perpetual Service* to his Country; which it is a great Controversy, whether any of the *former* ever did, since the Creation of the World; but no Controversy at all, that Ninety-nine in a Hundred, have done Abundance of Mischief' (*PW* x. 141).

125 *Ideas*: Plato's archetypal patterns, of which all individual objects are imperfect copies. PT.

Entities: in scholastic philosophy, the essences or existences of things, as opposed to their qualities or relations. PT.

Transcendentals: in Aristotelian philosophy, things transcending the bounds of any single category. PT.

as to Ideas . . . Heads: the satiric strategy of expressing wisdom as simplicity, obtuseness, and ignorance is used with devastating misanthropic effect in Part IV in the Houyhnhnm Master's reaction to what he hears about humankind. The satirized Laputians in Part III are absurdly and dangerously given to abstraction and theory. The King of Brobdingnag, the Houyhnhnms, and More's Utopians are like the Ancients and lack the scholastic philosophy and abstract conceptions which More, like Erasmus, mocked. Swift may ironically recall a satiric passage in *Utopia* which in turn was indebted to Erasmus: 'while they equal the ancients in almost all subjects, they are far from matching the inventions of our modern logicians. In fact they have not discovered even one of those elaborate rules about restrictions, amplifications and suppositions . . . They are so far from being able to speculate on "second intentions" that not one of them was able to see "man-in-general", though we pointed straight at him with our fingers, and he is, as you well know, colossal and bigger than any giant' (*Utopia*, 64).

No Law: it was one of Swift's maxims that 'IF Books and Laws continue to increase as they have done for fifty Years past; I am in some Concern for future Ages, how any Man will be learned, or any Man a Lawyer' (*PW* iv. 246). Few or no laws are a feature of ideal commonwealths, see Plato, *Republic*, iv. 425C–D; Plutarch, 'Lycurgus,' xiii. 1–2; More, *Utopia*, 82. The expanding body of legislation in the Hanoverian state was a topic of Jacobite satire. Recommending few laws and the example of Lycurgus, the Duke of Wharton remarked 'that *Jacobites* ludicrously say, in one Sense, the present Government is *Law-full*' (*The True Briton*, no. 61, 30 December 1723, in *The Life and Writings of Philip Late Duke of Wharton*, 2 vols. (London, 1732), ii. 521–3).

125 *Art of Printing*: the Chinese printed the teachings of Confucius from woodblocks in 932. PT.

Libraries . . . not very large: an index of a good society in *GT*. Swift wrote that: 'A great Library always makes me melancholy, where the best Author is as much squeezed, and as obscure, as a Porter at a Coronation'. Swift's 'own little library' contained nearly 500 titles in 1715 (*Corr.*, iii. 231, 232 n. 11).

Their Stile: in accord with Swift's own prescriptive views rejecting a florid for a simple, plain style (see e.g. *PW* ix. 65–8), cf. the linguistic simplicity and propriety of the Houyhnhnm conversation in Part IV where 'nothing passed but what was useful, expressed in the fewest and most significant Words'.

126 *Nature was degenerated*: the idea that humans used to be larger is as old as Homer (*Iliad*, xii. 447–9) and seemed to have biblical support (Genesis 6: 4; Numbers 13: 33), but was particularly popular in the seventeenth century (Gough, 377; PT). A French dissertation (1718) argued that Adam was 123 feet 9 inches high, Eve, 118 feet and 9¾ inches, Moses 13 feet, and Alexander only 6 feet (Eddy, 123). It was almost a topos in voyage literature texts to report the presence of giants or how the histories and excavations in remote countries indicated that there were giants in the past (for many examples, see D. F. Passmann, *'Full of Improbable Lies': Gulliver's Travels und die Reiseliteratur vor 1726* (Frankfurt am Main: Peter Lang, 1987), 166–82).

confirmed by huge Bones and Sculls . . . dug up: the voyager Jan Huyghen van Linschoten reported that 'the *Peruvians* say, that . . . in times past, there dwelt great men like Giants'. The traditional tale was proven when 'certayne places' were 'digged uppe, where they found so great bones and ribbes, that it was incredible to bee mens bones, but that they found the heads lying by them, the teeth thereof being three fingers broad, and foure fingers long, and five quarters square, which were sent into divers places of *Peru*' (Linschoten, 270). Gulliver brings back from Brobdingnag 'a Footman's Tooth' which 'was about a Foot long, and four Inches in Diameter' which helped 'confirm all I had said' about giants.

Tile falling: a familiar illustration of the precariousness of human life, e.g. Juvenal, *Satires*, iii. 269–74; Lucian, *Charon* (Lucian, 83). PT.

made up of Tradesmen: support for a militia rather than a mercenary standing army was an Opposition shibboleth. The Country platform of Tories and Old Whigs in the 1690s called for the disbandment of the army. In 1697 Robert Harley, later to be leader of Queen Anne's Tory government of 1710–14 and a friend of Swift's, moved to disband all the standing forces raised since 1680. William III and George I preferred a professional standing army to a militia. Robert Walpole thought the army more reliable than the militia in controlling popular disturbances (see Cruickshanks, 83–4, 98). More's Utopia is basically pacifist, but men and women undertake military training and can form a citizen's army if the need arises (*Utopia*, 85).

Manner of Venice: the ballot was used in the election of the Great Council in Venice from 1297 onwards. The secret ballot and annual elections are a feature of Utopia (*Utopia*, 48). The Venetian secret ballot was being recommended as a means of ensuring free elections in the crypto-Jacobite Tory press, see Nathaniel Mist's *The Weekly Journal or Saturday Post*, no. 175 (7 April 1722), 1047; *Fog's Weekly Journal*, no. 285 (20 April 1734).

127 *Imagination can Figure nothing so Grand*: but see Milton, *Paradise Lost*, i. 663–6: 'He spake: and to confirm his words, out flew | Millions of flaming swords, drawn from the thighs | Of mighty cherubim; the sudden blaze | Far round illumined hell' (*Paradise Lost*, 100).

the same Disease: a commonplace. The necessity of a balance of power between 'the *Kings*, *Lords*, and *Commons*' such as in '*Sparta*, in its primitive Institution by *Lycurgus*' is stated in Swift's *A Discourse of the Contests and Dissentions* (1701), *PW* i. 200. Cf. Chevalier Ramsay's *The Travels of Cyrus*: 'To establish an even Ballance of the Kings and Peoples Power, which lean'd alternately to Tyranny and Anarchy, *Lycurgus* instituted a Council of . . . Senators; whose Authority being a Mean betwixt the two Extremes, deliver'd *Sparta* from its domestick Dissentions' (*Cyrus*, i. 212).

Composition: agreement. This was the lost political alternative to the Revolution of 1688–9 proposed in Jacobite compounding tracts: a 'composition' between lawful king and people, replacement of a mercenary standing army with a 'militia', and a balance between 'the monarchical, aristocratical, and democratical particles of the composure' of regular government (see Charlwood Lawton, *The Jacobite Principles Vindicated*, in *Somers Tracts*, x. 536, 527; *Honesty is the Best Policy*, in *Somers Tracts*, x. 212, 213).

128 *like . . . Canary Birds*: slavery was a fate for many contemporary English mariners whose vessels had been shipwrecked or hijacked. 'Canary Birds' was contemporary slang, the modern equivalent would be 'jailbirds'. Cyrano is kept literally in a cage (Eddy, 21). Contemporary reports of the marriages of court dwarfs and unsuccessful attempts to multiply the breed may have suggested the passage. PT.

128 *even*: equal.

129 *wistful melancholy Look towards the Sea*: possibly a mock-heroic version of
     Odyssey, v. 151–8, where Odysseus sits weeping on the shore of Calypso's
     (= Glumdalclitch's) island, gazing out to sea and longing for home. PT.
     Throughout *GT* Gulliver's moments of interiority are presented as
     mock-pathos.

     some Eagle: Cyrano is carried off in his cage by a roc (*Histoire*, 339; Eddy,
     129). PT.

     like a Tortoise: Aeschylus was said to have been killed by an eagle which
     mistook his bald head for a stone, and dropped a tortoise on to it (Gough,
     378; PT).

130 *Squash*: splash.

     I was fallen into the Sea: possibly suggested by the fate of the dwarf John
     Wormberg, who was drowned at Rotterdam (1695) when the porter
     carrying his box fell into the river (A. M. Taylor, *TSE* 7 (1957), 30).

131 *better*: more.

132 *by all that was moving*: as movingly as I could.

133 *to rights*: completely.

     Passages: incidents.

     make: get to, arrive at.

136 *Phaeton*: in Greek myth, the son of Helios, the sun-god. Phaeton
     attempted to drive the sun's chariot, he lost control, nearly burned up the
     earth, was struck down by Zeus, and fell into the river Eridanus. The
     familiar story exemplifies pride before a fall.

     Tonquin: Northern Vietnam.

     New-Holland: Australia. Gulliver is sailing along the north-west coast.
     The east coast of Australia was unknown to European mariners at this
     time.

Part III. A Voyage to Laputa

139 *Laputa*: from Spanish *la puta* meaning 'the whore'. Swift may be alluding
     to a proverb in his Spanish dictionary: 'Beware of a whore, who leaves the
     purse empty' (PT). In Part III, Laputa suggests the Hanoverian English
     Court and the British metropolis. A contemporary political critique iden-
     tified the Flying Island with the royal prerogative (Abel Boyer, *Political
     State of Great Britain*, 33 (January 1727), 27; Lock, 90 n. 1). In his Irish
     tracts, and particularly in the *Drapier's Letters* opposing the grant of a
     patent to William Wood to mint copper coins for Ireland (written in
     1724–5; Swift was at work on Part III of GT in 1724 and finished a draft
     of the whole book by September 1725, see *Corr.*, ii. 487, 606), Swift
     represents Ireland as robbed by Britain. Jacobite polemic represented
     Britain post-1688 as a 'whore' and its court made up of thieves (*POAS*
     v. 59). Condemning the prostitution of Britain to William III and the

Dutch in 1688–9, the Irish Anglican Jacobite Charles Leslie asked 'Whether Dame *Britannia* were not less culpable in being forc'd to endure a Thirteen Years Rape from *Oliver* and the Rump, than by living a Five Years Adulteress now by Consent?' (*A Catalogue of Books of the Newest Fashion* . . . (London, 1694), 8). Laputa also satirizes pure science and intellectuals, so the name may derive from Latin *putō* meaning 'think', 'reckon', or 'consider', hence Laputa may mean 'the country of the thinkers' (Cecil C. Seronsy, 'Some Proper Names in "Gulliver's Travels" ', *N&Q* 202 (1957), 471). Principal satiric targets in Part III are pure science, and absolutism which is identified with the Hanoverian court and Walpolean ministry.

141 *William Robinson . . . Hopewell*: a William Robinson captained a ship called the *Adventure* (the name of Gulliver's ship in Parts II and IV) in 1710. There are naval records of three contemporary ships named *Hopewell* (see Quinlan, 413) and at least four ships of that name are mentioned in Purchas (Real/Vienken, 518). An account of the voyage of David Middleton to Java and Banda in 1609 describes 'a Hollander' on the 'Island of Bangaia' who lived near 'Amboina': 'This one Hollander bore such a sway, that never a man left upon the Island durst displease him' (Purchas, iii. 92–3). Middleton's English ship is called the *Hopewell* and is constantly threatened with being taken and boarded by the Dutch (Purchas, iii. 102–10).

Thirst . . . seeing the World: Raphael Hythloday was 'eager to see the world' and on his last voyage does not want to return but to stay at the remotest point which 'was altogether agreeable to him', although, like Gulliver on his last voyage, he does return, on a Portuguese ship (*Utopia*, 10–11).

proposed: anticipated.

Fort St George: Madras or Chennai in southern India; the East India Company established its base there in 1640.

142 *tyed Back to Back*: the Dutch method of murder of English crews made familiar in Tory and Jacobite polemic, cf. Charles Leslie, *Delenda Carthago. Or, The True Interest of England, in Relation to France and Holland* (1695): '*causing them to be tied back to back, they were cast into the Sea . . . the* Dutch . . . *went aboard the* English *Ships, and served every Man in the same manner*' (pp. 4–5).

strict Alliance: the English and the Dutch were members of the Grand Alliance (1701) in the war against France, but were bitter commercial rivals. Accounts of English–Dutch animosity are ubiquitous in the south seas voyage literature Swift drew upon in *GT*.

143 *Longitude 183*: contemporary maps place Gulliver in the Pacific, east of Japan, south of the Aleutian Islands.

144 *vast Opake Body*: PT compares the approach to the moon in Lucian's *The True History* (Lucian, 253): 'we sighted what looked like a big island

hanging in mid air, white and round and brilliantly illuminated'. An analogue to Swift's use of the flying island was contemporary political satire in the voyage-to-the-moon genre (see Eddy, 23–4; Daniel Defoe, *The Consolidator: Or, Memoirs of Sundry Transactions from the World in the Moon. Translated from the Lunar Language, By the Author of The True-born English Man* (London, 1705)).

144 *shining very bright*: the bottom of the Flying Island is later said to be of adamant and scientists used the word for diamond as well as for loadstone. PT

Island . . . as they pleased: there was great popular interest in the possibility of flying machines and flights to the moon, and flying machines were an enthusiasm of prominent members of the Royal Society, early advocates including Robert Hooke, secretary of the Royal Society, and Bishop John Wilkins. The preoccupation was a favourite target of sceptical satire (see *Memoirs*, 167, and notes pp. 332–4).

145 *polite*: polished, refined.

Italian: the Italian-sounding Laputians obsessed with music and mathematics associate Laputa with London and the Hanoverian court (George I was a patron of music and Italian opera, and the Royal Academy of Music's composers included George Frederick Handel, Giovanni Bononcini, and Attilio Ariosti). John Gay informed Swift in February 1723 that 'As for the reigning Amusement of the town, tis entirely Musick. real fiddles, Bass Viols and Haut boys . . . Theres no body allow'd to say I Sing but an Eunuch or an Italian Woman. Every body is grown now as great a judge of Musick as they were in your time of Poetry. and folks that could not distinguish one tune from another now daily dispute about the different Styles of Hendel, Bononcini, and Attilio' (*Corr.*, ii. 446). In Swift's virulent anti-Hanoverian poem 'Directions for a Birth-Day Song', the Whig panegyrical poet when the 'Song is done' is directed 'To Minheer Hendel next you run, | Who artfully will pare and prune | Your words to some Italian Tune' (*Poems*, ii. 469).

146 *neither . . . Debt*: I paid them back in their own coin. Gulliver is as astonished as they are.

Mortals so singular: cf. Ned Ward's satire in *The London Spy* on the unworldly, mathematics-obsessed intellectuals of the Royal Society in London: 'we came to . . . Gresham College . . . stepped . . . into a spacious quadrangle, where . . . we saw a peripatetic walking, ruminating, as I suppose, upon his entities, essences and occult qualities . . . His countenance was mathematical, having as many lines and angles in his face as you shall find in Euclid's *Elements*, and he looked as if he had fed upon nothing but Cursus Mathematicus for a fortnight' (Ward, 52). PT observes that the satiric device of putting unworldly intellectuals literally up in the air can be traced back to Aristophanes (*Clouds*, 218 ff.), where Socrates is suspended in a basket. The appearance of the Laputians has been compared to an emblematic picture of 'Mathematica' in the *Icones*

Symbolicae of C. Giarda (Milan, 1626) where Mathematica 'wears a tunic patterned with compasses, stars, numbers, and musical notations. She carries geometrical instruments, and (a more definite link with the Laputans) the lid is closed over one eye, while the other looks directly upwards' (Kathleen Williams, 'Swift's Laputans and "Mathematica"', *N&Q*, NS 10 (1963), 216–17; PT).

Taction: touching, contact.

so wrapped up: alluding to the traditional tale of Thales falling into a well while gazing at the stars. Swift's satire perhaps recalls Montaigne, *Essays*, ii. 12 'Apology for Raymond Sebond': 'I feel grateful to the Milesian wench who, seeing the philosopher Thales continually spending his time in contemplation of the heavenly vault and always keeping his eyes raised upward, put something in his way to make him stumble, to warn him that it would be time to amuse his thoughts with things in the clouds when he had seen to those at his feet ... As Socrates says in Plato, whoever meddles with philosophy may have the same reproach made to him as ... to Thales, that he sees nothing of what is in front of him' (Montaigne, 402). There may be personal satire on Sir Isaac Newton with reference to contemporary anecdotes about his absent-mindedness and impracticality (Gough, 382). Newton was loathed by Swift and the Tories for his activities as Warden of Mint (it was said that Newton would be the first Whig hanged at a Stuart restoration), for approving the quality of William Wood's copper coinage, and as the symbol of Hanoverian patronage of mathematics: 'one *Isaac Newton*, an Instrument-Maker ... and afterwards a Workman in the Mint, at the Tower, ... knighted for making Sun-Dyals better than others of his Trade, and was thought to be a Conjurer, because he knew how to draw Lines and Circles upon a Slate, which no Body could understand ... an obscure Mechanick' (*PW* iv. 122–3).

147 *Kennel*: gutter.

Before the Throne ... Mathematical Instruments: alluding to the Hanoverian court and its patronage of mathematics. George I is reported to have expressed great satisfaction at having Newton as his subject in one country and Leibniz in another. PT.

Strangers: foreigners. Xenophobic anti-Hanoverian propaganda complained of George I's patronage of Hanoverians in England, cf. Swift's poem to his friend Charles Ford on his birthday in 1723, commenting that in London 'you have told us from Experience, | Are swarms of Bugs and Hanoverians' (ll. 49–50; *Poems*, i. 313).

148 *Floating Island*: Sir William Temple had referred to English foreign policy and to England as a 'floating island' (Firth, 232–3).

the true Etymology: possibly a parody of any number of Richard Bentley's philological conjectures. Bentley was a satiric target in Swift's *A Tale of a Tub* and *The Battle of the Books*.

149 *happening to mistake a Figure*: a satire on recent attempts to determine the

altitude of the sun, moon, stars, and mountains, both lunar and terres-
trial, by quadrants and other instruments, perhaps also containing a reference to a mistake by Newton's printer in adding a cipher to the distance
of the earth from the sun (Nicolson, 120; PT).

149 *King . . . Musical Instruments*: a satire on George I, who had given Handel
a pension and had contributed towards the establishment of the Royal
Academy of Music. Members of the Royal Society such as Dr John
Wallis had contributed several papers on the analogies between music
and mathematics (Nicolson, 120–3; PT).

stunned with the Noise . . . Musick of the Spheres: PT suggests a parody of
Cicero's *Somnium Scipionis* (x–xi).

Packthreads were let down: PT suggests the system is modelled on a passage in *Icaromenippus* (Lucian, 127–8) where Zeus removes the lids from
a row of holes in his palace floor and receives supplications from all over
the world below.

150 *Intellectuals*: mental capacities.

judicial Astrology: cf. the ridicule of judicial astrology (that is astrology as
divination by the stars, as in the modern sense; astrology could also mean
astronomy in this period) in More's *Utopia* (p. 65). In 1708 Swift 'killed'
a high-profile contemporary astrologer, an anticlerical Whig by the name
of John Partridge. Calling himself Isaac Bickerstaff, a rival astrologer,
Swift in a sequence of premeditated pamphlets predicted Partridge
would die on the night of 29 March, gave a circumstantial account of his
death, and, when Partridge claimed to be alive, published a vindication of
Bickerstaff's veracity on the fact of Partridge's death. This April Fool's
Day hoax captured the public imagination (see *PW* ii. 139–70).

Disposition . . . Politicks: Swift frequently comments on this disposition in
the English people (see e.g. *Corr.*, i. 147; *PW* v. 79; *PW* xv. 14).

same Disposition . . . Mathematicians: Isaac Newton was a strong Whig
and the German mathematician Leibniz actively supported the Grand
Alliance (Gough, 384–5).

151 *conceited*: opinionated. Swift proceeds to satirize contemporary
astronomical speculation and theory.

that the Earth . . . swallowed up: alluding to Newton's analysis of planet-
ary motion in *Principia Mathematica* (1687) and his warning that any
disturbance of the earth's velocity in relation to the sun would be disas-
trous and lead to the earth falling into the sun. Newton was optimistic
that this would not happen as the loss of velocity was inappreciable even
over a vast tract of time (Nicolson, 125).

That the Face . . . Effluvia: during the early years of the eighteenth
century the *Philosophical Transactions* of the Royal Society accorded
much attention to the phenomenon of sunspots. It was suggested that
sunspots were caused by the eruption of solar volcanoes and that the
surface of the sun might become encrusted with lava (Nicolson, 125–7).

the last Comet: Halley's comet of 1682. Edmund Halley predicted its return in 1758 (Nicolson, 127–9).

will probably destroy us: William Whiston, in his *A New Theory of the Earth* (London, 1696), see esp. Book II, pp. 126–56, and in *The Cause of the Deluge Demonstrated* (1714) had concluded that the biblical Flood had been caused by a comet. Edmond Halley read a paper about Noah's Flood to the Royal Society in 1724 in which he described the earth destroyed and reduced to its ancient chaos (Nicolson, 131–2).

Perihelion: the point of a planet's or comet's orbit nearest to the sun. This parodies a passage in Newton's *Principia*, Book III, Proposition XLII, Problem XXII: 'The comet which appeared in the year 1680 was in its perihelion less distant from the sun . . . being attracted something nearer to the sun in every revolution, will at last fall down upon the body of the sun' (quoted in Nicolson, 132). Cf. the mathematical demonstration of the '*Perihelion*' in the orbit of comets in Whiston's *A New Theory of the Earth*, i. 37–47 ff.

That the Sun . . . annihilated: Robert Hooke had suggested the possibility that the sun was gradually burning itself up (Nicolson, 126–7). The idea of the sun dying or 'heat death', reinforced by the second law of thermodynamics, would later fuel theories of degeneration in the nineteenth and early twentieth centuries and would be a powerful satiric trope for Joseph Conrad, for instance, in his novel *The Secret Agent* (1907).

152 *want the same Endowments*: lack the same intellectual capacities as the Laputians.

Husband . . . Implements: conceivably a punning allusion to Juvenal's phrase for an unjealous husband: 'doctus spectare lacunar' (trained to stare at the ceiling: *Satires*, i. 56), *doctus* being made in this context to carry the additional sense of 'erudite'. PT.

married to the prime Minister: satiric allusion to the open infidelity of Prime Minister Walpole and his first wife Catherine Shorter.

English Story: 'Does not this resemble, Mr. Dean, the Case of the late *John Dormer* Esq; and *Tom Jones* his Footman? The whole of this Affair may be seen among those curious Pieces, intitled, *The Cases of Impotency and Divorce*, in five Volumes, printed for Mr. CURLL in the *Strand*' (*Key*, Part III, p. 12).

154 *its Diameter*: PT explains that the island appears to be modelled on the *terrella* (little earth) described in William Gilbert's *De Magnete* (1600), a loadstone ground to spherical form and used for experiments designed to investigate the magnetic action of the earth. Among the exhibits of the Royal Society was a *terrella* about four and a half inches in diameter; hence Laputa's diameter of four and a half miles. Swift is also probably alluding to estimates of the diameter of the earth by Newton and others. PT

as Naturalists agree: modern 'naturalists' would agree that *cirrus* can rise to a height of over 8 miles; but in 1729 J. T. Desaguliers gave 2 miles as the maximum height at which 'Vapour raised by the Heat . . . will settle' (*PTA* VI. ii. 68). PT.

154 *Astronomers Cave*: there was a deep cave at the Royal Observatory in Paris. PT.

155 *a Load-stone*: suggestive of the compass needle used in navigation, and as PT observes an imaginative transformation of the contemporary magnet-ized needle (used to indicate the direction of the earth's magnetism) which was capable of turning in a vertical plane about a horizontal axis. The heterodox Whig William Whiston's account in *A New Theory of the Earth* of the 'Power of Attraction belonging to the Loadstone' (i. 2) and calculation of the oblique motion of the heavenly bodies ('If a Body, as B, be moving uniformly along the line DC, from D to C; and another Body A be present, this latter Body A must draw the former B from its straight line DC, . . .' see i. 8 and *passim*) is probably one of the sources parodied by Swift in Gulliver's technical account and explanatory figure of the loadstone and the motion of the flying island. The Royal Society's *Philosophical Transactions* contain many papers of specialist mathematical discourse.

Weaver's Shuttle: 'the *Load-stone*, no doubt, is a just Emblem of the *British* Linen and Woollen Manufactures, on which depends the Welfare of those *United Dominions*' (*Key*, Part III, p. 15). The Flying Island is associated with England and the Hanoverian Court, and later in Part III there is allusion to that Court's arbitrary power and oppression of Ireland. For Swift a sign of that oppression was the Woollen Act (1699) of the English parliament which banned the export of woollen goods from Ireland to any destination other than England, where there were already prohibitive import duties. As PT suggests there is also a biblical allusion to Job 7: 6: 'My days are swifter than a weaver's shuttle, and are spent without hope'. An unprinted passage later in Part III valorizing armed insurrection, revolution, and regicide will suggest how the Irish may hope to end arbitrary Whig oppression.

157 *For, although . . . Clearness*: this sentence does not appear in the first edition, but was inserted by Ford, with 'an hundred Yards' in place of 'a Hundred', in his interleaved copy of the first edition in the National Art Library, Victoria and Albert Museum. In the later seventeenth and early eighteenth centuries tubeless telescopes were of enormous length, how-ever there was contemporary interest in small instruments with increased magnification. A refracting telescope described in the *Philosophical Transactions* of 1723 was 6 feet long and magnified up to 230 times (*PTA* VI. i. 133–5; Gough, 388; Nicolson, 123 n. 28; PT).

Catalogue . . . Stars: which beats John Flamsteed, England's first astron-omer royal, who only catalogued 2,935 stars. Flamsteed had made him-self obnoxious to Swift's friend and fellow Scriblerian John Arbuthnot, which may have been a reason he is chosen as a satiric target (*Memoirs*, 329; PT).

two . . . Satellites: Swift successfully predicted the satellites of Mars which were indeed discovered, in 1877. Mars's two moons, Phobos and Deimos, and their orbits agree closely with Gulliver's account.

158 *observed Ninety-three . . . Comets*: in 1704 Halley calculated the orbits of twenty-four comets. PT.

Estates: Swift wrote that 'LAW in a free Country, is, or ought to be the Determination of the Majority of those who have Property in Land' (*PW* iv. 245) which should be confirmed by the Royal Assent (*PW* x. 134). See Lock, 131, 138–9.

deprive . . . Benefit . . . Sun: PT points to a literary analogue in *The True History* where the victorious Sun-people coerce the Moon-people into coming to terms with them by cutting off their light supply with a wall of thick cloud, a total eclipse which effectively condemned the Moon to permanent darkness (Lucian, 258). The passage is usually understood to be referring to England's economic oppression of Ireland. In the *Drapier's Letters* Swift wrote that English trade restrictions imposed on Ireland 'denied the *Benefits* which *God* and *Nature* intended to us' (*PW* x. 141).

159 *About three years*: this passage which has been understood as alluding to the successful Irish resistance to the attempt by George I's Whig government to impose on Ireland the copper coinage manufactured by William Wood was among Ford's manuscript additions in his copy of the first edition now in the National Art Library, Victoria and Albert Museum. Swift wrote his pseudonymous *Drapier's Letters* to mobilize Irish resistance to the scheme. There have been many ingenious attempts to read the details in the episode allegorically. The references to 'four large Towers' and a 'strong pointed Rock', for example, while seeming to invite allegorical interpretation are sufficiently ambiguous or indeterminate as to resist precise identification, see Lock, 85–6, 101–2 on the problems of previous allegorical interpretations of the passage.

Lindalino: innuendo Dublin.

Immunitys: i.e. from prosecution.

Choice of their own Governor: in his 'Fourth Letter', the Drapier acknowledges the English King only because the Irish Parliament has accepted him as King of Ireland: 'For in *Reason*, all *Government* without the Consent of the *Governed*, is the *very Definition of Slavery* (*PW* x. 63). Swift routinely refers to Ireland as enslaved and the Irish as slaves in his writings.

160 *I was assured . . . Government*: the coded account of popular rebellion in which the citizens threaten to kill the king would have appeared militantly Jacobitical to the Whig authorities and was unpublished in Swift's lifetime. In September 1722 the Whig authorities received sworn information of an Irish Jacobite plot to kill King George (see Ian Higgins, 'Jonathan Swift and the Jacobite Diaspora', *Reading Swift*, 98). In the published *Drapier's Letters* Swift denied that Irish resistance to Wood's patent represented a rebellious desire for dynastic change (e.g. *PW* x. 61).

But this rhetorically violent, unprinted passage valorizes more radical ambitions and is an attack on the Hanoverian monarchy and Whig government.

160 *a fundamental Law . . . Child-bearing*: 'like the *English* Act of Settlement' (*Key*, Part III, p. 16). Swift alludes to the Whig government's repeal of the provision in the Act of Settlement (1701) forbidding the King to leave England without parliament's approval. There is also an oblique innuendo about princesses in the House of Hanover as both George I and his son were alleged to be illegitimate in contemporary anti-Hanoverian libels. Cf. the manuscript variant of 'Horn and Crown' in Part II of *GT* and see Swift's 'Directions for a Birth-Day Song' ll. 15–20, where there is an innuendo referring to the alleged sexual intrigue of Sophia Dorothea, mother of George II, with Count Königsmarck (*Poems*, ii. 461).

161 *very desirous . . . heartily weary . . . People*: cf. *The True History* where Lucian after watching a battle between two fleets of floating islands says he is rather bored with life inside the whale (his floating island) and wants to leave (Lucian, 270–1). PT.

Countenance: favour, encouragement.

162 *Munodi*: the name derives from *mundum odi* (I hate the world). He is an embodiment of the conservative dimension of the political and cultural stance in *GT*. In modern commentary he has been identified with various contemporaries as different as Midleton (a Whig), Carteret (a Whig), Bolingbroke (a Tory and sometime Jacobite), Oxford (Old Whig, Tory, and sometime Jacobite) and his early patron Sir William Temple (a friend and adviser of William III). Such particular identifications, all in some ways unsatisfactory, are assessed by F. P. Lock who concludes that he is principally 'a paradigm of the benevolent, conservative, country gentleman of Swift's Tory mythology' (Lock, 118–21).

163 *I never knew a Soil . . . Want*: cf. Swift's view of the Irish countryside, the 'miserable Regions' (*Corr.*, ii. 427) that surrounded the country houses of his Tory friends Robert Cope and Thomas Sheridan whom he visited while at work on *GT*.

Insufficiency: incompetence.

polite: elegant, cultured.

164 *about Forty Years ago*: the Royal Society received its first charter in 1662 and its second in 1663, 45 years before the supposed date of this conversation (or 44 by the 'Old Style' calendar, which counted February 1708 as part of 1707). PT.

PROJECTORS: inventors or planners of political, social, financial, or scientific schemes. It was pejoratively applied to schemes which were wild or improbable. Literary models for the Academy of Projectors include the House of Solomon in Francis Bacon's *New Atlantis*, the Court of Queen Whim in Rabelais, and an account of an academy in

Joseph Hall's *Mundus Alter et Idem*. The Tory satirists Ned Ward, William King, and Tom Brown had made the Royal Society and its transactions part of their satiric repertoire.

165 *All the Fruits . . . chuse*: cf. *New Atlantis*: 'And we make (by art) . . . trees and flowers to come earlier or later than their seasons; and to come up and bear more speedily than by their natural course they do. We make them also by art greater much than their nature; and their fruit greater and sweeter and of differing taste, smell, colour, and figure, from their nature' (Bacon, 241).

ill Commonwealthsmen: lacking in public spirit.

a ruined Building: the hydraulic elements in this story might be an allusion to a long series of experiments reported to the Royal Society by Francis Hawksbee and James Jurin investigating the ascent of water in capillary tubes and the effect on the flow of water at various heights, and accounts of experiments concerning running water in pipes (Nicolson, 150–1). The story may allude to the South Sea Bubble catastrophe of 1720 and to contemporary entrepreneurial projects involving water and mills, for which see Pat Rogers, 'Gulliver and the Engineers', *MLR* 70 (1975), 260–70. The story is also possibly a political allusion to the Act of Settlement of 1701 which had diverted the hereditary succession of the crown from the House of Stuart to the remote (but Protestant) House of Hanover. Munodi had complied with this Laputian act in 1701 (innuendo: the Tories had complied with the Act of Settlement), but the destruction of his 'mill' (innuendo: the English Stuart line: in contemporary political iconography, as, for example, in the Dutch print 'Qualis vir Talis Oratio' dated 16 October 1688, a windmill symbolized the Stuart Pretender, 'James III' to the Jacobites) and the deviation to a new one (innuendo: the distant House of Hanover) was ruinous for Munodi (innuendo: the Tory party). The Jacobite Matthias Earbery used the trope of water current and water-mills for dynastic political commentary in his edition of *Advices from Parnassus. By Trajano Boccalini*, no. III (May 1727), Advice XII, p. 54.

166 *I had . . . in my younger Days*: Swift was at least nominally a Whig in 1701. He was also the author of *A Project for the Advancement of Religion, and the Reformation of Manners* (1709) and had proposed an Academy for the English language in *A Proposal for Correcting, Improving and Ascertaining the English Tongue* (1712).

167 *Academy of Lagado*: scholarship has identified the targets of Swift's satire as the Royal Society in London, the University of Leiden (which Lemuel Gulliver attended), and the Dublin Philosophical Society. Swift's satire of the new science describes or is based on actual contemporary experiments reported in the publications of the English Royal Society (see Marjorie Nicolson and Nora M. Mohler, 'The Scientific Background of Swift's Voyage to Laputa', in Nicolson, 110–54). There were scholarly connections between the Royal Society and the University of Leiden,

which had a reputation for religious toleration and the Newtonian modern science. One of Swift's earlier satiric victims the anticlerical Whig Astrologer John Partridge (see Swift's Bickerstaff Papers, *PW* ii. 139–64) claimed to have studied at the University of Leiden. The Latin name of the University of Leiden, Academia Lugduno-Batavo, was commonly abbreviated in booklists and correspondence as 'Acad. Lugd.' (from which Swift possibly derived 'Academy of Lagado') and the physical description of the Academy has been thought to resemble the University of Leiden more than Gresham College, the home of the Royal Society (see Dolores J. Palomo, 'The Dutch Connection: The University of Leiden and Swift's Academy of Lagado', *HLQ* 41 (1977), 27–35). The Dublin Philosophical Society had external ties with the Royal Society and articles from the Dublin Society were published in the Royal Society's *Philosophical Transactions*. It focused on scientific papers and encouraged experimentation. William Petty, whose statistical approach to population studies is parodied in the conversation between Gulliver and the King of Brobdingnag in Part II, was first president of the Dublin Philosophical Society. In satirizing what he regarded as misguided scientific experimentation, Swift characteristically has multiple targets, but there is an underlying ideological consistency, and that is to discredit the Newtonian Whig intelligentsia which received the patronage of the Hanoverian court and to ridicule anything even remotely connected with the Dutch.

167 *largely*: copiously, in detail.

Continuation of several Houses: in 1710 the Royal Society occupied two houses in Crane Court, Fleet Street, but had acquired several more properties by 1724 (Nicolson, pp. 137–8, n. 52).

growing waste: become empty.

five Hundred Rooms: the size may be a satire on the Royal Society's ambitions for expanded accommodation (Nicolson, 137) or might have suggested the University of Leiden buildings (Palomo, *HLQ* 41 (1977), 29–30).

extracting Sun-Beams out of Cucumbers: over a period of years John Hales had reported to the Royal Society experiments on the respiration of plants and animals and on the effect of sunbeams and how they entered plants. Hales caught the respired sunbeams in hermetically sealed jars. Sir Nicholas Gimcrack in Thomas Shadwell's *The Virtuoso* (1676) bottles country air releasing it in his chamber in London (Nicolson, 146–8).

a horrible Stink: Rabelais (v. 22, p. 651): 'Panurge fairly threw up his food when he saw an archasdarpenim fermenting a great tub of human urine in horse-dung, with plenty of Christian shit. Pooh, the filthy wretch! He told us, however, that he watered kings and great princes with this holy distillation, and thereby lengthened their lives by a good six or nine feet'.

168 *Malleability of Fire*: cf. Rabelais (v. 22, p. 652): 'Others were cutting fire with a knife, and drawing up water in a net.'

most ingenious Architect ... Bee ... Spider: probably a satiric gibe at Sir John Vanbrugh, the anticlerical Whig dramatist and architect whose architectural achievement Swift regarded as ridiculous. The discourse on architecture in the four parts of *GT* can be and was construed as personal satire on this high-profile member of the Whig elite. The bee and spider were insects admired for their architectural skills, see Virgil, *Georgics*, iv. 178–9; Pliny, *Natural History*, xi. 5–6, 28. Cf. the fable of the Bee and Spider in *The Battle of the Books* (*PW* i. 147–51). Swift alludes to contemporary architectural experiments in which floors and bridges were proposed or designed without supports under them (Nicolson, 139).

a Man born blind: probably meant to reflect on Newton's corpuscular theory of light reported in the *Philosophical Transactions*, but is specifically based on Robert Boyle's account of a blind man at Maastricht who could tell colours by touch. Boyle believed he really did it by smelling (different coloured dyes had different scents). Martinus Scriblerus was the first to find out 'the *Palpability* of *Colours*' and could distinguish 'Rays of Light' (Nicolson, 140–2; *Memoirs*, 167; PT).

plowing the Ground with Hogs: cf. Rabelais (v. 22, p. 651): 'Others were ploughing the sandy shore with three pairs of foxes in a yoke, and losing none of their seed.' A paper to the Royal Society reported a custom in Ceylon where buffaloes were enclosed in a patch of ground and would be left there 'until the Ground be sufficiently dunged' (Nicolson, 149). PT. Pig manure is not a fertilizer.

Maste: nuts used for pig feed.

the Artist: cf. contemporary projects making silk from spiders' webs and deriving dyes from insect excrement when the insects had been fed certain foods (Nicolson, 143–5).

169 *place a Sun-Dial*: Newton 'was knighted for making Sun-Dyals better than others of his Trade' (*PW* iv. 122–3). Clocks had been attached to weathercocks and made to agree with the Sun's apparent motion (Nicolson, 139–40). Newton however would have been no match for Swift's astronomer.

Town-House: town hall.

Cholick: stomach or bowel disorder.

large Pair of Bellows: Swift uses the image in *A Tale of a Tub* when satirizing Puritan Enthusiasm and the Quakers: 'At other times were to be seen several Hundreds link'd together in a circular Chain, with every Man a Pair of Bellows applied to his Neighbour's Breech, by which they blew up each other to the Shape and Size of a *Tun*' (*PW* i. 96).

Experiments upon a Dog: cf. Cervantes, *Don Quixote*, ii, Prologue to the Reader, 484: 'There was in Seville a madman who developed the funniest and most absurd obsession that ever affected any madman in the world. And it was this: he made a tube out of a cane sharpened at one end and, catching a dog in the street or wherever, he'd hold down one of its hind legs with his foot and use his hand to lift up the other, and fit the tube as best he could in the place where, by blowing, he made the dog as round as a ball; once he'd achieved this, he'd . . . let it go, saying to the onlookers . . . "Do you think it's an easy task to inflate a dog?".' Cf. Rabelais (v. 22, p. 651) on artificial extraction of farts from a dead donkey. Thomas Sprat's *The History of the Royal Society* (London, 1667) records a notorious experiment by Robert Hooke in which artificial respiration was induced in a dissected dog by blowing into its windpipe with a pair of bellows (p. 232).

169 *the universal Artist*: Robert Boyle was an expert on these subjects and may be Swift's target here (Nicolson, 151–2).

171 *sow Land with Chaff*: cf. the satire on futile, fruitless projects against the order of nature in Rabelais (v. 22, p. 651): 'Others were ploughing the sandy shore . . . Others were shearing asses, and getting long fleece wool. Others were gathering grapes from thorn-bushes, and figs from thistles. Others were milking he-goats . . . Others were chasing the wind with nets.'

 true seminal Virtue: Nicolson comments that the ' "seminal virtue" of plants had engrossed English botanists since the discovery of Nehemiah Grew that plants possessed sex' (p. 149).

 propagate the Breed of naked Sheep: again satirizing the impracticality and futility of such projects which work against nature.

 a Frame: in *A Tritical Essay upon the Faculties of the Mind* (1707) Swift wrote: 'how can the *Epicureans* Opinion be true, that the Universe was formed by a fortuitous Concourse of Atoms; which I will no more believe, than that the accidental Jumbling of the Letters in the Alphabet, could fall by Chance into a most ingenious and learned Treatise of Philosophy' (*PW* i. 246–7).

 the most ignorant Person: for satire on short cuts to learning 'without the Fatigue of *Reading* or of *Thinking*', see *A Tale of a Tub* (*PW* i. 91).

172 *Custom . . . to steal Inventions . . . from each other*: alluding to the controversy between Newton and Leibniz as to who had first discovered calculus.

 School of Languages: politically charged proposals for language academies were in vogue. Tories like Swift looked to the French Academy as a model.

 shorten Discourse: for Swift this particular corruption was introduced in 1688–9: 'THE only Invention of late Years, which hath any Way contributed to advance Politeness in Discourse, is that of abbreviating, or reducing Words of many Syllables into one, by lopping off the rest. This Refinement . . . begun about the Time of the Revolution' (*PW* iv. 106).

 Diminution of our Lungs: cf. the argument of Lucretius (*De Rerum Natura*, iv. 526–41) that sound is made of physical particles, since too much speaking causes abrasion of the throat. PT.

173 *Words are only Names for Things*: Thomas Sprat's *The History of the Royal Society* (1667) reports that the Royal Society resolved to return to the use of a plain style of 'primitive purity, and shortness, when men deliver'd so many *things*, almost in an equal number of *words*' (p. 113).

Women . . . Vulgar and Illiterate . . . common People: Swift recommended consulting women and the vulgar on matters of word choice and style in sermons and indeed in learned treatises; see e.g. *A Letter to a Young Gentleman Lately entered into Holy Orders* (1721; *PW* ix. 65).

an universal Language: alludes to schemes for a universal language advanced in George Dalgarno's *Ars Signorum, vulgo Character Universalis, et Lingua Philosophica* (1661) and Bishop John Wilkins's *Essay towards a Real Character and a Philosophical Language* (1668); see James Knowlson, *Universal Language Schemes in England and France, 1600–1800* (Toronto: University of Toronto Press, 1975).

Cephalick Tincture: medicine for the head.

174 *Quantum*: quantity

Bolus: a medicine, larger than pills, to be swallowed.

175 *Professors . . . out of their Senses*: cf. *A Tale of a Tub* where it is recommended that inspection should be made 'into *Bedlam*, and the Parts adjacent' as the students and professors there have the talents for civil and military offices (*PW* i. 111).

ebullient: causing heat or agitation.

redundant . . . peccant Humours: an old theory of medicine held that health depended on the correct balance between the four humours or fluids in the body: blood, phlegm, choler, and black bile. A morbid or 'peccant' humour caused disease.

the Right: i.e. the hand that takes bribes and grasps at profit. PT.

Flatus: wind.

176 *Ructations*: belches.

Canine Appetites: 'a morbid hunger, chiefly occurring in idiots and maniacs' (*OED*).

Crudeness of Digestion: indigestion.

Lenitives . . . required: 'Lenitives': painkillers; 'Aperitives': laxatives; 'Abstersives': purgatives; 'Corrosives': caustics; 'Restringents': drugs to inhibit bowel movement; 'Cephalalgicks': medicines for headache; 'Ictericks': remedies for jaundice; 'Apophlegmaticks': purges for phlegm; 'Acousticks': cures for deafness.

178 *take a strict View . . . Excrements*: the passage alludes to the trial of Bishop Atterbury for Jacobite conspiracy; the government prosecution used correspondence found in the Bishop's close-stool.

Conjunctures: circumstances.

Tribnia: an obvious anagram of Britain.

178 *Langden*: an obvious anagram of England.

Evidences: witnesses.

The Plots in that Kingdom: Swift alludes to the arrest and trial of Bishop Atterbury for Jacobite plotting in 1722. The line taken in the contemporary Jacobite press was that the 'Atterbury Plot' was a Whig fabrication.

179 *Forfeitures*: the estates of those convicted of treason were forfeited to the crown. The estates of leaders in the Jacobite Rising of 1715 had been confiscated by the government.

Opinion of publick Credit: the credit rating, the price of government bonds.

a lame Dog: as PT observes: references in Atterbury's correspondence to a small spotted dog called Harlequin, which he received as a present from France, and which had its leg broken on the journey, were used at his trial as evidence against him. The reference to a lame dog was Walpole's main break in identifying Atterbury as the leader in the conspiracy, the 'T. Illington' in the coded Jacobite correspondence, for 'T. Illington' had been sent such a dog. For Swift's virulent ridicule of the Whig prosecution and its tools and methods, see 'Upon the horrid Plot discovered by Harlequin the B—— of R——'s French Dog' (1722; *Poems*, i. 297–301).

an Invader: after this word and before 'the Plague' in Charles Ford's MS corrections to the first edition there is: 'a Codshead a ——,'. The blank should be filled with 'King' (cf. the Tory satirist Ned Ward's *The Whigs Unmask'd: Being The Secret History of the Calf's-Head-Club*, 8th edn. (London, 1713), 8: 'a large *Cod's-Head*, by which they pretended to represent the Person of the King'). Codshead meant blockhead. Swift's application is to the Hanoverian King, and neither Motte nor Faulkner printed it.

the Plague, a standing Army: a topical anti-government political allusion to the Quarantine Act of 1721 and the clauses giving emergency powers to the government. A Jacobite tract of 1722 observed: 'because in Times of Tranquility, standing Armies might be thought a Grievance, a new kind of War was contrived, a Plague was denounced, Forces were decreed to be kept on Foot' (Lansdowne, 5). Swift may also be recalling More's hostility to standing armies in *Utopia*: '. . . an even more pestiferous plague. Even in peacetime, if you can call it peace, the whole country is crowded and overrun with foreign mercenaries' (*Utopia*, 17).

Buzard: a useless kind of hawk, suggesting stupidity or ignorance.

Gout, a High Priest: probably meaning obese bishops of the Low Church Whig party, but this affliction affected both sides of the political divide, Archbishop William King, a Williamite Whig, and Bishop Atterbury, a Jacobite Tory, were well-known sufferers.

Sieve: cf. Dryden, 'The Wife of Bath Her Tale', ll. 153, 155 in *Fables Ancient and Modern* (1700): 'our Sex is frail' like 'leaky Sives no Secrets we can hold' (Dryden, vi. 459). Henrietta Howard, a bedchamber woman to Princess Caroline and mistress to the Prince of Wales, signs herself 'Sieve Yahoo' in a letter to Swift (*c*.10 November 1726, *Corr.*, iii. 50).

Employment: a position in the public service.

Sink, a C——t: cesspool, a court.

Our Brother . . . Piles: if 'j' is counted as 'i' and if 'hath' in Faulkner's 1735 edition is emended to 'has' as in Motte's first edition and here, then this is a perfect anagram, as originally observed by Arthur E. Case (*PW* xi. 312; PT).

The Tour: the signature of the message. During part of his exile in France, Bolingbroke asked his friends to address him as 'M. La Tour'. PT (citing Arthur E. Case).

180 *North-West*: the map shows Luggnagg as south-west of Balnibarbi. On the problems the map-maker had with the maps in GT, especially with the map accompanying the Third Voyage, see Frederick Bracher, 'The Maps in *Gulliver's Travels*', *HLQ* 8 (1944–5), 59–74.

GLUBBDUBDRIB: this episode has a rich literary pre-history. The main models are to be found in the journey to the underworld in epic (*Odyssey* Book XI and *Aeneid* Book VI) and, importantly, in the related genre of the *Dialogues of the Dead*, and especially in Lucian's *The True History* and Boccalini's *Advertisements from Parnassus*.

181 *antick*: grotesque, bizarre.

182 *call up whatever Persons . . . name*: Swift is writing within the *Dialogues of the Dead* genre, cf. interviews with the famous dead in Lucian's *True History*.

not poisoned, but . . . Drinking: Alexander, King of Macedonia, conquered Greece and Egypt and defeated the King of Persia at the Battle of Arbela in modern Iraq in 331 BC. The story that he was poisoned is mentioned in Plutarch's *Life of Alexander* where he is said to have actually died of a fever after excessive drinking, although Plutarch quotes Aristobulus that the fever caused the excessive drinking (PT). On 29 February 1712 Swift was reading the Greek historian and philosopher Flavius Arrianus' *De Expeditione Alexandri*. He tells Esther Johnson in a journal letter to her: 'I came home early, and have read 200 Pages of Arrian, Alexdr the great is just dead; I do not think he was poisoned. Betwixt you and me all those are but idle Storyes, tis certain that neither Ptolomy nor Aristobulus thought so, and they were both with him when [he] died. Tis a Pity we have not their Historyes' (*PW* xvi. 501). See also *Library*, Part I, vol. i, 97–100.

not a Drop of Vinegar: alludes to the story (in Livy, XXI. xxxvii. 2–3) that the Carthaginian general Hannibal was able to cut through rocks obstructing his way in the Italian Alps by heating them and then pouring on vinegar to soften them.

just ready to engage: in the Battle of Pharsalia (48 BC) in which Caesar defeats Pompey.

182 *last great Triumph*: after his victory over the sons of Pompey at Munda in
Spain (45 BC). A triumph in Rome was a procession by the victorious
general and his army.

Brutus: Marcus Junius Brutus, tyrannicide, a close friend of Julius Caesar
who nevertheless was one of the conspirators who assassinated him in 44
BC. For Swift, as for many of his contemporaries in the early eighteenth
century, Brutus is viewed as a champion of liberty. Swift invoked Cato
and Brutus in a pamphlet of 1712 attacking the Duke of Marlborough
and the former Whig ministry: '*Cato* and *Brutus* were the two most
virtuous Men in *Rome* . . . those two excellent Men, who thought it base
to stand Neuter where the Liberties of their Country was at stake, joined
heartily on that side which undertook to preserve the Laws and Constitution, against the Usurpations of a victorious General, whose Ambition
was bent to overthrow them' (*PW* vi. 134). In Swift's *Drapier's Letters*
attacking the English Whig government over Wood's Patent to mint
copper coins for Ireland, the Drapier is given the initials 'M.B.' and King
George is Caesar (*PW* x. 21; see Jack G. Gilbert, 'The Drapier's Initials',
N&Q, NS 10 (1963), 217–18). Swift's praise of Brutus in *GT* seems
capable of different political interpretations. One interpretation is that it
expresses Swift's loyal Old Whig principles: 'Ever since 1688, an analogy
had been drawn between the defence of the Republic by heroes like Cato
and Brutus and the achievement of the English in the Glorious Revolution, who had won their fight against Stuart absolutism . . . many political writers of the age had come to view the Revolution principles in
terms of Roman republican values. These were the "Old Whig" principles' and Swift's choice of heroes reflects these principles (Passmann,
341). An alternative reading is that the meaning is seditious since Brutus
was praised in militant contemporary Jacobite propaganda aimed at over-
throwing the Hanoverian monarchy (cf. Richard Savage, 'Britannia's
Miseries' (ll. 99–104), in *The Poetical Works of Richard Savage*, ed.
Clarence Tracy (Cambridge, 1962), 23: 'Who cou'd behold such Noble
Virtues fall, | And not (like Brutus) own the Generous Call? | He
scorn'd (when Honour summon'd[)] Friendship's bond, | And from
oppression freed his Native Land. | His Friend he knew not, when a
Tyrant grown, | But stab'd that Cæsar that Userp'd the Throne'; cf. *The
True Briton*, no. 20 (9 August 1723) in *The Life and Writings of Philip
Late Duke of Wharton*, 2 vols. (London, 1732), i. 173: 'THE Great *Brutus*
who stabb'd *Cæsar*, is a Noble Mark of Publick Spirit'. For George
Granville, Baron Lansdowne in his militantly Jacobitical *A Letter from a
Noble-Man Abroad, to His Friend in England* (1722), '*Brutus* was an hon-
ourable Man' (pp. 6–7). A Whig writer observed in 1721: 'does not he,
who recommends the Assassinating *Cæsar* as an Heroic Action, encour-
age all those; who think they have as just a Cause to murder their King?'
(Matthew Tindal, *The Judgement of Dr. Prideaux* (London, 1721), 39).
The Life and Genuine Character of Dr Swift. Written by Himself (1733)
says that Swift's '*Travels, Part the Third*' is 'Offensive to a *Loyal* Ear'

(*Poems*, ii. 550), which implies that it was the seditious rather than loyal resonance that was expected to strike Swift's first readers.

183   *in good Intelligence*: on good terms.

Junius: Lucius Junius Brutus, who, after the rape of Lucretia by Sextus Tarquinius, led the uprising that expelled the Tarquins from Rome and so founded the Roman Republic. An iconic hero for Whigs as an enemy of tyranny (see Richard Steele, *The Spectator*, no. 508 (13 October 1712), in *Spectator*, iv. 304), but also for Jacobites (see Richard Savage, 'Britannia's Miseries' (ll. 105–6), in *The Poetical Works of Richard Savage*, 23).

Socrates: Athenian philosopher (469–399 BC).

Epaminondas: Theban general and truthful statesman (*c.*420–362 BC) helped make Thebes for a time the most powerful state in Greece. His military genius enabled his army to defeat numerically superior enemies.

Cato the Younger: Marcius Porcius Cato (95–46 BC), stoic defender of the Roman Republic against Caesar, a man of austere integrity who committed suicide rather than lose his freedom. Montaigne, *Essays*, i. 37 'Of Cato the Younger', lists classical tributes to him stating: 'He was truly a model chosen by nature to show how far human virtue and constancy could go.' Horace praised Caesar who subjugated the whole earth 'Excepting Cato's unrelenting soul' (Montaigne, 171, 172). The last line of Swift's 'Ode to Dr William Sancroft' praises the Archbishop of Canterbury, who refused to acknowledge William III as King after the Revolution of 1688–9 by saying that 'Heaven and Cato both are pleas'd' (*Poems*, i. 42, remembering Lucan's line from *De Bello Civilii*, i. 128: 'The Gods chose the victorious cause, Cato the vanquished').

Sir Thomas More: the author of *Utopia* was a martyr for the English Roman Catholic Church, executed for refusing to acknowledge Henry VIII as head of the English Church. Swift described him as the 'only Man of true Virtue tha[t] ever Engl[an]d produced' (*PW* v. 247). More is the only modern representative in the 'Sextumvirate' or group of six. More, Socrates, Epaminondas, and Cato appear in Swift's list of '*those who have made great* FIGURES *in some particular Action or Circumstance of their Lives*' (*PW* v. 83–4).

184   *I proposed that Homer*: Lucian questions Homer about his poems and hears what he thinks of his editors and critics in *The True History* (Lucian, 280–1).

his Eyes . . . piercing: traditionally thought to be blind, Lucian sees the truth about Homer: 'There was no need to ask if he was really blind, for I could see for myself that he was nothing of the sort' (Lucian, 281).

Didymus: of Alexandria (*c.*65 BC–AD 10), author of a commentary on Homer, nicknamed 'brazen-guts' because of his enormous industry.

Eustathius: Archbishop of Thessalonica (*c.*1175–94), author of a commentary on the *Iliad* and *Odyssey*.

they wanted a Genius . . . Poet: PT quotes Homer's remark in *The True*

History: 'The trouble about these wretched editors is that they've got no taste' (Lucian, p. 281).

184 *Aristotle was out of all Patience*: cf. Swift's comment in his 'Remarks' on Tindal's *The Rights of the Christian Church asserted*: '*Aristotle*, who is doubtless the greatest Master of Arguing in the World: But it hath been a Fashion of late Years to explode *Aristotle*, and therefore this Man hath fallen into it like others, for that Reason, without understanding him. *Aristotle*'s Poetry, Rhetorick, and Politicks are admirable, and therefore it is likely, so are his Logicks' (*PW* ii. 97).

Scotus: Duns Scotus (*c.*1265–*c.*1308), Scottish philosopher and theologian, scholastic commentator on Aristotle (the word *dunce* derives from his name).

Ramus: Pierre de la Ramée or Petrus Ramus (1515–72), a famous French opponent of Aristotelian philosophy.

Descartes: René Descartes (1596–1650), French philosopher and mathematician, who advanced a theory of 'vortices' of material particles in his theories about the universe; killed by Aristotle in Swift's *Battle of the Books* (*PW* i. 156).

Gassendi: Pierre Gassendi (1592–1655), French philosopher, astronomer and mathematician who revived the atomic physics of Epicurus in opposition to the systems of Aristotle and Descartes.

Attraction: Newton's theory of gravitation which replaced the Cartesian vortex theory.

185 *Mathematical Principles*: Newton's book expounding his theory is *Philosophiae Naturalis Principia Mathematica* (1687).

Eliogabalus: Roman emperor (218–22) notorious for luxury.

Helot: slave caste at Sparta.

Agesilaus: King of Sparta from about 398 (*c.*444–361 BC).

Spartan Broth: 'Of their dishes, the black broth is held in the highest esteem', and the capacity to enjoy it is an index of Spartan training in physical endurance. A king of Pontus bought a Spartan cook to make him some, but disliked it ('Lycurgus,' xii. 6–7). Martinus Scriblerus nearly dies from a dose of it as a baby (*Memoirs*, 106).

old illustrious Families: Swift's satire on the degenerate nobility has a family resemblance to the satiric exposure of the true genealogy of ancient families compiled in Burton's *The Anatomy of Melancholy*, II. III. ii. 1, pp. 136–42.

Polydore Virgil: Polydore Virgil (1470–1555), an Italian who became an archdeacon in England, the author of a massive history of England.

Nec . . . Casta: not a man was brave, nor a woman chaste. Swift is referring the reader to a twenty-six-volume history and other works for a quotation which apparently is not there.

Pox: syphilis.

186 *contemptible Accidents*: cf. similar satiric demystification of Henri IV and Louis XIV of France in *A Tale of a Tub* (*PW* i. 103–4).

secret History: PT compares Swift's 'Short Remarks on Bishop Burnet's History' (1724–34): 'THIS author is in most particulars the worst qualified for an historian that ever I met with . . . His Secret History is generally made up of coffee-house scandals, or at best from reports at the third, fourth, or fifth hand. The account of the Pretender's birth, would only become an old woman in a chimney-corner' (*PW* v. 183).

an Admiral: as PT notes, probably Admiral Edward Russell, Earl of Orford (1653–1727) is meant. Although in negotiation with the exiled James II in France and trying to avoid naval action with the French, he was engaged by the French fleet and defeated them at La Hogue (1692) which was a major setback to plans for a Franco-Jacobite invasion of England to restore James II.

187 *Actium*: sea battle in 31 BC in which Octavian (later Augustus) defeated Antony and Cleopatra. 'Antony at Actium when he fled after Cleopatra' is the first of the contemptible figures in Swift's 'Of Mean and Great Figures' (*PW* v. 85).

sole Cause of Antony's Flight: according to Plutarch ('Life of Antonius', lxvi) the real cause was Cleopatra sailing away with her sixty ships and Antony following her.

Court of Augustus: Swift's anti-Augustanism alludes also to courts in what was, and is still, often called the English 'Augustan Age'.

188 *Libertina*: a freed female slave. Prostitutes came from this class (cf. Horace, *Satires*, i. ii. 47–8).

Publicola: L. Gellius Publicola, commander with Antony of the right wing of Antony's fleet at Actium.

Agrippa: Marcus Vipsanius Agrippa (*c.*62–12 BC) was a friend of Octavian and held important military commands under him and was primarily responsible for the success of Octavian's fleet at Actium.

whole Praise . . . chief Commander: another satiric hit at the Duke of Marlborough.

English Yeomen of the old Stamp: in the 'Advertisement to the Reader' of the *Memoirs of Captain John Creichton* (1731) which Swift prepared for publication and probably wrote, the Jacobite Captain is described as: '*a very honest and worthy Man; but of the old Stamp: And it is probable, that some of his Principles will not relish very well, in the present Disposition of the World. His* Memoirs *are therefore to be received like a Posthumous Work*' which Swift offers '*in their native Simplicity*'. The man is distinguished by his '*personal Courage and Conduct*' (*PW* v. 121–2). Cf. the Duke of Wharton's Jacobite manifesto of 1726 denouncing the current Houses of Parliament corrupted by the Court and appealing to 'the old *English* Spirit' and to 'the Liberty of *Old England*' (Wharton, 6, 7).

managing at Elections: by corrupt influence, bribery.

189 *Dutch . . . that Kingdom*: as an anti-Christian measure after suppressing a
      Japanese Roman Catholic Christian revolt in 1637–8, Japan closed its
      ports in 1638 to all Europeans except the Dutch, who had assisted the
      Japanese against the Christian rebels.

190 *lick the Dust*: among the analogues for this image of prostration see Isaiah
      49: 23; Psalms 72: 9; Micah 7: 17. John Trenchard and Thomas Gordon,
      Cato's Letters, ed. Ronald Hamowy (Indianapolis: Liberty Fund, 1995),
      no. 105 (1 December 1722), 742: 'introduced into the presence of
      Dionysius . . . according to the custom of the court . . . fell upon his face,
      and kissed the oppressor's feet'. The episode evokes the image of oriental
      despotism and the abjection of subjects reported in voyage accounts. PT
      finds analogues in the description of the audience chamber of the
      Berklam of Siam and in an audience given by the Emperor of Japan
      which involves crawling on hands and knees in E. Kaempfer's *History of
      Japan* (1727). Swift may have been reflecting on William III's high-
      handed proceedings with the Protestants in Ireland after the defeat of
      James II, see Anne Barbeau Gardiner, 'Licking the Dust in Luggnagg:
      Swift's Reflections on the Legacy of King William's Conquest of
      Ireland', *Swift Studies*, 8 (1993), 35–44.

193 *Struldbrugs*: the satiric target is the desire for long life and an important
      antecedent is Juvenal, *Satires*, x. 188–288. Swift wrote in his 'Thoughts
      on Various Subjects': 'Every Man desires to live long: but no Man would
      be old' (*PW* iv. 246). There was considerable contemporary scientific
      interest in instances of longevity. PT.

194 *Happy . . . Happy . . . happiest*: an ironical echo of Virgil, *Aeneid*, i. 94–6:
      'O thrice and four times happy were those whose fate it was to die before
      their parents' eyes beneath the high walls of Troy!' PT.

195 *never marry after Threescore*: cf. the first of Swift's resolutions 'When I
      come to be old' (1699): 'Not to marry a young Woman' (*PW* i. p. xxxvii).

196 *lower and upper World*: earth and sky.

      Discovery of the Longitude: in 1714 Queen Anne's parliament offered a
      £20,000 reward for a satisfactory method of determining the longitude at
      sea (13 Anne c. 14). John Harrison (1693–1776) devoted his lifetime to
      the problem and solved it with the invention of his marine chronometer
      finished in 1759. Swift and his friends had Martinus Scriblerus put in a
      claim with the idea of building '*Two Poles* to the *Meridian*, with immense
      Light-houses on the top of them' (*Memoirs*, 168, 334–5, 343).

      perpetual Motion: there are what might be called prototype perpetual
      motion machines in Solomon's House in Francis Bacon's *New Atlantis*
      (Bacon, 240, 244). There was great scientific interest in the subject in
      the seventeenth century and into the eighteenth and it was also a
      long-standing subject of satire, see *Memoirs*, 332.

      the universal Medicine: the elixir of life which would cure all diseases and
      prolong life indefinitely.

198 *Courtesy of the Kingdom*: a customary legal right.

Meers: boundaries or landmarks indicating a boundary.

At Ninety: the list of disabilities corresponds with that in Juvenal, *Satires*, x. PT.

upon the Flux: in a state of flux.

201 *I do not remember . . . Travels*: in fact they were common from Pliny's *Natural History* onwards and had been parodied by Lucian in *The True History* (Lucian, 260). Swift's Struldbrugs give hideous corporeality to the idea of the degenerate nature of man.

I hope the Dutch: PT suggests an allusion to the *History of Japan* by Englebrecht Kaempfer (1651–1716), physician to the Dutch Embassy at the Emperor of Japan's court, which was published in 1727, after *GT*, but Swift may have known about the work which had been completed earlier.

red Diamond: a rarity.

Xamoschi: Shimosa or Ximosa on contemporary maps by Sanson and Moll, see Takau Shimada, 'Xamoschi Where Gulliver Landed', *N&Q*, NS 30 (1983), 33.

Yedo: old name for Tokyo.

202 *Low-Dutch*: Dutch. High Dutch in this period meant German.

Nangasac: Nagasaki.

trampling upon the Crucifix: *Yefumi*, the religious ceremony by which Japanese authorities attempted to detect Christians, who were forbidden in Japan. Compare the English version of John Francis Gemelli Careri's *A Voyage Round the World* in Awnsham and John Churchill, *A Collection of Voyages and Travels* (London, 1704), iv. 291: 'That the Christians might have no Opportunity of getting in under the name of other Nations, [the Japanese] were advis'd by the *Dutch*, who will have all the Profit to themselves, to lay a Crucifix on the Ground at the Landing Place, to discover whether any Christian comes under a Disguise, because any such will refuse, or at least make a difficulty to trample on the Crucifix to enter *Nangasache*, the Port of *Japan*. Thus the *Dutch* settled themselves in the Trade, excluding all others, perswading the *Japoneses* that they were no Christians, making no scruple for their Interest to trample the Holy Image of Christ, which the *English* refus'd to do' (see Takau Shimada, 'Possible Sources for Psalmanazar's *Description of Formosa*', *N&Q*, NS 30 (1983), 515–16); Charles Leslie, *Cassandra*, no. II (London, 1704), Appendix, no. V, p. 91: 'The *Test* in *Japan* for a *Christian*, is the Trampling upon the *Cross*. This is thought a Sufficient Indication, that he who do's it is no *Christian*. By this the *Dutch* Secure that *Trade* to Themselves.' For other sources of information about Dutch anti-Christian conduct available to Swift, see Hermann J. Real and Heinz J. Vienken, 'Swift's "Trampling upon the Crucifix" Once More', *N&Q*, NS 30 (1983), 513–14.

203 *Amboyna*: Ambon in Indonesia. This spice-island in the East Indies was controlled by the Dutch but the English had trading rights there. It was infamous for Swift's contemporaries as the site of a Dutch atrocity in 1623 in which Englishmen were tortured and killed (see William J. Brown, 'Gulliver's Passage on the Dutch *Amboyna*', *ELN* 1 (1964), 262–4). Swift's cousin John Dryden produced a play on the sensational subject, *Amboyna* (1673; Dryden, xii. 1–77, and p. 264 noting Swift's agreement with Dryden about the Dutch in Amboyna). The atrocity at 'Amboyna' was invoked in Tory and Jacobite polemic against the Dutch (cf. Charles Leslie, *Delenda Carthago. Or, The True Interest of England, in Relation to France and Holland* (1695): 'the Murder of the *English* at *Amboyna* . . . and other Depredations in the *East Indies* . . . their Breach of Treaties, and most *Barbarous* and *Perfidious* Cruelties upon the *English*' (p. 3)).

Theodorus Vangrult: the name must be ironical in the context of the anti-Dutch satire. Theodorus means 'Gift of God'. Vangrult, PT suggests, may be derived from the Greek *grulos* or *grullos* for pig. PT.

Skipper: probably a cabin boy is meant.

Part IV. A Voyage to the Country of the Houyhnhnms

205 *Houyhnhnms*: probably pronounced 'whinnims', suggesting the whinny of a horse. The mythic Houyhnhnms are horses, not humans; however, the homonymous similarity between 'Houyhnhnm' and 'human' and the fact that Houyhnhnm society is modelled on Lycurgan Sparta as described in Xenophon's *Constitution of the Spartans* and Plutarch's 'Life of Lycurgus', on the utopias of Plato's *Republic* and More's *Utopia*, on nations ruled by the laws of nature described in Montaigne, *Essays*, i. 31 ('Of Cannibals'), and on accounts of Golden Age primitivism, enables readers to understand them as pre-Christian 'Ancients' or utopians. The Houyhnhnms are mythic embodiments of what Temple in 'Of Heroic Virtue' described as the foundation principle of China's 'Prince of Philosophers, the Great and Renowned *Confutius*', an ideal of human aspiration: 'That every Man ought to study and endeavour the improving and perfecting of his own Natural Reason to the great Height he is capable, so as he may never (or as seldom as can be) err and swerve from the Law of Nature' (Temple, i. 200). R. S. Crane ('The Houyhnhnms, the Yahoos, and the History of Ideas', in J. A. Mazzeo (ed.), *Reason and the Imagination: Studies in the History of Ideas 1600–1800* (New York: Columbia University Press, 1962), 231–53) was the first to demonstrate that in presenting horses as rational animals Swift administers a cultural shock to his first readers by overturning a commonplace definition of man as a rational animal and the horse as an instance of an irrational animal given prominence in the logic textbooks of the seventeenth and early eighteenth centuries. The proposition 'rational' is to 'irrational' as 'man' is to 'horse' found in the third-century neo-platonist Porphyry's *Isagoge* had become a logical cliché. In one of Swift's favourite works,

Samuel Butler's *Hudibras*, Sir Hudibras who is 'in *Logick* a great Critick' would 'undertake to prove by force | Of Argument, a Man's no Horse' (*Hudibras*, I. i. 65, 71–2, p. 3). As a student at Trinity College Dublin Swift would have come across the definition '*animal rationale*' in the *Institutio logicae* of Narcissus Marsh (Dublin, 1679; reissued Dublin, 1681) and the particular formulation of the logical definition in this work was recalled by Swift when he stated in 1725 that his misanthropic intention in *Gulliver's Travels* was to prove 'the falsity of that Definition animal rationale' (Crane, 248–53; see *Corr.*, ii. 607, 623). Swift invents a fable where a hypothetical horse species are rational animals and humans generally worse than unreasoning brutes. PT observes that the idea of an intellectually superior horse goes back to Chiron, the centaur in Greek mythology, the educator of Jason and Achilles. Swift also draws on a tradition positing that animals provide humankind with exemplary patterns of conduct and are superior to civilized humans because they are more natural, a tradition of paradox drawn on by earlier misanthropic satirists such as John Wilmot, Earl of Rochester (see James E. Gill, 'Beast over Man: Theriophilic Paradox in Gulliver's "Voyage to the Country of the Houyhnhnms" ', *SP* 67 (1970), 532–49). The traditional view is that the Houyhnhnms are meant to be admirable, but a modern interpretation developed in the twentieth century has claimed that they are objects of satiric criticism. For the critical debate see: James L. Clifford, 'Gulliver's Fourth Voyage: "Hard" and "Soft" Schools of Interpretation', in Larry S. Champion (ed.), *Quick Springs of Sense: Studies in the Eighteenth Century* (Athens, Ga.: Georgia University Press, 1974), 33–49; Brian Tippett, *Gulliver's Travels*, The Critics Debate (Houndmills: Macmillan, 1989). For a rebuttal of the usual charges against the Houyhnhnms and emphasis on Swift's aggressive purposes in presenting them as the satire's positive, see Rawson, 14–15, 18–19, 24, 29–32.

207 *conspire*: shipwrecked in Part I, abandoned in Part II, victim of a hijack in Part III, in Part IV Gulliver experiences a mutiny and is cast out by his own men. Gulliver will remember this rejection by his own kind when he desires not to return to humankind at the end of his travels.

Yahoos: this '*strange Sort of Animal*' is of a different species from the Houyhnhnms, who regard them as savage animals or beasts of burden. They are not human but are humanoid. The satire works to conflate human with Yahoo. Travel books recorded an inland tribe in Guinea called '*Yahoos*' (John Robert Moore, 'The Yahoos of the African Travellers', *N&Q* 195 (1950), 182–5; Moore comments that the African Yahoos lived 'under more complete subjection to their masters than the Helots ever did' (185)) and the 'Yaios' of Guiana (Frank Kermode, 'Yahoos and Houyhnhnms', *N&Q* 195 (1950), 317–18). Swift drew on several sources for the Yahoos: accounts of the people of 'savage nations' in voyage literature and accounts of simians in voyage literature (see Frantz; Passmann, '*Full of Improbable Lies*', esp. pp. 186–94); accounts of the 'savage Irish' in Swift's and in English colonialist writings (see Firth,

228, and Donald T. Torchiana, 'Jonathan Swift, the Irish, and the Yahoos: The Case Reconsidered', *PQ* 54 (1975), 195–212); accounts of cattle-killing Irish houghers (law-breakers who hough or hamstring cattle) in 1711 (the year Gulliver enters Houyhnhnmland); accounts of the helots of ancient Sparta, serfs with pariah status who were periodically slaughtered (William H. Halewood, 'Plutarch in Houyhnhnmland: A Neglected Source for Gulliver's Fourth Voyage', *PQ* 44 (1965), 185–94). The Yahoos have also been seen to embody Christian symbols of Original Sin (Roland M. Frye, 'Swift's Yahoo and the Christian Symbols for Sin', *JHI* 15 (1954), 201–17). In a passage printed in the last chapter of the first edition of 1726, but not reproduced in Faulkner's edition of 1735, Gulliver speculates that the original 'two *Yahoos*' from which the race has degenerated 'may have been *English*' thus giving, Swift insultingly suggests, Gulliver's countrymen, who would claim a colonial title to Houyhnhnmland, a kind of native title as Yahoos.

207   *Adventure*: a common name of contemporary ships. The notorious pirate Captain Kidd sailed on ships with this name. Gulliver's men become pirates.

Captain Pocock: PT suggests the model for the Captain was Dampier, who spent three years with the logwood-cutters around 'the Bay of Campeachy', the southern part of the Gulf of Mexico, publishing an account of his *Voyages to the Bay of Campeachy* (see *Voyages*, ii. 107–225). On Dampier's dogmatism see Bonner, 8, 165. PT.

Logwood: the heartwood of an American tree (*Haematoxylon Campechianum*), used for dyeing and as an astringent in medicine, so called from being imported in the form of logs (*OED*).

a little too positive in his own Opinions: as Gulliver has been, cf. his opinion of the King of Brobdingnag's rejection of gunpowder technology as 'the miserable Effects of a *confined Education*', the 'Effect of *narrow Principles* and *short Views!*' (pp. 122, 124). Gulliver's conversion to Houyhnhnm opinions on humankind later in Part IV is presented as an enlightenment, Gulliver is convinced rather than credulous or indoctrinated (see p. 240).

Calentures: tropical fevers.

Barbadoes: the English sugar colony in the West Indies.

208   *Piece*: firearm.

Madagascar: the island off the south-east coast of Africa was a pirate colony.

Toys: trinkets.

209   *Animals in a Field*: the unsettling ambiguity about the Yahoos—they are animals (with claws) but also humanoid (they have human feet)—exploits accounts in travel books of 'savage peoples'. Cf. Dampier's well-known description of the Australian aborigines: 'The Inhabitants of this Country are the miserablest People in the world . . . setting aside their Humane Shape, they differ but little from Brutes' (*Voyages*, i. 453).

Their Dugs . . . walked: a standard travel-book description of the hanging breasts of native women, see *GGG*, esp. pp. 98–113, notes pp. 329–34.

maimed . . . their Cattle: in some Irish counties in 1711, bands of houghers were maiming and destroying the cattle of pastoralists and were regarded as committing Jacobite treason (*Corr.*, i. 415–16; *PW* xvi. 525). Gulliver fears he will be regarded as a hougher and, indeed, it is as a potential hougher who might lead Yahoos in raids on Houyhnhnm cattle that Gulliver will be deported from Houyhnhnmland, exiled as if he were a traitor.

210 *Excrements on my Head*: the high-profile voyagers Lionel Wafer and William Dampier both reported this experience with monkeys in Panama. Wafer, *A New Voyage and Description of the Isthmus of America* (1699): 'They are a very waggish kind of Monkey, and plaid a thousand antick Tricks . . . skipping from Bough to Bough . . . making Faces at us, chattering, and, if they had opportunity, pissing down purposely on our Heads' (Wafer, 66); Dampier, *Voyages to the Bay of Campeachy*: 'The Monkeys that are in these Parts are the ugliest I ever saw . . . If they meet with a single Person they will threaten to devour him. When I have been alone I have been afraid to shoot them, especially the first Time I met them. They were a great Company dancing from Tree to Tree, over my Head; chattering and making a terrible Noise; and a great many grim Faces, and shewing antick Gestures. Some broke down dry Sticks and threw at me; others scattered their Urine and Dung about my Ears' (*Voyages*, ii. 161).

211 *Magicians . . . metamorphosed*: possibly suggested by the *Golden Ass* of Apuleius, the hero of which turns himself by magic into a donkey. The same story is told in Lucian's *Lucius or the Ass*. PT.

212 *Passions*: feelings, emotions. The Houyhnhnms may be austere but they are not presented as passionless.

Chinese: comparing the Houyhnhnms' language with that of an idealized remote civilization, admired by Sir William Temple among others. Chinese was thought suitable as a model for a universal language by members of the Royal Society such as Bishop John Wilkins and it is admired for its permanence in Swift's *A Proposal for Correcting, Improving and Ascertaining the English Tongue* (1712; *PW* iv. 9). In contrast to the language of the Houyhnhnms, the language of a corrupt society like Luggnagg is said to be in a state of flux.

imitating . . . surprized: perhaps recalls Aristotle's statement (*Poetics*, 1448^{b}6–7) that 'man differs from the other animals in being the most imitative'. PT.

214 *Asses . . . Dogs . . . Cow dead . . . Disease*: the diet of the Yahoos (asses, dogs, cats, cows that have died, corrupted flesh of animals, weasels, rats) is described in Leviticus (11: 3, 27, 29, 39–40) as polluting. The Yahoos symbolize among other things the theological concept of Original Sin (Frye, 'Swift's Yahoo and the Christian Symbols for Sin', 216). PT.

214 *Wyths*: halters made of tough, flexible branches of willow or osier. PT.

215 *whereof they had no Conception*: the Houyhnhnms in having no conception of clothing represent unfallen nature or innocence, with nudity signifying simplicity, integrity, sincerity, and virtue in the classical and Christian traditions; see Milton, *Paradise Lost*, ix. 1052–9 (*Paradise Lost*, 531 and note referring to Horace, *Odes*, I. xxiv. 6 f.).

216 *a Sledge*: suggesting that the Houyhnhnms do not have the wheel, an indication that they are in a primitivist Golden Age.

   an old Steed: Burton, 'Democritus Junior to the Reader': 'To see horses ride in a Coach, men draw it', a sign of the world turned upside-down (Burton, i. 54).

   complaisant: courteous.

217 *how easily Nature is satisfied*: a commonplace. Praise of a simple diet is a stock theme in satires on luxury.

   no Animal . . . but Man: Pliny had written that civilized life is impossible without salt (*Natural History*, XXXI. xli. 88; PT). The English in Swift's *A Modest Proposal* (1729) are said to be willing to devour the Irish nation without salt (*PW* xii. 117). However, Gulliver, who is discovering that horses are the rational animals and humankind worse than unreasoning brutality, now finds that this utopian society based on the highest ideals of civilized aspiration, a life lived in accord with reason and nature, is without salt, a supposed defining commodity of civilization. It was also one of the spoils of the English maritime empire. Dampier describes the 'great Trade for Salt' and how at the island of Mayo the English 'have commonly a Man of War here for the Guard of our Ships and Barks that come to take it in; of which I have been inform'd that in some Years there have not been less than 100 in a Year' (*Voyages*, ii. 360).

   fare: Swift puns on the two meanings of the word, 'get on' and 'feed'.

218 *my Master*: the Houyhnhnm Master is perhaps analogous to one of Plato's Guardians or to one of the members of the highest class in Lycurgan Sparta (*Constitution*, ii. 2; 'Lycurgus', xvi. 4–6) with Gulliver in the role of obedient pupil.

   almost the same Observation: Emperor Charles V is supposed to have said that he would speak to his God in Spanish, his mistress in Italian, and his horse in German (Gough, 414; PT). '*German, Spanish* and *Italian*' are cited for their permanence in Swift's *A Proposal for Correcting, Improving and Ascertaining the English Tongue* (*PW* iv. 9).

219 *not the least Idea of Books or Literature*: ancient Sparta is said to have had no written literature but did have an oral tradition of poetry and song ('Lycurgus', xxi). Socrates (with whose opinions the Houyhnhnms are elsewhere said to agree) preferred oral poetry over written literature (Plato, *Phaedrus*, 274D–278B). Robert C. Elliott, *The Shape of Utopia* (Chicago: University of Chicago Press, 1970) observes that the abolition of books is a characteristic of utopian fiction (pp. 121–8). Swift could

express violent animus against books and book-burning was something of a Swiftian pastime (see Daniel Eilon, *Factions' Fictions: Ideological Closure in Swift's Satire* (Newark: University of Delaware Press; London: Associated University Presses, 1991), 123–39).

He knew it was impossible: as explained below, ideal or unfallen Houyhnhnm reason is cognitive rather than ratiocinative, when the Houyhnhnms have to deduce from apparent evidence they often get it wrong or cannot do it. The Houyhnhnms like the Spartans of Lycurgus are in a closed society cut off from the world and therefore from the corruption that comes from the luxury of maritime empires. Their ignorance is a sign of their bliss and primitivist virtue.

The Word . . . Perfection of Nature: the Houyhnhnms are represented as self-identical with nature. The venerable belief that Man was the most perfect creature in nature was also contested in *The Circe of Signior Giovanni Battista Gelli*. Tom Brown's 1702 version of the sixteenth-century Florentine's work, especially the seventh dialogue concerning horse versus man, was one of Swift's probable sources for Part IV (see Benjamin Boyce, *Tom Brown of Facetious Memory* (Cambridge, Mass: Harvard University Press, 1939), 84–5).

right: real, genuine.

220 *from the Hides of Yahoos*: cf. *A Modest Proposal* where it is said that the skins of Irish children 'artificially dressed, will make admirable *Gloves for Ladies*, and *Summer Boots for fine Gentlemen*' (*PW* xii. 112). On Swift's black humour, see *GGG*, esp. pp. 275–87.

those Parts that Nature . . . had given: Eve before the Fall protected in virtue needed no veil over her body (*Paradise Lost*, v. 383–4, p. 304). Gulliver's sexual modesty is a sign of fallen human nature (Genesis 3: 7: 'And the eyes of them both were opened, and they knew that they were naked; and they sewed fig leaves together, and made themselves aprons').

221 *All this . . . consented to*: the Houyhnhnms are not supposed to lie, and have great difficulty with the concept, but he has agreed to suppress the truth at Gulliver's request. The Houyhnhnm Assembly later deports Gulliver because he is a potentially corrupting influence in Houyhnhnmland and this episode would appear to be an (albeit comic) instance of fallen human influence.

223 *Nature of Manhood*: human nature.

224 *their Bodies . . . Prey*: a paraphrase of Homer, *Iliad*, i. 4–5. PT.

Wants and Passions are fewer: Swift produces a surprise effect as in emblematic and iconographic tradition horses signified Passion with the bridle signifying Temperance and the rider Reason (for examples, see D. W. Robertson, Jr., *A Preface to Chaucer: Studies in Medieval Perspectives* (Princeton: Princeton University Press, 1962), 30, 194, 253–5, 394, 476). An austere simplicity characterizes the Houyhnhnms but they are not said to be without passion. Swift's Houyhnhnmland like More's Utopia is influenced by stoic ideas that pervade the humanist tradition.

224 *Houyhnhnm Race*: 'race' is used in the sense of species or division of
     living creatures.

226 *flying from their Colours*: military desertion.

228 *our barbarous English*: in his writings on language Swift considers the
     English language as 'less refined than those of *Italy*, *Spain*, or *France*'
     (*PW* iv. 6). The corruption of the language is dated from 'the great
     Rebellion in Forty-two' and subsequent 'Usurpation' (*PW* iv. 9–10) and
     further decline in the language follows from the Revolution and start of
     William III's reign: '*the continual Corruption of our* English *Tongue;
     which, without some timely Remedy, will suffer more by the false Refinements
     of Twenty Years past, than it hath been improved in the foregoing Hundred*'
     (*PW* ii. 174). Swift laments 'a Tendency to lapse into the Barbarity of
     those *Northern* Nations from whom we are descended' (*PW* iv. 12, cf. *PW*
     ii. 175). He condemns 'those barbarous Mutilations of Vowels and
     Syllables' in the English language (*PW* ii. 176).

     Revolution: that of 1688–9.

     long War: that of the League of Augsberg (1689–97), soon followed by the
     War of the Spanish Succession (1701–13).

     Ambition . . . to govern: compare the scathing denunciation of French
     foreign policy, war-mongering, and the territorial ambitions of kings
     in *Utopia*, 28–31. Cf. also Rabelais (i. 33, pp. 109–13) satirizing King
     Picrochole and his advisers and their ambition of world conquest.

229 *Difference in Opinions*: Swift's satire on religious controversy, war, and the
     profession of soldier might be compared with the violent satiric denunci-
     ation of religious madness, war, and its causes compiled in Burton,
     'Democritus Junior to the Reader', i. 39–49. The sequence of subjects in
     Swift's satire in Part IV, chapters v and vi—war, law, money—is the
     sequence in Burton. As in *A Tale of a Tub*, Swift's satire on religious
     differences refuses to acknowledge that genuine differences in belief
     might exist. In his satire and polemical writings Swift endorses religious
     uniformity in the state.

     Whether Flesh be Bread, or Bread be Flesh: compare the satire on Roman
     Catholicism and the doctrine of transubstantiation in *A Tale of a Tub*.

     Whether Whistling . . . Virtue: under the influence of the Presbyterians
     and the Independents during the Commonwealth (1649–60), organs and
     choirs were removed from the churches. PT.

     Post: an image or crucifix. Swift satirizes Papist idolatry and Puritan
     iconoclasm, as he had in the characters of Peter (Roman Catholicism) and
     Jack (Calvinism and Puritan Enthusiasm) in *A Tale of a Tub*. Gough (p.
     415) and PT quote a Wycliffite saying that images had one use: 'thai
     myghtten warme a mans body in colde, if thai were sette upon a fire'.
     Swift satire recalls instances of iconoclasm during the Civil Wars and
     Interregnum, especially the Puritan campaign against crosses, often
     destroyed in public bonfires, see Julie Spraggon, *Puritan Iconoclasm
     during the English Civil War* (Woodbridge: The Boydell Press, 2003).

What is the best colour for a Coat: alluding to controversies over vestments and, as PT suggests, to disputes between Dominicans, Carmelites, Trinitarians, and Franciscans known by the colour of their habits, as Black, White, Red, and Grey Friars.

indifferent: of no consequence either way. The Greek word for 'things indifferent', adiaphora, was a technical term used by theologians to mean non-essential points upon which the Church has given no decision. PT. Swift's burlesque depicts some fundamental doctrinal disagreements among Christians as things indifferent.

Sometimes the Quarrel . . . Right: cf. *Utopia*, 29: where an adviser to the French King 'thinks a settlement should be made with the King of Aragon, and that, as a reward for peace, he should be given Navarre, which belongs to somebody else'. PT.

Dominions round and compact: a hostile allusion to the Hanoverian acquisition of Verden and Bremen at the expense of King Charles XII of Sweden, a hero of Swift's, and of 'James III' and the Jacobites who saw him as a potential Protestant supporter of their cause, see Lock, pp. 64–5; Ian Higgins, 'Jonathan Swift and the Jacobite Diaspora', *Reading Swift*, 100.

reduce: convert.

230   *many Northern Parts of Europe*: a manuscript variant in Charles Ford's interleaved copy of the first edition reads 'Germany and other' for 'many *Northern*', which makes the innuendo against George I as a beggarly prince who relies on mercenaries more explicit. Neither Motte nor Faulkner published the dangerously specific attack on the Hanoverian King.

Ignorance: this limitation in Houyhnhnm understanding is as elsewhere a sign of Houyhnhnm virtue and human depravity.

Art of War: the title of contemporary works in military discipline and technology such as *Military Discipline; or the Art of War* (1689); *The Art of War* (1707). An edition of *The New Art of War* was published in 1726.

Culverins: large cannons.

Carabines: firearms used by the cavalry, shorter than muskets.

Undermines: excavations under the walls of fortifications.

Countermines: excavations or mines made by the defenders of a fortress.

231   *he no more blamed . . . Hoof*: cf. Swift's letter to Alexander Pope, 26 November 1725: 'I tell you after all that I do not hate Mankind, it is vous autr[e]s who hate them because you would have them reasonable Animals, and are Angry for being disappointed. I have always rejected that Definition and made another of my own. I am no more angry with [Walpole] th[a]n I was with the Kite that last week flew away with one of my Chickins and yet I was pleas'd when one of my Servants shot him two days after' (*Corr.*, ii. 623; the blank is traditionally filled with 'Walpole', but also King George might be inferred, cf. the reference to 'kill the King' in the unprinted manuscript variant in Part III allegorizing Irish

resistance to the royal patent given to William Wood and to considerations about 'the best Way of murdering the King' in the plots passage of
Part III. Cf. Swift's correspondence in 1735 where king-killing is
imagined and approved, see Williams, iv. 337). The Houyhnhnms do not
blame the Yahoos for what they are but are pleased to consider their
extermination.

231 *Nature and Reason were sufficient Guides . . . Animal*: cf. More's Utopians:
'They define virtue as living according to nature; and God, they say,
created us to that end. When an individual obeys the dictates of reason in
choosing one thing and avoiding another, he is following nature' (*Utopia*,
67). Swift, like More, is using a conception of reason derived from the
Stoics, that of 'right reason' which enables instinctive apprehension of
the natural law. The Houyhnhnms are exemplars of stoic 'sociableness'
and hypothetical embodiments of the stoic-influenced state of nature
described in the 'Prolegomena' to Hugo Grotius' *De Jure Belli ac Pacis*, a
work Swift owned and recommended (see *Library*, Part I, vol. i, pp. 760–
6; *Corr.*, i. 615), where all obey what is enjoined by natural law without
the necessity of divine injunction, Church, or scripture (see Hugo
Grotius, *The Law of War and Peace. De Jure Belli ac Pacis Libri Tres*,
trans. Francis Kelsey (Oxford: Oxford University Press, 1925). Cf.
More's Utopians, who live in accord with reason and nature: 'Human
reason, they think, can attain to no truer conclusions than these, unless a
revelation from heaven should inspire men with holier notions . . . But of
this I am sure, that whatever their principles are, there is not a more
excellent people or a happier commonwealth anywhere in the whole
world' (*Utopia*, 74). The Houyhnhnms exemplify what the Jacobite
ideologist Chevalier Ramsay described as 'the Idea' of a 'State . . . con-
formable to reasonable Nature', the fictional 'Golden Age': 'IF Men,
would follow the Law of Nature . . . they would have no occasion for
positive Laws, nor exemplary Punishments: Reason would be the
common Law; Men would live in Simplicity without Pride, in mutual
Commerce without Propriety, and in Equality without Jealousy: They
would know no other Superiority but that of Virtue, nor no other
Ambition but that of being generous and disinterested.' Ramsay thought
'Self-Love' and the passions prevented humankind from living in such a
state (*An Essay upon Civil Government* (London, 1722), 36, 37). Swift
makes the same point, for the order of the Houyhnhnms is non-human.

I said there was a Society of Men among us: the satire on lawyers is much
softer in the first edition published by Motte (who was a publisher of
legal works). Ridicule of law and lawyers was a traditional satiric topos.
However, Swift's animus was undoubtedly intensified, as PT observes,
by the conduct of Lord Chief Justice Whitshed who, when Edward
Waters was prosecuted for printing Swift's *A Proposal for the Universal
Use of Irish Manufactures* (1720), refused to accept a verdict of not guilty,
sent the jury back nine times, and kept them for eleven hours; and who in
1724 dissolved the Grand Jury, because they refused to present Swift's

Seasonable Advice as a seditious paper. Gulliver's extreme claim that hereditary title in property is no longer recognized in law in contemporary England was a charge laid in the Jacobite press (e.g. Ramsay, *An Essay upon Civil Government*, 65–6). It is perhaps revealing of Swift's train of thought that Gulliver immediately starts talking about the arbitrary way treason trials are conducted after asserting that hereditary title to property is disregarded.

speak for himself: cf. *Utopia*, 82: 'As for lawyers, a class of men whose trade it is to manipulate cases and multiply quibbles, they exclude them entirely. They think it practical for each man to plead his own case, and say the same thing to the judge that he would tell his lawyer.'

232 *Practice*: puns on legal practice and 'machinations'.

Faculty: profession.

233 *sound the Disposition . . . Power*: cf. *Utopia*, 31–2, on how a king can work on judges to get decisions in the royal interest.

234 *under Queen Anne*: Ford's correction reads simply: 'A Continuation of the State of England. The Character of a first Minister'.

Use of Money . . . Metals: PT cites the ironical accounts of the power of gold in *Charon* (Lucian, 86–7) and in *Utopia* (60–1).

the rich Man . . . plentifully: cf. the condemnation of rich men in James 5: 1–6. The communistic practices of the Houyhnhnms are modelled on More's *Utopia*, which is itself inspired by the communistic practices of the early Christians (Acts 2: 44–5; 4: 32–5; *Utopia*, 93).

to seek: at a loss, unable to discover or understand.

this whole Globe . . . gone round: Swift's satire starkly contrasts with Whig celebrations of Britain's global trading empire and the importance of the merchant class and moneyed men. Cf. Joseph Addison's benign *Spectator*, no. 69, 19 May 1711: 'The Infusion of a *China* Plant sweetned with the Pith of an *Indian* Cane: The *Philippick* Islands give a Flavour to our *European* Bowls. The single Dress of a Woman of Quality is often the Product of an hundred Climates. The Muff and the Fan come together from the different Ends of the Earth. The Scarf is sent from the Torrid Zone, and the Tippet from beneath the Pole. The Brocade Petticoat rises out of the Mines of Peru, and the Diamond Necklace out of the Bowels of *Indostan* . . . Nature indeed furnishes us with the bare Necessaries of Life, but Traffick gives us a great Variety of what is Useful, and at the same time supplies us with every thing that is Convenient and Ornamental' (*Spectator*, i. 295–6).

235 *That, Wine was not . . . short*: not the attitude of King Lemuel (Proverbs 31: 6–7), nor of Swift who found 'wine absolutely necessary to support me' (Williams, iv. 469–70; PT).

I carry on my Body . . . Tradesmen: cf. Burton on luxury: ''tis an ordinary thing . . . to weare a whole Mannor on his backe' (Burton, III. II. ii. 3, p. 101).

236 *Mystery*: trade secret.

a Vomit: probably an allusion to Dr John Woodward (1665–1728), Professor of Physic at Gresham College, who prescribed long and severe 'courses of vomits' as the sovereign remedy for disease in his patients (*Memoirs*, 274). PT.

Clyster: enema.

237 *approve their Sagacity . . . Dose*: cf. *Verses on the Death of Dr Swift*, ll. 131–2: 'He'd rather chuse that I should dye, | Than his Prediction prove a Lye' (*Poems*, ii. 557). Cf. Juvenal, *Satires*, x. 222 on 'the homicidal tendencies of doctors'. PT.

Mind: real meaning or intention.

forlorn: forsaken, lost, doomed to destruction.

238 *Oath*: cf. Swift's *Examiner* (9 November 1710) on the 'Art of Political Lying' instancing the Whig Earl of Wharton who tags his lies with oaths (*PW* iii. 8–13) and thus exemplifies what Machiavelli admired about Pope Alexander VI in *The Prince*: he 'never dreamed of anything else than deceiving men . . . Never was there a man more effective in swearing and who with stronger oaths confirmed a promise, but yet honored it less' (quoted in *Utopia*, 83–4 editorial note).

Act of Indemnity: the Act of Indemnity and Oblivion (1660) pardoned all who had fought against the King in the Civil Wars or who had worked for the republican government, excepting some named individuals. Resented by Cavaliers as 'Indemnity for the King's enemies and Oblivion for the King's friends'. PT. As Tory Examiner, Swift was scathing about a 1708 Act of Indemnity that protected Whig ministers from prosecution (*PW* iii. 140).

Tunnels: secret passages; recalling, as PT observes, Juvenal, *Satires*, i. 36–43, on the sleazy routes to advancement.

239 *He made me observe . . . unnatural*: the colour hierarchy of the Houyhnhnms follows contemporary equine authorities in which the white and sorrel were ranked below the bay and the black. The dapple grey was regarded as the best kind of horse, see Richard Nash, 'Of Sorrels, Bays, and Dapple Greys', *Swift Studies*, 15 (2000), 110–15. The hierarchical distinction among the Houyhnhnms invites analogies with the caste systems in Lycurgan Sparta and Plato's *Republic*.

240 *managing*: treating carefully.

Truth appeared so amiable to me: possibly modelled on the remark attributed to Aristotle: 'I'm fond of Plato, and I'm fond of Socrates, but I'm even fonder of Truth.' PT.

241 *Reason . . . we had no Pretence to challenge*: i.e. we had no right to claim that definition 'animal rationale'. Swift's satiric project in GT was to prove 'the falsity of that Definition animal rationale', to reject humankind's claim to be 'reasonable Animals' (see his letters to Pope of 29 September 1725 and 26 November 1725, *Corr.*, ii. 607, 623).

242 *shining Stones of several Colours*: a travel book detail, cf. Linschoten's report of Amerindians in islands near Florida who gather from the sand 'certaine clear shining stones, yellow, blacke, and other colours' (Linschoten, 222).

That he had once . . . Experiment: as PT observes, the experiment is reminiscent of a passage in Defoe's *Colonel Jack* where young Jack, obsessed with hiding some money ('O! the weight of Human Care!'), hides the money in a '*foul Clout*' and puts his treasure in a hollow tree where it falls out of reach: 'I cry'd, nay, I roar'd out, I was in such a Passion.' But his despair turns to wild joy when he finds it again: 'I hollow'd quite out aloud, when I saw it; then I run to it, and snatch'd it up, hug'd and kiss'd the dirty Ragg a hundred Times; then danc'd and jump'd about.' He then checks that it is all there and goes away with the money (Daniel Defoe, *Colonel Jack*, ed. Samuel Holt Monk, introd. David Roberts (Oxford: Oxford University Press, 1989), 23–6).

243 *sordid*: in the sense of the Latin *sordidus*: 'miserly, avaricious'. PT. Cf. later references to the 'Greediness of that sordid Brute'.

Courts of Equity: courts (e.g. that of Chancery) designed to decide, on general principles of justice, cases not adequately covered by the common law. PT.

their undistinguishing Appetite: cf. voyage accounts of the undistinguishing diets reported of African peoples (see Linschoten, 75–6; Frantz, 53).

244 *their Language*: the Houyhnhnms'.

245 *had their Females in common*: an observation made of 'savage peoples' in voyage literature. The sharing of wives for eugenic purposes was practised in Lycurgan Sparta (*Constitution*, i. 7–10; 'Lycurgus', xv. 6–8) and the Spartan principle of sharing wives and children is adopted in Plato's *Republic* (457C–D). The Christian authors More and Swift modify the Spartan practice among the Utopians and Houyhnhnms, so while there is a communal allocation of individuals and goods between households and regions, the institution of marriage is preserved inviolate (*Utopia*, 54, 55).

Spleen: a fashionable neurosis, 'excessive dejection or depression of spirits; gloominess and irritability; moroseness; melancholia' (*OED*, citing Swift).

a Female Yahoo: traditional female tactics in literary pastoral, e.g. Virgil, *Eclogues*, iii. 64–5: 'Galatea, saucy girl, pelts me with an apple, then runs off to the willows – and hopes to be seen first.' PT.

246 *these politer Pleasures*: for the idea that 'unnatural' sexual appetites are the product of civilization, cf. Juvenal, *Satires*, ii. 162–70. PT.

247 *Sorrel Nag*: 'Sorrel' may be significant. The horse that threw King William III leading to his death, and so celebrated in Jacobite verse, was named 'Sorrel'. The name for Gulliver's Houyhnhnm companion, as Michael DePorte suspects, might be a dark joke at the expense of the monarchy ('Avenging Naboth: Swift and Monarchy', *PQ* 69 (1990), 429).

The Houyhnhnm called 'Master' by Gulliver suggests that horse's role as Gulliver's philosopher-teacher. Swift's own horse in the years that Gulliver is said to be in Houyhnhnmland was named 'Bolingbroke' after Swift's friend, Henry St John, Viscount Bolingbroke, the Tory leader and sometime Jacobite.

248 *the Red-haired . . . rest*: alludes to a pervasive sexual myth in seventeenth- and eighteenth-century Britain that red-haired people were lecherous, deriving in part from a medieval theory probably connected with the tradition that Judas (who according to legend committed incest with his mother) had red hair (PT), but going back to Aristotle and such spurious sex-manuals as *Aristotle's Masterpiece* (see Paul-Gabriel Boucé, 'The Rape of Gulliver Reconsidered', *Swift Studies*, 11 (1996), 98–114 (pp. 108–9)).

present: immediate.

softly: slowly.

a young Female Yahoo: the episode has been variously construed: as a bestiality scene of man-beast sexual contact, as a rape scene with the male as victim, as an evocation of the scenario of European male sexual encounters with native women, as an ironic adaptation of the 'Adam and Eve' bathing pools in Bacon's *The New Atlantis* where prospective husbands and wives inspect their intended mates nude (PT), and as a parody of Echo's wooing of Narcissus in Book III of Ovid's *Metamorphoses*. For detailed contextual analysis of the episode, see Paul-Gabriel Boucé, 'The Rape of Gulliver Reconsidered', 98–114; *GGG*, 92–182. As Gulliver recognizes, the main implication of this narrative episode is that it shows that Gulliver has biological kinship with the brutal, unreasoning Yahoos. He is recognized by Yahoos, as well as by the Houyhnhnms, as belonging to the Yahoo species.

249 *Eleven Years old*: Irish legislation concerning rape made carnal knowledge of a female under 12 a felony attracting capital punishment, see James Kelly, ' "A Most Inhuman and Barbarous Piece of Villainy": An Exploration of the Crime of Rape in Eighteenth-Century Ireland', *Eighteenth-Century Ireland*, 10 (1995), 78–107. There was an extreme disparity in age between Swift and his intimate friends Esther Johnson (Stella) and Esther Vanhomrigh (Vanessa) and some find in this episode of Gulliver and the under-age female Yahoo a grotesque parodic allusion to his relations with one or both of these women.

strikes you with immediate Conviction: the Houyhnhnms possess that cognitive reason aspired to by Seneca and the Stoics: reason as immediate perception of reality; reason that follows or is in accord with nature. Their world is that of 'unfallen Stoics'. Human reasoning, however, is of the ratiocinative or deductive kind (see A. D. Nuttal, 'Gulliver among the Horses', *The Yearbook of English Studies*, 18 (1988), 62–6). The Houyhnhnms embody what John Locke called '*intuitive Knowledge*' where 'the Mind is at no pains of proving or examining, but perceives the

Truth, as the Eye doth light . . . the Mind perceives, that *White* is not *Black* . . . This part of Knowledge is irresistible, and like the bright Sun-shine, forces it self immediately to be perceived, as soon as ever the Mind turns its view that way; and leaves no room for Hesitation, Doubt, or Examination, but the Mind is presently filled with the clear Light of it' (John Locke, *An Essay Concerning Human Understanding*, ed. Peter H. Nidditch (Oxford: Clarendon Press, 1975), Bk IV, chap. ii, p. 531).

249 *Reason taught . . . Houyhnhnms*: Swift saw liberty of opinion in the public domain as the radical political problem ('Ode to Sancroft', ll. 56–7, *Poems*, i. 36; *PW* ix. 263). The King of Brobdingnag articulates Swift's position on liberty of conscience when he urges outward public conformity: 'a Man may be allowed to keep Poisons in his Closet, but not to vend them about as Cordials'.

Sentiments of Socrates: *The Republic* 475E–480. Compare Burton, *The Anatomy of Melancholy*, I. ii. iv. 7, p. 364: 'What is most of our Philosophy, but a Labyrinth of opinions, idle questions, propositions, Metaphysicall tearmes; *Socrates* therefore held all philosophers, cavillers and madmen . . . because they commonly sought after such things, [which can be neither perceived nor understood by us], or put the case they did understand, yet they were altogether unprofitable . . . [We] are neither wiser as he followes it, nor modester, nor better, nor richer, nor stronger for the knowledge of it.' Cf. Montaigne, *Essays*, ii. 12, 'Apology for Raymond Sebond': 'Socrates . . . concluded that he was distinguished from the others, and wise, only in that he did not think himself so; and that his God considered the opinion that we possess learning and wisdom a singular piece of stupidity in man; and that his best knowledge was the knowledge of his ignorance, and simplicity his best wisdom' (Montaigne, 368). Cf. also *Essays*, ii. 12: 'The plague of man is the opinion of knowledge' (360) and 'The impression of certainty is a certain token of folly and extreme uncertainty; and there are no people more foolish, or less philosophical, than the "philodoxes" [people who are full of opinions of whose grounds they are ignorant] of Plato' (404). PT cites Plato, *Apology*, 19C–D; Xenophon, *Memorabilia*, I. i. 11 ff.; IV. vii. 6 on the sentiments of Socrates that certain knowledge of the physical universe was impossible and that ethics was the only useful subject of enquiry.

250 *where-ever he goes . . . at home*: cf. *Utopia*, 58: 'Wherever they go . . . they are at home everywhere.' PT.

ignorant of Ceremony: the Utopians live together in a friendly fashion, without ceremony, and respect those in authority spontaneously (*Utopia*, 82).

Fondness: doting, foolish affection. It was one of Swift's resolutions: 'Not to be fond of Children' (*PW* i. p. xxxvii).

same Affection . . . his own: cf. Plato's *Republic*, 461D. PT.

Nature . . . love the whole Species: cf. More, *Utopia*, 84–5: 'The Utopians think . . . that no one should be considered an enemy who has done no harm, that the kinship of nature is as good as a treaty.' PT.

250 *Reason only . . . Virtue*: as PT observes, a principle incorporated into the ethical system of the radical anarchist philosopher William Godwin in his *Political Justice* (1793). Godwin greatly admired the Houyhnhnms.

When the Matron . . . Consorts: according to '*Thebæus in many things a fabler*' there are 'Indian Philosophers called Brachmans' who 'live naked' and are vegetarian. They consort for 'fortie dayes with their wives' and when 'a woman hath had a child or two, her Husband forbeareth her altogether . . . And thus their number is but small' (Purchas, i. 240–1; Kermode, 'Yahoos and Houyhnhnms', *N&Q* 195 (1950), 318; PT). Cf. the rare meetings of the married couple in Sparta ('Lycurgus', xv. 4–6).

prevent . . . Numbers: cf. the regulation of households and population and relocation of children in Plato's *Laws*, v. 740A–741A and More's *Utopia*, 54.

In their Marriages . . . Breed: the practice of eugenics, education system, and social organization in Houyhnhnmland are modelled on ancient Sparta under the laws of the legendary Lycurgus as mediated by approving classical and later writers in the humanist tradition. The Spartan example is a pervasive presence in Plato's *Republic*, one of Swift's possible sources for state-controlled eugenics as for much else.

merely because . . . reasonable Being: cf. Swift's *A Letter to a Young Lady, on Her Marriage* (written 1723): 'I have always born an entire Friendship to your Father and Mother; and the Person they have chosen for your Husband hath been for some Years past my particular Favourite . . . I MUST likewise warn you strictly against the least Degree of Fondness to your Husband before any Witnesses whatsoever, even before your nearest Relations . . . Conceal your Esteem and Love in your own Breast . . . yours was a Match of Prudence, and common Good-liking, without any Mixture of that ridiculous Passion which hath no Being, but in Play-Books and Romances' (*PW*, ix. 85, 86, 89).

Violation . . . never heard of: PT compares Francis Godwin's *The Man in the Moone* (1638), 103. Antisocial passions like possessive jealousy and adultery were precluded from Sparta by the corporate spirit of Lycurgus' laws, 'adultery was wholly unknown among them' (see 'Lycurgus', xv. 6–9).

251 *thought it monstrous . . . from the males*: both sexes receive the same education in Lycurgan Sparta (*Constitution*, i. 3–5; 'Lycurgus', xiv), Plato's *Republic* (451E–457), and in More's *Utopia* (pp. 50, 63–4). Although Swift is progressive in arguing for the education of women, primary purposes of female education in *GT* are to produce good mothers and agreeable companions for men, cf. also Swift's 'Of the Education of Ladies' (*PW* iv. 225–8). The Houyhnhnm Master's sentiments were shared by contemporary women writers such as Anne Ingram, Viscountess Irwin, who comments in *An Epistle to Mr. Pope*,

Occasioned by his Characters of Women (1736) that in 'education all the difference lies' and 'No more can we expect our modern wives | Heroes should breed, who lead such useless lives' and approves 'the Spartan virtue' (ll. 33, 109–10, 117, in *The Norton Anthology of English Literature*, 7th edn., vol. i, ed. M. H. Abrams and Stephen Greenblatt (New York: Norton, 2000), 2600–3).

Representative Council . . . Nation: cf. 'the general council of the whole island' (*Utopia*, 48). In the Utopian general council or senate, which has representatives from each district, 'they first determine where there are shortages and surpluses, and promptly satisfy one district's shortage with another's surplus . . . Thus the whole island is like a single family' (*Utopia*, 59). The Houyhnhnms exemplify that 'rule of the law of nature' to abide by pacts and to conform to what the majority, or those upon whom authority is conferred, have determined (Grotius, *De Jure Belli ac Pacis Libri Tres*, trans. Francis Kelsey, 'Prolegomena', 15, pp. 14–15).

253 *Whether . . . exterminated . . . Face of the Earth*: compare Genesis 6: 7, the periodic massacres of the slave caste of helots in ancient Sparta ('Lycurgus', xxviii. 1–4), and Swift's own punitive extremism in works such as *A Proposal for Giving Badges to the Beggars* where 'strolling Beggars' from the country are said to be 'a most insufferable Nuisance, being nothing else but a profligate Clan of Thieves, Drunkards, Heathens, and Whoremongers, fitter to be rooted out off the Face of the Earth' (*PW* xiii. 138–9). On Swift's rhetorical extremism, see *GGG*, *passim*, but esp. pp. 256–66. Cf. in a comic context, Cervantes, *Don Quixote*, I. viii. 63: 'For this is a just war, and it is a great service to God to wipe such a wicked breed from the face of the earth.'

a Mountain: Milton places the Garden of Eden on a 'steep savage hill' or mountain (*Paradise Lost*, iv. 172, 226, see also the comparison with Mount Amara, iv. 280–5).

produced by the Heat . . . Sea: the two Brutes upon a mountain suggest a Yahoo Adam and Eve, however the Houyhnhnms, as PT observes, entertain a Lucretian theory of creation from the earth (Lucretius, *De Rerum Natura*, v. 791–8).

254 *cultivate . . . Asses*: the comparison of humans to asses was an ancient joke used satirically by Swift elsewhere, and frequently in *A Tale of a Tub* and *The Battle of the Books*. PT.

255 *this Invention*: the Houyhnhnms propose to do to the humanoid Yahoos what humans, as the Houyhnhnm Master has learned from Gulliver, do to horses. Proposals to castrate Irish criminals rather than inflict immediate capital punishment were being advanced in the 1720s, see e.g. *Some Reasons Humbly offer'd, why the Castration of Persons found Guilty of Robbery and Theft, May be the best Method of Punishment for those Crimes* (Dublin, 1725). See also *GGG* 230–1 for contemporary proposals to castrate Irish priests.

he was pleased to conceal: perhaps another sign of Gulliver's corrupting influence on the Houyhnhnm who again suppresses the full truth. The Houyhnhnm is presented as rather 'human' in not being able to break the bad news to Gulliver.

255 *In Poetry ... Mortals*: Houyhnhnm poetry and its subjects seem modelled on that in Ancient Sparta which had no written literature, but did have a flourishing oral poetic tradition. The subjects of Houyhnhnm poetry are what Lycurgus and Plato approved, and what Pindar celebrated ('Lycurgus', xxi; *Republic*, 390D; Swift's earliest poems were Pindaric odes. PT). Cf. also Montaigne, *Essays*, i. 31 (Montaigne, 158).

256 *the obscurest Places ... Grief*: Swift's Will contains a request to be buried 'as privately as possible, and at Twelve o'Clock at Night' (*PW* xiii. 149). He also expressed a wish to be buried obscurely at Holyhead (*Poems*, ii. 421). He seems to have made no public show of his very real grief at the death of his dearest friend Esther Johnson. The Utopians approve when people die blithely and they do not mourn such deaths, rather they celebrate such souls (*Utopia*, 96). The Houyhnhnm approach to death is what Montaigne admired and Montaigne points to the kind of significance Swift's account of the Houyhnhnms implies. Montaigne wrote (*Essays*, ii. 12, 'Apology for Raymond Sebond'): 'What they tell us of the Brazilians, that they died only of old age, which is attributed to the serenity and tranquillity of their air, I attribute rather to the tranquillity and serenity of their souls, unburdened with any tense or unpleasant passion or thought or occupation, as people who spent their life in admirable simplicity and ignorance, without letters, without law, without king, without religion of any kind' (Montaigne, 362).

upon returning: PT quotes Cornelius Nepos, *Life of Atticus*, xxii. 1–2: 'all this he said with so steady a voice and countenance, that he seemed to be passing, not out of life, but merely from one house to another'.

She died about three Months after: although she is outwardly stoical, there may be a subtle suggestion here that she dies of a broken heart.

258 *Honey ... mingled with Water*: a Utopian beverage (*Utopia*, 44). PT.

I enjoyed ... Enemy: cf. *Utopia*, 105 on 'the happiness of the Utopian republic, which has abolished not only money but with it greed! What a mass of trouble was cut away by that one step! What a thicket of crimes was uprooted! Everyone knows that if money were abolished, fraud, theft, robbery, quarrels, brawls, altercations, seditions, murders, treasons, poisonings and a whole set of crimes which are avenged but not prevented by the hangman would at once die out ...'. On Swift's lists and their literary contexts, and especially the influence of Rabelais, see Rawson, 101 ff.

Controvertists: controversialists.

259 *Virtuoso's*: scientific amateurs like Sir Nicholas Gimcrack in Shadwell's *Virtuoso*.

Mechanicks: manual workers.

Fiddlers: Swift once intervened to prevent a man from being pardoned for a rape commenting: 'besides he was a fiddler, and consequently a rogue, and deserved hanging for something else; and so he shall swing' (*PW* xv. 320).

descend: condescend.

most significant Words: cf. the laconic speech of the Spartans ('Lycurgus', xix). The Houyhnhnms reflect what Swift said in *Hints Towards an Essay on Conversation* were the 'two chief Ends of Conversation . . . to entertain and improve those we are among, or to receive those Benefits ourselves'. Swift condemned 'the Itch of Dispute and Contradiction' and 'telling of Lies' in conversation (*PW* iv. 92, 94).

Subjects: cf. 'Lycurgus', xii. 4, xxv. 2; Horace, *Satires*, II. vi. 70–6. Like the young people in Utopia, Gulliver is the auditor at improving table conversation and is drawn into the conversation with questions (*Utopia*, 58). Swift's principal satiric exhibit of debased conversation was 'at Court, and in the Best Companies of England', see his satiric anthology from a lifetime of collecting, *A Complete Collection of Genteel and Ingenious Conversation* (*PW* iv. 97–201).

260 *When I happened . . . Lake or Fountain . . . my self*: unlike Eve who liked what she saw (*Paradise Lost*, iv. 460–71) and Narcissus who fell in love with his own reflection in the water (Ovid, *Metamorphoses*, iii. 402–36), Gulliver hates the image of fallen humanity that he sees. Gulliver's abhorrence of the self he beholds has striking analogues in Christian rhetoric on humanity deformed by sin, see Frye, 'Swift's Yahoo and the Christian Symbols for Sin', 206–8. PT interprets the scene as 'an ironical adaptation of a stock passage in pastoral love poetry (Theocritus, vi. 34–8; Virgil, *Eclogues*, ii. 25–6; Pope, *Pastorals*, ii. 27–30) where the unsuccessful lover (Polyphemus, Corydon, "A Shepherd's Boy") looks at himself (in the sea, a "crystal spring") to check that he is not really so very unattractive. Gulliver has fallen in love with the Houyhnhnms, but feels a Cyclops to their Galatea.'

261 *ravenous*: plundering.

contrive some Sort of Vehicle: parodies *Odyssey*, v. 105–261, where Calypso receives orders from Olympus to send Odysseus away, and help him to build a boat. PT.

262 *renowned*: Gulliver assumes the fame of his book as no one has heard of the Houyhnhnms before.

263 *Wattles*: rods, sticks.

Stanch: watertight.

264 *But as I was going . . . Mouth*: Wafer reports how 'the *Indians*' adored him: 'some kissed my Hand, others my Knee, and some my Foot' (Wafer, 19). Swift's satiric deflation of this kind of voyager hubris elides into an insult to unworthy human nature.

265 *171⁴⁄₅*: until 1752 the new year in England began on 25 March rather than

1 January. So for dates between 1 January and 24 March both years were often given, 'Old Style' 1714, 'New Style' 1715.

265 *such a Solitude*: Gulliver's rejection of society had real-life analogues. Alexander Selkirk who was rescued after four years and four months on the Island of Juan Fernandez 'frequently bewailed his Return to the World, which could not, he said, with all its Enjoyments, restore him to the Tranquility of his Solitude' (*Englishman*, no. 26 (3 December 1713), 109).

266 *I arrived . . . South-East Point of New-Holland*: Gulliver seems to have reached the southern point of Tasmania. Swift is insouciant about precise geographical locations. Gulliver thinks he knows where he is, but the reader can have considerable difficulty finding him.

Maps and Charts . . . really is: parodies Dampier who suspects faulty charts and writes that New Holland (Australia) is further west than Tasman's chart indicated (*Voyages*, ii. 430–1, 432–3).

Mr Hermann Moll: famous Dutch cartographer in London. Moll's *A New & Correct Map of the Whole World* (1719) was a principal source for the maps in *Gulliver's Travels*, see Frederick Bracher, 'The Maps in *Gulliver's Travels*', *HLQ* 8 (1944–5), 59–74.

Knee: Wafer is wounded in the 'Knee' and confides to the reader that there is 'a Weakness in that Knee, which remain'd long after, and a Benummedness which I sometimes find in it to this Day' (Wafer, 4–6).

stood to: steered towards.

268 *Pedro de Mendez*: More's Raphael Hythloday is 'a Portuguese' and he returns to his country in a Portuguese ship (*Utopia*, 10–11). Mendez is the name of Portuguese sailors in the 1625 edition of *Purchas His Pilgrimes* which Swift owned. Swift had Portuguese cousins (Williams, v. 58). Dampier commented in *A Voyage to New Holland* that many of 'the Portuguez, who are Batchelors' have 'black Women for Misses' (*Voyages*, ii. 386), but Swift's Portuguese bachelor appears austere and chaste. The good generous Captain from a Catholic country offers a stark contrast to the perfidious Calvinist Protestant Dutchman in Part III. Mendez is a prominent patronymic among Sephardim (Jews who settled in Spain and Portugal), Marranos (secret Jews who appeared ostensibly Christian), and Jews who were Catholic Christian converts, and Swift may have chosen the name to suggest an outsider or a diasporic outcast figure who is the Good Samaritan to Gulliver (see Maurice A. Géracht, 'Pedro De Mendez: Marrano Jew and Good Samaritan in Swift's *Voyages*', *Swift Studies*, 5 (1990), 39–52).

269 *of my Veracity*: in the first edition the sentence continues: 'and the rather, because he confessed, he met with a *Dutch* Skipper, who pretended to have landed with Five others of his Crew upon a certain Island or Continent *South* of *New-Holland*, where they went for fresh Water, and observed a Horse driving before him several Animals exactly resembling those I described under the Name of *Yahoos*, with some other Particulars,

which the Captain said he had forgot; because he then concluded them all to be Lies.' These words were omitted by Faulkner in 1735, presumably to avoid a doubt about Houyhnhnm veracity, since they have told Gulliver: 'That no European did ever visit these Countries before me.' In the passage Don Pedro, like the Houyhnhnms, rejects out of hand the idea of a society where the roles of horse and human are reversed.

270 *backwards*: at the back of the house.

Inquisition: a parody of Dampier's fears recorded in *A Voyage to New Holland* about the Portuguese Inquisition in Brazil. Swift was informed that his mock-astrological hoax pamphlet *Predictions for the Year 1708* had been burned by 'the *Inquisition* in *Portugal*' (*PW* ii. 160). Gulliver's book might be understood by an Inquisition as blasphemy against Genesis 1: 27, 28 where it is said that 'God created man in his own image' and with 'dominion' over all living things on earth.

Rue . . . Tobacco: herbal cures for melancholy affliction in Burton, *The Anatomy of Melancholy*, II. IV. i. 3, p. 218.

no Commerce: contact, conversation, dealings.

271 *I fell in a Swoon . . . Hour*: a poem by Pope first published with *GT* in 1727 and included in Faulkner's 1735 edition entitled 'Mary Gulliver to Captain Lemuel Gulliver' exploits the comedy and quasi-pornographic innuendo in Gulliver's antics:

> Welcome, thrice welcome to thy native Place!
> —What, touch me not? what, shun a Wife's Embrace? . . .
> Not touch me! never Neighbour call'd me Slut!
> Was *Flimnap*'s Dame more sweet in *Lilliput*?
> I've no red Hair to breathe an odious Fume;
> At least thy Consort's cleaner than thy *Groom*.
> Why then that dirty Stable-boy thy Care?
> What mean those Visits to the *Sorrel Mare*? . . .
> Forth in the Street I rush with frantick Cries:
> The Windows open; all the Neighbours rise:
> *Where sleeps my* Gulliver? *O tell me where?*
> The Neighbours answer, *With the Sorrel Mare*.

(ll. 1–2, 25–30, 45–8; *The Poems of Alexander Pope: A One Volume Edition of the Twickenham Pope*, ed. John Butt (London: Methuen, 1963), 486–7).

suffer . . . presume . . . Bread . . . Cup . . . Hand: the echo of the Gospels (cf. Mark 10: 14; 9: 27) and the Church of England Communion service in *The Book of Common Prayer* (cf. 'We do not presume to come to this thy Table, O merciful Lord, trusting in our own righteousness, but in thy manifold and great mercies. We are not worthy so much as to gather up the crumbs under thy Table') indicates Gulliver's blasphemous pride and self-righteousness. Gulliver imitates the sound and trot of horses but he is hardly living a life of reason or imitating Houyhnhnm virtues of sociability, friendship, and benevolence. The Houyhnhnm Master did not treat his wife and family with contempt. In having Gulliver impudently acting as if he was God and in recoiling from 'Yahoos', Swift may be recalling Montaigne (*Essays*, ii. 12, 'Apology for Raymond Sebond'): 'There is not one of us who is so offended to see himself compared to God as he is to see himself brought down to the rank of the other animals' (Montaigne, 361). Swift's traveller boasts of his reason but from having looked on the light for a long time has become disorientated, blinded rather than enlightened. At the moment Gulliver cannot distinguish true reason and virtue from a prejudiced and bigoted monomania. In Gulliver's absurd antics Swift is making a further misanthropic point: even when shown a life of reason in accord with nature humankind is unable to truly imitate it.

271 *Stone-Horses*: stallions. Gulliver does not castrate his horses.

272 *faithful History*: cf. Lucian's *True History*.

wonderful Animals . . . Places: PT notes the similarity with More's *Utopia*; cf. the jaded remark: 'We made no inquiries . . . about monsters, for nothing is less new or strange than they are . . . but well and wisely trained citizens you will hardly find anywhere.' Hythloday, like Gulliver, 'told us of many ill-considered usages in these new-found nations, he also described quite a few other customs from which our own cities, nations, races and kingdoms might take lessons in order to correct their errors . . . he told us about the customs and institutions of the Utopians' (*Utopia*, 12).

273 *Nec si miserum . . . finget*: nor, if Fortune has made Sinon for misery, will she also in her spite make him false and a liar (Virgil, *Aeneid*, ii. 79–80). The Greek Sinon tells a famous lie which persuades the Trojans to take the wooden horse (full of Greeks) within the walls of their city and this leads to the destruction of Troy. Gulliver is Swift's magnificent liar who tells a gloriously false tale. His Greek-model (i.e. Spartan and Platonic) horses would, if their principles were introduced, destroy modern Troy (London). Swift elsewhere imagines the destruction of corrupt modern Britain. In *An Argument against Abolishing Christianity*, for example, Swift's sardonic irony supposes that the introduction of real Christianity would 'break the entire Frame and Constitution of Things' and 'turn our Courts, Exchanges and Shops into Desarts', and approves Horace's proposal to the corrupt Romans 'to leave their City, and seek a new Seat in some remote Part of the World' (*PW* ii. 27–8). Alluding to the *Aeneid* (ii. 311–12) in a letter to his friend Charles Ford, a Jacobite, Swift obliquely implies that his main worry if a Jacobite invasion takes place is that the flames in sacked Troy (Britain) might spread to his Deanry-house in Ireland (16 February 1719, *Corr.*, ii. 291).

Writings which require . . . Journal: PT compares More's similar statement at the opening of *Utopia* (p. 3).

274 *Cortez*: Hernán Cortés (1485–1547), Spanish conquistador who conquered Mexico terrorizing the population.

missive Weapons: missiles.

Mummy: pulp. Gulliver's fantasy of the terror Houyhnhnms could unleash on a European army recalls the terror the Spanish with their horses caused the South American populations.

Yerks: kicks.

Recalcitrat undique tutus: he kicks back, at every point on his guard (Horace, *Satires*, II. i. 20).

275 *distributive*: the kind of justice concerned with determining rights and distributing due portions (Gough, 425; PT).

their Princes tortured . . . Gold: Montezuma II of Mexico was kept in chains by Cortés (1519) until he handed over an immense amount of gold and precious stones. Atahuallpa, the last Inca of Peru, was murdered by Pizarro (1533) in spite of having paid a vast ransom in silver and gold (Gough, 425; PT).

convert: Atahuallpa was sentenced to be burnt alive, but earned the privilege of being strangled instead by allowing himself to be converted to Christianity at the stake. PT.

But this Description: PT cites the heavy irony of the praise of European diplomacy in *Utopia*, 83: 'In Europe, of course, and especially in these regions where the Christian faith and religion prevail, the dignity of treaties is everywhere kept sacred and inviolable. This is partly because the princes are all so just and virtuous, partly also from the awe and reverence that everyone feels for the popes.' Swift is also parodying contemporary Whig-speak praising British colonialism. The loyal Old Whig journal, *Cato's Letters*, for example, found English liberty exemplified in Britain's productive American slave plantations: 'the English planters in America, besides maintaining themselves and ten times as many Negroes, maintain likewise great numbers of their countrymen in England. Such are the blessings of liberty, and such is the difference which it makes between country and country!' (*Cato's Letters*, no. 67, 24 Feb. 172[2], 474, in John Trenchard and Thomas Gordon, *Cato's Letters or Essays on Liberty, Civil and Religious, and Other Important Subjects*, ed. Ronald Hamowy, 4 vols. in 2 (Classics on Liberty; Indianapolis: Liberty Fund, 1995).

liberal Endowments: as PT observes Swift supported his friend George Berkeley's 'Notion of founding an University at Bermudas by a Charter from the Crown' (Swift to Lord Carteret, [4 September 1724], *Corr.*, ii. 518).

276 *believed*: the first edition continued: 'unless a Dispute may arise about the two *Yahoos*, said to have been seen many Ages ago on a Mountain in *Houyhnhnmland*, from whence the Opinion is, that the Race of those Brutes hath descended; and these, for any thing I know, may have been *English*, which indeed I was apt to suspect from the Lineaments of their Posterity's Countenances, although very much defaced. But, how far that

will go to make out a Title, I leave to the Learned in Colony-Law.' Swift's final insult was to identify the Yahoos who resemble the 'Natives' of 'savage Nations' explicitly with the English, whom he would depict in another satiric masterpiece, *A Modest Proposal*, as cannibal oppressors who would eat the cannibal savage Irish. Faulkner omitted the passage. Swift may have thought that it seemed to contradict Houyhnhnm veracity, as they have said that no Europeans had been to their country, or Faulkner may have thought the insult to the English was too specific (after all, the idea that the Yahoos are partly based on the native Irish is never explicitly stated).

276 *Evidence*: witness.

277 *and therefore ... Sight*: Gulliver ends like Raphael Hythloday with a diatribe against 'one single monster, the prime plague and begetter of all others – I mean Pride' (*Utopia*, 106). Gulliver, who has, as he feared, relapsed into human corruptions since leaving Houyhnhnmland, here embodies the 'absurd Vice' as he preaches against it.

Women's Writing 1778–1838

WILLIAM BECKFORD   Vathek

JAMES BOSWELL   Life of Johnson

FRANCES BURNEY   Camilla
Cecilia
Evelina
The Wanderer

LORD CHESTERFIELD   Lord Chesterfield's Letters

JOHN CLELAND   Memoirs of a Woman of Pleasure

DANIEL DEFOE   A Journal of the Plague Year
Moll Flanders
Robinson Crusoe
Roxana

HENRY FIELDING   Joseph Andrews and Shamela
A Journey from This World to the Next and
    The Journal of a Voyage to Lisbon
Tom Jones

WILLIAM GODWIN   Caleb Williams

OLIVER GOLDSMITH   The Vicar of Wakefield

MARY HAYS   Memoirs of Emma Courtney

ELIZABETH HAYWOOD   The History of Miss Betsy Thoughtless

ELIZABETH INCHBALD   A Simple Story

SAMUEL JOHNSON   The History of Rasselas
The Major Works

CHARLOTTE LENNOX   The Female Quixote

MATTHEW LEWIS   Journal of a West India Proprietor
The Monk

HENRY MACKENZIE   The Man of Feeling

ALEXANDER POPE   Selected Poetry

The Oxford World's Classics Website

www.worldsclassics.co.uk

- Information about new titles
- Explore the full range of Oxford World's Classics
- Links to other literary sites and the main OUP webpage
- Imaginative competitions, with bookish prizes
- Peruse the Oxford World's Classics Magazine
- Articles by editors
- Extracts from Introductions
- A forum for discussion and feedback on the series
- Special information for teachers and lecturers

www.worldsclassics.co.uk

American Literature

British and Irish Literature

Children's Literature

Classics and Ancient Literature

Colonial Literature

Eastern Literature

European Literature

History

Medieval Literature

Oxford English Drama

Poetry

Philosophy

Politics

Religion

The Oxford Shakespeare

A complete list of Oxford Paperbacks, including Oxford World's Classics, Oxford Shakespeare, Oxford Drama, and Oxford Paperback Reference, is available in the UK from the Academic Division Publicity Department, Oxford University Press, Great Clarendon Street, Oxford OX2 6DP.

In the USA, complete lists are available from the Paperbacks Marketing Manager, Oxford University Press, 198 Madison Avenue, New York, NY 10016.

Oxford Paperbacks are available from all good bookshops. In case of difficulty, customers in the UK can order direct from Oxford University Press Bookshop, Freepost, 116 High Street, Oxford OX1 4BR, enclosing full payment. Please add 10 per cent of published price for postage and packing.